The Old Drift

'From the poetry and subtle humor constantly alive in its language, to the cast of fulsome characters that defy simple categorization, *The Old Drift* is a novel that satisfies on all levels. Namwali Serpell excels in creating portraits of resilience – each unique and often heartbreaking. In *The Old Drift* the individual struggle is cast against a world of shifting principles and politics, and Serpell captures the quicksand nature of a nation's roiling change with exacting precision. My only regret is that once begun, I reached the end all too soon'
Alice Sebold

'It's difficult to think of another novel that is at once so sweepingly ambitious and so intricately patterned, delivering the pleasures of saga and poetry in equal measure. *The Old Drift* is an endlessly innovative, voraciously brilliant book, and Namwali Serpell is among the most distinctive and exciting writers to emerge in years'
Garth Greenwell

'An astonishing novel, a riot for the senses, filled with the music and scents and sensations of Zambia. Namwali Serpell writes about people, land and longing with such compassionate humour and precision, there's an old wisdom in these pages. In short, make room on your shelf next to a few of your other favourites: Chimamanda Ngozi Adichie, Tsitsi Dangarembga and Edwidge Danticat jump to mind. It's brilliant. This woman was born to write!'
Alexandra Fuller

'*The Old Drift* is a stunning achievement: a novel of epic scope and powerful vision that also manages to be intimate, tender, and very funny. A truly important debut from a brilliant new voice'
Fiona McFarlane

'In turn charming, heartbreaking and breathtaking, *The Old Drift* is a staggeringly ambitious, genre-busting multigenerational saga with moxie for days . . . I wanted it to go on forever. A worthy heir to Gabriel García Márquez's *One Hundred Years of Solitude*'
Carmen Maria Machado

'*The Old Drift* is an extraordinary meditation on identity, the history of a nation, love, politics, family, friendship and life. Serpell's prose is dazzling. Darting back and forth through the decades and mixing different genres, Namwali has delivered an original, remarkable, magical work that both delights and challenges'
Chika Unigwe

'If, as she writes, "history is the annals of the bully on the playground" then in *The Old Drift*, Namwali Serpell wreaks havoc on the Zambian annals by rewriting the past, creating a new present, and conjuring an alternative future. In refusing to be bound by genre, Serpell is audacious and shrewd. This is a Zambian history of pain and exploitation, trial and error, and hope and triumph'
Jennifer Makumbi

'*The Old Drift* is a dazzling genre-bender of a novel, an astonishing historical and futuristic feat, a page-turner with a plot that consistently and cleverly upends itself. Playfully poetic and outright serious at once, it is one of the most intelligent debuts I've read this year. No matter your reading preference, there's something in it for you'
Chinelo Okparanta

THE
OLD
DRIFT

NAMWALI
SERPELL

HOGARTH
LONDON · NEW YORK

1 3 5 7 9 10 8 6 4 2

Hogarth, an imprint of Vintage,
20 Vauxhall Bridge Road,
London SW1V 2SA

Hogarth is part of the Penguin Random House group of companies
whose addresses can be found at global.penguinrandomhouse.com.

Penguin
Random House
UK

First published by Hogarth in 2019

penguin.co.uk/vintage

A CIP catalogue record for this book is available from the British Library

Hardback ISBN 9781781090497
Trade paperback ISBN 9781781090503

Typeset in 11.5/14 pt Dante MT Std
by Integra Software Services Pvt. Ltd, Pondicherry

Printed and bound in Great Britain by Clays Ltd, Elcograf S.p.A.

Penguin Random House is committed to a sustainable future for
our business, our readers and our planet. This book is made
from Forest Stewardship Council® certified paper.

For Mama

Meanwhile, at the far end of a valley, Aeneas saw
A remote grove, bushy rustling thickets,
And the river Lethe somnolently flowing,
Lapping those peaceful haunts along its banks.
Here a hovering multitude, innumerable
Nations and gathered clans, kept the fields
Humming with life, like bees in meadows
On a clear summer day alighting on pied flowers
And wafting in mazy swarms around white lilies.
Aeneas startled at this unexpected sight
And in his bewilderment asked what was happening,
What was the river drifting past beyond them,
Who were the ones in such a populous throng
Beside it?
          'Spirits,' Anchises answered ...

Virgil, *The Aeneid*, Book VI
(tr. Seamus Heaney)

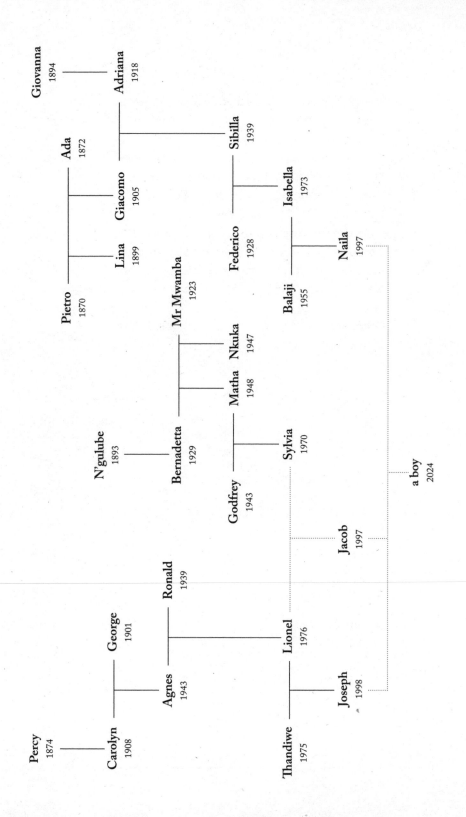

Contents

Zt. Zzt. ZZZzzzZZZzzzzZZZzzzzzzZZZZzzzzzzzzZZZzzzzzzZZZzzzzo'ona.

And so. A dead white man grows bearded and lost in the blinding heart of Africa. With his rooting and roving, his stops and starts, he becomes our father unwitting, our inadvertent pater muzungu. *This is the story of a nation – not a kingdom or a people – so it begins, of course, with a white man.*

Once upon a time, a goodly Scottish doctor caught a notion to find the source of the Nile. He found instead a gash in the ground full of massed, tumbling water. His bearers called it Mosi-oa-Tunya, which means The Smoke That Thunders, but he gave it the name of his queen. He described the Falls with a stately awe, comparing the flung water to British things: to fleece and snow and the sparks from burning steel, to myriads of small comets rushing on in one direction, each of which left behind its nucleus rays of foam. *He speculated that angels had gazed down upon it and said to each other, 'How lovely.' He even opined, like a set designer, that there really ought to be mountains in the backdrop.*

Adventure. Disaster. Fame. Commerce. Christianity. Civilisation. He was mauled by a lion that shook him in its jaws, he said, as a dog shakes a rat. His wife died of fever; his beloved poodle drowned. He voyaged over land and along endless waterways. He freed slaves as he went, broke their chains with his hands, and took them on as his servants and bearers. Late in his life, he witnessed a massacre – slave traders shooting at people in a lake, so many, the canoes could not pass. He despaired. He was broken, broke; Queen Victoria had forgotten him; the Royal Geographers said he was dead. Then a mercenary Welsh bastard named Stanley presumed, shook his hand, and sent word to London. And in an instant he was infamous, as if risen from the grave. Yet he refused to return to Merrie England.

Doddering, he drove deeper into the continent instead, still seeking his beloved Nile. Oh, father muzungu! *The word means white man, but it describes not the skin, but a tendency. A muzungu is one who will* zunguluka *– wander aimlessly – until they end up in circles. And so our movious* muzungu *pitched up here again, dragging his black bearers with him.*

His medicine box went missing – who took it? They never found out – and with it, his precious quinine. Fever hunted him and finally caught him. He died in a hut, in the night, on his bed, kneeling, his head in his hands. His men disembowelled him, planted his heart under a tree, and bore his corpse to the coast. The HMS Vulture *took his body home – what was left without the living was buried under stone in the Nave of Westminster Abbey. His people recognised him by the scrapes of the lion's teeth on his humerus bone.*

Such wonder at the resolve of his bearers. To travel with a corpse for months on end, suffering loss and injury, sickness and battle? Through blistering heat and blundering rain, beating off the taboo that to carry death is to beckon it? To come all the way to England, to face interrogation, to build a model of the hut that he died in? What faith! What love! No, no – what fear! That corpse, that body was proof. Without it, who would possibly have taken their word that a white man, among 'savages', had died of bad luck – a mere fever?

Men never believe chance can wreak great consequence. Yet the story of this place is full of such slips. Error, n., *from the Latin* errare: *to stray or to veer or to wander. For instance, the* bazungu *who carved this territory into a colony, then a protectorate, then a federation, then a country came here only because Livingstone did. They drifted in and settled the land, drew arbitrary lines in the sand, stole treaties from chiefs with a devious ruse: a 'Royal Charter' meant for business, but used for state. Waving flags and guns and beads to trade with, they scrambled rabid for Africa, and claimed it was Livingstone's legacy.*

Neither Oriental nor Occidental, but accidental is this nation. Would you believe our godly Scotch doc was searching for the Nile in the wrong spot? As it turns out, there are two Niles – one Blue, one White – which means two sources, and neither one of them is anywhere near here. This sort of thing happens with nations, and tales, and humans, and signs. You go hunting for a source, some ur-word or symbol and suddenly the path splits, cleaved by apostrophe or dash. The tongue forks, speaks in two ways, which in turn fork and fork into a chaos of capillarity. Where you sought an origin, you find a vast babble which is also a silence: a chasm of smoke, thundering. Blind mouth!

The Falls

It sounds like a sentence: Victoria Falls. A prophecy. At any rate, that's the joke I used to make until Her Royal Majesty Queen Victoria actually died in 1901, just before I landed on the continent. Two years later, I set eyes on that African wonder named for an English queen and became as beguiled as the next man. I came for the Falls, and I stayed for them, too.

What they say is true – the spray can indeed be seen from thirty miles off, the roar heard from twenty. The last part of our trek from Wankie was hard going and it was eleven at night by the time we made camp about a mile from the Falls, under a gargantuan baobab tree. Tired as I was, I could not let the need of sleep come between me and my first sight of that vast tumble. I left the others and made my way alone to look over the Falls from above, from the so-called 'Devil's Cataract'. I shall never forget it.

The night was luminous with moonlight. In the foreground was the bluff of Barouka island. Beyond it, veiled in spray, the main falls leapt roaring into the chasm four hundred feet below. The spray was so powerful it was hard to say whether the Falls flowed up or down. The shadowy black forest writhed its branches before them. The lunar rainbow, pale and shimmering, gave the whole scene a touch of faery. I was awed beyond words, as if standing in the presence of a majestic Power quite ineffable. My hat came off and for an hour I stood bareheaded, lost in rapture.

No. I shall never forget that nocturnal view of the Victoria Falls, full in flood and drenched in moonlight. I spent thirty-two years within a mile of that spot, and I'll be damned if that isn't still the best lookout.

✳

The next morning, I marked the occasion of my first encounter by carving my name and the date into the baobab tree: Percy M. Clark. 8 May 1903. This was unlike me but excusable under the circumstances. I set out for the drift five miles above the Falls, the port of entry into North-western Rhodesia. The Zambesi is at its deepest and narrowest here for hundreds of miles, so it's the handiest spot for 'drifting' a body across. At first it was called Sekute's Drift after a chief of the Leya. Then it was Clarke's Drift, after the first white settler, whom I soon met. No one knows when it became The Old Drift.

For two hours I sat alone on the southern bank, popping off a rifle at intervals. At long last, I saw a speck – a dugout coming from the other side. It seemed so far upriver, I wasn't quite sure it was coming for me; the river was so swift that a long slant was needed to bring the boat precisely to the spot where I waited. A dugout is a ticklish thing to handle in a strong current – a single crossways cough is enough to tip it over – but the Barotse are excellent river-boys. Standing to their work, they use ten-foot paddles to steer their primitive craft. They brought me back across and then my goods.

The Old Drift was then a small settlement of a half-dozen men – there were only about a hundred white men in all of the territory at the time. I stopped at a mud and pole store that served as the local 'hotel'. It belonged to a man who bore my surname, except his had the aristocratic 'e' attached. This would have been coincidence enough, but it turned out that he grew up in Chatteris in Cambridgeshire, practically next door to the university city I thought I'd long left behind. It seemed I couldn't get away from the old country, or its airs.

Fred 'Mopane' Clarke – a native moniker, for he was 'tall and straight and has a heart like a mopane tree' – had settled there five years earlier and become a forwarding agent, then started a transport service across the Zambesi. He later went on to great fortune building hotels and selling them off. But when I met him, we were simply two men making the best of it. Mopane was amused that I had tossed a coin to choose my new vocation – photography was a relatively new field in those days. I didn't bother to explain my ousting from the Trinity chemistry lab.

'The bollocks on you!' he said. 'Did you journey to Rhodesia on such a whim, too?'

'Yes,' I lied. 'Took up a post at a studio in Bulawayo. But toning and fixing is rather a chancy business in Africa, with the dust, not to mention the dust-devils. So I quit.' Another lie.

'But you've stayed on, it seems. Does life here in the bush suit you?'

'The settlers are a good sort. Honest, spirited. Don't turn their nose up at people. The Kaffirs are bewildering, of course, but seem pliable enough. The insects are rather an abomination.'

We exchanged bug stories. Tam-Pam beetles tugging at the hair, rhino beetles blundering into the knob, the putrid stink beetle and whistling Christmas bug. Scorpions, spiders, centipedes. Beasties all. I won the debate by telling him about the day I arrived in Bulawayo two years earlier. The sun vanished behind a black cloud: not a dust storm but a plague of biblical locusts! Then came the clamour: the frantic beating of pots and trays to scare them off. A hellish din, but effective.

'You shall face far worse here,' said Mopane cryptically. 'Do you intend to pioneer?'

'To wander. Pa always said, "My boy, never settle till you have to and never work for another man." Time to play my own hand, do a touch of exploring. I believe I shall be the first to follow the Zambesi from the Falls all the way to the coast,' I boasted.

'Like the good Dr Livingstone.'

'Oh. Yes, I suppose.' I shook off my frown. 'But without the religion.'

Mopane Clarke gripped my hand with a devilish grin.

※

I was ready for my escape into the wild. Leaving my camera equipment in Mopane's care, I set off for Kasangula, a kraal two and a half days away. It was bossed by a chief Quinani, a quaint old bird who squatted in the sun all day, snuffing, dressed in a leopard skin and a Union Jack hat. I hired five dugouts and fifty bearers from him, then set off upriver, planning to eat by the hunt.

The shooting was very good and quite varied back then. Partridge, pheasant, geese, guinea fowl, even wild turkey. The land abounded in game, from the stately eland to the tiny oribi. The first buck I bagged was a big black lechwe: it stared right into the barrel of my heavy-bullet Martini rifle. Next was an indigenous species of antelope that Dr Livingstone had dubbed the 'puku': a shy, crepuscular creature, bigger than the impala, similarly golden but without the telltale toilet stripes, and with a frowsy look to its fur. A native told me the name came from a local word for 'ghost': Livingstone had sighted it in dry season, slipping in and out of the high yellow grass of the veldt. Makes for a good steak.

For a year, I journeyed in a go-as-you-please sort of style with my petty fleet of dugouts. There were several obstacles between me and the coast. For one, the tributaries of the Zambesi simply teemed with crocs and hippos. For another, it was a right task just getting my boys to do their job. They were superstitious of my whistling – which I did merely because I had nobody to talk to. And they wouldn't pass certain spots without landing to make offerings to the dead and watch the witch doctor 'do his stuff', with animal tails and charms around his neck, bones and bangles around wrists and ankles. He was a fearsome sight – or thought he was. The Barotse were in fact a powerful nation, with many conquered tribes paying tribute. Penalties for missed payments were extracted in gruesome fashion: I saw natives with ears hanging by the cartilage, with noses slitted or removed entirely. This vengeful spirit erupted more and more among my bearers, too.

We had reached as far as Sesheke when a hippo upset a dugout and lost us some time. I suggested we get a move on to navigate the rapids before dark. 'Nothing doing!' the boys pretty much said. 'We'll see about that,' I replied and showed my .450 Webley, driving my personal crew one by one at gunpoint into a boat. I told the rest that if they didn't follow, they'd have to fend for themselves: 'No more skoff for you!' Off I went with my hostages and made camp at the foot of the rapids. When the others pitched up at sundown, I made them kneel and rub their foreheads in the dust and give the royal salute. That finished the 'indaba'. I had got them in the native's weakest spot – the belly!

With setbacks like these – plus veldt fires, squalls, reedy banks that made it impossible to land – I made little progress. The worst difficulty of exploration, I learned, is that it is a tormenting isolation. There was no chumming it up with the blacks, naturally, and the need for sympathetic company would have been unbearable were it not for the terrier bitch I'd been gifted at the Wankie colliery. That little wire-haired lady was my only pal, my inseparable companion. I sympathised with Dr Livingstone's affection for his dear Chitane, who drowned around these parts, they say. My Flossie had a marvellous nose and, though she could not save my journey, she saved my life in the end.

Late in my travels, King Litia, a sort of deputy to Lewanika, sent me a favourite chief of his to catch a lift. The most I can say for this chief, Koko, is that he had 'taking' ways. Unhappy over the tough barter I'd driven for his ride, he upset my dugout on a swift side channel of the river, unaware that I could swim like a fish. The consequences, however, were dire: I came down with a bout of 104-degree fever. I ordered a rest for me and my men. That night, feverish and half-asleep, I heard Flossie growling, and saw a dark figure crawling on hands and knees towards us. I gave a shout. The fellow replied that he wanted fire. Not plausible! There was a fire positively roaring on the other side of camp. It was plainly an attempt to knife me. I threatened to shoot, and he cleared. It was Koko – he had not forgotten the indignity of his own ten-foot drop into the water.

There are those who flatter themselves that they truly know the native. I would never make such a claim. The native is harder to understand than a woman. The more you know him, the less you know of him. The key is not to let his savagery in. To wit, I never whip a native unless he deserves it. A dog and a native are on a par: one should give them a good thrashing when they have earned it, but one should thrash neither until one's temper has cooled. So when we arrived at our destination, I kept my calm, tied Koko to a tree overnight, and turned him over to the new district commissioner at dawn. I released the few boys I had left – I had lost several to crocs and fever and run out of rations to feed the rest – and spent two days in bed, fighting my fever and awaiting trial.

During the hearing, darling Koko confessed at least five times that he'd have blotted me flat if luck had not contrived against him. The district commissioner, fresh from Oxford, was the sort who puts on a coat and cravat to visit a native queen. He asked me what I demanded for my trouble. Well, I demanded a hiding! The DC ruled thusly: ''Tis a trivial case. I shall dock his pay.' I am giving you this as an absolute fact. Remember, it was a young country with a native population preponderating largely over a sprinkling of white. So Koko had his pay docked – and he shortly received it back in kind by pinching from my boss boy the handsome leopard skin I'd received from his king Litia! Koko, as I say, was a daisy.

By then, the rains had arrived, in high dudgeon. I got back to The Old Drift two days later, famished and alone, soaked to the skin and flayed to the bone by a wet saddle. I headed straight for Mopane's hotel. He greeted me, kindly did not poke at the wound of my failed voyage to the coast, and fed me what was left of lunch – a hunk of bread and a tin of Vienna sausages. After my modest repast, a hut was provided for me. It will be gathered that I needed no lullabying into the deep sleep that ensued. I was completely done up. So much for imperial exploration! Was this place cursed? Or was I?

＊

I suppose I became a pioneer by default. When I first skittled here from Bulawayo, I had intended to settle across the river at Victoria Falls Town as soon as the railway bridge was complete – there would be great opportunities for those who got in early. I made my headquarters at The Old Drift for the time being. A year had passed since my first visit and the population was now fivefold but the place was still a mere trading post: a few wood and iron buildings and twice as many wattle and daub Kaffir huts.

The crowd, however, had become practically cosmopolitan. Van Blerk ran a store for a Bulawayo firm. Tom King ran a canteen for the Bechuanaland Trading Company. Jimmy, an American ex-cowboy, hunted hippos and started fistfights. A Greek made a living shooting meat – he once killed nine lions, mistaking them for boar. Mr L. F. Moore, the English chemist, edited the weekly paper, the *Livingstone Pioneer*. Zeederberg was a contractor for the post; the great event of the week, prefaced by a bugle, was sorting through a pile of His Majesty's mails, dumped from a Scotch cart onto the floor of a hut. A chap called 'The Yank' hung about, being lucky at poker, until his luck ran out. The only woman was the wife of a Dutch trader, an extremely jealous man and an expert in the use of a hippo-hide *sjam-bok*. He disfigured anyone who dared glance at his dour duchess.

There were two 'bars' where we drank and gambled away the hours. A gramophone screeched in one corner, while in another, merchants and speculators threw dice for drinks. In a third corner was a roulette table, the imperturbable croupier raking chips and filling columns of half-crowns, chanting: 'Round and round the little ball goes, and where she stops there's nobody knows! No seed, no harvest – if you don't speculate, you can't accumulate, and she's off!' There was a four-blind game of poker every night and sometimes a spot of *vingt-et-un*. Of other social life, there was none. No societies, no dance committees, not a dress suit in sight. A postprandial lying contest, chiefly concerned with lions and niggers, might take place, or we'd drum up a party for a hippo hunt.

Amusements aside, fortune flipped lives as the storm flips the leaves of a tree. A smithy gave up for lack of funds; a cotton-gin man died of sheer starvation; a Hebrew stopped through and played impressive card tricks until we ran him out, our empty pockets flapping like flags. Any old drifter might come along with a week's beard, months of wear to his trousers, and years of treading to his boots. He might leave in a worse bedragglement or he might depart in the finest of clothes, plus a quid in his pocket.

Men came and went. Those who stayed tended to die. The dry-season heat was oppressive, and the thirst it engendered required a sedulous slaking. During the rains, November to March, the place was a right swamp. The mosquitoes gathered in hordes, humming like a German band, their stings sharp enough to penetrate an elephant's hide: *Anopheles*, energetic and indiscriminate. Loafer, lord and lout were treated with strict impartiality in these parts, for the mosquito is a true democrat, and cares not what accident of birth has led you here, nor whether the blood it quaffs be red or blue.

Fever was so prevalent at The Old Drift, no particular attention was given to anyone down with it. No need to bother with a medico with a monocle and white bags creased as a concertina. Just feed the victim drops of champagne or of Schweppes with a feather, bundle him up, and let him sweat it out until the shakes subside. I once wrote an editorial for the *Livingstone Pioneer* and this was my warning: 'cursed is he who forgetteth his quinine o' nights, for the shakes and the pukes shall surely take him'. Out of the thirty-one settlers that season, no fewer than eleven died of black fever or malaria. The next year was far worse, with a loss of seventy per cent. Pioneering isn't all lavender.

We called the place Deadrock. There was a funeral about once a week. One of the survivors would serve as undertaker. We'd knock together a coffin out of old whisky cases, douse the departed in quick-lime, then encase him with black limbo or calico. The coffin was put on a Scotch cart hauled by oxen to the graveyard. The rest of the town marched behind, clad in slacks and rolled-up shirtsleeves, no coats. There were no Bibles beyond the mission, so the elected undertaker would recite fragments of the Burial Service, the other mourners filling in where they could.

Once, a coffin got stuck halfway down because the grave was too narrow. The undertaker leaned in to see what was the matter and tipped right on top of it. We hoisted him up, then the coffin, and set about digging a wider hole. It happened again when our chemist, Mr Moore, disappeared into the bush, delirious, and was found days later in a dreadful state of putrefaction. When we lifted him, he simply fell apart. The air was blue and thick enough to cut. At the burial, our appointed undertaker masked his nausea with gin, then fell in the hole because he was tight!

There was a lot of drink at The Old Drift – understandable, what with the boredom and the savagery to keep at bay, to say nothing of the competitive sports: gambling, prospecting, surviving. But high as our death rate was, we were a cheery camp. If only I'd known the greatest threat to our beloved Deadrock was the railway bridge I had long anticipated. Where once we lived as brave pioneers, things were soon to become 'civilised' in the worst possible way.

When operations began on the foundations in 1904, I crossed the Zambesi to see what was what on its southern banks. I am proud to say I ate the first meal ever served at the Victoria Falls Hotel. This was at the start a long, simple structure of wood and iron, with a dining room and bar. At the most it housed twenty men, at 12/6d per day. Its logo was a lion and a sphinx – Cape to Cairo, Cecil Rhodes's dream for a railway line that would run vertically up the continent.

The chef at the hotel was a Frenchman, Marcel Mitton, a hunter and a former miner. The barman was an American from Chicago – an ex-prizefighter named Fred who refereed our frequent brawls. Arabs and coloured men served the guests with a servility bordering on sarcasm, then sent the Kaffirs scurrying to do their jobs for them. Management was a man named Pietro Gavuzzi, a Piedmontese who had worked at the Carlton and the Savoy in London, and then at the Grand in Bulawayo before coming here. You'd think he would have been better suited for life on the railway frontier but he was the sort of man who grew his own strawberries to garnish the dinner plates.

While the bridge was being built, an outside bar called the Iron & Timber was set up for the workmen. A rough lot, even for the wilds, and they made the hotel uncomfortable for those more sedate and worldly. Gavuzzi was scared out of his wits by their antics. Whenever he came in sight of the Iron & Timber, he got chased round the premises. If caught, he was made to stand drinks all round. Once, the assembly collared him and tucked him up onto the mantelpiece, commanding him to sing. Warble he did, like a wood pigeon! Gavuzzi had not the knack of taking such fun fondly.

The Italians around here generally went the pious route. The Waldensian missionaries – the Coïssons and the Jallas – built churches and schools, then retired back to Italy laden with children and wealth. They never went full native, as we say. That sort of consorting was frowned upon. I once met a Jewish trader with four native wives and a host of salt-and-pepper children – people regarded him as pretty low down. Any overtures from native men in the other direction led straight to the gallows. Nothing seethes the blood of most settlers more than the thought of racial contamination.

Like most Europeans, Gavuzzi had brought a wife with him, an English girl. I knew at first glance that Ada was a shopkeeper's daughter. Always slumping around with a hangdog look, slinging her daughter everywhere with her. That girl, Lina, a lass of five, had a vicious streak – this place had clearly got to her, as I soon learned directly.

One night, I was in the hotel dining room, making friends with the top men on the bridge project – surveyors and engineers, that sort of personage. I was down with fever, but I had run out of prints, you see, and serving as forwarding agent for Mopane Clarke's trading business had not proved lucrative. I wanted to open a photography studio on this side of the river. Withstanding the trembles and blur, I stood the occasional drink, downed several myself, and tried to charm the gentler men. Things were going swimmingly when in waltzed Gavuzzi with his funny hat and vest, to see a man about a bill. Ada, who did the accounts, was behind him, holding Lina by the hand.

Now, it was a dizzy room already, tobacco smoke bitter in the air, half-naked Kaffirs careening about on errands, besuited Arab monkeys bowing over drinks trays. My fever was running amok, I was fagged out, and I could hardly hear – my head was a right balloon. Gavuzzi was an irritating man in the best of circumstances, and then he provoked me by cutting in. I shouted him off, he turned on his heel, and as he stepped away, I grabbed his hat, almost as a prank. It came off his head easily, but my grip went a touch too far and a patch of his hair came off with it, pulled up by the root!

I stared at it in my hand, wondering if it was a wig and we were in Parliament. Gavuzzi stood in shock, his pate turning scarlet, then sat on the floor with a bark. Ada rushed over quick as she could, given her condition – she was expecting – and left Lina in the corner. Most whelps would have wept but Lina shrieked with fury and when an innocent native boy rushed by with a tray, she struck him! Knocked him flat! He was never right in the head again. He became an imbecile, forever smiling at the daisies.

＊

So much for drumming up funds for a studio. But I managed to procure a contract to photograph the bridge during the stages of its erection. And that's how I ended up joining Sir Charles Beresford Fox, the nephew of the bridge's designer, on a voyage to the bottom of the gorge. We climbed down the workers' ladders and then along the face of the sheer wall. It was perilous going, rocky and thorny. We got to within twenty feet of the base, tied a rope to a tree, and slid down.

We wandered along the bottom, clambering over rocks the size of my childhood home in Cambridge. Then the gorge narrowed to a thin ledge hanging over a rushing torrent. No exit.

We parted ways, feckless Fox pushing on while I headed back, having taken the snaps I wanted and wishing to get home by nightfall. As soon as I lost sight of my companion, a terrific explosion went off, sending rocks in all directions, one squarely at my head! Thankfully it missed and landed with a crash fifty yards away. Workers on the other end of the gorge had apparently set off their final blast of the day. By the time I got to the rope, I was too spent to climb. Willy-nilly, I was spending the night in that gorge.

I tied myself to a ledge and settled in. It was weird beyond description to lie in the dark, sensing the Falls without seeing them. The spray condensed and ran over me in rivulets. The mist floated round, moaning and whining, a faint whisper, a deep groan, the great roar swelling to thunder then dying again to a sibilant hush. I've often wondered how the guttural shout of the Falls can sometimes break off to sudden silence, like a thunderclap in a clear blue sky.

I lay there, thinking of all I had accomplished in Africa and all I had not, of Sir Charles and Fred 'Mopane' Clarke and what an extra 'e' on a name can do, of the suffocating grace of the high-born. Climbing down here for a mere spot of money had nearly brought death upon my head. I won't say my life passed before my eyes that night, but I barely slept for bitterness. When dawn broke at last, I raced up that rope.

I staggered the half-mile to camp and demanded a whisky and Fox's whereabouts. Turned out he'd had a far worse time than I. He found our rope but his hands slipped and he fell about a hundred feet. Fortune snatched him from death's jaws – he landed on a ledge. They'd had to crane him out. No broken bones but an awful shock, from which he never quite recovered. Meanwhile, I had already been reported dead, and the news sent back to Bulawayo. A truer freedom I never knew! Far better to be a dead man walking than a man on the run. An American born in the Kingdom of Hawai'i eventually dethroned me as Orpheus of the Gorge. When he climbed down, he was actually struck by a boulder from a blast – it only crushed his foot but he died the next day.

*

The railway was completed in 1904, the bridge in 1906, and the years following brought a host of official settlers. The British South Africa Company – Rhodes's imperial machine – owned The Old Drift and decided to move it to a sandy ridge six miles away. A drier, healthier spot, to be sure, but more importantly, closer to the rail. They renamed the town Livingstone, marked out 200 stands, some for government and some for settlers, and christened it capital of North-western Rhodesia. We dislocated pioneers could choose land wherever we liked, 6,000 acres at 3d per acre, and five years to pay it off. I got a permit for 2,000 acres but not wanting to compete with crafty old Mopane, I set up a curio shop across the river at Victoria Falls Town.

Decades later, they moved the capital of what became Northern Rhodesia 300 miles north to another dusty old town. This one was called 'Lusaaka' after a village headman and was built on a place called Manda Hill, which means graveyard: rather a fall in stature from 'Livingstone', I'd say. I tried to take the old permit I had bought in 1904 to the Lands Department Office in that new capital city. Could I perchance have my land in Livingstone? They laughed me out of the building. Ruled out by statute of limitations. Hardly startling – the white man's reign in Africa was already dying out by then.

✳

After I set up my shop, I went back home to marry Kate. We'd known each other umpteen years but she insisted now was the time for the shackling. A poker game won me eighty pounds, enough for the fare home. I must say, the English countryside seemed cramped quarters after my years in the veldt. My siblings barely recognised old P.M., emaciated and with a face-fungus in patches, reach-me-downs hanging off me – a fairly disreputable wisp of humanity I was! I received strict orders to scrape off the beard and make haste to the outfitters, cash in hand. The assistants took a peek at my 'slops' and offered me the lowest price. 'Nothing better?' I asked. Up we went by degrees, the timorous Tims and I. Finally, it dawned on them: the tough had money to burn. Out came the luxury goods!

We married on 15 February 1906 at Great St Andrew's Church, Cambridge. Shock and dismay that the daughter of the Cambridge

Clerk of the Peace had tied the knot to my bedraggled self! The Zambesi may as well be the Lethe: one plumb forgets the millstone the question of money ties around the neck in Merrie Old England. I was in such a dither that I neglected to give Kate my elbow as we left the vestry, which I suppose only proved my 'country manners'. We honeymooned in Devonshire, but I was determined to sail back to Africa, where we could live in proper style.

When we arrived at Victoria Falls Town some months later, I learned I had once again been taken for a Johnny the Mug – the bloke I had hired to keep my shop and home had sold my belongings out from under me. I never caught the rascal. I was brought to tears by the kindness of my lenders. All but one – he knows who he is – forgave my debts.

Dear Kate had to build us a home from the ground up, from the very dust. My hutment was her hutment, misfortune be damned. At night, she curled close to me as the hyenas made the nights hideous with unremittent howling. One ached to hear them take two bars rest. Kate even shared my vigils when a leopard stole our chickens – we sat up, our nerves taut as banjo strings, hardly breathing until I shot the beast, fat as a stall-fed pig. Mostly she darned while I fished.

Once a week, we took a canoe across to Livingstone for a night out. Old Mopane had moved his trading company there and opened a bar and a couple of hotels. He always knew how to take advantage of a situation, even on shifting grounds. On our way to dinner or dancing, Kate and I would walk by his bar, and I'd peek in. The same old story: all classes from barrister to bricklayer tossing for drinks at the bar, singing raucous songs, and many a man laid out on benches. Naturally, I missed it, but ah, I was no longer a bachelor, roaming wide and handsome. I was a family man now, knee-halted and married – and happy! We were expecting, you see.

The great event drew near, preparations were made, and out popped a boy with a lovely head of black hair. He lived only a few minutes. Kate was nigh swallowed in grief. We kept tame guinea fowl in our yard and she often mistook their calls for his cry. We buried 'Jimmy' in the grounds of the Victoria Falls Hotel, there being no consecrated land. But remarks were made that touched us on the raw – I won't say who made them – so we reburied 'Jimmy' in our garden.

A year later, another child came early. There was a terrific storm that night, thunder trundling across the sky and a torrential downpour – seven inches in six hours! Staying dry was impossible: the thatch was an open net, the floor an ankle-deep swamp. Kate was feverish, I furious with anxiety. Time stomped on, heavy-footed. Well, the medico knew his job; my worry just made him seem slow. This time it was a girl. But we have two sons now, one named Victor to record our association with the Falls.

✳

With my curios and pictorial postcards, the shop did a roaring trade, and as the years passed, the flood of excursionists put us on a fair footing. I saw an opportunity and started some transport companies: canoe, cart, trolley, rickshaw. The Victoria Falls Hotel stole each of those ideas straight from my pocket! The Rhodesian Railway Company owned it now and management was an excitable Welshman, always fuming about. I liked to smoke my pipe in his office to fumigate him further – to my detriment. When I refused to lower my price of a half-crown per head, he bought the rickshaw company out from under me! They still have the gall to sell my guidebook in the hotel giftshop. I do seem plagued by the unpunishable crimes of others.

But luck comes with lawlessness, too, and I did finally earn my due. In 1907, a shooting club was formed at Victoria Falls Town. Government issued us rifles and ammunition at a cut rate and the prize was a silver cup for the best score over six months. Some of the shooters got wanderlust; others gave up or left; at the end of six months, I was the only one competing. I beat the top score in a rather amusing fashion. One afternoon, I was out hunting pheasants and I spotted a pig moving through the bush. Up went my barrel, and I let him have it. There was a yell, and a nigger jumped up in the air and disappeared. Here was my 'pig'! I saw at once what was what. The boy had been sent to cut grass but he had been loitering in a *donga*, or ditch. Fearing I'd report him, he had cut for it, stooping low to escape notice, but not quite low enough – just about as low as the back of a young pig.

I found the boy unconscious, a crowd already standing around. I patched him up and sent for a doctor and set off for home. I soon became aware that a pair of native police constables were walking behind me.

'What the blazes are you on about?' I demanded.

'We were told to bring you in to the police station,' came the stilted reply.

This got my goat. Native police are never sent to take in a white. Had they no respect?

'You had better get,' I yelled, 'unless you want to get shot too!'

They got. Naturally, I reported to the colonial police myself. By the greatest of good fortune, I was not asked to produce my shooting licence – I didn't have one! Anyway, the boy suffered no great damage. Native hide is thick and the shot hadn't penetrated any vitals. The medic didn't even bother to remove the shrapnel embedded in the skin of his back, which left a pimply sort of rash. There followed months of ribbing *me*, however. 'Who shot the pig? What's the price of pork?' As it turned out, by the strangest coincidence, the native's name was 'N'gulubu', which means none other than 'pig'!

Skip ahead two years, and a native boy walks through my front gate. All a-grin. Familiar.

'Go round the back!' I shout – natives were not allowed to use the front entrance.

He stays where he is, grinning to the wind like a numbskull. It's the village idiot, I realise. The one the Italian girl, Lina, had struck down in the dining room. Imagine this:

'I'm N'gulubu,' says he and turns around to show me the Braille in his back.

'Oh, are you?' says I. 'Well, here's ten bob for you.'

Off he goes, fit as a fiddle and just as merry. Everyone was satisfied. Certainly I was: I had peppered a nig for ten bob – and got a shooting cup for it! It just goes to show – if I hadn't been down with the shakes in the first place, I'd have never snatched Gavuzzi's wig, Lina would have never struck that boy, he wouldn't have misjudged his crouch, and I'd have nabbed neither pig nor prize!

✳

Every manner of visitor has braved the establishment of 'Mr Percy M. Clark, ARPS, FRGS, FRES', the oldest curio shop at Victoria Falls. Colonel Frank Rhodes and I talked long hours about his father, whose funeral procession I had photographed. In 1916, I was appointed official photographer to Lord Buxton and two future governors: Sir Cecil Rodwell of Southern Rhodesia and Sir Herbert Stanley of Northern Rhodesia – the two lands were finally divvied up. Sir Stewart Gore-Browne paid us many a visit – a strange man, and too free with the blacks by a mile, but our hospitality was well worth it: he helped us find sponsors for the children's education in England. I don't know if they will return, but Africa is in their blood.

I have seen this continent pass into dire civilisation. Where once one might hump one's blankets and step into the unknown, there's no unknown no more, as they say. Where once one might tramp toilsomely to gain a few meagre miles a day, now the motor car speeds by and the aeroplane growls overhead. Months stride past in an hour. There is no romance left here. I have seen moving pictures of the once shy and unapproachable Pigmy tribes of the Congo riding around in lorries. This new Africa may be of interest to those who frequent the closer-packed, noisier places in the world. But a greater, more profound noise rings in my ears just across from where I write – the Victoria Falls still keeps her vast and unchanging glory.

As for The Old Drift, which once had the dignity of a place on the map – well, it has been swallowed by swamp. I have chosen to put down roots at Victoria Falls Town, and here I will rot. But I still visit the old stomping grounds across the Zambesi now and again. All that remains is the cemetery: a dozen tumbled-down gravemarkers in the bush, dated between 1898 and 1908, some of the inscriptions eaten away by rain. It is a queer thing to wander the stones and call the roll of the dead and think on those poor crumbling sods. I read their names as warning shots:

Georges Mercier! John Neil Wilson! Alexander Findlay! Ernest Collins! Miss E. Elliott! Samuel Thomas Alexander! David Smith! Unknown! Unknown! Unknown! Unknown! Unknown! Unknown! Unknown! Unknown! Unknown! Unknown! Unknown! Unknown! Unknown! Unknown!

Miles south of Livingstone's final abode, above the Falls he renamed for his queen, just before the river takes its furious plunge, lie the stillest waters of the Zambezi and the stilled bodies of those who dared settle there. Ah, Ye Olde Drifte! Over the years, it went from passage to place and eventually gave way to a grave. This is where we live: on the tip of the tongue of the air, full of secrets – black fever, marsh fever, tertian ague *– and more than eager to squeal them.*

And who are we? Thin troubadours, the bare ruinous choir, a chorus of gossipy mites. Uncanny the singing that comes from certain husks. Neither gods nor ghosts nor spirits nor sprites, we're the effect of an elementary principle: with enough time, a swarm will evolve a conscience. Thus we've woven a worldly wily web, contrived a hive mind, if you will. Spindle bodies strung in a net of spacetime. Interested. Hmming along.

We've been needling you for centuries untold. Or perhaps we should say centuries told: you certainly love your stories. Your earliest tales were of animals, of course, beastly fables carved into cave walls. Well, it's time to turn the fables, we say, time for us to tell you what we know. A swarm is but a loose net of knots. We hang, an elastic severalty. Our song is the same: the notes we sing, like a plaintive erhu, *form a weird and coordinate harmony.*

All together at once is how a swarm sees but you humans go beginning to end. And so we recount each act in its turn: pace by pace, cause and effect, each and every flutter and tumble. Be patient and listen, no hurries, no worries, point by point, we outline the doctrine: to err is human, and that is your doom and delight. Even frivolous fairy tales *come from* fae, *from* fata *('the Fates'),* fatum *(Fate), 'the destiny which they have spoken'.*

You have now heard the note of one Percy M. Clark, a wanderer, a brute, a cad, the forefather who started it all. He called himself an Old Drifter but he didn't learn our lesson – his hand grasped a tad too tight. A slip and a clutch, a cry and a fall, and one child strikes another. That tiny chaos, like one of our wings, sets in motion the unwitting cycle: it will spiral across families for generations to come, spurring Fate's furious cataract . . .

I
The Grandmothers

Sibilla

1939

At first, they didn't know. It was disguised by the motley silt of the womb, those red strands marbling the white scud of the vernix, and they were distracted by the baby's cries and the task of severing the twisty blue link to its mother. The midwives passed the baby to its grandmother, whose name was Giovanna. She held it, noted that it was female, and used her pinkie to swipe a cross into its grimy forehead. Only then did Giovanna peer closer – what's this? Hair. Long, dark, sticky swirls of hair all over the stippled skin of her first and only granddaughter.

The midwives were still circling the mother's shipwrecked body, tending to her, murmuring like the sea, the child's cries like that same sea breaking. Giovanna swaddled the baby in elaborate folds and handed the burden to its bearer. The mother, whose name was Adriana, looked down at the hairy little face and promptly fainted. Giovanna grabbed the baby just before it tumbled off the bed. The midwives laughed. Such drama! The wool would fall out. The whelp had just forgotten to eat it in the womb.

Adriana woke to firm entreaties that she breastfeed. She took the baby into her arms. The hair seemed to have already grown longer and darker. Through it, she could just about see a purple hole opening and closing, letting out a mewling sound. Fine. Go on. Her fingers wrangled with the baby's lips over the nipple until it latched. The baby sucked noisily. The hair on its face shivered with the pulse of its mouth and Adriana stroked it, crying softly at its warmth.

Giovanna and Adriana bundled the baby up, bundled it home, and kept it there. They waited. But despite the midwives' promises, the hair didn't fall out or wipe away. So they began to cut it, Giovanna with great avidity, Adriana with cowed carefulness. It grew back thick and fast, as if unravelling from the knot in the belly or the cowlick on the chest, a dark drain into which Adriana's eyes often spiralled as she breastfed, wondering who or what was to blame for this curse.

*

The child's father was a man named Giacomo Gavuzzi and there were reasons to suspect that he carried hectic blood. In 1888, his father, a hotelier named Pietro Gavuzzi, had sailed from Italy to England to learn the trade. He'd picked up a wife in London and carted her off, pregnant, to the middle of Africa in 1899. Lina was born on the way, in the middle of the Kalahari. Giacomo was born six years later. After stints at the Grand Hotel Bulawayo and then at the Victoria Falls Hotel, Pietro had hoisted them all up again and dragged them around the world for a time – the Savoy in London again, the Plaza in Buenos Aires. The Gavuzzi family had finally returned to Piedmont in the early 1920s.

So much migration at such an early age lent the Gavuzzi children a slapdash worldliness. They had money but their education was poor, their manners poorer. When Lina came of age, she married a local governor in Alba and moved into his family estate, Villa Serra. Her younger brother Giacomo never quite settled down. Rootless, restless, he became a professional malingerer. Like the other men in Alba with empty heads and idle hands, Giacomo spent his days drinking and recovering from drink, mostly at his sister's home, where he knew he would be waited upon in style. That was how he met Adriana, who worked there as a domestic servant. It was not a serious affair and everyone knew Giacomo had left his seed in more than one woman in Alba. Of these, Adriana was the only one who had birthed a baby covered with hair.

Maybe Giacomo Gavuzzi was not to blame. But Adriana vowed that she would not name their daughter, as was customary, after his mother, Ada – not an Italian name, anyway, and too recognisable in a town as small as Alba, and suspiciously like her own name besides. Instead, Adriana named the baby after an oracle card, the kind that you use to read Tarot. She found it at Villa Serra while washing dishes. It was stuck to the base of a wine glass, which she had upturned to pour out the syrupy remainder of Barbera. The card was large and creased and had a sketch of a stout dame in a feathered hat rebuking an aristocratic fellow. In florid script across the top it said *Contrarietà* and, across the bottom, *Dispiacere*.

The moment Adriana read it, she felt the sharp knuckly clutch of her first contraction. She gasped a curse and crossed herself. She took a breath and continued to wash dishes as contractions quaked over her until it became clear this was the event she had been anticipating. It was time to head to the house on the outskirts of town where midwives served the less fortunate. As she shuffled towards the back door of the kitchen, Adriana decided – or rather the decision made itself. To name a child Displeasure was obviously to ask for it, so she chose the word on the back of the card. *Sibilla*.

*

Little Sibilla grew up well loved and close-kept. She lived with her mother and grandmother in an old hunting cabin in the woods, which she was not permitted to leave. The cabin was only one small room but for practical reasons, Sibilla slept in her own bed, with a white sheet that grew webbed each night and a pillow that rose with her every morning, her tangles having netted it like a fish. Her hair, as it grew, was thin and straight and dark, a brown that yearned to be black. It gave off warmth and shine and smell – a mixture of the food they ate and the lard soap they used.

By the time she was four, Sibilla had learned the general pattern of her hair's growth. The hair on her crown and face were the same, as if her scalp simply continued down her forehead and cheeks, skirting the eyes and the lips. The hair on her arms, legs and torso was longer. Every day, it grew until it matched her height – if you suspended it from her body, it would form a sphere. Sibilla had some hairless patches, which she cherished, counting them off every night as she went to sleep, a rosary of mercy: navel, nipples, ears, soles, palms, the spaces between the toes and the fingers. She did not realise it yet but her genitals were bare too.

While Sibilla's mother was at work, her grandmother took care of her. Giovanna washed Sibilla and fed her, pruned her like a zealous gardener and burned the daily pile of hair outside to fertilise her tomato garden. Giovanna taught Sibilla numbers and letters and everything she knew about what was visible from their one window: the Lanaro river; the hulking Castello di Monticello d'Alba with its square, round and octagonal towers; *le Alpi* in the distance. Giovanna told her granddaughter stories about Gianduja the peasant, with his tricorn hat, red and brown jacket and his *duja* of beer, lovely Giacometta always sitting on his knee.

As Giovanna aged and her mind and eyes began to cloud, she often forgot to cut Sibilla's hair. Instead, she would place her granddaughter on the floor between her knees and oil and comb and braid her hair for hours on end, humming folk songs. Sometimes, she would part paths into the overall scalp and string the hairs out to the furniture to make a web, Sibilla a placid spider in the midst of it. When Adriana found them like this, she would glare sulkily at them and proceed to make their meagre dinner. 'Games,' she would mutter with longing and disgust.

＊

Towards the end of the war, a resistance army swept into Alba and formed a Partisan Republic against Mussolini. The Partisans – *paesani* and defected soldiers – took over the wealthier homes and during a drunken brawl at Villa Serra, Signora Lina's husband ended up skewered on the tip of a dagger. Lina fell into a terrible, self-consuming grief. The *domestici* drifted away – all but Adriana. She needed the pay and she felt attached to the family: Giacomo wouldn't admit it, and Lina never mentioned it, but little Sibilla had Gavuzzi blood. So Adriana continued to clean at Villa Serra and to care for Signora Lina until the widow climbed out of her mourning.

After the short-lived Partisan occupation, the Fascists retook Alba and they too invited themselves into the villas for hot food and clean women. Being forced to serve as a hostess once again – for the other side this time – revived Lina's spirits. She had no political convictions to speak of so she gladly took in the well-heeled Fascists, who lavished her with finery and flattery. When the war ended, she kept on throwing parties at Villa Serra. It was a way to forget. Four years on, Signora Lina lived solely for the taste of whisky and the pleasure of watching strangers desultorily destroy her home every night. Adriana patiently set about resurrecting it every morning, righting overturned furniture, wiping wet puddles, scraping dry ones. Life would have gone on this way if the Signora had not, with a casual remark, upset the balance.

Adriana was cleaning the parlour one morning while Lina swanned around, lazily hunting for a cigarette, the bottom edge of her green robe sending toppled wine glasses rolling in circles.

'You,' said the Signora, pausing her perambulation to peer curiously at her maid. 'You do not smile any more?'

Adriana was tugging open a burgundy curtain and she hid her sigh under the humming cloth and the rattling rail. She considered. When had she last smiled?

'Your job is the same. You clean.' The Signora picked up a dirty fork from a table and carried it to another. 'My job is the same. I make things for you to clean.' She picked up a dirty plate from the second table and carried it to the first. 'It is a good system, sì?'

'Sì, Signora.' Adriana thought of the rotting duck she'd found in the toilet earlier, the line of ants investigating it, joining one by one a tiny floating raft of their dead comrades.

'So.' The Signora plopped herself in an armchair. 'More mopping, less moping.'

'Sì, Signora.' Adriana knelt to wash the window.

'You are looking fat as well.' The Signora's voice sharpened: 'Did you have a baby?'

'Sì—' Adriana paused. Her lower lip folded into her mouth.

Sibilla was now nine years old. It was one thing to pretend the girl was not a Gavuzzi but ... The Signora was now murmuring a string of old grievances – that her husband had been killed by those rough men and ... Adriana's arm mechanically wiped the window as she looked out at the valley. It was furry with forest and blocked with houses, half erased by mist. She thought of Sibilla's eyebrows, which were darker than the rest of the hair on her forehead and the exact same shape as Giacomo's – and the Signora's, for that matter. Adriana lowered her arm and closed her eyes. Was it possible that the Signora didn't know that Sibilla even existed? Unconsciously, Adriana swayed forward and her forehead hit the window with a small thud.

'Oh!' said the Signora with surprise.

Adriana opened her mouth to speak but a broken cry came out instead. She began to sob.

'Oh,' said the Signora with irritation.

Adriana hastened to apologise but the Signora was already on her feet and stalking from the room, the sweeping train of her robe knocking over a bowl of hazelnuts. There was no room in Villa Serra for anyone else's grief. Adriana wept anyway, fiercely, freely, relishing the privacy. When she wiped her eyes and blinked around, noon had filled the room.

Adriana jumped up and cleaned the rest of the parlour. She finished with the writing desk, polishing it until its scratches were scattered needles of shine. Then she searched in its drawers for pen and paper and wrote a note.

> My most beloved Signora,
>   Yes I did have a baby she has nine years but she is un-formed not a child of the Lord Almighty Our Saviour so I do not smile but my behaviour distressed you I did see so I beg of you to let me remain in your employ.
>   Yours in obedience,
>   Adriana

Adriana stared at the note, then folded it several times, trying to make it as unobtrusive as possible, but the more she folded, the thicker and stupider it seemed. Finally, a paper-cut finger in her mouth, she backed away from the damp lump dumbly reflecting itself on the desk.

*

As for the un-formed herself, Sibilla had begun her day as usual. She woke to the sound of her grandmother's snores and to the sight of a blur that slowly crystallised into a thicket. She got out of bed, stepping out of nets of hair, then wrapped it around her waist and rustled over to the hearth. Her mother had made breakfast before leaving for the Signora's. Sibilla sat down and tucked the hair from her face behind her ears. She took mincing bites of her porridge to avoid swallowing any hair and stared out the window. It was ... raining? Sibilla peered and blew upward – a waft of breath would lift her hair and grant her a better glimpse.

Sibilla had observed hair on other people. Nonna had kinky white curls that crept outward from her head when it rained, haloing her frowning face. And Mama got hairier when she washed their clothes, the fuzz on her arms darkening with that first plunge into water. This was reassuring. They have hair too, Sibilla thought. Mine is just longer. But Sibilla didn't like her hair. It felt like a part of her but also apart from her. Which was what Nonna had said when Sibilla had asked where babies come from. This was more helpful than what Mama had said, which was 'You don't want to know.'

But Sibilla did want to know. She wanted to know everything. Over time, she had learned to put together the things she already knew, to see how they fit. Like: Mama didn't smile and she worked all the time. Or: Nonna couldn't see well and Sibilla couldn't see well, but not for the same reason. Or: there were day dangers and night dangers and both came from outside. But Sibilla still yearned to go outside, more than anything. She asked Nonna every day if she could, hoping her pleas would one day slip between the widening cracks in the old woman's mind.

Today, for example, Sibilla wanted to know if it was in fact raining out there. She turned to ask but Nonna was still asleep, eyebrows raised in faint surprise, wrinkles ashiver with every whistling snore. Sibilla pushed porridge around her plate. Her grandmother didn't usually sleep in this late. But last night, Nonna and Mama had had a seething fight. Sibilla had woken to them whisper-shouting across the room. It seemed that Nonna thought Sibilla ought to spend more time outside; Mama thought this was too risky. *Danger, danger, growing girl, sun and air, never ever, don't you know, of course I know* – the voices rose and rose and broke – *you have no idea what they would do to her ...*

Sibilla looked through her hair darkly, putting some things together. Outside the house was the same as inside the house, just not as safe. But if Nonna thought she could go outside, it couldn't be *that* dangerous ... Sibilla found herself at the door of the cabin, as if transported.

She stared at its rough surface. The key turned (a click, a glance backward). The handle turned (a creak, another glance). The door swung open. Sibilla and the world met for the first time.

✳

Villa Serra was ripe with the smell of conquered rot. Adriana gathered her coat, her bag and her thoughts. These last, as usual, were of her daughter – she sometimes felt as if Sibilla was still inside her and she often dreamt of the birth: the midwives pulling the baby out, the long black threads from which it hung like a puppet slowly lengthening ... Adriana shuddered and shook off the image as she locked the back door and stomped heavily down the steps – she *was* fat. When had that happened?

Outside Villa Serra, the trees had started to tantrum, shaking their bushy heads – a storm was coming. Adriana cursed quietly, touching her fingers to her head and each of her breasts in turn. She never cursed out loud, only under her breath, and she always made the sign of the cross to nullify it. She'd been doing this since she was a girl but nobody had ever noticed it before Giacomo.

She had been working at Villa Serra for a few weeks when she first ran into him at the butcher's. Giacomo had been leaning against the pole of the stall, smoking. Adriana greeted him with the deference due to the Signora's brother, and though he greeted her back, she saw a vagueness in his eyes – there were many young maids at Villa Serra before the war. She began to haggle with the butcher over a rind of meat. When he refused to lower his price, Adriana cursed softly, her pursed fingers dabbing her forehead and chest. Giacomo noticed and laughed.

'This is very charming,' he slurred at her from his lazy lean. That was the beginning.

The end came months later and it was wretched. It was the usual story: Giacomo drifted away; Adriana tried to keep him. She even resorted to spells, each more desperate than the last. She wrote his name on a slip of paper and put it under a rock. She collected his semen, baked it in a cake and ate it. She stood between a candle and a wall and spoke an incantation to her shadow: *all other women are like mud, I am as beautiful as the moon.* She plucked out her hair and stole his and braided it together.

Adriana didn't like to remember this last piece of sorcery: secretly culling the strands from his comb when he was in the other room, her hairline retreating to pale cul-de-sacs, the gentle braid of love turning to a ball of fur in her pocket. Worst of all was the horror in his eyes when he found it – which turned into a kind of peaceable regret when she confessed to him that she was pregnant.

'You cannot leave me,' she whispered, gripping his arm. 'You cannot leave your child!'

His eyebrows rose, then lowered. 'What child?' He turned away and lit a cigarette.

＊

Sibilla paused on the threshold of the cabin, looking at the sky. It was a piercing blue with a few lowhanging clouds, each edged with the blaze of the sun. She was mainly struck by how big the sky was. It didn't seem that big from the inside. The wind stroked the hair on her face, then tickled her, then suddenly snuck around and blew at her from behind, raising the hairs on her body until they were streaming in front of her. She stood stock-still, arms locked at her sides, as her hairs flurried ahead, tugging at her, pulling her trotting along until she was outside the house.

She could see so far! To the right was Nonna's tomato garden: knobs of red and yellow and green flesh dangling from vines. To the left was the valley: terraced villas and tangles of hazel trees in the distance. The sun spun its fingers through the clouds. As if beckoned, Sibilla stepped forward. And as if in reply, the door swung shut behind her. She spun around and pulled its handle but it stayed shut – it needed to be pushed from this side. But how was she to know that, having never been on the other side of the door – of any door – before?

Sibilla groaned and pulled to no avail. Above her, the sun curled its fingers back inside a cloud and darkness fell over the valley. She turned around with frustration and found herself in the midst of a cyclone. Spiralling gusts sent hair whipping back and forth, under and around her. She squatted down, gathering to her naked body what hairs she could.

❋

As Adriana reached the switchbacks in the road to the forest, she pulled her collar high against the wind. The Signora had given her this coat. Adriana would probably pass it down to Sibilla someday and they would have to string the girl's hair through the sleeves so it spilled out at the cuffs like the *spaventapasseri* that scared the birds from the tomato garden. Adriana tutted. What a waste!

She loved this coat: it was woollen and warm and had purple satin lining. Sometimes, in the brief amnesia of waking up, she would catch a glimpse of its insides gleaming from where it hung on the cabin wall and her eyes would slide hungrily along its surface. It reminded her of Giacomo's slippery inner lip. Had this been her downfall – this desire to touch beautiful things with her hand, her tongue? Maybe it was her arrogance, the idea that she had the right to touch anything at all.

The rain came. Pulling her collar over her head now, Adriana ducked under the cover of the trees, glancing warily at the terraced vineyards above the road. The rain could easily make precipitous mud out of the soil. She thought of the fable Giovanna liked to tell Sibilla, about the *villa* and the *borgo* near the Castello di Monticello, how one year the rains were so heavy, the roads had turned to liquid mud that coursed down and seeped into the peasants' homes, and the rough mud-dwellers and the rich bean-heads had shouted at each other all night until ...

Adriana stepped in a puddle. She cursed and crossed herself. As she walked on, water squelching from the hole in the toe, she began to calculate if she could afford the cobbler, her fingers twitching with ghostly enumeration. Everything cost so much these days. The war had swelled the world with want. It had made everything rare and therefore precious.

❋

Sibilla's chest was heaving. She wanted to go back inside and wait for Nonna to wake up, but she was afraid to stand up in this fierce wind.

Sometimes, hair would flap out from her body and she would slowly reel it back in. After a while, it wasn't so bad to crouch in the wind, waiting. She examined the blades of grass between her feet, which were different from the wilty clumps her mother had brought inside to show her. The sky was grey now but this outside grass was the greenest green she'd ever seen, and it shivered in the wind like Nonna's sleeping face.

When the wind finally died down, Sibilla stood and wrapped her hair around her waist, crossing her arms to keep it taut. Then she stepped forward gingerly, trying not to trip over the hairs ambushing her feet, and followed the trail of grass. At first she looked at the ground, but as she gained confidence, she began to look up, to smell and hear more. After a few minutes of walking, she found herself in a grove of tall trees with rough bark and spiky branches. She circled one. It exhaled a peppery scent. She parted the hairs on her face so she could lick its bark.

She only noticed the raindrops pattering the crown of her head when a heavier one struck her there. She looked up and saw three sets of lines crossing each other: her hair, the tree needles, and rain. Again something struck her, this time on her back, then fell to the ground. But if rain was hard, why didn't the roof of the cabin break, or the window?

'*Mostro! Mostro!*'

Sibilla looked over her shoulder. Between the tall thick trees of the grove were four shorter skinnier trees. She peered as they melted into stumps and then rapidly grew again, their branches spinning wildly. Her eyes sprang wide as she saw the stones whipping towards her.

✳

If war had introduced the rich to the panic of an empty stomach, survival had bred a new luxury among the poor. After Signora Lina's husband had died, when the other servants had left Villa Serra and the rations had begun to run low, she had come to depend entirely on Adriana. Adriana knew how to squeeze the last droplets from a cow's teat, how to combine them with an egg for a meal, how to make gruel from the grains the Signora had once scattered for the birds. The Signora compensated Adriana for these skills with beautiful, inedible things: the coat with the purple satin lining, the watch with a spiral face that lay on Giovanna's wrist like a snail, the necklace of bluegreen glass beads that Adriana kept inside her pillow, an oriental vase that held in its belly dust and an awful silence.

This secondhand collection had become stained and chipped over the years but Adriana kept them stored in her mind with their original shape and integrity. She sometimes played a game in her mind, in which she would have to choose one of these objects over another, or over all the rest, or over a member of her family. Of course, Adriana would never really relinquish a person for a thing. It was just an amusement. But this *gesto di bilancia* arose more often these days, beyond her will, almost the inevitable punctuation to her thoughts when she was alone.

Once, in exchange for four baked roots, Signora Lina had handed Adriana a lump wrapped in wax paper. Adriana only dared unwrap it at home. Giovanna stood beside her, peering at Adriana's hands. Little Sibilla stood beneath them both, sniffing upward, hair pulsing into her nostrils. Adriana peeled open the paper, the scent of spice and lavender pouring out, and after a pause, they all reached for it, six hands clashing. It tumbled to the floor, denting itself there. Sibilla, closest to the ground, grabbed for it but couldn't get a grip – it caked the hair on her hands and sprang away again. Adriana swooped down with a *tsk* and picked it up as gently as she would an egg.

'*Non sai come tenere le cose belle,*' she snapped. 'You don't know how to hold nice things.'

✳

'*Mostro!*' the boys shouted and bent to pick up more stones.

Sibilla turned and ran, wincing as hair caught under her tread. The wind sent strands down her throat as she panted and she could barely see, but she could tell that she was running downhill and that the ground was softening. Her feet abruptly went ice cold and wet. She gasped and hopped backwards and turned. The boys were walking towards her. She knew they were boys but stared at their clothes with curiosity – she had only seen trousers and vests in a picture book of Gianduja. Two of the boys were carrying big branches. They stopped a few feet away from her. One boy's branch lost a piece of bark and it fell in the leaves with a rustle. Sibilla willed herself to stop shaking.

'*Mostro*,' one boy said again and the others laughed, their breath feathering the air.

Then she realised that she wasn't the only one shaking – they were, too, their laughter was shaking. They are feeling what I am feeling, she thought, and just then her hair began to rise.

✳

The truth was, Adriana had claimed the soap for herself before it even fell to the floor. It was impractical to use anything but tallow on Sibilla, and a waste to use it on a wrinkled old woman. Adriana kept it for herself, using it sparingly: birthdays, saints' days, at the end of her menses. She would drag the metal tub behind the cabin and fill it with heated water. Then she would strip off her clothes and lower herself into the steaming bath and spin piles of ornate lace with the soap, making baroque circles over her body with her palms. Like a woman, she would think. Like a real woman.

Over time, the soap dwindled and dulled and formed cracks like a desiccated fruit seed. It grew so thin that it slipped between her fingers into the water, where it would lose even more silky layers, a cycle of diminishment that filled her with anguish. To use it was to lose it. How strange, she thought now as she reached the short uphill path that led through the woods to the cabin. That soap had once seemed an extravagance – a thing that smelled like *gianduja* chocolate and felt like satin lining and gave you licence to touch your own skin and still feel clean. How had it become a need?

✳

Long strands of hair streamed out from Sibilla's body. She could see better like this and she noticed that the boys' hair sat greasy on their heads. The trees in the distance were not stirring, either. So what was lifting her hairs up this way? She saw the boys wonder the same thing. They glanced at each other and slowly began to back away, their eyes widening as her hair rotated to the front of her body until it was pointing directly at them. They stepped backward faster and faster until one of them stumbled over a root and cried out. Then they all turned and ran.

Sibilla's hair was streaming before her as it had when she had first stepped outside that morning. But this time, rather than drag her forward, it swung back and roped her into the water behind her. The shock of cold squeezed her eyes shut. When she opened them again, she saw the metal grey sky through the water. It warped under the cascade of a wave, then a swathe of her hair soared across her vision, languid as *melassa*. Individual threads of hair came into view, bubbles stringing each strand like Mama's glass bead necklace, each bubble bearing a miniature reflection of Sibilla's face. The small Sibillas blinked in unison.

Just then, the sole of her foot touched the riverbed and instinct sent all her concentration into her ankle. She bent her knee and propelled herself up, hair streaming down with the force of her skyward dive. Her head broke the surface and she gasped for air but her mouth was stoppered. She shook her head until there was enough of a crack between the thick falls of hair to breathe, then grabbed at a branch and pulled herself out of the water. She felt her hair tugging her back in so she began hauling it towards her, lock by lock, before it tried to swim off or drown her.

When she had finally lugged it all out of the currents, she found herself kneeling on the shore of a tumbling river. This must be the Lanaro. Nonna had pointed out flashes of it from the cabin window. Sibilla parted her hair with shrinkled fingers to examine herself in its surface. The water was choppy but she didn't notice the zigzag. She was mainly struck by how small she looked in her reflection. She didn't feel that small from the inside.

✳

When Adriana arrived home that day, she found her mother seated on a chair by the hearth and her daughter kneeling on the floor beside her. Giovanna was rocking and sobbing. Sibilla was silent, stroking her grandmother's knee with a heavy-looking paw. And they were both surrounded by a muddy, gritty spill of hair, more hair, Adriana exclaimed, than she had ever seen, though in truth that was what she often said when she came home from a hard day at work.

Sibilla told the story in bursts like gunfire: the door, the wind, the boys, the river. The rest of the evening was consumed with washing the girl's hair – with fetching water from the well with a tin can that bled drops from a hole in a fixed beat that counted the seconds till dawn. Guiltily, Adriana used the rest of the fancy soap to wash it. Sibilla and Giovanna both tried to help but the young girl's fingers were too involved and the old woman's too shaky. Eventually, they both fell asleep.

Adriana alone sat up late into the night with Sibilla's hair across her lap, extricating pine needles and rocks and dead insects from it. By the time she was done, the hair was huge with handling, fluffy and grey as smoke. She felt an urge as strong as a contraction to reach inside and pull her daughter out. Instead, she watched through the window as the sun rose behind the mists of Alba. Then she woke Sibilla up, wrapped her in sackcloth, and took her to Villa Serra.

1948

The Signora's green robe wafted gently over the threshold. She was calling over her shoulder down the corridor behind her. 'I'll be right back, Colonnello Corsale. I cannot imagine who is visiting so late. Or so early, rather,' she chuckled. The Signora turned. 'Oh, hello.'

'Signora.'

'But this is the front door—' The Signora's chin lifted. 'And what have we here?'

Sibilla looked up through her hair at the women exchanging words and gestures over her head. Mama had been forceful on their walk here, but now that they had arrived, she seemed fearful. She kept plucking at the sackcloth covering Sibilla. Impatient and hot, Sibilla tossed her head to unhood herself, and blew a puff of air to clear her vision. The Signora started. Her eyes went green and wide, then black and thin.

'I see,' she said curtly. 'Come on then.' She spun and walked back into the house.

Adriana and Sibilla followed her down a corridor to a room the size of their entire home. This room was dimly lit – the curtains were drawn and only a few squat candles guttered in the corners – and it looked like a storm had passed through, knocking things over, scattering mess everywhere. Sibilla was ordered to sit on a velvet stool before a velvet chair, in which was seated the largest person she'd ever seen. He looked like a taller, thicker tree than the ones who had thrown stones at her, or as Mama was now calling them, *i demoni*. The big man listened, his black moustache teetering with curiosity. This was reassuring, as were the bright buttons on his jacket, and the way his fingers massaged the air when he spoke. For some reason, Sibilla desperately wanted to sit on his knee. As if sensing this, he turned to her.

'Do you know,' he said in a deep voice that made his moustache buzz, 'whenever a draught blows through here, your hair is like the ribbons of a Chinese dancer.'

'What is a Chinese?' she asked.

'Ah! What a question! You know,' he remarked to the Signora, who was stretched out on a chaise longue. 'It really *is* a question now, after the war.'

The Signora murmured vaguely, then stood up and wandered off, stepping casually over the mess on the floor. Sibilla wanted to ask more about wars and ribbons and the Chinese but the man was too busy admiring the Signora from behind as she departed, and Mama was no longer Mama. She had become a blinky, twitchy thing, rising halfway from her seat when the Signora returned with a tray of drinks. The Signora handed Sibilla one filled with something clear and sweet and fizzy. It bit Sibilla's tongue and stranded ticklish bubbles above her lips and her interest narrowed to figuring out how to drink it politely. By the time it was finished, her fate had been decided.

Sibilla would live at Villa Serra with the Signora, for 'safety', and she would help her mother clean every day, for 'personal development'. On his part, the Colonel would write to a doctor friend of his about her 'condition'. Sibilla was about to ask about her *nonna* when the Colonel stretched his hand out to her. She extended her hairless palm to shake. But then his other hand rose and he reached them both towards her face. Sibilla glanced at her mother, who nodded gravely. Her fists at her sides, Sibilla tipped her face up to the Colonel. He put his palms to her cheeks and smoothed the hair back. She could see his eyes glinting from the caves under his bushy eyebrows, a mole winking from behind a fork of his moustache. He grunted and stretched her hair back harder, pulling it tight across her face. Sibilla winced and exhaled bravely.

'Yes,' the Colonel's moustache buzzed. 'Now I can see you.'

'Enough,' the Signora flustered between them. 'It is time to show the girl her quarters.'

These were in the kitchen larder, a tall, narrow room that smelled of wheat and coffee and vinegar. There was one window high up and a door with an outer lock. The Signora tossed a pillow on the floor, a square thing with a complicated pattern that the Colonel called '*orientale*'. This was to be Sibilla's new bed. She tucked her hair under her bum and sat on it. Her mother knelt before her.

'Sleep,' she whispered to Sibilla.

And she did. It was still morning but Sibilla was exhausted from yesterday's adventure. She dreamt of the Colonel, his moustache and eyebrows growing thick and wide until they covered his face completely.

※

Sibilla never saw her *nonna* again. A month after Sibilla had moved to Villa Serra, Giovanna sat up with a bolt in the middle of the night, waking Adriana up with a strange jumble of words about *prezzemolo*. Years ago, during the last months of her pregnancy, Adriana had developed a craving for it, and Giovanna had started growing it in the tomato garden to save money, collecting leftover hair from the *barbiere* to fertilise the soil. Only now did Giovanna realise what she had done, she said. She had planted the hair in the ground along with the seeds. And as Adriana had devoured sprig after sprig to satisfy her craving, she must have swallowed the fur right along with the parsley.

'I put the hair right in your belly!' Giovanna cried. 'Sibilla was bound to end up a *tarantola*!'

Then she crossed herself, lay back down, and fell asleep. Assuming it was a spot of senility, Adriana said nothing of it the next morning. A few days later, while harvesting tomatoes in her garden, Giovanna sat down and died. Adriana buried her with the help of their neighbour, who thus atoned for the stones his sons had thrown at Sibilla. Adriana mourned her mother sporadically, in between all the tasks she had to tend to – for her own sake and for her daughter's.

At dawn, Adriana would arrive at Villa Serra, unlock the larder, and wake Sibilla. The girl would urinate in the outhouse and wash her face in the basin, then they would proceed together to the doors of the grand salon. Adriana would throw them wide and they would pause a moment, riveted. What devastating thing happened here every night? Adriana would sigh, Sibilla would blink, and they would begin. Sibilla's hair was an asset for this line of work. She could dust without a duster, mop without a mop. She didn't even need to wash the tool of her trade – at the end of the day, she cut off the dirty ends and tossed them in the garden behind the kitchen.

For years, Sibilla worked at her mother's side, fondling Villa Serra's chipped and tattered insides with care. Later, when she thought back on her childhood, this is how she remembered her days. Her nights were a different story.

Shortly after she arrived at Villa Serra, Sibilla woke to the sound of the larder door bursting open.

'Come!' the Signora exclaimed. 'There is no more wine! We need entertainment!'

'Where is – ow!' Sibilla pried the Signora's high heel off her hair and stood. 'Where is Mama?'

'Your mother?' The Signora snorted. 'She isn't here. It isn't morning. Well, it *is*. But it isn't.'

Sibilla stared at the Signora through her nest. The Signora stared back a moment. Then 'Come!' she said again and stalked out of the kitchen, her heels stuttering. Sibilla followed.

As they approached the salon, a low roar rose, jazz frothing along its edge. When they reached the doors, the Signora opened them and, with a grandiose sidestep, disappeared into the party. Sibilla looked around. A short man was dancing with a tall woman, who seemed entranced by a candelabra. Behind them stood a group of women in all white with no mouths – oh, it was just their gloved hands covering their lips. A bald man was asleep on a divan, an empty glass perched on his chest in the centre of a red stain. His bare feet lay in the lap of a woman wearing a sky-blue gown. She was counting cards, copper ringlets trembling with the motion of her fingers. Was this what she and her mother spent their days washing away? This disaster in progress was far preferable to its aftermath. Everything in the salon was transformed by the glow of the chandelier, which was the most transformed of all, its dusty dewdrops alive with light.

Sibilla drifted towards the centre of the room to look at it, her train of hair dragging behind her. She felt herself catching on gazes, as if sticky strings tied her to the eyes in the room – wherever she went, they went. For the first time in her life, her hair felt like insufficient cover. Finally, a familiar face! The Colonel. He sat in the velvet armchair and on its footstool sat a young man with a ponytail, gesturing so wildly that the Colonel, scowling with concentration, seemed a statue by contrast. The statue melted – he smiled and reached for her.

'*Ragnatela!*' His voice bristled her scalp as he pulled her close. 'You have joined us at last,' he grinned. 'I've been scolding Lina for keeping you away.'

He put his hands on her cheeks and stretched the hair tight, as he had when they first met. Sibilla's relief at seeing him congealed in her stomach. Her hair seemed to stir under his palms, tingling with static, waves of which would sometimes attack her and leave her feeling like she had drunk too much espresso. He let go of her to introduce her to the young man with the *codino*.

'This is my brother,' said the Colonel.

'Sergente Corsale.' The young man bowed slightly.

'*Sergente?!*' The Colonel rolled his eyes. '*Sergente* of the Partisan Army of 1944 maybe! Or should I say the Partisan Army of the tenth of October to the second of November 1944 . . .'

As the Colonel continued to mock his brother's military service, Sibilla swept the hair from her eyes and extended her hand. The young Sergeant ignored it with a frown and bowed again. She couldn't tell if he was scared to touch her or expected her to curtsy instead. She let her hand and eyes drop. Colonel Corsale was expostulating about Abyssinia now, about *il Africa orientale* – nothing Sibilla had ever heard of – gesturing to her every once in a while as if to demonstrate something.

An old woman approached, white powder coating her cheeks and chin in unseemly patches. Sibilla cocked her head to one side by way of a greeting. The old woman yelped in reply, then reached up and tugged at the grey bun on top of her own head, undoing it. The wispy hair wafted down. Sibilla was annoyed by the gesture – it was like crouching to see eye to eye with an animal. But the old woman's eyes reminded her of her *nonna*, so she smiled. The old woman grinned back, her teeth stark as gravestones in the expanse of gum. Then she took Sibilla's arm and began to dance.

At first, Sibilla went along with the marionette movements of reluctance – jerk-sway, jerk-sway – waiting for an opportune moment to let go. But then someone else grabbed her other arm – it was the pretty card counter with the blue dress and the copper curls. The women danced, passing Sibilla between them. Her feet scraped, then tapped, then bounced against the floor, and soon enough she was bounding along, drawing near one dance partner, then the other, letting them spin her. The Colonel took notice and began to clap loudly to the beat from his seat. The Sergeant leaned against a wall, his wine glass pressed to his collarbone.

Sibilla could see! Whenever she spun, her hair would whirl up and out from her body, dissipating into a mist of suspended strands. The music jiggled and jumped. Sibilla spun and spun. A vortex seemed to deepen and clarify in her belly, as if this were simply the natural acceleration of a spinning that had always been inside her. The party guests circled her, clapping in time. The ends of her hair thudded across corduroy, whispered across satin, pittered against badges. Splotches of faces bloomed towards her and wilted away. She caught a glimpse of Signora Lina's scowling face and just then the spinning started to feel uncontrolled. Sibilla was no longer turning in place – she was orbiting a lopsided loop in the centre of the room.

But how to stop? Sibilla closed her eyes. Between spinning and stopping was a chasm. How to cross it? She heard dilating laughter and tumbling music. Only a plunge of nausea told her that she had finally stopped. As she swayed, something stirred over her – it was her hair wrapping around her – once, twice, encasing her completely. There was an airless pause, everyone caught in a gasp. Sibilla opened her eyes.

Oh! How soft! A dark cocoon, dreamy and warm, the still-spinning room striated in a spiral of strips, the way Nonna used to peel an orange. Sibilla could see a grey moustache, a red dress, a green eye.

Oh! How soft and beautiful! But now the cocoon was filling with heat, a vast vibration was swelling. The slivers of colour peeled away and a massing, swarming burst revealed all the capillaried flesh that hides behind the skin of the world. Sibilla fell into darkness.

She woke up in someone's arms. She blinked and the Colonel's dark moustache came clear, then his eyes. Over his shoulder she saw his brother, the Sergeant with his *codino* striding back and forth like a caged beast. She felt the hot wetness on her back before she felt the sting of the cuts down her spine. Later she learned that the Colonel had pulled out his hunting knife and cut her out of her hair, his blade skimming her back and opening a dashed line of gashes.

Now, he stood her upright on the shaggy rug of hairs that had fallen with his rescue. She looked down at the staticky pile, its uneven lengths reaching up her legs. Her back pulsed and trickled. The sliding violins started up again and Sibilla was picked up and carried across the room and laid on her side on a chaise. She felt wrung. I might fall asleep right here, she thought with a woozy giggle, and just as a cool damp cloth touched the top of her spine, she did.

The next day was a misery. Sibilla had to clean Villa Serra beside her mother as if nothing had changed. She wore a shift to conceal the marks on her back from the Colonel's knife, but she could not hide her fatigue, and she kept glancing up at the chandelier – the salon looked even shabbier now that she had seen it glowing under those dewdrops of light. That evening, Sibilla asked her mother to leave the larder door unlocked, just in case she needed the outhouse. She lay in the blue-lit room, kicking impatiently at her pillow, waiting.

When the moon peeked its head in through the small upper window, Sibilla crept out and down the corridor and stood before the wooden doors of the salon. She pressed her ear to the grain of one. The sounds of the party were so muffled they seemed to be coming from inside the door itself – the wood's tale or the woodworms' ruckus. She knocked and the door snarled open at once. The Signora peered around it. Her eyes widened green, then narrowed black.

'*Benvenuta*,' she said wryly. 'You will once again be the bright star of our constellation.' Then she opened the doors wide, her palm floating in sardonic welcome.

This became what Sibilla did every night. As soon as she entered the salon, the air took on a quiet frenzy, a withheldness, as everyone waited for her to spin. Was that why she came? Or for a respite from the weight and shade of her hair? Or was it for the brothers Corsale with their steady hands? Every night, Sibilla would spin and stop and faint and wake to them – the Colonel with his moustache, the Sergeant with his *codino*. Every night, one would cut her from her soft tomb and the other would tend to her wounds. Afterwards, Sibilla would lie in a daze and ponder the difference.

✳

For years, Sibilla's nights glowed and blurred, tintinnabulary with the sound of wine glasses, while her days remained cracked and dirty, gritty and grey as mopwater. Then one morning, when she was fifteen, her nighttime stepped into her daytime and undid the dichotomous pattern. She had dragged a bucket of laundry outside to hang on the clothes line in the garden. During the occupation, her mother had planted all manner of vegetables here to feed the king's men. But since the war, it had languished and nothing grew here now but a midden of kitchen scraps.

Today – the first day of winter, the last day of autumn, a sunken bridge between seasons – even the trees were bare. They looked gawky and sheepish, caught with their leaves down. Despite the shift she wore and the hair beneath, Sibilla was not warm enough. She wished she had borrowed her mother's coat, though its purple lining had shredded to webbing. She quickly grappled the wind-tossed linens onto the line, the cold speeding her fingers. As she hurried back inside, she noticed a shape in the corner of the garden – it was a man, squatting with his back to her, his hair in a stringy tail. The Sergeant. She knew him, and she didn't. He had dabbed a wet cloth down the knots of her spine every night for years, but they had barely exchanged a word.

She dawdled over to him, twisting the ends of her hair. He didn't notice her at first. He was busy raking the dirt, mumbling. Once in a while, he would touch his ponytail and sniff his fingers, then grabble at the earth again, rocking with the effort. She listened for a moment.

'Is *what* growing?' she asked finally.

'Hair!' he said, blinking at her, seeming not the least surprised by her presence. Mortified by this direct allusion to her condition, Sibilla made to leave but the Sergeant grabbed at her and caught a fistful of her locks. Hair rose on her arms.

'You see?' He let go of her and extended his palm. 'Hair! From the ground.'

Sibilla crouched beside him and watched him stir a little pile of dirt and stones and, yes, hair in his hand. She intruded her finger into the clutter and their fingers touched on his palm. They looked at each other.

'*Sì*, it is hair,' she said, pulling her hand away.

'Is it yours?'

'*Sì*, it is mine,' she said slowly, savouring this new flavour of power.

'But why is it coming out of the ground?'

'I cut it every day and scatter it in the soil. It makes things grow.'

'But then why—' He gazed at her. His light brown eyes looked gold and silver at once, the colour of sunlight behind a cloud. 'Why,' he shoved his palm under her nose, 'is some of it *green*?'

Sibilla smiled. 'Because those, Sergeant,' she looked up into his eyes, 'are pine needles.'

They stood up and walked through the dead garden together, her hair like filigree around them. He told her that when he had come out to relieve himself this morning, he had been surprised to feel hair prickling his ankles. His first thought had been of the girl who spun in the parlour each night: that she had died and been buried, that the hair marked her hasty grave, that they hadn't even managed to cover her up properly. It was like the sloppy graves dug during the Partisan War – storms often washed up bones in these parts. He was so pleased, he said, to discover that she was still alive. She was pleased too, Sibilla conceded.

The hairs he had plucked from her putative grave were a few centimetres long. As they walked and talked, he carried them in his hand like the headless stems of flowers. There were no real flowers in this garden, just blighted brakes muttering a brittle ditty. Sibilla could smell it in the air – the steely harbinger of winter. When they reached a corner of the garden, they turned and walked along the other wall. The moment of parting encroached upon them, and each step was a vanishing arrow they shot towards it. He was telling her about his mother's sewing box.

'White with red and yellow and blue flowers, round. Like this.' He put his wrists together and mimed a hinged lid. 'And she kept her pins inside. She wouldn't let me touch them.'

'And so you did?'

'*Certo*. So, one day, she was cooking a meal. My mother never cooks! This was for my brother. He had just come back from Abyssinia. I could smell it: the mud on his boots, his sweat, the blood caramelising. Venison!' The Sergeant closed his eyes dreamily. 'Now, my mother always takes her time cooking. Hunger is her only spice. So I say to myself, "Federico, here is your chance!"'

Sibilla mouthed the Sergeant's name to herself. It was like a charm – when she turned to look at him again, it was as if he had become clearer and sharper.

'—silver sewing pins,' he was saying, 'I pour them out and they go *skitti-skitti-skitti* on the table.' His hand scrambled across the air. 'I roll them back and forth. I put one on my tongue.' He glanced at her. 'Then two, then three. Three pins tastes different from two. The best is four.'

'Why?'

'*E beh*, the sound.'

Sibilla considered this and nodded.

'So this is how it felt to me,' he continued. 'Your hair. Like those pins.' He opened his hand to show her the hairs once more. But the frozen bits of soil had softened and grown muddy in his palm, and the hair was now serpentine. 'Or it did,' he said apologetically. 'Before.'

Sibilla smiled. They'd reached the end of another wall. She walked off, gesturing ruefully at the linens on the line and picking up the empty laundry basket – the day was young, there was work to do. He watched her go. At the kitchen door, she gathered her hair like a skirt, and trotted up the steps. Then she paused and turned.

'And how do they compare?' she called across the swiftening air. 'My hairs, to your delicious pins?'

'I will taste them now!' Federico cried out, raising the fist that clutched her hair. Sibilla smiled and closed the door but not all the way. She peeked out through the crack, watching him open his fist and bring his hand to his lips. But before he could put those thin strands to his tongue, the wind nudged them, frazzled them, and snatched them clean away.

✳

The kitchen door shuddered open. Adriana turned to it from her potato peeling. It was Sibilla, with her new teenagery smell. The yawning and dragging feet were bad enough. But the change in her daughter's odour irked Adriana the most. No mother dislikes the smell of her child, which is generally within the spectrum of your own smells – a shade here, a riff there, like your breath when you've tried a new food. But as she had matured, Sibilla's smell had grown rank and legion. Even when she wasn't in the room, it curled from corners where stray hairs had knitted, a melony-lemony-biscuity scent that Adriana found both puerile and daunting.

It seemed worse than usual today. Adriana plopped the last potato in the boiling water. Maybe it was because Sibilla's shift was hanging half off her and her time in the windy garden had teased her hair to a tangle. She was still standing at the door, peering out through a crack, her back to the room.

That was when Adriana saw it. She marched over, grabbed Sibilla by the neck, dragged her to a window, and pulled the collar of the girl's shift down. Under the light, Adriana examined her daughter's scars – the white stitches, black buttons and red and gold medallions running down her spine. Then she turned Sibilla to face her, bent down, and with the presumption of motherhood, parted the curtain of hair between the girl's legs. Nothing unusual, though it was no longer bare there and the sickly sweet musk grew slightly stronger. Adriana tilted back up and demanded an explanation.

Sibilla knew better than to lie to her mother so she spoke honestly about the nightly soirées at Villa Serra, using a monotone to temper the revelation. She obviously had no idea how familiar these parties were to her mother, even beyond the dread archaeology of cleaning them up every morning. When Adriana had first started working for the Signora at Villa Serra, she had in fact attended these very same soirées. She had mostly stood in the corner, dressed in borrowed clothes, too drunk on the spectacle to bother with the wine. She could still picture the salon in its glamorous heyday, the burgundy curtains lush as blood, the chandelier's bitterbright jewels. She still remembered Giacomo's eyes the night he recognised her from the butcher's stall and asked her to dance ...

As Sibilla spoke, this elaborate tapestry of memory was weaving itself in the steamy kitchen air before Adriana. Sibilla, on the other side, could of course only see its back: knots and strings and washed-out colours giving semblance to the barest of shifting shapes. She did not seem aware that something other than her own little story was happening here in the Signora's kitchen. She prattled on, dribbling out her little stories about spinning and hair, freedom and softness. Then she said something about the Colonel and his hunting knife, and as if it had appeared in the flesh, in the very mettle, the word 'knife' pierced it all – the tapestry tumbled.

Oh how Adriana wept! Oh how she castigated Sibilla for her recklessness! But even as she ranted, Adriana was not thinking of her daughter, but of the Gavuzzis. Adriana no longer loved Giacomo. She had barely mourned him when he died, a casualty not of the war, but of the flu that had swept through Alba in '43. He had merely been a conduit for something beyond Adriana's cuttingly narrow life to enter her world – something as big as a war and as small as a man. She had always known deep down that he was a trifling person. And as for the Signora, Adriana could see now that it had just been a piece of amusement for Lina: to invite maids to parties they would be obliged to clean up.

This blip in the Gavuzzis' relentless pursuit of distraction had been the peak and the tragedy of Adriana's life. And now the curse that had issued from it was standing before her, smelling up the kitchen, boasting about the bright nights on the other side of their drudge days. Did Sibilla not realise that she was not a guest at those parties, but a sideshow? Adriana knew now that the Gavuzzis would never accept her daughter. It was time for Sibilla to come home.

Had they left Villa Serra immediately that day, perhaps things would have turned out differently. As it was, there was still work to be done, so Adriana locked Sibilla in the larder to wait until nightfall. It was several hours before she came back to fetch her daughter for the journey home. As Adriana unlocked the door, she found herself oddly nervous – ashamed in advance for what she was about to do – and so she started chattering about the mess she'd had to clean up today.

'A brassiere clogged a drain and the Colonel, you cannot imagine, he brought the Signora the most bizarre gift, some kind of African bird. Grey, dirty. What noise! What shit!' Adriana bustled into the larder. 'What—' She stopped short. Sibilla was kneeling on her oriental pillow, facing away, gazing up at the one high window. And she was completely shorn, her head bald, her arms and neck a little patchy. She looked like a penitent in her shift.

'But how—?' Adriana stuttered. She felt a pang as she saw the rusty old knife on the ground next to a mound of hair. How much pain Sibilla must have endured to shave and scrape it all from her body! How raw! Adriana shook her head. Was this what she had always wanted? The daughter without the curse? Sibilla did not look more human for it. Her skin was greenish and shadowed with tiny black holes, almost the texture of the snowflakes that were now falling steadily across the high window of the larder.

Sibilla stood and turned around. Adriana's pity bled briefly into anger – was the girl trying to punish her with guilt? But no. Sibilla's gaze was kind, gentle even. Christ, she was beautiful! You could see the planes of her face, how articulate it was in the language of form.

'Don't preoccupy yourself, Mama,' Sibilla said mildly. She looked casual, her hands in the pockets of her shift. 'It will grow back.'

✳

The moment Adriana trapped her daughter at home, she lost her forever. Sibilla had become a servant and service does strange things to a person. It denies you a sense of self even as it frees you from taking hold of yourself. It stills the mind by busying the hands; if those hands are then stilled, the mind erupts. What will I do? Sibilla fretted as she stalked the cabin. What will I do with my hands?

She began each morning by cleaning the house. Her hands knew how to do this. Then she cut the ends off her hair. It sprouted faster than ever these days, as if to spite her, the locks slithering through the grip of the shears even as she closed them. Her daily trim took almost an hour. She put the leavings in a pail for her mother to scatter in the garden. She ate lunch. Then she sat and stared at the locked door, waiting.

Over the course of their final walk from the Signora's – Sibilla stunned by the cold, her numb fingers barely managing to unspool the hair from the pocket of her shift – Adriana had tried to replant seeds of fear in her daughter's mind: *boys and rocks, torture and drowning, old partisans who had acquired the taste for guns and women, the world is no Villa, you know, they'll set you aflame like a beast, they'll burn you up quick as a blink.* Yes, and then? Sibilla thought. Until then, what will I do with these hands?

To have nothing to do was like having your fingernails pulled out, one by one. Sibilla examined them. They were spatulate, each tipped with a quarter-moon, clouded by fur from her fingers. Were fingernails dead or alive? What about hair? What was the exact nature of these felt but unfeeling edges of her body, where the inside met the outside? The Colonel had told her once that human hair keeps growing after death. He had seen it on corpses in the deserts of Abyssinia during the war. Did that make hair the ghost of the body? What did it mean then that Sibilla was covered with it? Better hair than fingernails, she supposed.

She stared out of the small window at the drifting snow, as if the night sky were sloughing its stars. It was winter now. Mama would be home soon. And still he had not come.

✳

It took Sergeant Corsale a while to notice that Sibilla was gone. Everyone was distracted by the Villa's latest amusement: the Signora's African grey. Federico found the parrot repellant – it was scrawny and dishevelled, its beak like a witch's toenail – but it was amusing to listen to its drawling echo. The guests at the Signora's parties snickered about the secrets it would spill. Only after the novelty had worn off did anyone think to ask where the spinning girl had gone.

'Sleeping.' Lina tossed her head dismissively. '*Puttana pigra.* Come, Sergeant. Let us fetch her.'

Federico picked up a candelabra and followed his hostess as she zigzagged out of the salon, bouncing between guests like a bee drunk on springtime. When they finally reached the kitchen, they found the door to the larder open. They stared at the rumpled, dimpled old pillow. Not a trace of Sibilla to be found. Except – Federico leaned down with his candelabra and pointed – 'A hair!'

Lina rolled her eyes. 'Of course there's hair. The girl sheds like a dog. Too many animals in this house, what with my little Paolucci ...' She turned, already bored with the missing girl, and trotted back to her sotted guests.

Federico stayed. He knelt on the floor of the larder and pulled the hair from the pillow but it caught. He tugged. Aha! It was several hairs, braided together, and tied to a heavy jar on the floor of the larder. From there, it hooked around the corner of the entrance and snaked along the kitchen floor, all the way to the back door – he opened it – and down the steps into the garden, the wintry garden where just a week ago, he and Sibilla had walked and talked together.

Federico was too drunk to pursue the thread that night. But the next morning, he picked it up and followed it out through the creaky garden gate. He discovered that the braid, or rather the series of braids – Sibilla had cleverly knotted them end to end – continued into the distance, wrapped around tree stumps and posts, as the road switched up and back, climbing the hill to the forest.

※

Being trapped in the cabin made Sibilla's hair restive. It undulated like gracile tentacles, and sometimes pythoned around her when she wasn't paying attention. She knew it wasn't out to destroy her, though. It protected her, kept her from coming undone, formed a roped arena for the spinning she had discovered inside her in the Signora's salon. If that inner whorl was a tornado, her hair was the vault of the sky – it held her to a horizon. But as her days of confinement dragged on, the tension between inner force and outer constraint grew. Waiting made it worse. Anticipation was an enchantment: every creak was a footstep, every birdcall a greeting.

Her mother's arrival each night was a terrible deflation. Adriana would stomp in complaining about her job. She had become obsessed with the Signora's bird: a luxury too far! An animal that ate human food! And gave nothing back but noise and shit! Sibilla said nothing. She just nodded and served the meal she had cooked for them and washed their bowls. But her silence gentled as the evening went on. It was almost companionable when they went to bed. By that point in the night, Adriana's empty chatter had come to seem soothing, a kind of company, like sitting by a babbling brook. It was a version of family better than most.

※

Longing for a better coat, Federico doggedly tracked the trail of hair through the snow, from tree to sapling to fence post to rock. Between these poles, the braided line hung suspended, fallen snow clinging to it in little triangles like the banners of a medieval battle – all white, all surrender. Sometimes he would lose the thread under a snowdrift. Then he would find it again and chuckle. He was so charmed by the trick of it – though in truth he was half-charmed by his own charm. He had always loved a quest, the sparkle it sprinkles on a mystery.

Federico had lost his faith in the church as an adolescent, the moment that he had compared what he knew of sex with what he had been told about God. A little while later, he lost his faith in war. When he was a boy, war had seemed like the only way out of a standstill life in the landed gentry. As the youngest son of a titleless *nobile*, he was too rich to work, too poor to play. The military seemed ideal: a balance of work and play. But with a myth for an older brother – the Colonel always away in Abyssinia or Libya – Federico had developed a rather abstract image of war: an exalted space of pure momentum; a blur of racing legs and spinning wheels; fire and smoke curling across a map.

Then, on 10 October 1944, nearly eight years after Mussolini joined the Axis, 2,000 members of the Allied resistance came down from the hills of Piedmont. They swept through Alba, retaking the puppet government of Salo and establishing a Partisan Republic. The bells of the town's nine churches quarrelled clamorously. The townspeople stood in the streets, applauding with fervour or fear. The Partisans marched through in their motley outfits, gathering whores and cars and petrol, knocking on the doors of registered army officers and emerging with guns and gear – Federico recognised the insignia of black and yellow frogs from his brother's old uniform. Drunk on courage, he signed up as a *badogliani* the next day. He was only sixteen years old but because of his education, he was promptly promoted to the rank of sergeant.

It turned out that, in practice, being a soldier resisting the Nazis meant late-night foot patrols, dull days of shooting practice, and a great deal of waste: good soil ploughed up by bullets from the machine guns, casings strewn everywhere like the husks of seeds. Farms and houses were taken over by lazy, uncouth men, the buildings reverting to wood and stone, the men to animals. There were shallow graves everywhere – any step you took was as liable to land on a corpse's hand as in a pile of shit. Worst of all was the stink of futility. After just twenty-three days of occupation, the Fascists took the city back from the Partisans and held it until the Armistice the following year.

Federico felt distraught, listless. He had not served, he had only waited. There was nothing to do once the war was over but commiserate with his older brother, who had been injured in brave but minor fashion in the second Abyssinian campaign. Upon his return to Alba, Colonel Corsale had dabbled at farming and local politics, but it suited him better to spend his days limping through the forest shooting for sport and his nights telling old war stories at Signora Lina's parties. When Federico pitched up at Villa Serra after the Armistice was announced on the radio, his brother opened the door in full regalia and gave him a slow salute.

'Welcome to Limbo!' the Colonel cried, clapping Federico on the back. 'It's even worse than Inferno.'

The parties at Villa Serra were indeed depressing. In a rage of boredom, Federico often found himself prodding his brother to argue with him. Federico wanted to talk about the war, the ideals it had gestated, the deformed monsters it had birthed – like the colonies, which were now roiling with revolution, intent on independence. But the Colonel just laughed at these philosophical questions. He had long ago decided that the world was only tolerable if you could find the humour in it. Federico glared at him bitterly. How could you laugh when glory had proven a mutter? When democracy was stillborn?

The broken promises of the church, the Partisans, the war: Federico had become a man always sighing in the ruins. Though it be a melancholy song, a sigh is a song all the same. It was not that he had lost his faith entirely but rather that he had been blessed with a dolorous faith – a faith premised on loss, and thus endlessly renewable. When he had first seen the hairy girl spin in the Signora's salon, he had felt his ribs stretch near to splintering. The Colonel had muttered something crude in his ear of course, but Federico had just waved him off and watched.

The girl's tresses dove and fluttered as they whipped around her, her pale form gleaming under the smog of hair. And when she stopped and her hair kept going, when it bound her so tight that it smothered her, when his brother cut her loose and raised her like Lazarus from his bindings, and when he himself wiped the blood from her back – then Federico Corsale knew faith again. It flooded him now, as he reached the top of a hill, and saw a thread of her hair vanish under the door of an old hunting cabin.

✳

Sibilla was sitting on the floor, her eyes closed, listening for the sound of her inner spin, its whir like the throaty coo of a dove. A knock on the door lifted her to her feet before her eyes were even open. She raced to it and shouted instructions and waited while he found the key in the tomato garden and unlocked the door. They stood facing each other across the threshold. She was grinning at him, choked with joy. The Sergeant, measled with snowflakes, shivered happily at the sight of her, or maybe at his own sense of triumph. 'I found you!' he kept saying as she led him inside and sat him on a chair by the hearth and fixed him a cup of chicory coffee.

He sipped and talked and talked and sipped, giving her a detailed account of his discovery of her absence, and the trail of hair, and his journey through the snow. His mouth was like an *automa*. She sat on the floor and watched it open and close for some time. Then, to their mutual surprise, she interrupted. She told him her version of things, about how at first, locked in that dark, smelly larder, she had plucked out her hair, one strand at a time. How she had found an old knife under a sack of polenta and sawed wretched swathes of hair off herself, her skin flaming red then cooling white. She'd had to twist her arm over her shoulder to sever the hairs from her back. But she had made sure to pull out enough to braid into a firm thread. She had spooled it into a ball and trailed it from her pocket as her mother dragged her back to this cabin where, if he hadn't come, she would have been trapped forever ...

The Sergeant's mouth was open, his eyes wide. Sibilla was breathing so heavily that her hair pulsed with it. The fire smacked its lips. The Sergeant smiled.

'*Certo*,' he said. On the journey here, he lied, he *had* wondered how she had managed to make such a long thread for him to follow. But he had decided that she must have used the cut hair from the garden – the hair in the ground, remember? Sibilla did remember, and she said so, and smiled at him, relieved that he remembered too. She wasn't a fool after all.

'And how is Villa Serra?' she asked shyly.

'Oh. Well. There is a terrible bird that my brother gave to Lina. It talks and you—'

'It talks?'

'It says what you teach it,' he laughed. 'Lina, of course, has neglected its training ...'

He removed his jacket as the fire warmed his bones, freeing his arms to gesticulate as he told her all about the social intricacies of the salon at Villa Serra. She slumped and examined her hands.

'... going on and on about the damned babies in—'

'Babies?' She looked up.

'My brother, the Colonel, was boasting,' he scoffed. 'That in Africa they would string up babies over a long fire.'

'*Dio*, that's terrible,' said Sibilla, her eyes alight with revulsion.

Federico nodded seriously. 'And they would sit there and just watch them burn.'

'I cannot believe Italians would do such a thing,' she said.

'No, no!' Federico clucked. 'The natives!' His disgust soon found a new object. 'Even after we brought them our "God" and our "civilised ways". It is an abomination what we did to the *ascari*, to make them fight their own brothers ...'

'*Ascari*?'

'Black soldiers,' he murmured. 'War is a nightmare, Sibilla,' he said, gazing solemnly out of the window. 'It is a sickness, no matter the colour of the hand that grips the weapon.'

'What kind of weapon?'

'Guns, *sicuro*.' He frowned. 'In Africa they use *assegai*.' He glanced at her. 'I've heard.'

Her eyes glowed behind her hair like eggs in a nest. 'What is an *assegai*?'

Thus began a coincidence of four lips. In the beginning, those lips opened and shut across the room as Federico and Sibilla chatted. As the weeks passed and Federico continued to visit, they moved closer together until one day, those lips were opening and closing up against each other, silently, urgently. They mouthed blindly, spoke in tongues, each scandalised by the other's willingness to go further. Her hair writhed and knotted, tangled between them. Once, she tugged away from him and whispered: 'Does it repulse you?'

Federico's lips were still mouthing the air. He closed them and opened his eyes. 'What?

'My hair. Does it—'

Federico pulled her to him and kissed the top of her head. She nestled into his shoulder and her hair seemed to soften, as well.

'Good,' she said. 'Let's talk about the plan.'

'What plan?' Federico murmured into her skull, his voice humming through the bone.

'To leave this place.'

✳

One night a few months later, Sibilla woke to the sound of the key scraping the lock. It was still dark but on the verge of dawn, that briefest spell when even the insects are asleep. The cabin door opened and Sibilla heard her mother curse as she tripped over the doorsill. Sibilla turned onto her other side. Then she heard more sounds: a snort, feet stumbling, whispers, a glugging bottle, the hollow whistle of lips across its mouth. It sounded like two people, laughing at each other, hushing each other, laughing at the hushing and hushing the laughter and so on. A stupid game: the cabin was too small for secrets. Sibilla sat up.

'I can hear you,' she said.

Her mother squealed. The man buried his guffaw in something soft, skin or cloth.

'Come!' he finally wheezed. '*Ragnatela!* Join us. Let me take a look at you!'

Sibilla reluctantly slid off the bed, wrapping a sheet around herself, and lit a lamp. Their figures flickered to life. The Colonel was sitting on the chair. His shirt was unbuttoned, revealing his thick neck laced with greying curls. His eyes shifted back and forth between Sibilla and her mother, who was sitting on his knees. Adriana wore an unfamiliar dress that was either a stained white or a faded brown, and the bluegreen glass necklace Signora Lina had given her. Her hair was down and resembled an old mop. Sibilla realised she hadn't seen them together since that morning a decade ago when she first went to the Signora's. Neither had changed much – her mother a little thinner, the Colonel a little thicker – but things between them had clearly changed profoundly. Sibilla thought of Nonna Giovanna's fables. The Colonel was the puppet Gianduja, Adriana the Giacometta on his knee.

'Bring us water!' Adriana demanded from her throne.

Sibilla's hair bristled, but she complied. She walked over to the jug and poured water into two tin tumblers and handed them over, then sat back on her bed. Adriana kept licking her lips after every sip, an oddly sensual gesture though she was probably just trying not to make a mess.

'We have not seen you in our grand salon for quite some time, *ragnatela*,' the Colonel said. 'Let me take a look at you. I will miss you when I'm gone.'

Sibilla's eyes darted towards him. Gone where?

'Why don't you show us a trick?' Adriana slurred knowingly. 'Why don't you *spin* for us?'

'Yes, that would be jolly, wouldn't it?' the Colonel said, his eyes glinting in the lamplight.

Adriana laughed with relish, tipping her head back. Sibilla had never seen her mother's neck curve like that, a sapling bent by the wind, her bead necklace glittering like dew.

'Dance for us, *ragnatela!*' The Colonel began a stentorian clap, stomping his foot in time. Adriana giggled awkwardly, struggling to stay upright on his bouncing knee. When she managed to adjust her balance, she added the thin slap of her palms to the percussion.

Sibilla stared at their bared teeth and expectant eyes as their advance applause began to speed up. It was set to trigger the whorl in her. She despaired. Would she always spin like this for others, like a record, their needling gaze slipping into her grooves? Sibilla turned from the riot in their eyes and walked out of the cabin, closing the door behind her.

She sat in the cool grass under the trees behind the cabin, her arms around her knees. Had Federico – his unhurried, unworried courtship – given her the will to leave? No. He had a thirst for her too, the same kind she had seen in their eyes, and that she could hear her mother and the Colonel slaking together now inside the cabin. By the time their last cries clashed with the first birdsong, dawn had uncorked the sky and spilled white gold over the valley.

When the Colonel came out and limped off down the hill, Sibilla went back inside. Her mother glowered at her from her tousled bed.

'Just one night. After all this time.' Adriana sat up and pulled a slip over her head. 'A little pleasure . . .' She turned to look out of the window. Her cheek was creased with lines, though from the years or the sheets, Sibilla couldn't say.

Spring came. It darkened Federico's skin and brightened his hair. It blanketed the valley with luminous green leaves and white blossoms. Sibilla vibrated with restlessness.

'Take me somewhere,' she begged.

Federico demurred. 'You are the only journey I wish to take, my Giacometta.'

'Don't call me that.' She gave him a sharp look. 'Fine. Let me take *you* somewhere then.'

Despite the heat, Sibilla put on her mother's old satin-lined coat. She took Federico's hand and led him on the route she had taken as a child. Here were the peppery trees! Here was the root she had tripped over! Here was the Lanaro river!

'This isn't the Lanaro,' Federico laughed. 'It's just a creek.'

She shrugged. It was still hers – but what a difference the weather made! This wasn't a brown river under a stormy sky. Sunrays dove into the water and pulled twisted ropes of light out over the stones. The green trees overhead hushed fondly. Federico complained about the bites but even the *mosche* looked lovely in their glinting throngs. Sibilla tossed the coat aside and stepped barefoot into the water. Her hairs puckered its surface, drifted drowsily. Federico took off his boots to join her. They smiled at their underwater feet. Then he leapt onto the bank.

'*Che cos'è?!*' Sibilla asked. 'A snake?'

A school of fishes. She could feel them biting her ankles too now. Federico was already putting his boots back on, grumbling about the dangers of barefootedness. She looked down at the translucent creatures swarming her feet, darting in and out of the tangles of her hair. Were they hungry? No. Biting is just an expression of curiosity for those without hands. But she had the feeling that, left to their own devices, they might nibble her to the bone.

Sibilla shuddered off her footmaidens and stepped out of the creek. She spread the coat out and sat, waiting for Federico to stop talking. Finally, he looked at her. She looked at him. Her hair trembled.

As is usual for the first time between a man and a woman, the woman was dissatisfied, the man satisfied too soon. Federico rolled onto his back. Sibilla's hand was still on his wrist and his pulse ticked faintly, erratically, like cooling metal. They lay there for a while on her mother's coat, in the seep of his semen and the creep of the gloaming, looking up at the trees above nuzzling their leafy heads.

'Try again?' she whispered, and he did.

1956

Ding dong, said the bird.

The brothers Corsale were in the Signora's salon. The other guests had not yet arrived. The Colonel was sitting in his velvet chair, poking into the grey parrot's cage as it hopped about, squawking its echoes. Lina stood by the fire, pouring drinks into tumblers on the mantel. Federico was pacing furiously, his ponytail swinging like a whip as he speechified.

'The Italians *forced* the Africans to fight one another. And for what? For ideals utterly beyond their comprehension. The native has no notion of empire or democracy or the future.'

'No sense of time at all,' the Colonel muttered. 'Kaffirs are always bloody late.'

Bloody, bloody! said the bird.

'You've missed the point!' Federico exclaimed. 'Abyssinia was meant to be our greatest achievement. To take Fort Ual-Ual was one thing. But when we used the *ascari* for the invasion, we lost our souls, our dignity. We set them on each other like . . . like cannibals.'

'They're already bloody cannibals! Curse of Ham.'

Ham! Ham!

'Shhhh, Paolucci,' said Lina indulgently. 'It isn't true,' she said to the men. 'When I was in Rhodesia as a girl, they did not eat men. Other disgusting things – caterpillars, rats. But not *men*.'

'They eat the enemy's brain to ward off evil.' The Colonel turned from the bird cage and grinned. 'It's a sacrificial culture.'

'But that's what we did to *them*,' said Federico. 'We forced them to sacrifice—'

'I always say,' the Colonel was musing, 'that the only way to kill a cannibal is to spice him up for the next cannibal. Poison for poison.' He tipped his whisky glass back with a wink.

'We are the ones who used poison! Mustard-gas bombs, against the Geneva Convention—'

Poison mustard!

The Colonel groaned. 'Your righteous cynicism is extremely distasteful, Federico.'

But Federico kept talking about the colonies, about the loss of land after the war. *L'Impero Italiano* was being burned to the ground. 'They are like embers touched by the winds of change, these uprisings against us.'

Lina smiled. 'But France and Belgium and Spain, their empires are falling too.'

'It is always like this,' said the Colonel. 'How children fall asleep: slowly, then all at once.'

'The natives *are* children,' said Federico. 'They think they're at war with Europe, with the Queen. But they're throwing tantrums. Running their own nations?! Children playing house.'

'Children!' the Colonel exclaimed. 'Is that what you would call the Mau Mau?'

Mau, said the bird. *Mau. Mau. Mau.*

'You've turned my bird into a cat,' Lina scolded the Colonel. 'Aren't you afraid to go back?' She drifted over to him, carrying a candelabra with only a quarter of the candles lit.

'No, no,' the Colonel dismissed the air with a flat palm. 'Those brutes don't scare me.'

'What are you saying?' Federico frowned. 'Going back?'

'Our dear Colonel,' said Lina sadly. 'He's leaving us for Africa. What a misery!'

Misery!

'I've secured a position.' The Colonel leaned back and laced his fingers. 'With Fiat.'

Fiat!

'They have formed a civil engineering unit with Impresit. They are building the biggest dam in the world on the Zambezi river. And in six months, I will be there to oversee it.'

'Six months!' Federico exclaimed. 'So soon?'

'Yes, Lina has worked a miracle with her father's old friends in Northern Rhodesia. So you see, Federico,' the Colonel smiled, 'the empire isn't really dead. Even as we speak, it is rising from the ashes.'

Ashes! Ashes!

*

Every night now, Colonel Corsale came knocking. Sibilla would sigh and put on her shift and let him in on her way out. She would sit in the outer dark, letting him and her mother enjoy their little pleasure. Then the Colonel began to arrive earlier in the evening, before Adriana even got home. He'd lounge about, or pace with his rocking limp, regaling Sibilla with stories about hair. He showed her a picture of a Negress with a towering headdress woven out of her lover's hair. He told Sibilla about Chinese girls in the seventh century who embroidered pictures of the Buddha with their hair, and about the elaborate sculptural poufs Marie Antoinette had worn.

'Don't you ever wonder,' he asked once, raking his fingers down the air and trembling them as if to mime rain, 'why you are this way?'

'No,' she said curtly.

'Not curious?' The Colonel cocked his head. 'Well, I have been corresponding about your condition with Herr Doktor Klein – quite an expert, I met him in '42 – and he says . . .'

Sibilla had no interest in these hairy tales, which always felt like bait. She had grown to despise this bulky man, with his opinions and commands. *Spin for me*, ragnatela. *Talk to me.* He even brought the Signora's bird with him one time, to amuse her. At first, she had been intrigued by the idea of a talking bird. In reality, Paolucci was ugly and loud. Like the Colonel. He was always going on about his African adventures past and future: Kenya and Libya and Rhodesia; the lions and tigers and elephants he planned to kill. His talk stirred her, made her feel staticky. She preferred Federico with his blunt body and borrowed stories, the way he treated her hair as a charm rather than a curiosity. She kept the brothers' visits secret from each other.

'Isn't it grand?' the Colonel would say. 'To have a little wife hidden in the woods!'

Sibilla resented his presumption but said nothing. It was as if all those years ago, when he had flattened his palms over her face the better to see her, Colonel Corsale had somehow taken possession of her.

'What if it passes down to your child?' he asked now, sprawled grotesquely on her bed.

'What do you mean?' Sibilla snapped. She was seated at the hearth of the cabin, polishing the old spiral-faced watch the Signora had given her mother.

'Don't you know how it works? There's you. And a man. And when you *kiss* . . .' he grinned.

She clucked at his vulgarity. The Colonel started droning on about a man named Mandelbrot, about heredity and genes. Sibilla was curious, especially about what he called 'the paternal line', but too anxious to pay attention. She glanced at the door. Federico might arrive any moment. Recently, he had started hectoring her to marry him. Rather than run off, he had said, why not stay in Piedmont, have some children, settle in a small house, some place private of course? Sibilla was irritated by this – she wanted to escape this cabin, not just shift to another.

'... wrote to another friend,' the Colonel was saying, 'a scientist. And *he* believes ...'

Sibilla pictured the brothers staring at each other over the threshold. Often, when she lay beside Federico in the forest, pine needles itching her skin, his hands distracted in her hair, she longed to turn to him and say: 'You know, your brother comes to see us.' Or, 'I met that stupid parrot.' But confessing the secret would mean confessing how long she had been keeping it.

'... asked for a photo of you,' the Colonel said. 'I provided a sketch instead and—'

'A sketch!' The watch dropped in Sibilla's lap. 'How dare you!' she hissed.

✳

Federico did not come to the cabin every day. If he stayed away too long, he would find Sibilla in a huff, her eyes dim and slightly crossed behind her hair. This short-focus trick bothered him. Her attention was precisely why he came to see her. It was like a hammock – swaying, flexible – where he could rest the thoughts running amok in his head. When her eyes retreated behind her thicket, he drew her out with war stories, his own scant collection, but more often, his brother's: dark, violent tales that made her eyes return to him. But soon the Colonel would leave for Africa, taking with him his store of stories.

What could Federico tell Sibilla today? Maybe an anecdote about the Signora's parrot? He was walking along the switchbacks towards the cabin, enjoying the autumnal bluster. The sun was being fickle: darting into view, shying behind clouds, then announcing itself grandly. The breeze whipped left and right, casting chaos and roving shadows over the valley, as if a giant hand were mussing the fields. Federico ran his own hands over the dry stalks of wheat that had crept outside a fence. Their wispy burrs made him think of feathers and, again, of Paolucci.

Last night, someone had doused the parrot's feed in grappa. It had started hopping in circles, rattling off vulgar replays. Puttana! Pompinara! *Bring the wine! Bring the whores! Liar! Ashes!* Vaffanculo! Federico shook his head and absently broke a stalk of wheat. *Spin, ragnatela!* Che cazzo! *I spit on your father's grave! I spit on your mother's cunt!* Federico peeled the stalk to clean his teeth as he marched along the switchbacks. Silly beast. *Spin,* ragnatela! He stopped, the stalk dangling from his mouth. *Spin,* ragnatela? But the bird had arrived at Villa Serra the very day that Sibilla had left. How did it know the Colonel's nickname for her? Federico broke into a trot. How had it echoed his command? Federico began to run.

✳

'*Che cos'è?*' The Colonel's moustache lifted with surprise, as if its ends were tied to his eyebrows. He stood up and limped slowly towards her. 'I'm going to all this trouble to find a cure for you, *ragnatela.* You could even come with me ...' He paused to light his cigarette. 'You know,' he mused, 'there are others like you in this world.'

'Like me?' She didn't recognise her own voice. 'Where?'

'*Ragnatela!*' He swung to face her, blowing smoke in her eyes. 'I knew you were curious! Don't you want to know what the doctors call you?'

Sibilla stood and walked across the cabin, her hair slithering in the cracks of the wooden floor. She placed the watch on the table. 'I never asked for a doctor. Or a name.'

'Dear *ragnatela,* we cannot always know what we want ...'

'I know what you want!' Her hair rose, hackle-like. 'You want to swallow me!'

They stared at each other. Holding her gaze, the Colonel limped over to the table and reached into his vest pocket for a piece of paper.

'Sibilla.' Her real name sounded strange in his mouth. He always called her *ragnatela.* '*This* is who you are.'

The paper was folded but when he tossed it on the table, it sprang open. Sibilla stared at it a moment. Then she snatched it and ran to the hearth and threw it in the fire. The flames crunched into it. The

Colonel wobbled after her and grabbed her arm. He wasn't trying to save the letter – he had read it, it was gone – he wanted to hurt her. She glared at him, then they both glanced down at his grip on her forearm – her hair had slipped over his wrist. With a grunt, he twisted his hand and seized a rope of it. With his other hand, he spun her roughly – once, twice – into her locks until she was bound inside them. She tried to turn back but he held her fast.

As the familiar warm smother began, Sibilla heard an unhappy plucking sound, like a broken mandolin. She knew how sharp the Colonel's knife was, how swift and sure his stroke had been when he had cut her out of her nightly cocoon in the salon. As her breath and consciousness waned, she realised he was using its hooked back instead of its keenest edge, running it slowly down the hairs wrapped around her, playing a warped melody as he decided whether or not to set her free . . .

*

Federico knew what was happening the moment he burst through the cabin door. He grappled his brother off Sibilla, then straddled him and punched his face, over and over. When the pain in Federico's fists finally rose above the one in his chest, he stood up shakily, snatched up the knife on the floor, and stumbled over to Sibilla. He lifted her in his arms. His brother was rolling desultorily side to side, laughing through his bloodied moustache. The Colonel's fly was still open, the raw pink flesh there like a baby bird's neck. 'Take it. Take her,' he spat between thick, wet chuckles. 'I got what I wanted.'

Federico looked down at Sibilla, unconscious in his arms, though her hair was still moving. He carried her outside and laid her carefully in the tomato garden. Then he strode back into the cabin, straddled his brother again, and gutted the pockets of his uniform – slashed them open and took out the Colonel's identification papers, his wallet, his lighter and cigarettes. Federico spoke fiercely to the bleeding face beneath him, recounting all the things he was taking.

'Your name. Your job. Your honours,' Federico hissed out his list. 'Your future.'

He left only one thing: the hunting knife – in the middle of the Colonel's chest.

✳

Sibilla woke up outside in the tomato patch. Federico was crouching beside her, pecking her forehead mechanically. The smell of fresh soil bloomed all around them. The cabin door was open. Where was the Colonel? She looked at Federico but he avoided her eyes as he helped her up. He was sweaty, his clothes soiled. He put his arm around her shoulder as he hurried her down the path away from her home. She was shivering. Her hair felt electric.

As they stumbled along under the blustery bright sky, Federico explained the plan. They would travel by car to Naples and spend the night there. The ship for Suez left in the morning. They would touch down at Aden, Djibouti and Mombasa before they reached Dar es Salaam and travelled overland to Bulawayo. His brother had been talking about the itinerary of his African enterprise for so long that Federico knew it by heart. It was laid out like a destiny. They just had to reach out and take it. A new life! They would have to take precautions, of course. Sibilla would have to shave her face completely, every day. He would have to cut his *codino* and grow out his moustache. And she would have to call him by a new name. He was no longer Federico. He was 'Colonel Giuseppe Corsale'.

Sibilla assented to the plan in a kind of fugue state. Every time she called him by his brother's name, she saw double, the Colonel's face floating over Federico's like a spectre. The further they got from Alba, the closer they got to the dubiously named 'Federation' where they were to make their home, the more Sibilla, too, felt like a double of herself. It became a kind of itch under her skin that competed with the real itch over her skin from shaving her hair every day – at least thrice a day – during the journey.

Concealment was a constant preoccupation. Every door that opened led to yet another close-walled space – a hotel room, a ship cabin, a vehicle, a caboose. Some were less sturdy than others, some better lit, some shook or rolled or dipped, but they were all a suffocation of planes and corners. It seemed that the world was one giant house and

Sibilla was trapped inside it, doomed to traverse it – even its vastest oceans – via a series of connected rooms.

She finally got some fresh air once they reached Tanzania three weeks later. She stepped out onto the balcony of the hotel room in Dar es Salaam. It was night. Without her usual veil of hair, the moon was like stripped bone. The buildings and roads of the city looked clean and institutional under it. Only the smell of smoke and salt, the heat and the sounds – of birds and insects and the sea – told her she was in a new place. She heard a familiar ring: a bicycle bell. She looked down at the road below as a man wheeled by, a temple of bananas on his back. He paused as he met a pedestrian, a man wearing a turban – was he Arab? After a brief chat, they both glanced up at her. Sibilla waved. They did not wave back. She put her hand to her bristling face.

✳

Federico had finally put his military training to use. But even as he'd led a trembling Sibilla away from the cabin, even as he'd designed an escape plan and executed it, an image had niggled his mind. It was like Chinese acupuncture – that subtle, that potent. When he had first rushed into the cabin and seen those two too-familiar bodies entangled, Sibilla's hair had been slithering and twining around the Colonel's limbs – as if suffused with desire. The image haunted Federico, mocked him from the mirror in the shape of the moustache he was growing as a disguise. It hovered before him all the way to Africa.

Between visits to a lethargic Sibilla in their tiny single-portholed cabin, Federico stood on the lower deck and watched this immense, enigmatic continent slip by. Sometimes the African coast seemed featureless, monotonous, blank. Other times, it grinned, drooped, raged. *Come!* it beckoned. *Go!* it boomed. The sea obeyed. Beyond the white line of the surf, colossal rainforests loomed, so dark green they were almost black. Grey specks of civilisation were here and there embedded in the gloom, an occasional flag flying to pronounce that the white man had at least landed here. Federico felt the majesty of it, but also the futility. Those settlements, over a century old, had made barely a dent in the untouched expanse of the inner continent. So much for the cause of progress and reason in Africa.

He realised how mistaken he was when they made their way inland to the Federation – a slow and difficult journey on the southern access road to the dam construction site. The West *had* arrived in the interior, but it had brought its worst tendencies with it: bureaucracy, venality, banality. The European labourers drank local beer and smoked bush pipes. They hunted for food rather than for sport. They walked around with their shirts off, insulting and ordering and punishing *i negri* to fluff their egos. The Tonga workers, paid a pittance, were impenetrable, with their opaque skin and broad smiles and nodding deference. The dam workers were altogether as coarse as the *paesani* who had worked the fields and vineyards in Piedmont and joined the Partisan War. Federico was in the same position he had occupied then as a sixteen-year-old sergeant: anxious that they did not respect him, yet unwilling to stoop to their level.

While the other head engineers spent their time out on the site, mingling with this hoi polloi, Federico elected to stay in the office all day. This surprised his superiors: they had hired Colonel Corsale under the impression that he enjoyed being outdoors, hunting and fighting. Federico begged off. His old war injury was acting up, he lied, and he even began to fake a slight limp. Plus the sun here in the Gwembe Valley was far more vicious than it had been in Abyssinia, he noted. As rainy season approached, the temperature rose daily to 110°F. The office was smotheringly hot too but Federico swore otherwise.

He became a living filing cabinet for green folders of blueprints, schedules, orders, receipts, the edges of the pages curling from the humidity, their interiors riddled with holes from the ants. He shuffled and rifled and slid them around energetically, as if building the dam with thin flat slices. Every night, he went home, drank gin and made love to Sibilla to dissolve the clutter to blankness. And every morning, he encased himself in his unnecessary suit and went back to his stacks of paper.

＊

The Africans in Siavonga were politer than those in Dar es Salaam, but Sibilla suspected they had no choice about it. The township for the dam labourers was divided into segregated housing. The Italians and the Brits lived at the top of a steep hill, in simple houses that were nevertheless palatial compared to the hovels at the bottom of the hill for the blacks. The other expat wives bonded over trying to do their domestic duties in this rocky, hot wilderness, over having to race with lifted skirts and swinging buckets to beg water from the trucks that wet the road. But as a chief engineer, 'Colonel Corsale' had been assigned a maid, a cook and a guard.

Sibilla had been a servant herself for most of her life, but she was baffled by the African workers, by their mixture of subservience and hauteur. They did not seem bothered by her odd clothing: the loose dresses and shawls she draped over herself to conceal her hair. But whenever she automatically picked up dishes or wiped up spills or reached for a knife to chop vegetables, the young maid, Enela, frowned and lifted her nose. The girl practically snatched the plates and pots from Sibilla's hands and took offence at any offer of help, as if Sibilla were scolding her by doing her job for her. As the months passed, Sibilla learned not to linger in the kitchen, and to apply her tight-wrung energy to other tasks, like learning how to speak English and be a wife.

Sibilla and Federico had finally married. Shortly after the diluvial floods in 1957, the dam workers had imported a bell from Italy, set it up in the African church at the top of the hill, built a circular tower around it, and renamed it Santa Barbara. The day before it opened, Sibilla and Federico stood inside the barely dry concrete walls, under an unpainted cross, and exchanged vows before an Italian priest. The rituals felt half-wrought, attenuated by their distance from home. But there was some pomp at least: Federico had persuaded another engineer to bring some silk charmeuse and bridal illusion from abroad; Sibilla had handsewn the one into a dress, the other into a veil.

She flinched only once, when the priest said the name: 'Colonel Giuseppe Corsale'. Was that why Federico was marrying her? To seal the deception in a legal document – to make it official? Standing there in that half-built church, Sibilla gazed through her double veil at her double man: Federico, with the false name, gait and moustache of his brother. And she was two Sibillas too: the one twitching uncomfortably in her dress, and the one who swooned under his worshipful hands every night. The one who loved him and the one who was afraid of this man who had both rescued her from death and buried his own brother's corpse in a tomato patch.

✳

OPERATION NOAH, the memo said. Mrs Makupa, the native woman whom Federico had been training as a secretary, had brought it in. She was tall and thin and dark. Her hands were forever occupied with knitting wool – always black, despite the swelter of this place.

'Who sent this? Smith? Did he say it was urgent?'

Mrs Makupa shrugged, hands still rotating. Federico waved her off and scanned the memo, which was dated the previous month, September 1958. Now that the dam was nearly complete, the river was flooding earlier than usual in the season. This memo proposed to relocate the wildlife whose habitat was soon to be underwater: lions, leopards, elephants, antelopes, rhinos, zebras, warthogs, even snakes. A Noah's Ark indeed. Federico shook his head. Disaster had already come – to human life.

He looked out of the poorly cut window in the concrete wall of the office. It was raining again. In the distance, he could see the dam's broad curving face topped with a racket of scaffolding, the white plastic pipes like worms. Despite the rain, it was crawling with men, fly-like amongst the beetling machines. It looked like a mammoth corpse, half-dissected or half-rotten. They had already lost so many men to it. Twenty-seven had died in a collapsed tunnel – the survivors living off Coca-Cola and beer for three days. Seventeen had plunged seventy metres into wet concrete when a platform collapsed – this incident had led the Africans to strike until Baldassarini, the site agent, raised their pay to sixpence an hour. During a shuttering, an Italian had looked up at a passing Royal Air Force plane and plunged to his death.

Then came the floods. Last year, they'd barely had enough time to get out of the way. The men had scrambled to move the machines and to break part of the cofferdam wall to divert the river – but then the water had just seeped in a fault line and flooded it from the inside anyway: a swirling thrusting deluge, red as blood because of the copper in the dust here, a crane they hadn't managed to move swivelling wildly in the gushing torrents. Bergamosco, a chief engineer, had stood on the banks raging at the Zambezi, yelling *puttana!* as if Mother Nature were insulting him personally with this hundred-year flood.

Mrs Makupa came in again and handed Federico another memo without seeming to let off knitting – did she have a third arm in that bundle of black limbs? She waited while he read.

'Smith is here now?'

Mrs Makupa nodded, still knitting.

'Well, send him in then!'

✳

A few months after their wedding, Federico had surprised Sibilla with a *viaggio di nozze*.

'The seventh wonder of the world is only 500 kilometres down the river!'

They stayed in an old colonial hotel, a broad white structure with hammerhead wings and red tile roofing. It was so close to the Victoria Falls you could hear their faint roar in the distance. The lawns were perfect green carpets, the pool an unreal blue. The ceilings were high with slowstirring fans and pristine chandeliers, the churchly doors and windows topped with wooden arches. Sibilla eyed the fringed rugs sceptically – that just made them harder to clean. Black and white photographs lined the corridors, depicting the hotel's famed history.

Walking down one of those corridors after a tipsy night at the Rainbow Room bar, rubbing their stubbly faces against each other, Sibilla finally learned the truth about her family. She and Federico were drifting from frame to frame, staring at the photographs, trying to parse the captions in English beneath – neither of them were fluent yet. They were going backwards, so first came the boring conference rooms – 'Where the Federation's fate was decided,' Federico said. Here was a bejewelled woman – Princess Elizabeth in 1947. Here was a sleepy-eyed Indian man – he must be the Maharaja. Here were trolleys carting guests in floppy white hats to the Falls. Here was a train, the original Cape-to-Cairo.

Federico swayed ahead in his wrinkled suit and paused.

'Sibilla, Sibilla,' he called urgently. She approached, trying not to scratch her itchy face.

'Look.' He pointed at the portrait. Sibilla smiled at the man's vest and hat – so charmingly old-fashioned! Like Alba. She read the caption. The first hotelier. Gavuzzi.

She frowned. 'Was that not the name of . . . ?' She turned to Federico and they shouted out at the same time:

'The Signora!' she said.

'It's your grandfather!' he exclaimed.

They both laughed and stumbled on down the corridor. But after a moment, Sibilla grabbed her husband's shoulder and turned him towards her. 'Wait. What did you say?'

Nobody had ever told Sibilla that Signora Lina was her aunt, or that the Signora's brother Giacomo was her father, or that this man – Pietro Gavuzzi, who had apparently run this hotel in the middle of Africa – was her grandfather. Standing frozen before his portrait, trying to see her face in his, staring at the hat on his head, Sibilla was speechless as Federico explained her illegitimate life to her, insisting all the while that he'd assumed that she already knew.

Only later that night, as she lay with her back to Federico in their fancy hotel bed, did the tears come, the stubble on her face deviating their path. Sibilla didn't care that her father had abandoned her or that her aunt had made her work as a scullery maid. She didn't even care that her mother had kept all of this from her. She cared that Federico had known, and that she hadn't. Of all the torturous secrets between them, this was the one she could not brook – her husband had blithely let her believe that she was a bastard child with no past.

※

'What does this have to do with me, Mr Smith? I'm in charge of the dam, not the natives.'

'Yes, of course. We just thought it might help if they could set eyes on it.'

District Officer Smith was a tall Scotsman with a craggy face and a painstaking manner. He had once told Federico that he came from a family of fishermen, and Federico couldn't help feeling that it was beneath his dignity to report to him.

'The Tonga see the dam every day,' Federico shrugged. 'They certainly hear it.'

The two men were silent a moment, listening to the fray of construction on the dam: the thudding drills eating away at the rocksolid gorge, the creaking of the cranes, the rumble of the water coming through the diversion tunnel, the pitter of dust against metal, the droning worksongs of the blacks.

'Not all of the Tonga,' said Smith. 'These ones from Chipepo do not understand even the basic workings of a dam. They don't believe their village will be flooded. A demonstration—'

Federico laughed. 'Did they not see the riverbanks overflow after the rains last year?'

'The river floods every year, up to a point. They're quite used to that. But they have not been persuaded that within the next few months, this entire valley will be underwater.'

'Persuaded? The dam is already happening!' Federico pointed at the scurry of work beyond the window. As if in response, rain spattered feebly against the glass. 'Why do you not just round them up and move them again?'

Smith's pointy chin clenched. This was a sore spot for the British colonial officers. 'That was a last resort. The black nationalists agitating for independence – you've heard of the African National Congress?'

'*Sì*, I know them,' Federico snorted. 'They organised the dam labour strike last year.'

'Well, they told the naïve villagers that if they stayed put, then the dam wouldn't happen, that we would just give up. Our hands were tied – we had to send in the police.'

Federico thought the police should have been sent in sooner. Somewhere in the passage from Europe to Africa, from Sergeant to Colonel, he had lost his idealism. Why did the British keep treating the natives like wayward children? They held long *indabas*, gave them money, took them to parcel out their new land – all to no avail. As if the Tonga, with quills in their noses and clay in their hair, with their topless women who knocked out their front teeth for fashion, weren't destined to live off the land anyway. What did it matter where that land was?

✳

With Federico at the dam all day, Sibilla had too much time and too few tasks on her hands. These days, when he left for the office after break- fast, she would linger in her robe at the crude wooden dining table and ruminate. Why had he wanted her to keep thinking she was beneath him, like Cinderella? Why had he let her believe that she was of poor birth, that she had no father, that he had saved her from his brother? If even one of them was not true, could she be sure of the rest?

Young Enela was traipsing in and out of the room, clearing the plates. Sibilla reached into her robe and pulled out the postcard she'd bought at the hotel gift shop. It had become a talisman for her, its edges ribbed with fretting. She stared at in wonder. This was her grandfather, Pietro Gavuzzi (1870–1945), in his jaunty hat and vest. He stood arms akimbo before a crude building with a peaked roof and a wrap-around veranda – the original hotel – beside a giant sign that said VICTORIA FALLS. She had considered inscribing the postcard, sending it to her mother or to the Signora. *Dear Aunt Lina . . .* But that was not possible. Sibilla and Federico often lay awake all night calcu- lating how long they could pull off this theft of the Colonel's life. It was only a matter of time before someone found that corpse in the tomato patch.

Sibilla turned the postcard over and read the copyright: *Percy M. Clark, 1904.* She sounded the name out loud. It did not seem Italian.

'*Oh-oh*, you know that one, Ba Kalaki?'

Sibilla looked up. Enela was standing next to her, a set of plates bal- anced on her forearm. She had overhead Sibilla say the name.

'No. Do *you* know him?'

'Yes, please! Ba Kalaki had a shop those sides at Mosi-oa-Tunya. And my uncle, he was working for him . . .' The words faded as the girl waltzed into the kitchen with her tower of dishes.

The natives here seemed to refer to every male in the community as a father or an uncle or a grandfather. But regardless of his relation to Enela, if this 'uncle' of hers had known the man who took the photo- graph, Mr Clark, maybe he had known Sibilla's grandfather, too. The maternal line had been severed, but maybe she could trace the paternal line after all. Enela came back into the dining room, wiping her hands down her apron.

'Can you take me to your uncle?' Sibilla asked.

'To Bashi Bernadetta? *Ah-ah*? For what?' But before Sibilla could reply, Enela's frown released and she abruptly relented. 'Okay, it's okay. We can go.'

An hour later, they were bumping along a dirt road in one of the Impresit vehicles, Sibilla clad in gumboots and swathed in shawls. The driver's presence seemed to mute Enela. As soon as they got out and began the last stretch to the village on foot, however, she raised the topic of dam displacement. Sibilla knew, from Federico's scattered remarks, that the Tonga did not want to leave their homes. Enela explained that, while most of the villagers had agreed to go after the police had come, the old people still wished to remain. They had the right, they said, to stay with the dead, even if they would all be drowned when the river flooded.

'The dead?' Sibilla asked.

'The dead are the spirits,' said Enela. 'But we also have the white God. And other gods – the animals. And Nyami Nyami, that is the god that is swimming in the Zambezi . . .'

As Enela described this rivergod, with its serpentine body and whirlpool head, Sibilla's hair bristled under her shawls. She knew the African witch doctors sometimes decorated themselves with raffia. Did the Tonga think *she* was some kind of fetish, some animal spirit to be worshipped? Sibilla's suspicion grew when they reached the village, a cluster of mouldy thatched roofs held up by wooden poles, bundled goods here and there, ready to be transported.

Enela cleared their way through the throng, speaking in Tonga, a heavy language that freighted the air with ceremony. The women, naked but for their string skirts, averted their eyes but the men lay on the ground and rolled side to side, clapping their hands against their thighs as a sign of respect. Sibilla longed to ask them to get up – the rains had already kneaded the ground to red dough – but she refrained, knowing they'd find it condescending.

A plank was laid over the mud for her to enter one of the huts. An old native man in Western clothes was sitting on a wooden stool – this must be Enela's uncle. He beamed as Sibilla approached but fumbled over her hand and she realised that he could not see – his eyes had the blueish tinge that Nonna Giovanna's used to have. Sibilla sat on a stool and Enela introduced her as the wife of the *bwana* at Kariba. Only then did Sibilla understand that she was here not as a demi-god but because of her husband. The Tonga wanted her to serve as an emissary for the suicidal elders. Enela bowed and crouched out of the hut backwards.

Sibilla let her shawl fall away with relief – it was hot and fetid in here. The uncle grinned at her. He had no teeth, but she couldn't tell if this was age, health or Tonga custom – many of the women out-side were also missing their front teeth. Rain rustled the thatch roof. A mosquito looped ringingly round. Not for the first time, Sibilla was glad for the protective net of her hair.

'My name is Sibilla Gavuzzi,' she began.

'Mmmmm!' The old man clapped and smiled. 'Me. I am N'gulube.'

*

'They shot them,' Smith said after a moment. 'Eight Tonga men died on my watch.'

Federico looked at him, puzzled. 'Sì, but the Tonga declared war against your queen!'

'War?' Smith laughed bitterly. 'The villagers beat drums and threw rocks. They nailed misspelt manifestos to trees. They marched up and down in bare feet, imitating our police squadron, carrying spears on their shoulders as we carry rifles. Do you know how many spears were thrown? Hundreds! Not one policeman was injured. But eight bullets found their mark in the civilians.' Smith stood, put his hands in his pockets, and strolled over to the window. 'I dare say, Colonel, it was quite like Cain and Abel. Brothers murdering brothers.'

Federico started, then gave a forced chuckle. 'You think the blacks are our brothers?'

Smith turned to frown at him. 'No. The policemen shooting them were natives too.'

'Ah.' Federico tried to divert the topic from fratricide. 'Well, if you think a demonstration of the dam will help—' He was interrupted by the sound of a horn. It came in deafening blasts over the racket of construction and rain. Federico jumped up from his desk and ran to the window.

'The high-water signal!' he shouted over the din. 'It's too soon!'

But Smith was staring at him, shouting something incomprehensible.

'What?!'

'I thought!' the Scotsman shouted, pointing down at Federico's leg. 'You had! A limp!'

Federico shrugged, but panic was hammering through his body. The horns were still blasting. There was nothing to see out there – the floods had not yet come – but to distract Smith, he gestured out the window. And as if he had conjured her, there, suddenly, was his wife.

Sibilla was standing on the edge of the gorge, on a rocky outcropping. There was a crowd of people around her, natives, it looked like, some wearing traditional Tonga dress, others in Western clothes. Smith saw the villagers too – he put his hand to the glass as if out of fatherly concern. But Sibilla was neither their captive nor their leader. She simply stood among them in the static of the rain, her wet black hair encasing her, the Zambezi raising its red hackles behind her. Then the wind came and it started to roil.

We meet you wherever there's standing water. You like to treat us like beasts of the wild but civilisation suits us fine. A puddle, a tree hole or a lake works well; so does a tyre, a gutter, a pipe. You see, whenever you collect water – stand it in jars or gutter your roof or build a great dam to contain it – you're cupping an amniotic crib for us. We doomed the Panama Canal twice this way – the Chagres river flooded its banks and swamped you with all sorts of fevers. So of course we know the secrets of the biggest man-made lake in the world.

The tale of a place is the tale of its water, and Kariba Dam is no exception. The bantu wished to dam the Kafue but the bazungu chose the Zambezi instead.

'We're making a dam,' they told the Tonga. 'A kariba, a trap for the river.'

'You can't trap a river,' the Tonga replied, 'much less the mighty Zambezi, which is ruled by a god with the head of a fish and the tail of a snake. Nyami Nyami will undo your work.'

Omens unheeded, the bazungu proceeded with their foolish and damnable plan. They rescued the animals – 'Operation Noah' – then drove the Tonga off in tightly packed lorries. The people were banished from their homes to a land with no marshes, no river – the soil full of lead, the wood full of smoke, the ground as hard as a rock. Nyami Nyami's curse had barely begun.

The dam half-built, the fat rains came, and the Zambezi rose up and charged. It knocked the dam aside and swallowed some workers. The Tonga said, 'Nyami Nyami is hungry.' They killed a black calf and threw it in the river and the bodies washed up where it vanished. The feckless bazungu continued building the dam. When the flood came again, it lifted four men, plastered them to the dam like insects. The concrete was wet; the workers were dead; in the end, they built the dam around them. Strange tomb!

Now listen close to the first of our lessons: Federico did this too with his love for his wife; he swallowed her up in his faith. Yet he denied this same choice to the elders of the Tonga: the relief of total belief. No drowning for the natives, Federico declared, Sibilla's intercession be damned. This, and his betrayal – one secret too many – would sever their bond completely. You cannot contain the manifold fury of a people, a river, a woman!

Agnes

1962

Once upon a time in a faraway land, there was a princess and she played tennis because that was all she knew and *she was very good*, she was the best in all of southern England, minor newspapers characterising her style of play with words usually reserved for ornithology or engineering, *and she received many gifts* – there were trophies and cloth ribbons that rivalled the ornaments and jewellery she grew up with, prizes that paid for more vases and necklaces than she could possibly fill with flowers and throats – *when one day, out of the blue*, out of the clear blue sky, which she made herself gaze at until she could make out its colour every day up to the very end, *she went blind*, her vision bleeding away in droplets of sight over seven months until she couldn't see anything at all *and that was the end of the princess's dreams* – she knew she would never win Wimbledon, never celebrate on camera.

And so *she spent her days in her castle*, dressed in wool trousers and jerseys, eating half a cold dinner in the dining room, *walking the corridors, the echoes alone persuading her that the walls still existed, stalking the parapets and* slumping up and down stairs, she repeated words from the shiny reviews of old tennis matches, *singing a sad song to herself*, until finally spring came – the heat in the air, the heady smell of blossoms, birdsong loud enough to wake you.

One day, she put on her tennis shoes, tightened her racket strings, and began to collect them, *gathering as many dreams as possible* – the old tennis balls *from their hidden places around the castle*, from under the sofa and behind the fridge, above and between books, all the nooks where they had been abandoned to wither and soften like kiwis. *She made her way to the Grand Court*, her white stick tapping the starkest soundtrack as she walked along the stone path to the unkempt lawn.

She inhaled deeply *and she began to dance* – she rolled her shoulders, plucked a ball from the bag at her feet, tossed it in the air, and waited for it to rise ... remember gravity ... and fall into the rushing swing of her racket, *because although the princess could not see, she still knew how to lean, reach and spin.*

And so she danced by herself, serving until the bag lay empty, all birthed out. Then she picked up the empty sack, walked to the other side of the court, and crawled around, scavenging for the scattered balls and thus she played solo, *tracing that space alone* for two long months, a dead, knee-scraped time *until* ... One day, *the princess felt a tap on the shoulder and,* sensing that someone was standing above her, *she asked, 'Who's there?' The silent stranger took her arm;* she tensed, *smiling* with the complacent grimace of a trained circus performer, she groped for her racket, and she served. As soon as she heard the ball skimming the net, *she curtsied; he applauded;* she felt a hand on hers, then a furry little globe – someone had handed her what she was seeking, *and that is how the blind princess met the silent stranger.*

✳

Little circles of blankness had appeared one by one, first in the left eye, then in the right. Agnes could only tell that her eyes were failing at different rates when she closed one or the other. For each drop of sight that disappeared from her view, a small bump of the same size formed under her skin – on her forearm, her back, her cheek – like an insect bite but without the itch. She didn't notice this strange and gradual pox; she didn't connect the dots. Indeed, it took three losses in the autumn season before she casually mentioned to her mother that sometimes, when the tennis ball came speeding towards her, it simply vanished as if into a pocket of air.

Agnes was still in denial when her mother insisted they go to see their old family doctor that winter. Agnes sat on the edge of the examination table, her mother's hand trembling on her shoulder. Her father was seated in the corner of the room. His figure was blurry but she imagined he was in his usual posture – legs and arms crossed, keeping himself contained behind Xs. She could hear his incessant murmur of *hmms*, the static of his agreement burring her conversation with Dr Lemming, which was beginning to sound like something that Agnes's thespian cousin Jane might rave about: a modern existential drama, all questions and answers on a dark stage.

'Can you see this?' A faint beacon spun across Agnes's visual frame.

'Yes,' she said.

'And this?' A peripheral flicker, like a light bulb dying behind her.

'Yes!'

Her mother patted her shoulder to reassure or reproach her for her promptness.

'Has a ball ever hit you in the head or face?'

'No,' she scoffed. 'I'm ranked eighth in Surrey. *Eighth.*'

'Mm, of course.' A waft of onion. Did Dr Lemming keep a tiny onion under his tongue? Agnes had wondered this as a child, too, with more conviction in its likelihood.

'And can you see this?'

She heard a click but saw nothing. After a pause, she replied: 'Yes, of course I can.'

Her mother's hand lost its quicksilver tremble on her shoulder, became leaden. Agnes felt a sudden fury, hot and wet, behind her eyes. If nothing else, *this* would blind her, her mother's hand sinking its weight into her shoulder, her father no longer murmuring in the corner, everyone waiting with bated breath but not the way they'd once waited for her flat serve.

'Are you sure, Agnes?'

Nothing, nothing, a Venn diagram of nothing.

'Yes! I can see it, I'm sure, I'm fine. I'm fine, yes I can see it ...'

'Alrighty now.' Her mother gripped her shoulder. 'He turned it ... the torch isn't ... nothing to ...'

Dr Lemming grunted and cracked his knuckles. Agnes shivered. She had always been wary of her doctor's hands. As a teenager, she had noticed with horror why they seemed so misshapen – Dr Lemming had bitten his nails down nearly a half. Did he still bite them? Was he musingly gnawing away at them at this very moment? But no, Dr Lemming was uttering dry words – *scotoma, macular, retina, optic* – that her mother was wringing for a drop of hope: 'Money not a ... Anything we can ... Is there ...' The slightest creep of a cool shadow, another waft of onion, Dr Lemming's rough palm on her arm.

'Agnes, can you describe what you see? What does it look like, exactly?'

Agnes had never witnessed the burning of a photograph but she must have seen it in a film or read it in a book because this was what she thought to say. It was as if someone had held all that she could see over a flame until tiny holes appeared, then merged to form larger ones until her whole picture of the world had curled away. The strangest thing – the holes were not black. They were just places she couldn't see, the colour of nothing.

This wasn't what she said to Dr Lemming, though. What she said was:

'Terribly sorry, I don't know what it *looks* like. Because according to you, I can't *see*.'

Her mother clucked softly. Agnes hung her head, embarrassed by her stagey petulance, then rolled her head in a neck stretch she used to do before matches. This was comforting.

'Your sense of irony is admirable under the circumstances, Agnes,' Dr Lemming said flatly. 'It shows pluck.' He tapped her knee with a rough finger. 'But it won't make you see again.'

Agnes felt a snag in her throat as he stepped away, his shoes chirping on the parquet.

*

Agnes had always been a shallow, chatty girl. Going blind did not deepen her but it did shut her up somewhat, mostly because she found it hard to tell whether someone was speaking expressly to her. At first she insisted that everyone in the family preface their remarks with her name if they wished her to pay attention to them. But then she grew weary of hearing her name all the time (bloody condescending!), so she decided that they should raise their voices instead. Several rather shouty breakfasts later, it was clear that this would not do, either.

'Christ, Mum. No need to bellow!' Agnes shouted. 'I'm not *deaf*.'

'Oh dear,' Carolyn murmured, 'we'd better ... shall we ... the tea should ...' and escorted Agnes from the dining room to her bedroom, the doleful girl banging her shoulder purposely against every door-jamb on the way. Since the visit to Dr Lemming, Agnes had made every little crisis an excuse to throw a tantrum and stay locked up in her bedroom for days. She would pee haphazardly into a bedpan and eat mechanically from a laptray that Carolyn herself restocked. Now, Agnes slumped onto the bed and patted the side table until she found a plate of stale toast congealed with honey. She crunched into it, know-ing it would irk her mother.

'Dear Agnes, must you ... always said ... chewing ... I suppose ... but really, it's ...'

'And you, dear Mother.' Agnes spewed crumbs. 'Must you speak so gappily?'

Carolyn had developed this habit of speech when she'd married George in the early 1940s. Even back then, he'd had the aristocratic habit of interrupting people with encouraging noises: *Mmm ... yes ... yes ... of course ... yes ... mmhmm*, he would murmur loudly, some-times closing with an enthusiastic *Well!* If you responded to his cues by falling silent, you faced his expectant stare. Over the years, Carolyn had learned to accommodate her husband's intrusions by speaking in waves, which also had the advantage of disguising her less refined accent. She had been educated in England but could not shake her foreign-born roots. Carolyn's ellipses had grown especially lengthy lately, as she fretted over her daughter's waist and marital prospects.

'Sweetheart ... food is ... duvet cover ... crumbs all ...' Carolyn dribbled out minor chastisements as she tidied up the mess around Agnes, who lay like a queen in her litter.

'Nope. Sorry, Mummy. Can't *see* crumbs.' Agnes wiped honey from the cul-de-sac above her lip with a delicate pinkie. 'Blind, enn eye?'

Carolyn, helpless, retreated from the close-smelling room. Agnes lay down and took a nap. She dreamt she was playing tennis with two slippery, bristly balls that turned out to be her eyes. They stared up at her from her palms, blue and white and unblinking. *But if they're in my hands, how can I see them?*

She woke to a knock at the door. Her mother bustled in with her gardenia perfume.

'Your father ... out and decided ... a cane!'

Carolyn placed Agnes's hands on it. Agnes took it, held it cautiously away from her body, felt along its length.

'Is it ... white?'

'Mmm? ... oh, yes.'

'I've never thought about it really, but – are they *always* white, do you know?'

Carolyn did not know. Agnes stood with her cane and tested out movements. Swing it in circles? Tap it either side like a metronome? Trace figures of eight? Hold it hovering above the ground like a divining rod?

'Well, I suppose you ... the most important thing ... whatever ... comfortable?'

Agnes put her hand on her hip and held the cane out like a challenge, then lunged forward and brandished it, duelling the air and surprising them both into laughter.

'Well ... I suppose!' Carolyn summed up triumphantly.

Agnes lowered the tip of the cane to the floor. 'Yes,' she said softly. 'I suppose.'

This was improvement. Agnes had left her bed. After a few days, she began to leave her room as well. When she moved around indoors, she still preferred to count steps and feel for the furniture with outstretched arms, her hands floating, fingers undulating like seaweed, radiating openness to touch. But when she ventured outside, she used her cane. Its pittering sound, like the tick of a nervous watch, seemed to comfort her.

'It's certainly got her out of bed, hasn't it, *hmm*,' George said to Carolyn, smugly drawing his lips to one side.

Carolyn smiled and pushed his lips back to the middle of his face with a gentle finger. She knew, as every woman in the household knew, that it wasn't the cane but Agnes's monthlies that had finally prompted her to leave the dismal swamp of her bed.

*

The first task Agnes learned after her diagnosis, apart from getting food into and out of her body, was how to use a sanitary belt by feel. Mrs Wainscroft, the cook, whose manner was as forthright as her menu, assisted while Carolyn quivered outside the loo, making patchy suggestions:

'You might ... with the ... is everything?'

Agnes growled for silence.

'Such a complinckated garment,' came Mrs Wainscroft's high voice. 'Toss a towel in the girdle and be done with it, I say.' Then clapping hands and a raucous laugh – 'Righty-o, go on now. That'll keep you from staining another skirt all chocolatey!'

Most of Agnes's clothes were white, a habit from her tennis days, though she rarely wore her gear now – the collared short-sleeved shirts, the pleated skirts with their deep pockets. Some days, she would sit on the floor of her closet, enveloped in sartorial history. She would reach up and run her fingers over the garments and sniff up at the whispering polyester, the wooden hangers clucking with pity. Other days, she would take out her rackets and pull wanly at the strings like a piano tuner. To be so young, on the edge of greatness, only to suffer a fate as ancient and weighty as blindness! No end to the slings and arrows, and they were all aimed at Agnes.

But even misery gets boring after a while. Her parents were soon accustomed to her condition. George, a local MP, was busy being re-elected and Carolyn was busy worrying about it. When spring came, Agnes found herself itching to play again. She longed for the looping relay, that back-and-forth of human relation. The maids were too skittish, and she daren't ask Mrs Wainscroft: with those biceps and Agnes's blind eyes, a concussion on one side or the other seemed likely.

So, one day, Agnes clambered out of bed, put on a musty tennis suit, grabbed a racket and a bag of balls, and made her way to the old lawn by herself. She walked its periphery – more of a lozenge than a rectangle – trampling the overgrown grass, then felt along the net in its centre, wincing as she fingered the new holes in it. She took ten steps away and turned to face it. She pulled a ball from the bag and served. It was gratifying to feel the racket make contact until she heard the ball *fwip* weakly against the low stone wall on the other side. She gritted her teeth and served again. *Fwap!* Much better.

Ronald was a student of engineering at the University of London's Institute of Education. He was being sponsored for his degree by Sir Stewart Gore-Browne, who took an interest in any young man who had done exceptionally well at the school on his Rhodesian estate. Gore-Browne still kept in close touch with family and friends in England and had sent brusque but effective letters of introduction ahead for Ronald, who now rotated from estate to estate from one term holiday to the next. His fifth holiday had landed him at George and Carolyn's home in Surrey.

Ronald pitched up at the train station in late spring, besuited and carrying a clutch with two changes of clothes and his textbooks. Ignoring the chauffeur's sly-eyed sneer, he slid into the back seat of the Silver Cloud, admiring its wood panels and stitched leather and chrome fittings. The Rolls coasted around tarmac roads – small bright sedans swimming around this slow-moving shark – for nearly an hour before turning off onto a gravel drive whose stones gurgled affably under the wheels. The drive into the estate itself was cosseted in a lush, leafy canopy and twice interrupted by tall iron gates.

When they arrived at the manor, the chauffeur released Ronald into the custody of a maid, who was far more polite. She curtsied and gestured him through the large wooden doors into a tall, dark vestibule, a single skylight piercing down from above. They mounted the marble stairs and walked along a corridor, the walls of which were covered with oil paintings of aristocratic ancestors. His suite was enormous, with floor-to-ceiling windows through which you could see the flat green lawns and in the distance, a glowing haze of bluebells at the edge of the woods. Everything in here seemed drowned in heavy cloth: blankets, curtains, pillows, thick rugs. Even the washroom was carpeted. Amongst the jumble of decor, he noticed two ebony busts of African slaves, a man and a woman carved in European style, their profiles thin caricatures of negritude.

The maid left him and he unpacked, hanging his two thin suits in the armoire, and stacking his four thick books by the bed. Then he took himself on a tour. As usual, he fell immediately into a fever of class anxiety as he wandered around, peeking into the countless rooms. Torn between envy and gratitude, he compared this estate with the last, then compared both to the incomparable original, Shiwa

Ng'andu. Sir George was apparently an MP – was that different from a baron? How was he to be addressed? Ronald always worried he would neglect some custom or another: English etiquette was as rigid and inconsistent as English grammar.

At least this estate had a well-stocked library, he thought as he strolled around a gloomy room with a tomb's worth of tomes. The books were in variable states of wear, their pages either leathery with use or so brittle they crumbled at the touch. It looked like mostly legal theory with the occasional glance at ancient history: Pliny, Thucydides, Herodotus. There was no modern science, which was a relief. Ronald often felt obliged to read those books first, less out of interest and more because his hosts, knowing that he studied engineering, would inevitably quiz him on the only science they knew. He finally found a trove of novels and a few translated works of mythology – Greek, Roman, Norse – in a corner. These proved to be Lady Carolyn's – was that her title? – which was rather less useful to him.

At dinner that evening, his hostess demurred his efforts at conversation, offering him endless dishes instead, accompanied by apologies – 'must be ... taste so different ... wish we could ... well ... suppose ... best we can.' Ronald knew by now to thank her profusely and pretend that the rich sauces did not cloy his taste buds, that the overboiled vegetables did not caulk every cranny of his mouth. Sir George seemed to have a cold. He kept clearing his throat, *hmming* and *hrghing*. He spoke just once and then only to say: 'Our daughter. She's ... ill, or rather, hrmm, *indisposed* at the moment. She sends her regards.' Ronald expressed his best wishes for her health, then wondered if he had been too forward in alluding to her body at all. He gave up on conversation altogether and for the rest of the meal took recourse to smiling and nodding at Sir George, a great nodder himself, their bobbing heads as if on either end of a scale.

✳

When Ronald finally set eyes on this indisposed daughter, he was reading on a bench by the side of the tennis lawn – the best place, he had discovered, to avoid the strenuous labour of being a guest in a British manor. He had just turned to a chapter on aerodynamics in his textbook when he heard an insecty hum followed by a hollow pock, like a drop of water falling down a drain. He looked up and saw a ball bounce off the low wall beside him. He stopped it with his foot and smiled and waved at the tall girl in white holding a racket on the other side of the lawn. He was a little offended when she didn't wave back.

Instead, she tilted her face up to the sky and took a long sniff. The sunlight hit her eyes, turning the lids translucent, and that's when he saw that they were closed – she hadn't seen him. Was she winking now? No, just a flash of light from the edge of her racket as she raised it and pressed a ball against the strings with her other hand. Eyes still shut, she tossed and leaned and swung with a grunt. The yellow ball flew like a comet through the air, hit the short wall again, bounce-bounce-bounced and stammered to a stop.

Ronald closed his book and watched for a while. He considered the uses of blind play as a training technique. It would attune the player to her body, and hone her instincts so that sight was not the sole arbiter of when to strike. He grew puzzled again when the girl walked to the other side to gather the balls. The way she moved around on her knees, the way she patted the blank spaces between balls – oh, she couldn't see at all! This was not the blindness he knew from home, eyelids bulging or welded shut with pus, begging hands outstretched. Nor was it the kind he knew from the London Underground, people walking into him as if he were a pole that had popped up in the middle of the moving stairs.

The blind girl started to serve again, from his side of the net now. It was a relief to watch someone, himself unwatched. Her legs were exquisite, long and thick and white like the trunks of the silver birches on the eastern edge of the garden. Her face, collecting droplets of sweat like a cold glass of water, was not beautiful, but solid and cool. Her mouth never curved or opened. Her brow never clenched. As she grew warmer, flush dusted her cheeks with pink and yellow like the magnolia blossoms he'd seen in Kew Gardens.

Ronald sometimes had the impression that he saw eyes in her skin – or rather, felt them there like a watchful presence. She seemed both weak and imperious, helpless yet haughty. In a word: British. Right before she swung the racket, when she arched, raised up on her toes and leaned back, he would feel an urge to run to her, to encircle her waist and catch her before – but, of course, she never fell. He still wanted to hold her there, though, to lower her slowly, letting her bend like a bow until her long ponytail grazed the grass . . .

*

Every morning, after a strained and greasy breakfast with Carolyn and George, Ronald would take a stroll in the gardens, sniffing the flowers most foreign to him – honeysuckles and poppies still drooling with dew – then walk through the bluebell-infested forest to the stable to visit the horses, shiny as polished wood, their long heads as elegant as those of the *lechwe* at Shiwa. In the fields beyond, sullen cows sometimes approached, not to attack him, he learned from Carolyn, but expecting to be milked.

He visited the dairy only once. Encouraged by the grinning farmhand there, who mimed instructions as if not quite believing that a guest so exotic spoke English, Ronald stuck his pinkie into a newborn calf's mouth. He enjoyed the sucking caress until he remembered that his new tic of chewing his cuticles essentially made them open wounds. For days, Ronald obsessed about infection and henceforth avoided all farm life at the estate. He had not travelled so far in distance, years and education only to subject himself to diseases of the hand, mouth and foot.

After he first caught sight of the blind girl playing tennis, Ronald figured out which bedroom window belonged to her and began to pause outside it after his morning walks. Hiding behind a manicured hedge, he'd furtively pluck its leaves to make an aperture to see her through. This soon became the goal towards which his day was pitched: spying on the sleeping beauty until, weather permitting, she sat up and searched with nimble toes for the shoes beneath her bed. Then he would hurry to the tennis lawn, avoiding the maid blinkingly shaking a rug or casting out slops behind the kitchen, and sit on his bench with his textbook on his lap.

He felt smitten with pity and a kind of fear as he watched this pale, mad girl serve to no one, then rummage on her knees for the balls she had scattershotted, collecting them in her skirt and tumbling them into a canvas bag that, like the sky, slowly greyed as autumn approached. One day, it simply became unbearable to see her crawling around with those bright fuzzy spheres eluding her, drifting off at the touch of a finger. So Ronald stood up and went to her and gave her what she was grasping for.

*

It took a week of Agnes serving tennis balls and Ronald collecting them before they managed a proper interaction. They couldn't play – he didn't know how and she could no longer teach – so they exchanged words squatting on the lawn, tennis balls bumping between their ankles. At first there wasn't too much to say: he was a student, she was Agnes; he was Ronald, she used to play tennis really, really well. After a few days of empty chat, she gave in to a desire she had never confessed, not even to herself. She wanted someone to describe the world she could no longer see. She would never think of asking anyone in the house. They were all dreadfully inarticulate in one way or another, which had become clearer to her now that she relied so much on voices.

But Ronald spoke a straightforward, mellifluous English, lapsing only occasionally into malapropisms and odd idioms. Agnes could ascribe these to neither class nor region. Her parents had offered only the vaguest words about their guest's background: 'his sort', her father said; 'such innocent people', her mother said; 'substandard culture', her father said; 'in his nature', her mother said. Too bemused to enquire further, Agnes took any strangeness in Ronald's manner of speaking as a sign of personality or fashion – what did she know of hip lingo, isolated as she was from swinging London? She relished the lack of clutter in his sentences. None of those bloody *ers* and *ums*.

'Would you describe ... the sky for me?' she asked one day, a little hesitantly.

'I would say partly cloudy with a chance of rain, Madam.'

'There's always a chance of rain here,' she snorted. 'And don't call me Madam! Unless you want me to call you Mister!' She paused. 'I suppose you could call me *Mad* – short for Madam. And I'll call you *Miss* – short for Mister!' Her laughter died alone. Had she just insulted them both in a single drollery? She willed her voice to be softer, *coyed* it.

'And these clouds you mention. Are they white? Or grey?' she asked in a way that presaged a witty remark about variously coloured clouds.

'Oh? I am sorry, it was a lie. There are no clouds today.'

Agnes thought he was being facetious and felt a little daunted.

'Fine then,' she said, smiling bravely. 'Is the sky blue? Or is it *blueblue?*'

'It's blueblue. Like your eyes.'

'Oh dear, are they open? I try to keep them closed, but ...'

After an awkward pause, she asked him if he liked it here.

'Ah, it is very fine. Merrie England.'

She'd meant Surrey but now he was asking her if she liked it, and they were off again, talking about what they liked and what they hated: at school, at dinner, in cities and outside of them. She explained to him the rules of tennis, which he found baffling.

'Why do you call it *love* when you have zero points?' he asked.

Surely this was just an excuse to talk about romance. He sounded earnest, though.

'It comes from the French word for egg, *l'oeuf.* Because a zero is the shape of an egg.'

'Oh-*oh?*' he chuckled. 'But I thought the English hated the French.'

'Oh, we do, but we steal from them mercilessly. It's sort of our thing.'

✳

A few weeks later, Agnes was feasting on honeytoast and tea in the kitchen. Mrs Wainscroft was with her, offering backhanded admiration:

'A blessing, Miss Agnes, to have such lovely pale skin ... *pallid* skin, I've heard 'em call it, must be nice!' Mrs Wainscroft often pretended to greater illiteracy in order to make her point. It was her version of irony. 'So fascinating to see it against that Mr Ronald, you know, with *his.*'

'Hmm?' Agnes murmured through a mouthful of tea-soggy toast. She was feeling her knees under the table, wondering if they looked as rough as they felt.

'Never saw nothing like it. A chessboard or somethink.'

The week after that, they were discussing how Agnes would fare in London, whether she was ready for a shopping trip. Could she cross the streets on her own at the lights and at the—

'Why is it, d'you think, they call it a *zebra* crossing?' asked Mrs Wainscroft.

'The stripes, obviously,' said Agnes, her head in the closet as she felt along the seams of her old clothes, trying to discern by hand what textures she preferred.

'But where does *zebra* come from? Are they black with white lines, or white with black?'

'Doesn't matter, dear Crofty,' said Agnes. 'I can't make out lines anyway.'

Her voice was strained with patience. One of the great burdens of blindness was having to help other people remember it. But Agnes was growing reconciled to it. Time was passing, softening the rocks against which she once thought her life had foundered. And flirtation – the sheer possibility of romance – had stirred up a glorious hormonal buzz in her. It drowned out just about everything else.

When Ronald had first touched her arm on the tennis lawn, Agnes had felt a shock of warmth in her stomach: embarrassment combined with the recognition that he had been there all along. He was that metallic smell in the air singing like a high note over the cut grass and the rubber balls. He was the reason that, after serving, she had so often found herself waiting, as if the ball were on its way back. Now that they were spending more time together, his smell had become a comfort, even coated with his cheap men's spray.

There were other, more practical advantages to Ronald. He was monstrously witty, though she couldn't always judge his tone. He had a ludicrous name, and he was short, but neither of these flaws was his fault, after all. And he was a university student, which promised upward mobility. Besides, they didn't need money – she had her trust and her prize earnings. They would get a house, a small one with a tennis lawn, and maybe a corgi, like the Queen.

＊

When the epiphany came, it was like the jerk that wakes you from a dream of falling. Agnes had put on her nicest dress and invited Ronald to tea. They sat on the patio with the bird fountain. The birds were babbling. The fountain was chattering but not quite like rain – the pattern slightly more predictable. They were discussing family and Ronald mentioned something about his mother. The name was so exotic, especially compared to his, that Agnes simply had to ask.

'Well,' he replied, 'she is from the east. They mostly speak Chichewa there.'

'East ... Anglia?'

Ronald slurped his cup of tea and swallowed. 'No,' he said warily. 'The eastern part of Northern Rhodesia.'

'Oh ...' Agnes murmured, paging through her limited knowledge of geography.

'Oh?' she said, hitting upon a map of Africa, then on Grandpa Percy's finger pointing at a jigsaw piece inside it.

'Oh!' she exclaimed.

'Oh God,' she whispered.

The fountain splattered, the birds sang, the sun sunned down.

Agnes burst into laughter – thick, riotous, frothy laughter.

It wasn't that Mrs Wainscroft's hints hadn't conveyed the message about Ronald's race; it was that Agnes had chosen to hear them vaguely, to let them leave the impression of a certain swarthiness, a Byronic charm. It had never occurred to her that the object of her passion was of the darker persuasion, was Negroid, was *African* – a *nigger*, a *Kaffir*, Grandpa Percy's words bounced around her head unwittingly.

The revelation set Agnes vibrating with the force of a waterfall uncovered by the shifting of a great stone. In this flood was a current of amazement that this was possible: the not-knowing of it, the bloody *blindness* of it. There was flotsam of intrigue, jetsam of revulsion. Elation, a flurry of bubbles. Fear, rocks glinting under the water. Mrs Wainscroft's pointed comments resurfaced. A chessboard! What was the other one? Something about day and night, shadow and light? 'Those stripy horses' had been invoked at one point. Agnes laughed even harder. And now, floating above the momentous epiphany, like mist over the falls, relief: despite the cook's clumsy euphemisms and petty misgivings, the old biddy hadn't told Agnes's parents. Yet.

'That was a jolly laugh,' said Ronald, sounding slightly disconcerted.

'Yes, it was, wasn't it?' Agnes sighed and they each took a slurp of their tea.

*

Their first time naked together was a kind of miracle. Ronald seemed cautious at first, but when he realised she was letting him undress her, he responded eagerly. They tussled with their clothing, with their legs – so many legs, his in between hers or on either side or alternating – and finally he took her hand and guided it to his centre. Agnes knew what she would find there, and that it would be soft or hard, depending. But she had somehow never considered the transition from one state of being to the other. At her touch, it rose, and this independent action, a clock's hand moving towards noon or midnight, that rise to fullest tallest splendour, made her marvel.

'Oh dear!' she said. 'How lovely!'

Then came the blunder and blur, the pain and the pleasure, and the crying out, their voices like bells striking a rough harmony to announce and seal their union.

They were in the old shed behind the tennis lawn, surrounded by the smell of rusted tools. The wind shook the thin walls and whistled through the cracks in them. As they lay in that gusty, musty aftermath, Agnes asked Ronald to describe the room. He said the window was glowing green from the light coming through the trees outside, which made watery shadows on the walls. She asked him to describe her body. He spoke about *density*, which, because of his distinctive pronunciation, she mistook at first for *destiny*. But no, Ronald was speaking like the engineering student he was, about mass: how it felt when he lifted her thighs, how heavy her hair was despite its fineness. He analysed the bridge of her nose. He didn't mention skin colour.

The funny thing was, Agnes couldn't remember the look of *black* and *white* any more. When she concentrated on the words, all she felt was a vague sense of contrast, a drama of darkness and light. Why should colour mean so much? Oh, the slings and arrows! Agnes decided to loosen like the strings of a racket, to let the flung orbs get stuck, to grow around them. People would stare. Let them! She wouldn't see their eyes anyway.

She thought of Althea Gibson. The black American with the power drives and the gangly reaches, the Negress who had triumphed at Wimbledon even though it had reached 39°C, who had kissed the Queen's hand and sung jazz at the Astor. That was the future of race relations. Yes, Agnes had always been rather shallow, but as is often the case, this turned out to be rather an advantage when it came to love.

＊

There was no way to climb the thorny wall that sprung up between Agnes and her parents when she told them, however. They didn't even know about whom she was speaking at first.

'Oh ... delightful! An engagement! He ... where did ... ?' Carolyn sounded flustered.

'Here, of course,' said Agnes. 'He's very kind, as you know. Quite serious. Awfully witty.'

They were sitting in the conservatory, tea cooling in china cups. Agnes was lying on a bench, feigning a casual posture, a hand propping her head up. On the wrought-iron table, there was a breakfast spread – scones and blackcurrant jam, a jar of rustling cereal, a jug of fresh milk.

'Ahem,' George cleared his throat. 'Agnes, darling, did you say you met here?'

'Yes, your visitor, Papa. Here for the holidays? The engineering student.'

'Roland?' George asked, perplexed.

'Who?' asked Carolyn. 'Goodness ... not *French*, is he?'

'Dear God, no!' Agnes said automatically, then paused. 'Well, he is ... non ... British.' She breathed in the scent of her mother's perfume and the sugary tea and the roses unwinding from their buds. 'It *is* Papa's visitor,' she said. 'But his name is *Ronald*. And we're in love.'

'Hmm ... hrm?' George murmured like a record that has stopped but has yet to be turned.

'Technically, you're from there, too, Mummy. Northern Rhodesia. Lovely place, apparently. Didn't Grandpa Percy know Ronald's sponsor, Sir Stewart?'

'Christ!' Carolyn sputtered. '*Rhodesia* ... dear child ... You have no ...'

'I know you never talk about it – you barely lived there – but Grandpa Percy told me stories when he visited. When I was a girl.' Agnes smiled. 'About the hotel and the Italian man they put up on the mantel to sing like a bird and the great waterfall, one of the seven wonders ...'

'Victoria Falls, hmm,' George said distractedly.

'George!' Carolyn admonished.

'But Papa, you married a schoolteacher!' Agnes said. 'You always said love is blind!'

'Not *that* blind,' George murmured with an awkward laugh.

Agnes hung her head, trying not to weep. Her parents' silence swelled and reddened and seemed to suppurate like a wound. Finally, in a voice Agnes had never heard before – gapless, as if no longer needing to accommodate her husband or as if they now spoke as one – her mother issued their final words on the matter:

'You have disgraced us. Your grandfather would roll in his grave. You had better pray that this Kaffir has not yet laid a finger on you. Because if he has, I promise you, he will hang.'

1963

They got on a ship and sailed away. It wasn't easy. Ronald was largely unfamiliar with British bureaucracy; Agnes could barely manage a meal on her own, much less a voyage to Africa. They found an unlikely ally in Mrs Wainscroft, who was more delighted than dismayed by all the drama. 'Your dear mother has some nerve, given where she's come up from!' she said. Crafty old Crofty knew her business. She helped Agnes withdraw money from the trust that had come into effect two years earlier. She accompanied them on their train to Liverpool and arranged for tickets for the next voyage on the *Braemar Castle* to Mombasa – Agnes in First Class, Ronald in Third. 'Common enough to have a Negro porter,' she said. 'Just don't act like you're equals.'

For two weeks, Agnes and Ronald travelled in parallel across the Indian Ocean, conversing discreetly, eating separately. When the ship docked in Mombasa, they met as planned at the exit. Ronald bowed slightly, 'Madam,' he said, and guided her down the plank and off the ship, his hand lightly grazing her arm and her back. They were both thrumming with joy. It was a relief to be in contact again – they had just reached that stage of love when bodies become mutually addicted. They stood a moment on the bustling dock together, the murmurous rumble of the city before them, the low roar of the sea behind.

In between the pinkening passengers disembarking, brown boys raced around calling out their services. Ronald whistled for one. Though he was sweating and uncomfortable in his new suit – ordered specially for him at Hogg's, Sir Stewart's London tailor – he was glad to have it on. He felt his body relax into the familiar gestures of hierarchy. He pointed, instructing a boy to carry their trunks as he steered Agnes by the elbow through the motley crowd towards the cars cross-hatching the square directly in front of the docks. He secured a Model T Ford taxi and negotiated the price with the driver as the boy loaded their trunks into the boot. He paid the boy in British shillings – docking his tip for his open-mouthed stare at Agnes, whose sweat had drenched her dress transparent – and helped her into the cracked leather interior.

'Old Town,' he said to the driver, who had taken up the boy's stare as if they had simply changed shifts. Ronald shut his door with a creaky bang and off they went, slowly navigating the throng.

After one night here in Mombasa to recover from the long sea crossing, they would take a car to Nairobi and fly to Mpika. Then they would pick up his cousin's car and drive west to Shiwa Ng'andu, the closest thing to a British estate in all of Northern Rhodesia. There, Agnes could be wined and dined and cocooned in English custom, smoothing her transition into Africa. Ronald also felt obliged to express his gratitude for the bursary he had received from Sir Stewart Gore-Browne to study in England, to express how honoured he was to be one of the great man's 'sponsored boys'. In truth, Ronald was keen to stage a prodigal son's return. His white bride-to-be would be like a trophy on his arm as he mounted the hill of cypress trees and entered through the gates to Shiwa Ng'andu.

'But what *is* it?' asked Agnes. 'I know it's your family home, but what is the history of this ... She-war Nigandoo?'

During his time at university, Ronald had learned that 'history' was the word the English used for the record of every time a white man encountered something he had never seen and promptly claimed it as his own, often renaming it for good measure. History, in short, was the annals of the bully on the playground. This, he knew, was what Agnes would expect to hear. So Ronald skipped the real story: the southern migration of the Bemba tribe from the north in the seventeenth century, the battles with other tribes and the bargains with Arab slave traders that had left only a straggling group of warriors wandering the great plateau with its many lakes, carting around a wooden carving of a crocodile, their *chitimukulu's* totem, until one day, in the valley at the base of a circle of rocky hills, they came across a sapphire lake, *shiwa*, with a dead crocodile, *ng'andu*, on its shores – a sign that they should settle there. Instead Ronald began the story with a white man, one he knew Agnes would recognise from her Grandpa Percy's stories.

'No!' she exclaimed. 'The most famous man who ever lived in Africa? *He* died *there?*'

The driver, so pimply it looked like his cheeks were crammed with seeds, gawked from the rearview mirror. Ronald gave him a look, mentally docked his tip too, and took her hand.

'Yes,' he said. 'Dr Livingstone died near Shiwa, a little bit south. He even wrote down in his diaries that he had received his death sentence there! Because that was where his favourite dog had died.'

'Oh, dear!' she said. She paused. 'What sort of dog?'

'What sort of—?' He thought. 'A poodle, I believe.'

'Oh!' she said. 'I had no idea that they had poodles in Africa. It died of … the heat?'

'Chitane? No, he was eaten by a crocodile.'

Agnes laughed but Ronald was not joking.

'They buried Chitane there,' he said. 'You can even hear his barking in the night.'

'How dreadful!' Agnes looked genuinely distraught, sweat bubbling on her upper lip, streaks of red across her forehead. 'Wait. If he was eaten, what on earth did they bury?'

But Ronald had already moved on to the next great white man of Shiwa Ng'andu.

'Sir Stewart Gore-Browne came to Africa in 1911 to trace the borders between the Congo, Tanzania and Rhodesia. He followed the maps and built tall wooden beacons to mark the borders. And after he finished parcelling the land, Gore-Browne travelled deep into ...'

'... the heart of darkness,' Agnes inserted dreamily, bringing him up short.

'Hrm? No!' Ronald protested. 'It is not so dark. There is bush, yes. But these hills have some pinkish rocks. And at times the sand, it can be white, like salt. Very bright.'

'Oh, I just meant—'

'Yes, it is true in a way, it was a voyage,' he remarked. 'Gore-Browne was tracing the footsteps of Dr Livingstone's last journey. But he was also looking for land to settle.'

'Why?'

'Why does a man settle? Every man in this world must stake his claim!'

'But why in Africa?'

Ronald paused. One rumour was that Gore-Browne hadn't had enough money or clout to make it as a landowner in England, so he had decided, like many men of that generation, to go where pale skin and a small inheritance went a great deal further. Ronald decided to tell Agnes the other rumour.

'They say he was heartbroken. There was a woman. Lorna.'

'Ah,' Agnes smiled knowingly, in all her twenty-year-old wisdom. 'I see.'

'At any rate, Shiwa Ng'andu was the most beautiful place Sir Stewart had ever seen. He saw it first at sunrise. There were animals on the shore – zebra, kudu, reedbuck – and the lake was shining. It was a paradise.'

'Hmm, yes,' Agnes murmured. 'What's that poem again?'

Moved by his own words, Ronald was now caught in a cascade of memories. He had spent his childhood on the shore of that lake, he and his friends dipping their amateur canoes in the water, more concerned about crocodiles and hippos than the view. His adolescence had transformed the castle up on the hill into a second home. He became the lucky student who could roam the dark corridors, pluck books from the shelves, eat fancy dinners served by men twice his age – his own uncle once – and gaze idly through a turret window at the two blues beyond: the sapphire lake under the turquoise sky ... The car jolted forward and broke Ronald's reverie.

'On his first night by the lake, Sir Stewart received a sign. He saw a rhinoceros.'

'Marvellous!' Agnes crooned. 'I've always loved the look of them. Pyramid on the face.'

'Some people say the spirit of this lake, Ng'andu, it resembles this animal – a smooth dark body and one horn of ivory. But the black rhinoceros, it is very dangerous. *Chipembele*. It was the first one Sir Stewart had ever seen in Africa. Very big. He shot it—'

'Oh no!' The pulse in Agnes's collarbone fluttered.

'—brought him the big horn. That is why we call the old man Chipembele.' Ronald cleared his throat, declining to mention the other reasons for the nickname.

'Chee-pem-BERRY … Chee-PEM-bellay …' Agnes was trying to pronounce the word.

'*Chipembele*,' he repeated. 'So, Sir Stewart decided he must build a house above the lake. An English estate. And a place with a dairy, shops, school, tailor, post office, clock tower—'

'Oh!' Agnes laughed. 'Like a village!'

'Ah, yes,' he smiled. 'You see. We both have villages in our countries!' He squeezed her hand. 'After the First World War, he came back and bought the 2,300 acres from bee-sack.'

'Berserk?'

'No, *bee sack*,' he said, then spelt out the acronym. 'B-S-A-C. The British South Africa Company. That is who was selling the land at that time.'

'Not the Crown?'

'The Company,' he said. 'Cecil Rhodes's company. Rhodes is the one who bought the land from our chiefs. Many of them did not understand these bargains. They gave away their mineral rights for trifles: blankets and guns mostly. But in the end,' he shrugged, 'what can you do? They sold the land to Mr Rhodes. And Mr Rhodes sold the land to Sir Stewart.'

'Hrmp,' said Agnes – the universal sound for 'I am satisfied with this story but I still have questions' – and leaned back in her seat. The taxi was stuck in traffic, surrounded by the running patter of touts and hawkers selling maize, rabbit (live, skinned, pelt), wallets, fruits, cigarettes. Ronald wondered what Agnes would think if she could see these young boys threading around the dusty vehicles, forming a shifting tangle of humans and things. He looked out of his open window at the sights of almost-home: flame trees competing with jacarandas and bougainvillea for beauty. Flashes of brown skin that made him want to jump out and walk among the people, descend into that warm bath of personhood. And the sun! The sun in its constancy, hot and high in the sky, neither anticipated nor avoided. Just there, not even worth discussing.

When they arrived at their hotel, it turned out that crafty old Crofty had booked them separate rooms. Ronald grudgingly admitted that this was safer. Kenya was a newly independent nation and there was no need, as he told Agnes, 'to be canarying in the coal mine of racial equality'. He promised he would sneak into her hotel room later. But by the time he had found it, let himself in and crawled under her mosquito net, Agnes was asleep, her tousled head the picture of fluster and flush. For a moment, he thought he saw an eye opening in the middle of her forehead – no, it was just the moon flashing through the parted curtains. He kissed her where the moonlight had flickered and left her to her beauty sleep.

Because Ronald was Agnes's 'caretaker', as he informed the busybodies at the Nairobi aerodrome, brandishing a Wainscroftian letter of confirmation, they could sit next to each other on the flight to Mpika. The rest of the passengers fell into their accustomed segregation, but no one batted an eye when he slid in beside Agnes. She seemed sleepy in the way of a baby who wants to forget the danger it's in. But Ronald still found the motions of aeroplanes disturbing – like being in a canoe, except you might rock one way and never rock back, and you never see the waves coming. More to distract himself than to amuse her, he regaled Agnes with more Shiwa Ng'andu stories, shouting over the engines' buzz.

Ronald Banda had grown up in the staff compound, in a brick house with a chimney, under the shade of the imported blue gum trees. Every day, he went to Timba school, where he was taught English, Latin, maths and agriculture, with selected doses of British 'culture': drawing, hymns, a Christmas play for the chapel service. After their lessons, the Shiwa kids were free to roam. They pushed tyres with sticks or kicked patchwork balls made of plastic bags or old rubber. They climbed trees and hunted *kalulu* and jumped through the spray from the gardeners' hoses and played field games like tug-of-war and egg-and-spoon. They loitered in the shop to bother the Indian shopkeeper Mr Shem, or in the office to bother the Jewish bookkeeper Ba Fritzi.

The best times were when they gathered in the welfare centre to watch films. Ba Golo, as they called Gore-Browne, had brought a projector from England in the 1940s. The machine, with its rattling hot glow, had screened boring films at first: *English Gardens, The Queen's Guards*. Then the westerns came, with their horses and guns, low-slung voices and twanging music. The first time a Shiwa audience saw John Wayne die, the women started up a fanfare of mourning like he was a long lost relative. When Wayne came back to life in the very next film, the audience erupted again.

'But why?' asked Agnes. 'Were they happy?'

'No!' Ronald laughed. 'They said it was cheating!'

Treats like cinema night were rare. The boys were expected to work. Ronald helped in the lime and orange orchards, the trees like brides with their white flowers and jewels of fruit. He would fetch logs from the woodpile to be fed into the boilers, tip piles of orange blossoms into the big copper vats where they would be pulped into a sludge through which steam would pass. There they would condense, leaving behind their precious, fragrant residue. Essential oils had been Shiwa's primary source of income until the sadness disease came and killed the citrus trees.

'Sadness disease?' asked Agnes.

'Yes, a fungus called *tristeza*,' said Ronald. 'Ah, but sometimes I think Shiwa is cursed!'

The pitch of the aeroplane's engines changed. The captain announced their descent.

꙳

The drive from Mpika to the estate was identical to the ones in Kenya – tediously bumpy – except for the newly paved Great North Road, which felt as smooth as the tarmac in England. Agnes, her head out the passenger window, took in the smells: sunbaked earth, the coppery funk of untempered sweat, a sprig of fruit, the rot of rubbish, woodsmoke, the green smell of green leaves. She tried to match these scents with the images she had of Africa from books: little round huts and little black men and flat trees and elephants and dust. The only thing she could confirm thus far was the dust. And the heat, which was positively melting. It was all terribly exciting, nonetheless. And what bliss to touch Ronald again. Every time their skin brushed, a wave crashed through her, a thrilling crest of anticipation. They would be alone together again soon.

Ronald turned onto a bumpy road and a new scent came through the car window. It was medicinal and pure, singing out from the other smells like an oboe in an orchestra.

'What is that smell?' she asked.

Ronald sniffed. 'Eucalyptus! We are almost home.'

The borrowed Fiat stumbled along, navigating roots rather than potholes now, the air growing cooler as the trees stretched taller around them. Ronald began to narrate their surroundings to her. There was the lake, flashing in the distance. Here was the old bulky Fowler steam engine, which the children called Chitukukututuku. And now the workers' buildings. Children running and waving. A woman sitting on the stoop, grinding millet.

'And here is the gatehouse to the estate of Shiwa Ng'andu!'

Agnes sniffed. 'What *is* that smell?'

'The cypress trees,' he said as the car began to ascend a slope, 'they are imported from Italy.'

'No, not cypress. Something unnatural . . .'

'And there is Peacock Hill!' he said. 'Just to the side of the house, we can see it now.'

'Oh, are there peacocks here?' Agnes brightened. She had an affection for their eye-riddled train of feathers.

'There used to be,' he said. 'But this hill is named for a man, Mr Peacock, who died here in a car accident. He was pinned upside down in a ditch, with his head in a puddle of water – just a few inches, but enough to drown. He was buried on that hill.'

'Goodness,' Agnes shivered. 'The place is overrun with graves.'

Ronald began describing the manor, his excitement chopping the images to fragments: red bricks – arched windows – iron lattice – vines on the walls – orange and pink flowers – a big wooden door – the Union Jack. Where on earth am I? Agnes suddenly wondered. *Northern Rhodesia*. A storybook land. Named after the great Cecil Rhodes. They may as well have called it *Northern Cecilia*, she thought hysterically. What was the name of that poem again? The title bit the bait, but she could not reel it in. It thrashed under the surface of her mind.

Ronald opened her door. Agnes stepped out, grass tickling her sandalled foot, and the next thing she knew, she was immersed in a hot pool of sunlight, swamped in that strange smell.

'Lady Agnes,' a voice intoned, thunderously British. 'Welcome to Shiwa Ng'andu.'

She reached out her hand to shake and flinched when a kiss squelched on it instead.

'Stewart Gore-Browne,' boomed the British voice again. 'Very pleased to meet you.'

'Ba Golo,' Ronald said shakily, 'I mean, Sir Stewart. We are so honoured to be home.'

✳

Apart from Agnes and Ronald, Sir Stewart and his butler Henry Mulenga, there were a Lord and Lady Vyvant, and someone's niece, a Miss Higgins, here for dinner. This small party was immediately subjected to a tour. Every room of the manor was a new world of sounds and smells. The entrance hall: mouldy carpet dust, the slight spice of old wood. The sitting room: burnt stone, the animal scent of leather, oil-paint resin, the brush of velvet against glass windows. The kitchen: an oniony halo, the funk of dried meats, the tang of cooking oil. The chapel felt the most familiar, the most English: shoes slapping the flagstones, a floral scent from the hymnals, the creak of the pews.

The upstairs library felt the most alive. A gramophone was playing opera. A fire was licking its chops in the hearth, giving off a woodsy perfume. Agnes tracked it by its heat and ran her fingers over the engraving in the mantel, reading the misspelt, ungrammatical Latin:

Ille Terrarum Mihi Super Omnes Angulet Ridet. Could she read it because of her brief Braille training, or because Ronald had described it to her so often? She turned around, seeking his voice. It seemed everyone was out on the library terrace now, murmurous with pleasure that the tour was over and dinner about to begin.

She stepped outside and Ronald was beside her, his hand on her elbow. She heard percussive insects, the sliding whistles of the birds, an occasional howl that she could not identify. She sensed more bodies out here. Ah, the servants. A cocktail glass was pressed into her hand. She whispered thanks to the air as a slinky coolness slipped over the rim and ran down her wrist. Sir Stewart began a long toast – this was apparently his favourite drink, the Montmartre. Agnes sipped it. It stung her tongue with citrus. Ronald's hand stiffened on her arm. His return to Shiwa had not been mentioned in the toast, and neither had their imminent nuptials.

At the dinner that followed, under a tinkly chandelier, Ronald's sense of neglect seemed to deepen, his mood darkening – a gloomy cloud to her left – as the meal progressed. Agnes kept still, listening intently to the server's whispers in her ear – what on earth was guinea fowl soufflé? – and calibrating her movements with the sounds on her right, where Miss Higgins was sitting: the clink of a ring against the glass, the plop of jelly as it slid off a spoon, the scrape of fork tines against the plate. The conversation pinged around like a game of billiards, repartees bouncing off each other on purpose, or unexpectedly, abruptly sending someone into a pocket of silence. Sir Stewart held the cue for much of the time, telling them the history of the estate.

'Imagine! A seventy-mile march across the Congo. My boys winding through the swamp, carrying an English country estate on their heads. Trunks full of china, crystal, curtains, cushions, paintings, guns, a telescope. This very chandelier. I've always maintained that if one is going to do it, one ought to do it properly. The moment one gives up the niceties is the moment one stops being an Englishman.'

'And do not forget the Union Jack!' This was Henry Mulenga, the butler.

'I was received by the Bemba chief, Mukwikile.' Sir Stewart said the name with the lilt of a native speaker. 'A wise man, that one. Incredibly old and benign, like a creature from an ancient world or a black-faced drawing of God in a children's book. His people ... your people, Ronald' – Agnes felt Ronald soften at the notice – 'welcomed us with a great show. Drumming and ululation, girls dancing bare-breasted'– his voice vibrated over the taboo – 'though of course there's nothing like that nowadays.'

'Do you get the *Daily Mail* out here?' asked Mrs Vyvant. 'It seems so terribly isolated.'

'Yes, it was very lonely,' Sir Stewart mused. 'Absolutely no one to talk to. Two men came out early on – men I'd met in the war, you see. One was the son of a draper, the other a farm boy, no-nonsense men – I detest insincerity above all else – but they were not quite what one would have chosen for companions. One used to taunt me mercilessly about the servants' white gloves and so on. He kept going on about that damned Coleridge poem. Eventually ...'

'Christ,' came a whisper to Agnes's ear. 'At least someone noticed.'

'Noticed what?' Agnes whispered back to Miss Higgins.

'Madamu,' the server said in Agnes's other ear. 'Saddo of Hearty Beast.'

'Oh, yes, thank you,' she said. She had not quite finished her soufflé, which tasted like a gamier sort of pâté, but she let him replace her plate. She tapped the new dish with her knife, wishing she could use her fingers. She sliced into whatever it was – the heart of a beast? – and put a forkful in her mouth. It was gamey, too, but the sauce – a sour sweetness, cherry? – was divine.

'I'm sorry,' Agnes swallowed and turned back to Miss Higgins. 'You were saying?'

'"In Xanadu did Kubla Khan a stately pleasure-dome decree,"' whispered Miss Higgins.

'"Kubla Khan"!' Agnes exclaimed. The fish tugging at her memory was finally caught – she had learned that Coleridge poem in primary school. She mouthed the lines to herself: *And there were gardens bright with sinuous rills, / Where blossomed many an incense-bearing tree; / And here were forests ancient as the hills ...*

'... utterly withered away,' Sir Stewart raised his voice imperiously. 'Choked with weeds. Neglect, plain and simple. And beastly stories to cover it up! The Bemba are not lazy—'

'Isn't that *precisely* what they are?' Lord Vyvant expostulated. 'Present company excluded, of course.'

'But no, you are correct, us Bemba, we are lazy, good sirs,' said Henry Mulenga cheerily. Agnes kept imagining the native butler as a kind of doll, so silly and mechanical was his chatter. 'You must teach us, please. You must ... *Iwe!*' he erupted at a server. 'Are you blind like a bat? You are spilling on my cravat!'

'Yes,' Sir Stewart was saying. 'I suppose the Bemba are like children, easy to please and so open with their emotions. I have always loved to hear them singing as they work. A harmony that matches *La Bohème* in sophistication. They just need to get beyond this mud-hut mentality.'

'The native will never change his spots,' said Lord Vyvant.

'Hear, hear,' muttered Lady Vyvant across the table.

'There is work to be done,' Sir Stewart conceded. 'There is much to teach the black man, beyond tossing him in the mines. I always thought it a good exchange: my knowledge for their labour, my protection for their loyalty. A very desirable sort of socialism. Young men like KK, whom I sponsored to study – just like Ronald here – they are ready to take the reins. But ...'

'Who is KK?' Agnes asked quietly.

'Kenneth Kaunda,' Ronald said in one ear.

'Kubla Khan,' Miss Higgins whispered in the other.

Agnes stuck her empty fork in her mouth to stifle her giggle. Miss Higgins's jokes were not original but her tone was irresistible, teetering between irony and sincerity.

'The enterprise often feels like heartbreak,' said Sir Stewart. 'My wife Lorna ...'

'Ah, the infamous Lorna!' Agnes said under her breath to Miss Higgins, pleased to contribute something to their rebellious little complicity.

'Which Lorna do you think he means?' Miss Higgins replied in a droll tone.

'... brought them lovely sweaters,' Sir Stewart continued. 'But the blacks used them as rugs! Lorna wept over that, the poor thing. I often thought about that, long after she was gone.'

Oh! When had Lorna died? Ronald's distinctive pronunciation of the woman's name – like 'loner' – had made Agnes picture a thin, pale woman. Perhaps she'd fallen ill.

'No, we have not got any nearer to the right solution of the racial problem. The blacks are still subjected to such indecency. Henry often has to sleep in the car when we travel to Lusaka.'

'Indeedy!' said Henry. 'I have even had better treatment in Piccadirree than in Chinsali!'

'Hrm yes, Piccadilly, I'm sure,' Lord Vyvant sneered. 'So, Sir Stewart, I hear you have been speaking publicly against the colour bar? Are you going native on us, old chap?'

'No,' Sir Stewart laughed. 'I have resigned. I *am* resigned. I'm an old man now. I have grandchildren. What a joy it is to see them running around Shiwa! Natural hunters. The other day, our grandson Charles told us that he was going to kill all the lions in Africa!'

'Hear, hear!' Henry Mulenga gave a chuckle as flat as old tonic.

'The grandchildren live in a post-racial paradise,' said Sir Stewart. 'They are fluent in Bemba. Lorna is so proud of them. She sends her apologies, by the way – she's in the Copperbelt.'

Agnes frowned and swallowed a lump of meat. 'But I thought—'

'Gentlemen,' Sir Stewart boomed. 'Shall we retire to the library for port?'

✳

The segregation of the sexes sent Agnes to the parlour with Miss Higgins and Lady Vyvant. Miss Higgins guided Agnes around the furniture to a sofa, warning her of the cobwebs. They sat down together, wiping the sticky strands from their cheeks, spitting softly. Lady Vyvant stood in the doorway, giving instructions to the server, and Miss Higgins took the opportunity to spill the beans.

'There are *two* Lornas,' she said. 'Mother and daughter.'

'Ah! That explains it. I was quite puzzled. And the mother is dead?'

'*Shhhh*,' said Miss Higgins. Lady Vyvant had approached. There was a rustling pause as she sat across from them. Agnes imagined that the other two women were also smiling blankly.

'I believe you've left out a Lorna, Miss Higgins,' said Lady Vyvant finally, her voice like fingers running through gravel. 'There are three in total.'

'*Three?*' Agnes asked. She felt Miss Higgins wilt at her side, her gossip having been scooped.

'When he was a young man,' Lady Vyvant began slowly, 'Sir Stewart fell in love with a woman named Lorna in England. But she married another man, a doctor, and they moved to South Africa. They both died of malaria. It broke Sir Stewart's heart and he came to Africa—'

The door opened. Agnes listened to the server's footsteps, the knock of three glasses onto the table and the short rising notes of the liquor being poured. The footsteps receded, the door closed, and Lady Vyvant continued.

'A few years later, Sir Stewart went to a funeral back in England and saw Lorna's daughter there. And a week after that, he asked her hand in marriage.'

'Mmhm,' snarked Miss Higgins. 'But *this* Lorna was twenty years younger than him.'

'Yes, she was,' said Lady Vyvant matter-of-factly. 'She had grown up in South Africa with her parents, and desperately wanted to come back to the continent after they died. She essentially married Sir Stewart for homesickness.'

'And did the young Lorna look anything like her mother?' Agnes asked.

'Quite.' Lady Vyvant took Agnes's hand and placed it on the stem of a glass.

'Thank you.' Agnes paused. 'But did she know? That he had loved her mother?'

'Some say that she didn't. She was very young. Others say she went mad when she found out. She started playing a violin in the turret, taking to bed at all hours, having tantrums in public.'

'She ought to have figured it out,' said Miss Higgins. 'There was a poem about it, for Christ's sake. "The Two Lornas". By Thomas blooming Hardy.'

'Well, now there are three Lornas, as they named their daughter Lorna as well.'

'*The shadow of the dome of pleasure,*' Miss Higgins murmured.

Agnes shook her head and sipped her drink – sherry. It seared her throat with bittersweet warmth.

'So, Agnes,' said Lady Vyvant. 'Tell us about this charming protégé of yours. Ronald?'

'Oh! You mean my fiancé,' Agnes smiled.

There was a pause. 'I'm afraid you've been misled, dear child,' said Lady Vyvant, her tone as cool as ever. 'Marriage is not legal for Africans here in the Federation.'

'Oops!' said Miss Higgins and laughed.

✻

Meanwhile, the conversation in the library was revolving around suitably male questions – the quality of the cigars, the prospects of hunting, and now, politics. Ever since Northern Rhodesia, Southern Rhodesia and Nyasaland had been consolidated into the Federation, the educated black elite – the veterans and the trade unionists – had begun to agitate for independence from Britain.

'The colour bar between whites and blacks has risen higher,' said Sir Stewart. 'Infuriating business. Herding blacks like cattle on trains, making them queue for hours to receive their goods through a hole in the wall. This "off the pavement, boy" business is simply uncouth.'

'What choice do we have, old chap?' said Lord Vyvant. 'The natives cannot govern themselves.' He muttered his caveat in Henry Mulenga's direction: 'Present company, et cetera.'

'The problem,' said Sir Stewart, 'is that the natives were not even consulted about forming a Federation. At least one African should have been invited to the Victoria Falls Conference.'

'Oh tosh,' Lord Vyvant snorted. 'Do you remember when they demonstrated against federation with those signs? "Down with *Ventilation*"? Preposterous.'

'Well, now they are nailing placards on trees here at Shiwa,' Sir Stewart remarked, lowering himself into a leather armchair. 'These ones simply say FREEDOM. They are not wrong.'

The fire shuddered in its stone cave and the cigars puffed like chimneys and the glasses of cognac cast copper on the walls. Henry Mulenga spoke up from the sofa.

'Ah, but it is not okay for them to result to violence, *bwana*.'

Ronald clucked quietly at the man's broken English. Why on earth was this *muntu* butler here? Henry was taking advantage of Sir Stewart's generosity or perhaps his senility. But Ronald said nothing – to do so would beg the question of his own presence among the guests.

'These Cha-Cha-Cha animals are holding the country hostage!' Henry was expostulating now. 'Even these Luwingu riots! Too much disrespecting!'

'What happened in Luwingu?' Ronald leaned up from the fireplace mantel with a frown.

'That lunatic, Nkoloso!' Henry laughed scornfully.

'I was in London with Kenneth at the time,' said Sir Stewart. 'He shared the telegrams they sent from Luwingu with me and some lords in Parliament. The colonial officers tortured Eddie Nkoloso, nearly drowned the poor man. Kaunda made great use of it rhetorically, of course. He's an articulate man, whatever you think of his politics. A true wordsmith.'

'Words and sticks and stones!' Vyvant spat. 'Kaunda's political party is out of control now that he is out of gaol. Bloody firebombs! They set a car on fire with a white woman and her children inside!'

There was a silence as they stared at the fire, imagining a car with three bodies inside it.

'At least the children survived,' Ronald said softly. 'And before she died, did she not ask that the European settlers seek peace rather than revenge?'

'That utopian nonsense is what led to Mau Mau! Violence is in their blood,' Vyvant growled then glanced around. 'No offence meant to those present,' he mumbled into his cognac.

'Yes, you never know,' Sir Stewart laughed, his monocle blank in the firelight. 'African politics is a risky business. Do not sleep too deeply, my dear friends. They may just slit your throat in the night.'

✳

'I should have known,' Ronald fumed. He and Agnes were lying in her bed. It had irked him to have to sneak into her room. It wasn't hard to find – he knew the corridors of this manor like the lines of his palm – but he'd had to traverse too many of them to reach her. His own room was alarmingly close to the servants' quarters, where the bowing and scraping *muntus* lived, with their hats like upside-down buckets and their shirts like folded serviettes, those dogs standing on their hind legs, those fools who waited in a line every night for their measly glass of port. It was all so excruciating. When he thought of what Sir Stewart had said at the end of the evening in front of that racist *muzungu* and that jabbering *muntu* – 'Tell us about this charming patron of yours. Agnes?' – Ronald felt the humiliation might swallow him whole.

'Why do they say we can't marry here?' Agnes warbled tearily.

'Of course we can,' he grumbled. 'Not officially, no. But that is just a matter of time.'

'It was – awful – Ronnie,' she said, the words coming out in wet bursts. 'The girl – Miss Higgins – I thought – we might – be friends. But then—'

'We will find other friends, darling. We do not need these ... these hypocrites!'

'But why did you say you were my protégé? Are you ashamed of us?'

'Never!' he said angrily. 'I told you. I wrote Sir Stewart a letter announcing our engagement. They were expecting our arrival today, so my letter must have come. Bloody Henry Mulenga! He's the one who receives the mail now and reads it to the old man. He's become very free with his position. He must have changed my words! It's plagiarism!'

'Libel,' she corrected miserably.

'I should have known,' he said again. 'Ba Golo speaks with two tongues.'

'But you said he was a kind man. You said—'

'Kind? Ha!'

Now he told her the other reason the workers had given Sir Stewart the nickname Chipembele, The Rhino – how often Ronald himself had seen the *bwana* marching around the estate, shouting furiously, beating the workers with his big black stick, choking them. In the old days, he had even smashed their heads against trees. *Chipembele abuta-bele abamkombo mkwa*, they called him. The rhinoceros who comes and destroys everything when you're away hunting.

'He seemed so forward-thinking,' she murmured.

'Do you not see how we were given separate rooms? Like a colour bar? We are not welcome here.'

'But Ronnie, where will we go? If marriage isn't legal, then we're not safe here either.'

'We will go to Lusaka. I have people there.'

'Your family?'

'Aggie. You are my family now.'

He ran his fingertip over her closed eyelids, purplish and smooth and quivering, like Lake Shiwa on a windless day. He kissed her forehead, then her lips. They made lonely and hushed – and therefore heated – love. Afterward, they fell asleep in her bed, their limbs entwined.

*

When Ronald woke up the first time that night, his elbow was strung with pins and needles.

'Do you hear it?' Agnes hissed.

'What?' he winced, pulling his arm out from underneath her and stretching his fingers.

'Lorna's violin! In the turret. I think—'

'That's just the hyenas,' he mumbled and went back to sleep.

The second time he woke up, she said her leg was itching. He lit the kerosene lantern and examined her calf under its spooky light. It was covered in pink bumps with white centres like little eyes. He tucked the mosquito net around them more tightly and went back to sleep.

When he woke up the third time, she was gone. He checked the en suite, but she wasn't there. The light in the bedroom was the colour of 5 a.m., maybe 6. The morning drums would begin beating soon. He pulled on his sweat-stiff shirt, dust-cuffed trousers and tight dress shoes.

He opened the door, looked left and right, and raced down the dark corridor, trying not to skid on the flagstones. A rectangle of light glowed before him like a door to heaven – the courtyard. He ran towards it, then he saw Ba George and slowed to a trot. The old butler was wearing a suit, a bow tie squeezing the hanging skin at his neck, and holding a spotty tray. His carriage was painfully erect.

'*Mwashibukeni*, Ba Lonode.' Ba George bowed his head fondly.

'*Eyamukwayi, bashikulu*,' Ronald panted. 'Do you know where Miss Agnes is?'

'Mm?' The old man frowned. 'Ah, *mwebantu, katwishi*. I do not know.'

They walked together a few paces. Ba George asked after Ronald's parents.

'We have not gone to see them yet, but I will take her to the village soon.'

'That is very good,' Ba George said in a disapproving tone, as if he suspected that Ronald would do no such thing. Ronald smiled stiffly, eager to leave the conversation.

'Ah, look!' Ba George pointed. 'There is your Missus Aganess.'

Ronald was so relieved that he didn't even hear Ba George's 'your', the butler's kind acknowledgment. But he felt it – that Agnes belonged to him – as he looked out into the old courtyard.

It was a ruin: riven pavestones, piles of broken rocks, ancient hydrangeas clinging together in cracked pots. Barefoot, in her paisley dress, Agnes was standing in front of the birdbath, which was a statue of a woman, head tilted, one knee bent, the hem of her robes curled upward to form the basin. There wasn't much water inside, and what was there was bluegreen with mildew.

Some tiny creature had decided, nevertheless, that it was sufficient to its needs. It fluttered in the water, strumming up and settling down, sending a spray into the air as fine as the mists of Surrey. Agnes's face was carved in a look of concentration, her hands raised as if holding a small bowl up to the statue. It took Ronald a moment to understand that she was cupping the air around the winged creature, touching its motions, reading its splashing since she could not see it.

The sun rose an inch and cleared the horizon, sending a ray into the courtyard that touched the droplets that had collected on her forearms, making a flashing rash in her skin. Argus. Ronald remembered it from one of Carolyn's mythology books. A monster covered with eyes.

'Did you see that?' He turned to Ba George. The old butler was frowning and peering at the woman in the courtyard. He slowly nodded his head. But when Ronald looked back at Agnes, the light had shifted, or she had. The eyes in her skin were closed. Agnes brought her cupped hands together and the flurry above the birdbath ceased.

Ronald walked across the flagstones and touched her shoulder gently. Agnes turned to him and cracked her hands open slightly. 'I think it's a butterfly.'

He looked inside. It was not a butterfly but a dragonfly – no, a pair of dragonflies, locked in sexual congress, their iridescent wings still spinning in the pink cage of her fingers.

1964

Agnes woke with a start. Something was gripping her ankle – a cold, wet hand. She shook her leg free and turned on her side. She had been dreaming of a forest of blueblack trees – the ones at Shiwa? Lurking in the hollows of their roots was a crouched presence, a hand reaching through the dark. The stretching tendons. The grip. Agnes shivered and patted for the other pillow. Ronald was gone – already at work probably. What time was it? She heard doves cooing and a scratching sound, moving in mesmeric loops. She stretched out her leg and there it was again – a hand closing around her ankle. She sat up.

'Who's there?' she whispered.

The scratching sound ceased. '*Mwauka bwanji*, Madamu?'

'Grace?' Agnes smelled the girl's familiar odour now – Strike soap and Sun Beam polish and beefy sweat. 'What on earth are you doing?'

'Me, am just creening, Madamu.'

'*Ka*-leaning,' Agnes said irritably and collapsed back onto her side.

Grace's English irked Agnes to no end. The girl called the *kitchen* the *chicken* and sometimes forced Agnes to get up so that she could wash the *shittybeds*, which Ronald had explained was the local word for *bedsheets*.

'Do you think your fixation on the girl's pronunciation is a latent sign of *coroniarism*?' he had deadpanned.

When Agnes got the joke, she was mortified. Just because she was British and had moved to Africa – to be with him, mind you! – that did not make her a *colonialist*. She was nothing like Grandpa Percy, who, yes, had occasionally said things about the 'lower races', and used uncouth words like 'nigger' and 'Kaffir', and treated his time in Africa as a sort of jolly jaunt.

'Am velly solly for creening, Madamu,' Grace said now. 'But it is late. Past twove o'crock. The peepo are coming for the patty *pa* aftanooni. *Bwana* says I must shine the floze—'

'Why?! Why must you perpetually shine the floors? They're already a bloody hazard!'

Agnes did not appreciate such tokens of luxury as reflective and hygienic floors. She had wet her socks. She had slipped. It was easier to blame the maid than face her true terror of hurting herself in this unfamiliar place. Agnes had already gathered posies of bruises on her legs and arms, not just from stumbling over furniture but also from tripping over Grace herself, who was always underfoot, *creening* things. Once, Agnes had walked straight into the girl, standing fully upright in a doorway.

'Waiting!' Agnes complained. 'For me to crash into her! She's up to something.'

'She is up to nothing,' Ronald snorted. 'This house is never properly clean.'

'Then fire her!'

Ronald did not. Grace came with the house, which came with his job. He was on the planning committee for the country's first national university, a highly prestigious position. He had taken on the assignment with energy and aplomb, as a member of the elite in Lusaka, the capital.

Life here had been a rather more difficult adjustment for Mrs Agnes Banda, however. There was so much to adjust to. The extra oil in the food, the dearth of salt. The shower that was either freezing cold or blazing hot but never comfortably warm. (Ronald had laughed: 'How is a woman familiar with English weather baffled by this?') The night-time racket was unbearable. Dogs accusing each other across town. Mosquitoes dive-bombing her ears. A demented rooster that couldn't distinguish sunlight from street light and announced the dawn every hour to cover its bets. ('Don't worry,' Ronald had said, 'that chicken will get eaten or that light will get broken.')

Easy enough for him to say. He always slept right through the nightly cacophony, while Agnes lay there, vibrating with pique. This upended their balance: he woke a few hours after she had finally dozed off, parallel universes staggered by twelve hours. She often slept late into the day, getting up in time to join him for one of Mr Sakala's elaborate lunches – crumbling chicken fricassee or ersatz beef Wellington, bland and congealing. Marriage, career, Africa itself – something had exposed the many ways they were at odds. Alone and aggrieved, at home all day, Agnes often caught herself berating the workers, ranting over trivialities. A princess shouting at the pea under the mattress.

'This is not the time to *creen* the bedroom,' she hissed at Grace now. 'I'm sleeping.'

The words deflated like punctured balloons as they left her lips. *I'm sleeping*: what a self-defeating thing to say. Grace did not reply but the scratching sound started up again, just slightly softer. Agnes sighed and reached out from under the covers to turn on the radio beside the bed.

'Lusaka calling,' the broadcaster purred. He announced a radio play about *wamunyama*, the local word for vampires. Then came the world news, which was mostly about the prospect of a second Clay vs Liston fight. A dulcet voice advertising Palmolive. Satchmo growling like a pleased honeybear. Cutting through his song came a yawning sound – the front door opening.

Grace stopped polishing. Her bare feet pittered across the floor. She cracked the bedroom door. The two women listened to the voices knocking about the walls of the house. Agnes identified Ronald's tenor, a man's wheezing voice, and the kind of laugh that belonged to a big woman.

'Madamu, they are *hee-ya*. You must get up now.'

Agnes dragged herself vertical. Her toes fumbled under the bed, seeking her slippers. Grace snatched her to her feet and pulled her away from the bed.

'No, Madamu, you must be looking nice!'

They stepped over to the wardrobe together and Agnes rifled among the hanging clothes for a decent skirt and shirt. She changed into them and accepted Grace's adjustments.

'*Iye*, Madamu, but this *ka* blouse is small-small. Too much *nshima!*'

'What? Oh, yes, well. I didn't eat lunch today at least,' said Agnes, diving into the jumble at the bottom of the wardrobe, feeling for the mules with the block heel and the bow over the toes. She sat on the bed so Grace could strap them onto her feet with fingers still sticky from floor polish. Grace was perfunctory with Agnes's body and matter-of-fact about her blindness. In this sense, at least, she was preferable to Mr Sakala, who served Agnes's meals cut into child-sized bites and never failed to remind her that his wife was praying for the return of her sight.

'Do not forget the ling, Madamu,' said Grace, placing the cold band in Agnes's palm.

The Marriage Ordinance had finally been changed to allow Africans to marry, which meant that Agnes could marry her African, Ronald. They hadn't bothered with a church ceremony, but he had brought home a licence and a ring – copper with a malachite stone, he'd said.

Agnes slid it on and stood. Her heart sank. Talking to Grace was one thing. Talking to Ronald's sophisticated friends was another. There would be no hiding behind her Englishness.

'Come with me?' she begged, reaching for Grace's hand.

Grace squeezed it peremptorily and let it drop. 'Ah no, Madamu, you must go, *you.*'

*

Agnes felt her way out of the bedroom, Grace's scorn – or was it pity? – washing up her back. She moved slowly towards the sitting room, her hand slipping from the wall every so often to adjust her skirt. When she reached the corner, she paused, nerves twinkling in her stomach. How absurd it was! This trial of being a wife to a man. The flat pat of Ronald's step approached.

'Darling.' He kissed her cheek. He took her elbow and escorted her into the sitting room.

'This young man is Rick,' he said, directing her attention to the right.

'How d'you do?' Agnes reached for the proffered hand and tried to curtsy the Zambian way Ronald had taught her – her left hand cupping her right elbow, both knees bending a little.

'No, no,' came a British voice. 'We're equals here! None of this grovelling business.'

'And this is Phil, my colleague,' Ronald redirected her attention to the left. Feeling admonished, Agnes reached out and shook this hand firmly, no curtsying this time.

'*Hm?* Ronald,' said Phil. 'Is this woman of yours a chair that her legs do not bend?'

'Philemon is correct,' came a booming voice. This was apparently Mercy, the big woman Agnes had heard from the bedroom. 'She must show *rispect*. She must even go bare-chested to the parents!'

'And last but not least is Sue,' said Ronald.

'My *name* is Masuzio,' a lovely contralto voice objected in a singsong.

'Ah! *Imwe!*' Ronald exclaimed. 'We have become Africanised?'

'Why should I use a nickname? Just because the British cannot pronounce my name?'

Agnes swallowed. 'So nice to meet you,' she said, '*Mazoozio.*'

'Good effort!' Masuzio laughed. 'Top marks.'

Agnes sat, trying to keep track of the names attached to the four voices: Phil and Mercy, Rick and Sue – no, Masuzio. They were all African except for Rick, a British researcher. Ronald had told her last night how Rick and Masuzio had met. Masuzio, fresh out of secondary school, had been leaning against a wall at the *boma* in Chinsali, wearing a miniskirt. Rick had been riding his bicycle through town, wearing shorts. They had both looked at each other and thought: Nice legs! Agnes had been scandalised by this story until Ronald reminded her that he had first seen her in a tennis skirt.

'Cheers!' he said now, placing a drink in her hand. 'To Agnes!'

Agnes smiled bravely and held her glass in front of her, waiting for the clinks to come.

'So,' Mercy spoke in the loud voice of someone who mistakes blindness for deafness. '*Did* you bare your breasts to your mother-in-law before the wedding?'

Agnes choked on her gin and tonic.

'Oh, for crying out loud, Mercy,' Rick muttered.

Agnes cleared her throat. 'I haven't met Ronald's parents,' she said. 'Not yet, anyway.'

There was an awkward silence. Agnes felt as if she were floating in a chilly sea of sweat.

'Well, when you do,' said Mercy, 'and you *will*, the custom is to take off your shirt—'

'Must we perpetuate these primitivities?' Masuzio cut in.

'Ah, you, Sue!' Mercy groused. 'To bare the breasts is not primitive. It is even political! Mama Chikamoneka bared her breasts to the colonial secretary and she is a heroine!'

Agnes had heard about this on the radio. In 1960, the British colonial secretary, Ian Macleod, had flown in for a state visit and found a crowd of protestors at the airport, carrying signs that said things like THE DAYS OF MISRULE ARE NUMBERED and NO ROOM FOR WHITE SETTLERS. Some older women in the protest had stripped to their waists to shame him.

'Ha!' Phil wheezed. 'That was not politics. It was scare tactics. Swing those knockers, as the Yanks say, and knock the man out!'

'Sonny Use-Your-Left Tit!' Ronald joked redundantly. 'They made that poor man cry.'

Macleod had indeed wept to see the native women naked. The scene had struck Agnes at the time as utterly lacking in dignity and grace, the absolute opposite of Althea Gibson kissing the Queen's hand at Wimbledon.

The conversation had moved on to the nation's new name.

'I do not know why we do not just call it "Zambezi",' said Phil.

'Kapwepwe has chosen a nice name,' said Masuzio. '*Zam-bia!* It rolls off the tongue.'

'Yes. Now there is a freedom fighter with a genuine sense of African grandeur.'

'They should have just been calling it Zambezia,' Mercy complained. Her accent was much heavier than the others. 'Just think about it. ZAMBEZIA! The extra singable is much better!'

'You mean *syllable*?' asked Masuzio.

'You know what I am talking about!' said Mercy. 'Always scrutinising others for mistakes. Your *muzungu* husband has given you this correcting-correcting habit. The British have broken our backs. Me, I am just breaking a few words, eh—'

Agnes smelled cigarette smoke and heard ice – Ronald was refilling drinks. As the group continued to banter and hoot, a low voice came from beside her.

'So, Agnes.' This was Rick. 'What do *you* think of this election, this great transition?'

'I don't know enough about it,' she admitted. 'But as Macmillan says, the wind of hope is sweeping—'

'Wind of change,' Rick murmured. 'Yes?'

'Yes, of course, change. Erm, either way, it seems to me that self-government for the African people is inevitable.'

'You do realise that you and I will be among them,' he laughed.

'Whatever do you mean?'

'Everyone who is here on Independence Day will become a Zambian, even us Brits.'

'Oh that!' Agnes laughed as if she already knew this. 'I mean, it is only proper,' she reflected. 'A sign of courtesy and grace. Do you know the tennis player Althea—'

'Naturally one wishes to stay in good graces,' said Rick. 'But on this side, of course, the demand is for freedom, not courtesy. The foot on the neck doesn't feel the cramp.'

Agnes felt flustered. What did he mean by this side? A foot on the neck? What a horrid image! She tried to think of a reply but by the time she had come up with one – something about turning the other cheek – and rejected it as too stupid, Rick had been reabsorbed into the conversation.

They were now discussing the details of the coming Independence Day celebrations. Brass bands and jazz bands were coming from abroad, and so was Princess Royal Mary, who was due to arrive two days before the big day: 24 October 1964. A golden dress and coat had been designed for Mrs Betty Kaunda. She and the new President Kaunda would arrive in a Chrysler Copper Car, on loan from America to celebrate Zambia's lucrative mining industry.

Out of context, it all sounded to Agnes like superficial minutiae, as if this were just an unusually lively meeting of a planning committee for a bridge party. Bored and a little angry, she sat back and waited for the guests to leave. She had been worried that Ronald's hip, elite friends wouldn't like her, but now she faced an even worse proposition. What if she didn't like them?

＊

Independence was upon the nation. *Kwacha! Ngwee ... The sun has risen! Light falls across the plains ...* Every morning now, Grace used polishing the floors as an excuse to sneak into Madam's bedroom and listen to the radio chatter about 'Z Day'. The final touches were being made to a giant copper pedestal where the Independence Flame would burn. Grass-green Independence flags had sprouted across town. Workmen were chipping away at the fabulist British crest over the high court – a lion and a unicorn – which would be replaced by a realist Zambian one: a man and a woman on either side of a shield with wavy white lines on a black field, a pickaxe and a hoe crossed above it. Mr Kapwepwe, the Foreign Minister, had been sighted in his toga, practising with traditional dancers for the celebration.

Grace was not naturally given to joy. But she had never felt so proud to be African – no, *Zambian*, that word on everyone's lips. *Tiyende pamodzi ndim'tima umo*, she sang under her breath as she mopped the floors. The *bwana* insisted that she wear a blue frock and a silly white hat but as Z Day approached, she started tying her patriotic *chitenge* wrapper around her waist too, the one with a pattern of Kenneth Kaunda's face. That perfect brown oval with its widow's peak, grinning cheeks, twinkling eyes and teeth, was everywhere these days: on posters and on flags and even – Grace rotated her hips in subtle circles – on her own two buttocks.

She hadn't had the chance to vote for Kaunda. Only married women could vote, and the law had only just been changed to allow Africans to marry at all. But Grace had jealously examined her Aunt Beatrice's red-stained thumb – those who could not write their names had voted by dipping their thumbs in ink and rubbing them on the roster. Grace had exhorted Ba Agnes to vote, too, believing Madam's choice of a black husband would surely lead her to the correct decision. But Madam had begged off, saying she did not feel that she had the right. In the end, it did not matter. Kaunda's United National Independence Party, UNIP for short, had swept the African vote.

On Z Day, Lusaka was overflowing with bodies and vehicles – coaches and trains had been secured to bring people in from the provinces – and Grace was among them. Fallen jacaranda blooms carpeted the roads in purple, flame trees lined them in red, and the whole city flickered with little green flags. It was a joyous fete of dust and ululation, Independence Stadium at its centre. The crowds swarmed towards it down Great North Road, passing word along as the ceremonial events unfolded. Someone listening to the radio would tell someone else who would shout it out to the others, who would recount it to those behind them. Waves of news – 'The president has arrived!' 'The dancing has started!' – cascaded this way across town, fading to simpler language and softer cheers as they went along.

By midnight, Grace found herself huddled with a group of students around a saucepan radio. They hushed as the announcer intoned: 'We see the British flag coming down. We see the Zambian flag going up!' A thunk, a whistle, a bang – an umbrella of fire opened in the sky. Everyone looked up, gasping as one. The bright spots of light dilated into teary hexagons in Grace's eyes. Zambia was born.

Spent with emotion, she threaded her way through the partying crowd towards home. A parked bus ahead was visibly bouncing up and down. Grace shook her head and shifted her path to avoid it. She was not against happiness per se, but she disdained any excessive display of it. Then something pale caught her eye – a hand gripping the sill of an open window of the shaking bus. Grace stared at it, trying to work out why it looked so familiar. Then she saw the ring on the fourth finger. Copper with a green stone.

'Madam?' she murmured. 'But it cannot be.' She squeezed through the crowd towards the bus window and reached up to tap the pale hand. It vanished like a startled spider.

'Madam! Ba Agnes!' she shouted. Madam's face came into view, framed by the jolting window. It looked like a puddle of Maheu malt drink, shivering and yellowish.

'Grace?' Madam squeaked.

The bus hiccupped to life, then growled.

'Madam, but you do not belong here! Where is *bwana*?'

'Oh, Grace.' Madam reached her hand out of the window and Grace grabbed it. 'I'm so glad you found me. I had absolutely no idea how on earth I was going to get home and—'

The bus belched and rolled forward. They both cried out and Grace started jogging alongside, their grasped hands tethering her to the bus. As it picked up speed, she banged at the side of it with her free hand, shouting for it to stop. She heard Madam shouting too. Their wrists were sliding painfully on the edge of the sill. The bus finally lurched to a stop, engine still running. Grace bent over, one hand on her knee, the other raised to clutch Madam's hand.

'You can let go now, Grace,' Madam said breathlessly. 'They're letting me off.'

As they walked along under the orange street lights, catching their breath, Madam explained that she and *bwana* had received invitations to Z Day from Sir Stewart Gore-Browne, who was there in an official capacity as a former leader of the first African political party. Madam had decided to come to the celebrations alone – the workers had the day off and Ronald had abruptly left for the village without her.

'He has been worried about his parents ever since they joined the Lumpa Church.'

Grace was so gripped by this – the *bwana*'s family followed that madwoman? – that she forgot herself and started asking questions. Agnes and Grace had been listening to the news of this rebellion on the radio for the last few months, but they had never discussed it. A woman named Alice Lenshina had started a religious cult. Her followers, thousands of them, had built their own settlements and refused to pay taxes, showing allegiance to neither the colonial government nor Kaunda's party. As soon as he had won the elections, Kaunda had sent in troops to quash the Lumpa Church rebellion. Last July, the confrontation had turned deadly – reports said that at least 1,000 of Lenshina's people had been gunned down.

'Mm, but I think it is good,' Grace opined. 'You must show the mighty of the lion. Kaunda is a proper leader! These Lumpa-Lumpa are just causing mischiffs!'

'Yes, I suppose. But it does seem frightful to bring in guns so soon.'

'Oh, was the *bwana*'s family hurt in these shootings?'

'I'm not sure,' said Agnes, rubbing her sore wrist. 'Ronald has kept it very private.' She couldn't answer Grace's personal questions, so she offered some vague opinions about the political situation. Grace responded in kind. Fireworks stunned the sky smoky behind the two new Zambians as they walked, chatting back and forth, working at about the same level of ignorance, but with a near equal measure of interest. They had walked almost two miles before they remembered to flag down a car.

*

This was the start of a new relationship between Agnes and Grace. It was more like family than friendship, forged through proximity and dependence rather than affinity. It coincided with the opening of a chasm in Agnes's marriage. Ronald had become the Incredible Invisible Husband. At first he was away for weeks at a time, travelling north to tend to his mother, who refused to leave the Lumpa even after losing two children and a husband to the massacre in '64. Then he took a staff development fellowship to become a lecturer at the newly minted University of Zambia. This meant three years in Scotland to finish his degree. Ronald insisted Agnes stay behind in Lusaka. No need to uproot her life again – besides, it wasn't like they could stay with her family.

When Ronald declared that he was staying for two more years in Edinburgh to finish his PhD, Agnes was bewildered. Her husband had drifted into some realm that she could no longer access. On his infrequent trips home to Lusaka, they still made love – Agnes sniffing fervently, hunting the scent of other women and desperate for his own – but they barely spoke. And after a week, he'd be off again, to collect samples in the field or to dig in the archives or to present his findings to his dissertation committee in Edinburgh.

Grace tended to Agnes in his absence. Assuming her Madam would want to be around people like her, Grace carted her off to the places where all the expats congregated in Lusaka: the Ridgeway Hotel, the Polo Club, the Tennis Club. The colour bar had been banned but pockets of white life remained, places where money made the difference that the law no longer did. Agnes didn't question Grace's choices. She thought this was just what one did in Lusaka. As long as her aide was with her, she was fine. Grace was a wet blanket, but she was a blanket nonetheless.

There was near-constant physical contact between the two women, especially after Agnes got pregnant during one of Ronald's brief visits home. She had dire morning sickness and Grace spent weeks guiding her Madam from bedroom to bathroom and back, wiping up the splatter when she missed the bowl.

'I'm too old for this,' Agnes moaned between gushes. She was not quite thirty.

'No, no,' Grace clucked. 'My aunty, she even had a baby when she was forty-sickisty!'

Agnes spat miserably. 'That is a lie, Grace.'

'*Bwana*, he will come back soon.'

But Ronald did not come back to Lusaka when Agnes went into labour. And so in May of 1972, Agnes gave birth in the maternity ward at the University Teaching Hospital with only Grace there to wait patiently as she shrieked and pushed and wept and finally, held a nine-pound baby girl in her arms. In a fit of hormonal sentimentality, Agnes named her daughter Carolyn after her mother. She wrote to Surrey with the news but never received a reply.

'Never mind,' she said to Grace. 'I suppose we are family enough.'

'Yes, Ba Agnes. She is so brown, I can even call this one my daughter!' said Grace.

＊

Agnes couldn't picture her daughter's skin but she could feel her hair, which spiralled gloriously into itself, curls thick as thieves. Sitting by the pool at the tennis club or in front of the telly, Agnes would place Carol on her lap and work her fingers into that warm, springy halo for hours on end. Agnes loved this; Carol loved this; this was how they loved. But when the time came for the girl to start nursery school, Ronald, who had returned from the UK, said enough was enough. It was not acceptable for a child of Carol's status to run around Lusaka with that matted mess on her head. So one day, Grace took her to get her hair done and left Agnes by herself at the club. And that was how Agnes met Lionel Heath.

She was sitting alone at the junior courts, listening intently to the thuds and pocks of an ongoing match. Too embarrassed to play by feel in public, this was the only way for Agnes to revisit her lost vocation. She had learned how to discern the speed and direction of the ball by the sound of the rebound from the rackets and the echoing steps of the players. This was far more enjoyable than the other games of observation that expats played at the Lusaka Tennis Club: who was slighting whom, who was shagging whom, who was destined for a divorce or an abortion.

Today, the tennis players she was observing had just achieved a satisfying volley, a percussive chanty of grunts and thwaps, when someone sat next to her on the bench.

'I've never understood tennis,' came a man's low voice.

Agnes smiled blandly in his direction and turned back to the game. Why sit here then?

'So many . . . moving parts.'

She frowned. 'It can seem complicated,' she conceded. 'But it's really rather elegant.'

'Elegant? Elegant in what way?'

'Well,' she said. 'It works in threes.'

'Threes. Fascinating. Go on.' His voice, the deep vibrato of a tall man, sounded sincere.

Agnes explained – three points to take a lead, six to end a set, three sets to make a match – and then, carried away by pedagogy, she said: 'Do you know why they call a zero point *love*?'

'Is it not sheer British condescension to the loser? "You *poor* love," et cetera?'

'Oh dear, no!' she laughed. 'It's from the French word for egg – the shape of a zero. *L'oeuf.*'

'Loaf. Like a loaf of bread?'

'No, no. *Oeuf.*'

'Oaf? As in a fool?'

'*Errrf*,' she dragged the word out.

'Ooooof,' he echoed and she finally heard the tease in his voice. This was no Ronald – of course he knew the French word for egg, and the origin of *love*. He just delighted in wordplay – when she told him her name, he tossed it around a bit and ended up with another *jeu de mots*.

'Pleasure to meet you, Eggnest.' He took her hand off her knee to shake it. 'I'm Lionel.'

'Well, I suppose I shall call you the Lion then!' she said, a flush rising up her neck.

'Touché,' he said and she could hear the smile in his voice.

By the time Grace returned with a sore and sulky Carol in tow, Agnes felt that Lionel knew everything about her – except, apparently, that she had a child. She was mortified by the omission, but Lionel didn't seem surprised by Carol's existence, nor by her skin colour. He greeted the girl seriously and cheered her up with jokes and compliments about her hairdo – thin French braids with softly clicking beads on the ends. Grace repacked the bags as Agnes stood there, listening to her daughter's shrill trill and Lionel's bass rumble. Why was it so easy to talk to this man? Maybe because he wasn't like the other expats at the club, with their casual contempt and vestigial racism – calling the staff 'boys' and snapping their fingers. But he wasn't like Ronald's *apamwamba* friends either, with their intellectual insults and inside jokes. He certainly wasn't like Ronald. For one thing, he was tall.

✳

When they met again several months later, Agnes was seated at an outdoor table at the club bar, waiting for Carol to finish her swim lessons. To pass the time, she was chatting with an Austrian couple. Hans was here to conduct research on birds in Eastern Province, and Greta was here to accompany him. They were new to Lusaka, which made them somewhat tolerable, though they didn't speak English well. Agnes was trying to describe Ronald's research in simple terms.

'It's about testing the Kariba Dam. It's important to have a sort of switch to turn it ... *off*—'

'Eggnest! Are you boring these people with your little *l'oeuf* story?'

Agnes sputtered happily. She couldn't believe he'd remembered. Lionel explained the *l'oeuf*/love joke to the couple, who laughed in a puzzled, half-understanding way.

'Might I have a cigarette with you?' Lionel asked them. 'I am hiding from my wife.'

So he was married too. Agnes felt more relieved than disappointed.

'But naturally!' Hans said. 'Have your seat!'

Lionel sat next to Agnes, lit a cigarette and handed her his pack of Pall Malls.

'Trying to cut down,' Agnes demurred, patting her belly. Ronald had been appointed dean of engineering at UNZA. He had celebrated by promptly getting her pregnant again.

Greta squealed into Agnes's ear: 'Another baby? Oh, it is so good! It is a boy this time?'

While Hans asked Lionel what he did for work, Greta dove into a covetous conversation with Agnes about how far along she was (four months) and whether her 'condition' would be passed down (Agnes was finding Greta less tolerable by the minute) and why 'the blacks' here insisted on using cloth nappies instead of disposables. Agnes tried to engage in good faith but the topic was too dull, Greta's English too blunt ('how they getting the shit off?'). Agnes longed to hear more of Lionel's rumbling voice. She caught snatches of his work history – a position at Leeds, a stint in Tanzania – and when he said he was teaching at the University of Zambia, she turned to him, interrupting Greta mid-sentence.

'UNZA? That's where my Ronald works! I mean, my husband. He's in engineering.'

'Ah. Well, I'm in humanities and social science. We're unlikely to run into each other.'

'You belief in these different classes?' Hans butted in.

'Dear Hans, class is everywhere,' said Lionel. 'Look around. We're at a tennis club.'

Hans gave a forced laugh but pressed his point. 'I refer to classes of *study*. You belief . . .'

Greta resumed chattering about babies and bums and rashes and creams. Agnes sank back in her chair with a wan smile. She had almost given up when Lionel leaned in and whispered in her ear.

'It's all a bit Evelyn Waugh in Africa, isn't it?'

Agnes giggled. She had never read Waugh but she knew what he meant about the Etonian atmosphere – wealthy whites sipping Pimm's Cups and G&Ts, complaining about the sun and the service. 'There isn't much else to do, though, is there?'

'Well, actually. I have a sort of ... social club going at the university,' he said. 'Perhaps you'd like to join us? With your husband, of course.'

✳

Ronald claimed he was far too busy in his new deanship to join some trivial little club. Agnes was too embarrassed to bring Grace – both by the girl's illiteracy and her own dependency on her. So, the following Friday, Agnes put on one of the two dresses she could still fit and a cloche hat and asked the driver to take her to campus alone. She didn't often come to UNZA but she knew the route well. She could tell when they were on Lubumbashi Road (potholes, the crêpey rustle of bougainvillea); when they were passing through the back gate (a pause, a creak as the barricade rose); and when they reached the Goma Lakes (eucalyptus trees that sounded like the sea and smelled like Shiwa Ng'andu).

Agnes got out with her cane, wandered over to a group of chatting students and asked if someone might guide her to the right classroom. A young woman led her through what seemed like a concrete maze: up and down sets of stairs, along open walkways, through dank corridors. Finally they arrived. Agnes thanked the student and stepped tentatively into the classroom, removing her hat. She heard chairs scraping and papers rustling and whispering giggles.

'Welcome!' Lionel boomed warmly from the front of the room. 'We're just starting.'

Agnes smiled and felt for the nearest chair, sliding her cane under it as she sat. She was handed a solid rectangle – an unusually small book. She slid a finger inside its pages, which were as thin as onion skin. Was this a Bible study group of all things?

'Let's begin with where we left off,' said Lionel. 'Mao's concept of contradiction.'

A voice broke in. 'We must first go back to the idea of the dialectic, Prof.'

'Ah, yes, we ended in the middle, or should I say the *muddle*, of the dialectic last week, didn't we? This is in fact the nature of the dialectic, always in motion, surging forward and racing back, like the sea.'

Agnes perked up, thinking of the sound of the eucalyptus trees.

'But Prof!' a woman's voice called out this time. 'We do not know about the sea here in Zambia! We are landlocked. You must kindly deploy another metaphor for us please thank you.' A laugh.

'You're right, Stella. Awfully Eurocentric of me. Let's use a mathematical language – it's more universal. So, if we have a plus and a minus. Thesis, antithesis, what does it . . .'

Agnes heard the hollow scratch of chalk on a shuddery chalkboard. She sank back in her chair. The classroom was frightfully cold. Her stockings felt wet and dry at once. Jolly good Ronald hadn't come. To think, Lionel's club was some kind of communist collective! She couldn't sneak out unnoticed now, and she couldn't find her way back alone to the Goma Lakes where the driver was parked. Agnes sat in a misery of itch and sweat, waiting for the meeting to end.

After a few minutes, she was handed a sheet of paper. It was soft and slippery – a photostat.

'. . . transcript of the conversation,' Lionel was saying. 'Let's read it aloud. I shall be Mao. Who wants to be Kaunda?' A hand must have gone up. 'Thanks. Now remember, this is in translation. Mao begins: *"We hope that the Third World will unite. The Third World has a large population!"*'

'*That's right,*' said a wheezy male voice, ventriloquising Kaunda. The voice sounded a bit old for a student, and familiar somehow. They went on, alternating the lines of dialogue.

'Mao: *Who belongs to the First World?*'

'Kaunda: *I think it ought to be the world of exploiters and imperialists.*'

'Mao: *And the Second World?*'

'Kaunda: *Those who have become revisionists.*'

'Mao: *I hold that the US and the Soviet Union belong to the First World. The middle elements such as Japan, Europe, Australia and Canada, belong to the Second World. We are the Third World.*'

'Kaunda: *I agree with your analysis, Mr Chairman.*'

'Let's pause here,' said Lionel, 'and discuss the implications of this dialogue for Africa.'

'Ah, Prof,' came a voice from the corner, 'it is a simplification to knit us together like that. One Zambia, One Nation? Maybe. But One Africa? One Third World? I don't know.'

'And now,' a woman's voice chimed in, 'Kaunda has even instituted a one-party state. Is that true socialism? Or is it just fascism? He is becoming just another African dictator!'

An exclamation from the back; a clash of disagreement; a harmony of voices arguing the same thing in different words; a racket of shouts and laughter. As the conversation crescendoed, Agnes thought again about the sea and about coincidence – or had Lionel said contradiction? – wondering how likely it was for two things to meet one another in the sea, given the fact of waves. Before she knew it, the meeting was over. Agnes stood, thrilling with proximate knowledge as the other members of the group shuffled out of the room, chatting.

'I did not expect to find you here,' said the wheezy voice that had play-acted Kaunda.

'Yes, hello,' she frowned, reaching out to shake hands. 'Small world, I suppose.'

'Were you not listening?' the man laughed. 'The Third World is a *big* world!'

'Indeed.' Lionel joined them. 'The Third World is the majority of our world.'

'Yes, Mr Chairman. Your analysis is very pertinent and correct,' the man said, exaggerating Kaunda's sycophancy and that's when Agnes realised who it was: Ronald's friend, Phil, from that first house party over a decade ago.

'I must admit, it's all a bit beyond me,' she said feebly. 'The Third World – it sounds like something out of Tolkien.'

'A token?' asked Lionel.

'No, no, Tol-*keen*. He wrote—'

'Dear sweet Eggnest,' Lionel said, putting his hand on her forearm. 'Have you heard of this brilliant new invention? The British came up with it a few centuries ago. It's called irony.'

'The British?!' Phil protested. 'Irony is a French invention!'

'Hrm, second-rate irony perhaps,' said Lionel.

'Second World irony, you mean?' said Agnes.

There was a pause. Then they all laughed, Lionel loudest of all, and her heart was a sun in her chest.

✳

After that first meeting, Lionel rarely spoke to Agnes. She lingered after each session, like a fool, but he was always stuck talking to Phil or to a student, untangling some knot in whatever web the group had been spinning for the hour, some analysis of Hegel, or was it Engels? It really was beyond her. Most of it anyway. She could follow the history: the ravages of colonialism, the hut tax, the displacement of the Tonga during the building of Kariba Dam. And she quite liked Zambian Humanism, Kaunda's version of socialism – his idea that 'a person becomes a person through the people'. It was a philosophy, which had always seemed to her more supple and sophisticated than a politics.

During her sixth meeting, in a fit of excitement, Agnes crowned herself secretary. Ronald had bought her an expensive tape recorder so she could leave instructions for the workers, most of whom could not read. She offered to bring it to campus to keep track of what was said. Lionel thanked her profusely. Recordings of these meetings would be very helpful, he said.

Agnes sometimes played them back to herself at home, pressing her ear to the speaker as she lay in bed or gave Carol a bath. She adored the *ooh* sound of the African socialist concepts from Tanzania and Kenya – *uhuru* and *ujamaa* and *ubuntu*, words for freedom and family and humanity. She believed in all those things, too. It was so obvious that they were true and good, especially when conveyed by Lionel's rich voice and when applied to actual oppression of actual people, the Bantu. Agnes quizzed Grace about her cultural beliefs. What was it *like* to be Bantu? To come from an ancient tribe so naturally inclined to socialism that its name simply meant 'people'.

'Ah, you must ask the *bwana*,' Grace would stutter vaguely, 'I do not know such things.'

But Agnes never talked to her husband about meetings or radical ideas or anything any more, really. Ronald the dean had retreated completely – self-serious, self-important, and far, far away.

A couple of months after Agnes joined, Lionel's Marxist club – they called themselves The Reds – put aside abstract questions of ideology and turned to what was literally in front of them: the university. What, in short, could be done? There was the perennial question of bursaries. There was a student housing shortage. And, though it seemed to Agnes a mundane question, there was the curriculum, which was Eurocentric to a fault. There weren't many African fiction writers to choose from, but there was a new line of books – the Hyena Man series? – that everyone seemed to know about. The Reds started there and put together a new core sequence that would be more relevant to black Africans: Lenin, Marx, Memmi, Fanon.

The trouble began when a group of lecturers calling themselves the Zambian Caucus caught wind of this new syllabus and wrote a letter of complaint to the administration. Compared to lecturers from America and Europe, the caucus said, Zambian lecturers were second-class citizens: they received a lower salary, fewer opportunities, and had no say in big decisions. Case in point? The Reds' curriculum, which had been written by foreigners 'playing politics' on campus.

The Reds were furious. What foreigners?!

'Are we not all Zambians in this room?' someone said at the start of the next meeting.

'Not all of us,' Lionel said softly.

Agnes touched her cheek, fondling a pregnancy pimple. It felt as if everyone was staring at her, either because she was white or because she was married to a dean.

'That is besides the point,' a young woman shouted. 'Are we not trying to free ourselves from imperialist, colonialist frames of thinking like "foreign" and "national" in the first place?'

The Reds hummed in agreement. The question now was how to fight back against the Zambian Caucus's letter of complaint. Another, bolder syllabus? A counterletter?

'We can send letters,' Phil's wheezy voice came from the corner. 'But will they kindle a fire? *Mwebantu*. Let us show that we are not just a paper revolution. We are not just stooges!'

Stronger suggestions began to swirl in the room. *Boycott classes! Denounce Kaunda! Block Great East Road!* Agnes tried to focus, but her cheeks felt fiery and her fingers slipped on the tape recorder. As soon as the meeting was over, she stood up and walked towards the front of the classroom to speak to Lionel. But he was already engaged in a fierce whispering argument.

'There are spies in these meetings!' Phil was seething. 'Eyes-eyes-eyes all over.'

Agnes stopped.

'The ones who you think are not watching?'

Agnes turned.

'Those ones are the most dangerous.'

Agnes walked out.

She knew how to find her own way to the Goma Lakes by now. She walked slowly, pensively tapping her cane. The irony of it! The idea that *she* was a spy, some kind of 'foreign agent'. Was she not Zambian? Had she not been bestowed that honour on Z Day? A rain shower began as she reached the car park outside the student bar. The driver jumped out to help her into the car, fussing with an umbrella. Africans and their fear of water! In protest, Agnes rolled the window down a quarter and rested her head against it, letting the cool rain spray her hot scalp.

At home, she went straight to her bedroom, cracked the window and lay on the bed beneath it. She wanted just that much rain, enough to nourish her self-pity, not quite enough to drown it. When he got home from work, Ronald found her there, her cheek sprinkled with water.

'What happened?' He stroked the damp hair from her face. 'How was your club?'

She frowned. Ronald never asked about her meetings. 'Did you know your friend Phil is in The Reds?'

'Philemon? Of course,' he laughed, so knowingly she felt slapped. 'Why?'

'No reason,' she mumbled. Was Ronald a member of the Zambian Caucus? Had he got his friend to force her out? 'I'm not going back anyway. I'm exhausted.' She rolled onto her back.

'*Mmm*,' he rumbled with pleasure as he rubbed her protuberant stomach. 'Our son is making you *bulge*.'

She shooed him off. 'You don't know that it's a boy this time.'

'Yes, in fact, I *do* know,' he said, tipping his head onto her thigh. 'My mother even predicted. "Your second child must be a boy," she said.'

This sounded to Agnes more like a command than a prediction, but of course she hadn't been there – she had never met Ronald's mother. Rather than open that old wound, she ventured a possible name for the baby, if it did turn out to be a boy.

'Don't you think it sounds rather regal?'

'Regal?' He rose up, sputtering with disbelief. 'My child will have an African name!'

'Carol doesn't,' she scoffed. '*You* don't even have an African name, *Ronald*!'

'I do!' he shouted. 'It has just been rubbed out. That will not happen to my children!'

She heard the door click shut behind him.

＊

Sitting in his study the next day, Ronald pressed play on Agnes's tape recorder. The voice that came from the speakers was as polished as the wood of his desk.

'... no surprise the Labour Party sponsored Kaunda and published his calls for freedom ...'

Ronald shook his head. Of course, Lionel Heath would be blind to Kaunda's opportunism.

'... arrested for possession of communist materials that, like Mao, drew parallels between capitalist and imperialist oppression. This is the bedrock for revolutionary thinking in Africa ...'

Ronald let out a sound of disgust and pressed stop. Why did white men think they knew better than the black people they presumed to save? Ronald had once had faith in Great Britain's dignity and even its superiority – Shiwa had cultivated it in him, with its traditions and its airs and Sir Stewart's young delicate bride, Lorna. Even marrying Agnes had seemed like progress, as if her pale legs were pillars to climb. But during his time in the UK, Ronald had seen other pale legs, dozens of them, a forest of them stretching out before him in those years in Edinburgh.

Like any red-blooded man away from his wife, Ronald had sought out women that he could pay to touch him. He often thought of one in particular, with black hair, green eyes and thick creamy thighs. He remembered looking down and seeing her lips stretched over his penis, her head bobbing like a piston. She had gagged a little and he had almost stopped. But then he remembered that he had already paid her, so he closed his eyes and finished anyway. And that was when he had finally understood. White women were just women.

The study door opened and in strode his wife, just another woman, with her pregnant belly.

'Have you seen my tape recorder?' she asked querulously.

Ronald glanced at it on his desk. 'No,' he said. 'Why?'

'I'm about to go to my meeting. I simply cannot find it and neither can Grace.'

He peered around her, but the servant girl with that permanent frown hooked into her face was not with Agnes. 'I thought you had given up on your little communist meetings.'

'No,' said Agnes sniffily. 'I've decided to persist. They need me.'

He was quiet a moment. 'A letter came for you yesterday,' he said. 'Shall I read it to you?'

Her lips tightened like a drawstring. This was no Lorna. No one had applauded him for marrying this white woman. Sir Stewart had banished them. Ronald's mother, under the sway of Lenshina's cult, had refused to meet his 'half-caste' child. If they *were* his children – what had Agnes been up to here in Lusaka while he was away? She certainly never guessed what he had been up to in Edinburgh. Ronald didn't know when she had met this Lionel fellow, or how far their little friendship went. He pulled the letter from his pocket and unfolded it.

'"Dearest Eggnest,"' he began, then looked up. 'Egg. Nest?'

She nodded, blushes poxing her neck. He went on, trying not to smile at her discomfort.

'"Dearest Eggnest. First, I want to thank you. Your presence has meant so much to us. Sadly, we have decided that it would be best if you no longer attended our meetings."'

She inhaled sharply. Her red splotches seemed to bulge like eyes, glaring at him.

'"Your material contributions have been invaluable. You may keep the books but please forward the tape recordings of the meetings – discretion is advisable, given the situation ..."'

※

When Agnes was ousted from The Reds, she took to her bed. She ate honeytoast and tea and told tales to her belly. *Once upon a time in a faraway land, there was a princess ...* Grace was the one who washed and dressed and fed little Carol, walked her to and from school. Between these tasks, Grace placed flannels on Agnes's forehead and rubbed her ankles while they listened to the radio.

News of the mounting campus demonstrations came daily, announcers roundly denouncing The Reds' protests against the UNZA administration and then against Kaunda. *Three hundred students have blocked Great East Road! Hooligans! Is this what decent citizens pay student bursaries for? Today, the Ministry of Home Affairs arrested six foreign lecturers, including Lionel Heath. Serves them right for interfering in Zambian business!*

Campus was shut for weeks. Ronald worked from home, grumbling about the inconvenience to his research. Agnes was unsympathetic. She still fantasised about being a member of The Reds. She would have visited Lionel in prison, secreted his letters out to publish in the *Times of Zambia*. She would have held hands with students as they marched down Great East Road. Like Mama Chikamoneka, she would have bared her swollen breasts and stomach, shaming the uniformed men making arrests.

One day in February of 1976, Grace was kneeling on the floor, rubbing Agnes's ankles, when the radio remarked, almost in passing: 'Today, it has been confirmed that the UNZA lecturer Dr Lionel Heath, his wife, and his two daughters have been deported back to the United Kingdom.'

Agnes gasped.

'Madamu?' Grace asked worriedly and dropped Agnes's ankle.

For Ronald to divide Agnes from The Reds, from her only friends, was one thing. Even Lionel going to jail could be countenanced – forcing arrests was after all a standard practice in civil-disobedience campaigns. But to get the man ousted from the country? Ronald had betrayed her and trapped her at once. She could not confess to her hurt without confessing to her feelings.

'Ba Aganess?'

'It's alright, I'm alright, Grace.'

He had tied her hands but she would take her revenge where she could.

'I thought I hurt you doing this thing.' Grace resumed wringing Agnes's ankle.

'No,' said Agnes firmly, hand splayed over her belly. 'It was just little Lionel kicking.'

First there's the twinge, the harbinger of ache. You shiver, then suddenly feel faint. You're hot, then cold, then both at once – sweating yet parched, bone-dry yet soaked, like water from a twice-smitten rock. Paroxysm is the technical term for what follows next: the grip and release of the ague. You grow shaky and fevered, your retinas whiten, delirium sets in with a vengeance.

You find yourself drowning alone in a sea. You grasp a boulder to stay above water. Three men in white robes say you cannot cross here, but then God tells the angels to save you. They cast a rope out and you pull yourself over to the other side of the sea. You enter a city, a splendid musumba, *where the angels check the Book for your name. When they do not find it, they teach you new hymns, give you passports to heaven, send you back to spread the word to the people. You awaken from death with two Books in your hands – one black, one white; one sky, one ground – both aflame with the spirit of God.*

You gather the people like a flock of wild birds, they come to you 1,000 in a week. You give them new names, touch their foreheads with water, build a church beyond churches: the Lumpa. Your foes steal your Books and demean your wise teachings, but you're a prophet, a queen. Regina! They send the White Fathers to call you the devil, to mock little Alice in Wonderland. They send chiefs and kapasus *to demand your taxes. You say: 'Why must we render to Caesar?' They send Kaunda's men to denounce you as savage. They say: 'Drown the Lumpa forever.'*

You light the match and set it to thatch. You repel all invaders, the white and the black. You defend your churches with bow and axe – and spirit, of course, which streams in your veins, the burning white gold of the sun. Guns rise to the sky or merely shoot water, their bullets can no longer pierce you! But only your body is safe. Your people lie around you, scattered in heaps, mowed down by the hundred, riddled with holes, draining blood.

We drained yours first, only a little, but enough to cause cerebral malaria. Oh Alice Lenshina! Our own Joan of Arc! So many dead at the birth of this nation and all from a single, stray bite!

Matha

1953

For as long as she could remember, Matha Mwamba's life had been entwined with Edward Mukuka Nkoloso's, like the serpent that curls around the staff in the symbol for medicine. They came from the same Bemba village, Luwingu, in the north of Northern Rhodesia. Matha first met Nkoloso when she was still a child. At the time, her father was teaching farming at Lukashya Trades Institute in Kasama and her mother worked as a cleaner at a nearby Catholic mission. Matha's older brother, Mulenga, attended the lower school at the mission, but he was in danger of failing. Everyone knew that Mulenga had blundered too long against his mother's pelvic bone during labour and come out sweet and smiley and a bit vague. But Mr Mwamba was desperate for the boy to improve. Education was paramount for black people.

Edward Mukuka Nkoloso had just returned home after fighting abroad for the British in the Second World War, and he was teaching at Lukashya Trades too – maths, English, Latin. But bucking colonial restrictions against native-led schools, Nkoloso had decided to form his own Roadside Academy, as he called it, to teach science. Nkoloso sounded like someone who had seen the future so Mr Mwamba decided to send his son to the Roadside Academy. His teaching brought in enough to pay for extra lessons, especially since his wife, a fiery Tonga woman named Bernadetta, insisted on keeping her job at Lwena Mission.

Bernadetta had spent most of her girlhood caring for her father, who hadn't been right in the head ever since he had been struck down by a white settler when he was a boy. After her father died, she moved as far away from Siavonga as possible, to Northern Province, and before marrying Mr Mwamba, she had acquired a taste for work. She had come to believe that a job was not just a right but a necessity, like water or shelter or the touch of another. But with both Mwambas working and Mulenga at school and lessons, there was no one at home to watch the girls. Matha and Nkuka could not go to school – they were too young and female, besides – and they had just reached that ungovernable age: too heavy to be *papu*'d on Bernadetta's back as she worked but too small to watch each other. So, when the time came for her son's first lessons at the Roadside Academy, Bernadetta brought her daughters along as well.

✳

Nkoloso raised his army helmet and frowned down at the three Mwambas, aged ten, six, and five. Mulenga's attention was already wandering, wriggling like a litter of puppies from his grasp. Nkuka stood stock-still, gaze locked on her dusty feet. Matha, the youngest, looked up at him with unscratched eyes – virginal white and deep brown, like the coconuts he had first cracked open in Mombasa on his way to the front in Burma. This was two more students than he'd expected. 'They'll be quiet,' their mother had promised him in a tone that also commanded her daughters, then run off before he could protest.

No other students had shown up to the Roadside Academy, which was squeaky new, so Nkoloso led the three children to a table under a muombo tree outside his home. He sat Mulenga on a stool beside him and put the girls on a log on the other side of the table. Nkoloso took off his helmet and opened the mammoth King James Bible he had set on the table.

'The Bible has everything,' Nkoloso explained to Mulenga. 'This is how the White Fathers taught me. Latin, theology, science.' He looked up at the sky. 'Fig trees! Fishes! Even mathematicals, although they are not always exact. Let us see how well you can read.'

But Mulenga was staring not at the book but at a spider skittering up the muombo tree beside them. Nkoloso pincered the top of the boy's skull, turning it so his eyes fell on the page. 'Genesis 1:1. In the beginning . . .'

Each lesson began this way, with Nkoloso steadfastly coaxing Mulenga to read. Eventually, Nkoloso would grow bored with the boy's stilted recitations and start explaining forms of logic to him instead.

If you can see the tree, you can go to the tree. Here to there. If this, then that, and the same with the other. Soon, the lesson had become an exercise less in literacy than in analogy. Every parable, every event of Christ's brief life, was an occasion for an exegesis of Nkoloso's. Reading, writing, 'rithmetic and a touch of revolution.

The Lord called Lazarus from his grave and raised him from the dead.

'Just so,' said Nkoloso, 'white settlers dug up our graves to make way for the line of rail!'

Thou tellest my wanderings: put thou my tears into thy bottle: are they not in thy book?

'The colonialists set the hut tax in 1901 and sent our men to the mines to pay it, leaving their poor wives to weep many tears like the fugitives from Poland during the war.'

The Lord took five loaves and blessed and broke them to fill the bellies of five thousand.

'How many loaves would Christ have used to feed starving Africans in the famine of 1916?'

The Lord went unto his disciples, walking upon the sea.

'You know,' Nkoloso smiled at the sky, 'on my first aeroplane flight, from Bombay to Burma, I asked the pilot to stop so I could step out on the clouds. He refused, the monkey!'

Christ on the cross had asked his Father, Why hast thou forsaken me?

'"Is that you, Edward?" That is what my father cried when we ran into each other by chance in Mombasa. He was already quartermaster on tour of duty with the Northern Rhodesian Regiment,' Nkoloso mused sadly. 'He didn't know I had also been conscripted.'

As their mother had promised, the Mwamba girls were quiet during these lessons, though in different ways. Nkuka gazed ahead unseeing, rigid and quivering as a stalked hare. Matha seemed awestruck too, but she was by nature a laughing girl, squirmy in her seat. At the end of the hour, she was often kneeling on the log, leaning over the table, her neck stretched forward like a turtle. Sometimes, as Nkoloso guided her brother through the reading of a sentence, the student's drone lagging behind the teacher's booming recitation, Matha would issue a squeak from her hover above them. Nkoloso would look up from the Bible, fixing her fiercely until she tumbled back onto her bum, covering her giggling mouth with her hand, coconut eyes wide.

Nkoloso would smile at her – he was gentle, in truth – and quote 1 Timothy 2:11.

'Let the woman learn in silence,' he'd say, patting the *mukule* plaits furrowing her hair.

Then he would turn back to Mulenga, but the boy was always already staring at a cloud or a leaf or his hand – anything other than the page in front of him.

After months of these futile lessons, Nkoloso lost his patience. The boy seemed built of indifference, impervious to knowledge or interest of any kind. Nkoloso decided to set a trap for him. They were in the middle of reading the story of the fig tree that Christ curses to barrenness.

'Now in the morning as he returned into the city, he hungered,' Nkoloso read aloud.

'... *the seedy he angered* ...' Mulenga echoed in his muddled English.

'And when he saw a fig tree in the way,' Nkoloso continued, 'he came to it, and found nothing thereon but leaves only.' He was peering at Mulenga as the boy mumbled along. 'And said unto it,' Nkoloso laid his trap: 'Let every fruit grow on thee henceforward forever.'

Poor Mulenga fell right into it. '... *let heavily flute glow* ...' the boy began.

Nkoloso was about to correct him – 'It says *no* fruit, not *every* fruit!' – when he heard a low chuckle. Matha was hanging over the Bible, giggling.

'And what is so funny, Miss Matha?' Nkoloso frowned.

At this, Nkuka's eyes widened and she kicked her sister under the table. Matha stopped laughing with a wince, but she couldn't stop smiling.

'You!' Nkoloso stuck his finger in her face. 'You have rememorised this passage?'

Matha slowly shook her head.

'*Ah-ah*, so what is it, little girl? You think you can read?'

Matha slowly nodded her head.

'Okay, you must show us then!' Nkoloso turned the Bible around so it was facing the two girls. He pointed at the passage he had just intentionally distorted. Matha looked down at the page, then up at him.

'No – you said you can read it. So read!'

Matha glanced at her sister, who shook her head fretfully, then at her brother, who shrugged languidly. Matha knelt up onto the log. With effort, she turned the heavy Bible around so that it was once again facing Nkoloso. He sucked his teeth, about to launch into a lecture on not wasting time, when he heard a high, soft sound he had never heard before. It was Matha's voice.

'... fig tree with-hard away. And when the dee, dees-seep,' she faltered, then pushed through, *'dee sigh polls* saw it, they maravelled, saying, How soon is the fig tree with-hard away!'

Her finger was on the page, scanning from her right to her left above the words. This was how the book had been oriented for months, so this was how Matha had learned to read. Upside down.

'Speak up, child!' said Nkoloso, rising to his feet with astonishment.

'Be thou leemoved, and be thou cast into the sea. It shall be done,' little Matha piped, her voice reedy and confident, her finger inching slowly up the page. When she reached the top of the page – 'whatsoever ye shall ask in prayer, believing, ye shall' – she stopped and looked up at Nkoloso expectantly. Man and girl gazed at each other across the table, their lines of sight cutting slantwise through the air.

'But you are only five,' Nkoloso breathed. 'But you are a miracle!'

Matha giggled and covered her mouth with her hand.

When the Mwamba children arrived for lessons the next day, the two stools were placed next to the log on one side of the table so they could all face the Bible together. When Mulenga complained about this unprecedented inclusion of the females – 'they are feebo-minded,' he bluntly echoed their father – Nkoloso gathered them close and told them a story.

As a mission-educated boy, Edward Mukuka Nkoloso had wanted to join the priesthood. But he had been chosen instead for that grand disaster, the war. The war had been a giant mirror: you saw white men die across from you, as equals. 'Yes, we were all willing to die! Death or victory, but victory is sure!' Nkoloso had realised that death is a purifying fire, like *chitemene* – no matter the height of the crops, no matter how green or brown the leaves, the fire razes them all to the same level black.

'Equality!' he cried. 'You see? Only from level ground can you grow new crops. The war taught me that all men are equal before death, black and white. And yesterday,' he shrugged, 'Miss Matha showed me that this equality thing probably includes the females, too.'

✳

Nkoloso tutored the three Mwamba children at his Roadside Academy for a year. Then in 1954, he was transferred from Lukashya Trades to a school in the Copperbelt. When Nkoloso left Luwingu, Mulenga continued skating by at the mission school, but his sisters' education lapsed entirely. Left without childcare for her girls, Bernadetta simply absorbed them into the orbit of her labour. They became her minor satellites at Lwena Mission, circling her with their little buckets of water, in which they wet rags to wipe the chalkboards and wash the windows.

Nkuka seemed to take comfort in the orderliness of this work, as ready for rules as a soldier. But Matha was restive, her neck craning as she cleaned, her eyes peering over the boys' shoulders at their exercises, her ears almost sprouting from her head as she strained to catch the lessons echoing from the mission walls. Bernadetta noted this behaviour in her youngest with frustration. She often thought of what Nkoloso had told her before he left the village.

'Matha is very bright. You must nurture that brain! Do not let it rot.'

Her husband had no patience for this sentiment: 'There is no use in educating females!' he said. 'Everyone knows that.'

But looking over the rows of mission boys every day, those dullards with their shaved skulls, their scalps marbled with ringworm, Bernadetta felt choked with helplessness. She decided to take things into her own hands.

✳

One morning, Matha woke to the chill of a blade on the back of her neck. She flinched.

'Stay still,' her mother whispered.

Matha obeyed. Her brother and sister were still asleep in a heaving tangle beside her. Their father was snoring on a mat by the door. It was dawn. The sunlight coming through the thatched roof was reddish, like when Matha's fingers covered her eyes to count for hide-and-seek. Wood pigeons coolly greeted each other outside. Lying on her side on the packed mud floor, her mother's hand pinning her down, Matha listened to the birds and to the scrape of the knife rising up the back of her skull, shaving the hair from her head.

Two hours later, she was sitting in the back of a classroom at Lwena Mission. How different it looked from behind a desk! Instead of hunting the corners for rubbish and ants, or coralling the soapsuds you were splashing across a floor, you could just sit and look around: at the big blackboard awaiting its daily scripture, at the white walls carving the world into wedges of shadow and light. Matha blinked, tugging at the itchy neck of her brother's old school uniform. She forgot her discomfort as soon as the teacher came in and began shouting lessons at the students, who shouted right back. Matha soon grasped the pattern of call-and-response and added her voice to the throng. How pleasing to count in counterpoint! What a happy sound a shout could be!

This was nothing like the shouting between her parents. Those fights usually began as a back-and-forth, too, but they soon overlapped and eventually crowded into a chaos of mutual interruption. These arguments sent Nkuka into a shivery ball, hands over her ears, and Mulenga into a rigid knot, his skinny arms around his bony knees. Matha alone would sit cross-legged on her mat, listening, her head tilting to and fro like a bell as she tried to follow along. Her parents argued about the size of women's brains. They quarrelled about whether Bernadetta had inherited her father's feeble-mindedness and passed it on to Mulenga. They bickered about whether witch doctors were any more rational than priests and whether the European census-takers were really blood-sucking *wamunyama* and whether a chief had more power than a queen.

Their most recent debate was about the Federation. The white settlers had unilaterally decided to combine Northern Rhodesia, where the Mwambas lived, with Rhodesia to the south and Nyasaland to the east. The black nationalists – educated men, veterans and radicalised miners – had vehemently protested against this. Rhodesia was a colony, Northern Rhodesia a protectorate: this merger would drag the country into greater subjugation. The African National Congress had demanded that the Federation be dissolved, that the colour bar be struck down, and that the British grant independence to Northern Rhodesia. Mr Mwamba was on the side of the Federation, believing the British knew best; Bernadetta was on the side of the Congress. 'Freedom!' she seethed with her bitterbright eyes. Matha pictured Federation and Congress as forces of nature: an unmovable mountain and an unstoppable flood pitched against each other.

But more and more, her parents' arguments came down to a single, very human, figure of contention:

'You know Ba Nkoloso has been fighting our cause in the Copperbelt,' Bernadetta would say.

'That man is very foolish! He is biting the hand that feeds him, going against the British!'

'They are the ones who swallowed his hand! After he fought their war!'

Matha thrilled with the very mention of his name. Ba Nkoloso had been her first teacher, and Matha loved learning so much that she thought learning *was* love. As the years passed, she hoarded each shiny shred of information that blew through Luwingu about him. Some said he was selling medicine and toiletries to miners in the Copperbelt, that he had a job with Lever Brothers. Others said that this was just a ruse. Nkoloso was organising strikes among the miners and had led his new school on a march to the district commissioner's office to protest the digging up of African graves for European settlements. 'That man, he cannot resist resistance!' they said.

For three years, Matha attended the Lwena Mission School in secret – eventually, an open secret among the students. When she turned eight, her dimples deepening by the day, a group of boys dragged her behind the geyser and yanked down her shorts to confirm their suspicions. They pointed and laughed. Matha stared at them, unfazed, legs straddled wide to keep the shorts from falling off. Cowed by the lack of shame in her eyes, the boys resorted to extortion.

'Listen here, *Matthew*,' one said, 'we will keep your secret from Father Superior Deslauries and the teachers. But you must give us the answers to the maths exercises.'

Matha handed them over without rancour. She learned to temper herself in class: she never spoke up, never raised her hand to go to the board. She even inserted a few errors into her work, which only proved her cleverness – it's not so easy to be believably wrong. She sat in the back of the classroom, absorbing lessons and rumours, a quiet unsmiling repository.

Then one day, Matha sat up in her chair. The two boys in front of her were whispering.

'Ba Nkoloso has been let out of Bwana Mkubwa. He is coming home ...'

It was 1957. It seemed that the colonial government was sending Nkoloso back to Luwingu because they could no longer invent reasons to keep him behind bars. He would be under a loose sort of house arrest. Over the next month, Matha overheard more rumblings. Ba Nkoloso was apparently still acting as a surreptitious Congress leader, holding secret meetings in beer halls, telling people not to pay their taxes or work for the whites. He had even instructed the villagers in Luwingu not to pay respects to their chief Shimumbi, who he claimed had 'sold us to the Europeans!'

This was considered a terrible betrayal – to turn black people against each other. But Matha believed her former tutor would do it, and she believed he was right to do so. She still remembered the righteous conversations he used to have with her mother when she came to fetch them from the Roadside Academy. About the war, imperialism, democracy, 'one man, one vote' – which he had amended to 'one *person*, one vote' after Matha had revealed that she knew how to read. She longed to see her old teacher again, to witness his fiery speeches.

Then one day in August, the rumours about his resurrection in Luwingu took physical form and entered her classroom, like a proof. Ba Nkoloso's sister Ernestina, a Sister at the mission, appeared in the doorway holding the hand of a boy.

'This is *mwana mwaume*,' said Sister Ernestina, 'and he will be joining your class.'

The boy scanned the classroom with a defiant smile. Matha recognised him immediately. She had only met him a handful of times during the Roadside Academy years. But this was definitely Ba Nkoloso's son – you could see the resemblance in the bullish forehead. What was it like to have a father so struck with divine brilliance that people called him John the Baptist? Just then, the boy's eyes caught hers and his smile quivered. Matha dropped her eyes to her desk.

*

'Rudiculous!' said Mr Mwamba, stomping across the hut. 'John the Baptist?!'

Bernadetta sucked her teeth. She was squatting on the floor, serving a burnt supper to the children. 'Ba Nkoloso is not the one saying it. It is the people. They are ready for a leader!'

Mr Mwamba put his hands on his hips. 'Is he not baptising them like he's a priest?'

Bernadetta chuckled. 'Yes, he dunks them in the river, and ...'

Mr Mwamba bent over and put his finger over his wife's lips. 'Brasphemy!'

Bernadetta spat his finger off indifferently, continuing to adorn the rim of the pot of *nshima* with little round *ntoshis* for the children to pluck off when they had cooled.

'Yes, he splashes them in the Mupombwe river,' she said. 'Then he sends them off with a Congress card!' She laughed, deep and low and knowing, as she handed Nkuka a tin cup.

Later that night, Matha woke to the sound of that same laugh, but quieter. The door to the hut was open, the moonlight like spilled *mukaka* on the floor. She stood and waded through it as if in a dream, tugged outside into the yard by the sight of her own silvered feet. A breeze passed and she shivered and looked up. There was a woman's body swinging before her.

No. It was just an empty dress. The washing was still on the line overnight because, as Matha's father often reminded them, Bernadetta was a terrible housewife. Matha heard her mother laugh again. Then she saw her, silhouetted on the other side of the hanging wash with another woman. *Chitenge* wrappers had turned their legs into tree trunks. *Chitambalas* peaked their heads with leafy ears. The wind blew against the wash. Their shadows wriggled and writhed.

'If they think that they can lead a donkey to a muddy pool and make it drink, they are doubly wrong!' Matha's mother was saying. 'They simply cannot go on beating people. Arresting them, imprisoning them without trial!' Her voice splintered with rage.

'That is correct.' Matha was surprised to hear a deep voice coming from the other woman. 'Banning the African Congress cannot stop the people from rising!'

The moonbright clothes flapped. Their shadows weaved and nodded.

'Bernadetta,' the booming voice went on, 'are you ready to join this fight for freedom? Can you commit the way I have committed, even disguising myself to work underground?'

'Yes, Ba Nkoloso.'

Matha covered her gasp with her hand. But why was he dressed as a woman?

'Only the beaten body makes its cries heard,' said Ba Nkoloso. 'It is time to stage our rebellion.'

✳

There was trouble in Luwingu. Fires were burning. Riots were raging. The mission school felt the tremors too. Students sang protest songs at break, pretending they were just games. Mr Chiliboy taught *Antigone* in the upper school. News of Ba Nkoloso's subversions flickered along the rows of Matha's grade four classroom like *chitemene*, which was itself the spark of the trouble. Chief Shimumbi had sent orders to burn the crops for cultivation. Ba Nkoloso had told the people to refuse. Chief Shimumbi had sent his *kapasus* to set fire to them anyway and called for the insurrectionist to be arrested.

The next morning, after Mass, the other students clustered around Nkoloso's son in the open courtyard outside the chapel as he recounted what had happened next.

'My father started walking towards the police and colonials and the *kapasus*. He said, "Then hangcuff me!"' The boy stretched his arms forward in pantomime. 'My father was ready! For the hangcuffing. But then,' he paused, a natural dramatist, 'the cloud came! The people said *ati* why should this man, my father,' he put his palm to his heart with an earnest frown, 'why should he be hangcuffed? And not the chief! Eh? And so then from there, it was rioting—'

'Who was rioting?' Matha stepped forward. Her mother had come home late last night, her voice and skin and clothing all dirty and scratched. Had she been in that crowd?

'*Ah-ah!* It was all of the people,' Nkoloso's son scowled, displeased at the interruption.

Matha nodded, tugging at her tight collar. The boy stared at her.

'Who are you?' he asked. 'What is your name?'

'Matthew,' Matha said, lowering the pitch of her voice.

The other boys glanced warily at each other. No one had let the new student in on Matha's secret or their arrangement with her. He was too closely connected to the mission – his aunt, Sister Ernestina, was married to a teacher.

'Matthew?' he murmured suspiciously. 'I know you from somewhere.'

'*Iwe*, tell us what happened next,' another boy spoke up. 'Who threw the first stone?'

Matha scurried away from the courtyard, searching the grounds for her mother. They did not usually speak at school for fear of discovery. But Matha desperately wanted to set eyes on her. Last night, Matha's mother had come home and lain down on her mat without even washing the soot from her face. The usual back-and-forth between Matha's parents had been fearfully one-sided. Her father had run out of breath trying to fill the silence. He had shouted and cajoled and threatened to beat the words out of his wife, raising his fist over her only to lower it slowly under her mute animal glare . . .

There she was. Bernadetta Mwamba, disguised in her plain smock and bare feet. She was stooped over a patch of the garden with a girl, their hands busy in the soil. The girl picking vegetables looked up, sensing Matha's eyes. It was Nkuka, also in a smock. She had just turned ten. She raised her hand in a slow, questioning wave. Matha was waving back when she heard a shout. The girls both turned. Another shout. In the distance, three Land Rovers rolled into view, lurching up and down as they traversed ditches. Matha's mother stood up, her hands pulling Nkuka to her side and her eyes pulling Matha into her line of sight in one fluid movement. More shouts. Boys began to spill out of doorways, swarming towards the commotion. Matha ran back to the courtyard and met her mother and sister at the entrance.

Matha's mother gave her a look – *I'm here* – then shoved Matha by her bald head in amongst the other students.

✳

The schoolchildren were instructed to sit on the courtyard floor. Teachers in short trousers strutted about like secretary birds, hovering over them, wagging their fingers. The female cleaners and cooks, dressed in smocks and *chitenges*, stood near their sons, forming familial clots here and there. The White Fathers, in long soutanes, floated calmly towards the newcomers: the three *bazungu* officers in white shorts and socks and helmets who had stepped out of the vehicles with a host of black *kapasus*. Had one of the teachers committed a crime? Were they rounding up Congress? Matha glanced over her shoulder at her mother.

The other students sat calmly, as if they were at assembly or Mass or watching each other perform a drama by Shaka Spear, or was it Shaka Zulu? Matha could never keep the two straight. Stage left, Father Superior Deslauries was speaking to an officer, a tall *muzungu* with sick-looking skin. Centre stage, a short *muzungu* waved his hands and barked orders at the black cadets. In the backdrop, through one of the courtyard archways, you could see the *kapasus* chasing after a handful of men, zigzagging across the veldt.

Father Superior Deslauries stepped forward, and as he did at every Mass, spread his hands to bless the students with silence. He gave a curt introduction: 'Mr Walsh,' he said and walked off with downcast eyes. The tall *muzungu* stepped forward and raised an indignant finger.

'A man has been arrested!' he cried. 'We have brought him here because some of you children have been overheard singing insurrectionary songs and praising your Congress chief!'

The schoolchildren blinked. Congress chief? There was only one chief of Luwingu, Chief Shimumbi, and he was the one who had put out a warrant to arrest the Congress leaders.

'Bring him out,' Mr Walsh barked over his shoulder.

There was a scuffle as two *kapasus* wrangled a man to the front. He was wearing an oversized black suit splattered with mud, a tie loosely noosed around his neck. His hair was long and matted and wet. He trudged forward, his chin to his chest. He hung between the two *kapasus* as if suspended from their grip under his arms. Mr Walsh pointed at him and spat sarcastically:

'*Ecce homo* – behold the man! Behold your Congress chief!'

A *kapasu* grabbed the bushy locks to pull the man's head up. Matha gasped. Ba Nkoloso! He looked out at the students, swaying with every beleaguered breath.

'This bedraggled rat,' growled Mr Walsh, prowling the stage, 'this ... puppet dictator has been terrorising your district for months. Causing fires. Starting riots. He is *not* your chief!'

Mr Walsh strode over to a cluster of *kapasus* and pulled a man from amongst them. Matha gasped again. Chief Shimumbi! He was wearing his royal robes, holding his headdress in his hands.

'*This* is your chief!' Mr Walsh screeched, pointing at Chief Shimumbi, who rose a bit taller, and as an afterthought, fitted his headdress on. 'Do you see the difference now?'

Mr Walsh strode from the chief back to Ba Nkoloso.

'All of you!' He swept his hand over them as if stroking their heads. 'I want you to tell this *rrrat*! Tell him what he is.' He jabbed his finger at Ba Nkoloso as he cried out: 'Traitor!'

The schoolboys, trained to respond with verve to such calls, echoed the *muzungu* instantly: 'TRAITOR!'

Matha looked around, shocked. These same boys had been singing Congress songs just yesterday, songs about the downfall of the Federation and the rise of African freedom. Her eyes locked on Nkoloso's son, squatting at the edge of the audience, his head bowed with shame.

'Liar!' cried Mr Walsh, jabbing his finger again.

'LIAR!' the schoolboys shouted.

Ba Nkoloso hung heaving between the two *kapasus*. Sweat or blood dripped from his temples into the dust. Mr Walsh stepped forward and fingered Ba Nkoloso's tie with a melodramatic sneer, as if the cloth were rotten. The schoolboys laughed with the eerie mechanical sound of hyenas. Chief Shimumbi now mustered his courage and stepped forward. He spoke in Bemba and he too commanded the students to decry Ba Nkoloso. Walsh stepped back. Ba Nkoloso panted, his eyelids fluttering sluggishly like moths in the rain. Chief Shimumbi was working himself into a froth, insulting Ba Nkoloso's manhood and ancestors, calling for his death.

In a burst of passion, the chief stretched his hand out to a *kapasu* for a stick. He grabbed it and hit Ba Nkoloso across the stomach. A knot began to form in Matha's throat as Chief Shimumbi beat Ba Nkoloso about the shoulders, the back, the chest. Ba Nkoloso fell to his knees – the *kapasus* holding him up had dropped him, freeing their hands so they could join the beating – then tumbled onto his side. Some of the boys in the audience rose onto their knees to see better. But they said nothing. The teachers said nothing. The Fathers said nothing. All was quiet but for the thudding blows, the *kapasus'* big sticks flinging up and down like the *ibende* that women use to pound maize for *unga*.

When they finally stopped, Ba Nkoloso lay still. The short *muzungu* called for a pail of water and splashed it over him until he startled awake. Then a black *kapasu* lifted him onto his knees and started to shave his head with a pair of scissors. Ba Nkoloso flinched as blood trickled down his cheek. The *kapasu* bent down with a grin and picked up a tuft of hair, sniffed it, made a face, and leaned forward to hand it to a student. The boy reached for it with a smile and just as he touched it, a cry rang out.

Matha, her face wet with tears, looked around. It was her mother, racing between the rows of kneeling children, pushing them aside like stalks in a field. In a flash, Bernadetta had reached the *kapasu* and knocked the scissors from his hand: 'How dare you! Have you no shame!?'

The *kapasu* laughed and shoved her face forward onto the ground. Matha stayed seated, her heart pounding.

'Is this man your husband? Should we give you his dick?' the *kapasu* said in Bemba and spat on her. Bernadetta tried to get up. The *kapasu* stepped on her back.

'No, let her stand,' said the chief. 'Let them see what a Congress whore looks like.'

The *kapasu* raised his boot. Bernadetta stood shakily, her eyes darting to Nkuka amongst the cleaning women, then to Matha amongst the schoolboys. The look in their mother's eyes was impossible: it begged them to run to her immediately and it begged them to stay exactly where they were. Matha's eyes fled this torment and landed on Ba Nkoloso's.

He was looking right at her, his eyes like stones under water. And then – before Bernadetta and Ba Nkoloso and the other accused rioters were handcuffed and shoved into the Land Rovers that buckled away from the mission like a line of lazy buffalo – just then, Ba Nkoloso smiled at her. And she knew. No matter what happened to him or to her mother, to the Federation or to Congress, Edward Mukuka Nkoloso and Matha Mwamba would find each other.

*

All three of the Mwamba children were banned from the mission due to Bernadetta's crimes. Mulenga started cultivating vegetables to sell. Nkuka cooked and cleaned and managed their small household. Matha forlornly reread her old exercise books, trying to eke more knowledge out of the everfading pencil marks.

Four years later, their mother died in Bwana Mkubwa prison. Dysentery from bilharzia, the authorities claimed. Mr Mwamba fell into a hole of grief. He had been throwing himself against the wall of his wife for so long that when she suddenly vanished, he fell right over the edge. While he took the long way out, with the help of his younger sister and a renewed religious faith – 'God is in control,' he would intone with dead eyes – his care of his children languished.

In the hazy period after her mother's funeral, Matha slipped away to Ba Nkoloso's home. She knew his wife and his sister were preparing to move to Lusaka, where the cadres of the African National Congress – which had been renamed the United National Independence Party, or UNIP for short – would protect them until Ba Nkoloso was released from prison in Salisbury. Waving a letter of permission she had forged in her father's hand, Matha managed to persuade the two women that they needed her help caring for Nkoloso's children. They travelled by car to Ndola, then took the train down to the capital, a dusty, smelly three-day journey. Matha spent most of it squeezed up against an open window, watching the country roll by under the immense unmoving sky. She was thirteen years old.

Matha loved Lusaka. She felt for the first time that the rhythm of her body matched the rhythm of her surroundings. The thick press of pedestrians fit her soul like a glove. Her pulse beat in time with their feet. Her breathing rate followed the pace of the cars on those unpaved arteries with their grandiose names: Cairo Road, Great East Road, Great North Road. Double-decker buses called Giraffes trundled along them – the ticket checkers made Matha wrap an arm over her head to prove she was old enough to ride.

For a year, Matha essentially ran the household in Matero while Ba Nkoloso's sister worked, his wife sought assistance from UNIP, and his children attended school. Ba Nkoloso's eldest son was the same age as her, but he lorded around, temporary master of the house, while Matha swept and washed and cooked and mopped. She finagled her own small recompense. She befriended stray cats, feeding them scraps and naming them after Christ's disciples. And every morning, she woke before dawn and sat over the boys' schoolbooks, learning their lessons until the chickens began their chuck-chuck-chuckling and the breakfast *mbaulas* swarmed the air with specks of ash.

When Ba Nkoloso got out of prison in 1962, the family threw a big party – chicken and goat on the *brai*, crates of Mosi and Coca-Cola, friends and comrades spilling in and out of the house in Matero. Matha spent the day cooking behind the compound with the other women and only went to greet Ba Nkoloso in the evening. He was sitting in an office chair outside in the yard, wearing his old army helmet. It was dented and dulled with age, but Matha thought it sat on his head like a crown. He grinned gappily – he had lost a tooth somewhere along the way – joking about how the prison in Salisbury had been a map of the continent, every nation in a different cell block, except it was a Scramble for Soap rather than for Africa!

Matha knelt at his feet.

'*Ah-ah!* Can it be?'

'It *can.*' She shyly touched her hair. She had a little afro now that she no longer had to keep it shorn. Ba Nkoloso asked after her studies, quizzed her on maths and science.

'You've grown, my dear.' He shook his head happily. 'You are like the moon, eh?'

The men around them laughed, thinking he meant her newly round body. Matha glanced down at the curves that had emerged the moment she turned fourteen – they couldn't be denied. But when she stood up, excusing herself, Ba Nkoloso caught her hand and pulled her close and explained what he had meant.

'Your mind is still shining, Miss Matha!' he whispered. Then he reached down, picked up a book from under his chair, and pressed it into her hands. 'You will be *my* moon.'

*

A few weeks later, Matha was in a lean-to behind the Matero house, hunched over the book Ba Nkoloso had given her. The pages were polkadotted with mould and barely legible where his scrawled marginalia had spread like weeds over the text. On the floor before her were some basic household items: a glass bottle, a polishing cloth, a small plastic bottle. Matthias slunk around purring, trying to distract her. The sun was setting, making the lean-to glow red. Matha sat in that emerging emergency light, learning how to make a Molotov cocktail. The instructions were simple – something breakable plus something flammable plus something combustible ...

She heard a honk. She covered the book and the items with a *chitenge* and stood up, brushing the dirt from the seat of her black skirt. She let herself out and locked up. Ba Nkoloso's pickup truck was wheezing at the back gate, his scattertoothed grin hovering in the driver's window. Matha climbed into the bed of the pickup, joining the other four UNIP Youth cadets there – Bambo Miti, Fortunate Nkoloso, Reuben Simwinga and Godfrey Mwango. They were wearing all black, too, and sipping Mosi from bottles, which they raised in greeting.

The pickup jolted into motion and Matha heard a loud bleating sound. She thought Ba Nkoloso was honking the horn again but then she saw it: a goat kneeling in the corner of the pickup bed, its eyes rolling with fear. She looked around but the other cadets just shrugged at her with conspiratorial smiles. Godfrey handed her a Mosi. She sipped it, queasy with anticipation. After a twenty-minute drive, the pickup turned off Cairo Road and parked behind a low concrete building.

They all hopped out, Godfrey lifting Matha out like a child. They walked up to a door with a sign that said LUSAKA MORTUARY.

Ba Nkoloso knocked softly. After a moment, the door opened, releasing a fog of white light around a black head. Ba Nkoloso quickly slammed the door against the man, pinning him to the wall inside, his round spectacles tumbling down his nose. The mortuary assistant resisted at first but Ba Nkoloso's five-shilling note was very persuasive, more so than his promise of a house 'when Independence arrives with its celebration of our nation's new hegemony!' Independence was still two years away at least, far too long for a promise to hold in Lusaka.

'Just one body?' the *malukula* asked, staring at the money in his hand.

'Just one.' Ba Nkoloso patted the attendant on the cheek. 'But it must be a white woman.'

After a few minutes, the *malukula* reappeared, wheeling a gurney bearing a covered grey oblong. Ba Nkoloso cut the cloth open to see the face and nodded. The four male cadets stepped forward, lifted the body onto their shoulders – it hung between them like a *machila* – then carried it to the pickup and slid it feet first onto the bed. Godfrey tugged the sack off and they all stared a moment. The woman's skin was mapped with green veins. Her lips were pulled into a grimace. Her breasts were half-empty sacks, one nipple drawn down as if melting. Her frozen pubic hair looked windswept.

Matha had grown up in a village, so the killing of the goat was less shocking than what they did with its blood. Bambo gripped the shuddering beast between his thighs and clamped its jaws shut with his hands, pulling its head up so its neck stretched tight. Ba Nkoloso knelt before it and slashed its throat, holding a tin bowl under the cut until it was full of the thick, dark liquid. Then he carried it to the truck and poured it over the dead woman's pale chest and neck. The blood puckered and bubbled – its heat reacting to the skin, cold from the mortuary ice blocks. Something about the blood, its foreignness to the body it touched, made Matha sway weakly. Godfrey put his hand to the back of her neck to steady her.

Ba Nkoloso wiped his hands brusquely on his trousers. 'Now she looks freshly murdered!' he laughed as he climbed into the cab of the pickup.

The cadets clambered in the back, squatting against the edges, as far from the corpse as possible, keeping it in position with their feet as the pickup swivelled its way through Lusaka. The corpse lay face up, the goat's blood glistening darkly on her chest. The frilly shadows of the jacarandas on either side of the road made it seem as if she were underwater, thready waves passing over her. The label affixed to her big toe fluttered in the wind. Her teeth glinted grimly in the passing headlights. Whenever the pickup slowed, the smell would be upon them – cold rank flesh, coppery goat's blood, the sour hops of spilt Mosi. A sense of wrongness began to swell like a swarm of angered bees. Matha's nostril hairs curled. The back of her neck tingled.

The pickup finally slowed and turned into the drive of the Ridgeway Hotel. Ba Nkoloso found a parking spot near the entrance. The pickup stopped with a lurch and the body slid back, its skull ringing the metal siding like a dull bell. The cadets flinched away from it but Ba Nkoloso got out of the cab and slapped the side of the truck to make it gong again.

'Let us show these *bazungu* who they are dealing with!' he shouted, black eyes gleaming.

The cadets hopped out. As the men prepared to heave the corpse onto their shoulders again, Ba Nkoloso instructed Matha to go in and find the bellboy, who had been paid in advance. She ran in through the glass doors, blinking at the brightness of the lobby after the long drive in the dark. She found the young man waiting for her inside, dressed in a lime-green suit. Without a word, he turned and led her to the restaurant.

Matha had never been inside a hotel before, not only because she was poor, but also because she was black: the Ridgeway still had a strict colour bar. As they rushed along, her eyes bounced around, taking in the dizzying decor – a black and white chequered ceiling, floor tiles fitted in a staircase design, striped ferns in silver planters, a curtain printed with bundles of twigs, a chandelier that looked like a model of the solar system.

As she and the bellboy neared the restaurant, she heard voices and the tinkle of metal striking glass and porcelain. They stopped at the entrance and peeked in. Matha saw a dozen round tables, decked out in white tablecloths, littered with candles and plates of half-eaten food, the meat undone into messy bones and flesh. The *bazungu* guests were eating and drinking and smoking, speaking a thin piping English, as if sucking their words through straws. Hearing a slight commotion, Matha turned. The other cadets were careering down the corridor towards her, the white corpse on their shoulders, Ba Nkoloso leading the charge. The sweat on their foreheads looked like royal Bemba scarification under the electric lights.

'Bwela,' said the bellboy and pulled her around the corner. There were four switches in the wall. The bellboy nodded at her, reaching for two. She put her hands on the other two.

'Now!' Ba Nkoloso yelled.

They flipped the switches down in concert. Everything went black. A pause. Thuds. Glass breaking. A shriek. Matha groped her way back around the corner to the entrance. A soft glow was coming from the restaurant – the candles on the tables were still lit. She peeked inside again. The *bazungu* guests were on their feet, their faces fixed in stark masks of fear and disgust. Ba Nkoloso's back was to the door but Matha could see his silhouette, topped by his spouting mane of dreadlocks. He pointed at the corpse at his feet, its legs spread crookedly, the tag on its toe like a little flag.

'White men!' Ba Nkoloso shouted. 'Your time is up! We have had enough of this *muzungu* governor Welensky, with his Boer rules and violent antics!'

He stepped on the chest of the corpse. There was a collective gasp.

'We have killed his wife!' he declared. 'And now, we shall pounce on *you!*'

The cadets pressed forward into the room, jeering and shoving the hotel guests, poking them in the chest. The whites stumbled past Matha at the threshold, their shoes slipping on the corridor floor. She watched them go. Giggles roiled at the base of her spine, then rose up her body and spilled out of her mouth, with the faintest taste of bile. She felt the ground drop from beneath her feet – someone had whisked her up into the air and placed her over his shoulder.

He carried her into the restaurant, skirting the fallen wicker furniture and the marauding cadets, who had broken into song: *Tiyende pamodzi ndim'tima umo!* He lifted her onto the bar, sending glasses and bottles rolling. Matha winced as an ice spill seeped through the seat of her skirt. She blinked up at her rescuer. He bent and kissed her on the mouth.

'Welcome to the Academy,' Godfrey Mwango said, a scar on his neck gleaming in the candlelight.

1964

The headquarters of the Zambia National Academy of Science, Space Research and Philosophy was in Chunga Valley, a forested area west of Lusaka, where the edge of the city bled into the edge of the bush. Minister of Space Research Edward Mukuka Nkoloso walked among his cadets, patting shoulders, adjusting capes, igniting cheer. As usual, he wore an army jacket and had covered his dreadlocks with his combat helmet, both preserved from his service in the Northern Rhodesian Regiment. But today he had festooned this sartorial drabbery with colour: green silk trousers and a heliotrope cape. The cameras would be filming in black and white, but it was important to suit oneself to the occasion. The Zambian Space Programme was about to make its television debut.

It was September 1964, the height of the Cold War. The news that a fledgling African nation had joined the space race had hit the rest of the world like a scandal, pinging across the oceans, relaying around the planet like the very satellite that Nkoloso was shooting for.

'We will put a Zambian on the moon by the end of this year,' he had solemnly promised at the first press conference. 'The technical details must remain secret. Some of our ideas are way ahead of the Americans' and the Russians'. Imagine the prestige value this would earn for our new nation of Zambia. Most Westerners don't even know whereabouts in Africa we are.'

But they did now, Nkoloso smiled to himself. He had put his country on the world map by joining the race to leave it altogether. He looked around at the reporters who had flown all the way to Zambia for the test launch. These *bazungu* in shirtsleeves and spectacles looked like yams roasting on an *mbaula* – red and wet and bursting from the skin. Strangely reluctant to talk to people unless the cameras were rolling, the reporters were busying themselves with things instead, setting up tripods and scratching notes on paper and snapping photographs of *Cyclops I*.

Nkoloso admired his rocket from a distance. The ten-foot copper cylinder was propped on its end in the grass, listing peaceably, its bottom quarter singed black from pre-launch testing. The take-off had been disappointing from the point of view of spectacle – *Cyclops I* had only risen six feet before it crashed to the ground. The *mukwa* wood catapult he had been considering would not be powerful enough; the *mulolo* system, while ideal for training cadets to withstand weightlessness, would never swing far enough. Turbulent propulsion was the only way forward!

He walked over to confer with a Canadian cameraman, who was panting like a dog in the heat. Nkoloso asked if he could look through the viewfinder. The Canadian stepped aside and Nkoloso took his place behind it.

'How do you zoom?' he asked.

The cameraman wiped his brow and fiddled with some knobs. As the square bloomed fuzzily before his eyes, Nkoloso almost lost his balance. He started back from the camera.

'Does it turn things upside down too?'

No, the cameraman laughed and pointed. Godfrey Mwango, the star astronaut of the Space Programme, was upside down in real life. He was practising handstands to impress Matha Mwamba, the other star astronaut, a star that much brighter for being the only woman on the team. Nkoloso examined them through the lens. Matha was seated with her back against a tree, her legs stretched in front of her. Godfrey stood at her feet, facing her. He placed his palms on either side of her legs and tilted up again into a handstand, his arms forming a bridge over her shins. He settled into his balance with a stagger. Matha was giggling and stroking the cat curled up against her thigh. Another cat began making figures of eight around Godfrey's wrists and Matha's ankles, binding them to each other with a slinky invisible chain.

Nkoloso frowned. This was not the kind of weightlessness and star-gazing of which he approved. This was not the kind of revolutionary vision that his Academy demanded.

*

Her fingers deep in Judas's purr, Matha was laughing and wincing. Bartholomew's paws tickled and scratched the skin of her ankles as he tumbled over them in mesmeric wander. Upside-down Godfrey canted back onto his feet and grinned at her, the round black moons of his shoulders curving against the noon-blue sky. Bartholomew ceased looping Matha's ankles, gave her a look of disgust and sauntered off. Judas scampered after him. Always a follower, that one.

'Come, Sister of the Heavens. We are starting just-now,' said Godfrey, pointing at the SPACE banner. He reached down and pulled Matha to her feet. She tugged down on her leather bomber jacket, a gift from Ba Nkoloso. She was wearing it despite the heat because it set her apart from the other girls here, the hangers-on and would-bes. Some of them had babies on their backs – as if one could properly space-train with such a burden! Those girls teased Matha – they said she wasn't serious, that she laughed too much. But while they were busy wiping poo and snot and spit and piss from their babies' wet holes, Ba Nkoloso had taught Matha how to drive a car, fix an engine, and put together a circuit board with a handful of wires and an old battery.

Matha gave the girls a pitying look now as she and Godfrey jogged over to where Ba Nkoloso and the other cadets were lining up in front of the SPACE sign. There was a camera facing them: a square black box with a tightcurled horn, balanced on three long thin legs. Behind it were the reporters, microphones and notepads dangling from straps around their necks. With their dull stares and occasional flicks of the hand, they looked like a dazed herd of cows.

Ba Nkoloso led the cadets through their drill exercises: jumping up and down and back and forth, clapping and singing. He paced in front of them, his voice booming vigorously: 'Nkoloso watemwa malaila wateka nsongo tapema.' He had revised the Bemba warrior song to include his name. Matha wondered if the reporters had any notion of what the cadets were singing, or of its relevance to the fight for freedom. Probably not. These men didn't seem to grasp the political situation here at all. They kept asking the same obvious questions.

'Mr Nkoloso.' A British reporter with a goatee stepped forward now, the camera rattling on its legs behind him. 'I understand that you have a rocket. Where is it?'

'Yes,' Ba Nkoloso said with his wry smile. He pointed at *Cyclops I* in the distance. 'That is my rocket, and with it, we will go to the moon.'

'And who will be the first Zambian on the moon?'

'You have come at a most propitious moment,' Nkoloso grinned. 'We have just decided which of our astronauts will have the place of honour in the space capsule for our historic moon shot. Mr Godfrey Mwango has demonstrated an outstanding ability to walk on his hands.'

'Walk on his hands, you say?'

'That is the only way a man can transverse the moon, given the gravity conditions.'

The reporter nodded, his neck tendons straining like tree roots.

'Mr Mwango has also passed the acid test of any aspiring astronaut,' Ba Nkoloso continued, 'simulated recovery from a space capsule following a landing on water. A fearsome test for a young man who has only just learned to swim! We must now prepare him for our anti-gravity drill.' Ba Nkoloso bowed slightly and marched over to the training drum.

The reporter turned and spoke directly into the camera. 'To most Zambians, these people are just a bunch of crackpots and from what I've seen today I'm inclined to agree.'

Matha giggled at his nasal voice. What did he mean, cracked pot? Something broken and useless? Or something sharp and dangerous, something that explodes on the fire like a bomb? These *bazungu* all spoke a strange and unwieldy English, an English that brokered no other tongue. Matha could barely understand them, especially the American, who was now beckoning her over to his permanent spot under a thorn tree.

When she reached his station in the shade, he smiled at her, sweat hanging from his upper lip like a veranda after the rain. He introduced himself – Arthur Hoppe – and asked her questions with his hilly, hairy accent. Her name (Matha, she spelled it out carefully), her age (sixteen), her level of education (Form I). His next questions were harder. She ran each one through a sort of thought experiment: What would Ba Nkoloso say? What would be best for the Academy?

'I hear you have been training to go into orbit. Is that so?'

'Yes, please,' she said politely. 'It is so. I am the one going to Mars.'

'You're way ahead of us!' Hoppe grinned. 'We don't have any girls at NASA.'

'Oh-*oh*? Is *it*?' she giggled, covering her mouth with her hand.

'Miss Mwamba,' he leaned in confidentially, 'I hear you have been raising twelve cats as part of your training? What is their function?'

'Yes, please. They are to give me companionship on the journey. But they are also' – she took a deep breath to get the pronunciation right – 'technological accessories.'

'Technological accessories?'

'Yes, please. When I arrive on Mars, I will open the door of the rocket and I will drop the cats on the ground. If they survive, we will know that Mars is fit for human habitation.'

Hoppe laughed. 'And what will you and your cats do on Mars?'

This answer she had memorised: 'Our telescopes have shown us that planet Mars is populated by primitive natives. A missionary will accompany me on my trip but the missionary must not force Christianity on the Martians if they do not want it.'

Hoppe squinted at her, his smile wavering. He cleared his throat. 'And do you find space training thrilling, valuable or merely routine?'

She thought for a moment. 'It is a bit worrisome.'

'Miss Mwamba, how did you become an astronaut? When did you meet the director of the ...' he checked his notebook, 'Zambia National Academy of Science and Space Research?'

'And Philosophy,' she added. 'Me, I have known Ba Nkoloso a very long time.'

＊

'A-okay?' said Ba Nkoloso, thumping his fist against the steel drum lying on its side in the grass.

'A-okay!' Godfrey's muffled voice echoed from within. The cadets were gathered around a forty-gallon oil barrel, *Cyclops I*'s darker, dented twin. Reuben was holding the ceremonial spear aloft; Bambo clutched Ba Nkoloso's overstuffed briefcase against his chest; Fortunate was busily waving the new Zambian flag. The British photographer bent down and snapped a picture with his Kodak, its flash casting a silver glow over the measled inside of the drum and giving them all a glimpse of Godfrey's sweaty, smiling face.

'All systems go!' Ba Nkoloso shouted. 'Countdown!'

'Ten ... nine ... eight ...' the cadets chanted like schoolchildren.

Matha's heart beat in double time. She knew all too well the stuffy dark smother inside that drum, the reverberation of voices outside it – a buzzing echo in the metal and skin – the gentle rocking of the cylinder against the ground, like a canoe about to capsize.

'Two ... one ... Blast off!' the cadets cried.

Nkoloso gave the drum a shove with his boot. It began to roll and the cadets began to applaud, but the decline was too shallow and Godfrey taller and heavier than the average Zambian. The drum rocked to a stop, balanced against a tuft of scrub. The applause pittered out, a rain shower changing its mind. The photographer stood up from his crouch, lowering his camera. Reuben and Matha glanced at each other, then ran forward and gave the drum a four-handed shove. Now it rolled freely, picking up speed as it bounced down the hill before bumping to a stop against a tree. Everyone ran after it – the reporters, the cadets, even the girls with babies on their backs, ululating with the thrill.

Matha got to him first. The drum was banging with hollow booms as he righted himself.

'Wow!' he was saying over and over, or maybe 'Ow!'

'Are you fine?' Matha asked as his head crowned from the dark cave.

'What a ride!' he shouted as he crawled out of the drum. His uniform was smeared with brown streaks from the remnants of oil inside. 'Your turn, Miss Mwamba!' he grinned, swaying a little as he touched the back of her neck, setting it aglow with anticipation. She glanced at Ba Nkoloso for confirmation. He was busy speaking into the American's microphone, his lips grazing its perforated silver head.

'This is how we are acclimatising to the space travel,' he was explaining. 'It gives my cadets the feeling of weightlessness, of rushing through space.'

'Do you think that this training session has been a success?' the British reporter sneered.

'We have learned a great deal,' Nkoloso replied with a twinkle in his eye that Matha recognised as preface to a punchline. 'For one thing, we are going to need a bigger barrel!'

＊

Matha was swinging. The ropes hanging from the tree were creaking; the branches to which they were tied were creaking; the birds in the leafy canopy above were creaking; her bomber jacket was creaking. Matha tipped her head back and laughed, delighting in this questing sound of things moving, stretching, on their way. The other cadets were watching her swing, their heads pivoting back and forth as if the wind were tossing their skulls to and fro. Godfrey gave her an occasional shove to keep her going. Ba Nkoloso, standing a few feet away from her, rattled out his explanation to the reporters, the words fading in and out as she swung.

'*Mulolo* ... swinging technology ... ahead of the Americans and ... greater thrust to soar ... deep abysmal heavens ... theories of Diocletes ... flew towards the sun ... obscure flights of birds ... yes, fishes too! ... way forward ... turbulent propulsion!'

Matha had heard all this before, the way Ba Nkoloso blended together science and fable, African technology and Western philosophy. It confused others, but she had learned to see the world through his double vision. It was as natural to her now as the air through which she was swinging. She turned to face the television camera. She knew its square black mouth was quietly eating a picture of her. The British reporter stepped in front of it, his back to her. As she swung towards and away from him, she caught snatches of his commentary:

'Zambian astronaut ... finally airborne ... self-styled indigenous ... far-sighted if unconventional ... toothless space enthusiast ... Zambia's village idiot ... an amiable lunatic who ... a manifesto that ... "Wherever fate and human glory lead ..."'

We are always there, Matha whispered the end of the Academy motto, opening her eyes to the tilting, untilting world. Would the white men believe Ba Nkoloso? Would they give him the money he had requested for his Space Programme? Or would his plan for revolution backfire?

*

It was time for the water landing. Godfrey and Matha faced each other. He slid his hands under her armpits and lifted her up, trying to hide the strain of it – she was a heavy girl now. The oil drum was already in the stream, Reuben and Fortunate holding it in place as Godfrey lowered her inside. As soon as Matha's feet touched the bottom, the drum bucked violently. She gripped the sides and Godfrey gripped her shoulders.

'Are you fine, Sister of the Heavens?'

'I'm fine,' she smiled. He let go and gave the drum a push and off she floated. The cadets waved. The reporters stared. The cameras gnashed their teeth.

As she wobbled from the shore, Godfrey's figure receding in the distance, Matha giggled. Who would have thought she would end up being an astronaut? When Ba Nkoloso had invited her to join his new revolutionary academy, she had assumed it would be like entering combat. There were uniforms, yes – the bomber jacket she wore, the metal helmet that Ba Nkoloso wore – but they were more like costumes, and the battlefield more like a theatre of war.

The drum spun and dipped as it neared a rock in the stream. She leaned out and grabbed a branch jutting from a tree on the shore. She steadied the barrel, keeping it wedged against the rock so the reporters could take some footage. The sound of the river beating against the steel was like a giant *kalimba* – the plonking and plinking made her ankles hum. Matha gazed up at the sky, trying to look contemplative, but the trees above tangled her view.

Yes, serving as a cadet in the Zambia National Academy of Science, Space Research and Philosophy involved quite a bit of drama. It meant waking at dawn to paint signs – DOWN WITH FEDERATION! AFRICAN FREEDOM NOW! – on the colonial governor's house.

It meant staging sit-ins at all-white venues in Lusaka like the Rendezvous café and the Ridgeway Hotel. It meant writing protest songs with Godfrey, who had formed a band – the Just Rockets – to play at freedom rallies. It meant making homespun bombs with paraffin and cloth, and sometimes with wires and triggers. It meant crouching behind bushes at roadblocks to throw them at cars and sneaking out at night to plant them under bridges.

And sometimes, it meant pretending to be an astronaut, giving interviews about cats and rockets and technology to white men with squinty eyes and sweaty lips, trying to convince them that Zambia would land a man on the moon before America or Russia. Matha thought of Ba Nkoloso's words: *This is a guerilla campaign and a propaganda campaign. This is Cha-Cha-Cha! We will make the white men dance to our tune!*

Matha smiled at them now, the white men. The reporters were packing up their beastly camera. One had wandered off to sit under a tree. Another stared at her, his head tilted to one side. She heard a crackle in a bush on the shore. Godfrey had come to help her disembark. He splashed into the stream, grabbed the edge of the drum, and dragged it onto the bank. He lifted her out of the drum and she swayed before him, the ground see-sawing beneath her. He glanced over his shoulder, then pulled her behind a bush and stepped closer. He slowly unzipped her bomber jacket halfway down.

'Comrade,' said Godfrey, by way of greeting.

'Comrade,' said Matha, smiling against his lips.

＊

Edward Mukuka Nkoloso lay on his back on a bench at Independence Stadium, looking up. The sun had set and the moon had risen, a fingerprint smudge in the greyblue sky. Below it was the round rim of a stadium lightshade. And below the shade he could see Matha's forehead and cheekbone in silhouette, curving above the round of her breast, which in turn curved above the mound of her stomach. The moon, the shade, the rounds of Matha standing above him – each sphere darker than the last, each overlapping, moons on moons. Nkoloso sighed. The spheres were eclipsing. Apollo 11 had landed.

Nkoloso directed his grief at Matha's belly. Once, he thought he saw the tiniest of spheres, a tear, slip down her cheek – a rolling movement, a flash – but it was an illusion. He had summoned her here to discuss the Academy's misfortunes – both external and internal – but she had offered neither apology nor reassurance nor consolation.

'But what is *it*, Ba Nkoloso?' Matha said instead, her brow crumpled in frustration.

'WHAT IS IT?!' he thundered back, his voice echoing in the empty stadium.

'What do you want me to say?'

Nkoloso exploded to his feet and marched back and forth on the bench, steps ringing out.

'*Cyclops* could have been launched from this very place' – he waved around at the stadium – 'nearly five years ago. Z Day, 1964. But no, they said the rock-bang would contaminate the heavens. Now the Americans have beat us to become Controllers of the Seventh Heaven of Interstellar Space! They even promised me two million dollars. But these imperial neocolonialists, they have delayed payment because they are scared of our space knowledge. And now we must disband the programme. The revolution is over.'

'No, Ba Nkoloso, the revolution, it cannot be over,' Matha protested feebly.

'Pah!' he groused. 'It is finished! Apollo has landed.'

'Ba Nkoloso, you did not seriously believe we would get there before the Americans?'

He stared at her, dumbfounded. 'What was the Space Programme about for you, Matha? You and that Mwango boy were busy looking at each other. You should have been looking at the moon!' He jabbed a finger at the sky.

✳

But Matha was no longer listening. She didn't understand why Ba Nkoloso was going on about the Space Programme as though it were real. She wondered, not for the first time, whether he had in fact lost his mind like all the newspapers were saying. He was still pacing back and forth, his purple cape wafting as he raved about the cadets and their ingratitude, about the death of his dream to reach the moon, which Matha had always assumed was dead on the ground to begin with – a political ploy, a prank like the others. At some point, night fell and the stadium lights clunked on, lighting Ba Nkoloso from behind – a freeze-frame, an explosive black shadow backed by screaming white light.

Was this what James Brown would be like? There were rumours that the American musician was going to perform at Dag Hammarskjöld Stadium in Ndola next year. Godfrey was dying to get tickets. Ever since he had heard James Brown on the radio and seen pictures in *Jet* magazine, the Just Rockets had gone electric. Their afros and reper-toire and the ankles of their trousers had all gone shiny and round. There was a new shimmer to Godfrey too, as he squealed into the practice mic – a stake in the ground with a *chimanga* husk strapped to it – as he twirled in his silver cape, dropped into the splits, and bounced back up like the handle of a water pump.

After another hour or so of withstanding Ba Nkoloso's plaints, Matha left him nursing his wounds at the stadium and went in search of Godfrey. The Just Rockets practised in a shed behind a shebeen in Kalingalinga, but she didn't hear their crunchy, wailing Zamrock sound tonight, just Congolese rumba twinkling into the air, duelling with the crickets outside.

Matha braved the gauntlet of lewd, smelly men at the entrance to the shebeen, and waited for her eyes to adjust to the dim. There he was. Godfrey was sprawled in a chair, his silver cape lousy with sweat stains. Reuben stood over him, holding forth about Jimi Hendrix. Godfrey tried to take a swig from his Mosi, then held the empty bottle complainingly to the light.

'Is this where you've been hiding?' Matha laughed as she walked up to him.

Godfrey stood up with a grin, swayed towards her, and ran a finger along her jaw.

'The Americans reached the moon,' he remembered, his grin dwin-dling. 'Tragic, man!'

'Not you too.' She rolled her eyes.

'Your cats,' he said. 'Where will your cats go now, Matha?'

She ordered a Mosi and they went and sat under a tree outside to share it. He took a thronging gulp and passed it to her. She sipped it shyly though they both knew it was far from the first time she'd had a beer. She was being shy to show her love, being small to make him big.

'So, what did Dr Nkoloso say?' he asked.

'That we should have been studying the moon and not each other.'

'But Matha,' he slurred. 'You are my moon! You are my star and my sun and . . .'

'The sun *is* a star, Godfrey.'

'Oh-*oh*?' His eyes twinkled at her. 'Is *it*? Ah, you are too bright for me.'

'Ba Nkoloso also said we are mistaking ourselves for stars. With the band and whatnot.'

Godfrey harrumphed. 'Asking to make a little money is only fair after five years!'

'He says we have disrespected him and traded glories for pittances. He's angry about the Just Rockets. *Ati* he didn't teach us to defy gravity so we could dance for imperialist tourists.'

'*Ah-ah*, but he is the one who taught us how to perform tricks for *bazungu!*'

'Oh, mind you, he now says the space stuff was serious! Can you believe?'

'Ha?'

'Yes! *Ati* it was our true mission all along. The man has truly lost his mind.'

'So now we were really-truly going to the abysses of outer space?' Godfrey grinned. 'Not secretly rescuing our nation from' – he imitated Ba Nkoloso's voice and diction – 'bondage and the pangs of misery and the eternal tantalising agony of slavery, serfdom, servitude, imperialism and fascist colonialism?!'

They laughed together, their shoulders bouncing off each other. Godfrey sighed to a stop.

'Where will you go now, Matha?' he slurred, leaning back against the tree, his eyes sliding shut.

'Mars?' she chuckled wryly and took a bigger swig of their Mosi.

But hearing Ba Nkoloso's scolding come out of her own mouth had only made her feel worse. Why had he shamed her for love? And why had Godfrey not said 'where will *we* go?' just now? It was a sad scene altogether. Matha cheered herself up with busyness. She paid the drinks bill, bundled the two former astronauts into the back seat of Reuben's car, and slid into the driver's seat. As she drove down the dirt road away from the shebeen, laughter began to wriggle in Matha's belly. Blundering in and out of the ditches like this reminded her of the good old days, rolling down hills in drums for anti-gravity training. She looked in the rearview mirror to say so, but the men were both asleep, Reuben snoring like a warthog, Godfrey's silver cape making him look like a big robot baby.

✳

By her own lights, Nkuka was the only Mwamba who had made something of herself. After their mother had died in prison, and Matha had run away, their father had moved to his younger sister's farm outside Kasama. By then, more schools were opening their doors to the female sex, and the neighbours were sending their daughters to be educated. Mulenga was clearly a lost cause. So Mr Mwamba sent Nkuka in her brother's place.

Each morning at dawn, Nkuka walked two miles to the new Kasama Girls Secondary School. Nkuka was not as clever as her sister, and she was older than the other students, and there was one term when she had to drop out for lack of funds for the uniform and exercise books. But although Nkuka still despised Ba Nkoloso for ruining her family, her old tutor had taught Nkuka an important lesson at his Roadside Academy. He had shown her how to think like a *muzungu*.

When they put the 1965 Standard Exam in front of Nkuka, with diagrams and questions that made you choose from a list, she heard his voice clearly in her head. *If you can see the tree, you can go to the tree. Here to there. If this, then that, and the same with the other.* Nkuka found that she could pierce the clutter on the page and see the patterns beneath it. She was one of only three girls at Kasama Girls who passed that year.

Nkuka was eighteen years old by then. She had grown into her timidity, learned to infuse it with energy so that her shyness became coyness, her silence a kind of grace. And she knew how to present herself, how to keep her clothes clean and her hair and skin oiled. Her civics teacher began to take an interest in her. Mr Mwape was in his twenties, a thin, snivelling man who wore two oversized suits on alternating days and had bald patches in his afro like a diseased plant. One day after school, Nkuka brought him *finkubala* as a snack and asked if he needed any help. Soon, she was cooking his lunch and washing his two suits for him.

Mr Mwape convinced the headmaster to hire her for part-time domestic work, and her father to let her move from her aunt's farm to the dilapidated quarters behind the school. Nkuka shared it with four girls, but she had her own tiny room, which Mr Mwape could now visit. She accepted his overtures, canny enough to keep it quiet and to keep it going, knowing that this skinny man, with his hang-em-highs and spotty afro, could give her a way out. And he did.

Two years later, Mr Mwape smudged some numbers and used his connections in Lusaka to procure a job for himself and admission for Nkuka to the secretarial course at the Evelyn Hone College of Further Education. Previously a whites-only facility, it now admitted a few dozen freshly minted Zambians.

It took Nkuka four days, a car, a train and two buses to get from Kasama to Lusaka – a *chongololo* journey, as slow and segmented as a caterpillar. By the time she arrived, she was too exhausted to be impressed by the height and span of the main campus building off Church Road. She did notice the clock attached to its outer facade though. Nkuka had seen clocks before, of course. But this one was not bound inside a circle; its numbers were its frame. This was wondrous to her, less because she cared about time or technology, and more because it was her first encounter with a design that made her *feel* something. It made her feel free.

The Pitman's secretarial course was easy: typing, shorthand, filing. This kind of work – training the fingers to sally and sort – suited Nkuka well. Mr Mwape gave her a stipend for food and for lodging in a city council hostel – a small bedroom shared with one student, the kitchen and bathroom shared with six. Cookie, as the other girls immediately nicknamed her, spent the rest of her allowance keeping herself in fashion. Mr Mwape visited on Sundays when his wife and children were at church; the only condition of their arrangement was that Cookie not get pregnant.

Most of the other girls at Evelyn Hone – they called themselves the Eves – were *apamwamba*, the black and brown daughters of government officials and civil servants. Cookie took advantage of their fancy magazines and wardrobes for fashion ideas. She would match these to the closest McCall's sewing patterns, which she reused by tracing them onto newspaper. For material, she had the leavings of stain-and-fade-resistant Dacron, waxed cotton and Crimplene that the rich girls bought at Mistry's. And when she couldn't borrow someone's Singer sewing machine, she sewed her outfits by hand. Her stitches were so neat, her designs so clean, that she was soon taking commissions and receiving payment in kind.

Cookie was the first Eve to start wearing trouser suits (McCall's #2087 and #2169). The trousers were so long and wide that the cuffs dragged, collecting detritus that orbited her ankles. As soon as she came back from class, she would take off her flares and replace them with a withered *chitenge*. Staring through the gridded window above the kitchen sink in the hostel, she would scrub the bottoms of her flattering trousers, then drape them on a wire over the sink. She would carefully dry her hands and coat them with Vaseline. And only then would she join the other Eves at the kitchen table, painting their nails with infinite coats of polish, reading out the raciest passages from withered Mills & Boon paperbacks, drinking cup after cup of tea, and humming to the soul music scratching out of their blue Supersonic radio.

*

When Matha pitched up at the hostel one evening, her bedraggled boyfriend in tow, Cookie sighed, welcomed them into the kitchen, and put the kettle on to make them some tea. She had no choice – Matha was the only family member who knew that a married man was keeping Cookie in comfort, school and fashion. Matha was wearing dusty *maliposa* and an old, cracked bomber jacket over a *chitenge* wrapper and a sweat-stained UNIP t-shirt. The sleepy dude standing behind her, whom Matha introduced as Godfrey, was decked out in an absurd silver cape. Ba Nkoloso's work, Cookie thought bitterly.

That lunatic had killed her mother, undone her father, turned her brother to drink. But worst of all, Ba Nkoloso had reduced her little sister – lovely laughing Matha – to this. This boyfriend of hers was a common *muntu*. Tall and handsome, sure. But ignorant. Rabble. Godfrey had vegetable-dull eyes and an *mbanji*-slow tongue and a thick keloid scar on his neck, a lump bursting through the skin that reminded Cookie of a knot in baked bread. She couldn't stop staring at it as Matha let her tea go cold, explaining in great detail why the Zambian Space Programme was over. Good riddance! thought Cookie until she turned from the scar to look at her sister and realised that Matha was asking for a place to stay.

It was tight and tenuous living in the hostel. Cookie paid her room-mate with a Wrap-A-Rounder Dress (#9119) to find another bed so Matha and Godfrey could use it. Their furtive coupling, their chatting and canoodling, kept Cookie up all night; in the mornings, her washing and rattling woke them up. The room felt ruffled, night and day trading off in a noisome relay.

About a week after Matha and Godfrey had moved in, Cookie came home from Typing II class to find a troop of young men in green outfits lounging in her tiny bedroom. They were propped at different levels of the room – on her desk, her floor, her bed – like monkeys in a tree, smoking cigarettes and drinking beer and fingering instruments, imitating the notes of a song plinking out from the Supersonic, which they had filched from the communal kitchen. Godfrey flashed his big white grin at her from his perch on her pillow. '*Shani, mulamu?*' he said, then went back to pick-pick-picking at the strings of his guitar.

'Not your sister-in-law,' Cookie muttered as she stomped out of the bedroom and down the corridor, pushing past a dreadlocked guy dabbling on what looked like an electric *kalimba*. In the kitchen, three Eves were at the table, sulking over their homework. Matha was standing at the stove, whistling obliviously. She had tied a *chitenge* under her arms for an apron and was clutching a big flat wooden spoon. The *nshima* in the pot before her was roiling and leaping like a rowdy crowd. Matha glanced at Cookie as she recklessly added more mealie meal to it.

'Howzit, *sisi?*'

'Who are these *muntus*, Matha?'

'The Just Rockets!' Matha laughed, then her eyes softened. 'Friends, Nkuka. Comrades!'

'We are not supposed to have males in the hostel,' Cookie huffed. 'You know that.'

Matha gave her a look. 'Really, Nkuka? You are one to talk about having males – ow!' She winced as a bubble on the surface of the *nshima* burst onto her thumb.

'*Ach,*' Cookie sucked her teeth as she crossed the kitchen in two strides and grabbed the spoon. 'You were always so bad at this,' she said and took over stirring the thick porridge.

She couldn't say more, not with the Mwape situation, and certainly not with an audience – the Eves in the corner were already staring and whispering. Matha smiled sweetly around the singed thumb she was sucking as she backed out of the kitchen, then darted out into the corridor. As soon as she was gone, the Eves in the kitchen launched into a griping session. It was too loud in here, it was too crowded, how could they study? Cookie placated them by inviting them to the party. The Eves glanced at each other, then giggled and ran off to change clothes.

Cookie seethed as she continued to prepare the food, her sweat making her trouser suit (#2120) feel even heavier. But muscling her way through the cooking lit a spark in her marrow. By the time she served the meal – *nshima, kalembula* and *kapenta* on shared plates to be held on the laps and palms of the guests crowding the hostel – Cookie was flushed and tingling.

Watching with pride as everyone stuffed their faces, she drank a well-earned Castle and looked over the new arrivals in her bedroom: Youth Brigaders and musicians and a few students from the fancy new University of Zambia. Debates leapt back and forth across the room, arguments bouncing about as if this were a football pitch, the question a spinning ball. The two beds had been propped on their sides to make more room, and several Eves were dancing between them, hips circling in loose loops, lips between their teeth.

Big Gold Six played 'Ti Chose Smith Bampando', which tumbled into 'Four Year Plan', which gave way to Spokes Mashane. Alick Nkhata's voice honeyed out from the wireless and the rock musicians rolled their eyes as the Eves closed theirs dreamily. When the Dark City Sisters came on with 'Langa More', Cookie opened another Castle and joined the dancing. The *wayaleshi* did its best, bleating out those swaying, rocking soul songs, songs that stretch the time of courtship to accommodate comings and goings, lingering and touch. The guys and girls danced with coiled control, brushing the tips of their shoes and bumping the edges of their hips. The brink was the point.

The music receded from an event to an atmosphere as the smell of *mbanji* drifted into the air, a gift from the radical UNZA students. Thoroughly tipsy, Cookie wandered into the kitchen to work on her sewing plans, which coincided with her romantic plans in the form of the perfect wedding dress: McCall's #2020 pattern but with lace, tulle and beaded wrists. She was deep in a flow of tracing bow patterns from an old issue of *Vogue* when she heard a booming voice within the party's cacophony. She looked up from her sketches. The voice boomed again. She jumped up and left the kitchen, squeezing past the bodies corrugating the corridor.

She stood in the threshold to her bedroom, craning her head around a tall bearded guy in a striped sweater. Godfrey was fast asleep in an armchair, Matha on the floor at his feet, her head tipped back onto his knee, his hand casually draped across her throat. The other guests, wilted by the weed and the late hour, were leaning around the room, gazing at someone in its centre, nodding their heads with furrowed brows, trying to seem sober. Cookie ducked around the tall guy and that's when she saw that telltale helmet, blatant and ancient and stained as a full moon. Edward Mukuka Nkoloso was speaking, or rather, speeching, the gap between his front teeth issuing an occasional whistle whenever his vehemence took his own breath away. He poked a hole in the air with his finger. Sweat poured from under his helmet like his face was melting.

'... appreciate this celebration, which is very important to recognise the triumphs we have achieved in the struggle for liberation. But I must castigate you youthies as well! You have been lazy! You have been slouching, eh? Where is your passion? Where is the unflinching resolution and unbending dedication to freedom and justice? I call upon you, especially the girls! You must think, eat, sleep and dream the struggle for freedom! You think you are already free?'

The party guests clucked and shook their heads in agreement. The bearded boy next to Cookie turned and scolded her, 'You are not free, *ba* sista, you are not!'

'How can we be free if we are squabbling like monkeys over a mango? We must unite! I call upon you, the youth, to join me at the African Liberation Centre, safe house for freedom fighters from our neighbouring countries!'

Here several of the guests clapped. A drunk Eve on the floor let out a languorous ululation like a glugging drain. Matha had stood up and she was beaming at Ba Nkoloso, nodding fervently at his words. Cookie's feet grew slippery in her *patapatas*.

'Revolutionary youth! In death, revolutionaries are solidly immortalised into a battling ram! Let us tighten our belts and let us be prepared to die in the ranks of the liberation struggle!'

Applause erupted like thunder. Praise rained down from the very ceiling. Even the Eves – these young women whose mouths pursed around their proper English, who carried their books in navy British Overseas Airways Corporation bags to flaunt their families' flights to London – even they began to channel their mothers. They danced and sang the old songs, bending forward, raising their arms, trembling their fingers, shaking their heads in a fury of joy. The two men on either side of Ba Nkoloso lifted him up so that his fist could punch even higher.

Cookie pushed through this delirium of patriotism to the centre of the room, where Ba Nkoloso was rising like a column. She shouted up at him, and then screamed, and when all this still went unnoticed, she tore off her suit jacket. She did not go topless. Cookie was no Mama Chikamoneka. But she was wearing a mere camisole beneath her jacket and this drew attention. Young men and women backed away from her, their eyes locked onto the nipples poking through the satin. The noise in the room simmered to a murmur. Ba Nkoloso's bearers lowered him in front of Cookie.

'You,' she whispered, her eyes quivering.

'Nkuka?! Is that you?' He smiled broadly.

'*Iwe!*' she said louder and poked him in the chest. The room gasped. This was horrifically rude. Ba Nkoloso raised a hand. 'It's okay. This one is like my niece. She is unruly, like her name. Hottest part of the flame: Nkuka! The ember! Her mother was a martyr of our revolution—'

Cookie leapt forward at the mention of her mother. 'You let her die like a dog! You took her from us!' – Matha wrapped her arms around

Cookie from behind, hugging her away from Ba Nkoloso before she could strike him. But Cookie kept shouting from the prison of Matha's embrace: 'And you stole my sister. Now the whole world is laughing at us! Space Programme!' She spat. 'They called my mother a whore and now they are calling my sister a fool! Why were you lying to people, telling them she is going to Mars with a cat—'

'Twelve cats,' Matha corrected matter-of-factly.

'That one?!' Ba Nkoloso pointed at Matha, his black eyes glinting as he guffawed at the ceiling. 'Matha Mwamba is launching nowhere. She is carrying two! She is above take-off weight!'

There was a terrible silence. The party averted its eyes. A few guests began to mumble about how late it was getting.

'Your sister and her boyfriend? They have dishonoured our Space Programme,' Ba Nkoloso went on. 'That is why it has collapsed. We could not face our sponsors with a pregnant girl! The rumours have squashed us. And so now it is time for African liberation!'

But Cookie was no longer listening. Her mouth hanging open, she slowly turned within the ambit of her sister's arms until she was facing her. She looked into Matha's eyes.

'A baby?' Cookie asked.

Matha nodded, then glanced over Cookie's shoulder. Cookie craned her head to follow her gaze. Ba Nkoloso had moved on. He was rebuking a Just Rocket for neglecting the Space Programme, while also trying to recruit him for the new African Liberation Centre. Cookie looked past them at Godfrey, who was still in his chair, asleep, dream-sealed from the room. She turned back to Matha. The sisters kept their arms around each other.

'Godfrey doesn't know yet,' Matha said quietly.

'A baby!' Cookie exclaimed.

'Ya, it's a bit worrisome.'

'A baby,' Cookie whispered. Then she turned her head to one side and vomited.

✳

Later that night, when the party was over, Matha and Godfrey had a fight. The beds were back on their feet, a catastrophe of dirty plates and glasses on the floor between them. Across the way, Nkuka was passed out on her bed, limbs splayed, wig askew. Matha watched her sister snore for a while then turned towards Godfrey, who was on his back beside her. Having napped through most of the party, he was now wide awake, composing a new song in loops, trying to get the notes right.

'Godfrey?' She leaned up on her elbow.

Godfrey smiled at her but did not cease his ellipsing hum.

'I think if we ask, Ba Nkoloso will forgive us and give us jobs at the Liberation Centre.'

Godfrey frowned at her. She stared at the scar on his neck, the shape of a bullet.

'Zambia has its independence now,' she said. 'It is only right to help our neighbours in the struggle for freedom. And we need a proper job now if . . .' She put her hand on her belly.

Godfrey's hum stopped. 'I have a proper job.'

'What,' Matha snorted, 'the Just Rockets?'

He looked at her, hurt crumpling his brow. 'Think of Hugh Masekela,' he said earnestly. 'He was just another trumpeter until he went to America. Now he has his own *sound* . . .'

'You think you are going to go to America?' Matha laughed.

'Isn't that what Ba Nkoloso used to say? That only the Americans understand what it means to dream and that is why they would get to the moon first. And he was right!'

'Oh gosh.' She eyed him. 'You didn't believe in those space dreams, did you?'

'Maybe I believed, maybe I did not,' he shrugged. 'But the idea of it was a work of art! It was inspiring for Zambians to dream about going to the moon. That is how real change happens.'

'That is how craziness happens! The goal was to make real change, political change. Revolution! Not art! Missile rockets, not Just Rocketing around like some African Jimi Hendrix—'

'You are one to talk about craziness! With your mother? And your Bashikulu N'gulube?'

Furious, Matha jumped out of the bed, stepping right onto a greasy plate. With nowhere else to go, she stomped off to the communal kitchen where she paced for a while, fuming, waiting for Godfrey to come after her. But he didn't. Eventually, Matha fell asleep seated at the table, her cheek resting on her crossed arms like a lazy student.

✳

She woke up to her sister sitting across from her. Cookie looked freshly bathed. She was wearing a polyester suit and a full face of make-up. She took Matha's hand and calmly explained that she and Godfrey could no longer stay here. The Eves, Cookie said, had assembled as a group to issue a complaint about the party this morning. Matha and her boyfriend were no longer welcome.

In fact, despite their initial reluctance, the Eves had been quite taken with both the party and the Party. The space cadets, the Brigaders, the UNZA students, even Uncle Nkoloso with his dented helmet – these visitors had made the Eves realise that their generalised dissatisfaction with the world, their itch to complain about their conditions, could be turned into a political weapon. Within months, the Eves would be protesting everything from the shoddy food in the college canteen to Ian Smith's white minority government in Rhodesia.

But Matha never got the chance to see these radicals blossom. Her stay at the hostel had drawn her no closer to the girls studying at Evelyn Hone, including her sister. Matha was just as smart as they were, if not smarter, but she could never grasp their slang, their gossip about holidays at Lochinvar and Lake Malawi, about imported sedans from Germany and Belgium, about fashion labels from Milan and New York. Cookie took advantage of this class divide when she lied to her sister. She said the Eves looked down on Matha and the Just Rockets.

She never divulged her real reason for sending her sister away. Cookie had come to realise that everything in her life felt borrowed: her schooling, her clothes, even her man – they were all on loan. But Matha, somehow, owned her life. And watching Matha waltz around here with everything she had earned for herself, paltry as it was – a shabby man, a child out of wedlock, a zany politics? It made Cookie ill. Only a sister, an alternative self, could inspire such a sordid mix of disgust and envy.

'But where will I go?' Matha asked, clutching her sister's hand.

'Go home, Matha,' said Cookie. 'Lusaka is not for everybody, you know.'

1969

But Lusaka *was* for Matha. The city still felt like a second skin to her. But neither Ba Nkoloso nor Nkuka would help her, and she was fed up with Godfrey. Matha was down to her last resort – the aunties. She made her way alone across town to a formidably large brick bungalow in Rhodes Park. This was home to Matha's Aunt Beatrice, her father's eldest sister and the reigning matriarch of the Mwamba family, though she no longer bore the surname.

In the 1950s, Aunt Beatrice had married a civil engineer from Abercorn, who had taken her to England while he pursued further training. Though she had done nothing there but keep house, it was widely believed that this stint abroad had bestowed her with great wisdom. Aunt Beatrice, who could not read or write, was thus considered an authority on most things. She spoke a flashy broken English, gemlike words strung on a thin grammatical string. She'd had six children, two of whom now lived in England, mostly for the purpose of mailing home the necessities to which the family had become accustomed during its time there, including Cadbury Whole Nut, Walkers shortbread, and packets of white bloomers from Marks & Spencer.

Upon their return, Aunt Beatrice's husband had grown rich off the copper mines so, in the African way of familial socialism, she took care of their less fortunate relatives, calling upon this brood to offer gratitude and obedience in return. Her children endured marital and financial advice. Her grandchildren were paraded before her, squirming in hand-me-downs that smelled of disinfectant and the sweat of their siblings. Her extended family – the children of her siblings and cousins – drifted wishfully around the fringes of their luxurious home.

Thus, when Matha arrived to make her case, she joined a long queue of supplicants, kowtowers and spongers on the steps outside the

Rhodes Park bungalow. As the hours passed, the sunshine went from shy to cheeky to downright insolent. By noon, it was rudely glaring down. Matha took off her bomber jacket and rocked herself to relieve her joints from sitting for so long. The dogs kept coming to sniff her, hoping she had changed her mind about them.

'*Futsek, futsek,*' she said irritably. '*Ach, iwe.* Go!'

There were three of them, pure Rhodesian ridgebacks the red colour of the dirt when the rains begin. They were enormous and friendly, as were their tongues. But they were dogs and Matha missed her cats. Ba Nkoloso had released all twelve from the lean-to in Matero when he disbanded the Space Programme and, instant traitors, they had not returned. Matha longed for their soft fur and their hard eyes, and most of all their soothing indifference, the way they gloried in solitude, as if alone even with their owners. If only she could be so cavalier when it came to providers of food and shelter. Matha was not looking forward to the ordeal of pleading ahead of her. All she needed was a place to stay. Nothing fancy. Maybe a small loan.

It was late afternoon when a servant finally shook Matha's shoulder. She blinked awake, sat up, pulled on her bomber jacket and trotted past the others waiting on the veranda steps. The sitting room she entered was snug, carpeted in fuzzy orange and curtained in heavy pink. An ornamental fireplace took up much of one wall. Ceramic sheep grazed on its mantel. A wooden giraffe listed affably at them. Christ hung forlornly above. Aunt Beatrice sat in a recliner, leaning to one side, her elbow on the armrest, her cheek resting on her palm. Her skin was the blackbluesilver of burning paper and her hairline had faded from forehead to midhead, as if cowering from her stern brow. She was dressed like an overgrown schoolgirl in a high-necked grey dress, white stockings and Mary Janes. Six aunties sat with her, three on either side, cheeks in their hands as well.

Grumpy with humbling, Matha crouched before each aunty in turn to shake hands, her left hand cradling her right elbow. The greetings made a lilting round:

Mulishani mukwayi
    Eyamukwayi
Mulishani mukwayi
    Eyamukwayi

Matha settled herself on the floor before the semicircle of women. All was quiet but for the chatter coming through the open doors to the veranda – birds, dogs, a diesel generator – and from the radio in the next room announcing the shifting coordinates of a cricket match.

Finally, Aunt Beatrice tilted vertical, lifted her cheek from her hand, and spoke. She had a tremulous voice, words scrambling like spiders from her mouth and across the room to shiver up the spines of her audience. She presented the charges against Matha Mwamba steadily, one by one. Running *off* from the farm in Kasama. *Politicking* with *cadres*. Loitering with *space* gentlemen. Prancing around *out* of wedlock. The other aunties wordlessly concurred. They clapped their hands past each other, they shook their heads, they hummed descending staccato notes: MM. *Mm*. Mm. Aunt Beatrice concluded with a plea to the Lord to heal this waywarding child, which was followed by a general nodding of heads, a smattering of *Amens*.

Matha despaired. She had come to ask for help. How had news of her Lusaka life reached the aunties? How had this turned into a trial? Her fingers writhed like caterpillars in her lap, then metamorphosed into winged creatures that fluttered up to her face as she explained. About wanting to continue her education, about wanting to participate in the struggle for independence, about joining the national cause ...

'Child. Are you not *with* child?' Aunt Beatrice interrupted.

This question harrowed a ditch in the middle of the room. The air rushed into it as the aunties turned to stare. Matha's mouth fell open. Only Nkuka knew she was pregnant. When had she told them? Matha cast her eyes down and nodded. The aunties came to life, twittering and twisting their heads this way and that.

'It is seeming to me,' Aunt Beatrice intoned, 'that you are in need greatly for assistance.'

Matha scrunched her nose, allergic to this humiliation, but too trapped to protest.

'It is highly appropriate that, in exchange for this assistance, you must be granting us the opportunity to dictate the well-being of this child's life, given that in the foreseeing future ...'

A tear of rage slid down Matha's cheek. She had not come to bargain with her unborn child.

'... at the proper timing we will be sending the child for appropriate schooling. But for now ...'

Aunt Beatrice pursed her lips. The other aunties turned to her – yes, yes, their eyes said, but for now ... what was her verdict?

'You must voyage to your father's farm in Kasama. You will be bearing the child there.'

Aunt Beatrice tilted over, laid her cheek onto her hand, and closed her eyes with finality. The aunts exclaimed their amazement at this beneficence. Some even reached out and patted Matha's shoulder, grinning as if they were giving a gift rather than doling out a condolence. Matha fumed. She should never have come. The aunties were already concocting a plan to secret her to Kasama as soon as possible, before her pregnancy began to show. Matha had no choice but to go – she wouldn't even have time to send word to Godfrey. But she vowed she would never hand their child over to this shivery witch, even for something as valuable as an education.

✳

To her father, Matha's pregnancy meant that her prospects for marriage and employment, not to mention life on heaven and earth, were ruined. Mr Mwamba had always been a congenital worrier, a man who took Pascal's wager as a motto: *Let Us Live As If.* The experience of losing his wife to politics had bestowed him with a permanent distrust of the world. He had retreated from it entirely and now ran the family farm in Kasama with his younger sister. She was a widow, too, with a brood of children. They were cut from the same cloth, those two. They prayed together and worried together and quarrelled peaceably about farm problems: money and drought and equipment.

Mr Mwamba had put his previous life to rest with relief. Bernadetta had always been too *much*. Too eager to work, too bitter, too angry, too quick to blame the *bazungu*. The children she had left behind all seemed tainted by her too – Mulenga was as dim-witted as Bernadetta's father had been; Nkuka had been happy to abandon him as soon as he was done paying for her education. And Matha! When he received a letter from his eldest sister Beatrice in Lusaka about Matha's situation, Mr Mwamba had been disappointed but unsurprised. He had always suspected something bad would happen to his youngest. She had a cursed way about her. Always laughing.

When Matha pitched up at the farm three months pregnant –
two burly aunties on either side of her like bodyguards – she looked
up from her squat of greeting to see resignation rather than anger
grooved in her father's face. He had already slotted the news about her
into an old story. The story went like this: no matter how the world
shifts to accommodate her, this kind of woman finds a way to disturb
the peace. This kind of woman is the *nganga* that sits at the top of the
stream, kicking her feet to make it roil.

✳

This was not entirely untrue. If village life had ever suited Matha
Mwamba, it certainly no longer did. She sulked as she worked the
fields with Mulenga – her *dwanzi* brother finally living the pleasant,
listless life he'd always been destined for. She hung her head as she
plucked squeaky *visashi*, sucked her teeth as she gathered hairy *chibwabwa*, sighed as she shelled groundnuts and pounded maize. Hot and
hungry, doubly so because she was pregnant, she moped around in a
state of perpetual irritation, as if the very air were laced with stings.
In a sense, it was: there were swarms everywhere – why had she never
noticed them before? The sky looked like the greyish pages of her old
exercise books, the insects like a script of equations – commas and
dashes, full stops and slashes – the way maths looks in a dream.

Often, Matha begged nausea or fatigue just so she could sit in the
kitchen and listen to the Saucepan radio, the programmes barely
quenching her parched curiosity. She missed Lusaka, its hectic streets
and clamouring newsboys, the disgruntled Giraffes and Zinglish pat-
ois. She missed the Academy and Ba Nkoloso, and she even missed
her sister and the Eves. But God, she missed Godfrey! As soon as she
had arrived, she'd written a letter to him in Lusaka, apologising for
their fight, telling him about the pregnancy, pleading for him to come
to Kasama. Two weeks later, she received his reply. It was cluttered
with spelling errors but run-on with joy – about the baby, and the Just
Rockets, and his training to become a truck driver. *Am gona driv to com
and see you!*

Matha resigned herself to withstanding this hell in the countryside
until then. She wrote him letters in the meantime, but after Godfrey's

first reply, no more came. She lumped around, sulking, biding her time. But discontent was in her nature and it grew over the next three months, swelling with her belly, until one day, a conspiracy of chance events sprang a door wide and she found herself running through it.

✳

It all began in the queue at the Boma in Kasama. Matha and her father had driven into town from the farm to purchase a new sprinkler. They were waiting their turn in the queue, standing in the shadowed vestibule, the sun-drenched courtyard glowing behind them. Mr Mwamba had worn a suit for the trip to town and Matha was wearing her bomber jacket over a floral print dress – the latter a concession to her aunt, who ached for Matha to look more respectable, given her condition. Bored as ever, Matha was absently scanning the signs pasted to the walls of the Boma as they inched forward, absorbing the words in the shallow way of literate but distracted eyes – not reading exactly but registering shapes and sounds and general wordliness.

POUNDS … STERLING … CURRENCY … KWACHA … LAST DAY … !!!

As they reached the counter, Mr Mwamba extricated his spectacles and the money for the sprinkler from a worn grey satchel, the sole remnant of his teaching days. Just then, the meaning of the words on the signs flooded Matha's synapses.

'Ba Tata?' she gasped.

'What is it?' her father grumbled, putting his spectacles on. Visiting the Boma always made him irritable.

'It says it's the last day to trade in the …'

'Oh God!'

Mr Mwamba, too, had now read the writing on the wall. His face crumpled and he dashed out of the queue towards the exit, his satchel flapping like an elephant's ear. Matha raced after him. Outside, she saw him clambering into the battered Peugeot he had purchased from a farmer's widow – midnight blue, edged with orange rust. Matha managed to jump in the passenger side as he turned the key. The vehicle woke with a cough that gave way to a wheezing pant as Mr Mwamba drove back to the farm.

'These people!' he ranted. 'They do not give you adequate and fair warning! What is the time? Oh God, almighty saviour, please do not let these people close the bank before I come back ...'

Mr Mwamba did not normally use the Boma bank. Handing his money over to other people had never brought him much luck, so he had invested his earnings in the safest place possible: land. The Mwambas had held on to their farm property for decades, refusing to sell to white settlers, colonial administrators and government developers in turn. Whenever he had cash, Mr Mwamba put that into land too. Literally – he buried it. No need for a bank when you can use the ground for a vault, he always said.

But today, Mr Mwamba needed a bank. The colonial currency that he had been burying in the earth for the past ten years – the British pound and the Federation pound – were about to become obsolete, replaced by the proud new Zambian kwacha! The sun had risen! One Zambia! One Nation! One Currency! The new government would let the Zambian pound circulate for a few more years and they had stretched out the process of colonial currency extinction to accommodate the rural provinces, but according to the signs in the Boma, today was officially Mr Mwamba's last chance to trade old money for new.

The Peugeot lurched to a stop at the farm and Mr Mwamba gangled out without even turning off the engine. He ran to the field behind the house, snatched a spade from Mulenga's hands, and started digging. Matha's aunt was on the veranda, twisting water from a rag. Seeing her brother's unaccountable actions, she cupped her hand to her forehead, then started running towards him, holding the edge of her *chitenge*, shouting: 'What are you doing?'

Matha stayed in the car, watching the drama through the windscreen. The Peugeot panted around her. Outside, she could hear a woodpecker making its hollow, intermittent racket. In the distance, she could see her father bent over in the middle of the fields, which were bursting with green leaves and, now, mounds of red soil from his digging. When Matha's aunt reached him, he stood up straight and they accosted each other, their shouts as vague as a distant waterfall. Hired hands gathered around to watch. Mulenga wandered over, a puzzled look on his face. High on *mbanji*, no doubt. A mosquito whined piteously. Matha's eyes darted around the inside of the car, hunting it, then landed on her father's old satchel on the floor.

Now, Matha had loved driving from the moment Ba Nkoloso had taught her during space training. She loved how the mere step of a foot could send a vehicle zooming forward, its weight magically dropping away into speed. So she felt a little giddy as she slid into the driver's side of the Peugeot, undid the brake, put it in drive and chugged down the dirt road away from the farm. She laughed even as each rut in the road added another bruise to her bum. She was going home! Home was not these old people shouting in a field. Home was Godfrey, his hands gripping a microphone, wailing for love and for country. Stealing the car, driving it off, the money for the sprinkler in the satchel on her lap as her father dug up the rest of his livelihood in the rearview mirror – all of this freedom shook Matha up, filled her with giggles like bubbles in a Coca-Cola.

※

The bubbles burst when she hit Great North Road. What had she done? The dual carriageway was still mostly dust and gravel, widely known as 'Hell Run'. Trucks and lorries raced by, terrifyingly close, sending violent sprays of stone against her windows. The Peugeot's shudder over the rough road was so intense that when she hit the new tarmac at Kapiri Mposhi, the skin on the backs of her thighs began to itch, as if lingering in vibration. She finally pulled over under a pitch-black sky, the headlights barely grazing the darkness. In that eerie glow, she battened down in the back seat, her bomber jacket for a blanket, the satchel clutched to her stomach.

She woke at dawn, cold and hungry and disconcerted by the sight of the windscreen. She had been staring through it with such concentration the day before, she hadn't noticed it becoming almost opaque – streaked with mud, scratched with pebbles, blotted with bird droppings and the ashes of butterfly wings. She got out of the car and peed behind a tree. She cleaned her teeth with a stick, ate the four bananas she had bought at the petrol station in Kasama, and wiped off the windscreen with a leaf. When she got back in the Peugeot, it wouldn't start. She had left the headlights on the whole night and the battery was dead.

She managed to hitch a ride in a van packed with passengers, the air thick with their breath and sweat and palpable judgment about the tight stretch of her dress over her stomach. The sun was setting when they reached Lusaka. As she disembarked, Matha pressed a crumpled Federation pound from the satchel into the driver's hand. When he complained, she realised that she too had missed the currency deadline. She stuffed the bills in the pockets of her bomber jacket and bartered for her ride with the satchel itself – good, strong leather even if it was old.

She zamfooted to the shebeen in Kalingalinga to find Godfrey, shivering at the thought of seeing him, and hoping he had the connections to go back for the Peugeot and trade this outdated cash. They would need money and transport if they were going to navigate this baby situation. But she bounced at the shebeen. And she bounced at the old shed behind it where the Just Rockets practised. No Godfrey. No lazy smile, no sleepy eyes, no kiss to her belly. She stood there staring at the bare shed, the stake in the ground bereft of even its cornhusk practice mic.

Matha made her way slowly through Kalingalinga. Where would she sleep for the night? Then she remembered that an older cousin of hers lived here now, having been ostracised from the Mwamba family for a crime no one remembered any more. Matha asked around the compound until she found it – a five-foot-square cubical shack shaped by wood and metal sidings, a *chitenge* hanging over a gap in the facade. She knocked on the metal siding and a woman of about twenty-five poked her scowling face around the curtain.

Matha hadn't seen Grace in years. She had grown into a tall, sullen woman, with a frown so deep it looked like a scar. Matha reminded her of who she was and launched into an explanation: about Godfrey, and the baby, and why Kasama was no good for her, and why there was a Peugeot on the side of Great North Road awaiting jump leads, and how the Just Rockets' practice shed had been empty, and how she just needed a place to sleep for the night because she would surely locate the father of her child tomorrow. Grace stood with her arms crossed, an old Kaunda *chitenge* wrapped around her waist, listening in silence to this saga, her eyes lingering over the bulges in Matha's pockets. When Matha was finished, Grace nodded and beckoned her inside. She gave Matha the leftovers from supper, laid out a sleeping mat for her, then lay down on her own and curled away like a provoked *chongololo*.

＊

Matha woke to an empty shack. She felt ruffled – or rather, rifled. The obsolete bills she'd stuffed in her jacket pockets were scattered around her mat, several of them crumpled in little balls. Grace had apparently discovered the useless stash. Matha got up, washed at the communal taps, and began the hunt for her lover. The same round of places, the same dearth of Godfrey. Nothing. Zee. No sign of him, she complained that night as she wolfed down the remainders of Grace's supper. Grace hitched an eyebrow and picked up her sewing.

The following week, Matha managed to locate Godfrey's Just Rockets bandmates, who had started a new band called Dynamite Rock without him. Reuben told her not to worry. Godfrey had probably just gone to see his family in the Copperbelt. But Godfrey was not back the next week, nor the week after that. Matha gave up on retrieving the Peugeot. It had surely been stolen or stripped by now, she told Grace as she wiped down the *patapatas* she'd borrowed from her cousin. Grace shrugged and resumed her sewing.

Matha mailed a letter to the Ndola Boma looking for him. No reply, she complained two weeks later to Grace as she beat the dust out of her sleeping mat. Grace sucked her teeth and bit through a thread. Matha stayed up all night drafting a missing-person notice to print in the *Times of Zambia*.

Late the next morning, she woke up with an itch on her nose. She batted it off, thinking it was a mosquito, but there it was again. She blinked her eyes open to the sight of a brown blur. She swivelled her head back like a chicken and the blur clarified into a rough weave. It was a sack. Several sacks, in fact, stitched together, hanging from the ceiling. Matha sat up and poked at it. It swayed. Over the last month, Grace had sewn a wall of old *unga* sacks, dividing the shack in half, making their banishment complete even unto each other.

＊

Matha finally quashed her pride and went to see Ba Nkoloso at the African Liberation Centre. He was in his office, at his desk, typing a memo.

'Miss Mwamba!' he announced without looking up.

'*Shani*, Ba Nkoloso,' she said, cupping her hands and curtsying. 'You are busy?'

'Yes.' He squinted at the typewriter. 'Our neighbouring nations have not achieved independence, so we are vigilantly pursuing ...' He looked up. 'I thought you went back to Kasama.'

'I am here now. I am looking for Godfrey.'

'Oh, my *star* astronaut?' said Ba Nkoloso, rifling roughly through some papers. 'The only chap in this nation fit for moonwalking? The *star* of the Just Rockets?'

'Yes, that one of it,' she giggled. 'He seems to be missing. It is a bit worrisome.'

'Worrisome!' Ba Nkoloso slapped the papers against his desk. 'If I was you, Miss Matha Mwamba, I would be more worrisomed about what he left behind!' He pointed at her stomach.

Matha glanced down, putting her hand protectively over it. Smarting from her family's rejection; living in poverty with a frowning cousin who despised her; not just bearing, but actively resisting Godfrey's absence – his persistence in not coming home to her – had already strung threads of hurt in Matha's throat. Ba Nkoloso's words strummed across them, making them vibrate. She swallowed.

'When the baby comes,' she ventured, 'maybe I can join your work here?'

'You? Here?' he laughed bitterly. 'This is revolutionary business, Matha. Serious business. Not for girls who cannot keep their ...' He broke off.

Matha looked at this man she had known her whole life, this small man who had always had such power, such force in his booming perorations. She felt like she was hearing his real voice for the very first time. She divined the store of disappointment inside it, like a cave hidden by a waterfall.

'Do you know what they said when you started to grow that baby in your stomach?'

The threads in her throat thrummed.

'They said that I was the one who put it there,' he said softly, angrily.

A tear rolled down her cheek. Ba Nkoloso shook his head. 'The Academy could never survive that.'

Matha turned and stalked out of his office, dashing the tear from her face, but it was useless. Tear after tear slid down her cheeks as she trudged back to Kalingalinga, a dribble that gurgled into a stream, then gushed into a great heaving flood as soon as she was inside the divided ramshackle cube that was now her only home.

＊

In the beginning, Matha Mwamba sobbed on her back, eyes clenched, breath skipping like a record. When the fit ceased, she turned on her side, facing the old *chitenge* over the doorway – a pattern of birds in a thicket. As she lay there, tears collected in the cove between her eye and her nose. She blinked and the pool brimmed over and plopped in one big droplet onto the new *chitenge* she'd folded into a pillow. The droplet sat for a moment on the waxed threads, a clear sphere catching the sunlight that flashed inside whenever the curtain lifted from the door. Matha briefly forgot herself, forgot why she was even crying, as she gazed at that little globe of light. Then it collapsed to a stain like a shadow of itself. She blinked again. The next tear that fell was long and continuous. It grew the stain until her whole pillow was wet shadow.

For days, Matha cried. She lowed and keened and fell silent and wept. For days on end, she watched, through the warped lens of salt water, the dawning and setting of the curtain over the door, the pattern of thicketed birds dissolving as night fell and emerging line by line when the sun rose. Her eyes and nose grew swollen. Her cheeks were hot and taut, webbed with dry salt. The threads in her throat were an utter tangle. She relinquished herself to gravity, the cradle of its heavy arms.

As if from a great distance, she could hear her cousin coming in and out of their home. A couple of days into the weeping, Grace's bustling sounds abruptly stopped. Between sobs, Matha heard an audible sucking of teeth. A minute later, a ripple moved along the rough *unga* curtain dividing their lives, and a tin plate of cooked samp appeared underneath it. Matha took it up and ate it eagerly – she was pregnant after all – salting the meal with her tears. With food came scraps and with scraps came insects, the cockroaches and flies and fleas and ants. They conquered the crusty remnants on the plate, and the pot she had been squatting over as a bedpan, and her damp and tender skin.

On the third day, she pulled herself together enough to throw out the soured remains and stinking waste, and to sweep the insects away. Then off she plodded through Kalingalinga, tears pittering from the overhang of her chin, seeping into the neck of her dress. In Zambia, crying is private and communal: women come together behind walls to wail. Matha's public, personal grief seemed odd, rude even. Women stared and clucked. Men avoided her path. Schoolboys laughed at her. Matha spat in their direction and kept weeping as she made the hour-long trek to the hostels near Evelyn Hone.

✳

As soon as Cookie opened the door, Matha collapsed onto her knees.

'What's wrong?' Cookie asked as she crouched beside her sister. Matha's belly was as big as a village pumpkin now but she had lost weight. There was a sandy scrim on her cheeks, which were usually as dark and shiny as the backs of beetles.

'Godfrey's gone,' Matha croaked.

Cookie rolled her eyes. 'Well, thank your lucky stars for that,' she said as she dragged Matha back onto her feet, led her to the kitchen and plopped her in a chair. Cookie set about making them some tea.

'Where is everyone?' Matha hiccupped, glancing around.

'Protests,' Cookie waved dismissively. 'The Eves have caught politics like the flu. The canteen served chicken feet and the girls want to know where the rest of the chickens went. As if government is now hoarding breasts and livers.'

Matha nodded blankly.

'Where have you posted up?' Cookie asked.

'With Grace. In Kalingalinga.'

'You're living with Dis-Grace!?' Cookie's laugh died in her throat. 'Okay, okay, sorree.' She sat down across from her sister and willed herself to ask. 'So what happened now?'

Matha let out a sob. 'I can't find Godfrey,' she began, 'and with the baby on the way ...'

Cookie listened and offered occasional reassurances cribbed from Mills & Boon, about love triumphant, dreams and passion, visions and hope. She didn't believe any of it, of course. As Matha went on with her sob story, Cookie tried not to yawn, her eyes tracing patterns in the fastfading stains of the tears falling onto her sister's dress: triangles and diamonds and stars. It's always hard to imagine another person's pain, especially a pain as abstract as heartache.

'... why did you tell them?'

'Hmm-what?' Cookie blinked up from her mesmeric pattern-making. Matha's face was covered in a sheen of tears that glinted under the new fluorescent bulbs in the kitchen.

'Why did you tell the aunties that I was pregnant?'

'*Ah-ah*, but I didn't,' Cookie lied without hesitation.

'But—' said Matha. The sobs ratcheted up again. Cookie sighed but did not offer to take her sister in. While Matha was away in Kasama, Cookie had made some calculations. She would graduate soon, and Mr Mwape was on the verge of leaving his wife, she could just sense it. He would never marry Cookie if she was carrying the baggage of an unwed sister *and* her unborn child. The prospect of Cookie's 'patron' stopping by to see her, only to find a shorter, darker, prettier version of her, with a belly out to here? No. As far as Cookie was concerned, Matha had squandered all her gifts – her intelligence, her beauty, her sunny disposition – while Cookie had churned out profits from the scraps. She would not give them up for mere heartbreak.

'... if you hadn't told the aunties,' Matha was blurbling, 'they wouldn't have sent me away to Kasama and then Godfrey—'

'Godfrey what?' Cookie scoffed. 'He left you, Matha.' She sipped her tea and lied again. 'Everyone knows that while you were in Kasama, he was hopping from bed to bed.'

※

Kalingalinga, named for the bell on the door of the shop of the man who owned the land where the shanty town first squatted, was a busy pocket of the city. Men went to work weak and came home drunk. Women droned hymns and bemoaned the drunkenness of their husbands over a maze of hands shelling beans, grinding grain, selling things and buying them. Babies tied to their mothers' backs sucked their thumbs and napped and stared. Teenage boys in borrowed clothes stole things and made jokes. Teenage girls cooked and danced, cleaned and flirted. Children built toy cars out of wire and pushed old bicycle tyres along with sticks. The compound buzzed and swarmed and lived and turned its head from Matha Mwamba.

She faded as her pregnancy swelled, her legs and arms thinning as if her flesh were gravitating towards the hub at her centre. Grace still left plates of food at the foot of her sleeping mat and emptied her bedpan each morning. But Matha's connection to other people diminished as her crying continued unabated, as she wept on for her compounded losses.

Even as she slept, tears slid into her ears, seeping into her sinuses. Soon the inner membranes became so cushioned with salt that everything started to sound like pebbles clicking at the bottom of a river. Her lashes grew so tangled that they planted themselves in the pores of the swollen flesh around her eyes until, like Venus flytraps, they looked sewn shut. She could barely make out shadows and light through the mesh.

Eventually, the weeping stole her voice too. Matha was dreaming that she had found Godfrey at last, and he was drinking the tears she'd been collecting in empty Coca-Cola bottles. A stream of words issued from her lips – 'Drink, you must be so thirsty, I hope it's not too sweet, I hope it's not too salty' – but then her sleeptalk came apart, breaking into letters, which became like clusters of insects trying not to drown, knotting themselves together. When Matha woke up, there was a crawly lump lodged in her throat, like a hairy Adam's apple, and if she tried to speak, her voice was but the barest scrape of sound.

*

When the baby came, Grace made sure to fetch the midwife. The old woman stayed only long enough to catch and smack it, cut the cord, and rattle a prayer over the two sticky bodies. She knew new mothers sometimes fell into a spell of unbanishable sadness, but this was excessive and premature. This was, in a word, witchcraft. The midwife gathered her toolkit – a razor, scissors, thread, Dettol – and as she left, she cursed in Nyanja. '*Mfwiti!*' she spat. The cube was ripe with the human tang of amniotic fluid, urine and blood, cut with the chemical smell of baby oil and Dettol. The sack curtain was raised – they had needed the whole room. Grace was washing the floor, muttering about the fate that had her cleaning not only the messes of *bazungu*, but those of her useless relatives as well.

The useless relative herself, lying half-naked on the doubled sleeping mats, barely registered these complaints through her muffled senses, dulled by the herbal anaesthetic she'd been fed. The baby was where the midwife had left it, curled up wetly on her stomach, slowly oozing up towards her breasts. Matha felt as hollow as this empty room, her thoughts eddying around like smoke. The midwife's parting curse scythed through it like a flash of light. *Mfwiti*. Witch. The baby finished its crawl and tried to latch. Matha helped it along, grimacing at the sharp tug on her nipple.

They had called her mother a witch, too. As a girl, Matha had always seen her mother as an ideal woman – the fury, the industry, the permanent sense of grievance. *This world is not enough*, Bernadetta had said, reaching her fingers through the wire fence the one time their father had brought the children to visit her in Bwana Mkubwa prison. Mr Mwamba had scarcely been able to look at his wife that day. It was true that everything about her was disgracefully ragged: her hair, her clothes, her face. But when her mother had clawed at the fence, Matha had grabbed her fingers with pride, clutching the fervour there. *This world is not enough*. Matha had always resolved that she would turn the world right over, for her mother, *as* her mother.

The baby unlatched and began to cry, its halting breath cool against Matha's damp chest. She tried to bounce it, jiggling it up and down. At the prison, Bernadetta had pulled Matha towards her – so close that Matha's ear had pressed painfully against the wire fence – and she had whispered: *Go to Ba Nkoloso! Find him!* Matha had followed those instructions to a tee. She had hitched a ride to Lusaka with Ba Nkoloso's family, waited for the great man to be released, joined his Academy, and become a star astronaut in his Space Programme. She had become the revolutionary in disguise that her mother had been. And now?

The baby started to cry again. Matha had never considered that being female would thwart her so, that it would be a hurdle she had to jump every time she wanted to learn something: to read a book, to shout the answers, to make a bomb, to love a man, to fight for freedom. She had never thought Ba Nkoloso, Godfrey and Nkuka would each abandon her in turn to poverty and lone motherhood. Matha bounced her baby in vain. *Go to sleep, baby*, she whimpered. *Shut up, baby.* She had never imagined that to be a woman was always, somehow, to be a banishable witch. Now, as her baby wept for hunger and as she herself wept distractedly – weeping was just what she did now, who she was – Matha felt that dawning shock that comes when you look at yourself and see a person you once might have pitied.

Dear old Eddie, Afronautical whiz! Like us, a most righteous whiner. No matter how powerful the machine may be, never doubt the old squeaky wheel. Hark his pleas: Let me see! Give us free! He obeyed his own statute of liberty. If Livingstone was our white father, Nkoloso was our black prince – Bemba royalty, they say. Equally smart, just as possessed, abrim with the will to explore . . .

Born in a village, he was schooled at a mission and sent for the Catholic priesthood. But the British stole his future and sent him to Burma to fight their Second World War. On his very first flight, they say he spoke up and asked to step onto the clouds. This early release into the wide, wide world had pierced the bold man with wanderlust.

He came home from the war and started a school, but the colonial powers refused him. So he started a riot, a real revolution, then escaped to the bush to hide out. When the kapasus found him, he promptly came forward, and stretched out his wrists for the cuffing. They netted him, near-drowned him, tortured him, jailed him. Behold the dumb beast! they cried. But nothing they did could stop this man. Talk about freedom of mind! In a prison in the bush in the middle of Africa, he penned missives to the Queen of England!

After his comrades finally gained independence, they too tied his hands with red tape. They wrapped him in respect, sinecured his feet. He looked out at the land, then up at the sky, and said it was time for the moon. No brakes, they said. Too free, they said. Had the revolutionary lost his mind? Was he just playing games or was he just playing tricks? Was he a conman or a madman or a visionary seer? Should we praise or mock the stars in his eyes?

There is no way to tell, but as flyers ourselves, we claim him as one of our own. Mukuka Nkoloso, the ultimate bug – needler of conventions and rules. But in the end, he succumbed to custom. They shamed him with scandal, they humbled his hubris, they said, Don't get too carried away now! It's true that freedom can fling you too far, that ambition can burn too bright. Just ask Nkoloso's star Afronaut Matha. Launch too quick, fly too high, and you might perish in the calamitous sun!

II
The Mothers

Sylvia

1975

But why does she cry? Which one? You know, whats-her-name. Mary?
Mother Mary is always crying in the pictures. It is like naming your
child Scissors – you will be getting what you have asked for. *Imwe*, she
is not Mary! She is *Ma-tha*. Oh-*oh*? Isn't it Matha who was washing the
feet of Our Lord Saviour Jesus Christ? No, that was the sister. Matha
was the one sweeping! *Aah*? Maybe this one is also making water to
wash the floors. *Ha!* The Bible tells me so: Put thou my tears into thine
botolo. It is for baptising! Is she not dying? *Awe*, you cannot die from crying. Maybe she is crying for the dead. Maybe she is like Alice Lenshina,
who saw a vision. Maybe she is Mama Afrika weeping for – *A-ta-se*, you
people! This woman is just a witch. That is the beginning and middle
and end-all of it. *Mwandi*, maybe she has a disease we have never seen.
Maybe she is the Queen of Chainama Hills.

Chainama Hills was Lusaka's mental hospital. Straightjacketed
inmates sometimes escaped from it, emerging over the hill with the
jerky crawl of *inswa* from the holes in the ground after the rains.
The escapees would stumble along Great East Road until an indignant or compassionate citizen managed to chase them down and
return them to the hospital. Matha Mwamba was not an escaped
inmate. Nor was she the mother of Christ, nor a saint, nor a witch.
But she was silent and unfriendly, and this served to confirm each
one of the reputations that floated around the crying woman of
Kalingalinga.

Aloof as her twelve cats had been, she would walk solemnly
through the compound every morning, her basket of vegetables on
her head, her baby on her back. She had set up a solo stall in a corner of the market between a woman selling dried mushrooms and

another selling dried caterpillars. At first, Matha's only customers were absentminded men or women softened by her sweet-faced baby. Then word spread about her produce. The *chibwabwa* and *lepu* and *visashi* were a little withered, but the tomatoes! The tomatoes were delicious! Practically pre-salted.

At first, Matha's baby girl would cry for this or that, but as time went on, even this natural language ceased. Sylvia might make plaintive noises or crease her brow like an irascible old man. But no tears would come, as if she were cowed by her mother's incessant crying, as if she had realised that if she did let a tear spill, it would be lost in the deluge anyway. Sylvia was a quiet girl in a quiet world. Her mother rarely spoke. Her Aunty Grace, chatty enough with their neighbours, fell silent as a stone whenever Sylvia and her mother entered the cube they shared.

Deprived of human voices, Sylvia took to touch. If an unfamiliar customer approached the tomato stall, she would scurry behind her mother and start scaling up to her back, where she belonged. When Sylvia grew too big to be *papu*'d, she wrapped her arms around her mother's leg instead. And when she grew too big to cling, she patted herself on the shoulder, rubbed the side of her neck, hugged her own knees or crossed them.

Sylvia did eventually find a friend. It turned out that the sun could make a whole other version of her, a flat, black Sylvia miming her every move along the planes and surfaces of the world. Together, she and her shadow took pleasure in small things. The crispy, crinkly sound of certain vegetables and pieces of rubbish. The reflection of her face in a bucket of water. The immensity and float of the sky. The jerky crawl of *inswa* from the holes in the ground after the rains.

*

One day, when Sylvia was five or six – her mother did not keep track of birthdays – her quiet life opened and sound and fury flooded in. Sylvia woke, as usual, to her mother sneezing salt. The sky beyond the raised curtain at the shack entrance was the colour of a rag that has been washed too often. Sylvia lay there, listening to the doves' song lilting *down-up-down, down … down …* until the sun finally stretched its arms overhead. She sat up and imitated it. Ba Mayo was outside, lighting the fire for breakfast. The *unga* sack curtain was still – Aunty Grace had already left for her job cleaning for an *apamwamba* family in Handsworth Park.

Sylvia loved this time of morning, when everyone was too inside their nighttime dreams or their daytime plans to pay any mind to the daughter of the witch at No. 74 Kalingalinga. Sylvia picked up her yellow bucket and padded outside, making her way to the communal latrines to pee, then to the tap to fill up. The tap had already grown its two tails – a tail of water snaking along the ground, and a tail of sleepy-heads in the queue. When she reached their conjoined head, she filled her bucket, lifted it over her head, nestled it onto her unkempt afro, and quickstepped home, the water rocking contentedly above her.

In the yard at No. 74, she swung the bucket down and set it at her mother's feet. Ba Mayo patted her head in thanks, then crouched to blow the coals of the *mbaula*. Sylvia padded back inside to fold up their sleeping mats. Why did so many insects die in the night? She counted a moth, a trail of fallen ants and four mosquitoes that had all drowned in a puddle of her mother's tears. Kalingalinga was still gathering its morning sounds – crowing, calling, complaint. Sylvia contributed the soft scratch of her handbroom as she bent double and swept the dead insects out, one hand behind her back.

When she stopped, she heard someone crying. Ba Mayo cried all the time but she was never loud about it. Sylvia went outside and found her mother standing over the *mbaula*, the pot of *nshima* porridge on the coals trying to bubble through its own heaviness. Ba Mayo's fists were on her hips, her head pivoting back and forth like a bird as she searched for the source of the noise. On the ground a few feet away, a woman with scruffy grey knots of hair was sitting, sobbing loudly, a big book by her side – it was their neighbour. Sylvia knelt in front of her and clapped her cupped hands in greeting. Then she helped the older woman to her feet and led her to her mother. 'Ba Mayo!' she shouted. 'It is Ba Mrs Zulu!'

The porridge on the coals had finally overcome its weight and was bubbling enthusiastically. Sylvia rescued it, pouring portions into three tin bowls. She took two over to the women, who were now sitting under a tree, and squatted nearby, sipping porridge from her spoon, watching them. It was Sylvia's first lesson in varieties of grief. Mrs Zulu fretted with the book on her lap as she howled, her tears diverted by her wrinkles. Ba Mayo's jaw jutted, her tongue exploring her teeth as tears slid steadily down her smooth cheeks. Punctuated by Mrs Zulu's hiccups, the quiet between them seemed quieter. Then after a few minutes, as if struck by an idea, Ba Mayo stood up, leaned over and slapped Mrs Zulu across the face. Sylvia sputtered. Mrs Zulu gulped. Ba Mayo disappeared into No. 74.

✳

Mrs Zulu had been deferred but she remained undeterred. She began posting hand-scrawled advertisements around the compound: ARE YOU CRYING? NOT TIPICO SAD PEPO, ONLY TRULLY SAD. WOMAN ONLY. SEE M. ZULU IN NO. 78 FOR INTAVEW. BEHIND THE BUTCHARY. It was rumoured that Mrs Zulu's application interview consisted of just one question: 'Is there a cure for your suffering?' If the woman nodded or implied that there was a balm for her misery, Mrs Zulu would erupt: 'Yes? Then no, I am not here to cure you. Go! Get your cure from somewhere-elsewhere!' Mrs Zulu seemed to believe that only incurable sadness would yield the miracle of Matha's infinite tears.

When Mrs Zulu next made her short pilgrimage from No. 78 to No. 74 Kalingalinga, she was armed with nine weeping women in a deferential queue behind her, ordered by height. Wielding her thick Bible in one hand, a raspberry shoot in the other, Mrs Zulu stood at the head of the line and rallied them to weep and hoot and holler. Then 'March!' she shouted, and off they went, Mrs Zulu sending her whip whizzing behind her like an equestrian whenever the keening slackened.

Soon everyone in Kalingalinga knew what it meant to see those thin horizontal tattoos gleaming white or pink on a mother's or a sister's outer thigh. The nine Weepers each had their own reason for crying. A philandering husband. A stillborn baby. An abusive brother. But Mrs Zulu did not care to hear why the women were sad and they did not dare share. As if they were at a neverending funeral, they just gathered together to sit in the yard outside Matha's home and cry all day long, their sobs beating through the air.

Neighbours rolled their eyes. Grace scowled. Dogs set to wailing in competition. But after a while, Matha herself grew reconciled to them. Indeed, she became downright gracious, welcoming them in for hot tea in tin cups and bread and butter sandwiches. Over the years, Matha's constant tears had aged her and isolated her. Now she found herself enjoying The Weepers' girlish banter, and the laughter that broke through their tears like a breeze on a humid day. She savoured the company of other young women whom she could chastise by wiping their tears with her shrinkled fingers or soothe simply by doing what she always did.

*

Maybe that's why Matha got distracted. Because, two months after Mrs Zulu gathered The Weepers and brought them to her like a wilting bouquet, little Sylvia went missing. Matha woke up with her usual salty sneeze. But when she rolled over to pat her daughter's head, the sleeping mat was empty. Matha sat up. Grace had already left for work. Matha fumbled around the shack, its dented, chipped objects tumbling here and there in the cyclone of her hunt. Her daughter was not inside. And she was not outside, crouching as was her wont over a small piece of the world, rapt in contemplation. Matha hurried to the toilets, desperately rubbing salt from her eyes. But Sylvia was not there either.

Matha cursed her tears for dimming her vision and choking her throat, which only clicked when she tried to call Sylvia's name. She knew that her daughter was too timid to go too far without her. Could Grace have taken her to work? Grace, with her scar of a frown, Grace who had ignored her niece except for exactly once, a close call with a lit *mbaula* when Sylvia was two? There was no kind of sense to be made of it but Matha had no sense left in her now anyway. Her mind was in the grip of panic.

She made her way to the neighbourhood where Grace worked. Going anywhere took a long time – Matha was banned by reputation from the buses because her crying infected everyone's mood – and she knew only that it was near the university. Matha spent the morning drifting around Handsworth Park, waiting at the gates of a dozen houses. Maids and gardeners shooed her off, thinking her a beggar or a lunatic. By the time she found the right address, the sun hung high in the sky, a bright blob.

'*Ah-ah*. So you are Grace's famous cousin who is crying all the time?'

Matha nodded at the skinny black blur topped with a squat white blur – a hat, she assumed.

'Your relative is always complaining about you,' he laughed. 'I am Mr Sakala, the cook.'

Where was Grace? Where was Sylvia? But Mr Sakala was still talking.

'It cannot be so bad, my dear. Have you had some tea?'

Was he trying to cheer her up? No, no, no – there was no time for such sentiments!

'It is very important to keep the body nice-and-warm. There is a special root I use for Dona Agnes. She is from abroad' – here he paused to measure job security against the relish of gossip – 'and she is *blind*. This root, it is good for the eyes. She is improving. I know she will play tennis again . . .'

Matha tried manoeuvring herself in around him. Mr Sakala stopped her, wedging her against the gate with a long wiry arm.

'You cannot come in!' he said incredulously. 'You will not find Grace here at any rate. She sent a message this morning to say she is not well.'

But my baby! Matha held her elbows and rocked them in the universal symbol.

'Oh-*oh*! That piccanin hyena is pregnant?! I've cotched her!'

Matha hung her head as Ba Sakala gloried in the prospect of a Grace further disgraced. He didn't understand who Matha was looking for and she could not explain. When she turned away from him, the light in the sky was already blunter. The day was retreating. Everything was running away from Matha, even time.

✳

Sylvia had been in the thick of sleep when it happened. Someone gently took her arm, raised her to her feet, and led her stumbling out of No. 74. Only when they were already on a bus, bouncing along the road, did she become aware of who had taken her. She immediately tried to slip from her grip, but Aunty Grace held her. When they got off the bus half an hour later, Aunty Grace dragged Sylvia, fiercely kicking the whole way, down a road and through the gates outside a tall concrete building, then up the outdoor steps to the second floor, holding Sylvia in a chokehold while she wrestled the key out of her pocket and into the lock. Once they were inside what looked like a kitchen, Aunty Grace kicked the door closed, threw Sylvia on the floor, knelt on her and started hitting her, so hard that Sylvia stopped resisting out of sheer shock.

After a few minutes, another woman came in the room. Aunty Grace was panting in the corner, Sylvia in a ball on the floor, staring between her fingers at the enormous purple trousers hanging from a line over the sink. The woman sat at the table, upon which, Sylvia now noticed, breakfast was arrayed: a glass of orange squash, a plate of golden *vitumbua*, and a bowl of *nshima* porridge that wafted a silky sweetness into the air, banana coins dimpling its surface.

'Your mother will be very happy that you're here,' the woman said in English.

'*Iwe!* You don't want *vitumbua?*' Aunty Grace shouted loudly from the corner, also in English. 'Show some thank yous! It is good food.'

'Come here, love. Sit. Eat.'

As the day went on, Sylvia heard many such words of comfort and promise from this new aunty, words about the toys awaiting her in the next room, and about the party they would throw for her tomorrow. But in the end, it was not the words that did it but the food, the squash and the *vitumbua* and the porridge and the unchecked decadence that followed: toffees and lemon drops and chocolates and mints. These were like stones that you could put in your mouth, where they would melt at different rates and with marvellously different flavours. At first, Sylvia had trouble distinguishing them from the brightly coloured presents in the bedroom – the little plastic bricks and the little glass balls with swirls in their centre. Aunty Grace frowned but New Aunty laughed and clapped her hands as Sylvia tore open the wrappings and placed the toys on her tongue, just to test, just to taste.

✳

After Handsworth Park, Matha's next stop was Rhodes Park. She was not welcome here either. Aunt Beatrice had paid to send Matha to Kasama, had offered to help with her child's schooling. Matha had refused it. Instead, foolish girl, she'd run away again, stolen a car this time, and cut off ties with everyone, all for a *muntu* who had disappeared anyway. And now, this crying-crying business? The servants looked at her sideways. Even the dogs disdained her. Matha sat on the steps of Aunt Beatrice's bungalow, awaiting a hearing that would never come, watching the sun set. She felt empty and rattled with loss, like a dried seed husk. Yet Matha did not barge her way in. She did not kneel beside those big red dogs and scream for Sylvia.

As the dogs began their nightly row across Aunt Beatrice's yard, Matha lay down instead. Truth be told, there was a tiny doubt in the midst of her grief. Over the course of the day, Sylvia's disappearance had become a temptation. Sylvia had always been a reminder of everything that Matha had lost. Every day, she woke up, felt her daughter's small squirming body beside her, remembered, and despaired. Yes, truth be told, before the panic had set in this morning when she found the girl missing, there had been another feeling – a flash of relief that, for once, there was no skin pressed up against hers. What would life be like without Sylvia? Lying there on Aunt Beatrice's steps, thinking on that question, Matha drifted to sleep. For the first time in a long while, she was at peace, alone and gladly dreaming.

She dreamed of a messy mass of blood slipping back inside her with a suctiony sound. A thick cord ravelled into tight loops. A baby clambered up feet first, bestowing weight and tightness to her belly. Her swollen breasts ebbed, their milky tide receded. Tears travelled up her cheeks, tickling into her eye ducts. There was a gradual, deep unwrenching. Then streams of pleasure surged together, imploding with a swallowing action. She hiccupped a moan as sperm sprang back into a penis, which withdrew from her and deflated. A pair of hands left her cheeks. A pair of lips drew away. Matha saw him clearly. Godfrey. Those lips as plump as her tomatoes, the keloid on his neck as thin-skinned, his tightcurled lashes like the tendrils on their stems. 'Comrade,' he whispered and vanished into the dark.

✳

Grace felt bored and distressed. She had been hired to put the little girl at ease as she was transferred from Matha's care to Nkuka's. But Sylvia's unexpectedly fierce resistance had forced Grace to slap her into submission in the kitchen. This had stirred up some long-forgotten curdle in Grace's stomach. It had felt both too bad and too good to strike a small person. Maybe it was because the small person in question was such a dullard. No surprise there. Grace had long thought that, while salt water was a fine thing – she longed to see the sea that her Madam Agnes was always talking about – it had to do funny things to a child to be soaked in it all the time.

Over the years, watching Matha dribble tears into her baby's mouth along with the milk, watching Sylvia toddle around Kalingalinga, playing pitifully with her own shadow, Grace had more than once thought about rescuing the child. But it had always seemed too much trouble, especially when The Weepers had started coming around No. 74 like some kind of cult. Grace had reconsidered only when Matha's sister, a decent and smart woman if a little snooty, had proposed that they save the child from Matha's abuse – and offered Grace money for expenses. Maybe if she did this favour for the family, Grace had reasoned, the aunties would finally forgive her for what she'd done all those years ago.

But now, watching Nkuka's face light up at Sylvia's stupid antics with her fancy new toys, Grace felt disgusted. The child needed a bath, she thought sullenly. *She* certainly wasn't going to give her one. Grace's job with the Bandas involved childcare – she was responsible for bathing baby Carol for instance – but Madam Agnes's daughter was clean and bright, not a dirty little *muntu*. Besides, hadn't Grace done enough? She had brought Sylvia to Nkuka. A strange sum but it added up: a neglected child plus a barren woman, a woman who was now whispering to Grace, asking whether Matha knew yet that her daughter was gone.

'I do not even think Matha will care,' Grace shrugged. 'She hates the girl.'

Sylvia looked up from the spinning top before her, but Nkuka distracted her by declaring that tomorrow, they would throw a birthday party, and wouldn't that be fun? Sylvia grinned and clapped her hands like a monkey. Grace rolled her eyes. Yes, she had done plenty for these two. And she had done it quickly, and quietly, without much violence.

She had done it in a crowded compound, without being spotted. Grace had always thought she would make a good spy.

✳

How great is the distance between what we are and what we think we are. Grace *had* been spotted, of course, by one of The Weepers. That morning, Bonita, a mawkish girl with the look of a goat – pointy-chinned, bony-legged – happened to be on the bus when Grace pulled a sleepy Sylvia onto it by the wrist. Canny enough to recognise wrong-doing in action, Bonita had trailed them. She'd got out with them at the Inters stop, and stood behind a tree to watch as Grace dragged Sylvia up the outdoor steps of the Indeco Flats and opened a door on the second storey.

As soon as she saw the door shut, Bonita took the next bus back to No. 74 Kalingalinga. Matha was nowhere to be found, so Bonita hurried over to No. 78. She found Mrs Zulu sitting on the ground, her granddaughter standing over her, tying her grey hair into knots.

'They have taken Sylvia!' Bonita cried breathlessly.

'What are you talking about?'

'The aunty has taken Sylvia. I saw it with my own eyes. Ba Matha is missing too – and No. 74 has been ransacked!'

Mrs Zulu rose, so slowly that her granddaughter kept trying to fin-ish the hairdo, her chubby arms rising up and up, until the head finally slipped from her grasp.

'It is a state of emergency,' Mrs Zulu declared.

She sent word to The Weepers to gather immediately. When all nine stood before her in various states of frowse and undress, she announced the situation. Someone wondered if Matha and her daugh-ter were together at the Indeco Flats? Mrs Zulu doubted it, she doubted it extremely! Mrs Zulu had her suspicions – she had always had her suspicions! – about that misnamed cousin of it. Grace! The Weepers clucked in concert. Should they go back to the flats? No. Not yet. Mrs Zulu decided they should camp at No. 74 Kalingalinga and wait for either the victims or the perpetrator to return.

None of The Weepers wept that day. And that night, scattered in groups in the dirt yard, none of them slept either. They sipped tea and slapped at mosquitoes and shared their blankets and kept vigil. And when Matha returned alone from Aunt Beatrice's the next morning, they rejoiced. They wrapped their arms around her and lifted her onto their shoulders. They sang her name in the melody of a hymn.

Matha did not protest. How was she to tell these loyal women that in the night, in the exile of Aunt Beatrice's steps, she had given up on her daughter? That she had followed in her mind a trail from Sylvia nowgone to Sylvia neverbeen? That she had come home this morning without even trying to search for her. Matha was too ashamed to confess. She let The Weepers carry her along, let them cry tears and sing songs on her behalf, as Mrs Zulu led the charge to the Indeco Flats.

✳

Sylvia woke up with a small person's hangover, a dizzy, fuzzy feeling born of sugar and adrenaline. Yesterday had ended in a way she had never thought possible. She had been permitted to bounce on a bed. An actual bed. With actual springs. Up in the air and down again and right back up once more! Sylvia had never felt so light, so tossed. She had never imagined a ceiling that she would want to touch. And New Aunty had not spanked her for any of this. This beautiful woman had just sat smiling on the other bed in the room – two beds! in one room! – and watched, spots of brightness in her eyes, as if she had just stopped crying, or was about to start.

Sylvia kept expecting New Aunty to cry, maybe because she resembled Ba Mayo – there was something familiar around the dip between the eyes. Plus New Aunty was doing all the things Ba Mayo always did, bathing Sylvia and feeding her and plaiting her hair into *mukule*. But although Sylvia kept checking all day, she never saw New Aunty cry. This was wonderful because when New Aunty wrapped her arms around her, it wasn't damp or sticky. But it was also confusing: wasn't crying just what one's mother did? All day, every day? This tearlessness was both a respite to Sylvia and a dry, empty space.

Sylvia soon forgot about it, though, so busy was she living her new life. There was the food she had never tasted – the sweets that stung her mouth with riotous pleasure – and the toys and the clothing in colours she'd never seen. She was still wearing the sparkling pink dress that had ballooned around her as she propelled herself up and down on this actual bed in this actual room that New Aunty had said could be all hers, hers alone. Sylvia assumed this was a lie – who in the world had a room all to herself? – but things like truth were starting to seem rather flexible. For instance: who in the world knew that she had more than one aunty?

＊

Cookie had got herself in a bind. Most girls run off as soon as they have taken advantage of an affair with a schoolteacher. Not Cookie. Cookie had kept track of Mr Mwape's promises (a Panasonic TV, a Sony hi-fi) and demands (no babies, no men) over the years, as if in a ledger. After she'd graduated from Evelyn Hone, Mr Mwape had found her a job at the National Registration Office and secured her an Indeco 'bedsitter', with three rooms and a full kitchen. Most of the tenants here shared flats, coming in and out of each other's rooms, cooking and cleaning together like village women, swimming in a stream of gossip. Cookie alone could insist on a flat of her own.

She had kept her 'arrangement' with Mr Mwape, borrowing her female friend's birth control pills when she ran out, washing her vagina with diluted bleach, getting her male friends to buy condoms for her. She'd only had to get an abortion once, a few years ago. After her period had skipped town for the third month in a row, she had taken herself to a stall in Luberma market with a sign that said: SENIOR HERBALIST. IF ANY PROBLEMS CONECT YOUR CONDITION, COME IN FOR AN EXAMINE. The abortionist had been discreet but sloppy, mixing traditional and Western methods without care.

When Cookie came to after the operation, the *banakulu* had told her bluntly that she could never have another baby and that she should refrain from 'cavorting' for at least two months. Cookie stared up at the thatched ceiling, wracked with pain, wading through her various feelings until she landed, gratefully, upon relief. No more tricks to prevent pregnancy – no more herbs or condoms or sponges. No more worries.

Until now. A month ago, Mr Mwape had announced that he could no longer afford to pay for two households. Maybe his wife had finally caught on. Maybe he was just bored of keeping Cookie, who was no longer a young girl but a twenty-eight-year-old woman. In any case, he'd pitched up at her flat, a bottle of conciliatory Red Door in his hand, and broke it to her: he couldn't support her any more. He needed the money for his children, who were coming of age, going to university. Cookie had been distraught but she had simply smiled and kissed him and led him to bed. Only when he left her lying there alone in the twisted sheets in the cool evening light did she sit up and put her head in her hands.

The irony of it all! She had gone to great lengths, for a decade, to keep from having this man's child. Now she needed one. Only a child of her own, it seemed, would balance the scales with his wife; only a child would compel Mr Mwape to keep funding Cookie's life and lifestyle. Blood was a stronger tie than any ring. Sitting in that damp tangle of sheets, the Red Door bottle like a brick beside her – Cookie knew what had to be done.

The very next day, she had gone to Aunt Beatrice and reported that her niece Sylvia was being mistreated. Matha was clearly mad – crying every day in the compound, gathering crying women into some kind of hysterical cult. Sylvia was stunted, malnourished, possibly mute.

'Mmm,' Aunt Beatrice had said. 'This thing is running in the family. Your grandfather was off on the head and Bernadetta was never the straightest spoon in the box either.'

'Yes, Matha is the same as our mother! We must take the child away. For the girl's sake.'

'Are they not living with that other one?' Aunt Beatrice had asked. 'The one who—'

'Yes, Ba Aunty. Her name is Grace. I will talk to her. I'm sure she will help us.'

✳

New Aunty was putting the final touches to the birthday cake. Sylvia was sitting on a chair before it. The only other guests at her party, Aunty Grace and a neighbour's son, were standing on either side of her. Sylvia, still dizzy from sugar and from spending so much of the last two days indoors, stared at her hands in her lap. Her fingernails had never been so clean. They gleamed against her pink dress, which was slightly worse for wear after a night and a morning of bedjumping. A chain of yellow streamers decorated the kitchen wall. Blue balloons bobbed next to a sign Sylvia had spent all morning colouring with felt-tip pens. HAPPY BIRTHDAY MUTINKHE, it said, as did the cake with its single twisty candle.

Sylvia was not in fact a dullard. She did not know her birthday but she knew her own name. She was too interested in this party to mind, though: the flowery smell of the icing and her own fresh skin, New Aunty caressing her back and calling her *Tinkhe, Tinkhe* – what a gentle bell of a name! – and saying, 'It's time to light your candle!' New Aunty pulled a match from a cardboard box and struck it with a zip. She held it to the candle and the flame straightened up from the wick, then rolled its head – the kitchen door had swung open, banging against the wall.

Mrs Zulu's face was in the room, pure rage, a crowd of shouting women behind her. The Weepers. What were they doing here? Were they here for the birthday party? No – the women began stomping around, yelling insults, smacking at the balloons, tearing down the streamers. Mrs Zulu leaned over Sylvia and spat on her cake. Aunty Grace and the neighbour's son were cowering by the kitchen door. And New Aunty was finally crying, her make-up dripping off her jaw onto the collar of her dress as she ran to and fro, shouting 'Stop! Please stop!'

There were so many people doing so many things that at first Sylvia didn't see her mother. Then a salty dampness hit the air, the flame sputtered out, and she knew Ba Mayo was here. Sylvia stared at the strand of smoke trickling up from the candle into the air. She felt hands slide under her armpits and lift her up and away from the cake with its dead candle and wrong name and icing of frothy spittle. Sylvia's legs wrapped automatically around the waist of her rescuer – it was New Aunty.

'Get out of here!' she was still shouting in a hoarse, shaky voice.

Ba Mayo stepped towards them. She was shorter and rounder than New Aunty, and New Aunty's skin was lighter, but face to furious face like this, Sylvia could see how much they looked alike.

'You cannot take care of this child,' said New Aunty, hefting Sylvia higher on her hip.

Ba Mayo said nothing, tears rolling steadily down her calm face.

'You are mistreating and abusing her. This is her first birthday party! Isn't it?' Aunty turned to Sylvia in her arms. Sylvia nodded. 'This is Mutinkhe's first party ever and ...'

Sylvia frowned at the name but burrowed her head into New Aunty's neck. It smelled like cooking oil and washing powder and butterscotch. New Aunty was still reciting her list of grievances when Ba Mayo reached out and grabbed Sylvia's arm. Sylvia flinched from her mother's familiar damp palm, but Ba Mayo gripped harder. Sylvia wrenched her arm away.

'I hate you!' she said.

Sylvia barely spoke English. Sylvia barely spoke at all. But from the safe, sweetsmelling compass of New Aunty's arms, she turned to her mother and tried out those three English words that she had recently heard coming from Grace's mouth. Sylvia thought she meant them, too, although she didn't know whether she hated her mother for trying to take her back now or for losing her in the first place.

＊

When Matha woke up the next morning she found the *unga* sack curtain rolled up beside her on the floor. Grace was gone, along with all of her possessions. Matha learned later that her cousin had moved into the *bwana*'s house in Handsworth Park. But Matha didn't really care what had sent that frowning cow packing. No. 74 felt positively palatial without her – Matha could roll twice over on her mat and meet no resistance. No, Matha would not miss Grace.

She would miss The Weepers though. Those young women, holding hands, telling secrets, arguing over who was sadder, crying like it was a hobby? They had rung the bell of her heart. They had made her feel like maybe she could love properly, that she could learn how to. But her new friends had abandoned her the moment she walked out of Nkuka's flat that day. They had muttered and sucked their teeth at her. Their eyes had said: *Are you not a mother?!*

Well. Maybe she wasn't. Everyone else seemed to know that you should not believe a child when it pushes you away. That when a little girl says *I'm not your friend*, and turns up her nose, you smile patiently and take her into your arms anyway. But when Sylvia had looked at her and said *I hate you* in that reedy little voice, it was one strike too many to the fragile, cracked glass of Matha Mwamba. It shattered her, and so she'd said it back. 'I hate you, too,' Matha had croaked at her daughter, as if she were still a child herself, as if her weeping had not made her grow old but made her regress. We're better off without each other anyway, Matha had thought as she walked out of Nkuka's flat empty-handed, brushing off The Weepers' protestations.

And now they were all gone, even that smelly old bat Mrs Zulu, who had marched away from it all, given up her faith with all the petulance of the disillusioned believer, leaving her Bible behind in No. 74 like a chastisement. Left to her own devices, Matha wept quietly as she *mukule*'d her own hair, propping up a shard of mirror between her feet to see. She wept gently as she cooked *kalembula* on the *mbaula*, adding the bean leaves to the spitting oil, then chopped tomatoes, then diced onions. She wept calmly as she washed her dirty pots with sand under the communal tap and shook them dry. Matha Mwamba was alone but this time her solitude was a choice, her grief a consolation.

'Tinkhe, darling?'

Aunty Cookie knocked on the door frame of the bedroom – Sylvia's bedroom, her very own. Sylvia was sitting on the floor with her legs wide, a pile of Lego in the fork between them. She looked up and smiled at Aunty, then saw a man standing behind her. He was wearing a hat, which he removed now as he stepped into the room. His hair cupped his head on either side, leaving the top bare. Aunty reached down and helped Sylvia to her feet.

'I want you to meet somebody,' she said.

The man stepped towards Sylvia and shook her hand. His felt limp and bony at once, like sticks wrapped in a rag. 'Hallo,' he said stiffly. 'I am your ... daddy.'

'*Anh?*' Sylvia asked.

The man was looking at her with confusion as well. Aunty rubbed Sylvia's shoulder firmly. 'Remember what I told you, Mutinkhe? *I'm* your mummy now. And this is your daddy.'

Sylvia considered. Then she sat back amongst her toys. 'Okay,' she said.

'*Wakwata imyaka inga?*' the man asked, peering down at her.

'Mutinkhe is five,' Aunty said. 'Like I told you!'

'She's so small!'

'Hallo, Daddy,' Sylvia piped up in English, trying to help. 'Me, am Sylvia. I like to play.'

'Let's leave you to play, then, *Tinkhe*,' Aunty said loudly. 'You can get to know Daddy later.' She stepped closer to the man. 'I think she got used to that Sylvia nonsense at my sister's,' she said under her breath as she guided him towards the door. 'In any case, you can see she looks just like you.'

'But are you completely sure, Nkuka?' Sylvia heard the man ask. 'Were you not careful?'

'Of course,' said Aunty with a smile, 'but with a man like you, with so much power, sometimes these things can break through.'

'Why did you not ask me for . . . assistance? Why did you not tell me all these years?'

'My relatives helped me out,' Aunty said sweetly. 'I did not want to bother you.'

'I do not understand how I could have missed the pregnancy . . . So many months!'

'You don't remember? When you took that work trip to Luapula? And then when you were back, I told you I was having problems so we could not . . .' Aunty glanced at Sylvia, who promptly lowered her head and concentrated on fitting two Lego pieces together.

'Yes, I suppose it is a possibility,' the man muttered, shaking his head. 'But—'

'Listen, big *bwana*,' Aunty said coyly. 'I am not having any problems now, so . . .'

She twined her fingers in his and pulled him through the open door towards the one across the corridor, her white high heels making pocking sounds, his black Bata shoes shuffling. Just before Aunty shut the door to the master bedroom, she leaned out and gave Sylvia a warning look, a finger over her lips. Sylvia smiled and turned back to her building blocks.

1984

In the fourteenth year of her life, Sylvia Mwamba fell in love three times. The first time, she was electrified with that desire that hits teenage girls as fiercely and randomly as a bolt of lightning. Sylvia, struck, had fixed her eyes on a boy at school named Mwaba. The only person she told about it was her best friend, Mutale, who was still in the dark when it came to desire. The girls were both in grade seven, but Mutale was two years younger. Sylvia had started school late, Mutale early – the reverse was true of their periods. Mutale was bright, smugly uncontested at the top of the class, and she looked the part: wiry, bespectacled, supremely indifferent as to the state of her hair. Sylvia, by contrast, was highly conscious of her appearance, though she couldn't afford to improve her clothes or hair. Aunty Cookie's patronage – the 'Mummy' act was only for Mr Mwape's visits – was strictly limited to food, shelter and school supplies. The muddled mass of students found Mutale too smart, Sylvia too poor; the girls talked to each other because no one else wanted to talk to either of them.

The day love's lightning struck Sylvia, the girls were sitting under the veranda outside a classroom during their ten-minute tuck-shop break. They ostensibly wore the same uniform: blue dresses, white knee socks, and black mules chalked with dust from the schoolyard stones. But if you zoomed in, you'd see that Mutale's shoes were Bata-bought, real leather with sturdy binding; Sylvia's were *salaula*, secondhand (or secondfoot), battered about the toes. Mutale's socks were grooved fields of pristine white; Sylvia's were grey, dimpled with stitches where she'd mended holes. Mutale's dress was starched to paper-doll starkness; the seams on Sylvia's sprouted threads like weeds from cracked pavement. To wit, Mutale Phiri lived in a three-bathroom house in Ibex Hill, with a gardener who watered the grass three times a week; Sylvia Mwamba lived in the Indeco Flats, where the plumbing often took sick days.

Sylvia sat with a bag of crisps in her lap, listening to her friend. Mutale generally gravitated towards two topics: her plans to become a nurse, and her new baby brother, whose bodily secretions were making her reconsider her choice of career. Today, she was expressing her wonder and disgust that an infant's poo smelled so much like whatever it had eaten. Sylvia knew the only way to make someone listen to your shit was to listen to their shit – or their baby brother's. But Mutale, mashed popcorn spilling onto her lips, was still going on about soggy nappies and a rainbow of poo and Sylvia hadn't even managed a preview of her own news. She had actually spoken to a boy! And he had spoken back! Her stomach dove every time she thought about it. Sylvia looked down at the tomato crisps Mutale had bought for her at the tuck shop. Sunlight bounced off the shiny red packet, casting a pinkish smudge on her socks.

'...just makes you think,' Mutale was shaking her head. 'How can I even be a *mother* when—'

The bell rang. Mutale finally noticed the dismal impatience in Sylvia's face.

'Pass me a note in fourth?' she offered.

*

Sylvia composed the note during third – physical education. For the fifth day in a row, she would not be allowed to participate because she did not have a proper PE uniform. Sylvia was too ashamed to tell her aunty she needed new shorts – her period had leaked last month, sealing the fate of the old ones, which were already thin as paper and torn in places. The PE teacher didn't even bother telling Sylvia off this time, silently directing her with a pointed finger to the side of the court. Sylvia sat on the ground, tucking her skirt between her thighs to cover her panties. She watched the netball game – shouts hitting the air, hands hitting the ball, bodies hitting each other – paying special attention to a bosomy girl named Nancy, her rival in romance.

Sylvia pulled her geography notebook out of her bag. The handwriting under each dated entry always started off fine, then gradually keeled forward, slanted flat, then straggled below the lines – she often fell asleep during class. Perched on her sentences like leggy red insects were the teacher's excitable marks, all exclaiming what Sylvia already knew: that she did not care for geography. She tore out a page from the back of the notebook to write the note:

> *Hi. Am feeling confused I dont no whats going on with me but am going a bit insaaaane. I wish I could freese the world jast to think. In the morning HE toked to me. I got a bit emoshanalll. Am not gonna cry but I want to do samthing crazy.*
>
>

XOXOXOX,
Sylvia

>
> *p.s. Thanx for the crisps*
> *p.p.s. Lok your lips and thro away the key*

This momentous incident had taken place that morning, while everyone was waiting for the morning bell. Mwaba, a precociously tall thirteen-year-old often seen with his arm around Nancy, had been standing at the back of a crowd around the car window of someone's older brother – cigarettes or beers were being exchanged. Sylvia had mustered up her courage and tapped Mwaba on the shoulder. He'd turned with a raised eyebrow. She'd mumbled a greeting.

'Okay, hi,' he'd replied, staring at her with a puzzled look, as if a chicken had suddenly turned its head to him and spoken. There was a long pause.

'Checkit, I'm gonna bounce,' he'd said finally and moved deeper into the cluster by the car. Sylvia had stood dumb, ringing with wonder, watching as he disappeared amongst the backs jostling in front of the older brother's Benz, joining in the collective sound of disappointment – 'Nooooo …' – as something fell outside the car window and landed with a thud.

✳

Sylvia handed the note to her friend at the start of fourth period, as they settled in their chairs before the hulking black typewriters at their assigned desks, Sylvia's directly in front of Mutale's. Mutale read the note, rapidly scrawled a reply, and passed it forward to Sylvia:

I need to open my typewriter before the teacher comes. What do you mean you want to do something crazy? Don't do anything stupid. It's just a (disgusting) boy!!!!!

God bless you and your family,

Love,

Muta

Sylvia's brow and stomach knotted. She shoved Muta's useless note beneath the corner of her typewriter as the teacher, a short fleshy woman strapped into a blue skirt suit, walked into the room.

Mrs Makaza taught all of the typing and secretarial classes. The students called her Yakuza and they feared her mightily. They removed the black plastic lids from their typewriters as Yakuza waddled to the front of the class, stiff-backed and regal despite all that juddering flesh. She smacked a stack of white paper onto her desk. The rustling in the room ceased. Then she faced the students and snapped her gaze up. Her eyes bulged under her thin-tweezed eyebrows.

'Begin!' she trumpeted.

The prefect bolted to her feet, ran to the front desk, fetched the stack of paper, and darted down the aisles handing the students two sheets each.

'Heads forward!'

Sylvia sat up straight. She imagined herself a soldier, one of the rigid bodies that stood in front of the Zambian White House when the national anthem played on TV Zed at 1700 hours each day.

'Put your peppas in!'

The shiver of the sheets slipping into slots.

'Scroh!'

A sound like fingernails on jeans as the students scrolled their sheets.

'Fingahs on the keys!'

A crowd of mice stomping in unison.

'Okay! Begin! A. Spess. A. Spess. A. Spess. A. Full-stop.' Yakuza began to stalk the aisles to the marching beat of the students' typing. 'S. Spess. S. Spess. S. Spess. Nexti-line.'

Overlapping *shwings* as the students hit the release levers, sending their carriages flying to the right.

'A-S-D-F. Spess. Semi-cologne-L-K-J. Spess.'

Now, individual letters rose ranks and became words, which became battalions of sentences.

'The red fox jamped ovah-the-fence,' Yakuza barked. 'Nexti-line.' *Shwing*.

Soon the typewriters were clattering, no longer in unison but for the cascade of metallic *shwings* at the end of each line. Sylvia fell into the rhythm, her carriage chuck-chuck-chucking, her typebars kicking high to land their feet on her page. It was a respite: typing strange sentences about animals she had never seen, being told what to do and being relatively capable of doing it.

Only when Sylvia smelt soapy sweat and dusty pantyhose did she realise that Yakuza was hovering over her shoulder. Sylvia kept typing but her chest rose with anticipatory pride. Her lines were perfect. Routine had done wonders for her spelling and not once had her typebars tangled. She was caught off guard when Yakuza abruptly snatched the note from under her typewriter.

Without preface, as if continuing her dictation, Yakuza read Mutale's note to Sylvia out loud: 'I need to open my typewriter before the teacher comes.'

Methodically, all the students except Sylvia and Mutale began typing it out. This was an unusually coherent sentence for Yakuza but it made a kind of classroom sense. One boy even smiled, noticing that all the letters in the word *typewriter* were in the top row of the keyboard.

But then Yakuza went on: 'What do you mean you want to do something crazy?'

The clattering of keys dwindled. The students blinked up. Yakuza strolled to the front of the room as she went on, even spelling out Mutale's punctuation – the parentheses and exclamation points in '(disgusting) boy!!!!!'

'So . . .' Yakuza murmured in conclusion. This was ominous. Yakuza never spoke below the volume of a shout. 'Who is this "disgusting boy", Miss Phiri?'

Sylvia was still facing forward but she could sense Mutale shaking her head behind her.

'Okay, fine. Let us ask the peppatrator herself.' Yakuza turned to Sylvia. 'Miss Mwamba?'

Sylvia cast her eyes down as titters fluttered across the classroom.

'Anybody?' Yakuza opened the question to the class. 'Who is the "disgusting boy"?'

Sylvia didn't even catch who said it, so deep was her shock when two voices shouted out:

'Mwaba!'

'It's Mwaba, Mrs Makaza!'

Everyone laughed. Sylvia turned and accused Mutale with a glare. Mutale shook her head and crossed her heart and mouthed 'Hope to die.' The other students grinned guiltily as the call and response with Yakuza continued: Oh, that one? He's handsome, eh? Ah, no, Mrs Makaza, he is *not*, she just does not know, this girl. Oh-*oh*? So it's not Mwaba Kashoki? *No*, it's the younger one, Mwaba Ndala. *That* one? Yes! The brother to Simon. Oh-*oh*? He is handsome? NO!

Good students, poor students, students who had never spoken in class before, students who were scared of teachers – they all joined in. They were excited to speak freely with Mrs Makaza, a teacher so formal that the first day of class she hadn't even introduced herself, simply writing her name on the board before launching into the first drill. Sylvia sat silently as the show went on. It was as if her heart were hanging in the air, as if her classmates were dogs lunging casually to shred it. How? How did they all *know*?

✳

Mercifully, school holidays came the following week. It was June, a season of hot dry days and cold dry nights. Dry in feeling all the time: Sylvia was soon dead bored. She had nursed her wounds. She had spent a great deal of time thinking about what she should have replied when Mwaba had said, 'Checkit, I'm gonna bounce.' Then she had passed more time elaborately 'forgetting' Mwaba by dwelling on his flaws. She had just about resigned herself to being loveless and alone for the remainder of her days when she fell in love for the second time.

Mutale had invited her to come to the Agricultural Show with her family. That morning, Aunty Cookie dropped Sylvia at the Phiris' house in Ibex Hill. The girls got ready in Mutale's gigantic bedroom. Sylvia borrowed her friend's white patent-leather pointy-toed sling-backs, stuffing tissue inside to make them fit. Then she handsewed a skirt out of an old bedsheet – the thread was a thicket at the hem, but it had swirly white buttons along the side. She pulled on a teal t-shirt she'd bought at *salaula* with tuck-shop money. She didn't like its bubble letter logo – a peeling heart – so she turned it inside out and tied a knot on one side to make it tight. For her part, Mutale wore stonewashed jeans that gaped like fins at her hips, red and black leather flats, and a red crop top that she concealed under a loose black shirt she planned to take off once they ditched her family at the show.

After applying make-up for each other, the two girls stood together in front of the full-length mirror. Sylvia could read the words of her own shirt, doubly reversed: inside out and reflected. *JumpRopeForHeart.* Mutale's outfit was nicer, but she wore it like a child – her breasts were just swollen nipples and her lip gloss made it look like she'd been eating fried *kapenta*.

'You look so much better than me, Muta,' Sylvia smiled, lying through her scarlet lips.

✳

Mutale was no competition but the other girls at the show certainly were. Wherever Sylvia's eyes landed in the ticket queue outside, she found yet more items to add to her 'Wishful List'. Silver hoop earrings. White leggings that hooked under the arch of the foot. Black fingerless lace gloves. Purple stretch belts with gold-rimmed butterfly buckles. As for the *butas*, it was Michael Jackson season, and every boy who could afford one was in a red leather jacket. Heady with aspiration, Sylvia barely noticed her friend's eagerness to get away from her family. As soon as they clunked through the turnstiles, Mutale grabbed her hand and dragged her into the murmurous crowd.

The Agricultural Show always took place at Showgrounds, a 140-hectare expanse of land off Great East Road bounded by white walls on all sides. These were painted with ads for Dettol and Lifebuoy and Strike, for Maltesers and Maggi and Milo. There were redundant ads for car dealers (BENZ BENZ BENZ) and unlikely ones for salons (ASTOUNDING INDIAN HAIR) and it seemed every other wall bore a black and yellow ad for Harvey Tiles, with some skew Zinglish analogy: A ROOF WITHOUT HARVEY TILES IS LIKE A FACE WITHOUT

A SMILE – IT MIGHT BE GLOOMY. A ROOF WITHOUT HARVEY TILES IS LIKE AN AEROPLANE WITHOUT A PILOT – IT WON'T FLY. A ROOF WITHOUT HARVEY TILES IS LIKE A SCHOOL WITHOUT TEACHERS – THERE WILL BE ILLITERACY.

In the off months, Showgrounds was an odd little leisure city. There were polo fields – sometimes green, sometimes brown – where in the old days, people had actually played that strange game that seems like a drunken bet about golf and horse riding. Next to the fields was the Polo Grill, an open-air restaurant specialising in sundowners, where over the years, whites and coloureds and blacks and now a motley crew of *apamwamba* drank and flirted away the afternoons. A handful of businesses operated year-round: a flower shop; a gift shop; a vet; the cylindrical Henry Tayali Art Museum; and the Gymkhana club with a peacock farm behind it – two species of preening males competing with each other. The grounds were otherwise empty, a concrete maze of stalls awaiting its annual *raison d'être*.

In the beginning, the Lusaka Agricultural Show had been literal: farmers from rural districts came to the capital to display their cows and goats, their bulldozers and sprinklers. Then the farmers started bringing their wives and children too, and the show became a fair. Candyfloss and popcorn vendors cropped up. A miniature train was imported, its tracks carving a long, twisty double scar across the grounds. Then radio stations began to set up dance floors. Alcohol crept in. The youth swarmed in to drink it. By 1984, the Agricultural Show had become a city-wide party.

Sylvia and Mutale held hands and walked around together. Mutale looked at the exhibits. Some of these were schoolish – signs and pamphlets with sciencey talk, unsmiling UNZA students giving brief lectures. Others were farmish – smelly, twitchy animals standing or kneeling in makeshift stalls. Sylvia looked at the people. Men in suits clapping each other's backs, their wives fluting 'hallos' as their eyes darted discerningly over each other. Toddlers greased with Vaseline trotted around in the dust, their weirdly adult outfits – skirts and suspenders, hats and bow ties – in various stages of collapse. Babies rode their mothers' backs, gazing at strangers or ducking their heads shyly. Sylvia focused mostly on the people her age, the young sweating bodies clad in shiny metal and bright colours, *featuring*.

A tall boy with skin dark as pencil lead walked by, his stride collapsing and catching itself in a 5/4 tempo. He glanced Sylvia's way with casual grace, then paused his stroll and looked back, running his hand over his fade. Mutale pulled Sylvia away from this situation so roughly that Sylvia left one of her borrowed shoes behind. They both caught their breath as it tumbled away in the dust. Mutale rescued it just before a man trod on it, but just after a little girl dripped a gob of ice cream onto it. Mutale sucked her teeth, picked it up gingerly by the ankle strap, and used a mango leaf to wipe the muddy pink mess off. She skulked back to Sylvia, who was now standing with her bare foot perched on top of the other shoe. To keep her balance, she was holding the tall boy's arm, which flexed whenever her weight shifted. '*Chops,*' she mouthed with wide eyes.

The boy's muscles were indeed on prominent display on either side of his black net shirt. His name was Daliso, he told them, then proceeded with a long and detailed chuffing routine, his voice dropping into false delays and slurred consonants in order to sound American: 'Am a deeshaaay, you know, riiide?' Daliso's bloodshot eyes looked like they'd been popped out, rolled around in the dirt, and popped back in. He smelled like *ma sawa sawa*. Otherwise, he was perfect. If only the shoe in Mutale's hands would disappear, Sylvia could keep holding his muscular arm and keep her feet in this sexy pose.

Naturally, Daliso the DJ had an entourage of boys, who crowded around as soon as they saw what his net shirt had caught. Sylvia had already been claimed; Mutale was now targeted. Too bewildered even to repulse their 'Hi swit-haats', Mutale stayed silent, tugging at the edge of Sylvia's hidden *JumpRopeForHeart* and making *let's go!* eyes. Annoyed by Mutale's reluctance, the guys started calling her a Jelita – the little girl who runs and jumps in kids' books. Sylvia laughed along with them. After a few more minutes of this flirtatious bullying, Mutale gave up and walked off alone, looking pitiably over her shoulder. Sylvia barely noticed. She had just met Daliso's brother, Francis, who had a hightop fade and a real leather jacket, and she was beginning to thrum with proximity to so much *maleness*.

For the rest of the day, she wandered around with this new crew, which lost and regrew members like a lizard as it moved deeper into the exotic delights of the show. At Lusaka's 58th Agricultural and Commercial Show, Sylvia Mwamba saw for the first time: a man in bumshorts and a boa; a headless woman in a dark tent; an albino woman walking around in a *chitenge* just like someone's mother; one zombie and his nation, dancing on a makeshift stage – a 'Thriller' performance; a woman who slapped a man's face, then gasped at herself, a smile stealing to her lips; and a live penis. This last was by far the most riveting.

The sky was a dusky rose by the time Sylvia and Francis sought some privacy between two stalls. In one, a man was emptying out unsold helium balloons. In the other, a young woman in a bow tie was selling groundnuts in front of a diagram of legume root systems. She sucked her teeth when Sylvia and Francis squeezed past.

'Sorry, *ba* sista,' Francis grinned. 'We just gonna rap for a beat.'

The alley smelled like urine and burnt nuts and helium. At their feet were the dregs of the day – a blue-stained lollipop stick, a red puddle of candyfloss vomit, a torn crisp packet, a trail of gumdrops. Sylvia could hear the rubbery whine of the draining balloons, the tired panic of vendors shouting out their clearance prices, and the wailing of babies, who always know first when it's time to go home. Francis was standing very close to her. She raised her eyes to his.

'Chillax, swit-haat,' he murmured. 'Iss arright.'

He kissed her. She let him, slightly bewildered by his inability to control his lips or his tongue. She started to kiss him back and the lightning in her began to melt and run liquid through her veins. After a minute or so, Francis pulled his penis out and put her hand on it. It was darker than she had imagined it would be, and it grew as she held it, as fast as a mushroom that springs from the earth during rainy season. It smelled like a mushroom too, a dank earthy scent, and its skin was as thin and soft as a mushroom's gills. Francis's eyes were closed. He had seemed strong when he had handed his penis to her like a gift or a greeting. Now he seemed weak. The springy weight in her palm was vibrating – his knees were trembling and his breath was uneven, as if secretly, without letting on, he was already running away.

*

Sylvia carefully penned her name and number on a piece of paper for Francis that night when he dropped her home at the flats. He never called. Nevertheless, she mentally pitted her two loves against each other for months. Francis was older but Mwaba was taller. Francis had kissed her but Mwaba sometimes smiled vaguely at her. She had touched Francis *down there* but she still got to see Mwaba's handsome face every day at school. Mwaba soon lost this advantage, however. Like most students in Zambia, Sylvia failed the national Grade 7 Exams that November.

'Foolish girl!' Aunty Cookie scolded her. 'Wasting other people's time and money!'

'I have tried, Ba Aunty,' Sylvia said. 'My brain is just not strong. I fall asleep too much.'

In truth, Sylvia was relieved to have failed out of school for good. She had never understood why the teachers taught what they taught. Sediment, tectonic, archipelago. Hypotenuse, equilateral, isosceles. What was any of it good for? No. She did not miss those useless lessons or her only friend – after the Agricultural Show, Mutale had shunned her, masking her hurt with a stagey disdain. But Sylvia did miss the casual crowdedness of school, the brush of skin on skin, the feeling of being amongst many people doing many things – typing or netball or even just standing in line at the tuck shop.

Without school, she grew lonely and listless. To step outside her aunt's flat was to be sent – the neighbours always had an errand for an unoccupied teenager – so she stayed in all day. She perused old *Ebony* magazines and painted her nails with polish eked out from old bottles. She waited for the cartoons to come on the Panasonic TV, staring at the prison of thick coloured bars until they dissolved at 1700 hrs. Sometimes she tried on the home-made dresses hanging in purgatory at the back of Aunty's closet. Too small for Cookie, who had put on a stone over the last decade, they fit Sylvia's figure beautifully.

One afternoon, she was turning and posing in front of the closet mirror, pouting her lips, when the bedroom door unexpectedly opened. It was Mr Mwape, his head hovering over her shoulder in the mirror. She stared at him. He stared back with frank admiration, then smiled.

'Are we being naughty?'

'No,' Sylvia said, refraining from rolling her eyes.

Mr Mwape was a familiar visitor at the Indeco Flats, but he had been stopping by more often recently. He was in his forties now, working for the Ministry of Education. He had started shaving his patchy afro, so he had a shiny bald head to match his taut round belly. Sylvia still called him Daddy out of habit but she had no delusions about this 'patron'. She watched as he sat on Aunty Cookie's bed with a proprietary air.

'Come.' He patted the duvet cover next to him, a twitch under his left eye.

Sylvia approached in her bare feet, her nipples scratching against the inside of the low-cut sequinned dress, its pleated skirt swishing at her thighs.

'Sit,' he said, shifting his patting hand from the bed to his knee as if she wouldn't notice the difference.

Sylvia looked at his pinstriped thigh. She looked at the oblong bulge where it joined his body. Her ears felt hot. She gingerly hitched herself onto his lap, not quite relaxing into a seat. Mr Mwape smelled of after-shave and pipe tobacco.

'Good girl,' he said gummily. 'You must show respect. You must not say no.'

Mr Mwape didn't do much that day, nor in the weeks that followed. But Sylvia felt torn about it: the sly touches, the near kisses, the nuzzling, even dressing up in Aunty's clothes, which she felt somehow obliged to keep doing because of that first time. She couldn't pinpoint why all of this felt wrong. She knew he wasn't really her father and, though he was an older man, he tapped a current of curiosity in her. Did he love her aunt? Did he love *her*? Could she love him the way she loved Mwaba and Francis?

*

Sylvia found herself avoiding the flat, ducking Mr Mwape since she could not quite bring herself to push him away. She hung around outside the complex instead, on the side of the road where various *kantemba* sold food to people who worked in that part of town – cleaners from the hotels down the way, taxi drivers, road repairmen. She would sit on a big flat stone, not really thinking, just letting life in, listening to the song of all this anonymous busyness: the authoritative shouts of unmonitored children; the relay and laughter of greetings and bargains; Michael yelping or Whitney belting from the *chimanga* boy's boombox: *How will I know . . .*

'. . . if he really laafs you . . .' sang a voice beside her, whirring as if from inside a bottle.

Sylvia looked up. The girl was tall and dark, pretty with a pointed chin. She had just ordered her lunch from the *chimanga* boy, who shook his brazier to keep the current batch from burning, then started peeling a fresh cob for her. A bulging plastic bag swung from the girl's fingers as she rocked to the music against the post of his stall. She wore a white t-shirt, a waxed wrapper, and *patapatas* – all shiny and pristine, even the rubber sandals, which gleamed like snakes on her feet under her *chitenge*. A crisp *chitambala* cut across her forehead.

'Nice polish,' she purred and stepped closer to examine Sylvia's sandalled feet.

The *chimanga* boy called out, thinking he was about to lose a sale.

The girl turned and spat, 'You can wait if you want my money, idjot!' Her hand slapped the air and rose vertical.

Shocked and pleased by the girl's rudeness, Sylvia smiled in solidarity. The girl smiled back, the kind of almost-smile that made you want to finish it for her, with a joke or a compliment or the tip of your finger if need be.

'I need to resurrect mine,' the girl said, raising her *chitenge* so that her foot emerged from its shadow. Her toenails were indeed a mess, the remnants of polish like the jagged outlines on the maps Sylvia had once gazed at blankly in geography class. But Sylvia was more struck by the fact that the girl was not wearing a skirt under the *chitenge* she had just lifted. She was so scandalised by that flash of smooth dark thigh that she almost didn't hear the girl's request.

'Borrow me your polish?'

Sylvia nodded and jumped up. The decision was simple, quick, and entirely obscure to her. She ran over to the Indeco Flats, wriggled between the locked gates, jogged up the outdoor stairs, pulled her key from the knot in her *chitenge*, and unlocked the door. She quickly found the polish – the rich colour of the darkest menstrual blood – in her stash of Aunty's old bottles, locked up again and ran back to the *kantemba*, smacking the thick glass bottle against her palm along the way, hoping the dregs weren't too dry.

The *chimanga* boy was back to droning his prices at passersby and at first Sylvia thought the girl had already gone. But no, there she was, hunched slightly, biting into the scorched maize inside the newspaper cone, wincing at its heat. Sylvia, a little out of breath, handed over the polish. The girl swallowed her mouthful, wiped her hand on her *chitenge* and took it. She held it up to the light, then picked up the plastic bag at her feet and sauntered off, *patapatas* flapping.

'Ta muchly! *Ciao!*' she sang.

I'll never see that polish again, Sylvia was thinking when the girl looked back over her shoulder with her incomplete smile: 'See you,' she called. 'And it's Loveness, by the way.'

✳

Sylvia never invited Loveness inside the Indeco Flats. Once, when Sylvia was eight years old, she had stayed out after sunset, playing with the neighbourhood kids around a street light outside. Under its orange glow, Sylvia had put her hands on the other girls' shoulders and circled her little hips, chanting: *two-by-two-cata-pilla-by-two!* Aunty had discovered her there, snatched her up by her collar and walloped her buttocks. Not for dancing like a grown woman, but for consorting with the poor. Sylvia made sure to keep her new friendship confined to Loveness's abode.

This was an old security hut behind the Indeco Flats – a kind of open-air brick closet. Loveness had cleverly constructed a roof by lashing old plastic bottles together and weighing them down with stones. The light that came through that roof was murky, but sometimes spun with rainbows and when it rained, it sounded like you were inside a giant *silimba*. Loveness kept an *mbaula* outside, where she fried *vitumbua* to sell. She told Sylvia she had chosen this place after running away from her uncle's house.

'I just left,' Loveness said with a toss of her plaits, which she had been on her way to get done when she met Sylvia – the bulging bag had been full of wig. 'I got tired of that man making moves. Anyway, he was too big for me. Ouch!' Loveness giggled. 'Pass the ciggies?'

Sylvia handed over the box of Pall Malls. Loveness lit one, inhaled, then blew out a steady stream of smoke. She offered it to Sylvia, who declined.

'You know, in this life' – Loveness sucked musingly on the cigarette – 'all you really need is love.'

Sylvia nodded, wondering whether to tell her about Mr Mwape or Mwaba or Francis.

'That's why I changed my name.' Loveness tilted her head and smiled as she sang it out: 'Loveness!' She always pitched her voice higher when she said it. 'Doesn't it suit?'

Sylvia nodded again, looking at the cigarette. She had never seen a girl smoke. Impulsively, she plucked it from between Loveness's fingers and sucked on it softly – *puff puff puff* like a toy train.

'No,' said Loveness, plucking it back. 'Hold the smoke in your mouth, then breathe it in.'

She demonstrated, then placed the filter between Sylvia's lips. Sylvia inhaled, holding the smoke in until it seared her lungs. Sylvia coughed and coughed. Loveness laughed and laughed. The coughing fit opened Sylvia's bloodstream to the nicotine. The buzz hit like a swarm and she canted back, her head bumping gently against the wall of the security hut.

✴

With Loveness's tutelage, Mr Mwape became more manageable. The girls prepared for his afternoon visits in advance. Inside the security hut, Loveness would pinch Sylvia's nose to make the hill a peak; plait a labyrinthine *mukule* into her hair; rub pink lippie into her cheekbones; paint her fingernails for her; and dab baby oil behind her ears in lieu of perfume. Sylvia would head inside the Indeco Flats, Loveness waving at her from the gates. There, in Aunty Cookie's bedroom, she would choose a dress to wear, and wait for Mr Mwape to arrive.

After a few weeks of this, the girls resolved that Sylvia should skip the dress entirely and go straight for the satin lingerie Aunty Cookie kept in the back of a drawer. Sylvia had to tie a knot on the side so the panties fit her hips and stuff tissue into the cups of the bra so it wouldn't sag. But when Mr Mwape found her in this get-up, sprawled out on Aunty's bed, the tic under his left eye went manic, twitching like a moth against a lit bulb. He panted and sweated, his hands like animals trying to escape, his trousers tighter than they'd ever been. Despite all this strain, however, he did not pull off Sylvia's borrowed panties that day.

'What does he mean, I'm still a little girl?' she complained to Loveness that evening.

'Maybe you haven't pulled enough,' Loveness shrugged.

'What do you mean, pulled?'

Loveness told her all about it. How you have to pull your *malepe* until they stretch – as long as your thumb – so that with the right stimulation, they swell with blood and grasp the man's *mbolo*. 'It's simple,' she said.

Sylvia stared at Loveness. 'Show me?'

And she did. The girls took off their *chitenges* and panties and sat facing each other, knees bent, thighs spread. 'Like this,' said Loveness. Later, she showed Sylvia how to use Vaseline and *umuthi* juice from *impwa* to ease the pulling, and gave her a splitted stem to wedge the labia open. Sylvia was late to this and it burned at first. But it soon became her favourite game: to sit knee-to-knee in the sweet, yeasty funk of the brick hut and pull with Loveness, gazing at her lips, the pink inner flesh bared like a fruit bursting from its peel.

If a customer came by for a *chitumbua*, the girls would pull their clothes on in a fit of giggles. They would emerge from the shadowy chamber and perform tasks in silent coordination over the *mbaula* – ladling the lumps of dough into the vat of oil, exchanging cash and change, draining the crispy golden balls, wrapping them in newspaper and handing them over with a '*zikomo kwambili*'. Loveness was uniformly languid in her movements, aloof and drifty, and she'd often sell *vitumbua* with her head turned the whole time, as if looking at something infinitely more interesting.

✳

The lingerie did wonders: Mr Mwape started to bring Sylvia gifts – a bottle of perfume; a new, better-fitting bra. She was on the verge of making specific requests from her Wishful List when they got caught.

One afternoon, the bedroom door banged open and Aunty Cookie was there in the room in a powder-blue trouser suit, home early from work. Sylvia expected to be cursed at or beaten, but Aunty barely looked at her. Keeping her eyes fixed on Mr Mwape, who was trying to cover himself with a frilly pillow, Aunty simply stretched out her arm and pointed at the exit. Sylvia hastily wrapped herself in a *chitenge* and hopped through the door, which was promptly slammed in her face. Sylvia pressed her ear to it.

'. . . long have you been plotting this . . . this . . . this *sheer perversity*?!' Aunty cried.

'*Ha!* How old were you when you seduced me in Kasama? Fourteen?'

'Eighteen! The girl calls you *Daddy* for goodness gracious me!'

'And whose fault is that?'

'Are you saying that I raised this female *for you*?!'

'Female?!' he scoffed. 'Don't you mean blackmail?'

Sylvia snuck across the corridor to her bedroom and closed the door, her heart bouncing unhappily. She put on her pyjamas and lay there watching the sun set outside her window. After an hour of shouting, she heard the front door to the flat slam. A moment later, her bedroom door opened, letting in electric light. She leaned up but she couldn't see Aunty Cookie's expression with the brightness behind her head.

'Sorry, Ba Aunty—' The door shut before Sylvia could finish.

When she woke up the next morning, the flat seemed the same as usual. Aunty Cookie had already gone to work at the National Registration Office. Traffic on the main road honked and rushed by. Sunlight flickered in through the curtains. The cornflakes box sat on the table, with that rooster in the colours of the Zambian flag. The only difference, it seemed, was that Aunty's bedroom door, with its treasure chest of womanly things, had been locked. Sylvia bathed and got dressed and went to find Loveness.

Her friend was asleep inside the security hut, curled around the *mbaula*, which she had dragged inside to keep warm. Her skin was coated in an undisturbed blanket of ash and there was dried blood in the cracks of her big lips. Sylvia didn't wake her. She took the *mbaula* outside and lit it and fried up some buns. Loveness emerged, squinting and sniffing. As they chewed their greasy, salty breakfast – Sylvia's second of the day – Loveness explained the blood on her lips. To do that, she had to explain the man who hit her – who he was and how they'd met. By the end of the story, Loveness had retraced all the staggering steps between running away from her uncle's house and the bruises on her face and neck.

'Me, I must also run.' Sylvia shook her head. 'Ba Mwape is like your uncle. He's sick.'

'*Awe*, no!' Loveness swallowed the lump of *chitumbua* in her mouth. 'Mr Mwape is a soft man! He brings you presents. He takes care of you. Pampering is very good!'

'But these men you talk about – they also bring you presents! Me, I can do what you do.'

'No, Syls.' Loveness stared into space, picking at her cuticles. 'You cannot do what I do. It's dangerous. Have you not seen that the police are rounding us up again? All these *tuma* "unaccompanied women" raids. No, you must stick to your Mr Mwape.'

'Mwape is small potatoes. I want the big potatoes. From the hotels.'

'You're too young for that.'

'We're the same age.' Sylvia rolled her eyes. 'You just want the customers for yourself.'

A smile snuck onto Loveness's face and Sylvia stuck her tongue out and then they were giggling. The two girls spent a lazy, happy day together: frying buns and selling them, crooning into paper cones, devising their futures. Someday, they would open a hair salon, maybe combine it with a nail parlour. Sylvia had no patience for market money, the baffling accounts of who owed so-and-so such-and-such, tiny numbers fluctuating like the *udzudzu* over the trashy ditches between stalls. They decided that Loveness would keep track of the business side of things while Sylvia worked on choosing styles and products. Between them, they finished two Mosis and six Pall Malls trying out names. *Hair Today, Gown Tomorrow. Up in the Hair. The Hairport.*

Sylvia swayed up the stairs at the Indeco Flats as the sun set, wondering what punishment Aunty Cookie had in store for her at home. The silent treatment? Sylvia pulled her key from the knot in her *chitenge*. No TV time? The key slid into the lock, but it wouldn't turn. She pulled it out and examined it. Extra chores? She slid it in again and twisted in vain. Only then did she realise that the look on her aunt's face yesterday had not been one of anger or disgust. Sylvia had stolen Mr Mwape from Aunty Cookie. There was no punishment equal to that humiliation. Sylvia didn't even bother knocking.

*

One warm Thursday night, a month after she moved into the security hut with Loveness, Sylvia decided it was time to try her luck. Under the eerie underwater light of the plastic-bottle roof, she gathered her tools: a lace camisole, a white blouse, a skirt she had sewn from a men's t-shirt, and *salaula* stilettos that set her ankles spinning. Using a child's pocket mirror, she applied foundation, rouge and red lipstick. Then she began the mile-long march from the Indeco Flats to her destination.

A Lusaka evening: a purpling sky, woodsmoke from supper fires, mosquitoes singing delirious rounds, the clapping and chanting of a church meeting, the bitter smell of car exhaust. Sylvia teetered through it, so anxious it felt like she'd eaten something still alive and rotating. She had chosen to make her debut at the Ridgeway, knowing that Loveness went to the Pamodzi on Thursdays. But the two hotels were precariously close to each other – kittycorner across an intersection – and the party girls who worked them would definitely report it to Loveness if they saw Sylvia. By the time she reached the Pamodzi, her stilettos were dangling from her fingers by their ankle straps and sweat had seriously compromised her make-up. She wiped her feet clean in the cool grass under the neon hotel sign, squeezed back into her heels and stepped wincingly into the hotel.

Avoiding the bellboys, she made her way through the gauntlet of *apamwamba* guests in the lobby – a businessman sitting with legs crossed reading the *Times of Zambia*, a *muzungu* with a rotting nest of dreadlocks smoking a cigarette, a young woman in glasses reading a book – wait, was that … ? It was. Mutale was wearing jeans and a bulky sweater – that girl had never taken proper advantage of having the money for fashion. She was probably here for a fancy dinner with her parents. As if sensing eyes on her, Mutale looked up from her book.

Sylvia pulled her plaits forward to hide her face behind the swinging curtain and picked up her pace as much as her heels would allow.

She hadn't spoken to Mutale since abandoning her at the Agricultural Show and hadn't seen her since leaving school. As Sylvia reached the exit to the poolside area, she glanced over her shoulder and saw a tall figure approach Mutale. Was that ... ? It was. Mwaba! Sylvia hustled outside, feeling a clutch of shock in her throat. But then it released – something had shifted. She smiled to herself. Those two were just schoolchildren.

It was a warm night. The Ridgeway swimming pool glowed smooth and white under the big moon. As Sylvia moved towards the outdoor bar, she felt eyes following her and her confidence began to grow. She had deliberately worn clothes that showed you what to do with her body. Her loose shirt drooled off her shoulders and gasped open at her cleavage. The folds of her skirt grasped her hips and caressed her thighs as she walked, cloth fingers inviting human ones to join them. She propped herself on a bar stool, tossed her plaits and ordered a Mosi.

The bartender gave her a wary look but caved easily to the kwacha she waved at him. This cash – saved from sales of *vitumbua* over the last few months – was the only reason Sylvia could be at this luxurious hotel instead of at a shebeen. She cast her eyes around. Tourists, local businessmen, a few wives, no party girls just yet. She closed her eyes and listened to the subtle music of affluence: swishing palm trees, tinkling ice cubes, murmurous conversation, and a certain absence of sound, too – a lack of urgency, of complaint. She felt a swell of resentment at Loveness for keeping her from ...

'Cheers.'

Sylvia opened her eyes. A grizzled *muzungu* in a limp suit had slid onto the stool beside her, holding a tumbler of whisky towards her. She clinked her bottle of beer against it and sipped.

'Vhut is your name?'

'Wouldn't you like to know?' Sylvia pouted at him.

She was not supposed to smile. *I never smile for free*, Loveness always said. *No smiles until he buys me a drink.* The man laughed and went ahead and told her his name, then where he was from. He bought her a drink, then another. After two more hours of pouting and drinking and eventually not just smiling but laughing, Sylvia found herself stumbling along a corridor, her shoulder glancing off walls rocky with framed paintings. The grey-haired *muzungu* (Dutch? Danish?) walked ahead, intermittently turning back to wave her on with a beer bottle.

He closed the door to his hotel room behind them, pulled her into a hug, and said, 'Hello,' as if they had not already greeted. She extricated herself and stepped further into the room, which was clammy with air conditioning. She sat on the bed, took off her shoes and her skirt, and stretched back. The bed was like a bowl of *vitumbua* dough, soft and firm and creamy. She hadn't slept in a bed since she'd been kicked out of Aunty Cookie's flat, and she'd never slept in one like this. The man knelt over her on it and began fumbling his mouth over her skin, using his fingers to tug at her plaits and her nipples and her panties, as if they were all the same sort of object.

When he finally put his thing inside her, it hurt but not as much as Loveness had said it would. Sylvia turned her head away from his astringent breath, wondering whether sex had been painful for Loveness when her uncle had first 'started' her. Sylvia closed her eyes and tried to picture the big fat man bouncing on top of the skinny little girl – Loveness before she was Loveness. Was she in the middle of doing this exact thing, at this very moment, across the road at the Pamodzi? At the thought, Sylvia felt a purring heat inside the pain below ... The Danish-Dutchman interrupted her by cramming two crooked fingers into her mouth. Did this count as kissing? She wasn't supposed to kiss customers. Sylvia decided that it didn't and remembered to make some noises. The man responded immediately – bucked hard once, twice, stopped.

There was a strained silence as he rolled off her and reached for a pack of cigarettes on the nightstand. Sylvia asked him for one and he lit it for her. She sucked gently to draw the ember to life, then lay back on the damp pillow, trying to recall the price she had whispered in his ear at the bar. The exact centre of her body was ringing with a stinging, smarting sweetness. She was still drunk – a corner of the ceiling dove repeatedly, in a loop. She felt a double feeling: she missed her friend and she hated her friend. Sylvia took another drag, held the smoke in her mouth, then inhaled until her lungs burned.

'Vhut is your name again?' asked the Danish-Dutchman.

'Loveness,' she exhaled just as the buzz swarmed in.

2007

Back when Lusaka was a dusty old town, before it became the capital city, propeller planes would stutter down the dirt runway at City Airport, bearing expats and dry goods into the country. After Independence, after the big international airport was built 25 kilometres east, the Zambian Air Force took over the old runway, and now only the rich and powerful landed their private planes at City Airport: soldiers, industrialists, bankers, politicians.

Government built a fence around the perimeter and sprinkled some seeds at its base. Over time, bougainvillea spread along the wire mesh, dabbing like a paintbrush on canvas until the fence was a messy wall of green and pink. It shielded the wealthy and the foreign from having to see the local destitution across the road in Kalingalinga compound. For their part, the compound mothers forbade their children from going anywhere near those fences. 'Who knows what those rich people are tossing?' The *bazungu* especially, so temperamentally irritable, so red in the face for nothing, seemed capable of dropping anything out of the windows: books, diseases, car parts, bottles, cutlery, their own bodies even. But fences can rise only so high. People in the sky could see Kalingalinga from above – the roofs of shacks weave such a pretty patchwork! – and people on the ground could gaze up at the big silverbellied creatures flying overhead.

As soon as the compound kids heard a roaring in the distance or felt vibrations in the ground, they would start running. 'TEKAS TO AMELIKA! TEKAS TO AMELIKA!' they would shout up at the plane as it buzzed above them. They would try out flight themselves, outstretched arms tilting to imitate a shaky lift-off, noses humming to make engine noises. They would run in a horde, throw their palms onto the ground and flip over, their thudding feet like a giant thrumming its fingers. Yes, all the Kalingalinga kids loved aeroplanes, but only Sylvia Mwamba's son was obsessed with them. Long after the plane had passed and the other kids had moved on, Jacob alone would sit cross-legged, ground-bound, looking up.

※

Every day, the compound kids who didn't go to *sukulu* followed the pattern of the rich in cities: they started off in the centre but, eventually, the promise of freedom and wider spaces had them moving towards the outskirts. That's how, one afternoon, Jacob found himself with a group of six boys, walking beside the *verboten* airport fence. The boys were chatting about the electric pulse that supposedly throbbed through it now to keep them out. Mabvuto, the eldest, witty enough to appreciate the irony of his 'Kiss Me, I'm Irish' shirt, said this had to be a rumour. Who would bother making an electric fence in Lusaka?

He reached out to touch it, then began thrashing around wildly. 'Zzz-zzzz! Aahhh! Aaahh!' He paused and patted the leafy fence dramatically. 'Ah?'

'PAWA CAT!' the other boys shouted and laughed.

Power cut or no, the fence was clearly safe enough to climb. Mabvuto hoisted himself up one of its metal poles. He didn't get far – the peeling white paint got under his nails and there was razor wire at the top – but he got a glimpse of the airport grounds before he dropped down.

'There is construction just there!' he exclaimed as he healed the leprosy of paint on his thighs with picking fingers. 'There are materials!'

The boys' eyes sparked entrepreneurially. They often scavenged in the dump to find scraps to sell to Kalingalinga residents looking to add a new roof or wing to their homes.

'But we cannot go in there!'

'How can we even cross the razor wire?'

'I know a way in,' Jacob said, his voice dropping like a stone into their excitable chatter.

The other boys glanced around at each other daringly. Mabvuto gave an authoritative nod, as if this was all his idea, and off they went. Jacob led them along the fence to a tree that had grown enmeshed with its metal loops. The tree's crown barely crested the fence but its roots, in their tumbling sprawl, had partially unearthed the base. Jacob had tried in vain to wrench the warped weave back by himself last week. Now, six pairs of hands finished the job and six pairs of legs wriggled through into the airport grounds.

A few metres away they could see an entrance road, a straight grey bridge over a yellowbrown sea of grass. Just beyond it were the materials Mabvuto had spotted. In the distance gleamed the tarmac runway where, they knew, aeroplanes dozed and landed and, astoundingly, took off. But between there and here was a roadblock: a metal bar with red and white diagonal stripes lay across the road, supported by squat pillars. There was no way to skirt that bar or hop the fence on either side of it – there were two guards sitting outside a hut, monitoring it. They wore green uniforms and knee-high boots, and casually propped beside one, and over the lap of the other, were big black rifles.

The boys approached cautiously, crawling in a ditch beside the road. Shading their eyes, they saw a red sedan drive up the entrance road and slow to a stop. One of the guards sauntered over to it, gun swaying from his shoulder strap. He scanned the sky as if rereading protocol, then leaned down to talk to the driver. The *muzungu* passenger closer to the boys looked out of her window but did not seem to notice the crop of brown heads in the ditch. She turned back to face forward and suddenly Jacob was running. *Chipolopolo!* Fast as a copper bullet.

In seconds, he was squatting under the car's back window, as if he'd mushroomed from its side panel. His friends could see the white woman's profile, chin lifted, her skin blue inside the car. Below it was Jacob's profile, chin tucked to his chest, his skin metallic in the sun. He was hidden from the guard, but the boys stirred uneasily at the thought of angry *bazungu*, an angrier *muntu*, plus a car, plus a gun. The guard stepped away and raised the candycane bar. The car pulled forward, a parasitic Jacob clinging to its side. Still hunched over, he broke into a trot as the car accelerated, then darted behind a bush on the other side of the roadblock. The car sped on. The guard went back to his post.

In their ditch, the boys whispered their boasts. Each boy claimed he would be the next to try Jacob's trick. They were just waiting for a bigger vehicle to hide behind. A Land Rover, maybe. Or a lorry.

✳

Jacob raced on, his head down. He kept to the side of the road, looking for a safe place to stop. The sun was simmering like a coppery soup, the trails of woodsmoke like its steam in the distance. His panting breath competed with his thudding feet and the creaking chorus of crickets in the grass until all sound was engulfed by a roaring deluge from above. He froze and looked up but he couldn't see the plane. He headed in the direction of its rushing sound.

At each step through the sea of yellow grass, the crickets sprang forward in overlapping arcs, reminding him of drops splashing from a puddle. Furry whips of grass lashed at his legs, embedding seeds in his skin, like the worms that burrowed into his feet and that his mother plucked out with tweezers. Would she be worried? She didn't pay much mind to his whereabouts these days but he'd never strayed this far from home. Jacob was just considering turning back when he caught sight of the monstropolous beast.

He slowed and crept up to it. Its gargantuan nose, an orange cone with a black tip, pointed down like it was sniffing the ground. Above the nose were four square eyes, one intact but clouded with sunset sky, the other three empty. As he neared, one of those blank eyes gained sight: a black oval appeared, balanced on its bottom edge. The eye blinked and the oval vanished – it was a crow. Jacob tracked it as it took flight, beating its wings up and up, going from a splotch to a cross to a speck to nothing. Then he turned back to the beast that it had fled.

It was a wreck. Not the whole aeroplane, just the cockpit. The body and wings must have been cleared away already. The grass around the plane was short and black and stubbly. Jacob stepped carefully over it, picking through ruptured, melted metal, burnt seats, white stuffing, fragments of plastic, a plastic pamphlet. He found a blue seat belt with a silver buckle, which he tied around his waist. He was strong and limber for a ten-year-old, but he slid down several times before he managed to scale the nose. Finally, he smeared spit and dirt on his feet for grip, backed up to get a running start, and dashed up the incline. Just as he was about to slip off again, he grabbed the frame of a broken window. 'Tchah,' he winced as the glass cut his palm, but he kept his grip and clambered gingerly inside.

The floor of the cockpit was a nest of grass and wire and glass. There were dirty puddles and green and white bird droppings everywhere and a blue curtain fluttered in the back. The pilot chairs sat like thrones before the array of buttons on the console. Jacob sat in one, damp seeping into his shorts, the cuts in his palm whistling with pain. He looked straight ahead, surveying the land before him and the sky above. The sun had been swallowed by the ground but its last gasps of light were turning the clouds a neon pink. Jacob tapped at some crudded buttons, pulled at a rusted lever, and roared ...

An echo from below: a shout. Jacob stood and looked down. Two men stood in the black grass underneath, looking up at him grimly. One of them was pointing a gun.

⁕

Dr Lee Banda got tangled up with the missing boys by accident. He had stopped by the Kalingalinga clinic to see to an infected mother whose infant had croup. Lee showed her how to feed the baby with the dexamethasone syrup, angling the spoon past the lagoon of saliva-snot around its mouth. Lee fought the urge to wipe the baby's face – Musadabwe had scolded him fiercely the last time he had shamed a mother this way. Instead, Lee turned to the patient and asked after her older son, who was Virus-negative but had looked malnourished the last time Lee had seen him.

'Mabvuto? Ah, who knows?' the woman said sadly, then went on to complain. 'He acts up when he is not at *sukulu*. He runs around! How would it be if only I had money for the school fees?'

The baby barked softly in commiseration. The question the woman was asking had an answer – it was in Lee's pocket. Out of a misplaced sense of indignation, he offered a different one: 'Why don't I go and look for Mabvuto and bring him home in time for supper?'

'Oh-*oh*? Okay, thank you please,' his patient replied with dull eyes.

He left her soon after and walked around the compound, making a survey of the place – the church, the woodyards, the dump – but there was no sign of Mabvuto. Lee was walking back to his pickup, resigned to doling out charity money to his patient, when he came across a circle of worried mothers. Their boys were missing too. Mabvuto was no doubt among them. They directed Lee to the airport, the source of all their fears, and the likeliest temptation for the boys.

Lee's triumph at finding the runaways in a ditch on the side of the entrance road into the airport wilted the moment he learned that one was still missing – the boy had somehow jumped the roadblock. Lee put his hands on his hips and scrutinised the sky. It looked like tea-time and his stomach thought so too. He was beginning to wish that he had paid his Hippocratic tax and been done with it. To save time, he stashed the other boys in the bed of his pickup and drove to the security hut. He leaned his head out of his window and grinned. The guards remained unamused until he obliquely offered them a bribe and even then, one of them insisted on accompanying him.

The sun was setting and Lee's indignation with Mabvuto's mother had festered into irritation – the low crackling burn that regret kindles – by the time they found the boy inside the aeroplane wreck. There was nevertheless some pleasure to the finding. *Cotched!* Lee thought. That was what he and his friends had said back in the day at Falcon, with that double glee of the hunter and the snitch. Just then, out of the corner of his eye, Lee saw the guard raise the gun.

'Hey, hey, he's just a kid, man,' he frowned, reaching out and pulling the barrel down.

The boy skittered down the nose of the plane and slunk up to them. He wore what looked like a seat belt low on his hips, but he was otherwise empty-handed. He had a quiet intensity about him. Lee and the guard walked him between them to the pickup, where he climbed in the bed with the others. Lee drove back to the roadblock, where he dropped off the guard, resorting to another bribe to prevent what would no doubt have been a pointless, bullying interrogation.

Lee drove out of the airport and directly into the compound, leaving dust and curiosity in his wake. As soon as he braked, the boys leapt out of the back. But before they could run off, they were swarmed by gloating good girls, who began wringing their hands so the index finger snapped the knuckles, chanting: '*Halifogali*, nevah said a sorree, jumped in a lorree ...' Weary as an embattled soldier, burdened with his own good deeds, Lee pushed his way through the crowd of compound dwellers. He walked each of the boys to their respective homes, staving off rewards of tea and beer from their poor, grateful mothers.

✳

Lee dropped off the one who had found the crashed plane last. The boy led him to a one-storey building painted in coral pink, with 'HI-FLY HAIRCUTTERY & DESIGNS LTD' in big green letters on the facade. Beneath the sign was a list of services and prices offered.

A series of severed heads demonstrated the patterns you could have your hair plaited into: S's and X's, cul-de-sacs and labyrinths, exclamation points and question marks, hedgehogs and horns, antlers and antennae. An English garden of possibilities, Lee's mother would have said. Lee walked up the short set of steps ahead of the boy and knocked on the wooden door.

A woman – young, pretty – opened it, tightening her *chitenge* at her waist. It was patterned with tea kettles, as was the *chitambala* tied casually around her head.

'*Bwanji?* Can I help you?' she asked.

'*Bwino, bwanji?* Does this belong to you?'

He pulled her son from behind his back, gripping him by the head. Lee was pleased to note that the boy's skull fit within the span of his palm. But the woman, still leaning against the doorjamb, did not seem impressed or even surprised to see her son. She remained motionless but for a slight lift of her eyebrow. 'And where have you been?' she asked.

Was she talking to him or to her son? Lee and the boy looked at each other.

'Hmp,' she said. They looked back at her. Lee saw now that she was, in fact, neither young nor pretty. She was in her thirties and beautiful. Indeed, her beauty had reached its richest hour. Her upper lip was two soft hills, her lower lip their reflection in a lake, blurry along the bottom edge.

'Go inside,' she said, pulling the boy to her and then patting his buttocks to embarrass him in. She turned back to Lee.

'I know you,' she said, tilting her head musingly.

'No, you don't,' he laughed.

'Yes. Actually. I do,' she said matter-of-factly, her head slowly traversing ninety degrees until it was tilted the other way. The breeze picked up. Litter fluttered against Lee's ankles.

'How?' he asked.

'We had sex. On your birthday.'

Lee chuckled and told her exactly how impossible that was, turning the back of his hand towards her to show his wedding ring. She lifted her eyebrow a millimetre higher.

'It was some time ago,' she said. 'Maybe ten years.'

'Well. If it happened, I must have been cut.'

'Oh, thank you. Very flattering.'

'No, that's not what I – I mean, I don't recognise your face, so I must have been—'

'Maybe you would recognise other parts.' Laughter glimmered in her eyes, but the rest of her face was as placid as a gazelle's.

'You're very forward, you know,' Lee said. 'You've got no brakes.'

'And what is the point of brakes if you do not have petrol to drive?'

'What?' Lee sputtered, struggling to keep up.

'Shame. You've forgotten paying me as well?' The woman shut the door in his face.

Lee closed his mouth. He slowly turned around. He stared at the spot in the sky where the sun had burnt out, slate clouds drifting there like ash. He rifled through memories of nights out on the town: him and his *butahs*, slapping hands, slapping car bonnets, slapping asses. He tried the files from both clinics – the old one and the new one here in Kalingalinga – the nurses and the cleaners, the Virus patients and their morose daughters. But still he could not find her.

A breeze dragged the smell of rubbish into his nostrils. Lee thought of his wife. Across the compound, women were clapping and singing a hymn. Lee thought of his work. Flies buzzed around him, black bits of life rebounding off the invisible planes of the air. A bicycle bell rang halfway, closer to a click than a ring. Lee turned back to the door of the salon and knocked again.

Once Sylvia had forced Loveness's hand and proven herself capable of withstanding the trade and its occasional brutalities, the two women had joined forces. For years, they'd worked the high-end hotels together: Ridgeway, Pamodzi, Intercon. When their faces had become too familiar, too *faded*, they'd shifted to less fancy places – Ndeke, Chachacha Backpackers. Once they had run even these tourist hubs dry, they'd decided that their best bet was to catch the *apamwamba* as they flew in and out of the country. So despite Sylvia's reluctance to move back to a compound, one where her mother lived, no less, she and Loveness had chosen to land in Kalingalinga, across from City Airport. And with the help of an unexpected patron, they had finally opened their hair salon.

Hi-Fly Haircuttery & Designs Ltd was essentially one large room, a *chitenge* curtain hanging across it to set off a private area in the back where Sylvia and her son Jacob slept. In the front, the salon girls blow-dried and hotcombed and slathered lye on recalcitrant kink. They held lighters to the ends of braided wig extensions to keep them from unravelling, rolling them between spit-dampened fingers. The whole place reeked of burning – electrical, frictional, chemical – Sylvia's girls sifting varieties of incineration as indifferently as demon drones in hell. There were usually five or six of them in rotation – Loveness had an itchy firing finger – but there always seemed to be more, as if multiplied by the mirror that took up one wall of the salon. The customers would sit before it and the girls would stand behind them facing the mirror, chatting to them – strange conversations where you lock eyes with someone with her back to you.

Jacob's punishment for his airport excursion was to stay in the salon, all day, every day, 'helping out'. This was a torture to a boy built for roaming. Grounded, he sat in a corner watching sulkily as the girls cultivated their hairy crops, carving scalps into neat *mukule* rows and shelling beads from braids. The girls barely noticed him. Jacob was just the boss's son, courier of tools and creams and the fuel of their labour – endless cups of tea. The girls danced to the radio, showed each other their new panties, freely discussed their periods and lovers, giggled at dirty jokes over his head.

Jacob liked the washing days better. In the yard behind the hair salon, under the jacaranda tree he sometimes climbed, the girls would set out the metal tubs, fill them up and do the washing together. Church and radio songs bounced around the air, notes like motes. Brown fingers sloshed about in the frothy water. There were always several mumbly conversations going between the girls, who stored wooden pegs between their teeth as they pinned clothes to the line. Jacob loved those pegs, their carved rivets, the mechanics of their snap and hold. He'd clip his lips shut with them and waddle around like a duck, to make the girls laugh, to make his mother notice.

'Too nice,' she would chuckle. 'A child that shooshes itself? I should have named you Chongo!' Then she would kiss his head and go and stand next to Aunty Loveness, lean against her, their fingers linked like children.

Yes, at Hi-Fly Haircuttery & Designs Ltd, Jacob was around many people, but not necessarily with them. This was one kind of loneliness. The other kind came at night, when his mother was out with Aunty Loveness. Jacob would drag the dry linens off the line and press them with the hot iron that had given off an eggy smell ever since he took it apart to see how it worked. He would fold alone, pinning sheets to his chest with his chin, draping them over his forearms, hands moving together and apart like ground control for air traffic.

✳

Lee Banda had always been beautiful. It was clear even in his baby pictures, where his lashes curled more voluptuously than his mother's. This beauty meant that Lee knew himself only through other people, who held up mirrors to him, different ones depending on the person. Women on the street wore their mirrors in their eyes and shiny teeth: *Pretty man. Chops. Fit.* His guy friends carried mirrors in shades of envious green. His father's mirror was cloudy, his mother's a sheer plane of gold. His son's mirror reflected his body parts in gargantuan proportion: shoulders beyond the frame, a bulbous Adam's apple, massive thighs on either side of an equine member. His wife's mirror reflected him exactly as he was.

Only the mirror that Sylvia Mwamba carried was in motion: it spun around in her long fingers, alternating images of his naked body and hers so rapidly that they seemed to merge together like a Kenyan sculpture or a Picasso painting: his eyes above her nose, her breast bulging from his stomach, his toe protruding from her vagina, a perverse quadralabial mouth. It was not beautiful, this image of their mating, but it was the picture of himself that most fascinated Lee, perhaps because it had not yet taken place. Or had it? He had mulled over that first alleged encounter between them. He had checked his records and found nothing. Maybe if they had sex now, it would come back to him, like when you retrace your steps to find a lost thing. But Sylvia was making him wait.

One time, he thought he remembered it. On a visit to the salon to scope out test subjects, he had lit a cigarette and she'd scolded him.

'You are busy burning fake hair, why can't I burn nature's leaves?'

'Do you not see these wigs on display? I cannot be selling hair that smells like old men.'

'I'm not old,' Lee huffed. He was thirty-one.

'You're not young, either.'

'You're six years older than me!'

'That's not the point. *Saat*. Put it out.' She sucked her teeth and walked off.

'Sylvia!' Lee called her back to the argument.

Still moving away, she glanced over her shoulder and answered vaguely: '*Anh?*' And in that moment, Lee felt he recognised her. Not from these past few months – not from his visits to the salon, their rendezvous at the shebeen, their lunch dates at Chicken Inn. No, Lee felt he recognised her from before. Behind that vision of a retreating shape, calling to him as a child might, was a memory. Of the first time they'd had sex? Ten years ago, on his birthday, as she claimed? Maybe it *had* happened – that difficult year before his wedding had been a druggy blur. Maybe it was déjà vu. Either way, it changed shape as soon as he grabbed it, like one of the morphing stone animals from his dreams.

Lee Banda was not a man to be swayed by visions. He needed subjects for his lab and Sylvia would give him access – her salon was clearly a front for a brothel. These were precisely the women who might have the genetic mutation he sought. As he courted her, he took samples from her and her girls, and sent them off to be tested. And in the end, he found his holy grail – not just one mutation but two. The instinct that had made him turn around and knock at her door had proven correct. Now he was getting impatient. Sylvia said *anh?* like a child, yes, but not an obedient one. She was the kind of child that says *no* just to say *no*, to suck on the word like a lemon drop.

*

Sylvia wanted to say yes, but she delayed. Holding it over Lee, out of reach, stirred a swarm of power in her. Despite his obvious desire for her, that sprung arrow thrusting towards her, Lee was not just another customer. He was a fancy, rich doctor. A real prize. And not easy to win. His marriage seemed unhappy but unassailable. He loved his children at home so much he even brought one of them to the salon sometimes, a sallow boy of about nine. Joseph always sat in a corner, as far away as possible from Jacob. The two boys were cagey around one another, as if each begged the question of the other.

Things had slipped many times during Sylvia's career – her resolve, her guard, the condom. Ten years ago, the police had again started cracking down on 'unaccompanied women' in the hotels. Loveness had fled east to work at a cousin's bar in Chipata. Alone in Lusaka, Sylvia had neglected herself, working only when she felt like it, and in a haze of alcohol. She remembered Lee, though. He'd been with a bunch of coloured med students at a bachelors' party at the Ridgeway – a sloppy night, everyone drunk and handsy.

There had been other men that night, that week. It didn't matter. Sylvia knew she just had to plant the seed of possibility in Lee's mind and see what sprouted. Clients had made propositions to her before, all with that temporary, almost impersonal passion that possesses men when they're fucking. But it would take a snare of a less obvious kind to capture Lee. So Sylvia stalled, holding just out of his reach something he believed he'd already had.

She knew he was hooked when, one day at the Hi-Fly, he confessed something seemingly insignificant to her, a trivial thing really. Sylvia was washing a customer's hair. Lee was sitting in a chair tipped back against the wall, smoking, his legs stretched out so that she had to step over them whenever she reached for the hose. Every time she passed, he grabbed at her with his free hand, and she flung droplets in his face. The customer kept sighing and complaining that the rim of the bucket of water was digging into the back of her neck. Sylvia didn't care. Her thighs were wet, her cheeks sore with smiling. She felt like a young girl again.

'You know, Silly,' Lee said, 'I have to tell you this story about my wife—'

'Heysh!' Sylvia glared at him.

The customer raised her head, her look somewhere between mortified and mortifying. Sylvia murmured a reassurance and pushed her head gently back over the edge of the bucket.

'A couple years ago,' Lee went on, 'my wife had this rotten tooth. It was *bad*. You could smell it on her breath.' He shuddered and took a drag of his cigarette. 'She had it pulled—' Here Lee became so overcome with laughter he couldn't speak, spurts of smoke puffing from his nostrils, ash raining over everything. 'So now,' Lee chuckled and wheezed, 'now all her other teeth are starting to shift! And she has a gap in the front.' He dissolved again into laughter, tears bejewelling his lashes. The customer shook her head subtly.

'*Ah-ah*, that's your story?' Sylvia snapped. 'Rubbish, that's not even funny.'

'But you, my *dahrring*,' he swiped at her bum and she swivelled her hips out of reach, 'you have beautiful straight teeth. Shiny and white. No gaps!'

Sylvia sprang water at him with her manicured nails. 'Ach, stupit,' she said softly.

But that evening, as she closed up the salon while Lee waited outside in his pickup, Sylvia caught a glimpse of her face. It was dark inside but for scattered glints across the room from the pickup's headlights. She stepped towards the mirrored wall into a sliver of light and gingerly lifted her upper lip. It was neither a smile nor a grimace. She looked coolly at her perfect teeth. Lee honked the horn and started a round of compound dogs barking. She let her lip drop. Her left eye quivered. She watched herself decide.

✳

To Jacob, the Hi-Fly often felt like a ship floating on a lake of boredom, its crew shifting about restlessly. The day wove and unwove itself across the salon in rays of light and shadow as the girls plaited and unplaited their own hair to pass the time. Any customer at all was welcomed in with giddy relief, especially the old white woman, Ba Sibilla. Every few weeks, she crouched in through the doorway, covered in a hijab's worth of shawls, and one of the girls would rush off to fetch the boss. Mummy would hasten in to give Ba Sibilla a queen's welcome, placing a stool for her feet, fixing her a cup of rooibos, radiating grace while Aunty Loveness sent the other customers grumbling away, their hair in various states of disarray.

As soon as the salon was empty, the girls would gather around and unveil Ba Sibilla, revealing the long white hair stringing down her body like a Nyau dancer's raffia. The girls would grease her hair with the special olive oil she always brought with her and pull combs through it until it was a smooth, silvery sheet cascading over her. Mummy would carefully cut it, leaving wavy piles on the floor. When she was done, Ba Sibilla, a tiny creature without her hair, would shake herself off, wrap herself up, and make her exit.

Jacob sometimes helped the girls gather up the hair on the floor and carry it out to the yard behind the salon to distribute between three big buckets. Mummy would come out with her precious hair-dye kits, Clairol and Crème of Nature, black-market boxes with battered corners. She would pour the chemicals with their searing smell into the buckets, one for each colour: brown, red, yellow. Wearing thin plastic gloves, the salon girls would stir the hair with the dye for ten minutes, rinse it, then string it on the clothes line to dry. The next day, Jacob would wake to find it already wrapped in plastic for sale on the counter.

*

At first Sylvia was irritated by the way Lee clambered onto her like a boy, his fingers and tongue jabbing. But as soon as they were both naked and his erection made him serious, she loved him. She loved his worried face hanging over her, his frown lines twitching, his eyes elsewhere but somehow still present, his body fraught as he moved in and out of her. Tricking him with delay, she had tricked herself – the relenting was too sweet. It overwhelmed her with a feeling she'd never had before with a man: mutual desire. This sex-love spilled over to afterwards, when Lee became like a boy again – his damp head on her sternum, his lips parted and wet on her breast.

She let him sleep for a while. Then she carefully extricated herself from under him, replacing herself with a pillow, and tiptoed over to the dressing table. They were at his house in Thorn Park, in the master bedroom, his wife away with their son on a trip to Harare. Mrs Banda's smell still hovered over this part of the room, a sugary musk, and the makings of beauty were laid out on her dressing table: bottles of foundation, a smidge lighter than the one Sylvia used on her own bleached skin; tubes of lipstick, pinker than the ones Sylvia used; mascara and eye make-up in green shades that would never work on Sylvia's skin. Sylvia plonked herself naked in the dressing chair, pleased to feel Lee's semen seeping out of her into the cushion. She rolled her hand over the tubes and bottles on the table, stirring them out of place.

In one corner, a red wig sat on a styrofoam head. A child's hand had defaced the bust – it was pitted with bitty holes and graffitied with a felt-tip. Sylvia pulled her own plaits forward, feeling their brittle tug on her scalp, and ran her hand over the thin silky ropes. She had always assumed that Lee's coloured wife would wear natural curls or maybe the straight perms that were so popular these days. It appeared that Lee's two women had this in common – hair like a pet that you buy and groom and comb. Sylvia reached out to finger Mrs Banda's wig and saw the reflection of the man in bed behind her. Lee's eyes were open. She gazed at his face in the mirror, at her own face, at their reflections above the clutter of make-up. They were both so beautiful. How strange that such love should be born in the midst of such trifles.

※

When a real man walked into the Hi-Fly with whichever *galifriend* he was treating to a hairdo that day, the salon girls turned sweet and fey, cooing softly as Mr Mistah handed the cash over to Loveness. Of course, as soon as he went to wait at the shebeen next door, Miss Galifriend became just another head, pulled this way and that. Teeth were sucked, eyebrows raised over the negritude of her hair. Her head was subjected to a swarm of fingers like brown mice nibbling at her scalp. By the time Mr Mistah got back, reeking of beer, Miss Galifriend was exhausted, eyes dazed under a shiny forehead. The girls chimed sugary praises.

'Now you see, she has hair that talks! *Ati zee-zee-zee . . .*'

Miss Galifriend tossed her head feebly to swish the fine, straight strands, hers or someone else's.

'Me, mine is KWY-YET,' Mr Mistah said, patting the archipelago of baldness on his crown. 'Instead of *zee-zee-zee*, it just says *Zee*. Nothing!'

The girls fluttered and tinkled. Jacob seethed in his corner, wanting to burn it all down. The only other person who received such treatment was Uncle Lee. With his bold jaw and muscles like snakes twining his bones, Uncle Lee would swing his enormous presence into the salon, trailed by the scent of expensive aftershave. He'd kiss Jacob's mother on the top of her head. Then he'd sit with legs sprawled and regale them with stories of Jo'burg and Addis and Nairobi – the places his work as a doctor had taken him – or enquire about the salon girls, their 'habits', mostly.

Jacob's mother gave curt answers to his questions but the corners of her mouth betrayed her. She let him swab her workers' cheeks once, the girls giggling awkwardly around the long Q-Tips. Jacob had participated too, just to have something to do. Uncle Lee sometimes brought his son with him, a skinny coloured boy named Joseph, who sat in a corner, reading a book, wrinkling his nose at the smells in the salon. Jacob wrinkled his nose back, at the book. Bored as he was, he refused to play with that *apamwamba* boy, and he did not take kindly to another competitor for his mother's attention.

✳

A few months into their affair, Lee's head between Sylvia's breasts, he turned his head up to her and asked about her mother's condition. Perhaps because he was a doctor, he always asked after people's health – her son's, Loveness's, the girls'. He had even brought a needle to one of their early dates at Chicken Inn. A vaccination, he had said, though it seemed like he was drawing blood rather than dispensing medicine. An odd 'gift', but Sylvia had just chalked it up to the ways that men expressed affection to women like her – always a little protective, always a little violent. She was surprised to hear that Lee knew about her mother's crying, though. It turned out he had heard about it from Joseph, who had heard about it from Jacob.

'Jacob?' she frowned. 'He doesn't know about my mother. They've never met.'

'So she cries constantly? She has depression?'

'Ah! No. That's just what you Westernised doctors like to think.' She pinched his arm.

'Ow!' he flinched, grinning. 'I *actually* think she has an autoimmune disorder.'

'Auto-*what*?'

'Autoimmunity. It's when the system that protects the body turns against it, attacks it. Tears wash out foreign bodies – like dirt – from the eye but it can go too far. Your mother's condition might be due to genetic abnormalities—'

'Ya,' she said coldly. 'She's even blind from this disease. But it's just – she *chose* that.'

Lee's complicated words always made Sylvia feel bad about not finishing school. She stared at his arm where she'd pinched him. His skin was so light that she had left red marks. She felt self-conscious about the skin-lightening cream she had been using for years on her face and neck and arms. Those parts of her body were taupe, but all the rest was brown, the contrast as sharp as tea with and without milk.

'You're saying the heartbreak queen of Kalingalinga is faking it? Crying on cue?'

'Ha! You should go and tell her that,' Sylvia laughed. 'Loveness says that if you are going to insult your *mamafyala*, you may as well go all the way and just kill her.'

'Well, she's not my mother-in—' He stopped.

Sylvia cut her eyes at him. Lee reached over and stroked her breast, as if to soften what he'd said, to persuade her that it was in fact a good thing that Matha Mwamba was not his mother-in-law.

'She was never a mother to me anyway.' She faked a yawn. 'Why do you care about her crying?'

'I don't.' Lee put his hands behind his head, his elbows winging his thick skull. 'I care about *you* and it's possible that you inherited something from her.'

Sylvia rolled onto her side away from him. She wasn't like her mother. She had no auto-tears to give. She had never cried for a man, not once, not even when they had broken her heart, her bones, her spirit. Cha! Occupational hazards! Sylvia was feeling ready to retire. Her whole life had been preparing her for Lee: someone who would take care of her ...

'And Loveness?' Lee startled her from her musings.

'*Anh*?' she said mechanically, looking over her shoulder at him. Then she remembered that she had never used her 'professional' name with him – he was referring to her friend. 'What about Loveness?'

'You know that she has The Virus as well?'

She frowned. 'What virus?' she asked, though of course she already knew.

✳

At Hi-Fly Haircuttery & Designs Ltd, time was ticking away under the tapping of fingernails on the countertop. The girls were sitting on the floor scratching dandruff out of each other's hair. There was a low sizzling from the corner – Jacob was trying to fix an electric fan he had found in the dump. A plump coloured woman walked in, wearing heels and a skirt suit, and carrying an expensive handbag. Her face was fully made up, her auburn bob so shiny it was like a polished bowl. She stood at the threshold of the salon, blinking.

'Would Madam like a perm today?'

'*Mm,*' said the woman. 'I want the boss.' Her tongue slithered over the word – she had a slight lisp.

The salon girls glanced at each other. Aunty Loveness shouted to Jacob in the corner:

'*Iwe,* get your mother.'

He stood up from his project reluctantly and ducked behind the *chitenge* to the back of the salon. The customer stepped deeper inside but a shadow remained behind her – there was someone with her, a boy. The girls raised their eyebrows – it was the son of Sylvia's dude, Lee. Joseph looked even sulkier than usual, his eyes on his green trainers as he dragged his feet over to a corner to sit. Sylvia flung the back curtain aside and stomped barefoot into the salon, knotting her *chitenge* under her armpits.

She had been out late last night drinking heavily with Lee and his colleague, Dr Musadabwe, celebrating some new discovery of theirs. She had spent all morning in bed behind the back curtain, sipping at water with Eno and Disprin dissolved in it, and thought she had made it clear to everyone that she did not wish to be disturbed.

'You cannot tell people that I'm bathing?' she groused at Loveness, then turned and shouted to Jacob in the back. 'The water will get cold, just drain it.'

She marched over to stand behind the customer, who was now seated before the mirror.

'I am the boss here. My name is Sylvia Mwamba. But my girls are very good, Madam,' she said to the customer's image. 'You do not need special services from me—' Sylvia stopped. She had noticed the reflection of Joseph sitting in the corner behind them.

'I'd like—' Lee's wife croaked. She cleared her throat. 'I'd like a relaxer, please.'

Sylvia swallowed and nodded. Mrs Banda removed her auburn wig as gracefully as possible, revealing a reddish afro underneath. Loveness stepped forward to take the wig and stretch it over a wire bust to keep its shape. When Sylvia looked up from the terrain of kink to be conquered and saw that copper helmet sitting on the stand, she blinked for a moment. She reached under her own *chitambala* and scratched. Then she called for Jacob, still in the back, to bring a box of Dark & Lovely relaxer from the stash there.

After a moment, he came in with it, wearing the exasperated look of a child who has been given too many instructions in a row. His eyes immediately found Joseph, who had started picking through the entrails of the electric fan that Jacob had been trying to fix.

'*Futsek, iwe!*' Jacob seethed as if Joseph were a dog.

'Go outside with that boy and play,' said Loveness. Jacob's eyes bulged and he started to protest. Sylvia cut him short with a look as she struggled thin plastic gloves over her fingers.

'It's okay, baby,' Mrs Banda said to Joseph. 'Go on and play.'

Jacob turned with disgust and swept through the curtain to the back, where there was a door leading to the yard behind the salon. Joseph followed, his feet dragging.

Sylvia gave Mrs Banda a tight smile – solidarity in motherhood at least – and began parting the reddish afro in horizontal lines from ear to ear. After the harrowing of those trenches came the dabbing of cool white fire into them, then the gentle combing to spread the chemical agent across the battlefield. Mrs Banda closed her eyes. Sylvia did her job. Loveness counted kwacha. The salon girls stood in a cluster across the room, watching and whispering, classing and contrasting.

This one even has green eyes. *Iye.* But look at how big the other one's eyes are. And the eyelashes? Maybe she *is* Maybelline! *Kikiki!* You people, light is right. *Ah-ah,* but they are the same colour! Almost, yes, but Ambi-light and coloured-light are different, *mwandi.* Nooo!

Same-same. Ambi it works very well. It means Africans May Be Interested. *Hehehe!* But on Bana Joseph, you can see *tuma* dot-dot-dots like a *muzungu*. Fleckos? Me, I think she just has too much face. Mm*hm*, and with those skinny lips. Did you see the gap in the teeth? Bana Jacob has such a nice figure. This other one is fat. But look at her high heels, they are very spesho and ...

And so it went, the salon girls trying to solve the mystery of a cheating man by trying to see with his split vision. Loveness finally disbanded their gossipy circle by snapping her fingers at them. They scattered about, attending to pointless tasks – polishing bottles, cleaning brushes. The room brimmed with silence. Even the two boys outside in the back were suspiciously quiet. When the lye was fully applied, Sylvia pulled a shower cap over Mrs Banda's whitesmeared hair and released its ruffled edge with a conclusive snap.

'Sylvia,' Mrs Banda began.

Everyone turned their eyes towards her.

'*Anh?*' Sylvia said, very quietly.

Just then, there was a commotion at the front door. Everyone turned their eyes towards it.

'*Odi?*' The greeting was muffled. A shadow crept over the threshold. 'Anyone home?' called the hairy white woman as she rustled into the Hi-Fly, holding a little brown girl by the hand.

WeeeeeweeeEEEEweeeeeeEEEeeeeeeEEEEEeeeeWEEEEEEeeeeeeEEEeeee. We.

On we drone, annoying on, ennuiing on with our wheedling onomato-
poeia. Udzudzu. Munyinyi. Vexatious pests! But better than your barking
with wet, pungent holes! We? We sing with our dry, beating wings. A plangent
vibration adrift in the air, a song as gracile as the swarm itself, our buoyant
undulant throng. Why do we sing? For love, naturally.

At dusk or at dawn – the tipping of the day – our males hover over a chimney or a steeple. Around this post, they form a grey haze, a swirling mass of
seduction. One by one, the females fly in, braving the entomological gauntlet.
With quickspinning wings, each strums a keen air as she swoops through the
chaos of men, and with their hairy antennae, they track her.

Then comes the chase, the grapple, the fall – you humans have these rituals,
too. The male on the bottom, the pair tightly lock, and after a minute or so,
they part ways. On occasion, her grip is too tight and he'll pay for a life with
his nethers! If he escapes unscathed, he'll do it again, six to eight times in his
lifespan. But the female is done now – she has loved and lost once – and she has
all that she needs for the breeding.

A puddle, a pond, a lake, a river: she moves over the face of the waters.
Hovering, she curtsies, and thrusts from her bottom a hundred fertilised eggs.
She dive-bombs the surface with babies-to-be until a battalion awaits there. She
gathers them into a small tapered craft, a canoe half the size of a rice grain.
Then with nary a glance, our mother departs, leaving us to hatch without her.

We are like Russian dolls of metamorphosis, each phase of us hatched
from the previous. Split the shell, breach the slit, then shed the old husk.
From egg to larva, the comma-shaped pupa, then the wingèd and wobbly
imago. Step onto the water with delicate feet. Pause as the soft spine stiffens.

Not too long! There are threats all around! It's a cesspool, this puddle of
Eden: birds and bacteria, fishes and ants, nematodes, whirligigs, lizards. One
of our species, Toxorhynchites – their larvae even eat one another.

Sylvia knows well, love can be hell: familial, romantic, maternal. Oh,
lovers are murder! They'll cast you aside, they'll run you out quick as
quicksilver!

Isabella

1984

Isabella was eleven years old before she learned that she was white – white in the sense of being a thing, as opposed to not being a thing. It wasn't that Isa didn't know that her parents were white. Of course with her mother, this was largely a matter of conjecture, as a layer of dark hair kept her face a mystery. Though as she aged, this blanket of hair would turn grey, then silver, then white, a definite movement towards translucence, Isa could never properly make out her mother's facial features. More distinct were her legs, the tufts of fur running like a mane down each thick shin, and her laugh like large sheets of paper being ripped, then crumpled. Isa's father, the Colonel, was white, but it often seemed more like pink and grey were battling it out on his face, especially when he was drunk.

Isa's parents had settled into life in Lusaka the way most expats do. They drank a lot. Every weekend was another house party, that never-ending house party that has been swatting mosquitoes and swimming in gin and quinine for more than a century. The Corsales hosted their sundowners at their one-storey bungalow in Longacres, under a veranda with generous shade. Isa's mother floated around in a billowy *boubou*, sending the servants for refills and dropping in on every conversation, distributing laughter and ease amongst her guests. Purple-skinned peanuts that had been soaked in salt water and roasted in a pan until they were grey cooled and shifted with a whispery sound in wooden bowls. There was soon a troop of Mosi beer bottles scattered around, marking the tables with their damp semicircular hoof prints. Full or empty? The amber glass was so dark, you had to lift each bottle to find out. Cigars and tobacco pipes puffed their foul sweetness into the air. Darts and croquet balls went in loopy circles around their targets, loopier as the day wore on.

The Colonel sat in his permanent chair just beyond the shade of the veranda, dampening with gin the thatch that protruded from his nostrils, occasionally snorting at some private or overheard joke. He was only in his fifties, but his skin was already creased like trousers that had been worn too long. Budding from his arms were moles so large and detached they looked ready to tumble off and roll away. And, as though his wife's condition had become contagious, his ears had been taken over by hair – the calyx whorl of each had sprouted a bouquet of whiskers.

The Colonel liked to drink from the same glass the entire day, always his favourite glass, decorated with the red, white and green hexagons of a football. As his drunkenness progressed, the glass grew misty from being so close to his open mouth, then slimy as his saliva glands loosened, then muddy as dirt and sweat mixed on his hand. At the end of the evening, when Isa was sent to fetch her father's stein, she often found it beneath his chair under a swarm of giddy ants, the football spattered like it had been used for a rainy-day match.

*

Isa had no siblings, and when the other expat children were around, she was frantic and listless in turns. Today, she began with frantic. Leaving the grown-ups outside, propping their feet on wooden stools and scratching at their sunburns, she marched three of the more hapless children inside the house and down the long corridor to her bedroom. There, she introduced them to her things. First to her favourite book, *D'Aulaires' Book of Greek Myths*. Second to the live, broken-winged bird she had found in the driveway two days earlier. Third, and finally, to Doll. Bird and Doll lived together in an open cardboard box. Isa stood next to it with her chin lifted, her hand pointing down.

'This is Doll. She comes from America. She has an Amurrican accent.'

Due to the scarcity of imported goods in Lusaka in the early 1980s, Isa was allowed only one doll at a time. This one had already gone the way of all Barbies: tangled-haired then patchy then bald. Ever-smiling Doll, denied a more original name by her fastidious owner, sat with her legs extended, one knee bent at an obtuse and alluring angle, a tiny plastic pink stiletto dangling from an arched foot. Her perforated rubber head tilted to one side. She seemed interested and pleasant.

Bird, also on its way to bald, cowered as far away from Doll as possible, looking defeated. Isa bent down and poked at it with her finger. Bird skittered lopsidedly around the box until, cornered, it uttered a vague chirp. Alex and Stephie, prompted by Isa, applauded this effort. But Emma, the littlest, thinking that Doll rather than Bird had made the sound, burst into startled tears. She had to be soothed (by Stephie) and corrected (by Isa). Isa felt annoyed.

So she sat the other children down in a row on her bed and taught them things that she knew. About fractions and about why Athena was better than Aphrodite. About the sun and how *it* wasn't moving, we were. But soon, Emma's knotted forehead and Alex's fidgeting began to drive Isa to distraction. Then came the inevitable tantrum, followed by a dark sullen lull. The other three children hastened from the room in a kind of daze. Isa sat next to the cardboard box and cried a little, alternately stroking Doll's smiling head and Bird's wary one.

When she'd tired of self-pity, Isa went to the bathroom and locked the door. She took off her shoes and climbed onto the edge of the bathtub, which ran parallel to a wall about two feet away. Only by standing on the edge of the tub could she see herself in the mirror on the wall, which hung at adult height. She examined her grey eyes, closing each of them in turn to see how she looked when blinking. She checked her face for hair (an endless, inevitable paranoia given her mother's condition) and with a cruel finger pushed the tip of her nose up – she felt it hung too close to her upper lip. Then she let herself fall into the mirror, her own face rushing towards her, her eyes expanding with fear and perspective until, at the last second, she reached out her hands and stopped herself. She stayed in this position for a moment, angled across the room, arms rigid, hands pressed against the mirror, nose centimetres from it.

Finally, bored of her own face, Isa jumped down and explored the floor. She unravelled the last few squares of toilet paper from the roll and wrapped the chain around her neck like a scarf. She opened the cardboard cylinder of the empty roll into a loose brown curlicue – a bracelet. In the musty dust behind the toilet, she discovered some of her mother's old plastic o.b. wrappers, which were twisted at each end like sweets wrappers. She stood them on their twists to make goblets. They were about the right size for a cocktail party Doll might host. Ignoring the knock at the door, Isa pretended to offer drinks to her bare toes, which wriggled with pleasure. The tentative knuckles against the door became a flat palm, then a clenched fist.

'OY!' came a muffled shout.

Isa flushed the toilet as though she'd been using it, then unlocked the door and emerged. Head high, bejewelled in white and brown, her tampon-wrapper goblets balanced on an outstretched palm like a tray, she strolled imperiously past the line of drunken guests waiting for the loo. Back in her bedroom, she made Doll sip from a goblet and modelled her jewellery for weary Bird. But it was too cold and dark to play in here alone. Reluctantly, Isa removed her makeshift jewellery – too childish for her mother to see – and made her way back to the party.

*

She stood in the doorway of the veranda, blinking the sunlight from her eyes. The other children were running around making meaningless noises in the garden. She decided to avoid them, choosing instead to be pointedly polite to their parents, who were sitting in a messy semicircle on the veranda, happily insulting each other. Isa picked up snack platters and shoved them under the noses of perfectly satiated guests. She refilled their mostly full beer glasses, tilting both bottle and glass to minimise the foam, just like her father had taught her.

Finally, Isa's mother told her to go and sit down over by Ba Simon, the gardener. He was standing at the far end of the veranda, slapping varieties of dead animal onto the smoking *brai*. Isa pulled up a low wooden stool. He reached down to pat her on the head in welcome but she ducked, ignoring his eyes and his chuckle. She didn't like how the sweet scent of his soap mingled with the smell of the burning meat. He was singing softly under his breath: ... *waona manje wayamba kuluka* ... Probably some *stupit* song from the shebeen, Isa scoffed, repeating in her head a condemnation she had heard a thousand times from Ba Enela, her nanny.

There are three kinds of people in the world: those who, when they hear someone else singing, unconsciously start to sing along; those who remain respectfully or irritably silent; and those who start to sing something else. Isa began warbling the Zambian national anthem. She heard it every day at 1700 hours, when the TV came on, as the brightly coloured bars gave way to an image of soldiers standing at full salute. *Stand and sing of Zambia, proud and free. Land of work and joy and unity.* Ba Simon smiled down at her and gave up on his song, shaking his head as he flipped steaks he wouldn't get to eat.

Ash from the *brai* drifted and spun like the children playing in the garden. Isa watched their gangly limbs with a detached revulsion, her elbows on her knees, her cheeks in her hands. Stephie was sitting in a lawn chair, depriving a grown-up of a seat, reading a book. It was Isa's *D'Aulaires*! Scandalised, Isa glared at Stephie for a while and then decided to forgive her – her nose had such a perfect slope. *Unlike* Winnifred's, which was enormous and freckled, almost as disgusting as the snot bubbling from Ahmed's brown button.

Those two were trying to play croquet under the not-so-watchful eye of Aunt Greta. Younger than most of the adults at the Corsale parties, Aunt Greta always spent the day chain-smoking and downing watery Pimm's and looking through everyone, as if she were endlessly making and unmaking some terribly important decision. Isa found Aunt Greta beautiful but looking at her for too long made Isa feel there were too many things that she didn't yet know.

Emma, who had cried about Doll, was all smiles now, sitting cross-legged on the ground by herself. Her eyes were slightly crossed as she observed something – a ladybird, it looked like – crawling along her hand. Emma was *so* small. Isa tried to remember being that small, but the weight of her elbows on her knees made it hard to imagine. The ladybird was even smaller. What was it like to be *that* small? But anyway, how could Emma have been afraid of Doll, Isa wondered, when she clearly wasn't afraid of insects, which everyone knew could bite and spread disease and were far more disgusting?

Isa had once retched at the sight of a stray cockroach in the sink. It had been a pretend retch. She'd heard from a girl in the class above her at the Italian School that cockroaches were supposed to be disgusting. But horribly, Isa's pretend retch had become real and had burned her throat and then she'd felt ashamed at having been so promptly punished by her body for lying. Enough time had passed by now to transform the feeling of disgust at herself into a genuine disgust about small, crawling creatures. She watched as Emma turned her cupped hand slowly like the Queen of England waving at people on TV. The ladybird spiralled down Emma's wrist, seeking edges, finding curves. Emma giggled.

Isa swallowed and looked away and saw a clutch of boys crouching in the corner of the garden near the low white wall. They were probably playing with worms or cards or something. Isa watched them idly. Every once in a while, the four boys would stand and move a little further away, then huddle down again. Isa grew curious. Were they following a trail? They inched along the garden wall towards where it broke off by a corner of the house. Just around that corner was the guava tree Isa climbed every afternoon after school. The boys stood and stepped and crouched once more. Isa grew suspicious.

She got up, absently brushing the ashes from her marigold dress, streaking it with grey. She looked down at the stains and bit her lip and squeezed one hand with the other, caught between her resolve to do a good deed and her need to change her dress. She glanced back at the veranda. The adults were roaring with laughter, slumping with drunkenness. Whatever wrongdoing was happening in her garden, it was up to Isa to fix it.

✳

She raced diagonally across the lawn in her bare feet. As she neared the wall, she slowed and stalked the boys, tiptoeing right up to their backs and peering over their shoulders. At first she couldn't see much of anything, but then she caught a glimpse of a thick-looking puddle at their feet. It was mostly clear but, as Jumani now pointed out in a hushed whisper, there were spots of blood in it. Isa's eyes widened. Blood in her own garden? She looked back at the party. Emma was interrupting Stephie's quiet read; Winnifred's freckles were pooling into an orange stain in the middle of her forehead as she concentrated on the next croquet hoop; Ahmed, snot dripping dangerously close to his open mouth, stared back at Isa but he seemed sunstruck rather than curious. She glared warningly at him and turned back. The boys had disappeared around the corner of the garden wall. Isa took a deep breath, circled the mysterious puddle, and followed.

She found them squatting at the foot of the guava tree – *her* guava tree, with its gently soughing leaves, its gently sloughing bark. Isa strode towards them with purpose, abandoning all efforts at sneakiness now. But the boys were too fascinated with whatever they saw to notice her. A whining and a rustling from under the tree drowned the sounds of her approach. Isa looked over their hunched shoulders, her throat tight. Lying on its side, surrounded by the four boys, was Ba Simon's dog.

Cassava was a ridgeback, termed thus because of the tufted line of fur that grew upward on either side of the spine. At the bottom of this tiny mane, just above the tail, was a little cul-de-sac of a cowlick. Ba Simon had named the dog Cassava because of her colour, though Isa had always thought her yellowish white fur was closer to the colour of the ivory horn her father had hung on the living-room wall. Today Cassava's fur was crusted over with rust, and her belly, usually a grey suede vest buttoned with black teats, was streaked with dark red.

The boys were whispering to each other. Isa's first thought was that they had poisoned Cassava and were now watching her die a slow, miserable death under the guava tree. But then she realised that Cassava's head was pivoting back and forth along the ground. Isa stepped to one side and only then did she see the oblong mass quivering under the eager strokes of Cassava's long pink tongue. The mass was the cloudy colour of frozen milk but the way it wobbled was more like jelly – or the layer of fat on gravy that's been in the fridge too long. It was connected by a pink cord to a slimy greenblack lump. Jumani reached a stick towards it to investigate.

'No!' Isa said in a hushed shout.

Jumani dropped the stick and he and the others turned to her. Cassava whined and licked faster, her tail sweeping weakly. Just then the oblong thing on the ground jerked. Isa pointed at it, her eyes wide. The boys turned back. Where Cassava was insistently licking, there was a patch along the oily surface through which they could just glimpse a grey triangle. It was an ear. Isa took a seat beside the boys in the dust, her precious marigold dress forgotten.

Perhaps out of fear, perhaps out of reverence, the children didn't try to touch Cassava again while her tongue continued to lap at the oblong mass. Occasionally a tobacco-tainted breeze would float from around the corner or laughter would flare up, crackling down to a chortle. But the grown-ups didn't come. The children watched in silence, gasping only once, when the outer skin finally burst, releasing a pool that crept slowly over the ground.

There it was, lying in a patch of damp dirt, trembling as Cassava's tongue grazed its sticky body. It was the size of a rat. It was hairy and pink. Its face was a skull with skin. Below its half-closed pink eyelids, its eyes were blueblack and see-through. But no, that was just the sunlight dappling through the guava tree leaves and reflecting off them. If you looked closer, you could tell those eyes were opaque.

The boys grew restless. Cassava was still licking but nothing was happening. The mystery was revealed, the thing was dead. What else was there to see? They got up and strolled off, already knocking about for other ways to pass the afternoon. Jumani offered Isa a hand up but she shook her head. Awed, resolved to maintain her dignity and her difference from the boys, Isa stayed with Cassava and the dead pup. She was so absorbed in that hypnotic tongue rocking the corpse back and forth that she didn't notice the girl until she spoke.

'He et all the bebbies?' the girl asked, then answered herself. '*Eh-eh*, he et them.'

Isa looked around and saw nothing. Laughter fell from the sky. Isa looked up. Ba Simon's daughter was sitting in a wide crook of the tree, head hanging to one side as she smirked down. Chanda was nine, close enough to Isa's age, but they weren't allowed to play together because of an unspoken agreement between Ba Simon and Isa's mother. Once, when they were much younger, the two girls had been caught making mud pies together. They had been so thoroughly scolded by their respective parents that even to look at each other felt like reaching a hand towards an open flame. Isa's entrance into the Italian School had made their mutual avoidance easier, as had her innate preference for adult conversation and her recently acquired but deeply held feelings about the stained men's t-shirt that Chanda wore as a dress every day.

Isa glared at Chanda's laughing face.

'He ate *what*? But anyway, it's obviously a *she*,' she said.

Chanda descended expertly from the tree, flashing a pair of baggy pink panties on the way down. Isa concluded that Chanda had been secretly climbing the guava tree during school hours and that she had stolen the panties off the clothes line. Chanda lowered herself to the ground.

'His stomach has been velly low,' she said. 'And then *pa* yesterday? He was just crying-crying the ho day. *Manje ona*, just look. He is eating the bebbie.'

Isa was horrified, then dubious. 'How do you know?'

Chanda, standing with her feet apart and her hands on her haunches in imitation of Ba Enela, nodded knowingly. 'Oh-*oh*? You don't believe. Just watch.'

Cassava's licking tongue had not changed its rhythm, but her teeth seemed to have moved closer to the dead-eyed skull. Isa shuddered and scrambled to her feet. Mustering all her courage, she stretched out her bare foot and kicked the dead puppy as hard as she could away from Cassava. It tumbled away into the dust, a guava leaf trailing it like an extra tail. Cassava growled ominously.

'Did she do that yesterday too?' Isa demanded, reaching behind her for Chanda's hand.

Chanda was silent. Cassava began scudding her distended torso across the ground towards the puppy. Isa glanced at Chanda's face, which, in reflecting her own fear, terrified her further. Cassava wheezed and growled at the same time. Her thin legs twitched.

'Let's go,' Isa said breathlessly.

And they did, their hands still clasped, Cassava baying behind them.

*

Isa felt buoyed by running, like it had released something in her. She let her legs go as fast as they wanted, relishing the pounding of her feet on the dusty path towards the servants' quarters. It had been a long time since she had visited this concrete building at the bottom of the garden. When Isa was a very little girl, like Emma, there had been an emergency. Her father had drunk too much gin from his bleary glass and tumbled to the ground, his football stein clutched unbroken in his hand. There hadn't been anyone to take care of Isa while her mother veiled up and drove the Colonel to the hospital. So Isa had gone home with Ba Simon for supper.

Instead of *spaghetti con carne*, they had eaten *nshima* and *delele*, the slimy okra dish that always reminded her of the shimmery snail trails on the garden wall. Ba Simon had been as kind and as chatty as usual, but the servants' quarters had been dark and cold and oddly empty, his wife and daughter hidden away despite having cooked the meal. Isa had been relieved to hear the soft shuffle of her mother's hairs on the floor later that night ...

Isa stopped with a cry – she had stepped on a sharp rock. Her halt jolted Chanda, who was still holding her hand. Isa let go and lifted her foot to examine the sole. It wasn't bleeding but there was a purple dot where the rock had dented it. An arrow of fear pierced Isa's exhilaration, deflating her back into her sulky self. She lowered her foot and turned to see how far they had run. The Corsales' garden was big enough to encompass a small field of maize and greens, which Isa glimpsed now through the tangle of mulberry bushes to her right, with their slight limbs and stained roots. She turned to look ahead. Another patch of green, the vegetable garden behind the servants' quarters, was visible in the distance, just beyond the avocado tree with the old tyre swing. She really ought to go and tell Mama about the dog.

When Isa turned to inform Chanda of this with her most grown-up voice, she found herself surrounded by three other children. There was a boy who looked just like Chanda, and two younger girls, toddlers, who looked just like each other. Isa stared at them. She had never seen twins in person before. They stood with their hands clasped behind their backs, their bellies protruding like they were pretending to be pregnant. Isa sometimes played this game in the bath, pushing her belly out as far as it could go until her breath ran out. But this did not seem to be what the girls were doing. A picture of Cassava's low stomach from last week flashed through Isa's head. One of the girls was probing the inside of her cheeks with her tongue. The other was making stuttery noises.

Chanda apparently understood her because she replied in Nyanja, pointing at Isa and shaking her head. The boy looked at Isa, smiling broadly. He stepped forward and held out his hand, making the same upturned tray Isa had made for Doll's goblets. Isa stepped back, unsure.

'*Bwela*,' Chanda implored. 'Come. Come.'

She pointed to the servants' quarters to show where Isa was meant to come. There was bluish smoke and the sound of splashing water coming from it. Isa relented.

✳

The children walked together through the tall grass towards the building. It was squat and grey and had no door, just a gap in the facade for an entrance. There were no windows, either, just square holes drilled into the concrete for ventilation grilles. As they approached it, the boy ran around to the back shouting something. A young woman Isa had never seen before appeared from behind the quarters, carrying a metal pot, her wrists and hands wet. She wore a green *chitenge* wrapper and an old white t-shirt. Isa noticed immediately that the woman wasn't wearing a bra: you could see the shape of her breasts and the dark outline of her nipples.

The woman smiled at Isa and waved, and called out, '*Muli bwanji?*'

Isa knew this greeting and replied in an automatic whisper, without smiling, '*Bwino.*'

When the woman reached Isa, she stretched her hand out to shake but didn't bend at the knee or touch her right elbow with her left hand as blacks usually did. Halfway through the handshake, Isa realised that she was the one expected to curtsy. She hurried to bend her knees but they seemed to be locked and she managed only a jerky wobble. The woman lifted her nose imperiously. She turned to Chanda and demanded something. Chanda shrugged and ran up the three steps and into the quarters, dribbling a forced giggle behind her.

'*Ach,*' the woman said and sucked her teeth. As she headed back to the rear of the building to finish her washing, she gestured for Isa to follow Chanda inside.

Isa gingerly made her way up the steps and into the velvety darkness within. The concrete floor wasn't dirty – it was polished to a slippery shine – but the dust on her bare feet rasped as she entered. There was a strong coppery smell of fried *kapenta* with a tinge of woodsmoke. As she pressed forward, the smell took on an acrid note that she dimly recognised as pee. It was so dark that she couldn't see anything except the gold grid on the floor where sunlight had squeezed through the ventilation grille. The fuzzy squares seemed more radiant for having been through that concrete sieve. As she moved into the lattice of light, it travelled up her legs until it was glowing on her stomach. She raised her hand into the light and it made her palm glow like the orange street lamps on Independence Ave ...

A chuckle from the corner interrupted her reverie. Isa looked around, concentrating on the darkness, willing her eyes to adapt until they could just make out three dark figures sitting in a corner. There was a young woman, younger than the one outside; an old woman, who was mumbling something; and Chanda, who sat cross-legged, fiddling with an ancient cloth doll with a familiar shape. Isa worked out that it was the faceless ghost of the doll who had preceded Doll. She felt a little shocked that it should be here then even more shocked that she had forgotten it to such a fate. She stepped towards Chanda with a notion of accusing her.

Only then did Isa see the baby sitting on the young woman's lap – she moved closer – and sucking on the woman's breast. Isa knew about breastfeeding, but she'd never seen it in action before. She couldn't tell whether the baby was a boy or a girl. It had short hair and was naked but for a cloth nappy. Isa wanted to turn away but she couldn't stop looking at how the child's lips moved and how the breast hung, oblong and pleated like a rotten pawpaw. The women were still deliberating, clearly about her. Chanda, who was responsible for this intrusion, for this straying, sat staring at Isa, absently twisting the old doll's arm as if to detach it.

The baby began to cry. It did not wail – this was an intelligent sobbing, like it wanted something. Isa stared at it and realised it was staring back. Its mother lifted it and bounced it on her lap. After a moment, the old woman started laughing, a rattling laugh that devolved into a cough and then rose back up again to the heights of gratified amusement. She said something to the woman. The woman laughed too. Chanda joined in with a forced high-pitched trill.

'What?' Isa asked.

They kept laughing. The woman stood, holding the baby so it faced Isa. She gazed at its sobbing face, which was distorted with wet concentric wrinkles, like its nose was a dropped stone rippling a black pool. The baby shrieked, wriggling its arms and kicking its legs. Was she supposed to take it in her arms? The room echoed with laughter and weeping. Was she supposed to laugh too?

'What?' Isa demanded.

The laughing woman began shoving the baby towards Isa's face in little jerks.

'What?! What?!' Isa shouted.

The baby's face came so close to hers that their noses touched.

'*Muzungu,*' the woman said.

As if at the flip of a switch, Isa burst into tears. She turned and ran from the building, tripping down the steps in her haste, her breath hitching on every corner of her young-girl chest. As she ran past the mulberry trees, the beat of her feet released a flock of birds from their boughs. They fluttered past her and flickered above her bobbing head, their wings a jumble of parentheses writing themselves across the sky.

✻

The night brought the breeze and the mosquitoes. The guests waned in number and spirit. Isa's mother planted bristling kisses upon their cheeks and sent them off to navigate Lusaka's roads and their drunken dramas on their own. The Colonel was still in the garden, dozing in his chair. One hand clasped his football glass to his belly, the other dangled from the armrest, swaying like a hanging man. In the old days, his wife had dragged him to bed herself. But over the years, his boozing had swollen more than just his ankles. These days, she just ordered Ba Simon to do it.

'*A-ta-se!* I'm not carrying that *cornuto* to bed. The man's *earlobes* are fat,' she grumbled, leaving her husband to the night, the breeze and the mosquitoes.

Isa wandered around the yard, yawning, picking up Mosi bottles of various weight under Ba Simon's direction. She hadn't told anyone

about the dead puppy yet, or about the residents of the servants' quarters – did they realise how many people lived there? – or about the
laughter and the baby and how she had been named. Isa felt tired and
immensely old, old in a different way from the times she played teacher
to the other children. Old like her father was old, a shaggy shambling
old, an old where you'd lost the order of things and felt so sad that you
simply had to embrace the loss, reassuring yourself with the lie that
you hadn't really wanted all that order to begin with.

She collapsed on the grass beside the Colonel's chair. The wicker
creaked in rhythm with his snoring. She put her fingers in his dangling
hand.

'Papa?' she said softly. '*Dormendo?*'

Isa spoke Italian to her parents only when she was very tired. The
Italian School had helped her recover some of the simple Italian her
parents had used with her as a toddler. But like most of the other
expats in Lusaka, the Corsales generally spoke some muddled version
of English at home. Isa slapped a mosquito from her shin.

'I went to the servants' quarters,' she said.

The Colonel's whiffling snore continued. Isa got up and went and
sat on her stool beside Ba Simon, who was vigorously scrubbing the
grill, singing the same tune from before: ... *waona manje wayamba
kulila* ... Isa could barely muster the energy to gainsay his song with
her own. She only got partway through 'Drive My Car', her mother's
favourite song, before she decided to ask him a question.

'What does *muzungu* mean?'

Ba Simon kept humming for a moment. 'Where did you hear that
word?' he asked.

Isa didn't reply.

Ba Simon hesitated. Then he made a face.

'Ghost!' he blurted, waving his hands about. 'Whoooo! Like that
katooni you are always watching.' He smiled and moved closer to her
with his hands still waving. 'Caspah the *chani-chani* ghost,' he sang in
the wrong key.

'The *friendly* ghost!' Isa sang back, giggling in spite of herself.

They chatted about nothing for a few minutes. Ba Simon wasn't
very clever, Isa thought at one point, and then promptly forgot. But
Ba Simon noticed her think it even though she hadn't said it, and soon

enough, he told her it was time for bed. Isa dragged her feet to the glass veranda door with the twisty white security bars. It gave an unhappy moan as she opened it. She looked back over her shoulder.

Ba Simon was getting ready to carry her father to bed. His body was pitched awkwardly over the sleeping man, his dark stringy arms planted beneath the Colonel's neck and knees. When he saw Isa watching, the strain in Ba Simon's face dissolved instantly into a smile.

'Go,' he whispered.

And she did.

1995

Everyone knew that Balaji sold the best hair products in Kamwala, the neighbourhood inhuska where the Indian traders and their families lived. The other shops in that six-street radius around the market specialised in *chitenges* or kitchenware or carpets or a desperately motley assortment of goods. Only Balaji specialised in hair. Wig packets lined the walls of his dark, narrow shop, Patel & Patel Ltd, Inc., making it look like a furry animal turned outside in. And inside the belly of that beast was everything you needed to care for your homegrown or purchased hair – tongs, brushes, combs, rollers, pins, clips, bands, oils, creams and a bevy of *just-in-cases*.

Balaji was widely regarded as a savvy businessman and a decent man. But he was over forty, for goodness' sake. The women of Kamwala, that chorus of wives and widows who determined the fates of every Indian bachelor in Lusaka, had given up on marrying him off. Whenever they discussed his profound eligibility with his Aunt Pavithra, they never called Balaji *single*. They said he was *unmarried*, a word moulded around the absence of what really ought to be the case by now.

Balaji treated the young boys who worked in his shop like sons, ordering them about and smacking their heads with a firm palm whenever they erred. They were all sorts, those shop boys, every shade and type imaginable. Sikhs with sparse beards and bobbling hair buns; Hindus who cursed Balaji's pubic hair when he made them stay late; blacks with bare feet and lambent eyes; coloureds with sulky charm and bitter eyes. Balaji fired them often for the slightest misdeeds, stories of which he would ebulliently recount to their replacements.

'That *muntu* shuffled my wigs, not even asking! I had them organised type-type-type – horse here, artificial here, human there – and the boy decides to line them up by colour! Like a bloody rainbow. Now if Mrs Tembo comes in and wants very-special-good horsehair, I can't tell the bloody difference – it doesn't *smell* like horse, and the labels on the packaging are faded from when that Chinese boy decided to steam the hair scarfs instead of ironing them and . . .'

The boys listened to his monologue as they wiped counters and changed price tags, their hands and eyes slow. The only reason anyone ever chose to work for Balaji was his endless cache of *mbanji*, which he freely distributed but of which he never partook. While his stoned boys orbited around him, Balaji held forth like a man at a bar, his voice a heavy ball rumbling over a wooden floor. That's how Isabella first encountered him: a broad-shouldered, square-jawed, moustachioed *mwenye* behind a counter, thundering on about the placemat a dullard coloured had sold as a doormat.

Isa had ended up at Patel & Patel Ltd, Inc. by chance. After picking her up from the new Shoprite in town, the driver had slowed down just past the bridge on Independence Ave and turned into the market area around the Hindu temple and the mosques. Her mother, the driver said, wanted them to pick up some hair oil. Isa sighed. She was twenty-two and jobless, certainly the right person to do the family shopping, but she didn't like the markets, preferring the fluorescent lights and clean parquet of the South African chains that had cropped up everywhere when Zambia had dropped its embargo after Apartheid fell. Although Kamwala had real shops, not just wooden stalls, and was chock-a-block with imported goods, she did not enjoy navigating the dirt roads and the shouting people.

Parking was a nightmare near the market, so the driver stayed in the car while Isa got out and searched for the shop that sold the special olive oil her mother used. She wandered for ten minutes before she located Patel & Patel Ltd, Inc. in a side street. Its outer wall was covered with a fading mural of products – scissors, brushes, combs – each with a thin shadow painted behind it. She stepped from the trashy bedlam of the road into the cool cave of the shop, relieved to escape the experience of walking outside while female. She wiped her hair off her forehead and brushed her hands down her denim skirt. Then she raised her eyes and realised the ordeal wasn't over.

The shop boys had locked on to her, their blunt eyes sharpening at the relatively unusual sight of a young white woman in Kamwala. Behind the counter, a large blustering Indian man was booming about a doormat. He paused when he saw her, then boomed on, slapping some of the heads that had frozen with her entrance, as if to jump-start them. The telephone rang and he interrupted himself to blurble into it: 'Patel and Patel Limited, Incorporated, Balaji speaking. No, no kettles here, sorry-sorry. Fine and classic hair products only ...' He was big-boned, but his eyes were light and skittish, flocking to Isa then fluttering off again.

She approached him and asked for the olive hair oil. He nodded and stooped behind the counter, lowering his thick body into the recessed space. She heard him shifting some things. The shop boys veered lazily around the store like flies around a piece of offal – erratic but curious. He stood up quickly.

'Very-very sorry, Miss,' he said, tilting his head equivocally. 'It has not arrived.'

'Oh. Are you sure?'

'Yes. Well? No.'

'You're not sure? Or it's not here?'

'What I am sure,' he said, leaning towards her, 'is that you must come back for it.'

The boy polishing combs to Isa's left giggled. Heat flurried into her cheeks and the corners of her mouth twitched, tugged by a tangle of competing strings – amusement, annoyance, attraction. Balaji smirked – his teeth were yellowish but she liked his pointy incisors. She smiled. He grinned. By the end of this hitching exchange, they were both beaming.

Embarrassment sent Isa scurrying out of Patel & Patel Ltd, Inc., but she returned the following week, when Balaji sold her just a little oil, so that it would run out faster and she would have to come back. When it didn't run out fast enough, Isa applied it to her own scalp so that she could come back even sooner. He never did tell her that he'd had surplus of it in stock the day that she first came in.

✳

Eventually, word of Balaji followed Isa home. It was like a mosquito, that word – invisible but unavoidable – and it even sounded a bit like one: *mwenye*. It whined around among the other words winging from the mouths of the workers in the Corsales' kitchen.

'*Heysh*, but what did they expect?' asked Chanda, whisking a broom. 'Sending her to the shop. Alone? *Cha-cha!*' A young woman now, Chanda was both deeply judgmental and deeply envious of those with greater liberty than she.

'At first, they didn't know,' Enela said, up to her elbows in dish-soap bubbles. 'Isa was supposed to be fetching hair creams, not *kawaya-wayaring*.'

'But Aunty, that area?' Chanda stopped sweeping. 'It is where all the young *mwenyes* work.'

'You don't know? It is not one of those shop boys. It is the owner of the shop himself!'

'*Ah-ah!* An old *mwenye!*'

'With a belly from eating the food he should have given to the children he does not have.'

'*Aaaah?* But that girl is very foolish!' said Chanda, wondering if she herself would ever have the opportunity to be so foolish.

'Shem. She is not becoming a wife, that one. She is becoming a widow.' Enela raised a soapy finger. 'He will fall on the ground before he can even fall into the bed.' They looked at each other and giggled.

Meanwhile, the widow-in-training, oblivious to these footnotes to her story, sat alone in her room, justifying her feelings to the mirror. Though she was no longer a child, Isa's bedroom had not changed much over the past decade. Her *D'Aulaires' Book of Greek Myths* still stood on an otherwise empty bookshelf, its pages now yellow and dog-eared, as if it had undergone one of the metamorphoses it depicted.

The cardboard box under her bed was crammed with a genocide's worth of Dolls.

Only the dressing table felt new. Simon the gardener had commissioned a carpenter in Kalingalinga to build it for her thirteenth birthday. It was heavy wood, painted in white, its table littered with make-up tools she liked collecting more than using: the bristly puffs and metal instruments; the severed fingers of lipsticks and mascara tubes; the iridescent crumble of eyeshadow staining the surface like butterfly dust. The dresser had a built-in mirror, in the glassy depths of which Isa was now pondering her face – bracketed, thankfully, by the straight, reasonable hair she had inherited from her father – and rehearsing the case for Balaji.

Balaji was the only person who listened to her. Balaji didn't care that she had no sense of fashion. Balaji was a respected businessman. Balaji was strong and kind. The measure of his strength was the stern voice he used with his shop boys. The measure of his kindness was the length of time his hand lingered in the hand of a begging leper: one and two and three and four and only then would Balaji let go, leaving a heap of ngwee in the fingerless palm. Isa looked away from her face in the mirror, down at her hands, when other justifications came to mind. The way his skin, the colour of the caramel inside a Twix bar, made her forget her own, which was the colour of the biscuit. The look in his eyes, the tremble in his lips, when he had kissed her for the first time last week.

They had been standing in the stockroom of his shop in Kamwala. Balaji had finally managed to convey to her through their casual banter that he was burdened with neither child nor wife. Then he'd made some excuse for her to join him in the back as he searched for a special comb he thought her mother might like. There, in the midst of the mess of things to be stored or sold or forgotten, he'd leaned forward and put his lips to hers, sending a fierce boomerang of desire pivoting into her belly and out again towards him. Isa had been startled by the look on his face when they parted. He had seemed almost offended by his attraction to her. His caterpillar eyebrows had bent their backs and she'd nearly heard him say it in a hoarse, indignant whisper: How *dare* you? It made Isa feel guilty and proud, as if, just by existing in the same world as him, she had done something of note.

Everyone else had ignored Isa all her life. Her parents were too busy distracting themselves to attend to her, and she never got along with the other expat kids. She looked down on them for fear of being looked down upon – a self-perpetuating cycle. As a child she'd felt connected to the workers, especially Simon, who would sing tunelessly to make her laugh, and beckon her with that lilting Bemba call that doubled her name: *Isa kuno,* Isa. But when she'd learned that black Zambians saw her as a *muzungu,* Isa had isolated herself from them, too.

As she matured into the not-quite-beautiful daughter of a truly beautiful woman, Isa's sense of self-pity only grew. Over the years, she had strung for herself a rosary of grievance, all the slights of her life clicking against each other as she counted them: not enough love, not enough attention, not enough praise for her perfectly adequate beauty. Balaji changed all that. He looked at her as if her beauty were complete, and more importantly, as if it were a threat to him. Now, Isa looked back up from her hands to her face in her dressing-table mirror and saw herself through his eyes. She almost gasped with wonder.

When the time came for Balaji to meet Isa's parents, she warned him in advance about her mother. Sibilla, knowing that her appearance often came as a surprise, wore her biggest *boubou,* swamping herself in its tented folds. But Balaji still exclaimed when Sibilla opened the door.

'Miracle of miracles!'

Sibilla demurred with a smile, stepping back so he could come in, her long train of hair slithering on the parquet floor. Balaji, in a crisp white kurta, clasped his hands and gave an ambiguous roll of the head, then followed her into the sitting room. It was decorated with a few knick-knacks – a little Leaning Tower of Pisa, a troupe of carved wooden hippos – but its walls were practically tiled with framed photographs: the Colonel stoical in a safari suit before a white gush of water; Isa climbing a tree in her school uniform; the Colonel in a t-shirt pointing at a bird in a tree; Isa smiling wanly over a birthday cake. There were none of Sibilla, the photographer. A skittery Isa, in a plaid blouse and an old-fashioned denim skirt, was sitting on the settee across from her father in an armchair. Tea was laid out on a low coffee table but the Colonel had eschewed it for his usual mug of gin.

'Welcome, Mr Patel,' said the Colonel without getting up.

'Oh, I am not Patel,' Balaji said affably as he sat on the settee beside Isa. 'That is just the name I inherited when I bought the shop.'

'Papa, I told you,' Isa seethed.

'Okay-okay,' Balaji placated with a smile. He was sweating profusely. 'We can now clarify: my name is Balaji. Just Balaji. My family is from a town called Tirupati in the south-east of India.'

'How interesting,' Sibilla said cautiously.

Overexcited by her attention, Balaji turned to her and leaned forward. 'I must tell you, mother-soon-to-be, you alone could feed the hungry scalp of Venkateswara!'

'What is vinka—?'

'In my town,' said Balaji, 'there is a temple called Tirumala. It sits in the seven hills – the seven heads of the serpent Adisesha – and it is dedicated to the Vishnu Lord Venkateswara—'

'What does your pagan god have to do with my wife?' asked the Colonel, waving his stein in Sibilla's direction and sloshing gin over his trousers.

'Sorry-sorry,' said Balaji, sweat spritzing from his moustache. 'Should have started earlier. Once upon a time long-long ago, Lord Venkateswara was struck in the head by a rock. A shepherd threw it or maybe some cruel kiddies. No matter. A princess, Neela Devi, saw the bald patch the rock left when it scarred him. And so in her pity for him, she cut off her own hair and planted it in his scalp.'

'Planted it?' the Colonel scoffed. 'Like a garden?'

Balaji shrugged. 'All we know is Princess Neela Devi gave her hair to Lord Venkateswara to cover the bald spot. And it was a great-great honour. Maybe she gave him a wig? That,' he brightened, 'is *my* line of business. Wigs-wigs-wigs. And I am still importing the hair from Tirupati.'

'What do you mean?' The Colonel was growing drunker and stupider, and because he knew it, angrier as well. 'They sell hair at this,' his fingers danced mockingly, 'Titty-Putty temple?'

'Tirupati is the town,' said Balaji patiently. 'Tirumala is the temple.'

'Tiramisu, tiramoola, *qualunque cosa.*' The Colonel waved his glass and gin rained over them again.

'Well,' said Balaji. 'As you may conceive, Tirupati is positively brimming with hair.' He explained that thousands of pilgrims went to Tirumala every day, inching along in winding queues to offer gifts to Lord Venkateswara. They gave their weight in money and jewels but mostly they gave their hair, through the practice known as tonsure. Devotees, young and old, crowded into the *Kalyana Katta* that dotted the hill below the temple to sit with bowed heads before barbers who shaved their heads and passed their hair on to the god. A young Balaji had picked up the trade from his father and quickly learned the importance of a sharp razor and a fearless arcing stroke from the base of the skull to the crown and forehead.

'But I had no real talent for barbering,' he admitted. 'And no real interest either. You see, I was a business*boy* long before I became a businessman.' His eyebrows danced.

When young Balaji had been caught selling scraps of hair on the side to wig traders, his precocious business acumen had been punished, then leveraged. As soon as he came of age, Balaji had been sent to live and study with his uncle, who profited off the leftovers, all of the masses of hair that Venkateswara didn't need.

'Big-wig business!' Balaji grinned, 'in South America and China and Hollywood, too. But the biggest wig biz,' he snapped his fingers snazzily, 'is with the blacks.'

He had grown up in Tirupati with his Uncle Andhra and Aunt Pavithra, then moved abroad with them, first to Kenya, then to South Africa, and finally landing in Zambia in the 1980s.

'Ten years later, and the Africans are still thirsty for hair. And Zambia is a good-good country. The politics do not interfere with business here.'

The Colonel, who had plenty to say about the political interferences he had suffered while building Kariba Dam, might have objected to this, but he had fallen asleep in his chair, his empty stein nestled in his lap. Balaji kept talking anyway. Isa nodded blankly beside him. Sibilla looked at the pair of them, her daughter with those grey eyes as vague and vacuous as rainclouds and this boisterous man nearly twice her age, riddling the air with his doublets and triplets of words. How funny that boring little Isa should have chosen such a man!

Isabella had been a sweet, cheerful baby. But she had grown into a sulky, haughty creature, neither Italian nor Zambian, and disdainful of both. Sibilla couldn't help but feel there was something pointed about the choice of a wigmongerer for a fiancé. Yes, an in-betweener like Isabella herself. But a man who made his money off the scalps of strangers?! Sibilla bristled at this more than at Balaji's age or ethnicity, though she knew Isabella was daring her parents by asking for their approval of an older Indian man. Everyone knew how the Colonel treated brown people and black people, despite his staunch humanism and liberal pretensions.

Sibilla had fought with her husband about this practically since they'd arrived in this country, from the moment she had tried to be an emissary for the Tonga villagers before the floods at Kariba. His callous dismissal of them, those old people who simply wished to drown with their gods, had made her see him in a new light. She had never tried to leave him – they shared too many secrets. What could she do without his protection? Where could she go? But Sibilla's marriage had long felt like a handbag that she had neglected to empty out, that she still carried around even though she kept her money, handkerchief and comb elsewhere on her person.

Perhaps it was just as well that Isabella had found this strong, capable man to take care of her. The girl was so helplessly subject to her whims and grudges. She hadn't been bright enough to make it into university, and now she skulked around Lusaka with nothing to do, and seemed to blame everybody else for it. Sibilla looked through the scrim of her hair at Isabella knotting her fingers, at Balaji bullying the silence, at the Colonel snoring in ginny slumber. Well, if the old man couldn't be bothered to stay sober long enough to pass his contemptuous judgment on this marriage, on his head be it. Sibilla stood and clasped her hands.

'You will make wonderful spouses,' she said to the couple, only half-believing it to be true.

Isa smiled cautiously, her gaze darting between her dozing father and her doting suitor. Balaji stood too, rattling off promises to take care of Isa 'forever-and-ever', his head wobbling solicitously. Sibilla walked him to the door, his apologies and thanks dribbling behind him in triplicate.

✳

Isabella Corsale, pallid, skittish and tense, strode through the house in a wedding dress. She had found it in the back of her mother's closet, behind the rainbow of *boubous* that Sibilla always wore to cover her hair. Isa had tried the dress on immediately, batting at the layers of frangible lace, holding her breath to zip it over her ribcage, plucking at the loose shoulders and rotating the twisted sleeves. It was perfect. She was rustling down the corridor to examine it in the full-length mirror in her room when a cleared throat stopped her in her tracks. She turned towards the open door of the study.

'The dress itself is good,' said her father, crossing his arms over his round belly so that his shoulders were level with his earlobes. 'Whether it *suits* you is another question altogether.'

It looked suspiciously like her father had been lying in wait for her. He was sitting in his study, but his chair faced the open door to the corridor, his haunches spilling out on either side of his seat, a fat ankle resting on his knee. Isa looked past him into the room. No books, no shelves, no desk for the chair. The only other piece of furniture in there was the sunken, rumpled bed where he lay from morning to night, sipping from his stein, swallowing his daily river of gin only to piss it out again in the loo next door.

Sometimes, that river would return more abruptly, in a spastic waterfall from his mouth that Simon would have to mop up. This was technically an inside-the-house job and should have fallen to Enela. But, '*Awe. Nakana.* I've refused,' the old maid would protest like a spoiled child, unwilling to touch any part of a *muzungu* who no longer bothered with bathing and reeked of fermented sugars. That smell lingered in the threshold now, hanging in the air with his pronouncements.

'This dress looks too bright,' he mused. 'Is white even a *suitable* colour for you?'

'Why are you so full of poison?' Isa cried, then turned and swept off down the corridor.

*

The Colonel had been making digs like this ever since Isa and Balaji had announced their engagement. He had missed his chance to express outright disapproval of the match, and this was his only way to let his feelings out. Those feelings were not kind. The Colonel had retired a decade earlier, after the North Power Cavern of Kariba Dam was complete and management had been 'Zambianised', which meant that most of the positions had been given to native Africans. He had resented being displaced by those men, most of whom he had trained himself. He had handed them all the technical knowledge about engineering that he had garnered over years of experience, and they had repaid him by pushing him out!

What did those idiots know of the delicate balance of stone and water? What did they know about watching your own work, your own men, get dashed to pieces by the terrible force of the Zambezi? Eighty-six labourers had died building Kariba Dam! Their names were still engraved in the wall at the Church of Santa Barbara. A worthy martyrdom for the largest hydroelectric dam in the world. The Colonel was still mighty proud of that dam, even if the country had robbed him of even that old man's prerogative: gloating.

Retirement had worked its peculiar lethargic magic on Federico. His wife had weaned him from her bed years ago. The servants treated him like a chore. His daughter pitied him though she had barely graduated from secondary school, had no job prospects, and was about to marry some wog trader. Federico had even given up on entertaining expats – no more parties for him to laugh or snooze or slosh his way through. Nowadays, he just lay around, festering in memories. These were mostly of Sibilla.

Sometimes he remembered her in the old country, the young girl who had spun in Signora Lina's parlour, who had plucked his heart and made him a murderer. Sometimes he remembered her here, when it was still an oddly shaped colonial territory in the middle of Africa, their wedding day in Siavonga: the Church of Santa Barbara redolent of fresh concrete, Sibilla's hair covered with the white tulle layers she'd sewn by hand, the very wedding dress which their daughter had just been flaunting. It *was* too white on Isa, Federico thought, patting under his chair for his stein. Not because she wasn't a virgin, though he doubted that she was. But because on her it looked nothing like the sensuous, smoky grey it had made layered over Sibilla's hair. He had noticed that its wrists were yellow now too – Sibilla's perfume must have stained them all those years ago. He could almost smell it: citrus, gardenia, a hint of something earthy.

He thought of their honeymoon at the Victoria Falls Hotel – the tremendous roar of the water around them like static. They had loved each other desperately then, or needed each other (was there a difference?), the secrets that bound them making their sex feel fraught, as if it were a means of survival. Federico felt the faintest echo of an erection, as far off as a cry over hill and dale. When had his wife stopped wearing perfume? When had she stopped spinning?

A flash of memory: Sibilla on the edge of Kariba Dam, surrounded by a black throng, some foolishness about saving the Tonga, or *not* saving them – letting them stay and drown? That was the day the floods came, the terrible floods – '57 or '58? Federico thought of his dead men. Edmundo who had requested the church bell. Giovanni the foreman. Pietro. He raised his stein to his lips, eyes gazing into the middle distance. Federico's skin was an empty suit now. He lived elsewhere, in the past, wandering in a ruin of his own making. Why bother being kind in the present?

*

Isabella was not a religious person, but she insisted on being married in a church, by a priest. The wedding would thus proceed without the colour and shine that adorns a Hindu bride and groom. No red, no gold, no purple henna. Balaji's Aunt Pavithra almost spat in his face when he broke the news to her. He had already thwarted years of community matchmaking by choosing this white girl-child. And now they would be forced to endure a white wedding to boot?

'That is the colour for a widow!' she cried. 'Here, at least, a red shawl.' She pressed it into her nephew's hands. Balaji refused it.

'Sincerest apologies, Aunty. But my bride will wear white-white-white,' he said, not without a smidgen of pride. 'It is what her father is wishing.'

This was to give the decision an air of authority. But who knows what Isa's father, the lifelong atheist, would have wished? Perhaps instead of that frothy white apparatus around Isa, the Colonel would have found gilded silks more *suitable*. Perhaps if he'd had the chance to run his hands presumptuously over Aunt Pavithra's gold-threaded sari at the wedding, he would have slurred in her gold-riddled ear: 'Isa should have worn your type of thing! Very exotic.' But the Colonel never got the chance to bond with his in-law or insult his daughter, because three weeks before the wedding, Simon's knocks to the study door, pokes to his cheek and shoves to his arm each in turn failed to wake the Colonel from his final sleep. His daily river of gin had reversed and drowned him.

They didn't postpone the wedding. They couldn't afford to change those bookings now that they had to pay for a funeral as well. The church service at the Catholic mission for the Colonel was short and only a few people were in attendance: six retired Kariba men, the family, Balaji and the workers. The burial at Leopards Hill cemetery was quick, too, a perfunctory transaction with the ground. Sibilla, a black veil over her hair, watched the groundsmen lower the coffin into its hole as Enela warbled a weepy dirge in Tonga and the priest splattered holy water over it. The Colonel would have hated this, but he'd left no instructions and these were the rituals. Besides, Sibilla thought with a hint of bitterness, he hadn't let the tribal elders die in Kariba as they wished, either.

Her mind was full of his name, his real name, not the one he'd stolen from his brother. *Federico*, she thought, *Federico, Federico*, repeating it with the mechanical exactitude of an insect. Behind the mourning veil and the fall of hair that doubly pixellated her view, Sibilla was settling into a great relief. She finally had permission to set her marriage down. She had loved Federico once, yes, completely. The momentum of that love had carried her all the way to this country only to come to a halt. Sibilla had often recalled their honeymoon at Victoria Falls, too, not with Federico's dreamy nostalgia but as the moment when their love had stalled in front of that portrait of her grandfather, Pietro Gavuzzi.

Over the years, this betrayal had eaten away at the ties binding her to Federico, wearing the strings down until, one day in 1972, they broke. They had just moved from Siavonga to Lusaka. Federico had started a desk job here and now that they weren't living out in the bush, Sibilla had finally allowed herself to get pregnant at age thirty-three. She'd been sitting outside on the veranda of their new home in Longacres, hunched over her big belly to shave the hair on her feet so that she could paint her toenails. And out of the corner of her eye, she had caught Federico looking at her from a window, his mouth open, his eyes narrow.

Before he saw her see him, before his face crinkled into a smile, Sibilla had felt three things at once. One was déjà vu: the threads of time went slack and two moments pressed against each other like cat's-cradle palms. The second was embarrassment: she thought she had been unseen in her awkward crouch over her belly. The third was an epiphany: she realised that her husband's love for her had absolutely nothing to do with her, that it never had. It was as indifferent to her as his brother's had been. This is not so strange. Love often turns out to be a test and a confirmation of separateness. Around then, Sibilla had started sleeping in another bedroom. She simply no longer wished to touch him.

No, Sibilla did not mourn Federico's death and only later would she come to mourn the loss of him over the years, the sense of something familiar receding millimetre by millimetre, like a warm bath draining around you. At the funeral, she felt sad only for Isabella, who had not been ready for him to die. Sibilla reached out and put her hand on her daughter's jolting shoulder. Isabella, in too-tall, too-shiny heels and an ill-fitting dress, was weeping ferociously. Her fiancé stood on the other side of her, offering her his big hand, which she alternated between gripping tightly and rejecting outright. Sibilla watched him endure. Balaji could do no right by Isabella Corsale. He would learn that soon enough.

Sibilla had decided that she liked her new son-in-law, or in any case, that she could tolerate him. She would be moving with Isabella into his home in Kamwala after the wedding, to help take care of the grandchildren to come. The house in Longacres that had come with the Colonel's sinecure with Kariba Dam was too large for a widow anyway. In truth, Sibilla wouldn't have stayed even if she could afford it. She wanted nothing to do with that house, or the stolen job – the stolen life – that had paid for it. She was done with mercenary secrets.

＊

The day before the wedding, Sibilla ran into Balaji outside Isa's childhood bedroom. He was closing the door, shutting off the racket of sobs within.

'Sorry-sorry, just dropping off *jalebi*. Our Bella is not well—' A muffled cry came from behind the door. Balaji looked distraught, a giant child who has lost his toy. 'She is crying the whole day—'

'Balaji,' Sibilla cut in.

'Yes, Madam?'

'Will you cut my hair, as you do in your town? I wish to go to your wedding without a veil.' She hadn't planned this request, but she realised now that she'd been harbouring the idea ever since he had first told them about the temple and the barbers and the carpet of wet hair on the floor.

'Are you sure, Madam?' he asked with his rolling nod.

'Isabella, she cuts it,' Sibilla explained. 'Or what do you say? Trim. Since she was small, she trims it.' She swept her hands over her face and neck. 'Could you trim for me? For the funeral – I mean, for the wedding.'

'As you wish.' Balaji bowed solemnly.

She led him out to the veranda. It was one of Lusaka's contrarian June days, when the sun is fire and the shade is ice. The lawn, bracketed by its low white wall, was patchy, already thirsty for rain. The fruitless guava tree juddered pitifully in the wind. Sibilla sat under the lip of the veranda, her tufty feet stretched out to reach the sunlight. Beside her was a small table that Enela had set out with scissors and razors and a bowl of hot water, its steam diagonal and hesitant in the wind.

Balaji fingered the instruments, then chose a pair of scissors. First, he cropped great swathes of hair from Sibilla's head and face. When he had got it down to a staticky afro, he wet the halo and carefully snipped it into commas that fell onto the embroidered chest of her *boubou*. Finally, he picked up a razor and deftly scraped the remaining bristle. They were close enough to inhale each other's breath, absorbed in the ritual. The fretful wind dried the cut hair, gusted it around their ankles. They did not see the grey eyes looking out through the bedroom window, bright with covetous tears.

✳

The wedding day was windy, too. The clouds looked buffeted and thin. As the hours passed, Isa's white dress picked up so much red dust it was almost the colour of a sari anyway. The wedding guests looked stifled in their dark suits and pastel dresses. Only Aunt Pavithra had held out and worn a glorious navy, gold and green sari. When she accidentally dropped the silk *pallu* draped over her torso, unveiling the delicious folds of her belly, she looked like a recently fed python, both substantial and exquisite. The older women envied her peaceably – at their age, another woman's beauty was no threat and indulging a little envy is a wedding pastime.

Isa herself was brimming with it. She had never cared much for the idea of marriage, which seemed too long and ongoing to comprehend fully, but she had always longed for a wedding: an event, a spectacle surrounding her, emanating from her. The church was cold, the priest spoke too slowly, the pews creaked as if they were in the overdecorated hull of a ship. Balaji kept clearing his throat as if he were about to cry. But Isa felt triumphant and calm and spellbinding. All eyes were on her. The priest pronounced them man and wife. Balaji crumpled his moustache against her nose. The audience applauded as they walked back up the aisle together and waited outside the church for the receiving line.

Only as the guests filed past to shake hands did Isa see that their eyes were wet with grief, downcast with pity – those eyes belonged not to her but to the Colonel, whose own eyes were buried under this red dust, though not yet dust themselves. Sibilla's envy shifted from her mother to her father – not for his death but what it had brought him: unanimous attention. Tears slipped down Isa's cheeks. The wind dried them to salt. Her guests inched past, whispering congratulations and condolences. In a fury of deprivation, she took their naked hands in her gloved ones, spitting red dust with her thanks.

✳

Perhaps because Isa and Balaji first met in a shop, haggling became the pattern for their relationship. If one went up, the other went down, as if they sat on either end of a restless scale, never quite on par, but thrilled with the tilt of it. Thus, he had determined where they would go for their honeymoon – Victoria Falls, like her parents – but she had decided that they would wait until they got there to have sex.

But then the long uncomfortable drive south tired her out: Great North Road was cratered with potholes and around sunset there was an accident, and though they waited for an hour for help to come, it eventually got dark and so they gave up and left money with a young boy to sit with the injured man and pay the hospital fees. Nothing too disastrous, but by the time Balaji and Isa finally arrived in Livingstone that night, their hotel had given their reservation away. The only room available was at JollyBoys, a new backpackers' lodge. They checked into a double – Balaji shoved the two single beds together – and went straight to sleep.

And so it was not until the second morning of their marriage, in a hovel for teenagers on a gap year, that Isa and Balaji had sex for the first time. Sunrise pinkened the cheap batik curtains. A ray of light slipped between them, took a stride over the floor, spotlit a dead cockroach – lending it a lovely amber glow – then stretched across their dual-carriage marriage bed. Balaji smiled and rolled over the crack between the two singles towards his bride.

Isa's face was so beautiful to him that morning, her skin gleaming in the dawn, her lips soft with sleep, her eyes blurry with weeping, that it would linger in his mind for decades, a lifelong hangover. Over the years, when confidants to his marital distress conjectured that his wife wasn't worthy of him, when other women came on to him, implying he deserved better, he genuinely believed them all to be wrong. His feel for Isa's face, the match of her form to his taste, had revised his eyes so he could see nothing else.

To wit, he had never had to work so hard in his life not to ejaculate. Balaji thought of Vishnu, of his Aunt Pavithra, of cricket matches. He closed his eyes and broke the skin of his lip with self-command. When he could bear it no longer, he finished with a great bellow. He opened his eyes and was only a little surprised to see blood on the sheets. Isa seemed overcome. Well, where there is some buying, there is also some selling, he thought. He kissed his bride's forehead, shuffled off her body, put on a bathrobe and slippers, and went out to fetch chai for them from the rickety table in the JollyBoys lobby.

※

Isa knew what sex was, of course. Her parents and their expat friends had not been ones to euphemise during their sundowner conversations. But she hadn't known that she would feel this way about it, dizzy with the debasement of it. Balaji started off slowly, pecking her lips, embarrassed by their morning breath. But in what seemed like no time at all, he was suddenly above her, hugely erect, crazed with restraint. A penned bull. That familiar resentment of his desire, the *how could you?* blazing in his eyes. Isa had never felt so beheld. He was awful. He was an animal ... and she wanted him. Because, as it turned out, she was an animal too.

When he pushed himself into her, she could barely locate herself inside the flood of sensation. She closed her eyes as they rocked and bucked together. Behind the buzzing in her ears, she dimly heard Balaji choking on his own roars. The moment he pulled out, the rush of loss sharpened into pain and Isa opened her eyes and instinctively reached for him. His face was gentle and cowering. She smelled the room, her own tang rounding out his alkaline residue.

'It is a little bit bloody, sorry-sorry.' His caterpillar eyebrows writhed smugly.

'Oh ... yes, that makes sense,' Isa managed.

Balaji grinned and heaved himself off her and went out to get them some tea. Raw and a little stunned, Isa turned on her side and breathed. So this was sex then. This would be marriage. Out of nowhere, it came to her: the car accident yesterday.

It had been late in the afternoon when they had come to a village, mud and thatch trickling into view on either side of the big tarmac road. The windscreen had been furred with dead insects and bird shit, but they'd both seen the drunk man at the same time. Isa could still recall the distinctive dance of the bicycle he'd been riding, the wobbling swoop of it into the road. It had happened suddenly: the bumper had made contact with the bicycle and the man had flown off it, landing awkwardly on the road, with a terrible sound.

Isa had screamed as the car had skidded off the road, tumbling into the pebbly dirt, the car nuzzling into some scrub before it had jolted to a halt. They had breathed a moment. Big brave Balaji had jumped out, telling her to stay inside. Isa, frozen anyway, had stared through the windscreen as the dust drifted right – or was the car drifting left? Up through the haze she had watched as her husband rose, a body in his arms ...

Isa shivered and pulled the thin sheets up over her body – they were still chilly with sweat. Balaji came back into the room with two steaming mugs and set them on the side table. She sat up and leaned back against the wall.

'Do you think that man will be okay?' she asked. 'The bicycle man. From yesterday.'

'Oh, yes-yes-yes, only a broken leg,' he tutted, nestling in next to her.

'You don't think he will come begging for money?'

'He'd better not,' he snorted. 'We left more kwacha than he's ever seen in his whole life.'

Balaji put his arm around her and she smelled the heady nutty scent of his armpit. She looked up at him and let him kiss her, waves of sick desire swallowing her worries. Within minutes, they were at it again, their mugs of tea cooling beside them. It was implacable, this sex, this marvellous, strenuous sex between Isa and Balaji. It would never cease, even as they underwent the general turmoil and fade of a long marriage. This was both a gift and a curse.

1997

Every family is a war but some are more civil than others. The first front in the war of Isa's new family was the Battle of the Mosquito Net. It appeared one night like a drowsy apparition, draped over the four-poster bed in the master bedroom of the house in Kamwala. Isa tried to start an argument about it right away but Balaji dragged her inside the translucent cube for their nightly bout of lovemaking. When they were done, panting beside each other, she gestured around them.

'This thing is ridiculous!' she said. 'We never used mosquito nets at home.'

'Hm?' Balaji murmured. 'It is to protect us, Bella. You can barely see it. Go to sleep.'

Spent, she did. But she was haunted all night by dreams about a woman sleeping above them, as if the roof of the net were a hammock. It was like being suffocated, she complained to him the next morning.

'By a woman?' Balaji grinned. 'Maybe she can join us next time.'

'It's like being inside a *cloud*,' Isa pouted. 'It's not necessary.'

'Don't be absurd,' Balaji said. Malaria was a real risk and he wasn't about to go without a mosquito net because of some fanciful dream.

They bantered about it for a few days, but when Isa had another nightmare – a giant spider weaving a web around them – she took it down herself, sneaking it out of the bedroom and stuffing it in a closet when Balaji was out at the shop. She was furious when it reappeared the very next day, dimpled with wrinkles, a shabbier, friendlier version of itself.

A silent campaign began. Isa took the net down; Balaji made sure it went back up. Isa raged; Balaji shrugged. Sibilla stayed out of it, protected by her own net of hair, which had always baffled mosquitoes. The servants found it amusing at first and even took bets on how long each *bwana* would hold out. But they soon grew weary of fobbing off the duty of hanging it up and taking it down. The mosquito net grew poxy and lax. Its holes widened.

One night, Isa managed to exercise enough self-control to stop Balaji in the middle of sex and force him to take the net down before she would let him back inside her. He gave in, then promptly fell asleep after his orgasm, as she knew he would, and so the bed remained blissfully netless until the morning. Isa woke to the open air and her husband kissing his way up her leg, rising from ankle to shin to knee to ... two kisses higher, he stopped. Isa craned her neck to look at him.

'Just playing connect-the-dots,' Balaji chuckled. 'Bite-bite-bite,' he pressed them like a series of buttons. 'You had better hope you don't catch a fever, nincompoop.'

He left her in bed to examine the delirious line of magenta spots in her skin. It was as if something small and injured had stumbled along her leg, dripping a trail of pink blood. Later, under the desultory drip of the shower, she found more bites, in all kinds of places. How infuriating – Balaji was right. She blamed Kamwala. She'd never had trouble with mozzies in Longacres. Then she remembered why.

In the afternoon, she walked from the house to Patel & Patel Ltd, Inc. Balaji looked up with surprise when she walked in – she hadn't been here since the wedding.

'My bride!' he introduced her to his boys as if they'd never met. The *dwanzi* boys smiled their marijuana smiles. Isa smiled back daintily, then turned to her husband to place her order.

Balaji laughed and shook his head. 'I shouldn't be selling anything to you,' he said as he counted out her change. 'This is *my* money. And you shouldn't be lighting fires in my house.'

Back at home, sitting on the floor of the bedroom, Isa opened the box and a green coil tumbled out and promptly crumbled into uneven pieces: apostrophes and parentheses and an @ sign. She wedged a semicircle into the flimsy metal stand, lit a match, and brought the flame to the green tip. She watched the thin thread of smoke dangle up from it. Then she went and sat by the open window, a novel in her lap. The rain came, bringing with it the velvety scent of wet soil. Isa stared out at it for so long that when she turned back to the page, the letters seemed to drizzle down it. In the corner of the room, the ember tip of the mosquito coil crept slowly along its arc, leaving the scent of myrrh and a pile of cinders.

When Balaji got home that evening, he came into the bedroom and closed the door. He inhaled and exhaled dramatically: 'Aaah.' They looked at each other across the smoky room. She smiled. He smiled. That night, while the net sieved a puddle outside the window, while drugged mosquitoes drifted around as slow and as light as the ash in the air, Isa was kind to her husband with her hands and mouth. And when she fell asleep afterwards, before him this time, her lips were curved in triumph.

The next morning, Balaji woke to the sound of rain strumming the window and his wife retching in the en suite.

'Okay-okay in there, Bella?' He tried the door but it was locked.
Silence. A croak, another gush.
'*Now* you get sick?' he said, his chuckle trickling to naught.

*

Isabella's first pregnancy was difficult. She vomited every day until the
second trimester. She craved fruits that weren't in season. Her skin was
a soupy mess, pimples bubbling up on her chin and brow. At night, the
baby often concentrated its weight into a blunt ache on her side. Balaji,
having now been promoted to Daddiji, was allowed nowhere below
her waist, for which they both suffered. The months passed by in hypo-
chondriacal waves as she conjured two-headed, hare-lipped, fingerless
nightmares to scare herself with – to say nothing of hairy ones. What
if Sibilla's condition reappeared, one of those genetic ghosts that skips
a generation only to haunt the grandchildren? Isa lavished cajolings
upon her belly, willing the baby to be normal. The baby responded in
the usual way, resolutely rotating, kicking stoically at its flexible walls.

Daddiji sat beside Isa in bed, listening to her worrying and feeling
with his hand the steady beat of the foot inside her. What a struggle!
he thought. The Battle of Schrödinger's Hairball. The strength of the
kicks secretly pleased him, though. He felt like a father, full of inex-
pressible bloodly solidarity. A boy, an ally! Finally, someone to adjust
the gender balance in this house.

He felt terribly guilty when Isa gave birth to a girl. They had not
learned the sex of the baby when they went for their scans at UTH – he
had just assumed. All those months of misaddress, like mispronoun-
cing a friend's name! Daddiji overcompensated for his error by loving
little Naila a little too much. He gave her secret treats and protected
her from her mother, who was often harsh with Naila as she grew into
a toddler, grabbing the girl at random to peer at her pores. But while
Naila's hair was lovely and thick and black, and grew faster than normal, it was largely confined to her scalp.

Once, when she was four years old, Naila fell asleep with bubblegum
still in her mouth. She woke with it tangled in her hair and ran straight
to her father, knowing his punishment would be less severe. Used to
shaving hair down to the skin for tonsure, Daddiji had left the child

near bald when he cut the bubblegum out. As it grew back into a page-boy, Daddiji finally got a chance to see what Naila might have looked like if she *had* been a boy. But even then, he realised, it was impossible that she could be anyone other than herself. She was Naila! How unwise, he thought, to love someone in advance of knowing them.

✳

It was inevitable that Naila would become a weapon in the next front of the war between her parents: the Battle of the Unborn.

'*Kwacha?!*' Daddiji would call to his daughter every morning at breakfast. *Dawn has come?!*

'*Ngweeee . . .*' she would respond, drawing it out like a true patriot. *Light falls over the plains . . .*

Daddiji would wink. Isa would roll her eyes. This rally call from Independence days was old and musty, as out of date as UNIP itself, which, after nearly thirty years, had been ousted by the Movement for Multi-party Democracy in '91. Four-year-old Naila just liked the sound of *kwacha!* and *ngweee*: the bassdrum prompt, the droning reply.

For Daddiji, it was all about the money – kwacha in particular, ngwee having long fallen out of circulation. The new president, whom Kaunda had dubbed 'The Four-Foot Dwarf', had rejected his precedessor's socialist principles in favour of privatisation and the free market. Despite somersaulting inflation rates (K4,000 to the pound by 2001), wig was (still) all the rage in Lusaka. The counter at Patel & Patel Ltd, Inc. was stacked high with limp towers of cash – kwacha in the thousands and millions.

Daddiji was trying to change Isa's mind about having another baby. She had been using lack of money as an excuse to postpone getting pregnant again. But there *was* money, plenty-plenty money, he insisted, and therefore no need for clumsy prophylactics or enforced abstinence. There are men who force their wives. Daddiji was not capable of this. Besides, Isa still wanted him, he could sense it when he held his hand above her skin like a dowser. And yet she pushed him away whenever he reached for her at night.

'No! We're not ready.'

'I am certainly ready, and if I can just . . . ah, yes, you are *quite* ready, too.'

Her eyes slid shut deliriously. She shoved his hand away. 'We have to be careful.'

'We *are* careful. *Full* of care. Look at how much care I have for you, just look.'

'We have other cares, too.' She tore her eyes from his erection. 'Naila's education—'

'Naila is *four*, Bella. And must we be million-billionaires to have another child?'

'All you think about is money.' Isa blew at the hair that had fallen over her eyes. 'You sit in your shop all day counting out your money and then you come home and fill our daughter's head with this *"kwacha, ngweeee!"* nonsense. Do you think you're teaching her business? Do you think *this* is business too?' She wrapped a hand cruelly around his member. 'You cannot put a price on everything!'

'Can't I?' He smiled grimly and placed his hand on her breast.

They glared at one another, each gripping the other's pound of flesh. Then their anger burst, releasing an energy that swirled quickly into desire. As always, much sighing and capitulation followed. Isa simply couldn't help the way her lust bloomed like a lotus flower on the surface of some internal swamp. At least this time she managed to get a condom on him first – or so she thought.

✳

A few days later, Daddiji was sitting at the head of the dining table when he felt a tickle under his palm. He lifted his hand and found a white card taped to the arm of his chair. *Chair K50,000*, it said. He glanced at Naila, who shrugged. Daddiji decided to ignore it and reached for his Coca-Cola. As he sipped, he caught a flash of white at the bottom of the glass. He went cross-eyed trying to make it out through the bubbles. He swallowed and raised the glass to read the tag taped to its base. *Tumbler K1,000*. Daddiji lowered his glass and looked around. They were everywhere. Little Naila watched as he walked around the dining room, collecting the diaspora of labels, detaching them from lamps and curtains and books until he had a heap of price tags – or were they receipts? He sat down as Isa came in.

'We are making a point?' he asked her wryly.

Isa said nothing as she took her seat but her lips twitched smileward. Sibilla, oblivious, came in with a steaming bowl of pasta and set it on top of the tags like they were a new sort of trivet.

The next day, more tags appeared around the house: on utensils and decorations and pillows, attached with string or Sellotape or a staple. Daddiji had to admit, his wife had a good business sense – the prices were the right value. He would know, having purchased these things, after all. He thought he understood Isa's message: 'Life costs too much to bring another child into it!' To convey his response – 'Love is free. Your efforts to block it are what is expensive!' – he taped a tag of his own on the packet of condoms in the drawer of her bedside table, capping the price with an exclamation mark.

It was a nice piece of rhetoric but Daddiji's victory didn't last long. Isa had two advantages over him: time on her hands and the need to be right, a need so intense that it often surpassed the original argument. Soon there was an infestation of numbers, everything in the house labelled with a price. The family lived like this for a time, as if the home were an extension of Daddiji's shop. They ate supper with labelled forks off labelled plates, swilled their drinks from labelled glasses. They brushed their teeth with tagged toothbrushes, laid their heads on priced pillows. The price tags flapped and flickered in the windy nights of dry season.

One night, Daddiji dreamt that they were chasing him, diving at his head, flocking onto his hands, biting his palms – a lifetime of papercuts in one fell swoop – then flying off, leaving him to stare at his bloodied stumps ... He woke with a start and stared at his alarm clock for a good three minutes before he realised the numbers there were not the unbudging time, but another price tag.

Casting a look of disgust at Isa still sleeping beside him, he sat up and went to take his bath. When he found yet another tag bleeding its ink into the soap, he decided to make a thorough sweep of the house. He gathered all that he could find and went out to the yard behind the kitchen, where he lit an *mbaula*. Pyjamas dampening in the dew, he dropped handfuls of price tags into the embers, humming 'Awaara Hoon' to himself as the curling, blackening action began.

✳

Sibilla had taken advantage of her grandmotherhood to resume doing some household chores, to let her body serve as it wished. She had gone outside to pluck some fresh eggs from the chicken coop for breakfast when she saw her son-in-law with his bonfire. She paused and put her hands on her hips, peering through her hair at him. What on earth was he doing? The smell of burning paper was pleasant but there was another smell, bitter as tarmac. Ah. Ink. He was burning the silly little price tags.

Sibilla felt a wave of pity for the man. Motherhood hadn't warmed up Isabella one bit. Even with the extra padding pregnancy had lent her figure, the woman's bones were still made of ice. As soon as Daddiji left for work, Isabella spent her whole day sticking numbers on things, the frenzy in her eyes somewhere between panic and glee. Now she seemed to have infected her husband with her mania.

Daddiji grinned stupidly: 'Good morning, Nonna Sibilla! Fine-fine morning, isn't it?'

'It is just okay,' Sibilla mumbled and proceeded to the chicken coop. Naila would be awake soon. The child needed breakfast – and protection.

Sibilla refused to intervene in a paper war, but she was growing concerned that, unbeknownst to her parents, little Naila was becoming obsessed with money. Sibilla had recently discovered a world globe covered in the girl's rickety scrawl – Naila had priced all the nations with a felt-tip pen. The prices were laughably off and Sibilla had been amused to see that Zambia was worth the most: K100. But Naila had started collecting stray kwacha, too – from the kitchen table, her mother's purse, her father's bedside table – and storing it in an old cigar box. Sibilla was disturbed by this – the bills were worth very little but it was still theft – yet she hesitated to tell the girl's parents. She wished to remain non-aligned in their peculiar Cold War.

※

The Saturday that this price war finally came to an end began with Isa at Shoprite doing the food shopping. Naila was at home with her *nonna*, Daddiji snoozing over a *Times of Zambia*. Isa wandered the aisles and compared the imported goods, running her fingers over the plastic-wrapped produce and the colourful boxes of cereal. The wheels of her mind were rolling along like the four wheels of her trolley – except only three of them were running smoothly. The fourth wheel stubbornly stuck and spun. Part of Isa's mind was fretting. This tag campaign could not last forever, and it was the only thing standing between her and another pregnancy.

The truth was, Isa's reluctance to have another child didn't really have anything to do with money. It had to do with an image she couldn't shake. It was from three years ago, when Naila had only just learned how to walk. That day, Isa had been standing in her underwear in front of her closet, trying to decide what to wear, when she felt a pinch. She winced and looked down. Naila was clutching Isa's calf, gnawing at her knee like a holy fool. She was probably just teething, rubbing her gums against the bone, but Isa frowned down at her in befuddlement. What a stranger this human still seemed to her.

Shaking her head, Isa turned back to her closet and caught a glimpse of herself in the full-length mirror. She stopped and stared at the unfamiliar bulges, almost architectural, that now carved her torso. In a flash, she thought: This child *did* this to me. And right then, in that moment of petty regret, Isa saw that she was bleeding, a splotch spreading up her white panties like a red hand cupping her crotch. When the pain came, it was so intense that she vomited.

She cleaned herself up, left Naila in her *nonna*'s care, and took a taxi to the doctor. He gave her an exam, told her she'd had a miscarriage, gave her a pill and sent her home. Isa told everyone she was having a bad menstrual period and a migraine and needed to be left alone. She didn't tell Daddiji what had happened, knowing that his caterpillar eyebrows would stitch into a look of concern that would only irritate her. And she dared not tell Sibilla, who had on more than one occasion made oblique comments about what an 'unnatural' mother Isa made. Isa felt vaguely ashamed, as if her body had betrayed her. While she healed, while she mourned the lack of a baby to mourn, she staved off Daddiji's nightly advances.

Things went back to normal and they dove back into their usual lovemaking. And then it happened a second time. Again, Isa went to the doctor alone and, again, nobody noticed because she always did things alone. She had kept it secret once, so it only made sense to keep

it secret this time too. After the third miscarriage, it became too painful to keep trying, to keep running up against her body this way. That
was when Isa started making Daddiji use contraceptives all the time
and arguing that they didn't have enough money to grow their family.
This was the true origin of the Battle of the Price Tags.

Somehow, by virtue of this domino effect of secrecy and subter-
fuge, Isa's life had become a closed circle. Even now, mingling in the
supermarket with other middle-class Zambian shoppers, she felt set
apart. How had her mother, a freakshow of a woman, managed to find
a sense of belonging here? How had her father, a drunk and a racist to
boot, managed to die surrounded by love and respect? Isa paid for her
groceries, ignoring the cashier's polite greeting, and directed the driver
to load the bags into the boot. She didn't speak as he drove them home,
staring instead at the traffic outside, the buyers and sellers on the side
of the road.

Isa was so focused on her own loneliness that she was doubly disconcerted to find a crowd of people outside her house when they got
back. As soon as the driver turned onto their road, they both saw the
cars parked up and down the driveway, some on the kerb.

'Ah, Madam, it must be a funeral,' he said, glancing at her in the
rearview mirror.

This seemed unlikely, but what if it was the prelude to a funeral – an
accident, an emergency? What if the spinning wheel in her mind had
been a premonition? Terror zoomed into the centre of Isa's chest. Oh
God, oh God, her pulse was chanting as she jumped out of the car,
pushed past the lingerers in the driveway towards the front door, and
started wrestling through the crowd of people inside. She found what
she sought in the kitchen: Naila sitting cross-legged on the floor over a
cigar box overflowing with kwacha. Isa swooped down and picked her
up. Daddiji strode into the kitchen, counting out change, joking with a
man who was clutching an old boombox.

'Welcome home, Bella!' he beamed at her.

'What's going on?' Isa looked over Naila's head at him. 'Who are all
these people?'

'All these people?' His eyebrows darted up and down. 'They're
customers! I put an ad in the paper. We're selling the things you
kindly-kindly priced for us.'

Everything went: the furniture and the cutlery and the plates and the books and even the little Lord Vishnus. That ought to have been the end of it: the house swallowed in emptiness, the mice in the ceiling now audible. Naila doing knobbly-kneed cartwheels across the parquet. The members of the family eating with their hands like real Zambians, sleeping on the floor like poor ones. Isa and Daddiji back to their nightly tussle.

But there was one final parry. It came after they had replaced all that was replaceable and properly forgotten all that was not. Naila had got a new bed, bigger than the one they had sold. Isa sat in a chair beside it, watching her daughter sleeping, Naila with her milk-tea cheeks, with eyelashes so thick and dark they looked wet. What would become of Isa's precious little girl if she were to wake up and look down and discover the final trump card in this stupid game between her parents: a blank price tag – or was it a receipt? – tied with a thread to her big toe?

*

It turned out Isa was already pregnant again, from that delirious night before the Battle of the Price Tags began. This time, it stuck. Seeing this as a sign, she gave herself over to the business of her children. Isa grew fat and recalcitrant over the next four years, a period that Daddiji called The Proliferation and during which she gave birth to three more daughters. In photographs taken around the turn of the twenty-first century, Isa's smile was hidden between plump cheeks, and no matter how Sibilla coaxed her to look at the camera, her eyes were either off seeking some child crawling or stumbling into potential danger, or gazing down at the one in her arms. She became addicted to the drug of breastfeeding – the smarting relief and the chemical high of locking eyes with her baby. Isa finally had the captive audience she had always sought.

'Everybody else lives *with* their children,' Daddiji grumbled. 'Must we live *for* them?'

They did seem outnumbered on Sunday mornings. Gabriella was picking her nose, preferring what she found there to her breakfast.

Lilliana was sitting in her high chair in her forest-green onesie, a vol-
cano of giggles and burps, dribbling a lava of scrambled eggs. Naila
was scraping hers across her plate, whispering 'kwacha' when she
pushed them one way, 'ngweeee' the other way.

'You will never know the depth of a mother's love,' Isa said indignantly, shifting baby Contessa from one breast to another, dripping
milk over her own plate.

'If you're such a loving mother, why are the workers in this household bloody legion?'

'Don't play with your food!' As Isa reached forward to scold Naila,
her nipple plopped out of Contessa's mouth, which opened wide with
surprise and then umbrage.

'Why so much shouting-shouting?' Daddiji shouted.

Contessa started wailing and that set Gabriella off.

'And where are your precious workers now when we need them?'
Isa yelled back.

'It's *SUNDAY!*' Daddiji bellowed. 'I think we can handle one day a
week without—'

Naila covered her ears and imagined her sisters' heads exploding
one by one – *plop! plop! plop!* – like overripe fruit. They were already
halfway there, with their big cheeks. The Proliferation had been hard-
est on Naila. She had been swaddled in the warmth of her parents'
attention for years. It felt as if a blanket once large enough to wrap
twice around her was now shared with fitful creatures who tugged and
yanked at it all night, leaving parts of her body exposed: her foot or her
arm or her back. This was the worst thing about being a sibling: you
never knew when you would feel the chill.

※

Isa relished her daughters' obedience but did not enjoy enforcing it. So,
after a few years, she created a regimented routine to rein them in – and
make them profitable. She named the family business Lovely Luxe Locks
Ltd. It turned out that, after all her worries, the girls had indeed inherited their grandmother's genes but in just the right proportion – their
hair grew at twice the normal rate. Sibilla refused to participate in this

enterprise, and the workers washed their hands of it, saying that it looked like witchcraft, that it was like inviting a curse to come inside for tea. Management therefore fell to the eldest. Naila was then ten years old.

Every morning, after their breakfast and bath, Naila ushered her sisters through a set procedure – shampoo, rinse, condition, rinse, air-dry, oil and comb.

'How long until harvest?' Gabriella would ask.

'Soon,' Naila would say, weighing the hair in her palm. 'You're almost ripe.'

'What if it runs out?'

'It won't,' Naila would reassure her sister, smoothing her tresses down her back.

When Naila had finished combing the other two girls as well, four-year-old Contessa especially squirmy, she would line them up by descending height in the corridor outside the master-bedroom door. Naila was at least two feet taller than her sisters, and from her viewpoint, their heads always looked like a shimmering black waterfall.

Mother usually emerged around 8 a.m. She was like a goddess to her girls, with her long skirts, her grey eyes, her red lips. Naila, Gabriella, Lilliana and Contessa would face her as she stalked the corridor before them, hands clasped at the base of her spine. Then she'd pause before each girl in turn and ask: 'What are you made of?'

Every once in a while, one of the girls tried to give a different answer: water, bone, snow, sugar, animal, vegetable, mineral. But Mother did not want innovation. She simply waited until each girl gave the correct sound-off.

'Hair.'

'Hair.'

'Hair.'

'Hair.'

Naila sometimes mentally echoed the question back: And what are *you* made of, Mother? She pictured Mother's lips turning down as she said: 'I'm made of veils.' This seemed the likeliest answer because of the wedding photograph on the bedside table in her parents' bedroom. Naila often snuck in to stare at it – Mother suspended in mist or dust, translucent layers with a sepia tint.

※

Naila asked about it once. Love Luxe Locks Ltd had managed three harvests thus far. She and Mother were packaging hair into packets in the dining room, wrapping it around cardboard and squeezing it into plastic rectangles.

'Where's the dress?' Naila asked.

'The dress?' Mother looked up from her busy hands but her eyes immediately skipped off to her other three daughters. They were playing quietly in the corner, their newly shorn heads making them look like little monks. Bald Gabriella made a zooming noise and bald Lilliana started beeping – they were being spaceships. Bald Contessa was near tears – she did not know what sounds to make.

'Your wedding dress,' Naila pressed, keen to take advantage of having Mother alone.

'Wedding dress.' Mother stared at the packets on the table. 'It was your grandmother's.'

'Nonna's?'

'Yes. She was beautiful in her day, you know.' Mother's voice was growing irritated. She began sewing hair onto a wig scalp – it was Gabriella's, the shiniest and thickest.

Naila knew her grandmother was beautiful in her day because she was still beautiful now – but it did take a moment to process the picture of Nonna in a white dress. Naila had only ever seen her in those big, colourful West African dresses with embroidery lathering the chest.

As if they had conjured her, Nonna Sibilla appeared in the doorway, removing the shawls with which she veiled her appearance outside the house. She was coming from the Italian School, where she spent a few days a week using fairy tales and puppets to teach the students how to speak the language of her childhood. She had offered to teach Naila and her sisters too, but Mother had declined the offer. The girls attended Namununga, a mixed school with mostly Indian teachers, English-language instruction, and a high tolerance for practices like tonsure. The way Mother saw it, why would they ever need to know Italian in Zambia, anyway?

Naila watched her sisters race to their *nonna* and throw themselves into the folds of her purple *boubou*. Nonna expertly feigned wonder at their shaved heads, running her hands over the fuzz on their skulls. Naila knew Nonna disapproved of the family business: she had tried to explain to Naila once why it was wrong, using words like *servitude* and *slavery* and *child labour*. But her sisters looked less like slaves and more like puppies to Naila, nestling up to Nonna, all giggles and warmth, exaggerating the force field of their love to prompt their mother's notice. Rather than hush them, Mother looked to Naila, who gathered them up and whisked them out, giving Nonna a peck on her hairy cheek as she passed.

In the sitting room next door, Naila organised her sisters into a new game, offering absentminded suggestions – they could devise an alien language or introduce a robot – until they were once again absorbed. Then Naila snuck to the door between the two rooms and cracked it.

'... least I finally have a job,' Mother was saying.

'This is a job?' Nonna Sibilla gave a throaty cackle. 'Using your children to pay your bills?'

'I have not harmed a hair on their heads.'

'Everything you do harms the hair on their heads! And poor Naila is made to—'

Naila held her breath at the mention of her name but Mother veered in another direction.

'They are not like you,' she said. 'It is not their *friend*. It's just hair. And it literally grows from their heads. An infinite resource. In fact, *you* could—'

'I could what?' Nonna interrupted. 'Join you? Give you my ... infinite resource? No. Just be happy that your girls didn't inherit this thing that I have.'

'But they did! They inherited the best part of you – their hair grows much faster than mine. Five centimetres a month! Do you know what kind of profits—'

'Profits! What has become of you, Isabella Corsale?'

'It is Isa Balaji now,' Mother said calmly.

'I considered this. Maybe it is a cultural difference?'

'Oh, stop!' Mother moaned. 'It's a business. I married a businessman, remember?'

'Balaji was always just a middling man—'

'A *middle*man, not—'

A cry erupted from the playing girls. Mother glanced at the door and Naila curled behind it, her pulse thudding in her ears. She raised her eyebrows at her sisters, and an index finger to her lips. They quieted.

'You hear them?' Nonna said. 'They are people. Not looms! Not things!'

'But they *are* things,' said Mother. 'They are the only perfect things I have ever made.'

Nonna was silent. Something cool passed over Naila's skin, raising goosebumps.

'Naila?' Mother called out.

Naila waited a beat before she stepped inside the dining room. 'Yes, Mother?'

'Come,' Mother said coldly. 'It's time to put price tags on these packets. Your *nonna* can watch the girls. Tell the maid to bring her some tea. She needs something to calm her nerves.'

⁎

Sibilla sat in the sitting room with her granddaughters, obediently awaiting her tea. Contessa was performing a wobbly dance for Gabriella and Lilliana. These three had landed in the family as if all at once, a bundle of limbs and affection and need. Only Naila stood apart. Perhaps it was because she had come earlier than the others but her mother had also cultivated that separateness. Isabella seemed to resent her eldest, for being Daddiji's favourite or for being less subject to her will. Once, coming across that ridiculous morning charade in the corridor – Isabella marching before her daughters like a matronly Mussolini, demanding 'What are you made of?' – Sibilla had caught Naila rolling her eyes and making shudder quotes with her fingers when she answered, 'Hair.'

Chanda came in with a tea tray. Sibilla smiled at her. She hadn't planned to bring all of her old servants with her to the Kamwala house like a lady with maids-in-waiting. But when Simon, the old gardener, had succumbed to TB, Sibilla had felt that she should take care of his daughter. Chanda had grown into a sweet, square-shouldered woman, who provided without complaint for both her fatherless son and her twin siblings. She knelt now before Sibilla and poured tea into a cup. She was wearing the uniform Isabella insisted on, a pink and white affair that made her look clownish under her magnificent headdress of long plaits – like a *kudu* in pantaloons.

'Myook, Ba Madam?' asked Chanda, holding the creamer aloft.

Sibilla nodded and turned back to her granddaughters. Lilliana was dancing now, like a robot it seemed – arms at right angles, neck stiff with concentration. If only they knew how much like robots they were, machines in their parents' hair factory! Sibilla wondered, not for the first time, whether she was to blame for this. She had vowed to stay out of the war between Isa and Daddiji. But she hadn't been able to help herself when it came to the Battle of the Price Tags. She knew she shouldn't have tied that blank tag to Naila's toe after the girls' parents had sold everything in the house.

'Chooga?' asked Chanda.

Sibilla nodded and held up three fingers, then four. They both laughed. Chanda's teeth glowed white. Her plaits danced as she handed the mug over. Sibilla sipped her tea. At the time, she'd thought it would be the ultimate rejoinder to Isa and Daddiji both: *You cannot put a price on a human being.* She'd reasoned that one of them would find it and blame it on the other and feel ashamed. Chastened. She had never considered the possibility that instead they would join forces and become allies, that they would end up collaborating on an operation that revolved entirely around putting prices on their children's heads.

'Contessa wins!' Gabriella yelled. She had apparently been designated judge of the dance competition. Lilliana began to whimper. Chanda turned to look, and Sibilla noticed that the wig braided into her hair was bronze, not black, and less shiny than her granddaughters' hair. So! The servants had boycotted Lovely Luxe Locks Ltd! Before Chanda could rush off to attend to the children, Sibilla reached out and grasped a bouquet of her plaits.

'Oops!' Chanda giggled and swerved back to accommodate the pull to her head.

'Where did you get this?'

'Sorry, Ba Sibilla.' Chanda looked down, thinking she was being chastised for disloyalty.

'No, it's fine,' Sibilla smiled and released her grip. She raised her voice over her granddaughters wailing in the corner. 'I just want to know. Who did this beautiful thing to your hair?'

'Ba Madam, it is just this *ka* woman *pa* market. She is a relative to Ba Enela.'

'Is she? And what is her name?'

'Ah? But I think they are calling her Loveness.'

✳

When Sibilla hunched into the stall of the Northmead market where Chanda had directed her, she was surprised to find a glow coming from above. She looked up and saw that the ceiling was a sloping raft of plastic bottles. It kept out the rain but let in the light. She was charmed by this resourcefulness – she remembered well using what you have to make what you need. There were two women on the floor inside, their shoulders pressed comfortably together, chatting and drinking beer. They were dressed well for market women – one wore a velour tracksuit with gold and pink roses, the other a tight lycra dress with what looked like deliberate wrinkles stitched in.

'Loveness?' asked Sibilla.

'What's up?' The darker-skinned woman looked up from her Mosi.

'I have a proposal for you,' said Sibilla, and removed her face scarf.

The women's eyes widened but they did not flinch. Local Zambians had always accommodated Sibilla's condition easily – they were so used to foreigners being strange, they had no expectations or judgments about the nature of that strangeness. Sibilla explained that she had come to offer her services – her resources. She wished to donate the long white hair that still spilled daily, endlessly from her scalp, so that they could package it and sell it as wig.

'So you are what?' Loveness laughed up at her. 'An NGO for hair?'

The other woman stood up and circled Sibilla, ran her fingers expertly over the product on offer. 'No, but it is good hair,' she said to Loveness with a shrug. 'We can use it.'

Loveness narrowed her eyes and requested funds as well, in the Zambian way – not asking directly but wondering aloud if there was any to be had. Sibilla reached into her purse and handed over what she had saved from teaching Italian. It would be just enough to build a salon, to fit it with a wall-length mirror, and paint it with a sign and a mural perhaps, to advertise their services.

✳

The Balaji girls were placed in the back seat of the blue Mazda. Drinks were placed in their hands, drinks that would be drunk too fast, held in too long, expelled among tall grasses on the side of the road. A climate pattern of bubbly colourful rain: gulped in through sticky lips, splashed out between sticky legs. In the spaces between, the journey. Sounds and insects and hot dusty air drifted in through the open windows, riding the spines of uneven breezes. A funk steadily grew: bodies sitting still in the midst of movement. They were off to Lake Malawi.

Daddiji was at the wheel, master of the Mazda and the road. Mother was in the passenger seat beside him. On either side of Great East Road, breeze blocks rose and fell, half-built and quarter-built houses, like Lego projects abandoned by baby giants. The car passed through a village every once in a while, the road filling with bodies and bicycles. Daddiji would honk and the pedestrians would scamper gingerly out of the way as if scalded, then stare at the passing car and catch the girls' eyes – a brief connection, severed by speed.

Potholes riddled the road, sometimes crowding into a sinkhole so cavernous its shadowed depths were as dark as fresh tarmac. Sometimes Daddiji would swerve too late and *thumpety-thump* they'd go. *Slow down*, Mother would mutter. *SLOW DOWN!!!* the four girls would echo-yell from the back, making Mother smile and Daddiji actually slow down. Sometimes there were too many potholes to avoid, and then a new sound joined the soundtrack of the drive: the *clackety-clunk* of a giant typewriter writing their journey eastward.

When the morning sun grew strong enough to scorch the breeze, they rolled up the windows and turned on the air conditioning, which smelled of frosted dust. The girls row, row, rowed their boat. They were animal, vegetable or mineral. They spied with their little eyes something beginning with ... Naila's back pressed into her seat as the road through the front windscreen began stretching upwards like a cobra. The car climbed swiftly, swallowing it, until it came up behind a putt-putting minibus, blue on the bottom, white on the top. It was bursting at the seams with people, their elbows jutting from the open windows. The car drew close enough to see the name of the bus painted in red on the window – CHE GUAVA – and the messages scrawled in the dust coating it: JESUS LOVES ME, I LOVE MARY, MARY LOVES KASONDE.

Daddiji honked and indicated, then sped up to overtake the bus. As they drove by, they heard the humming swarm – it was a song, each note swelling to capacity before it tipped into the next. Daddiji told the girls that the people on the bus were singing a hymn to ward off danger and mourn the dead. He pointed at the valley below, at the metal frames burnt black or rusted red there – a graveyard, a warning. Naila stared at the glinting guardrail, at the bends and gaps in it, until it slunk back into the ground.

Once they were past the minibus, Daddiji had to slow again behind a lorry struggling up the hill. Its bed was a barn: a cage of wooden planks brimming with sacks and crates and a chicken coop. A how-now-brown cow was pressed against the back slats, moaning loudly as the lorry climbed. Daddiji pointed and laughed. The girls laughed because he was laughing. Mother tutted. Daddiji accompanied the cow's moans with an excitable 'whoaah . . . whoaah . . .' The girls joined in – 'whoaah . . . whoaah . . .'

It happened all at once. The slats of the lorry splintered, then broke. The cow tumbled out of the truck, landing awkwardly on its front legs. Even with the closed windows, it was a horrible sound – nearly human. The girls shrieked as Daddiji swerved sharply off the road. The tyres tumbled off the tarmac onto pebbles and dirt. The Mazda skwerched to a halt, its front bumper nuzzling a bush. As always, emergency bred hierarchy: everyone fell into place.

'Wait!' Daddiji barked. 'Don't open the windows.'

Mother turned a stern face to the girls to reinforce his message. Naila squeezed Gabriella's hand. Lilliana stroked Contessa's hair. Behind their catching breath, they could hear the groaning beast and the heedless lorry chugging up the hill. Dust spun, surrounding them in cinnamon light, then drifted left, giving the illusion that the car was sheering right. Two men emerged from the haze. They were stumbling, dragging the unconscious cow between them. Framed by the windscreen, it was like a cartoon. One man's t-shirt was bullseyed with sweat. The other man, holding the thrashing tail end, paused to wipe sweat from his face. They vanished into the bushes and re-emerged on the other side, an awkwardly hobbling mass.

'Looky-look!' Daddiji roared with laughter. 'That was quick. At least someone got a supper out of it!'

Mother glared at him. He kissed her forehead, then manoeuvred the car back onto the road. To cheer his girls up, Daddiji launched into a story about the men and the cow, about their 'tribe', which he said lived at the bottom of the hill and caught all the things that rolled down it. The girls moaned.

'No! Daddiji, snot possible.'

'That doesn't even make sense,' Naila muttered.

'Okay-okay,' his head see-sawed in the rearview mirror. 'You don't believe Daddiji.'

'Ugh, *Daddiji*.'

'Just tell it, Daddiji.'

'Rightee-o. Once upon a time . . .'

In Daddiji's story, the tribe was called the Hilly Bottoms and one day, a lorry had stalled halfway up it and the driver had gone for help. As soon as he left, the Hilly Bottoms gathered at the base of the hill and deliberated. Then a breeze blew and the doors of the lorry swung open, just like arms opening for a hug. Twelve soft-drink bottles fell out. Some of them burst, making a sticky sharp carpet, but others went rolling unharmed down to the Hilly Bottoms, who cupped their hands with their knuckles to the ground to catch them.

The next time a lorry stalled, the Hilly Bottoms were blessed with bales of wheat. Then Bata shoes. Popcorn – blue, yellow and pink like at the Agricultural Show. Bunches of bananas. Ears of *chimanga*. Dartboards rolled down the hill, then rocked onto their split faces. Shoe polish. Mattresses. Daddiji never got around to the moral of the story – about opportunity? Ingenuity? Things coming to those who wait? Instead, he fell into a rhythm of naming the things that tumbled down from the lorries that paused on the slope of the Hilly Bottoms. Buckets. Marmite. Watches. Chickens. The girls sang along, adding to his list.

They drove east, away from the orange sun. It rotted behind them, leaving pulpy stains in its place. They reached Chipata just as night fell. By the time they had got through customs and immigration, the littler girls in the back seat were stacked against one car door like tumbled dominoes. Naila alone drowsed against the other door, her breath fogging a pulsing halo over the window.

'Do you remember when we went to Livingstone?' Daddiji asked Mother.

'Our honeymoon?' Mother murmured, turning her head to the back to check on the girls. Naila closed her eyes and feigned sleep.

'And the accident?' Daddiji asked. Naila could see the thick edge of his glasses. 'The drunk man. On the bicycle. Sometimes, I'm thinking-thinking. And just now. With the cow—'

'Yes,' Mother said sombrely. 'I thought of it, too.'

'What do you think happened to him?'

After a moment, Mother replied: 'It was just a broken leg. I'm sure he—'

'But do you remember his face? There was a hole in his face, Bella. In his cheek—'

'Shhhh.' Mother turned back again. Naila let her eyes slide shut. After a moment, she heard her mother say, ever so softly:

'We left that little boy with him. And money. Plenty of money.'

Behind her closed eyes, Naila saw the hole in the man's cheek, releasing red bubbles one by one. She saw kwacha floating up out of her father's pocket and her mother's purse, fluttering down over a group of villagers clapping with gratitude, clapping to catch the cash.

※

Sibilla had decided to take matters into her own hands. Sitting in the taxi on the way to Kalingalinga, she looked over at her granddaughter. Naila, in her Namununga school uniform, was in three-quarter profile, her head turned to look out of the window as Lusaka scudded by. The girl was twelve, still bone thin, her temples shadowed with soft fur. Her beige skin was darker than usual – the family had just come back from their annual holiday at Lake Malawi.

The girls were always excitable upon their return, bubbling with stories for their *nonna*: how the waves in the lake were big enough for surfing, how they saw the treetops waving in the game park – a herd of elephants silently passing through. This time, they were all agog about an accident with a cow. A cow? Yes, a cow that fell from a lorry and then two men stole it for the Hilly Bottoms! Oh, and they found a moth sleeping on the hood of the car – the size of Daddiji's hand! It was all very sweet and charming.

But later that evening, when the younger girls and their parents had gone to bed and Sibilla and Naila had stayed up watching *Idols South*

Africa together, Naila had told another story. About a drunk man and an accident and money falling like rain over the villagers and Daddiji driving away. And wasn't it funny, the bicycle? And wasn't it strange, the hole in the man's face? Sibilla had hidden her shock from the girl as she pieced it all together. They had left that man there. Not just Isabella, but Balaji, too. And in front of their children. This was what trading bodies for money yields, she'd thought: creature comforts, a life of family holidays and unworried purchase, and a man left to die on the side of the road.

Sibilla looked out of the taxi window. She had never got used to the flatness of Lusaka, so unsettling after the mountains of Alba. Here, it felt like there was too much sky pressing down on the levelheaded trees. She sat back and closed her eyes, relaxing into the peace of grandmotherly love, a love without need or resentment. Naila. Here was someone she could sway, someone she could teach. *You do not have to succumb to inhumanity,* Sibilla practised in her head. *It's not a question of power. It's a question of generosity, what is freely given, tossed from a window to help others. Do you know the story of Petrosinella?* It would be a small intervention, but ...

'You are sick, Madam?' the taxi driver interrupted her thoughts. She opened her eyes. He was looking at her in the rearview mirror with a frown.

'Sick? No, I'm not sick,' said Sibilla, puzzled.

'*Sick,*' he persisted. 'Like *mwenyes,* how they wear their hair ...'

'Oh!' Sibilla clapped her hands, the hairs on them shivering like tassels. 'You mean *Sikh.* No, I'm not Sikh. But my son-in-law, he is from India.'

'Oh-*oh?*' he said. Black Zambians always pretended to be shocked that people intermarried.

'Yes, this is my granddaughter.'

Naila waved at him and grinned. He waved back. Sibilla was about to ask how many Sikhs he knew personally when he slowed and turned into the compound. He inched into its busy inner recesses until there was simply no more road to traverse. Sibilla paid his exorbitant price as Naila stepped out, eyes wide. Sibilla joined her, breathing in the familiar smells of the compound. She felt comfortable here, among the poor. She understood the constant complaining that surrounded them like the droning of insects. They were right: it was all just luck, just circumstance.

She herself had grown up a servant in a tiny cabin in Italy only to end up a *bwana* in a big house in Zambia. Naila had grown up here in 'the Third World', but in a sheltered part of it. When she wasn't at school, she was at home with her sisters, helping their mother sell the dross of their bodies. It made sense that the girl would be skittish in Kalingalinga, her eyes darting and her shoes stumbling on rickety boards and broken concrete as they picked their way towards its centre.

Boys and girls dressed in faded school uniforms and *salaula* strolled by. Old women sat in the shade, shouting to each other as they adjusted their *chitenges* under spatulate breasts. Young women walked with babies on their backs and buckets on their heads, the water tower in the distance carrying its oblong crown with equal grace.

Sibilla used a swatch of her hair to chase the flies orbiting her head and some of her locks tumbled from their fastenings and dragged in the scummy water. As she watched her granddaughter duck her head bravely under wood and metal beams up ahead, Sibilla felt something stir in her chest – her internal spin. She hadn't felt it for decades. She sensed that same energy in this downy brown sapling of a girl. Naila: bright and curious and separate enough from her family that she could be pried away from her fearsome mother and that fascistic business.

'Look,' said Sibilla, pointing at the pink building with HI-FLY painted on it in green letters. As they walked up to it, Naila looked at her quizzically. Sibilla smiled and took her hand.

'*Odi?*' she called out the Zambian greeting as they stepped inside. 'Anyone home?'

Blood, blood, glorious blood! Nothing quite like it for sating the gut. Don't mistake our thirst for a catholic taste. In fact, it is rather selective. Only our females imbibe the red stuff, and only to nourish our ova. Nor are we wanton when it comes to bloodlust, just opportunistic and savvy. The more you brood and wallow about, the more we tend to devour you.

We have a hundred eyes, we smell your scent plume, we sense your heat as we near you. You might hear us sing as we wing through the dark, alighting on knuckles and ankles, but our feet are so tiny, we land without notice, the gentlest of natural surgeons. We use the thinnest, most delicate needles – our labia curl, our fascicle pokes, our stylets slide, then slice.

Counted in grams, the boon is a droplet, but it weighs up to three times our mass. Heavy, unsteady, it's not easy to fly but the risk of lingering is tenfold. Ducking the swat of a hand or a tail, we aim for a vertical surface. We hang there a while, and in just a few minutes, we've done our deft haematology, dripping away the watery broth and storing the solids for later. These we feed to our babies in need and thus you become our wet nurses.

And what do we leave you in kind recompense? A salivary trace, a gum to stop your blood clotting. It's harmless but foreign, and your body is foolish, so it attacks itself in dismay. Our gratuitous gift becomes curse in effect: it sparks a histamine frenzy. This is the curse of keeping too close, of binding and holding and steeping. To stay is to spoil; to settle, to stagnate; to protect, to become an ouroboros. Blood's thicker than water, too thick by far – it clots and it scabs and it turns on itself in a heartbeat.

Trust our biology, it teaches you better. If you grip too tight, you'll lose the fight. If you stay in one place, you'll fester and waste. When young ones grow full, they must drift from the pool, lest it turn to a watery grave.

The word generations *(from the verb* generare, *from* genus, gener-, *'stock' or 'race') is related to* genocide, genre *and* gender *– they all come from *gene-, 'to give birth'. Isabella's a brooder – she sulks and breeds and nurses her clutch. She reins in her young – and reigns over them. Sibilla at least set her granddaughter free and breached this cloying enclosure. Will Naila survive? Will she flee too far? What course will this shift set adrift?*

Thandiwe

1994

Tick. Tick. Tick. Tick.

Over the past year, Thandiwe had developed an internal clock for when the seat-belt sign would go off. As the plane's steep climb slowly tilted forward and evened out, she counted.

Tick. Tick. DING.

'Welcome,' the captain's voice smacked and crumpled over the intercom. Thandi unclicked her belt and got up from the folding cabin seat, which flipped up with an irritable thunk. She smoothed down her striped skirt, pulled back the edge of the pleated curtains and peeked out at today's flock. Some passengers had already dozed off from the heat and vibration of lift-off. Two businessmen were laughing – they would want a whisky or a G&T soon. The rest patiently awaited their feeding.

The captain signed off and the other stewardess, Brenda, unclicked herself from her folding seat on the far side of the kitchenette. She stood and picked up the intercom receiver to make the service welcome announcement, her voice sashaying like a teenager's. As soon as Brenda hung up, she and Thandi began rotating around each other, preparing the meal service. Their movements suggested efficiency – they had been working the HRE–LUN route together for months – but not ease. Rumour had it that Zambia Airways wasn't doing too well and was starting to fire people. Brenda had been with the airline too long, Thandi not long enough, and it was still unclear whether fresh or seasoned meat was preferable.

The same question could apply to lunch, Thandi thought as she pulled up a corner of the red striped foil over a tiffin of stew and sniffed.

'Cooked to kill the germs and the taste!' said Ghostfriend Brenda.

Thandi chuckled. She often had entire conversations with this imagined version of her co-worker – Brenda as she had been before so many years as a stewardess had chewed up her beauty and her patience. Ghostfriend Brenda was lovely and kind and quick to laugh.

'What's so facking funny?' muttered real Brenda as she kicked absently at the brake of the beverage cart and missed. 'Shit!' she seethed, rubbing her stubbed toe. Then she cast a sour look at Thandi and disappeared backward through the pleated curtains, pulling the cart after her.

Thandi sighed, then winced as a cramp clenched her stomach. She was on her MP and Brenda was too – their work schedule had synced their bodies, which were apparently indifferent to their mutual dislike. Thandi hated having her period on flights: on her feet for hours, timing her visits to the lav to avoid the rush forty-five minutes after meals (stomachs syncing up just as wombs do), all the while bleeding sporadically into the thick pad, its adhesive ripping her pantyhose or sticking to her pubic hair. Worst of all, even though Brenda was in the same situation, there was no commiseration to be had.

Thandi preferred it when they were not sunk in this animal condition, when they were both cool and mechanical, attaching only as needed, like the metal parts of a seat belt. It felt safer. Last year, a Zambian Air Force plane had crashed in Gabon, killing the entire football team, and Thandi felt more jittery than usual. She looked out of the porthole of the B-737 at the placid blue beyond. In a few hours, she would be in her hotel room, freshly showered, in a soft robe, on her back. She took a breath, undid the brake on the food cart, and pushed it through the curtains.

She rolled it down to First Class, where Brenda was waiting with the beverage cart, her smile as shiny and fixed as her manicure. Once their carts made contact, they caboosed up the aisle again towards the kitchenette, Thandi stepping back, Brenda forward. Their chanted refrains made an overlapping song – 'The chicken or the beef?' 'Would you like a drink?' – the stutter of shifting trays adding percussion, the glasses tinkling deliriously.

The passengers were obedient until row 23.

'The chicken or the beef?' Thandi asked a young man in 23C.

He paused. 'Is that all there is?'

'To life?' Thandi responded, surprising herself. Something about the way he'd said it – the tone of his voice or his smile – had made his question sound philosophical.

'To eat,' he laughed. He was handsome: broad shoulders, dark hair and eyes, a smattering of pimple scars like paw prints on his forehead. 'It's not a deep question,' he said.

The older gentleman sitting in 23D across the aisle broke in. 'The young lady must have been thinking of the question of the chicken or the egg.' He smiled stickily at Thandi.

'Mmm?' Thandi smiled back, suppressing her impatience.

'You know,' 23D adjusted his spectacles, 'that profound question: which came first, the chicken or the egg?' His accent was somewhere between English and Zinglish. He nattered on about poultry and embryos, snakes and tails, the problem of origins, the origin of species . . .

'But what if the first chicken *ate* the first egg?' 23C interrupted with a laugh, the diamond stud in his ear flashing as his head tipped back. Brenda leaned forward to look at him over the drink she was pouring for row 22. Her cart bumped Thandi's cart, which slid towards her. Thandi stopped it with her foot and set the brake.

'Nice move,' the young guy murmured.

Thandi smiled grimly. 'Chicken? Or beef?'

'Oh, ya, ya. Beef, please.'

She plunked a red-striped tiffin on his tray and turned to the other side of the aisle.

'Chicken,' said the older gentleman in 23D. 'And what is your name, young lady?'

Nerves tingled in the back of her neck. Name requests often preceded complaints. She pointed at her badge with pursed lips.

He squinted at it. 'Thandiwe! A good Ndebele name. I am Dr Bernard Phiri.'

She shook the doctor's hand, then promptly undid the brake and backed the cart. She had a job to do. So she did it, offering chicken or beef to a boy with his hand cocked into a gun; to a fussy woman who wanted fish; to a sleeping man she hesitated to wake up, so beguiling was his slumber. Thandi noticed that, when Brenda reached row 23, she leaned her bosom into the young man's view, poured him a double shot of whisky, let her hand linger on his wrist. Several rows later, Thandi could still smell his CK One cologne and Dr Phiri's tobacco breath.

These scents mingled with the gross puffery that came from the lavatory soon after, forming a thick aura in the kitchenette. Thandi and Brenda rotated silently through it, cleaning up, then sat in their separate folding seats.

*

Ding. A softer bell. Someone had pressed the call button. Still strapped in, Brenda turned to peer through the curtains, then unbuckled and jumped up. 'I'll get it!' she said peppily, her curvy body wobbling rapidly down the aisle. Thandi unbuckled and stood and peeked out, scanning the ceiling for the red nub. 23C. Brenda was already leaning over, smiling and tossing her hair weave. Thandi rolled her eyes. 'It's a bit much,' she snarked to Ghostfriend Brenda. 'The age difference alone ...' Real Brenda glanced at her and Thandi ducked behind the curtain. After a moment she peeped out – damn! Spotted. Brenda beckoned her. They walked towards each other in the aisle, Brenda looking slumped even under her shoulder pads.

'He wants *you*, of course,' Brenda clucked over her shoulder as they turned sideways to pass bum to bum. The 'of course' was about skin colour – Thandi and the young man were both coloured. Thandi frowned until she reached 23C. Then she turned and smiled with closed lips.

'Can I help you, sir?'

'Yaaa ...' he said, staring at Thandi's breasts as if willing her uniform to split open. His smile faltered as he took in her posture. He cleared his throat. 'Are you ... Zimbabwean?'

'Yes?' she said, wondering if he was. His tackies looked expensive.

'I'm just wondering if you've had passport problems—'

Thandi sighed. Not this again. Dr Phiri across the aisle caught her eye and shook his head.

'Sorry, sir,' Thandi said to the young man. 'But we cannot advise—' She saw the kitchenette curtains open at the end of the aisle. Brenda appeared, waving and pointing grumpily at her watch. Time to clear the trays. 'You can address any questions about your passport at immigration in Lusaka.'

'Um, actually—' He motioned her closer. She leaned in cautiously. His whisky breath was sweet and stringent, sugar cubes strung on a line of acid. 'I just wanted to tune you for a beat. Can I get your digits?' he whispered.

'I'm sorry, sir, I—' She shook her head stiffly.

'Ya, ya, no *warrries*,' he said, exaggerating his accent. 'It's cool, it's cool.'

She smiled with closed lips and stood up straight. Just as she stepped back towards the kitchenette, she felt it – a hand cupping her bum. It could have come from either side of the aisle. Thandi paused, staring at Brenda's irritable face framed by the pleated curtains. Thandi kept walking. She was used to this sort of incidental touch, the brushes she chose to brush off. She was nineteen years old but she had looked like this from the age of thirteen. She was well trained by now to unsee any look, unfeel any touch if it meant keeping her job.

Thandi had dreamt of becoming a Zambia Airways stewardess ever since she first saw that Flying Chair ad on TV as a girl: the orange Z in the logo that reclined into an airline seat that zipped a contented white man around the world, while a graceful black woman materialised like an apparition and served him a glass of whisky and a plate of fine cuisine. An infectious, optimistic jingle played at the end: *Zambia Airways ... We're getting better in every way ... We're getting better every day.* What elegance, young Thandi had thought, what adventure!

As soon as she reached the kitchenette, Brenda started whisper-shouting, accusing her of flirting. Thandi estimated that this was two parts jealousy to one part genuine irritation.

'Okay,' she cut Brenda off. 'Can we clear, please?'

Thandi shoved her empty cart towards the aisle, but it stuck on something. Brenda clucked and squatted, grimacing as she reached her manicured nails under the wheel and pulled a thin white thing off the textured floor with an unsticking sound and held it up to the light. It was brownish in places and twisted, like a dead frangipani petal.

'It is ... it is your pantyliner,' Brenda said with horror.

It was *not* Thandi's pantyliner. She could still feel the much thicker sanitary pad between her legs, already sodden with blood from the last half hour – Thandi's MP was way too heavy for a mere pantyliner. But if it wasn't hers, then it was Brenda's and the older woman clearly felt so humiliated that it had slipped and fallen from under her skirt that she was trying to fob it off.

'That's not mine,' Thandi said quietly. 'It must be a passenger's.'

'Oh please,' Brenda said, her lip curling. '*Sies*, Thandi. There hasn't even been passengers back here. Why are you denying? You know this thing came from your brookies.'

'Are you serious?' Thandi tilted her head.

Ding. A soft one. They glared at each other. *Ding*. Thandi parted the curtain and together they looked down the aisle. Another *ding*, and another, a commotion – passengers murmuring, trays clacketing. Thandi's heart rose up and beat in her throat: was the plane about to crash? A woman around row 20 stood and turned to them, gesticulating.

'Doctor!' she shouted. 'We need a doctor!'

Time split. Later, Thandi would think of it as a series of stills, like the paintings depicting the Stations of the Cross that she had once seen at the British Museum during a stopover in London. Here were legions of eyes watching her race down the aisle. Here was Dr Phiri – apparently not a medical doctor – hands up as if under arrest. Here was a woman stretched out in the aisle, bucking wildly, skirt hitched, petticoat plastered to her thighs, eyes closed, spittle in a lacy pile on her chin. Here was Brenda, mouth wide, lipstick cracking, dogteeth glinting, shouting for everyone to calm down. Here were Thandi's hands shackled around the woman's ankles, trying to hold her still.

And there – Thandi looked up – there was the young man from 23C, crouched with his hands cupping the woman's skull, the crotch of his baggy jeans spread like a skirt, his fancy tackies on either side of her head.

'She's having a seizure,' he said matter-of-factly and time moved smoothly again. The woman jerked and frothed. The young man gently rotated her skull to one side, took his wallet from his pocket and wedged it between her teeth. Thandi made a sound of protest.

'Trust me,' he winked (winked!). 'I'm a doctor.'

As the other passengers crowded around Brenda, a natural mother hen in the storm, Thandi kept her hands on the woman's ankles.

'You're good at this,' he smiled at her. 'Steady. What's your name?' He reached his hand over the woman's flailing body, like it was a plate of *sadza* or a cup of tea. Thandi looked at his hand and giggled, then stopped, shocked at herself. He nodded reassuringly.

'Thandiwe,' she said and let go of one of the woman's ankles to shake his hand.

'Nice to meet you, Thandiwe,' he said. 'I'm Lionel.'

'Lionel? Like Richie?'

'Ya,' he winced, then smiled. 'But everybody calls me Lee.'

✳

The belief in other minds – the realisation that other people have their own vibrant mental lives and are not merely projections of our own – seems to emerge between the ages of four and eight. This is also around the time we learn to read and begin to ask some version of the question: where does my name come from? It's as if, for the first time, we realise that the moment we're born, we all fall into a pre-existing net of words. Like characters in a story, we are *named*. No longer safe in our petty internal worlds, we're shoved suddenly to the outside. We look back at ourselves and wonder: who *is* that?

As a boy, Lionel Banda had always known where his older sister's name came from. Carol was Carol because their grandmother, a misty figure who lived far away in the mysterious Land of Ing, was Carolyn. As for his own name, Lee had always been a practical boy who thought in equations like: 'I'm Lee because I'm Lee.' Then one day, when he was seven years old, he had an accident at the supper table. His *ntoshi* missed his mouth and he spilled relish down his stripey sweater and his sister said his full name.

'Lie-NULL!' Carol shouted, imitating their mother's scolding tone.

Ba Grace, their mother's aide, leaned over and cleaned him up with a serviette. As they resumed their quiet munchery, Lee wondered something about himself.

'Why did you name me Lionel?' he mumbled through his mouthful of *nshima* and cabbage. There was a pause.

'It is a velly good name,' said Ba Grace. 'Strong. Like a lion.'

Daddy drank deeply from his glass of Scotch and laughed, but it wasn't a happy laugh. It shot out, *rat-a-tat-tat*, and Lee was surprised to realise that it was aimed at his own stripey sweater. Was he not strong? Lee wiped off the oil smeared around his lips. Is that what Daddy meant? The worst part of his father's cruelty was its inconsistency. Lee never knew when he was going to receive a cold look or a light smack or – and this hurt the most – a sneering insult.

'Lion is my favourite animal!' He grinned now, trying to laugh it off.

'We *know* that,' said Carol. 'And mine is *kalulu*. And he *tricks* lion, HAHAHA.'

'Not all the time! He tricks *njovhu* sometimes!' Lee argued bitterly.

He was too young to understand that his older sister was rescuing him. Carol often instigated 'argy-bargies', as Mummy called them, as a distraction from the darker rifts between their parents. Brother and sister debated the beastly tales until Ba Grace shushed them both.

After supper, still fretful, Lee picked a different fight with his sister, this time over a toy.

'It's mine, Daddy bought it for me!' Lee cried, trying to wrench the action figure from his sister's bigger, stronger hands. They were sitting on the floor of their shared bedroom.

'It's. My. *Turn!*' Carol groaned between gritted teeth. She was eleven, far too old to play with this kind of toy but still committed to the righteous ethos of Bags I. She tugged at He-Man's bulging legs as Lee tugged at his big-jawed head. The talking figurine slipped and fell with a clatter, then began its mechanical self-affirmation:

'I ... *have* ... THE *POWER!* I ... *have* ... THE *POWER!*'

'The battery's gonna die!' Lee yelled, grabbing He-Man by the sword and switching off his power. Lee glared at his sister, his vision sparkling with tears of protest, but Carol had frozen. She raised her index finger, her neck straining like a hare as she listened. Shouts were coming in muffled spurts through the wall that separated their bedroom from their parents'. Carol scrambled across her unmade bed to hear better. Lee joined her in the tousled sheets and pressed his ear to the wall, too.

The shouting had a pattern. Daddy would go first, his voice rising one indignant step higher with each word. Mummy would reply with a clipped sentence, calm and resolute. It was almost like he was calling out, 'I ... *have* ... THE *POWER!*' and she was responding with that conclusive reply: 'He-Man.' After a few minutes of this fight, during which Lee thought he heard his full name uttered more than once, there was a silence.

All of a sudden, Carol jumped on him and started pummelling. Lee fought back eagerly. Their cries as they punched and grappled were so loud that he didn't hear the door open or the stern voice asking what was going on. He just felt his sister's fists rising off his ringing bones and his mother's hands replacing them. Mummy lifted him, arms and legs scurrying in the air, and carried him over to his neatly made bed across the room, the smooth pond to his sister's messy waterfall.

Tears, more of injustice than pain, starred Lee's vision again. But he could still see Mummy's smile lines, and he could smell her powdery sweat like wet clay, and he could sense the liveness of her freckles, those tiny eyes in her skin that made it seem like she really could see, and that let him see himself in her – that brown speckling exactly the colour of his skin. My golden boy, she called him ...

'My golden lion,' she whispered now. 'My sweet boy. I named you for my dear friend, a wonderful man named Lionel Heath.'

＊

As the years passed, Lee learned to track the seasons of his father's animosity. Sometimes, Dad would lob insults like bombs with timers. The words would tick along innocuously – 'foolish', 'soft', 'small' – only to explode later into their full meaning: that his son was stupid and weak, a runt and a disappointment. Dad's cruelty was not restricted to Lee. He would sometimes be dismissive of Carol and sarcastic to Mum and rude to Ba Grace, dropping cutting remarks about 'the ladies' to Lee behind their backs. Lee was befuddled by this. He hated his sister and loved his mother and took Ba Grace for granted. The idea of treating them all with the same contempt made no sense. It especially wounded Lee to hear his father speak ill of his mother. Lee worshipped her. He wanted to be a doctor when he grew up, just so he could cure her blindness.

Lee only came to understand how tenuous his parents' relationship was – and to suspect he had a part to play in that – when he was thirteen years old. At the time, he was attending Falcon, a boarding school in Zimbabwe. Lee had grown more confident since entering that parochial schoolboy world, with its petty rivalries and incidental friendships. Coloured and foreign both, Lee felt superior to the black Rhodies, the majority in Zim but the minority at Falcon, and to the *bazungu* with chips on their shoulders and doubts about whether they were really smart or just rich. All the students wanted to talk like the coloureds – calling *howzit exay?* or *'sup own* as they slapped a hand into a grip – and to dress with their sloppy grace: half-rolled sleeves, neckties loose as nooses. Lee enjoyed being neither at the top nor the bottom – after all, even reversals of fortune pivot safely around the middle.

The September of his third year at Falcon, Lee's father decided to make a holiday out of driving him to school for Michaelmas term. The family would cross the border at Chirundu, then swing down to see the ruins of Great Zimbabwe before dropping Lee off in Matabeleland. Tours of the ruins had dwindled as President Mugabe had started to make his stance on foreigners clear. So the Bandas were alone as they panted up the Hill Enclosure and mounted the rocky set of steps inside. Their guide, wearing threadbare hang-em-high trousers, no socks, and businessman shoes, walked ahead of them, sending facts over his shoulder.

'This is the Great Stone House from which our nation, Zimbabwe, has taken its name. It was built in the eleventh century or somewhere there. You can see the stones are packed in this kind of ziggyzag pattern. No binding mortar.'

Lee looked around at the crumbling towers and corridors. The morning sun spoked through odd gaps here and there, rending the air with gold. Great Zimbabwe reminded him of his childhood hero, He-Man, and his fortress on the planet Eternia called Castle Grayskull – the same dull grey bricks, the same chaotic turrets and curving arches. Carol, standing next to him, her neon clothes casting tinted shadows on the walls, seemed bored. She stared at the guide, smacking bubblegum, her giant headphones humming like bees in a hive.

'You can see from the shape,' the guide said, 'this place was a palace. It quite definitely housed many kings, who had many cattle and many wives.' He grinned. 'Not to say that they are the same.' Only Dad laughed.

'The poorer villagers lived on the outskirts of the city down there.' The guide gestured to the valley. They turned. Carol grabbed Lee's arm, her head still bopping to the beat in her headphones, and pointed at a troop of vervet monkeys scampering around and staring from the trees.

'This architecture is very advanced. The archaeologists said it could not have been built by Africans,' the guide said bitterly. 'They said, no, the white man or yellow man must have built it.'

Something bubbled in the base of Lee's throat. *White man. Yellow man.*

'They even found art. *Shona* totems,' the guide said emphatically. 'Beautiful carved soapystone birds sitting on top of these monoliths,' he pointed at a man-sized column a few yards away. 'Cecil Rhodes stole our totems! Just like his *murungu* settlers stole our land.'

Mum whispered something to Ba Grace. Dad's eyes were hidden behind self-tinting glasses.

'But they could not carry away those boulders. That one with the sloped back, you see? It is also a Shona fish-eagle totem. Can you see it? That is our national bird.'

Lee frowned, trying to map the long neck and lion-like paws of the bird on the Zimbabwean flag onto the tumble of giant rocks. He could picture the little stolen birds – the shiny black statuettes glowering down from their plinths – but he could not make out this biggest, greatest bird, the one that had been left behind.

'What were the totems for?' Lee asked his father.

Dad raised an eyebrow sardonically. 'Probably had cameras in the eyes. Empire is always watching! You should know that from your *muzungu* mother.' He jerked his head at Mum.

She was standing behind them, oblivious, holding Ba Grace's hand, her hair plastered to her pale face. *Always watching. Muzungu mother.* Tick. Tick. BOOM. Bile stung the back of Lee's throat and instinctively, he spat. It zipped diagonally from his mouth and landed by his father's shoe in a frothy globule that sank slowly into the dirt. Lee looked up. Dad hadn't seen it but Ba Grace was staring at him, aghast at this rudeness. Lee smiled and strode away into the ruins, heart pounding. He knew Ba Grace would never say a word against her Madam's golden boy.

✳

But the presiding spirits of Great Zimbabwe were displeased. That night, beasts made of stone the same mottled grey as the ruins haunted Lee's dreams: giant birds and lions and even dinosaurs stood, ranged all around him in a game park – a conglomerate of all the game parks and zoos he'd visited with his family as a boy, Luangwa and Kafue and Munda Wanga and the one at Victoria Falls. Lee was puttering alone amongst these massive dream statues when they suddenly came to life and chased him. The enormous birds flew over him, looming stone bellies raising a wind over his head. The lions leapt after him, claws like hooks, teeth like scythes – swift stony creatures, their flesh crumbling to rocks as their paws slammed into the ground behind him ...

Totem. Lee woke up soaked in sweat, breathing hard like he really had been running, and with a painfully full bladder. He got out of his camp bed and made his way to the bathroom of the motel room the family was sharing, nearly tripping over Carol asleep on the floor. Her Walkman headphones issued a titchy hum – she was at that stage of life when music is a pressing need at all times.

Totem. It rang like a bell in Lee's mind as he stared down at his twining stream of piss. That was the word their guide had used, that impoverished scholar of Great Zimbabwe, so full of rage at the failed politics of his country that he had forgotten he was talking to a mixed-race family. But maybe this family was a kind of failed politics, too. Your *muzungu* mother. Wasn't that word an epithet? And why had Dad used that other word about Mum? *Empire.*

As Lee made his way back to his camp bed, he noticed the tumble of family suitcases spotlit by the bathroom light, which he'd forgotten to switch off. Mummy's bag was open and Lee decided to hunt for Cadbury Fruit & Nut, which she always brought for special occasions. That was how he found the book – small and red, its gold-lettered title crumbled to illegibility. He opened it. WORKERS OF ALL COUNTRIES, UNITE! He raised an eyebrow and turned the page. But after the portrait of a round-cheeked man with a Mona Lisa smile, the book was hollow. A rough rectangle had been carved into its pages, and wedged in that space with torn sides like the unmortared bricks of Great Zimbabwe was a cassette tape labelled with his name.

*

Thandiwe was not immediately charmed by Lionel Banda. It was at least four more flights before she could even take him seriously. He was younger than he looked – at eighteen, a year younger than her – and in his first term of med school at the University of Zimbabwe in Harare. He wasn't quite as stupid as his jokes suggested. She attributed his poor sense of humour to laziness at first, then realised that he reverted to boarding school behaviour when he was nervous, falling back on chummy banter and rough-and-tumble antics to cover it up. It was only bearable because he was so handsome.

Lee stole a first kiss from her in the middle of the third flight – not in the kitchenette or the lavatory but, humiliatingly, from his seat. When she leaned over him to clear his tray, he brushed his lips past hers, light and quivering and quick. If it weren't for the maroon smudge that her lipstick left at the corner of his mouth and his miserable grin afterward, she might have dismissed it as an accident, like the brush to her bum the day they had met. He still denied that it had been his hand.

'It was Dr Phiri!' he laughed. 'That lecherous old rat across the aisle!'

'Don't you mean Mr Phiri, PhD?' She rolled her eyes. 'Some doctor.'

Once it began in earnest, Brenda gave snide compliments about their affair, saying it was 'destined' – again, because of their skin colour. Yes, Lee and Thandi were both 'coloured', but not the same kind of coloured. Lee was Zambian, with a black father and a white mother. He had grown up in Handsworth Park, a suburb in Lusaka where university lecturers lived with their families, and was well off enough to rent his own flat in Harare. Thandi was Zimbabwean, a second-generation coloured: her parents were both *goffals*, her mother slightly darker than her father and with red hair and green eyes that she'd passed on to Thandi and her sister. Thandi had grown up in a middle-class coloured neighbourhood, Arcadia, as insular as Harare's white enclaves. After decades of oppression during the colonial period – denied citizenship, their pay docked, housed in Coloured Quarters – Rhodesian coloureds had turned inward, generations of genetic mingling yielding a population with light skin, emerald eyes, bronze hair and freckles.

To wit, Thandi had grown up with plenty of handsome coloured dudes with imported clothes and squeaky tackies and slick moves, fly *butahs* who took their beauty for granted and did all the usual coloured guy things – car races at homegrown tracks, bottle-service at night clubs, sundowners at *brais*. In short, Lee thought his body and mind were unique; Thandi knew they were not. His looks, his confidence, even the precious way he cupped her breasts and placed a pillow under her bum when they fucked: none of this practised connoisseurship appealed to her.

Thandi *was* interested in bodies, though, just not in the way you might imagine. She had been having sex since she was fifteen – everyone started that young back then, even if no one talked about it – and she had always been careful. She had used condoms until one of the Zambia Airways girls helped her get a diaphragm from a free clinic in London. It was messy but its curved shape – its bendy inversion – appealed to Thandi. She was an up-close person. She zoomed in. She traced the lines between the moles on Lee's chest and pressed the nobs on the pads of his fingers. She often asked him questions about anatomy. She liked his medical mind, the cold intensity that entered his eyes when he clicked into that mode of abstraction.

To Thandi, bodies were shapes. Her love for maths had ended in Form II with geometry but there was a parallel universe where she had become an artist – except she was no good at drawing either, and had never tried to paint. On stopovers in London to visit her sister, she would push through her jet lag and take the Tube to visit the Tate in Millbank. A battered, pen-streaked guide hanging limply from her fingers, she would stand too close to the paintings and sculptures, then step slowly backward, letting the shapes – the smooth intricate bodies of humans and flowers and fruits – fill her frame of vision.

*

Lee had gone straight from Falcon into med school at UZ in Harare. It was the 1990s and Zim was on the brink, the newspapers clamouring about strikes and land and Mugabe's lugubrious persistence. But Zim was always on the brink, after all, and life for a wealthy émigré remained eminently liveable. Lee continued to take comfort in his half-belonging, and started to enjoy his newly clear skin and towering stature and easy intelligence – he had finally come into his genetic inheritances. Med school itself was a blur of booze and blow and low-burning lights. Lee barely ate and went booting at Rumours or Circus and took his exams on three hours of sleep.

Testing his endurance became addictive, a way to empty himself so that he felt only the energy of pure skill – the haptic knowledge of syringe, scalpel, intubation – singing through his nerves. The same edgy emptiness possessed him when he took women to bed. Lee chuffed them like a machine, pulled them like a machine, fucked them like a machine, and was impassive as a machine afterwards. His buddies called him Automatic, or Vicious. Even after he met the beautiful stewardess on that Zambia Airways flight home to Lusaka, Lee kept pulling chicks.

One night, a few months after he and Thandi had started dating, Lee took a posh girl named Yvonne back to his studio flat in Harare. They sat on his leather sofa and drank Zima and smoked Pall Malls as R. Kelly's perverse, practised yowling issued from the stereo, cajoling them to bump and grind. Lee started a gentle snog, cupping Yvonne's face in his hands. He leisurely slid one hand up her shirt, the other down her skirt, expertly unlocking that complex apparatus – a clothed woman.

Within minutes, Yvonne was naked on the sticky sofa and Lee was hovering over her, thumbing her clit, mumbling at her nipples, the three springy protrusions hardening in tandem as her breath caught and released. She moaned his name – *Lee, Lee!* – her British accent evident even in that single syllable. He kept one eye on her breast, trying to stay erect for the big event, but his other eye kept darting to her chin. His stubble had rubbed her make-up off, revealing a rash of raised purple bumps there, almost like burns or plaques. Before he knew it, Lee was examining Yvonne like a patient, scanning through the encyclopedia of conditions in his mind as he brought her to orgasm. Finally, just as she came, he landed on a diagnosis: Kaposi's sarcoma.

❋

Thandi fell for Lee because he was a body that handled and understood bodies. And then she fell for his mother. They met on a sunny August day in Handsworth Park. After a brief introduction, Lee's father, Ronald – a short, dark man who smelled of expensive aftershave – left Thandi and Agnes to have tea in the garden.

'So. Tendeeway,' said Agnes. 'Tell me about yourself.'

'Um, well, I grew up in Harare. My dad works for the national electric company—'

'No, not your father.' Agnes tilted her head. 'I asked you to tell me about *you.*'

Thandi paused, then laughed. 'You know, no one has ever asked me to do that.'

'Really?' Agnes smiled, her bottom lip catching on a big tooth. 'How perfectly strange!' She was pouring tea into a cup, a finger hooked on the rim to check the level.

'These teacups are very pretty,' Thandi said, then hesitated. 'I mean, nice.'

'Are they? Won't you describe them for me?' asked Agnes. 'As *you* see them.'

'Oh. Um, they have these ridges going up. Like something pouring up, like shooting up . . .'

Agnes traced her cup with her fingers and nodded. 'Like a fountain?'

'A fountain, yes!' said Thandi. 'Like in Trafalgar Square.'

'Trafalgar Square? In London?' Agnes sounded surprised.

'Yes, my sister lives there,' Thandi explained. 'I pass through on stopovers. I love Trafalgar Square!' She found herself babbling about the little white pigeons and the big black lions and the strangeness of a place like that in the middle of London – at once so regal and so public.

'Did you go to the National Gallery?'

'Yes! I love the paintings by Mr Turner—' Thandi hesitated again, then went on. 'The sky and the sea and the light. The light especially. It looks like a body and . . .'

'How remarkable. Like a *body*, you say?'

'Yes, you know how they say "a body of light". An angel maybe?' Thandi tried to tame the thought. But Agnes pressed Thandi about how exactly light was like a body. Thandi obliged. Their words fell in together. The conversation between them grew rich and warm and delicious, like a stew they were both stirring, their laughter scattered here and there like spice.

✳

Lee was amused when Thandi told him how much she had enjoyed meeting his mother.

'Did she ask you why you think you're good enough for me?'

'Um, *no*.' Thandi rolled onto her back. 'We talked about fountains.'

'Fountains?' He snapped her bra strap. She always kept her bra on when they had sex, shy of the white bumps that studded her nipples. He had told her that this was normal – the bumps secreted oil to lubricate them for breastfeeding. But that just reminded her of how many breasts he must see as a med student.

'Ya, fountains,' she said. 'You know. Like Trafalgar Square.'

'With the big *tuma* lions?' He lit a cigarette.

'*Mmhm*.' She closed one eye then the other to make the ceiling switch perspectives.

'You know,' he said, 'I used to have dreams about giant animals. Like those lions.'

'Really? Lee Banda's icy brain can have *dreams*?'

'Ya,' he said, shy and indignant. 'It started with that bird totem at Great Zimbabwe.'

'I've never been to the ruins.'

'You youthies, you have no patriotism. That is the problem with this *kahntree*,' he said, adopting the complaining tone of an old man.

'*Ach*, shattap, men. Just because you went to school here doesn't make you Zimbabwean.'

'We are bluther nations! We were once the Fedallayshun!' He blew smoke from both nostrils like a cartoon bull. 'Didn't my dad tell you that? He's usually full of the good old days.'

'I didn't really talk to your dad.'

'Why not?'

The truth was, she had found Ronald curt and condescending. And she had hated how Lee acted around him when he came to pick her up from the house, like an abused puppy ducking for the inevitable blow. That kind of weakness repulsed her. But she didn't say this.

'I just like your mum. She's interested in my ideas.'

'What ideas?'

'Hm. Yes. What ideas?' She rolled her eyes. '*Teach* me about *Great Zimbabwe, bwana*.'

'I don't remember much. It was a long time ago,' he said, curling his fingers into a cone around his cigarette. 'But you know what? I found this weird tape on that trip.'

'A tape?'

'Ya,' he chuckled with a frown. 'We were staying at this motel in Bulawayo. And I saw this little red book in my mum's suitcase, so I picked it up ...'

'*Hallo!* Invasion of privacy!' Thandi smacked his arm.

'Whatever, man, listen. There was a tape *inside* the book. The pages were cut out to make a space, and the tape was, like, hidden inside. And, get this – it was labelled "Lionel".'

'Mmmm, *very* Sherlock Holmes.'

'So I listened to it on my sister's Walkman. And it was like – a play.' He shook his head. 'Or a performance? They were re-enacting a conversation between Kaunda and Mao.'

'KK and the Mau Mau?'

'Just one *Mao*, like China. Chairman Mao. I looked it up later and it turns out they met in 1974.'

'Huh,' she said. 'Who knew?'

'Anyway, on the inside cover, there was this poem. About the lion and the egg?'

'The lion and the mouse,' she corrected. 'That's a children's story, babe. Like *kalulu*.'

'Ya, maybe.' He shook his head. 'It was a bit ... off, though. The poem was addressed to my mum: "Dearest Agnes", it said. And it was signed: "With love, Lionel".'

'Whoah, who is this Lionel?' Her eyes widened. 'I mean, who is this *other* Lionel?'

'That's the question.' Smoke wreathed his smile.

'You don't think ...'

'Who knows?' He leaned over and crushed his cigarette in an ashtray. Then he grabbed her playfully by the shoulders. 'But don't let me catch you with some dude's poem in your diary, Thunder!' He flipped her onto her belly, pressed his chest to her back, and whispered in her ear, 'You. Are. Mine.'

Lee wasn't really a possessive man. But he often used the spectre of jealousy this way as an excuse to prove himself. Now, as ever, he proceeded to fuck Thandi with great precision.

✳

Brenda broke the news in the middle of their next airborne shift: Zambia Airways was about to declare bankruptcy. Thandi let out an uncharacteristic stream of curses. Brenda snickered.

'Should have seen it coming, my deeya. At least you have a fancy coloured doctor to marry.'

Some of the stewardesses would try to trap pilots or businessmen into an arrangement. Others might catch shifts on other airlines. Many would be left hanging in Zim or Zam, with their non-transferable skills. Would Thandi, in fact, have to marry her fancy coloured doctor? It had been a year and she was pretty sure she was in love with Lee Banda. She'd met his parents. But they were both still so young. The thought of marrying him made Thandi feel like there was something empty and frenzied in her chest, a bee in a tin cup.

The LUN–HRE flight that day felt apocalyptic. The lavatory was awash in disintegrating tissue. Passengers dropped ice in the aisle and snorfled their food and snotted through napkins. A newborn issued a piercing wail that made Thandi brim with self-pity. Brenda had shrewdly crammed a closet with passengers' extra baggage and pocketed the fee. The closet door wouldn't shut, but Brenda ignored its thin racket, flipping calmly through her magazine, cleaning behind her manicure with a toothpick, cooing over the intercom. Somehow, this glib consistency, Brenda's same-old-same-old reaction to the fact that they would all soon be fired, bothered Thandi the most.

When she let herself into Lee's flat in Harare that night, she dropped her bag on the trashy floor, took off her standard-issue green pumps, went to the bedroom and lay on the unmade bed. She fell asleep fully clothed. She woke in the dark. She knew Lee was still on his rounds, but she felt annoyed. He needed to come home so that she could refuse his comforting words, then let him seduce her. She padded around the flat, judging its blatant maleness. A stiff leather sofa, a scratched glass table, clashing electronic equipment. No light, no warmth, no round bodies or upward movement. In the fridge, she found two Tuskers and a can of rust-coloured tomato paste spotted with fuzzy white mould. She sneered at Lee's boxers on the floor. She spitefully reset his alarm clock. It didn't take long to find the book.

It was A4 size with a flimsy blue cover, like an exercise book from primary school. Inside was a list of names, all women's names, and dates both old and new. Thandi scanned mechanically, pausing only once, when she saw a name she recognised. It was her own, starting last year and appearing with more frequency amidst the others as the months went on. Her heart bobbing at the base of her throat, she put the notebook back and sat on the sofa, waiting.

Lee came in a couple of hours later, wearing scrubs, holding his keys and a file that said CONFIDENTIAL. Thandi began to accuse him, the volume and pitch of her voice rising steadily. Her jealousy, like his, was not real. It was an idea of jealousy, a tic picked up from films and friends. What she really felt was humiliation, like when he'd kissed her in front of everyone on the plane. How could he have *exposed* them like this? The stakes felt even higher now that she had lost her job. She didn't breathe a word of that, though.

When she was done shouting, she slid on her green pumps, picked up her bag and strode to the front door.

'Thandi, wait,' Lee called out. 'I need to talk to you about this.'

She turned to look at him. His eyes were on the file in his lap. His brow was crumpled, his lips curved down. This was the cringing face he wore around his father, as if his greedy entitlement had been replaced by fear. Disgusted, Thandi turned back around and walked out the door.

1996

'I can't believe you've never partied in the bush, man,' Scholie said in his mongrel accent, a voice like flipping through satellite TV stations. 'How long have you been in Livingstone? Six months?'

He touched the small of Thandiwe's back as he helped her onto the first bench of the Land Rover. He tucked a blanket around her like she was a child and she thought he might kiss her forehead with those plump lips of his. Instead he patted her knee, jumped in the driver's seat up front and started the engine. It thrumped like a dying animal, then accelerated to a screechy hum. They jerked forward.

'Oops,' Scholie said in his own voice and smiled back at her.

Thandi shivered and off they went. He drove out of the lodge and onto the smooth new tarmac, then along an older road pocked with potholes. After a few minutes, he turned the Land Rover onto the dirt road of the game park and the rumble of the tyres gave way to an uneven crunching, pebbles raucously raining up against the under-carriage. They paused at the gatehouse, where Scholie and the guard exchanged a laugh in lieu of cash. The Land Rover surged on, the guard leering through the dark at her as they passed.

The Land Rover was open on the sides and it was soon submerged in the sounds of the park: spiralling calls and burps and gurgles. The breeze grew satiny. An ongoing buzz sometimes whined louder and then thin wings would flick Thandi's cheeks. She held her blanket up over her mouth and stared out into the night. There would be animals out there. But she saw no signs of life, and if the headlamps now and again caught beady flashes on the horizon, she could not distinguish them from the stars. Her eyes were beginning to get tired when the Land Rover stopped, so abruptly she almost careened off the back bench. Scholie held his hand up and said, 'Shhh.'

Thandi reached for his shoulder but before she made contact, she was flung back in her seat as the vehicle leapt ahead at top speed, bump-ing up and down, the canvas roof scraped by low branches. Insects catapulted off her body. Her hair weave, carefully pressed that morn-ing, tangled in the wind. But she was exhilarated by the momentum, the blast of speed and air. She felt a sting in her right eye and rubbed at it. It only grew worse, coming in progressive stabs. Her blinking became like a seizure. Tears looped over her cheek, buffeted into odd paths by the wind.

Thandi screamed with frustration, and the wobble in her voice made her realise that she was shaking. Scholie glanced back, slowed the Land Rover to a halt and turned off the engine. He climbed swiftly over the division between them and turned on a small torch hanging from his key ring. He shone it in her face.

'Stop blinking!' he said.

'I can't!'

'I can't see what's wrong unless you stop blinking.' Torch in one hand, he used the fingers of the other to stretch her eyelids open, exposing the pinpricks of pain.

'There's an insect in your eye.'

'Oh God,' she stuttered, 'it's biting me from the inside!'

'Keep it cool, he's the one that's gonna die.'

He stretched her eyelids wider, pursed his plump lips, and blew against her eye with quick force. She blinked uncontrollably. Again, he tugged her eye open and his breath rushed against the tender cornea. The moment grew still and wide, so wide she could almost feel the individual beads of his saliva spray. She shuddered, tears welling from her eye socket.

'Why were you going so fast?' she snapped. Her eye was sore but the stinging was gone.

'I heard something,' he grinned. 'Can't be too careful in the bush.'

＊

When they got to the camp, Scholie helped her off the Land Rover in a showy way that annoyed her – as if she were not herself in the hospitality business. She stepped away huffily and promptly stumbled. He raised an eyebrow at her high heels and left her, striding towards the bonfire. She stood there, wishing she hadn't dressed up, eyeing Scholie as he slapped palms in greeting, his teeth glinting in the firelight. By the time she had navigated the ruts in the ground, he was sitting next to a white girl, an open beer bottle between his legs. Thandi paused, taking in the canvas tents that circled the circle of people, and the darkness that circled them all.

There were a dozen or so tourists, and scattered among them, three other Zambian game guides apart from Scholie. Thandi waved hi to them over the fire. They all knew her from JollyBoys, the new backpackers lodge where she'd been working this year – part of her job was to ring the guides to arrange drives or hikes for the guests. There were two local girls here, too, whinnying and tossing their plaits. Thandi was grateful for their presence – her outfit was tame by comparison – but she went to sit by Scholie nevertheless. She didn't want anyone to get the wrong impression.

Scholie didn't look up as Thandi levered herself down, negotiating her tight jeans. He was already in conversation with the white girl, whose laugh was surprisingly deep and throaty – a grandfatherly laugh. Thandi leaned forward to catch Scholie's eye. He smiled and winked, except the wink fluttered, teasing her. She shook her head but her pulse raced with the memory of his breath on her.

'Little TandyCandy,' he said. 'You were so cute. Shaking like a chicken in the rain.'

Scholie sounded more Zambian when he spoke to her, his accent shorn of the twangs and twirls he'd accumulated over years of trying to make his meaning clear to foreigners. Thandi smiled. He *would* like it that she had been so helpless in front of him. Their ongoing joke was that she was Kariba Dam and he was the water and, if he persevered, she would one day open her floodgates.

The white girl was looking at Thandi. Or through her: the girl's gaze was thick with drink and she scratched absently at the tattered bracelets strung on her wrist like scraps on a clothes line. Her hair was ragged as the flames and almost the same colour. Thandi reached across Scholie's legs to introduce herself. The girl gave her forgettable name in an American accent and as she clasped her hand, Thandi caught a whiff of her: tea biscuits on a tin plate in the midday sun.

The wind lifted, making the bonfire holler and the tents sound like clapping hands. Scholie and the girl resumed chatting. There was nothing for Thandi to do but stare at the fire's gradual, unruly death, and eavesdrop. Among the tourists, it seemed, nobody knew anybody but everybody knew everybody: recognisable knots in the informal net of backpackers draped over southern Africa. There was a group of Nordic creatures gleaming under the crisp of their sunburn; a gaggle of British girls who had already taken over the drinking, dictating its pace and quantity; a South African couple with limbs entwined; and the American girl next to Scholie, wobbly and giggly and all on her own.

She had apparently started drinking early – not at her hotel, but at a bar frequented by locals. Scholie asked how she'd heard of the place.

'My bungee instructor,' she smirked.

'He's Zambian? And who was that?' he asked, testing her.

'His name is something like Chungo?'

'Chongo! I love that guy, he's mal,' Scholie laughed. 'His name means *shuttup*.'

Thandi rolled her eyes at this translation-as-flirtation.

'So.' Scholie sipped his beer. 'When did you jump?'

'I bungee ... *jamp*?' the girl giggled. 'I mean, *jumped*, yesterday.'

'They only started doing it last year, this jumping off the bridge thing. It's madness!'

'Oh-my-god. Spiritual experience. It was like ... I was truly *alive* for the first time in my life.'

'Radical,' Scholie murmured. 'Have you seen any of the other waterfalls?'

'Oh, yeah,' she exclaimed. 'We went to that really tall one, Kalambo Falls? In Impala?'

Mbala, Thandi thought irritably, it's a town, not an animal. She got up and moved over to the other side of the fire, a few feet away from one of the Nordic tourists, who lifted a hand in greeting. Thandi smiled and smoothed her hair, subtly slapping the seam of her weave. She wished she had rescheduled her plaiting appointment for sooner. She would have to withstand this needling itch for at least two more days.

The Nordic tourist stood and walked over, handing her an open beer. She thanked him. He sat. They sipped in unison and conducted a pro forma interview: their names, where they were from, what they had studied at uni. His cool, keen curiosity reminded her of Lee's mother. She told him that she had gone straight from uni to Zambia Airways, then taken a job at JollyBoys after the airline went bankrupt and she was let go the following year. She had just asked whether his job suited his degree any better than hers did when she heard Scholie pitching his voice high – 'It's biting me from the inside!' – followed by his baritone laugh.

She glared at him across the fire. He was lying on his side now, his cheek propped on his fist, three empty Mosi bottles leaning against his thigh, a fourth in his hand. The Nordic tourist called out to him.

'Vhut is so funny over dare?'

'It's her story.' Scholie gestured to Thandi with his beer. 'She should tell it.'

Anxiety engulfed Thandi's irritation. Everyone was looking at her. She took a sip of beer and told the story quickly, mocking herself to temper it.

'It happened just now,' Scholie confirmed with a grin. 'I'm the one who saved her.'

'*Saat*. Shuttup, *iwe*,' she said, sucking her teeth under a smile.

Scholie goaded a guide named Mainza into telling another animal story. Mainza's voice rolled smoothly, his tone mellow with Mosi. His story about a pregnant hyena unfolded at its own pace and grew more and more amusing until everyone was fitting their laughter into his pauses. The stories that followed were the same as always, each trumping the last until the insect in Thandi's eye had led to Mainza's hyena, an elephant trampling in Zim, a mauled baby in Kasama, and a drowning in Lake Malawi ... This was apparently the cue for the two local girls. They made their exit with a lucky guide, each clinging to one of his arms as they teetered over to his vehicle.

'Wow, that's deep,' Scholie was murmuring about the drowning story. He was facing away but Thandi could see from a ripple in his shoulder that his hand was on the American girl and it was moving. The South African couple were snogging again. The conversation seemed destined to fragment. Then the American girl spoke up.

'I had this really intense thing happen a couple of days ago.'

'Ya?' Scholie said.

'Yeah, on my way to Livingstone. So, we were supposed to leave Lusaka at the crack of dawn, right? But we got totally wasted the night before so we didn't leave till, like, noon. Then we stopped at the Choma museum – whatever,' she shook her yellow hair, 'point being, the sun set at like six and it was pitch-black out and we hadn't arrived yet. This couple I was backpacking with, Jess and Matt, they were having a fight. So I was like, "Look, I'll drive." But then me and Matt, *we* start fighting. He's saying I should gun it so we can get to the hostel and I'm like, no, let's just pull over and sleep. I turn to ask Jess, who's in the back. And *bam*!'

Scholie sat up. '*Bam*, what? You hit an animal?'

'No, no, no,' the girl said hastily. 'We swerved off the road into a ditch. We literally felt the tyre blow, like' – she trapped her curled fingers behind her thumb and flicked them in a spraying motion – '*poof*! So we're in this ditch, the only light is coming from the headlights. It's like *pitch*-black. All we can hear is the seat-belt alarm and crickets. Jess is yelling – like, *what the hell is going on?* I'm totally shaking. Then we see these eyes glowing in the dark. Jess is like, *that is an animal . . .*'

Thandi frowned. So it was an animal story after all?

'. . . but it's this little African kid. He runs up to the car and knocks on my window. He's got no shoes on and he has that little pot belly, you know, from starving? He doesn't speak English and he's super young and I can't understand what he's saying but then he goes *come, come*, he knows that word. So I get out and my legs are like fuckin jelly but I go with him and he takes me to this man lying on the side of the road.'

Thandi's head tipped back slightly, like she'd been knocked on the chin.

'And I can see from our headlights, there's a bike a few feet away, totally mangled—'

'Wait, you hit him?' Thandi asked.

'No, no!' the American girl exclaimed, her hands spinning again. 'It was *not* us. Like I said, our tyre blew out.'

Thandi looked around to see if the others were buying this. They were rapt, silent. Maybe it was just the beery drowse but everyone looked like they had stumbled into a private room.

'Some other car hit him earlier.' The girl looked flushed. 'Broke his leg. And they just *left* him there.'

'My Goht!' said the Nordic tourist next to Thandi.

'Zambians,' Scholie shook his head. 'Typical.'

Thandi stared at him incredulously.

'So the kid is holding money in my face,' the American girl continued, 'like waving it around, like *that's* gonna help. There's no ambulance, we're nowhere near a phone – do you guys even *have* payphones out here?' She shook her head. 'Anyway, so this guy is out here alone in the middle of nowhere, in the middle of the night, bleeding out on the ground. I tied my t-shirt above his knee . . .'

'You should have made a splint,' Thandi muttered. She had received extensive first-aid training to become a stewardess. Scholie flapped his hand to shut her up.

'. . . kid is staring at me,' the girl was saying, 'because I'm in my bra. He's in fuckin shock, and I'm in fuckin shock, and his dad's bleeding out, and it's just a clusterfuck. Matt and Jess come over with a flashlight and, first thing, Matt takes off his t-shirt and gives it to me to cover up. I'm like, dude, someone's *dying* and this is your priority? With the flashlight, we can tell this guy's in bad shape. There's all this blood and a hole in his cheek where you can see through to the teeth. Matt says the guy's drunk on the local drink, um, it smells like rotting fruit?'

'*Chibuku*,' Scholie murmured.

'Yeah,' the girl blinked, 'he's totally wasted on that stuff, definitely too drunk to stand up or walk. So we decide I should stay with him because Jess is too scared to stay alone and Matt doesn't want to go for help alone. There's this construction site, half a brick house type thing, so we use a tent to make a gurney and carry him in there. Matt and Jess start walking to a town we passed a half hour back. And I stay behind and wait with the man and the kid and some beer to keep me company.'

'Now, *that's* bloody brave,' one of the British girls slurred.

The American girl described how the rest of the night went. How the boy fell asleep. How she cradled the man's head on her lap, and the blood soaked through her jeans, drying there. How she got a bit drunk and lost the feeling in her thighs. How the sun was already rising when the ambulance finally came. Thandi could see it all. The boy curled in the corner like a snail's shell, the waxy dawn sky, the man's blood blackening. She even knew how the story would end: a patched tyre, a race to the nearest hospital, a triumphant recovery. Perhaps there would be a quasi-adoption of the boy: sponsored schooling, intermittent donations, his pot belly diminishing as his fortunes grew. But the American girl trailed off before all that.

'The guy was fine in the end,' she said. 'But it was super intense. He had, like, a *hole* in his face. Not bungee-jump intense but, you know,' the girl laughed.

After a beat, her audience did too. Except for Thandi. Didn't it seem a little convenient that this girl had not caused the accident and had magically saved its victim?

'To life!' The American girl stood, raising a beer with a whoop. 'Let's fuckin dance!'

Someone pulled out a radio and soon an Ace of Base song was yelping out of it and everyone was up and dancing, as if on command. Thandi alone stayed seated by the bonfire, watching Scholie rock his hips in front of the American girl. Sex had arrived, with all of its tender collusion. The wind picked up, raising copper in the embers. The canvas tents applauded.

*

There had always been other girls around Scholie. That was why Thandi was so reticent. After finding Lee's callous inventory in his bachelor pad, she wasn't about to fall for another philanderer. But it was hard to resist Scholie – his dark, rich skin, his plump lips, even his slippy-slidey accent. He and Thandi had spent many nights partying after her shifts at JollyBoys, drinking at the hotel bars or dancing at the one nightclub in town, which had a full wall of mirrors. Thandi would back up against him and wind her hips as they stared in the glass, admiring themselves and each other under the roving blue lights. They never took it any further. Thandi knew that after he dropped her back at JollyBoys late at night, he often went out again and found another girl to take to bed.

But the bonfire at the bushcamp was the first time Scholie actually left Thandi to find her own ride home. She supposed it was his way of saying he would no longer besiege her dam wall. At dawn, just before he slipped into a tent with the American girl, he looked at Thandi and shrugged, his eyelid twitching at her. Teasing her? Mocking her? Hungover and sulking at her own passivity, Thandi climbed into Mainza's Land Rover. She almost wept with dismay when the troop of British girls from the bonfire clambered in after her. Just a quick drive, Mainza promised. These girls wanted a tour of the game park.

Thandi leaned her head against a cold metal pole in the back, three itchy blankets over her, as the British girls – shockingly spry after all that drinking – *oohed* and *aahed* and leapt up to take pictures of impala until they eventually realised that impala were as common here as deer in England. Thandi had almost managed to fall asleep in the jouncing vehicle when Mainza swung it into a small grove and parked.

The British girls thudded out, pulling up the waists of their boot-cut jeans to avoid wetting their hems in the dewy grass. Thandi stayed in the Land Rover, watching them follow Mainza over the grass. When he reached a cluster of grey rocks, he stopped, turned to them and opened his hands like a preacher.

'This is the Old Drift cemetery,' he said. 'The very first European settlers to this place came here in the 1890s. But they say this place was cursed and most of them died. From what?' He pointed at a girl slapping at her neck. 'From the same reason you're smacking yourself!'

'Mosquitoes?'

'Malaria, you twat,' her friend said.

'Yes!' Mainza said, pretending to be impressed. 'But in those days, they called it *black fever.*'

'OoOOoo,' another girl tittered. 'Is that like *jungle* fever?'

'That *ka* American movie?' Mainza pretended to be scandalised. Then he smirked and leaned towards them to murmur confidentially: 'I wish!'

The British girls giggled and glanced back at Thandi in the Land Rover. She avoided their eyes. She knew they were thinking of Scholie and the American girl at the bonfire. They had all seen him and Thandi arrive together. Mainza saved her by resuming his speech.

'Take a look around. Not all the headstones are marked, but you might even find one of your ancestors.' He swept his arm wide and stepped to one side as if welcoming them into the graves.

Thandi was completely exhausted by the time Mainza finally dropped her at JollyBoys. There was no time to sleep – she had only half an hour before her shift. She showered, climbed into her skirt suit as if into a torture apparatus, and took up her station behind the front desk. The clock said 6.04 a.m. The hostel guests who had booked a morning drive were already in the lobby, rustling around a table with an electric kettle, a basket of teabags, a jug of milk and a plate of biscuits. Thandi stared at the Italian woman with dark brown hair. Her husband, a big Indian man with a moustache, was handing her a cup of tea with a cloying solicitude.

The couple had checked in two nights ago, for their honeymoon. They had arrived at night without a reservation, flustered from a long drive. The man had carefully counted out cash for the room. Their mismatch – in age and in race and in accent – seemed worse now, wrong somehow, as wrong as Scholie's dark hand on that girl's pale back as they'd rocked their hips in tandem. Thandi snatched up the reception phone receiver. She bit her lip – she couldn't remember her sister's number in London or her parents' in Harare. Instead, she dialled the one number in Lusaka that she knew by heart.

✳

A week later, Thandi was sitting on the kerb, waiting to board the Mazhandu coach to Lusaka. The coach was expensive but she knew she couldn't withstand a minibus today, not with this hangover. The going-away party the JollyBoys staff had thrown her the night before had left her wrecked. She sipped on ice water, wishing she hadn't had her hair plaited with extensions yesterday. A tender, stinging force field now cradled her scalp – too much discomfort for a six-hour journey.

A group of tourists showed up at the coach stop around the same time as her. There was a group of guys who had stayed at JollyBoys: Thandi remembered their unplaceable accents. She smiled weakly and waved but they just looked at her vaguely. Now that they had checked out, they wouldn't bother with her – the young woman who spoke uncluttered English to them as she handed them keys and printed their bill. A girl sat with them, squatting on her bag, knees tenting her long batik skirt.

Thandi stared at the girl, an itch in her mind. She didn't seem attached to any of the men but she was enjoying their lazy morning revelry: coffee in flasks and *vitumbua* and morning-after stories. Then the girl gave a deep, raspy laugh that dredged up a memory from Thandi's mind: the night at the bonfire. In the daylight, the American girl looked nondescript. She could have been any girl from any time during the months that Thandi had spent in Livingstone. But she wasn't. She was that girl from that night and Thandi swiftly hated her.

The moment the driver had loaded the suitcases and opened the coach doors, Thandi boarded. She plonked herself in an aisle seat and her *kiondo* on the window seat. She was flabbergasted when the American girl pitched up in the aisle next to her and blithely asked if she could sit there. Thandi looked around. The coach was already nearly full.

'Ya, no, I guess it's available,' Thandi said sullenly. She slid over into the window seat, lifting her *kiondo* onto her lap. The girl smiled and slung her rucksack on the floor in front of her seat, her shoulder wrung red where its strap had bitten the skin. She sat down, her foot propped on it, her other leg bent under her like a half-collapsed chair. Thandi looked at the girl's shoe on her rucksack, each wearing its layer of grime patiently, in the way of martyred objects. The girl combed her fingers through her hair, filling the air with a candysweat smell as she pulled it into a ponytail that looked heavy in its lightness. Thandi reached in her bag for her bottle of ice water. Just looking at that hair the colour of unripe maize made her feel thirsty.

The coach driver strolled down the aisle, counting heads. The girl pulled a paperback from her rucksack – *Out of Africa*, of all things – and fanned herself with it but the pages released only a weak sugary must. She puffed her lips at Thandi to commiserate. She didn't seem to recognise her. Thandi nodded and sipped at her water bottle, the plastic crackling unhappily as the vacuum released. The chill crept down her throat, delicate and sharp, but as soon as the water hit her stomach, nausea rose like a demon. She swallowed and shut her eyes to fight it but it was slippery and coiling. She needed to eat something. She pulled her food warmer out of her *kiondo* and notched it open, hoping the shortbread biscuits the JollyBoys cook had baked for her this morning hadn't yet cooled. The girl looked over.

'Would you like one?' Thandi held out the container reluctantly.

'A cookie? Hell yes!' the girl said, taking one with her closebitten fingers. What was her name again? All Thandi could remember was that it had a cat-like snap and purr to it. Scholie would know, of course. But Thandi would never see Scholie again. And she would never ask him. Even if she did see him. Which she wouldn't. The girl bit into the biscuit and grinned.

'It's just like the ones on safari!' she said. There was a galaxy of crumbs over her lips.

'And what did you see on your safari?' Thandi asked with the exact rhythm and tone that she had been using at the front desk at JollyBoys for the past six months.

'Eland, rhino. Hippo. Monkeys, of course …'

The girl responded at length, crunching through Thandi's biscuits along the way. This was how all the tourists had spoken after a game drive, naming the animals one by one like children. Her forearms on the desk, Thandi had nodded and smiled, watching their wind-brightened eyes dim a bit more with each animal. Sometimes the wonders of the world are better left unsaid.

The coach gave a hitch and its bowels began to grumble. Thandi's bowels responded in kind. The air conditioning gushed down with the smell of scrubbed dust. Something was crawling up her throat. Saliva brimmed in her gullet. Biscuits or no, Thandi was going to be sick at some point on this coach ride. The girl had finished her nursery-room incantation.

Thandi swallowed. 'And how was your guide?'

'*Ah. Mazing.* I met him at this bonfire and he took me for a morning drive the next day, just us.'

'And did he teach you anything interesting?'

'Well, he told me about, um, the musting? You know how the bulls – the male elephants – go into heat? It kind of made me think of my period, you know – how it runs down their leg?' She grinned. 'He told me a joke about periods, too. Okay, so: what's an elephant's tampon?'

Thandi raised an eyebrow.

'A sheep!'

Thandi sneered with distaste. The girl rocked into her grandfather laugh. When she had sorted through it, thoroughly explored every cranny of her amusement, she put her hand on Thandi's shoulder.

'Come on, it's *hilarious.*'

Thandi glanced at the girl's hand on her skin just as the coach descended into a giant pothole in the road. The vomit rose, and Thandi turned away, her long plaits strumming the back of the seats in front of them. She had no choice – she opened the food warmer in her lap and puked over the remainder of the biscuits. Barely anything came up: a grainy mush, water, and something putrid yellow, the colour of a warning. Thandi wiped her mouth, closed the lid on the mess, and turned it to lock it.

'Oh my god, are you okay?' The girl stroked Thandi's back. 'I used to get car sick all the time growing up—'

'Just hungover,' Thandi croaked but the girl was already recounting her childhood and how and when and why she had vomited so much back then. The coach heaved and humped along. To stave off her nausea, Thandi fixed her eyes on the girl's nose, the smattering of freckles like make-up she hadn't rubbed in. What would happen if those spots grew in number, merged, crowded her skin with melanin? How differ-ent this girl's life would be, the one she was still stitching into a thread-bare story with her patchy memories of a small town in California. When the coach finally turned onto the smooth Great North Road, it felt like an exhalation. It gave Thandi an excuse to look out of the window. After a pause, she heard the rustle of the girl opening her stiff copy of *Out of Africa*.

Thandi closed her eyes and rested her head on the window, her plaits squeaking against the glass. She hated that this girl felt so free to talk to her and touch her. But wasn't that why Thandi had come to Livingstone? To meet new people? To befriend them in the name of that African mantra: opportunity-opportunity-opportunity? No. She had just wanted to flee Lee's cowardly eyes, to get out of that damned spot. But then she'd met charming Scholie, and so she'd stayed on, letting him charm her. And now, of course, she was leaving again, this time to get away from Scholie, so that when he pitched up at JollyBoys and said, 'Hey, man, where's TandyCandy?' they'd say, 'Ah, sorry, man, she's bounced.'

✳

When Thandi woke up from her nap, the coach was climbing a road, old car crash sites on the banks marked with white crosses. The sun made the scratches on the window glow and as her gaze receded from that bright cross-hatching, Thandi noticed her reflection: big eyes, small nose, big lips, small chin. She kissed her lips inward to spread her lipstick and saw the American girl's face behind her, looking not at the world outside the window but at Thandi. Their glances touched in the glass and the girl spoke.

'Are you feeling any better, you poor thing?'

Thandi felt obliged to turn. She nodded with a close-mouthed smile.

'I'm telling you, it's totally car sickness. I don't know if it's worse on a bus. This is my first bus ride in Africa, actually. We drove down from Lusaka to see the Falls.'

Thandi breathed. 'And what did you think of the Victoria Falls?'

'Oh-my-god. So. Fucking. Beautiful. I've seen a lot of waterfalls, like the one up in Impala and this incredible one in Cambodia. But this was, like – the perfect circle rainbow? *So amazing*. Lemme show you.' The girl reached down for her bag and her head bounced against the seatback in front of her. 'Oops,' she giggled. 'Good thing it's so soft,' she said, stroking the fuzz on the seat.

She was right. The whole coach was furry: the ceiling, the aisle, even the walls were coated with a coarse grey fur flecked with primary colours. An inside-out animal. Thandi's eye hit a mirror, a large disc above the driver. Rows of heads danced in its reflection and she felt another surge of nausea. The girl had pulled out a sheaf of photos – glossy and unbent – from an envelope and was scrunching closer, bringing the smell of her hair with her. She rifled through the pictures quickly, flashing a montage. Monkeys dangling and reaching for nuts. Livingstone's bulky, cartoonish statue. Another bloody sunset. A shoe-less boy. Arms and oars spoking from rapids. A girl in cargo shorts and a pink shirt floating upside down, arms extended like Christ, a cord scribbling across the sky above her ankles.

'Is that you?'

The girl turned to Thandi with a solemn look in her eyes.

'Oh-my-god, bungee jumping? It's a spiritual experience. I saw death coming straight at me, and then the bungee caught, and honestly, I felt truly alive for the first time in my life.'

She shook her head, moving through photos of the Falls now, all nearly identical – white clusters of chaos against a black-rock backdrop, with that lovely twisting torque that they get during the dry season – until she reached one of her standing on the footbridge.

'There it is,' she said with wonder, as if remembering what she had been seeking.

Thandi peered at it. The girl looked prettier than she was in real life, standing with her knee cocked and that prismatic halo around her – the rainbow unchecked by a horizon, free to make a full circle. Thandi had hurried through that rainbow herself only a month ago, too nervous about the slippery footbridge to pause until Scholie had put his arms around her and made her look. Thandi wondered for the first time if there was some justice in the choice that he had made at the bonfire. She opened the food warmer again and heaved, but nothing came up.

'Are you sure you're not sick?' the girl asked as she stroked Thandi's back.

'I'm fine,' Thandi said impatiently, spitting into the warmer. 'I just drank a lot last night.'

'Oh, I thought you had malaria or something!' The girl tapped the tip of Thandi's nose. Her finger smelled of dead cigarettes. 'I know the feeling. I had a *rough* night at that bonfire last week.'

'I know. I was there,' Thandi said shortly, surprising herself. She had assumed she would play out this farce until they reached Lusaka.

'Wait, you *were?*' The girl burst out laughing. 'Wait, of course, I thought I recognised—'

For a moment, relief bubbled up through Thandi.

'You know what?' The girl scrutinised her, then nodded firmly. 'I just remembered. Your braids! I loved the red then too! I've been wanting to get mine done like that. Do you know—'

'I didn't have plaits that night. I came with Scholie?' Thandi said pointedly. They exchanged a look.

'Wait. You're not *with* Scholie, are you?' The way the girl said his name was off, the 'o' a little too long, the 'l' too liquid. Thandi was tempted to lie but she smiled reassuringly.

'No. Don't worry. He tried, but.'

'Oh, okay,' the girl breathed, relieved. She cocked her head with a knowing smile. 'He must have been hard to resist. I mean, I was *super* drunk but that dude was *super* persuasive.'

Thandi had a flash of memory: two backs hunching to enter a tent. She looked out the window again. The last thing she wanted was a chat with her new mate about Scholie's persuasive moves – she wasn't inclined to confess that a rush of air to the eye was the closest she and Scholie had ever got. Outside the coach, the clouds were soft skirts pleated with slanting light. Concrete buildings slid by on Great North Road, iconic pictures advertising their purposes: carpentry, coal, hairdressing, drink. The side of the road thickened with people: pedestrians, women selling tomatoes stacked in pyramids, men on bicycles warping under firewood.

'So you heard the stories at the bonfire then?' The girl's voice sounded tight.

Thandi turned wearily. 'Yes. I was there.'

The girl was staring at the seatback in front of her. Her cheeks were pink, but that might have been the setting sun coming in through the window. 'So you heard mine then. Yeah, that was a pretty shitty night.' She paused. 'You know, I was *so* drunk. And I really thought he was dying.' Her voice cracked. It was like she was pleading, explaining something to a jury. 'It was *so* sad. And I felt like all he wanted was to be touched, you know? Like, held with love. Like, touched in that way.'

Thandi didn't know what to do with her face. What was this girl saying?

'He didn't say anything but I could tell, you know? From his hands and his eyes. I tried to say no, I was whispering so I wouldn't wake up the boy, but he didn't get it. He just kept touching my hair and face. And then he put my hand on him. I thought he was *dying*, you know? And I felt like I could give him this, like – gift. I thought if I touched him the way he wanted me to, he would understand. How sorry I was.' The girl turned to Thandi. She looked thin and torn. 'And I was right,' she said. 'He did.'

The girl's face was so close, Thandi could see the whites of her eyes, the jagged red lines in them. She wondered how old she was, this woman she kept thinking of as 'the girl'. Thandi had always thought of sex as an exchange – of love or power – or a prize to hold over someone or withhold from them. She had never thought of it as a gift. She didn't know what to say.

'I can plait your hair for you if you want,' she offered finally. She touched the hair wisping at the girl's temple. 'Your hair is too thin – it will fall out. But I can try.'

The girl smiled toothily and then they were like schoolgirls. The girl sat with her feet in the aisle and her back to Thandi. Thandi sat sideways with a knee hitched and her back to the window. She pulled out the scrunchie and the hair swept down, static lifting a blonde mist. She smoothed it and parted it. She threaded her fingers in it and rotated her wrists, twisting the rising mayhem into order. She was halfway done when the girl murmured, 'Just let me know how much you charge.'

Thandi's jaw tightened, but her hands kept on twiddling. The girl nestled sideways into the seatback beside her. Outside, the sky blushed then dimmed. The smell of woodsmoke seeped into the coach. By the time they had circled the roundabout under the Findeco House skyscraper, gone over the bridge, and turned into the bus depot, it was night, and the girl was fast asleep. The plaits in her hair were already loosening.

Thandi crept over her and queued up in the aisle behind the other bleary, yawning passengers. Under the orange street lamp outside, family and friends milled around chatting while they waited for the driver to haul their luggage out of the low belly of the coach. Thandi was sniffing her fingers to see if the girl's hair had left a scent when an older white woman with a cane stepped hesitantly towards the driver. Thandi felt pity rise, and relief. She went over and took the woman's hand.

'It's Thandi,' she said. 'I'm here.'

Agnes smiled warmly and pulled her into her arms. 'We are so glad you're home, Tendeeway,' she said, her lips vibrating against Thandi's ear. 'We have missed you so much.'

We. Thandi looked over Agnes's shoulder and saw the pickup across the street, his face framed in the window. Lee didn't wave or smile. He just looked at her, stern and beseeching and beautiful. His skin was in the shadows but she knew it was brown-brown-brown. Just like hers.

＊

A year later, Thandi was balanced on stilettos, hovering over a toilet seat, the skirt of her voluminous dress gathered behind her and tilted up so that the wire hoop rested on the cistern. She was releasing a copious volume of liquid from her bladder, legs aching in her squat – a unique paranoia, this mistrust of the backs of other people's thighs. She could already feel a knot in her forehead, harbinger of the hangover to come. But for now she was happy and tipsy – a four-glasses-in feeling – giddy enough to have brought a bottle of champagne into the toilet stall.

She picked it up and drank as she pissed, relishing the heft in her hand, the silky sting on her tongue, the amusement of concurrently filling up and emptying out. She swallowed the itchy sweetness, lowered the bottle, and then she saw it: a smudge of blood in the crotch of the panties stretched between her calves, a circle of red in the white, like the Japanese flag. She unrolled some toilet paper. She wiped and examined and confirmed. It was her period. On her wedding night. Settling hopelessly onto the dicey seat, Thandi wept. How had she timed things so badly?

After a few minutes, she pulled herself together. She shimmied off the panties – painstakingly chosen from a Victoria's Secret catalogue and sent from London – and peeked out of the stall to make sure the bathrooms were empty. She hastened to a sink to wash the stain out, scrubbing fiercely at the damn spot, lace threads popping inside her wringing fists. Back in the stall, she hefted her skirt, threaded her stilettos through the holes, and tugged the panties, reluctant with damp, up her thighs again. She didn't have a pad – she had left her bag in the ballroom – so she wrapped a long stretch of toilet paper around the crotch, where it settled into a papier-mâchéd lump.

Thandi tottered back to the wedding reception in the Ridgeway ballroom and sat next to Lee at the bridal table, shifting her hips to keep the wedge of toilet paper in place. He glanced at her, but kept his back turned as he continued to flirt with her mother. While Thandi had been weeping in the loo, he had castled their positions. She was now sitting next to his father, who had been strutting around all day in his boxy tuxedo and tinted spectacles, trailed by a cloud of cologne and cognac. Drunk enough to forget their mutual dislike, Ronald started telling her about UNZA, where he had been dean of engineering for twenty years. Thandi suppressed her yawns behind smiles as he regaled her with bureaucratic stories about hirings and firings, bursaries and hierarchies. She wished she were sitting with Agnes, who was chatting softly to her aide, Grace.

The reception moved in slow motion, chewing up the cake, draining the liquor bottles, swallowing time. Thandi stared out at the laughing, chatting, eating, drinking, blinking wedding guests. All dressed up and laid out before her, they seemed like strangers, passengers on a flight. Only when a child waved, or a man raised his beer bottle, or a woman clinked a fork against a glass to make Lee kiss her – which he did with dead eyes and great gusto – did Thandi remember that these were her friends, her family, her people, that she had chosen them to be here with her. All she wanted was to be at home in bed, curled in a ball, alone and quietly bleeding.

2006

Thandi's wedding-night mishap ought to have made her more adaptable. Instead, as time passed, she grew obsessed with always being prepared. Her life became a matrix of schedules – hers and Lee's and their son's. Her dainty handbag transformed into an African mother's handbag: a repository of unexpected need. Over the years, that leather sack accumulated tissues, nappies, dental floss, condoms, panties, a bra, a clip-on tie, tampons, sugar packets, ketchup packets, lozenges, mints, sweets, toothpicks, an interesting toy, an interesting book, bottles of perfume and of rubbing alcohol, plasters, scissors, and a sachet of sharp and tiny tools – paperclips, safety pins, tacks and staples. As a stewardess, anticipating needs was how Thandi had served people. Now it became how she loved them.

Her son's mere existence spurred a rage of solicitude in her. Marrying Lee had felt like a concatenation of compromises, with him and with herself. But Joseph was separate from all that, a beautiful accident – her blood pressure had skyrocketed during her pregnancy, and it had been a high-risk birth, an emergency C-section at eight months. The baby was underweight and prone to infection, colicky and mucousy. She stared for hours at his little face, a synopsis of his parents' storied ones – Lee's gold undertone, Thandi's green eyes. Only she could provide what her boy needed. She fed him often, monitored his growth like a nutritionist. She held him tight enough to crush his bones.

By the time he was eight, Joseph had learned that he could get her attention by moving ever so slowly, a milquetoast torpor designed to torture her. He spent most of his time in his room, which he kept meticulously tidy. Thandi would stand in the threshold, her hands cupped in front of her.

'Need anything, baby?'

Joseph, sprawled out on the bed, wouldn't even look up from whatever languorous task was at hand – thumbing the pages of a book or the buttons of some toy.

'Anything at all? Hungry?' Thandi would reverse her cupped hands, turning them over as if she held an hourglass with grains of patience retracing their path.

After an unbearably long pause, Joseph would raise his head, mouth slack, and shake it. Left. Right. Left. Thandi would turn and walk off so he wouldn't see her hands jerking open, the hourglass shattering, her patience running out.

'He's not *that* slow, Thunder,' Lee would say when she complained, chucking her under the chin. 'You're just too *fast*.'

Easy for him to say. Lee spent all his time at work or abroad at conferences or out with his friends. She couldn't really complain. After he had moved back to Lusaka from Harare and finished his medical residency at UTH, he had set up his own lucrative medical practice. They had moved into a large house in Thorn Park, with a freshly watered garden and two cars. They had a maid and a cook and a gardener and a driver, which Lee seemed to think was enough adult company for his wife. He would waltz in just in time for a meal or a bit of telly, then head straight to bed, belittling her impatience in passing.

'Mrs On-your-mark-get-set. You're just too *ready*,' he'd chide and then leave her alone once again.

Thandi *was* ready. Every night, she lay beside her husband in bed, White Linen perfume seeping from her neck and tickling her nose. For a long time, she had been too preoccupied with caring for her son to mind that Lee had stopped having sex with her. Now that Joseph was almost self-sufficient when it came to food, clothing and shelter, she was ready to make another baby, a new needy being. But in the meantime, her co-creator had slipped away. Their marriage had ceased to be conjugal; his body did not conjugate hers; there was no grammar between them.

This sometimes happens in a marriage, and with age, but Thandi was not done with sex. She was thirty-one, brimming with desire, haunted nightly with visions of men – rough men, hung men, sweet men, creative men – annoyingly, all slight revisions of her man. Lee had not been her first but he had been her best. He had set her sexual compass. How humiliating to lie on her back every night, nipples brushing her nightie with each breath, aching for him, while he lay on his side, snoring with a stringy whistle, his palms clasped and wedged between his knees.

He still slept with other women, she was sure of it. But what could she say? She had forgiven him in advance, hadn't she? She had found his little fuck-book in Harare, that cold list of names, and she had run off to Livingstone, and she had bounced right back to him anyway. They had never spoken about that book but it had revealed to her just how broad his tastes were, just how expansive the circle of his desire. When she had agreed to marry him, she had never thought that one day, she might be left standing outside of it.

Her ache for him spread through her each night, as if issuing from an unbearable throbbing in her upper left wisdom tooth. She eventually resorted to touching herself while he slept beside her. She would hitch one leg like a flamingo and fumble with her fingers, pondering what would happen if he caught her busy-handed, if he woke up and asked: 'What on earth are you doing, Thunder?' Would he believe her if she said she was scratching an itch? Would he roll on top of her with a cheeky grin? No. Whenever she turned to him and opened her eyes, she'd find him dozing through her solitary ministrations. It was a small death every time.

She began taking herself to the guest room to take herself in private. She would lock the door and lie on the bed. Eyes closed, breath catching, she would thrum and clench, automatic tears slipping down her temples, a rancid taste in her mouth. These excursions always put her to sleep and sometimes she didn't make it back to the master bedroom until morning. She would come in and find Lee awake, sitting on the edge of the bed, rubbing his eyes. 'Good morning,' he would say with a soft smile. He never asked where she had been, which felt like both a relief and an insult.

One evening, as she kissed her son goodnight, she saw Joseph wince and turn his head from her mouth. Only then did it dawn on her that her toothache might smell as rotten as it tasted. Was that why Lee was avoiding her? She started taking antibiotics, hoping to quell the infection. A month later, Mrs Thandiwe Banda found herself once again caught with her pants down, sitting on the toilet – her own this time – and wondering what she had done to deserve this. She scrutinised the canvas between her legs, trying to read the baffling stain, sniffing tentatively at it. It smelled like a bakery and it felt like one too – dry and hot as fire. Hellfire? Was this her punishment for her nightly visits to the guest room? Thandi was not a regular churchgoer, but she was well acquainted with flaws and their consequences.

Thandi said nothing to her doctor husband and she barely registered the pharmacist's matter-of-fact diagnosis – thrush – and how normal a condition it was, especially on antibiotics. She suffered in silence as she inserted the cool lozenges into her hot hole. She suffered as the prescribed medication destroyed the pearly legions of yeast inside her. She suffered a trip to the dentist, who peremptorily pulled the tooth. And she suffered when it was over, and she found herself back in bed, lying beside a beautiful man who still had no apparent interest in touching her.

Once Thandi gave up on pleasuring herself, she had more time to stare at Lee and think. To notice how his smell changed on certain days of the week, to parse its individual notes (bergamot, smoke, lye, gin). To try to deduce where he took their son after he picked him up from school. Yes, Thandiwe Banda became quite the scientist. She curled on her side and observed her husband, her palms, like his, clasped in prayer and wedged between her knees.

✳

Microorganisms are highly deceptive creatures. A virus, for example, seems weak by definition: it is classified as an *obligate* and its primary state is one of need. But a virus does not just hide inside its host like an animal seeking shelter in a cave, nor does it just hitch a ride in a cell and drop off elsewhere. A virus sneaks in and takes over. Some viruses, like Ebola, are effective because that takeover is so rapid and gruesome; but most of them, like the common cold, are powerful because they are relatively mild but ubiquitous. Lee chose to study The Virus because it is one of the most devious of obligates.

Its ultimate cunning is its choice of host, what's called its *tropism*. The Virus targets the immune system, infiltrating the white blood cells that usually direct operations to defend the body from invaders in the first place. It then uses those immune cells to reproduce itself, co-opting their mechanisms for genetic replication. The same is true, in a sense, of The Virus's main mode of transmission: sex. It takes advantage of the two engines of life – the desire to reproduce and the will to persevere. Sneakiest of all, The Virus vanishes into the cells it has usurped, making it invisible to the system that would seek to destroy it. It is the great pretender, a spy in disguise, an inner subverter. This makes it all the more difficult to cure, much less prevent.

'By the year 2000, fifteen per cent of the Zambian population was infected with The Virus – mostly women, mostly adults. And that was six years ago,' Lee said, shaking his head. The NGO workers and social scientists in the audience bowed over their scribbling pens. He could almost hear them thinking: Why won't these bloody *muntus* just stop fucking already?

Lee was delivering a talk at the Alliance Française of Lusaka, which was hosting a conference about addressing the needs of those infected by The Virus, as well as the orphans they left behind. The Virus had wrought an epidemic. Prevention campaigns had helped. Billboards all over the country proclaimed the virtues of safe sex and, more dubiously, abstinence. That looped red ribbon icon was now scattered over pamphlets and walls like a plague of red eyes. And unlike other political leaders in the region, Kenneth Kaunda had acknowledged The Virus as early as 1987, after his son Masuzyo died of it. There had been substantive advances in treatment since then: access to antiretroviral drugs, with the vehicular-sounding abbreviation ARVs, in the early 1990s; the approval of the first generics a few years ago.

But still, it was as if – and Lee said this now, turning away from the charts and graphs on his projected PowerPoint to gesture at the ceiling like a poet: 'It is as if a giant animal has crunched its teeth through millions of people. It has devoured an entire generation of this country. All the parents are gone.' He looked out at the audience of bobbing heads. 'We are a nation of orphans.'

This was mostly rhetoric. Lee needed to convey the magnitude of the epidemic to policymakers if he was to acquire the resources he needed for his experiments. But in truth, Lee was too pragmatic to weep for dying Zambians, and he was far more interested in the biology and epidemiology than the sociology of the disease. He turned to his next slide, an old one.

'This is the structure of The Virus.'

He only showed this one to non-scientists these days. The diagram was basic and oddly floral – a circle surrounded by spokes, the glycoproteins The Virus uses to attach itself to an immune cell. Lee looked at it admiringly.

'A vaccine usually works by giving the body a tiny dose of an inactive virus,' he explained.

This is like an invasion by a zombie militia – small-scale and half-dead, but unusual enough for the body to notice it, destroy it, and learn all about it in the process. When the real army comes, the immune cells are primed to attack. But The Virus thwarts this approach by targeting the immune system itself, by in effect infiltrating both the schools and the military bases of the body.

'To develop a different kind of vaccine, we have been looking instead into some promising studies about a group of sex workers in Nairobi,' Lee said. 'These women are obviously highly exposed to The Virus, and they test positive for it. But for some reason, it has not blossomed into the full-blown disease in this small population.'

A few bowed heads in the audience sprang up like maize kernels bursting into popcorn.

'As we've known since the 1990s,' Lee went on, 'human immune cells have receptors that The Virus uses to enter and infect them – CD4, CCR5, CXCR4. The hypothesis is that these prostitutes have mutations in the genes for one or more of these receptors. In short, these women may have a *natural immunity* to The Virus.'

Audience members whispered as he proceeded to the next slide. This research was not new – the Americans had discovered a Virus-immune patient with this mutation in 1994 – but social researchers seemed to know little of the scientific data being gathered in Africa. Yes, the studies were scant and suffered from a breathtaking lack of resources. But being here, in the midst of the crisis, ought to make you hungry for medical breakthroughs wherever they could be found. Lee was always a little surprised by the surprise he encountered at these conferences.

After his presentation was over, an older man, white hair stubbling his chin, approached him.

'Hex-cuse me, sah. But that was remakabo! Extra-extra-ordinary!' the man exclaimed, pumping Lee's hand energetically. 'Blirriant!'

'Thanks,' Lee murmured. There weren't many locals at this conference. The *bashikulu*'s suit was old-fashioned and scuffed, his hems as withered as his thin purple lips. He was wearing a stethoscope for some reason, and dusty white nursing shoes.

'Am Dr Patrick Musadabwe. We must link up, Dr Banda! You are velly implessive.'

Lee sighed internally, anticipating a request for money. He glanced around the room at the clusters of chatting *bazungu*, seeking an exit from the conversation.

'... must inform you that I have a velly-good population for testing this Nairobi thing.'

'What do you mean?'

'These women in Kenya.' Musadabwe leaned in with an eyebrow raised. 'You are aweya that we have these same women in Lusaka as well?'

'Yes, I'm aware.' Lee scratched his head and tried not to laugh or inhale – Musadabwe's breath was staggeringly foul.

'You must come to my clinic, just down the road in Kalingalinga. We can do velly-good resatch together.'

'Ah sorry, Ba Uncle.' Lee put on his politest Zambian manners. 'I have my own clinic.'

'But do you have the correcti peshents? Because if we transplantate these kinds of mutation thingies, pahaps through the stem cell transplantation—'

'You know about stem cell transplants?' asked Lee, peering curiously at this ragtag doctor.

'Of course!' Musadabwe exclaimed, issuing another cannonade of halitosis. He put his hand on Lee's arm. 'Come, my friend, come to my clinic. It has eveelithing you need.'

✳

Musadabwe's clinic, a squat blue and white building in the middle of the compound, did not have everything that Lee needed, not by a mile. It was empty inside but for an old wooden desk, its concrete floors speckled from the fresh paint job on the walls. Reaching up now and again to pat Lee on the shoulder, Musadabwe gave a tour of the rooms – 'andi this one will be for examinationing our peshents ...' If the patients were not poisoned by fumes from the paint, Lee thought, or from the good doctor's mouth. If he even was a doctor. Despite the string of titles after his name on the outside wall of the clinic, Lee wasn't quite convinced by Mr Malaprop over here.

Musadabwe seemed to know his stuff, though. They sat on the wooden desk and drank from a bottle of Scotch – the only bottle, the only chemical, in the place – lecturing each other on bone-marrow transplants and receptor mutations, on inherited conditions and antiretroviral resistance, on autoimmunity and genetic abnormality, on using what was available to make something new.

'Together, Dr Banda,' Musadabwe exhorted, 'we can vanquish this monster!'

As the sun sent its dying light into the hollow clinic, Lee thought it through. He had been having trouble recruiting subjects for his vaccination research at his private medical practice across from the International School. The Virus was still taboo and his wealthy patients sometimes seemed more desperate to keep their status under wraps than to stay alive. They paid him generously not just to administer imported ARVs, but to remain discreet about it too. Even the promise of anonymity hadn't convinced them to try experimental therapy.

Besides, if Lee wanted to replicate the Nairobi study, he needed to find a different kind of Virus patient – sexually active, asymptomatic, and willing to undertake great risk for money. This clinic was in a perfect location – a compound frequented by prostitutes and their clients. And Musadabwe, doctor or no, was the first person Lee had met who both felt the urgency of the problem and had the ambition to pursue a solution into the shadiest corners of Zambian society.

'Fine,' Lee said finally, swaying a little as he shook Musadabwe's outstretched hand.

'Yes, it is extremree fine!' Musadabwe grinned greenly at him. 'Velly-good.'

<hr />

At first, Musadabwe's One Hundred Years Clinic was simply a hole in Lee's pocket. Lee funded the entire operation – building the sterile examination rooms, importing equipment and ARVs – and keenly felt its redundancy: did he not already have a private clinic? It was like he had just built its poorer, shabbier cousin in the compound, and worse, for patients who could not pay. If anything, these patients opened the hole in his pocket wider with their bleating pleas. They wanted fees for schooling, food for sustenance, medicines for opportunistic infections and for everything else besides – colds, coughs, rashes. And still, the holy grail of study subjects eluded him.

Things moved faster when Lee discovered Hi-Fly Haircuttery & Designs Ltd by chance a year later. Plying Sylvia with dinners and stories, Lee took samples from her and all of her 'salon girls' and followed their leads to other casual sex workers in the community. He began a side project of his own, an experiment of sorts, based on a hunch. Musadabwe ran some tests and after a year of sorting the data and sending samples to their collaborators in Kenya and South Africa, they confirmed the results.

Some of these women, just like the ones in Nairobi, indeed had a natural gene mutation for an immune cell receptor. The Germans had effectively cured an HIV patient by giving him a stem cell transplant from a donor with a mutation like this – they were calling him The Berlin Patient. And in October of 2009, Lee and Musadabwe received a new report from the lab in Jo'berg: one very special woman had a second receptor as well. Zambia had a Lusaka Patient. It was indisputable: they had revolutionised the hunt for the Virus vaccine.

*

To celebrate the results, Lee and Musadabwe and Sylvia went to a shebeen next door to the Kalingalinga clinic and drank for hours. By the time Lee got home that night, he was falling-down, head-over-heels cut. He stumbled through three doors – out of a taxi, through the front door, into the master bedroom – kicked off his shoes, and collapsed next to his wife. Thandi was still awake, lying in the fetal position, hands between her knees. Her white nightie and *chitambala* looked silver in the gloom.

'And where have you been?' she asked.

This was new. He thought they had a silent agreement. He paid; she stayed. He didn't ask about Livingstone or her guest room visits; she didn't query his nightly whereabouts.

'Ah – work, you know,' he said, closing one eye to stop her from bouncing in his vision.

'Work.'

'A forum at, uh, UNZA. The Swizzerlandians, I mean the Swiss ...' He began to drop off.

'You smell like whisky.'

'Good nose.' He licked his chops sleepily.

'Work,' she said again.

Lee opened his eyes. Thandi's eyes glinted malachite. He looked away from them and saw her hip under the nightie, curving up like the moon on a horizon.

'Come here,' he growled and put his hand on it. He expected her to resist but instead, her breath caught and she bit her upper lip. She was lovely in the faint light coming from the clock radio, her skin purplish at the creases of the elbow and armpit and neck. Before he could stop himself, he had rolled onto his back and pulled her on top of him.

They lay pressed to each other for the first time in years. He felt himself grow hard against her pelvis. She had put on weight but she was still his Thunder – still quick and strong. He nudged his head towards hers and kissed her big, slippery lips. Her legs slowly parted and bent to kneel on either side of his hips, like a hesitant jockey. He cupped her breast – a mother's breast, lowswung but buoyant – and she moaned and hitched her nightie up, then her panties to the side. She worked him inside her and began to rock her hips. Lee's eyes slid shut. He forgot himself completely, forgot his resolve to keep her safe from his secret store of deviousness.

*

As soon as it was over, they fought. Lee was panting from his orgasm. Thandi was collapsed on him, vibrating, still pent up. Then he twitched. It was the slightest buck of the body, just enough to signal *I'm done*. Thandi scudded off him, sat up and exploded. She had not known that her mouth harboured such a reserve of vile clichés. She called him a faggot, a *dambe*, a drunkard with a useless dick. She threatened to leave him, to move to London to live with her sister.

'And I'm taking your fucking son with me!'

Lee sat up and raised his hand. He stopped himself – even drunk, there were too many checkpoints between Lee's mind and his body for him to lose total control.

'What, you're going to *hit* me now?' she spat.

He lowered his hand and lay back, chest heaving, a tendon in his jaw writhing like a maggot.

'At least you'd be touching me for once!' Thandi shouted. 'Fuck you, Lionel Banda!'

She got up and stomped off to the bathroom down the corridor. She peed and wiped, semen sopping the toilet paper, and turned her panties inside out before putting them back on. Her hands were shaking with rage. Instead of returning to the master bedroom, she went to the guest room, locked the door, and lay on the pristine bedspread. She grabbed a pillow and put it between her legs and humped it furiously, trying to put out the fire he had sparked in her. But after a while, her hips stilled and she pulled the pillow up to her face and wept into it instead.

She woke up a few hours later with crust in the corners of her eyes. She dampened her finger with spit to wipe them, thinking of Scholie, the vibration of his breath when that insect had flown in her eye more than a decade ago. Handsome, charming Scholie, Prince of Livingstone, blithely rescuing her, then abandoning her for some white chick . . .

Thandi felt a sudden touch of paranoia. Scholie had been a player for real. Wasn't it risky to spit in someone's eye like that? Wasn't it what Lee's Virus research papers called 'mucous membrane contact'? How would Dr Lionel Banda have handled that situation? A saline eyedropper? An antibiotic ointment? A pirate's eyepatch? Thandi realised she was smiling. She knew him so well. A throb of love for her husband – even still, even now – clutched her throat and raised her up and out of bed.

But when she crept back into the master bedroom, he was gone. It was early morning, the light in the room amber. Thandi disrobed, put on a shower cap, and took a hot shower. She towelled off and massaged cocoa butter into her skin. She put on clean underwear, a skirt suit and high heels. She sat at her dressing table and applied her make-up, priming her face like a canvas, then shaping its beauty with shadow and shine, line and glitter. Last of all, she lifted her wig off its decapitated styrofoam head. Joseph had long ago defaced the bust with a green felt-tip pen, but the Lovely Luxe Locks wig she had bought in Kamwala was exquisite, a shiny copper orb. Thandi crowned herself with it.

*

'Where does your father take you when he picks you up from school?'

Mummy looked so serious standing in the doorway to his bedroom that Joseph replied immediately. Dad had never expressly told him *not* to tell Mummy where they went. But as soon as Joseph told her the truth and saw her face go from shocked to sad, he realised both that it was indeed a secret and that he was tired of keeping it.

'He takes you to a hair salon?!' Mummy asked.

'Mostly,' he said as the tension released in his breastbone.

'Okay, then. You must show me where it is,' she said, and his breastbone knotted right up again.

As the driver manoeuvred the sedan into Kalingalinga after lunch that day, Joseph leaning forward between the front seats to direct him, he wondered why his mother was all made up, like she was going to church or one of Dad's work functions. And as he slunk into the Hi-Fly and went to sit in his usual corner, he wondered why she was standing in the middle of the room, cradling her handbag like a baby and demanding that the 'boss' do her hair. He watched the salon girls scurry around to attend to his mother's needs as she seated herself regally before the wall of mirrors.

Joseph wished he had brought a book. He had been so disconcerted by their conversation at home that he had forgotten. In his eleven years of life, this was the first time his mother had ever asked *him* for something. Bored, he looked over the bits and bobs scattered on the floor around him, lighting on a shallow wire basket that looked like a sun dial, part of a disembowelled electrical fan lying on its back. He found an outlet in the wall behind him and plugged in the faceless half of the fan. When it didn't start, he spun its blades with his finger. It probably belonged to Jacob, who liked to play with gadgets ... There he was now, skulking out from the back room, wearing that stupid aeroplane seat belt around his waist, and hissing at Joseph.

'*Futsek, iwe!*'

The woman with skin like carbon paper spoke sharply. Jacob protested, then fell silent.

'Yes, it's okay, baby,' Joseph's mother said. 'Go on and play.'

✳

The October afternoon was windless, the sun plunging steadily down a cloudless sky. The yard behind the salon was still but for the two boys and their shadows. The clothes line swooped over their heads with its flock of avian pegs. An *mbaula* sat in its ashes like a mourning thing, a crumple of rubbish beside it. The jacaranda tree was in bloom, its flamboyant crown and train glowing in the lowering light. Jacob carved into its bark with a knife. Joseph sat on one of its roots, using a stick to write and erase words in the fallen blossoms on the ground. After a few minutes, Jacob turned and leaned back against the trunk, arms crossed.

'Who have you come with?' He nodded at the back door of the salon.

'My mum.'

'Oh-*oh*? Why has she come?' Jacob picked at a scab on his elbow. 'To start a fight?'

Before Joseph could respond, a girl stepped out into the yard. She looked Indian, her skin a little lighter than Joseph's. She was about the same age as the boys but thin and gawky in her light blue school uniform.

'Howzit?' she said. 'I'm Naila.'

Joseph shrugged and drew lines in the dirt. Jacob yawned and overturned an old yellow bucket to sit on.

'O-kaay.' She looked around, then sat down on a root next to Joseph's. She played with her hair for a while, plaiting it loosely, then unplaiting it. After a while, she got up with a sigh, dusted the seat of her uniform, and began to climb the jacaranda tree.

'The branches will break,' Joseph warned, dropping his stick and standing up.

'No, it is strong,' Jacob called. 'I have climbed this one before.'

The girl's Mary Janes were skidding on the trunk. She sat on the ground and started to pull them off.

'Don't!' Joseph yelped. 'You'll catch tetanus!'

'*Ah-ah*, what is wrong with no shoes?' Jacob scoffed. He himself was barefoot. 'Some of us do not have rich daddies to buy Bata. Take them off! It will make the climbing better, believe you me.'

'Don't listen to him. He's not educated. Where do *you* go to school?'

'Namununga.' Naila's shoes now off, the edges of her skirt tucked into her panties, she placed her foot against the trunk like a warrior.

'I'm at Rhodes Park,' Joseph said with a measure of pride.

'What can school be teaching you about climbing?' asked Jacob. 'You are a softie, you.'

'And what would *you* know about the laws of physics?'

'Physico what?' Jacob frowned, then smiled with delight. 'Look!'

He pointed at Naila, who had started to climb again. The boys watched her rise. Her dress was like the sky, a pale flat blue. Her limbs were like the tree's, bent and beige, a little scaly. You could see fear only in her toes, which curled to grip the bark. She moved slowly but surely and soon disappeared up into the foliage.

*

Jacob knew well what a good climbing tree the jacaranda behind the salon was. Its bark was just rough enough, and its branches started low, forking with curving angles that did not require great leaps of effort or faith. Inspired, he took off his aeroplane belt, tossed it on the ground, and followed the *mwenye* girl up. He heard her panting above him and he felt the soft kisses of the blossoms against his skin and he sensed the tension in his legs and arms as he balanced himself in the familiar stages – here, now there, now here – of his zigzag up the tree. Halfway up, he looked down between his straddled legs and saw Joseph's face frowning up at him. The *apamwamba* boy was still on the ground, of course, with his hang-em-high jeans and fly green trainers.

Uncle Lee had always been nice to Jacob. He brought him the occasional treat or toy, and he made his mother laugh, softened her. But his son? This skinny, ugly, banana-coloured boy, reading all the time, and acting like a goody two shoes, as if there were rules about tree climbing – Jacob hated him. Staring down at that smug yellow face, Jacob felt a crackle in his throat, and without even thinking about it, he spat.

The glob landed squarely between Joseph's eyebrows. The coloured boy clutched his face, shouting in horror. Chuckling, Jacob scurried up the tree, pushing off its branches, ducking its shaggy purple locks, reaching away from the boy gagging and cursing below.

The girl came into view, facing away. She was sitting with one bum cheek on a limb, her other leg swinging. She was peering down intently, trying to make out what Joseph was shouting about. Her hair fell forward, revealing the damp back of her neck, the curls distinct as cuts.

'Bwanji?' Jacob shuffled himself along the limb towards her to sit.

'Bwino.' She turned with a grin. Her eyes widened. She was pitching forward. Jacob gasped and reached out for her, his hand sweeping through the air as if swatting a mosquito.

*

Joseph heard the boughs snapping before he saw the girl plunging towards him through the canopy. She caught at a branch, which broke, then another, which didn't, and for a breathless moment, she swung, safe as a monkey. Then she slipped. The silence as she fell through the air was terrible. The sound when she landed was worse. Joseph stepped towards her, his throat still sore from ranting, his brow sticky with spit. Naila was on her side among the jacaranda blossoms, her eyes closed, her hair splayed up and behind her in the shape of a splash. If it weren't for the moans pulsing from her lips like water from a hose, she might have been asleep in a purple bower.

Joseph crouched down and saw her cheek ballooning before his eyes, a slow hydraulic rise. Blood trickled from her nostril and curdled the dust. She cracked an eyelid. That was when he leapt back. When he saw the blood flooding her eye – that was when he ran. He bolted into the salon through the back door, pushed the curtain aside, raced past the women inside, yanked the front door open – slamming it against the wall in his haste – and fled into the compound.

Joseph didn't hear his trainers pounding, his breath snagging on the spikes of his sobs. He didn't hear the pedestrians shouting as he bounced off them or the cars honking when he darted into the road. Only one sound could penetrate the panic suffocating him. His name. When it came, he stopped and turned and everything surged at him.

It was as if he had pulled a plug. A river of colour and movement and smells and noise – life itself – washed over him: Kalingalinga with its brightly coloured signs and *chitenge*-patterned people, and in its midst, in the distance, a broad-shouldered man in a long white coat striding towards him.

Joseph put his hands on his knees to catch his breath and blinked down at his dirty trainers. Where had he been running? Was the girl dead? He stood up straight just as his father reached him, put his big hand on his bony shoulder, and asked: 'Joseph, where is your mother?'

⚹

Thandi was sitting in a plastic seat, her head ensconced in the rattling inferno of an old hairdryer. Her relaxed hair had been rinsed and wrapped around big plastic curlers, which vibrated in the blast of hot air aimed at her skull. She was vibrating too, with the adrenaline of looking Lee's mistress in the face, of boldly subjecting herself to the other woman's hands and the chemicals she had slathered on her scalp. But Sylvia had not pulled too hard as she combed. She had not left the lye in too long so that the hair would fall out in clumps later. Sylvia had been calm and deft and professional. Relax, her fingers had said. Relax, the cool rinse had murmured.

Sylvia and her girls were now clustered around a veiled woman who had just come in and sent a little girl outside to play with the boys – their boys. The scratches in the dryer shield made it hard to see them, as did the sweat rolling from her temples into her eyes, but it looked to Thandi as if the salon girls were unwrapping a mummy, the customer's shawls unscrolling and wafting to the floor. Thandi's vision began to water.

She gave up, slumping in the chair and closing her eyes. She suddenly felt exhausted. Asking her son about his father had been excruciating enough. Joseph was the only one who knew where Lee went when he was not at work. But still. The shame she had felt, stooping to bully her boy with questions, forcing him to betray his father – and the rage, too, at Joseph's sullen complicity, his disloyalty – something in her relationship with her son had ... *SLAM!*

Thandi opened her eyes and caught the back of someone running out through the front door. She couldn't discern more from within the buzzing cocoon of the dryer. The salon girls didn't seem bothered – they had already turned back to the new customer with scissors in their hands. Sylvia ignored it, too, going about her business, chatting with her partner – was her name *Loveness*? – who was counting cash at the counter. Standing beside her pretty dark-skinned friend, Sylvia looked washed out. Thandi judged her for bleaching her skin with Ambi but she had to admit that Sylvia was otherwise lovely, with high cheekbones and big eyes and a natural waist. Her impassive beauty had thrown Thandi off.

She had wanted to shame Sylvia simply by coming here with the unspoken truth etched all over her face: *I know. I know all about you.* But now that the thrill of confrontation was over, now that the salon had turned indifferently to the next customer, Thandi felt that she had just exposed herself to more humiliation. The hairdryer was like a machine of self-mortification. The noisy swarm of heat around her head was her own fear, her own anger made external, a ring of hell, accompanied by the smell of sulphur and ...

Smoke? Thandi's eyes sprang open. Swirling clouds of it were flooding the room. Coughing, she tried to pry the helmet off her head but it was locked in place. She slithered down in her seat until she could manoeuvre herself out from under it, accidentally knocking hair curlers loose in the process, sending them spiralling down. She jumped up and scanned the room. It was empty of people but filled with the racket of the dryer and a chaos of smoke.

She quickly traced it to a socket in the wall where the hairdryer and a broken electric fan were plugged in. The two cords were steaming and sparking. She grabbed a hand towel, wrapped it around her hand, and yanked at both: the dryer cord came out and it sputtered to a stop but the fan cord ripped out from the machine instead of the wall. Still plugged into the outlet, the torn end of the cord sizzled over the floor like a serpent with a lightning tongue. She leapt away from it and stepped into something soft – a pile of white hair on the floor. She stared down at it in a daze. It was as if the tangled skeins of smoke in the room had frozen in place.

Just then she heard a commotion – or rather two. One came from behind the curtain at the back of the salon, the other from its entrance. The curtain parted and Sylvia staggered in with a little Indian girl in her arms, trailed by her son, her workers and the girl's quailing *gogo*, the customer from before, who now had a shorn head. At the same time, the front door swung open and Lee and Joseph came rushing in. As if choreographed, the two calamities on either side of the salon crashed at its smoky centre.

Thandi watched Sylvia transfer the injured girl, bleeding and shaking, into Lee's strong, capable arms. Thandi saw that Sylvia and Lee did not greet each other – they did not need the hello, the entrance into a conversation, because it was always ongoing. She sensed the ease of their bodies, their muscles moving in tandem, their skin brushing. Overcome, Thandi looked down. She saw the white hair at her feet and the softly sparking cord of the fan. She saw the shapes and how they fit together. With a grunt, she kicked the serpent with its fiery head into that fortuitous kindling.

'Thunder.' Lee turned to her.

She stepped forward to help, her body blocking his view of what she had done. As she wiped the girl's bleeding cheek and fashioned a sling from a rag; as she and the others followed Lee out into the compound, carrying the girl to his pickup truck, Kalingalinga bystanders attaching themselves to the host in their wake; as she and her husband navigated this emergency as deftly as they had the one 30,000 feet up when they first met fifteen years ago, Thandi felt at peace. She had been brave. She had done exactly what she needed to do.

Lee the brave, the bold, the bright. Brinksman of love and of science. His ultimate aim is laudable, true: to free mankind of The Virus. But to do it that way, to play chromosomes, is to tinker with Nature's design. Foolish Pandora! Wilful Prometheus! Shirk primal laws at your peril! This is one topic to give us our due: we know far more virology than you do. Malaria, dengue, fevers yellow and black, West Nile, and the newcomer, Zika. Illness we know, in our blood and our spit. Parasites, viruses, wormy nematodes: you name it, we surely deliver.

Mala aria's the worst, she uses us both – that rank double agent – to make and remake her own kind. Hippocrates knew her, and Shakespeare, too, though he didn't know whence she came. Hear Caliban's curse: All the infections that the sun sucks up from bogs, fens, flats, on Prosper fall and make him by inch-meal a disease! But bad air's the wrong name – she doesn't waft from the swamp, she's carried by all of the swamp-dwellers.

Our proboscis, a needle that punctures the skin, is the devious, dark double carriageway. When we snack on your blood, we exchange a few fluids, and the parasite cells catch a ride. They go down to your liver, and stay there a spell, and grow exponential in number. Sometimes they rise to the top of the head and breach the wall of your mind. Either way, your warm body allows them to hibernate and this is when fever besets you.

Oh Her Highness, Queen Mal, she's an imperious imp and she's taken a fancy to travel. We're her gnatty waggoneers, trundling along, driving a swift team of atomies. Once in your veins, they gallop right through you, blistering your sweet lips with plague. But you humans have made it far worse, you know, by travelling so much yourselves.

Though a fidgety itch we occasionally give, this itch to run is your own. As exploration expanded and freedom went faddish, you took the pathogens with you. You carried us, too, as tiny stowaways in aeroplanes, in tyres, in soil. We got loaded on boats, shipped across seas, with a baggage of bad blood beneath us. Wherever we landed, we spread our thin wings, then we spread our Queen Mal's malcontents.

In this same global way, Lee's scientific play will scatter the hazard haphazardly. Though he did not tamper with bad air as such, bad blood is much harder to banish . . .

III
The Children

Joseph

2014

Dad was coming home to die, or at least that's what he had told them over the phone. He arrived on a Thursday. They were late to pick him up so they found him already outside the airport. He was waiting under the covered walkway to the car park, with its blue canopy and its white tent walls plastered with ads for Airtel and Standard Chartered and Digit-All. American suitcases, bedecked with buckles and pockets, sat on either side of him like guard dogs. Chinese passengers – their presence in Lusaka had swelled in the early 2000s – swarmed around him.

He wasn't yet forty but he could have been sixty. He had The Virus, as did Joseph's mother and younger brother, Farai. Only Joseph had escaped its clutches. But Dad had never shown the symptoms before. He was thin now – as thin as sixteen-year-old Joseph – and his beige skin looked leathery. In grey slacks and a flag-green golf shirt that rippled in the breeze, he looked like an old tree in rainy season, especially backed by the blue glow of the canopy.

Grandpa Ronald stayed in the car while the others got out to hug the prodigal son. Ba Grace loaded suitcases into the boot while Joseph helped Dad into the passenger seat. His arm felt light – Joseph thought again of parched wood – and his eyes glassy and blinky. When they were all in again, Gran leaned forward from the back and clutched the edge of his seat.

'How was the flight, darling?' she asked, her voice trembling.

'Not too bad,' he replied, turning so she could hear him. 'These days, flights feel like nothing. I have had more flights than I've had beers. Well, that's not true, since I've had beers on flights, but you know what I mean.'

He chuckled and inhaled expansively as they picked up speed, the breeze purring through the open windows. The outskirts of the airport whipped by. Men on bicycles stacked high with firewood seemed to zip backward as the car passed.

'You know what? I'm good,' he said to Grandpa Ronald, who had not asked, who was busy driving while old, his spectacles pincering the round tip of his nose. 'It's good to be home.'

Home. When he had called last week to tell them he was coming, he had offered to stay in one of the houses he owned in Lusaka. Joseph had overheard Gran's end of the conversation.

'How bad is it?' she'd asked.

Pause.

'What?' Gran had paced the kitchen in her *patapatas*. 'You ought to be with your family!'

Pause.

'One of your properties? No, please, darling, don't be absurd. Just come home.'

What home? Joseph had wondered then. *What home?* he wondered now, staring at the pale spotty rag of Gran's hand still clutching the edge of the passenger seat. The family home in Thorn Park where Joseph had grown up had been sold in 2012, after the divorce. Joseph had gone to stay with his grandparents in Handsworth Park while his mother took little Farai to London to get medical treatment. A few months had turned into a year, then two, as a series of infections haunted the boy's lungs. Mum had said it wasn't worth it for Joseph to join them until he was done with his IGCSE exams. The thread connecting him to her was going slack.

Dad had drifted away, too. He technically lived in Addis Ababa with his new wife, Salina – no one in the family had met her, no one had even attended their wedding – but he had spent much of the past five years hopping between international conferences and workshops about The Virus. Joseph had been deemed too young to travel alone to visit him. Their relationship these days consisted of terse WhatsApps, mostly about Joseph's studies: *How's Rhodes Park, how's exam prep? Fine, where r u?* New York, Cape Town, Beijing. Dr Lionel Banda was anywhere but Lusaka, spreading the word about his research on a vaccine for The Virus, which was now about to kill him – a world tour of futility.

This was apparently his last stop. Joseph didn't really believe his father was dying and he didn't understand why he would come back to Zambia if he were. Would Mum come home from England to help him die? What sort of preparation, what sort of entertainment does a dying man want? Last things? Joseph had no idea what those would be – he was still obsessed with first things.

When they got home from the airport, Dad's first thing was tea. To please Gran, of course. Except then, at the last minute, he chose coffee – 'I've become too used in Addis. Black as night, please' – and they all joined him even though it was late, and they would all have insomnia, bad dreams, a bad morning. Such toppling effects seemed inconsequential in the face of Death. Joseph stared at his father, trying to see if Death hung over him like a smell or a colour – egg-yolk sulphurous and yellow. But he was the same – tall, handsome Dr Banda, just thinner and darker, the colour of honey on toast. Was that from the Ethiopian sun? Or The Virus?

'Did the antiretrovirals stop working?' Gran asked then blew over her mug. She was always unwilling to ignore the elephant in the room. It was the least Zambian thing about her.

'The ARVs are still effective,' said Dad. 'It isn't The Virus that's doing it, it's the side effects of the vaccine.'

He shuffled off a rack of obscure technical terms to make his point: he was going to die; he was a doctor, he would know. Joseph sipped his bitter coffee. What else is like that? An obstetrician knowing she's pregnant? A priest knowing he's sinned? *Heal thyself.* Grandpa lit a pipe and changed the topic. Dad's laugh was still outrageously loud, his chin shirring as he cackled, but he fell asleep in the middle of their conversation. He had to be nudged and prodded and in the end, half-carried to bed.

'No, no,' he kept saying. 'I just got here!'

Dad slept in Joseph's bedroom and Joseph slept on the sofa. The tinny aqua light from the stereo turned the sitting room into a dull aquarium through which Joseph's eyes swam back and forth, thinking *proud prod prodigal prodigious*, until sleep finally drowned him.

※

When Joseph got home from school on Friday – he was in grade ten – he found his father napping in front of the TV, a red book closed in his lap. It was small but its musty smell perfumed the whole room. They shared a mango and laughed about Joseph's teachers. Joseph was at that stage of feeling superior to them. He was at the top of his class and auditing online MIT courses in his spare time. Dad was amused by this arrogance in a son he had always believed to be shy; Joseph was pleased that he had changed enough to surprise his father. They indulged each other for a while, bantering about biology and chemistry. Then they bickered over DSTV. Joseph wanted to watch *Mzansi Magic*, Dad wanted to watch Real Madrid: the dancing girls vs the kicking lads. Dad won. Joseph fell out of humour. Just because you're dying – he didn't say it but his father rubbed his head as if he had, as if condescending to his worry.

On Saturday morning, over breakfast, Dad announced that he was going golfing. They all stopped eating Ba Sakala's cold, rubbery pancakes.

'This is no laughing matter,' said Gran.

'Don't be foolish,' said Grandpa.

They refused to drive or accompany him to Lusaka Golf Club. Unflappable, Dad sent the gardener down the road to whistle for a taxi and took off by himself. He came back hours later, the ankles of his plaid trousers red with dried mud. He had hit par.

'A toast!' Dad said and sent Joseph for some liquor.

He hunted around the larder for a while but all he could find was an old bottle of Grandpa's cognac, which he poured into crystal glasses that he had to wipe clear of dust. The four of them toasted. Joseph sipped and winced at the thin sweet tang.

'Lusaka, you cannot compete!' Dad kept boasting. He was full of dirty jokes about the arthritic caddy, about his swollen knuckles. 'You know what they say about busy hands!'

'Oh, you're terrible, Lionel,' said Gran, sheepish about how anxious she had been.

'Don't be obscene,' said Grandpa, puffing his pipe.

'Don't play innocent!' Dad scoffed. 'I know how you guys did back in the seventies.'

Grandpa cleared his throat. There was an awkward silence. Joseph stared. The notion of his grandparents anywhere near sex was both self-evident and terrifying, like seeing a ghost.

✳

That night, Dad had a stroke or a heart attack or both. Gran stumbled into him lying unconscious on the bathroom floor, still in his plaid golf trousers. An ambulance would have taken too long, so they drove him to the hospital, Dad's head on Joseph's lap in the back. They arrived just as dawn chinked through the clouded glass of the sky. The doctors determined that it was best to leave him unconscious, in the hopes that the swelling in his head would go down.

They sat and waited. They alternated between speaking to him and about him, and pronouns and verb tenses began to muddle – *you are, he was*. His hospital bed looked more like a contraption than a place for rest. He seemed tangled in it, held prisoner by the machines monitoring him. At 11 a.m. or so, his eyes locked open, the tendons starting in his neck.

'Where is she?' he said, gazing around wildly.

Gran scrambled for his hand in the sheets. 'Lionel? Lionel!' She turned to Joseph and it seemed for a moment that her skin was blazing with eyes. 'Get the doctor, Joe! Now!'

But by the time the doctors had rushed in, Dad had closed his eyes and nuzzled back into his coma. Joseph's grandparents whispered about which 'she' he had meant. Before the stroke, Dad had asked after Thandi and Farai in England. But maybe he had meant his new wife Salina?

On Sunday afternoon, his lungs gave up and the doctors put him on a respirator. It took a while to adjust to the staticky sound of the breathing tube, and to the light spatter of tracheal blood visible in it. His bare feet were yellow and cracked and they would intermittently curl inwards as his shoulders rolled forward. The nurse came in and punctured their hopes. No, she said, this was not a sign of life. It was pronation, an involuntary convulsion of the body. Oh.

'It's time to gather the family,' Grandpa noted grimly, and went outside to make calls.

Tears rolled from Gran's unseeing eyes. She wiped them with her hand repeatedly, uselessly, a windscreen wiper in a tornado. Ba Grace cried with her, a brief squall. Joseph didn't yet feel his grief so he cried at a remove. He cried for his grandmother's crying, quietly, so as not to disturb it.

＊

Joseph's mother arrived early Monday morning, a small boy clutching her hand. Joseph hugged her stiffly and waved down at his three-year-old brother, whom he hadn't seen since Farai was an infant. Farai had inherited their father's golden skin and dark brown eyes but their mother's reddish hair. Hers was hidden now under a black *chitambala*, a sign of her haste. Joseph could tell that she had been weeping the whole flight over, too, even though on the call to London, he had only heard Gran say: 'Lionel's sick. Come home.'

Mum had learned that he was dead once she got to the house, once she had been settled with a cup of tea and Farai had been extricated from her lap. Joseph and Grandpa had driven to the hospital to pick up the death certificate, so they missed the drama. Ba Grace filled them in on how Mum had reacted.

'But Bana Joseph? She was cry-ying, *bwana*,' she said, making bee-like patterns around the room, bouncing Farai in her arms. The boy was weeping, his head kneading rhythmically into her shoulder. 'I was with this one so I could not help. That *ka* lazy *muntu*' – her disdain for the gardener was palpable – 'he was not around. So Madamu was the one who held her down. *Iye! Mwebantu*. Hm? *Hm.*'

Ba Grace made to *papu* Farai, adopting a precarious pose: her body bent perpendicular, with the boy balanced belly down on her back. She cast a *chitenge* over him like a sail, tied its corners in a knot over her heart, and rose with him strapped to her back. Farai slipped a thumb in his mouth and melted against her.

Gran came in and stood in the middle of the kitchen, stricken and silent. Grandpa went over and put his arms around her. Joseph realised he had never seen them like this. He almost laughed at the incongruous sight – the short black man and the tall white woman, gently rocking.

＊

The will seemed simple at first. Lee had named Agnes his executor, and everything was to go to Salina apart from some funds for his two sons' education. But it seemed Lee had neglected to update part of the document: his bank account and houses in Lusaka were still bequeathed to Thandi. This meant that the most complicated estate items – three houses in three different neighbourhoods – were now her responsibility. Thandi had started to build a new life in England. She had a job at a travel agency and was working towards right of abode for her and her sons. An inheritance in Zambia was more of a headache than a gift.

Salina apparently felt the same way. When Gran called to inform her of Lee's death, she sighed. 'I told him he would only reach death sooner if he went to greet it.' She was Virus-positive too but she had refused his experimental treatment. She told Gran she would fly into Lusaka for the funeral and went on to enquire about the new upscale Radisson Blu hotel in town.

'Typical,' Aunt Carol muttered. Her face was puffy from crying, her cargo pants creased at the joints. She had just flown in from Malawi, where she worked as a wildlife conservationist.

'I invited her to stay but she said she wouldn't want to impose,' said Gran, flustered.

Aunt Carol sipped her tea. 'They were only married for a year, Mum.' She herself was unmarried.

'They must have meant *something* to each other,' said Gran. 'But Salina did seem awfully calm to learn she was a widow.'

'It is very rude,' said Grandpa. 'She has dishonoured my son.'

They stared at him. He had always had a strained relationship with his son. Now that Lee was dead, Grandpa seemed unusually interested in honouring him, or at least in displaying that honour to others. Grandpa had six siblings, two of whom had had eight children each. Having long kept his life with his white wife and coloured children separate from this 'village', as he called it, he had recently reconnected with the relatives to organise the funeral. They had eagerly inserted themselves into the arrangements. They loved Lee with an assumed bloodlove and boasted of his successes – and there would of course be plentiful leavings, bones to pick, at a funeral of this calibre.

When his grandparents came home from choosing the coffin, Joseph could tell that they had argued. Gran looked bewildered, Grandpa fractious. Gran told Joseph later that it had been a madhouse at the warehouse in town, a dozen relatives vying for the honour of selecting the perfect box. In the end, Grandpa had bought a gold-plated coffin lined in white satin, the most expensive one in the place. The funerals, both the home one and the church one, would be opulent and grand. Dr Lionel Banda would receive all the ceremonial honours due to him.

✳

The home funeral came first. The mourners – relatives, friends, colleagues and patients – trickled into the house in Handsworth Park over the course of three days. Women knelt on the sitting-room floor and wailed. Men sat outside in armchairs and murmured. Joseph was sent to the TV room, where all the 'kids' – those under twenty – had been banished. The girls were heaped on the sofas, dabbling on their phones, chatting and laughing. The boys lay prone on the floor, gazing at the flat-screen TV, where Serena Williams and some white woman were driving a neon ball back and forth across flush green parcelled in white. The volume was up. Grunts and pocks and hushed British voices filled the room. Joseph sat in a corner and took out his phone.

'Joseph!' Ba Grace's voice came from the doorway. She was holding Farai by the hand. 'Please, you must take care of your bluther and give your mother some time.'

Joseph got up reluctantly and led the boy into the room by the hand, Farai looking forlornly over his shoulder at Ba Grace's retreating back. The two of them sat in the corner.

'You're my brother?' Farai asked.

'Yes.'

'Do you have a car?'

Joseph shook his head.

'A bike?'

'No.'

Farai proceeded to interrogate him about every vehicle imaginable: planes and motorcycles and vans and trains. Finally, Joseph collapsed onto his back and begged him to stop. Farai giggled and put his small heavy head on Joseph's stomach, sighing 'Hokay, hokay.' For the rest of the afternoon, Farai was content to sit next to him, his hand coiled inside Joseph's while they watched the tennis match.

When it was over, they went to the kitchen together to fetch a drink, Farai trotting at Joseph's side. The house had been rearranged, furniture shoved to the walls, bookshelves turned to face them, valuable items locked up. It didn't seem like home. They passed the open door to the veranda, where the men chatted quietly in *mbaula*-lit dimness. They passed the open door to the dining room, where Gran and Aunt Carol sat in silence at the table. Gran looked frail beside her muscular daughter, cowed by the traditional *chitenge* wrapper she was wearing. Their faces were human and sad in the evening light.

In the kitchen, Joseph took two Fantas from the battalion in the fridge, handed one to Farai, and searched for a bottle opener. One of Dad's colleagues came in and plucked a Mosi from a crate on the floor. Joseph felt intimidated until he zoomed in on the doctor. His white lab coat was wrinkled and stained; his afro was flat on one side and speckled with grey; a withered black stethoscope hung from his neck, a prop too far.

'You are the sons of the diseased?' the doctor asked.

'Yes.' Joseph stood taller. 'I'm Joseph. This is Farai.'

'Ah! Me, am Dr Musadabwe.' They shook hands. 'Your father was a great man! I heard a lot of goody things about you. Am velly-solly for your losses.' The man's breath was putrid.

'Thank you,' said Joseph. 'Did you work at his clinic?'

'Ah, no, I'm just a fellow student with your father from UTH days. A velly-good man.'

Joseph thought his father had gone to med school in Zimbabwe, not at UTH. He felt a tug on his hand and looked down. Farai raised his Fanta bottle, which looked oversized in his little hands and still needed opening.

'Give,' said Musadabwe.

Farai handed it over shyly. Musadabwe opened it with his teeth and handed it back. Farai broke his beaming smile to sip from it, then marched out of the kitchen.

'Your father?' Musadabwe turned back to Joseph. 'Was a blirriant man. A mind stretcha!'

Joseph nodded and fondled his own unopened Fanta.

'His resatch was just—' Musadabwe pursed fingers and lips and kissed them together. 'He was on the blink of blaking through to some other side. *Groundblaking*, I swear to Goad.'

'His vaccine research?'

'Yes! He was going to heal us. The Virus is getting worse with these viro multiplications . . .'

Two Chinese men in lab coats strolled in, speaking in serious voices. Musadabwe fell abruptly silent and turned away from Joseph, opening the fridge as if to contemplate its insides. Joseph excused himself to the man's back and went to look for Farai.

He found him outside the closed door to the sitting room. Farai wrapped his hand around Joseph's thumb as they both pressed their ears to the wood. Behind the door, the keening of the women accrued volume and insistence until one voice broke into a seething wail. The other voices climbed to meet it in staggered succession, as if up a ladder with missing steps. It had never occurred to Joseph that sadness could have such fury to it. The two feelings seemed so different, two bells of disparate size and swing. Now they chimed together and the hair on his neck rose up.

✳

Three days later, the family held a funeral service at the Cathedral of the Holy Cross. It was cloudy outside and the modern stained-glass windows – skew panes of lemon and menthol and cherry – looked like dusty coughdrops. The family sat in the frontmost pew, Grandpa and Joseph in suits, Ba Grace, Gran and Aunt Carol in *chitenge* outfits. Salina, who had arrived only yesterday, wore an Ethiopian garment, a rococo braid of orange and green winding down it, and a headwrap as tall as a bishop's hood. Thandi wore a black retro-1990s suit, the sort of thing that was so fashionable in London that it was old-fashioned in Lusaka. Farai, with a child's impunity, wore overalls.

The extended family, the village of Grandpa Ronald's relatives, filled the pews behind them, the women wearing matching *chitenge* wrappers over their church dresses. Meeting them all had been nightmarish for Joseph in a hall-of-mirrors way, the prominence of certain traits

– high cheekbones, trapezoidal noses – making it especially difficult to distinguish between the aunties. Scattered in the audience were about thirty doctors of various ethnicity, their white coats making them look like paper dolls among rag dolls. At one point in the service, they all rose on cue and began reciting in unison:

I swear to consider dear to me, as his parents, him who taught me this art; to live in common with him and if necessary, to share his goods with him; to look upon his children as his own brothers, to teach them this art. He will prescribe regimens for the good of his patients according to his ability and his judgment and never do harm to anyone. He will not give a lethal drug to anyone if he is asked, nor will he advise such a plan; and similarly he will not give a woman a pessary to cause an abortion. But he will preserve the purity of his life and his arts. He will not cut for stone, even for patients in whom the disease is manifest; he will leave this operation to be performed by practitioners, specialists in this art. In every house where he come he will enter only for the good of his patients, keeping himself far from all intentional ill-doing and especially from the pleasures of love with women or with men, be they free or slaves. All that may come to his knowledge in the exercise of his profession or in daily commerce with men, which ought not to be spread abroad, he will keep secret and will never reveal. If he keep this oath faithfully, may he enjoy his life and practise his art, respected by all men and in all times; but if he swerve from it or violate it, may the reverse be his lot.

Joseph followed along in the programme. The Hippocratic Oath. The contortions of translation made the xeroxed pamphlet seem almost archaic. Was this who Dr Lionel Banda was? Never doing harm? Keeping himself from the pleasures of love? Joseph kept turning back to the colour photo of his father on the front, an old one with full cheeks and shiny teeth and turmeric skin, a fallen eyelash on his cheekbone like a parenthesis. Joseph felt a prick in his chest. Dad was dead.

The feeling was short-lived. By the time the speeches commemorating Dr Banda's professional triumphs had gone on for an hour, Joseph had stopped listening. He felt bored and hungry – he hadn't eaten breakfast. When he stood up for yet another hymn, static burst in a loud hush behind his eyes. He felt light and heavy at once, as if gravity had reversed . . .

He woke to too many hands and eyes on his body – doctors trying to outdo each other in caring for the dead man's son. Ba Grace was at his feet, shouting instructions at random. His mother was at his head, Farai in her arms. She looked more annoyed than concerned.

'Y'alright, luv?' Her accent sounded oddly British. It was the first she had looked at him today, or since she had arrived, really. He nodded and sat up. Everyone clapped, which felt wrong somehow. As the crowd of people around him dispersed, Ba Grace helped him to his feet, admonishing: 'You must have tea in the morning so your stomach does not eat itself!'

'God is punishing you,' Grandpa Ronald whispered sardonically as he passed.

He meant for being an atheist. It was true that for the past many Sundays, while Grandpa and Ba Grace had gone off to church, Joseph had stayed home to read to Gran – the *Guardian* mostly, book reviews and editorials. This was more out of sloth than a firmly held position. But now, in the cathedral, Joseph felt so dizzy that he wondered if Grandpa was right. He sat on a bench against a side wall, his ears hot and blocked. *Foodlessness foolishness feint faint fatigue.*

The mourners began filing past the open casket. Joseph saw Salina go by, stoical and alone, casting barely a glance at the corpse. He joined the line behind Gran and his mother, Farai still in her arms. When they got to the casket, Mum buried her head into Gran's chest and pulled Farai's head into hers, making three nested curls of their bodies as they moved past. Gran couldn't see; Mum didn't look. Joseph stepped up to the casket. He was almost surprised to find his father there. Dad looked small in his fancy box, unworthy of all this spectacle, his face rubbery and shrunken, a pretender's mask.

＊

A week later, Joseph went with his mother and grandmother to the Barclays at Woodlands to sort out the burdensome inheritance. Salina had left. Most of the relatives had vanished, too, as soon as they learned that the deceased's distributable possessions were in Addis Ababa. At the bank, they found a long queue, so Mum asked for the manager, a woman she knew from Zambia Airways.

'Thandiwe!' said a plump woman in a tight business suit. 'Gosh, it's been ages.'

'Brenda, how are you?'

A flurry of air-kissing in a cloud of clashing perfumes.

'You've stayed so thin!' Brenda said admiringly.

Mum smiled wanly and introduced Joseph and Gran.

'Lovely to meet you.' Brenda's eyes lingered over Gran's white stick and closed eyes. 'So howzit, Thandi? I heard you moved to London, lucky fish! How's your handsome doctor of a husband?'

Mum cast her eyes down.

'Oh, my deeya. What has happened?' Brenda guided Mum and Gran into a booth.

Joseph sat by himself on a bench in the lobby, which stunk of mid-day torpor. Officious tellers ticktocked by in high heels while customers, mostly glum men in cheap suits, shuffled the queue along. Twenty minutes later, Gran and Mum reappeared with a stack of files.

It was lunchtime so they shifted to the Chicken Inn next door, Joseph guiding Gran by her upper arm, all loose jelly in thin skin, her freckles like tiny green eyes in the fluorescent light. She picked at a plate of chips while Joseph tore through half a chicken, his stomach slowly turning on itself until he was staring at the stripped bones in disgust. Mum ignored her plate of wings as she sorted through the papers she'd spread out over the table. An ancient printer had spewed them out – perforated side strips, faded ink – and spots of grease appeared on them, darkening as they seeped in, lightening as they dried.

'It's . . . it's,' Mum sputtered, shaking her head.

'Oh dear,' Gran said softly. 'He has left quite a mess for you, Tendeeway, hasn't he?'

When they got back home, they found Grandpa in the sitting room. He was still in his pyjamas, peering and jabbing at his new smartphone, a bulky plastic bag on the table before him.

'You're back!' he said with relief and scooched his glasses up his nose. 'The hospital sent someone with his things. I didn't know if they would be relevant. For the will.'

Grandpa seemed somewhat offended that his son hadn't named him executor. Gran sent Ba Grace to make some tea, then sat across from him. Mum went to check on Farai. Joseph knelt in front of the coffee table and looked through the things inside the plastic bag. He took out his father's crumpled golf clothes, the green shirt and the plaid trousers still spattered with mud. The little red book that his father had been reading the other day fell onto the table with a thud. Joseph put it aside and pulled out his father's wallet and iPhone, which was dead. He went to the wall outlet and plugged the phone in to charge.

The wallet was crammed with money in several currencies, an origami wedge of receipts, and four driver's licences from different countries. Joseph almost expected different names, too, but no, they were all for Dr Lionel Banda. His National Registration card was at the back, laminated corners sneering around a picture of a startlingly attractive young man. Joseph felt a stab of envy – he had inherited all of his father's bad traits and none of the compensatory ones – acne without the rugged scars, height without the muscles, yellow skin without the golden glow.

Over rooibos tea and Eet-Sum-Mor biscuits, his grandparents were discussing what they had learned about their son from the bank. There was a tangle of different accounts that each received regular transfers from his bank in Addis Ababa. There were other, shadier dealings in the bank statements, too: money going to commissioners, coming from drug companies, online purchases from URLs twisted around the words 'pharma' and 'Rx'. And there were six accounts receiving monthly infusions of cash from his main account in Addis, all vastly different sums. One account was receiving nearly four times as much as the others.

'Business partners?' asked Gran hopefully.

'Women,' Grandpa shook his head.

Gran seemed upset, but Joseph didn't understand why she was surprised. Even as a boy, he had picked up on the whiff of sexual drama his father carried with him when he had fetched him from school and toted him around Lusaka on his little 'visits'. Joseph remembered it well – those long, dull afternoons sitting in some woman's flat or hair salon or office, his eyes glued to his book as he waited for his father to finish. He wondered whether any of Dad's women had been in that mourning room at the home funeral, if the one who had wailed so furiously was one of his widows.

Gran ought to have known how her son was. Did she actually think he had contracted The Virus, passed it on to a wife and a son, divorced, remarried, and then *stopped* fucking around? Did she not realise that sex was what had killed him? The charging iPhone blurbled to life and lit the wall around the socket. Joseph walked over to it, his body brimming with an unspoken 'I told you so', that satisfaction that lays over disappointment like the play of iridescence on the surface of an oil slick.

*

The last thing Mum had to do before flying back to England was to visit the three houses she now owned in Lusaka. This time they left Gran behind and brought Farai – he had been grumpy that morning and Mum suspected Ba Grace had fed him something with groundnuts in it. The real estate agent they had hired sat in the back seat. She had apparently once been a model and her red skirt suit and plexiglass stilettos and heavy perfume seemed to confirm this. Joseph didn't have his licence yet but he drove, wanting to impress his mother.

The first house was very nearby, on Senanga Road. No one was home, not even the servants. They had to peek through the gap in the locked gate to see it. The glances Joseph caught – white bricks, a red-dust driveway, a boulder in the garden painted as a chessboard – stirred something in his memory, but his mother said this wasn't possible. They had moved out of this house just after Joseph was born. He must have been remembering it from photos.

They drove on to Munali to examine the second house, a bungalow with drooping eaves and a well-coiffed garden. Joseph and Farai sat on the warm boot of the car, the metal flexing around them with popping sounds. Only the cleaner was home this time. The estate agent and Mum stood talking at the threshold. The cleaner, in a faded tunic and bare feet, was nodding at the ground, waiting for them to finish their conversation so she could go back to work. His mother would have forgotten this – she had been abroad too long – and the estate agent didn't care.

They headed to Northmead to see the last house, Joseph carefully dodging potholes so as not to wake Farai napping in his mother's lap. They drove past the shopping centre, and just as they turned onto Paseli Road, the estate agent reached a sheet of paper forward between the front seats. Joseph glanced at it as she scraped a curved pink finger-nail down a column of numbers.

'You see?' she said to Mum. Pairs of zeroes, each pinioned with a full stop: o.o, a column of eyes. The car crunched into a pothole. Farai bumped his head against the window, woke up and started crying.

'Shit-sorry,' Joseph said and looked back at the road.

'That's where the payments should be,' the estate agent was saying. She had nearly wedged her torso between the front seats. Despite her perfume, Joseph could smell the Marmite on her breath. Farai was still whimpering.

'Almost there,' said Mum, hugging him close. She shrugged at the estate agent. 'We'll just boot them out.'

'*Hm*,' the woman frowned. 'Yes, but—' She leaned forward to say something.

But then they had arrived and she had to communicate in the pauses between Joseph honking the horn and the gardener opening the gate and the car creeping into the flagstone drive, where a white pickup truck was already parked – Joseph did a double take, it was Dad's old Peugeot! – but Mum didn't notice because once they were out of the car, Farai refused to walk on his own and she was picking him up and the estate agent was just repeating herself about the payments when the front door opened and a woman stepped out of the house.

She was in her forties maybe, wearing a shiny orange robe with no bra underneath, her nipples beading the satin, her uncovered hair in shrubby clumps. She was beautiful, nevertheless.

'Oh!' said Mum.

The woman knelt heavily onto the stone driveway – Joseph and the estate agent both instinctively reached towards her – and clasped her hands together. She began mumbling through tears, as if praying to Farai, who stared down at her with wide eyes from his perch in Mum's arms. Mum spun and stalked back to the car, her face frozen in an odd little smile, sudden tears leaving runnels in her make-up. Joseph touched her arm as she passed but her flinch held the quick of anger.

He turned back to the estate agent, who was already shouting questions, her manicured fingers pursed like she was aiming at a dartboard. When the weeping woman didn't reply, the estate agent clipped past Joseph to join his mother and brother in the back seat of the car. Helplessly, Joseph watched her shut the door. Through the open window, he heard her begin to explain that this woman was an illegal tenant, she had not been paying ... The estate agent turned and closed the window, the sunbright glass rolling smoothly up over the contempt on her face.

This time, when he turned back to the woman, he recognised her. It was one of Dad's mistresses, a hairdresser named Sylvia – God, he had called her Aunty Sylvia back then, hadn't he? The last time he had seen her was at her salon, the day Mum had questioned him about Dad's whereabouts and they had gone to Kalingalinga and the Indian girl had fallen from the tree. Dad had clearly continued his relationship with Sylvia after that if she was living in his house, rent-free. It came to Joseph again, the phone call he had overheard between his father and his grandmother about where Dad would stay when he came home to die. *One of your properties?* Gran had asked. Dad had wanted to come *here*. To this house. To her.

Sylvia's crying had taken on more momentum now, her sobs as rhythmic as a pulsing vein. There were two parallel purple marks on her neck – burns perhaps. It was disquieting to see her sealed off in her grief yet crying so publicly. She knelt there in a spotlight of sunshine, her face tilted up to the fresh blue sky, the folds of her robe shaking around her, her mouth stretched wide and her throat vibrating with the wretched urgency of a baby bird.

✳

Joseph saw the fire on his way to take his IGCSEs. Grandpa was driving, Joseph in the back with his textbooks spread out over the seat. He wasn't studying so much as calming himself, whispering words like one of his Aunt Carol's Buddhist mantras. He barely noticed the burning smell and the frustrated honks of the cars until Grandpa slowed to a stop. Joseph looked up.

'We can't be late today, Grandpa.'

'And where should I go?' Grandpa gestured at the windscreen.

Beyond the grey wash of old rain and scratched glass was a scene out of a BBC Africa Special Report: young men in old clothes running through smoke and dust.

'Hooligans,' Grandpa said and turned on the radio. The DJ, his voice an ungainly hybrid of Zinglish and American accents, bellowed over this month's ubiquitous Drake song. Grandpa tutted and pressed SCAN. The radio bumped from station to station: strident exhortation (*God! Is in control!*) to oldies (*out of my dreams! and into my*) to the smooth baritone news (*Ebola outbreak in Liberia will*) to more oldies (*candy-coated rayiyin dro-ops*) . . . Grandpa turned down the volume as the cars oozed forward again, pulling onto the dirt bank to bypass the burning pile in the road.

'Savages,' Grandpa said as he inched the car around it and back onto the tarmac.

Joseph turned to look out the rear window and saw a woman in a bathrobe standing on the side of the road, shouting furiously over a pile of charred objects at her feet. It was Sylvia – he recognised the distinctive colour of her robe, as shiny and orange as a naartje. It had been a month since his mother had found her squatting at the Northmead house. The bailiffs must have finally ousted her and put her belongings in the road. Someone had set them on fire – chaos to cover looting. This sort of thing happened often in Lusaka these days.

Joseph saw a young man dart out of the fray, carrying a black box over his head. At first, Joseph thought he was one of the 'hooligans' and 'savages', but his ventures into and out of the road had the methodi-cal rhythm of saving rather than the scattered logic of opportunistic theft. The young man placed the black box at Sylvia's feet, smacked his hands, and ran back in. Who was he?

Joseph's buttocks vibrated. He pulled his phone from his back pocket but the screen was black. He turned it off – it would have to be off for the exam anyway. He turned to look back at the fire again but a car had cut in behind them and hidden the scene from view. He felt another buzz to the bum. Oh, it was Dad's iPhone. He had been carry-ing it around with him out of a kind of nostalgia. He pulled it from his other back pocket. This screen was lit – a preview of a text. He tried to unlock the phone to read it but it asked for a code. He sank back and turned it off. He had only caught the contact name before the message preview disappeared. The Doctor. Doctor who?

2015

Joseph's exams went well despite his worries, or perhaps because of them – he secretly held a superstition that his anxiety fuelled his intelligence. He immediately began studying for his A levels – his father had left him money for university fees and Joseph wanted to go to Oxford. Waiting for his stellar international education to start was both irritating and boring, like that French word: *ennuyeux*. Then, one day, Gran mentioned offhand that his father's will had stipulated that Joseph's tuition money go to an African university.

'He was right.' Grandpa gave an approving nod. 'Too much brain drain nowadays.'

Joseph was furious. He resented this belated pan-Africanism – this petty swipe from the grave. He called his mother in London to ask if he could use some of the money from selling the Lusaka houses instead.

'Oh baby, there's none left,' Mum laughed sadly. 'Medical bills. Farai needed another operation.'

Joseph was not handsome, but he was clever and rich. And for a long time, that had been enough to dwarf the social marks against him: his pebbly acne, his *skinnymaningi* long legs, his fat banana feet. Now it turned out that being top of the class, cream of the crop, guaranteed him nothing. He fumed until he learned that the University of Cape Town had a study-abroad programme at Leeds. Surely that didn't count. It was not Oxford, but it would do.

✳

In between studying for his A levels, Joseph tried to unlock his father's iPhone. He kept it charged, an electronic memento mori, and it still buzzed all the time, Digit-All ads and messages flashing over the locked screen. But he couldn't unlock it and he didn't know how long he had before the SIM card expired. He had googled 'forgot iPhone passcode', but he didn't have enough of his dad's details to reset it. He tried to guess the code instead. 0000. 1234. Sets of four from his father's Reg card. His birthdate, his dad's, the nation's. Nothing. Zee. And for every ten wrong guesses, the phone locked for an hour.

One day, while he was watching *The Hunger Games* in the TV room with Aunt Carol – she had been visiting more since the funeral, to spend time with Gran and Grandpa – the iPhone buzzed on the table. He picked it up and saw the preview of a text – another one from the mysterious 'Doctor'. This time Joseph caught the words *vaxin* and *kalingalinga* before the screen went black. *Kalingalinga*. That was where that hair salon was – the one owned by Sylvia the Widow – but what did that have to do with his father's vaccine research? He clicked the phone back on, but the preview had been banished by the keypad.

'Shit,' he said. Locked out again.

'What are you up to?' Aunt Carol leaned forward from the sofa.

'Nothing.'

'*Children, children,*' Aunt Carol sang, then turned back to the movie with a chuckle. The rest of the nursery rhyme ran through Joseph's head as he left her and went to his bedroom.

Children, children?
Yes, Papa.
Eating sugar?
No, Papa.
Telling lies?
No, Papa.
Open your mouth.
Ha. Ha. Ha.

The whole point of that song, Joseph thought as he sat at his desk and opened his laptop, was to give the sugar enough time to melt in the mouth of the culprit. What was the name of that salon again? Some silly wordplay on aeroplanes? Right. The Hi-Fly. He googled and found an article from 2009 – the salon had apparently burned down – that gave the proprietor's full name: Sylvia Mwamba. Joseph found twenty or so Sylvia Mwambas on Facebook but none of them seemed old enough. Then he thought to search for her son.

Scouring through dozens and dozens of Jacob Mwambas, Joseph finally found a bitty picture of the young man he had seen rescuing electronics from the fire in the road last year. Joseph scrolled through the timeline: unsmiling selfies showing off Jacob's clear brown skin and bulging muscles; links to news sites – BBC, Quartz, AllAfrica – with tech articles like 'Flight of the RoboBee' and 'Facebook to Build Solar Drone'. Finally, Joseph came upon a photo of two women in cone-shaped party hats. It was fuzzy, taken with a camera phone, and nobody was tagged, but he recognised Sylvia's doe eyes and noted a glow from below – birthday candles.

Would Dad have been bold enough to use his mistress's birth date as his passcode? Joseph picked up the iPhone and tried the day and month from Joseph's Facebook post. No. Estimating Sylvia's age, he tried the month and year. No. Maybe she was older than she looked? Down the year went until he hit 1970. *Open Sesame.* The keyboard vanished and the iPhone's home screen bloomed with its neat garden of icons. Little red badges told Joseph that his dead father had 873 unopened texts and 5,012 unopened emails.

❋

Joseph was two months away from taking his A levels when the University of Cape Town erupted. 'Rhodes Must Fall!' the students cried, meaning the statue, not the man. Joseph googled. In the Wikipedia photo, the big bronze Cecil Rhodes looked thoughtful in his square throne, turquoise rust turning him geological. Protestors gathered in small crowds to throw shit at it and graffiti it and *toyi-toyi* around it. A month later, it was craned up and away. Joseph was annoyed and bored by this news. *Ennuyeux.*

The University of Zambia, the university down the road where Grandpa had been a dean for decades, had a statue, too, by Henry Tayali. *The Faceless Graduate* was a cartoony concrete thing with a graduation cap and Mickey Mouse shoes, its facelessness meant to symbolise education for all: rich and poor, men and women. To Joseph it just looked unfinished, and obviously male. Had female students ever protested it, crying 'The Graduate Must Fall!', smearing it with menstrual blood? Not likely. The Cape Town protests seemed gentrified to him – how nice for you, destroying history to make a point when some of us just want the chance to study it.

By the time Joseph received his A-level results – top marks but not quite high enough for a merit scholarship – the protests had mutated into 'Fees Must Fall!' Cape Town students built a shanty town on the library steps to protest the lack of adequate housing. They set cars on fire and lobbed a petrol bomb into an office. They cut the nose off Rhodes's memorial and spited his nameplate: CECIL JOHN RHODES became RACIST THIEF MURDERER. To the aspiring applicant, these protests all seemed nonsensical. For a *man* to fall and *fees* to fall were not the same thing.

'It's like they're protesting because of a pun,' Joseph complained at supper.

'You do realise that Cecil Rhodes named *two* African countries after himself.' said Gran. 'And he was not just an imperialist. He was a businessman, too, the head of a company.'

'The British South African Company!' Grandpa nodded, gravy oil glossing his lips.

'Decolonising education is not just about race,' Gran continued as she gently scooped up some cabbage with her *ntoshi*. 'It's about class, too. The university fees are so high precisely because of Rhodes's capitalistic ideology. Rhodes *and* fees must fall.'

'Wait, they're saying fees must go?' Grandpa asked as if abruptly remembering his opinion. 'These students, they don't understand that attending university is a privilege. It must be paid for!'

'Did you not receive a bursary from Sir Stewart?' Gran asked witheringly.

'It is not the same!' Grandpa snatched his *ntoshis*, smashed them into his relish, tossed them into his mouth. 'Why throw money at middle-class students when there are mouths to feed! This Marxist idealism of yours is not Zambian,' he garbled as he gobbled. 'It is imported.'

'Important, did you say?' Gran said icily. 'I couldn't hear you through your mouthful.'

Grandpa swallowed. 'Imported!' He took a swig of Mazoe. 'Do not correct my English!'

'It is a condescension—'

'Yes, it is! Do not forget I learned the Queen's English in *your* bloody country.'

'I was *saying* it is a condescension to say that Africa is not ready for free university education—'

'Oh, it is "Africa" now, is it?' Grandpa scoffed. 'The whole country of Africa?'

'You know what I mean,' Gran said tremulously.

The lights went out. They all paused, waiting for the generator to clunk and judder to life. Joseph blinked at the darkness. He could have sworn that right before the power cut, he had seen the freckles on Gran's skin flash open, tiny eyes glinting all over her. The lights stuttered back on and the low-grade electric whine of the household appliances swarmed up around them again.

'That is what people should be protesting!' Grandpa expostulated. 'I've told these ZESCO people that load shedding is the wrong idea. These power cuts have become a real noonsense!'

'Well,' said Gran calmly, 'you can't separate *power* cuts from political *power*—'

On it went, their banter about politics beating the protests in South Africa to flat abstraction. To Joseph, it was just a *noonsense*, as Grandpa would say. Where the hell was he supposed to go to uni?

✳

Joseph's first and only term at the University of Zambia was a torture to his ego. It had been easy to get in, with his marks and his Grandpa's old position, and at least he could live at home – there was no way he was going to stay on campus. Even the new Chinese-built student hostels were rumoured to have cockroach nests for wall insulation. Joseph still felt deprived and infantilised, eating home-cooked meals, reading the news to Gran, arguing with Grandpa over the remote. And on campus, his smart-alec arrogance was lost in a sea of conceited and talented students, most of whom were better looking than he was. The truth of the matter was that Joseph had left his heart in Cape Town. He constantly checked for updates on the protests and planned to transfer as soon as possible. In the meantime, he enrolled in UNZA classes on ecology and microbiology.

He couldn't stop thinking about his father's research, and he hoped learning about these topics would help him make sense of it. He had systematically read through all the unopened emails and texts on the iPhone. They confirmed what he already knew: that Lionel Banda had been on the cutting edge of the scientific search for the Virus vaccine. Joseph printed out the scholarly articles that Dad had emailed to himself but they prickled with unfamiliar abbreviations – CCR5, CCR2, SDF-1α, CXCR4, CD4, CD8, NK, T-cell, B-cell – the letters crowding together as if marching to battle, superscript numbers and punctuation perched like birds on their shoulders. Googling the terms didn't help; he grew lost in a labyrinth of internal reference.

Joseph felt pained. He had done well in his biology IGCSEs. He had imagined that, when Dad had come home to die and they had cracked jokes about Golgi bodies and the 'smooveness' of the endoplasmic reticulum in the TV room, they had been mutually impressed. Now he realised how out of his depth he had been, and how obliging his father. It wasn't a gap in intelligence, he assured himself, just in knowledge.

Despite the standard lecture style at UNZA (a skinny bespectacled man droning in front of an ashy blackboard), Joseph thrilled to the lessons. The Darwinian model he had learned for A levels was essentially a child's drawing: big fish eats little fish which eats littler fish. Now he learned that the very littlest fish, microorganisms, sometimes entered the little fish on purpose so as to be eaten by the big fish, which helped the microorganisms spread. This wasn't survival of the fittest. It was survival of the slyest. It began to make sense to him that his father, a man of subtle infiltrations, had chosen virology.

Indeed, the workings of animal biology seemed to mirror the workings of human society. Joseph's ecology lecturer introduced the students to three terms for how organisms coexist: '*Parasitism*,' he intoned, 'is when one organism benefits, while the other one is harmed – this is what viruses do. *Mutualism* is mutually beneficial, like when the plover bird cleans the crocodile's teeth of scraps. And *commensalism*,' he concluded, 'is when one organism benefits from another without affecting it, like the lice that eat human skin flakes or the vultures that trail lions for carcasses.'

Later that day, using the hotspot at the Mingling Bar campus cafe, Joseph googled the term *commensalism* on his phone and found out that it came from the Latin *commensalis*, or 'sharing a table'. He looked up at the open-air canteen, students clustered around square grey tables with red brick bases, sharing their meals under the concrete overpasses that criss-crossed campus like intestines. Here we all are, he thought, sharing our lives in a former colony, each of us filled with bacterial colonies whose edges are as fixed as the borders of the country – which is to say, not very fixed at all.

Joseph often found himself doing this on campus, positioning himself outside of the hubbub, observing the gestures and glances of social microcosms. No one really talked to him, anyway – he reeked of coffee and ethanol from the lab – but he told himself that he preferred to watch the world rather than be in it. Maybe that's why he noticed the thief before anyone else did.

⚹

He had headed into the student bar by the Goma Lakes for a quick snack – just a Mosi and a locobun. He was surprised to find the bar packed, the volume up, strobe lights wafting. Then he remembered – it was Friday. Well, he would finish his meal before walking home to Handsworth Park. He shouted his order to the bartender over the bass drum that was trying to reset his heartbeat. He paid, took a munch and a swig, leaned against a wall, and pulled out Dad's phone.

Dr Lionel Banda still received emails and texts and WhatsApps, but fewer and fewer as time went by – the shadows he had cast in the world were slowly receding. Joseph scanned through the latest messages and was in the middle of deleting invitations from Nigerians to take their money and from Russians to suck their nipples when a text bubbled up from 'The Doctor'. It read: *Pos CXCR4 mut in #11!* That abbreviation looked vaguely familiar.

Joseph looked up at the ceiling, trying to remember where he had seen it, and that's when his eye caught a movement across the room. A hand had vanished into someone's pocket. It reappeared again but he couldn't see to whom it was attached. It was small and light-skinned – it gleamed under the strobe lights – and for a moment, Joseph watched it dart like a silver fish in the murky abyss of the bar. Then he pushed off the wall and moved across the room, navigating around the dancing students, tracking the thieving hand.

When he got near enough, he grabbed the wrist above it. The girl turned with surprise, then smiled and began to dance with him, her wrist still in his grip. She was tall and thin but her hips were wide, built to carry a bum. Joseph was neither a good nor a willing dancer but the look in her eye plucked something in him, made it vibrate. He swayed side to side. She drew so close that he could see her shimmery lipstick and smell her scent, a dark bitter nut inside the fruit of her deodorant.

He felt his shirt catch. She was tugging at it, trying to show him something. She pointed across the bar to two guys dancing on either side of a girl with long gold and purple plaits, her hips spinning like a centrifuge. The guys had raised their arms over her with the Digit-All Beads in their fingers switched on to make a spotlight. Everyone was watching them, more for the technological novelty than the dance performance. The thief grinned at him, nodding her head to the music.

'I've never seen one of those Bead thingies in real life,' she called out, still bouncing her bum. She spun and dropped it, then pulled it back up, dragging it just inches from his crotch. She smirked over her shoulder.

'I'm Lila,' she shouted. Her breath smelled like freshly baked pound cake.

He bent slightly and spoke in her ear. 'You're a thief.'

She smiled and shrugged her shoulders to the beat. Then she pranced towards the exit, a finger beckoning him to follow. Once they were in the car park out front, she turned to him.

'Smoke?' she asked, her voice like velvet stroked the wrong direction.

'Nah,' he said.

There were four *butahs* leaning against the outside wall, wearing those new MC Hammer-style sweatpants – tight at the calves, loose at the thighs. She begged a cigarette off one of the guys, who lit it for her. She walked back to Joseph, fully aware of the smokers' eyes on her ass. Under the street lamp, Joseph saw that her tight black t-shirt had a white blur in the centre – an image of fogged glass with two words finger-scrawled in it: MANIC PIXIES. Under it was a unicorn with a dagger for a horn.

'It's an Iranian punk band.'

'Ah,' he raised an eyebrow and glanced away.

'You don't like?' She stretched it down and away so she could peer at it. 'It's *salaula*.'

'*Salaula*? You know that word?'

'*Ah-ah, ndine mu Zambia, iwe.*'

He laughed. Her Nyanja wasn't bad. 'You were born here?'

'Born and bred, *exay.*'

'But your parents are what?'

'Guess.' She spoked her fingers up into her hair – long, purpleblack, shaved on one side.

'I give up,' he said then tried anyway: 'Ethiopian?'

'You're mixed too, ya? Green eyes and that.'

'We say coloured here, but yes. Are you sure you're from Lusaka?'

'What kind of mutt are you?' She blew smoke from the side of her mouth like Popeye.

'*Muntu-muzungu.* I'm not exactly sure what proportion. You?'

'*Muzungu-mwenye.* Exactly half,' she said. 'My mum's Italian.'

'So basically *muzungu*,' he said.

She stepped back and scanned him. He felt spotty and sickly.

'With a Zambian passport, what's the frikkin difference, right?' She smiled and he felt forgiven. She gathered her hair, twisted it into a bun, and pulled two pens from her jeans pocket to pin it up.

'Wait. You were stealing *pens* in there?'

'Ya,' she laughed. Her teeth were insanely white, like an actress. 'You down with OPP?'

Without warning, she began sprinting towards the Goma Lakes. He ran after her. They raced across the stepping stones like kids and then clambered up a grass hill to sit. The eucalyptus trees drooped in the distance, ministering spirits. It was cool and clear – it was May, the rains were over and the moon was as big and fat and yellow as a sun.

'So, you a fresher?' he panted. The collegiate slang felt like mush on his tongue.

'Ya, you?'

'Ya,' he sniffed. 'But I'm gonna transfer soon. UCT.'

'Shit, men. I wanted to go there too.' She picked at an intentional rip in her jeans. 'I didn't get in either.'

'No, I'll definitely get in,' he said and hated himself.

'Why aren't you already there then?'

'The protests,' he said. 'It's crazy right now. End-times shit.'

She laughed so hard that it rocked her onto her back. 'Are you jok-ing?' she asked the sky. 'That's why I wanted to go! They're frikkin trying to *do* something! Fight the power and that!'

'How about fight the power *cuts*?' He was surprised to hear himself echoing his grandfather. 'Why make free education a priority when people still don't have food or electricity or running water?'

'They did it in Chile!' she exclaimed, sitting up again and crossing her legs. 'They made it completely free. Uni for everyone, paid for by those corporate oil companies and shit.'

'Are you sure you want to use Chile as the example of democratic progress?'

'Who said anything about democracy, men? Democracy's bankrupt. People from the West shout "democracy" but they're vampires, suck-ing our resources. Bloody capitalist stooges.'

'Stooges?' he chuckled. 'You really are Zambian. So what, you give all your money away?'

'I'm Marxist,' she said with disgust. 'I'm not stupid.'

There was an awkward silence. She plucked at the grass between her crossed legs. The music from the student bar thudded and crescen-doed like doom approaching. He turned to her but before he could speak, she swung her face at him and kissed him. It was awful. Her tongue was thick and musty, like the slugs he dissected in lab. His penis responded eagerly anyway and he kissed her back. She broke away first and looked across the lake and asked him a question about his parents. He blinked, nonplussed. This girl had no brakes. No steering wheel, either. He furtively adjusted the fly of his khakis and replied politely. When he said his father's name, she pummelled his arm with her fists.

'Whoa, whoa, whoa!' he said, flexing it instinctively.

'I know your dad,' she nodded, her high-crossed hair bun wobbling.

'What?'

'Yessss!' she seethed. 'Your dad's my hero. He saved my life!'

Something dug into his stomach. 'He *was* a doctor,' he began but she had launched into a story about a compound and a tree and a boy who pushed her, or actually, kind of *bounced* her—

'Wait. *Naila?*'

'Ya! Lusaka's a frikkin village, men,' she laughed. 'Wait.' Her face zoomed into his again. 'No. You're joking.'

'What?'

'You're the coward! You're the one who ran away like a frikkin weasel!'

He frowned. 'I – I ran for help. I'm the one who fetched my father. My father who *saved* you?' He stood up and dusted his seat off. 'Look, I have class in the morning. Good to meet you. Again or whatever.'

She stood up. Her eyes looked like black pebbles under water. Her lips had a duck-like pout and for a moment, he thought she might kiss him. Instead, she slapped him. Shocked, he put his hand to his cheek. She mouthed 'ows', wringing the impact off her hand, then turned and strode back towards the car park. 'Don't run off again!' she called over her shoulder. 'Coward.'

He stumbled after her. By the time he reached the car park, she was in the driver's seat of a blue Mazda, mugging for him through the windscreen. The passenger door was open. The smokers in front of the bar laughed as he got in. Benzes and Beamers still meant something in Lusaka, and the guys drove the cars, not the girls. But Joseph didn't care, and neither did his penis.

✳

He woke up in her narrow bed in one of the UNZA hostels outside Arcades – her roommate was out of town. Naila was awake, arms crossed over her bare breasts, glaring at him.

'What the hell, men?' She sucked her teeth. 'Do you have no manners?'

'What?' he asked, blinking the blur from his eyes. 'What time is it?'

She sucked her teeth and rolled over to check her phone. 'It's half five. Looky here, men. No handouts. This is a tit-for-tat economy. Give and take. Emphasis on give.'

He sat up and scratched his head. Oh, is that what she was on about? Early-morning light cast a coral shade over her messy dorm room.

'Girls don't come every time,' he said, picking his khaki trousers off the floor beside the bed and sitting up to pull them on.

'*Excuse* me?' She smacked her phone onto the bedside table. 'What did you say?'

She was kneeling topless in the sheets like a golden nymph in choppy white waves, her face contorting as she started shouting about gender equality and the right to orgasm and again, about poor manners. 'Frikkin amateur,' she concluded. 'Is this your first time or what?'

'What if it was?' he scowled as he stood up. 'Now who has no manners?'

She rolled her eyes. He saw his shirt on the chair and as he strode over to fetch it, he slipped on something. He caught himself by grabbing the edge of a rickety bookshelf and looked down. It was the condom, which he had neglected to knot before tossing on the floor last night. It had spilled its guts and he'd stepped right into them. He lifted his foot with revulsion. This was banana-peel stupid. Naila cracked up. He stepped back to the bed and wiped his foot down the edge of her mattress but she just laughed harder.

His phone buzzed in his trouser pocket and he pulled it out and sat on the bed, avoiding the streak of semen he'd just left there. It was a new message from the anonymous Doctor, an apology for yesterday's text: *sory rong numba*, it said.

'Ugh, I get spam all the time, too,' Naila commiserated. She was kneeling up behind him on the bed, peering over his shoulder at the screen.

He nodded absently, tapping a reply: *who is this?*

'You don't know your own doctor?'

'This isn't my phone,' he said. 'It's my dad's.'

'Oh!' She tumbled onto her back. 'You mean my hero, Dr Lionel Banda?'

She smiled, sprawled out in her green panties embroidered with – was that . . . ? It was. It was the Zambian flag. She had a *chitenge* pattern tattooed on her tricep, too. A true patriot.

'Dr Lionel Banda is dead,' he said and something small and hard began to buzz in his throat, like a dung beetle was trapped there. He had never had to say those words out loud before.

'Stop lying.'

He just looked at her.

'Oh,' she said softly, her eyebrows knitting. 'Sorry, men.'

'I'm trying—' He stopped and cleared his throat. 'I've been trying to figure out what he was working on before he died. He was doing some pretty important research. On The Virus.'

'Oh, wow.' She unconsciously covered her breasts with a forearm. 'Like, a cure?'

'Maybe. A vaccine, more likely. I'm still trying to find his lab log.'

'You don't have his . . . files? His experiments or whatever?'

'All I have is this.' He held up the phone. 'I found some articles he sent to himself, but—' The phone buzzed in his hand and he looked down. 'This Doctor guy keeps texting—' He broke off and laughed at the message. He turned the phone so she could read it: *WHO IS THIS?!*

'Shame,' she laughed. 'Probably thinks he's getting texts from a graveyard.'

She rolled off the bed onto her feet and stretched her arms overhead. She had small breasts but her ass stretched that Zambian flag taut. She wrapped a *chitenge* around her torso.

'Try Memos,' she said and flounced out of the room to the loo.

Of course. Joseph had only ever looked at the email and messaging apps on the phone. He tapped the microphone icon now and found a dated list of files, the most recent from the day before his father had died. He touched his finger to the screen. Dad's voice rose into the room, buffeted by wind:

'. . . question then is whether to modify the genome of the host or the genome of the vector, which—'

Joseph pressed pause, his whole body sprung with goosebumps.

Naila came back in and started tossing through the mess on her floor, murmuring, 'Now where are my frikkin keys?'

As she drove the Mazda along the empty roads towards campus, Joseph went through all the apps on the phone, one by one. In Notes, amongst to-do lists and logs riddled with question marks and exclamation points, he finally found what he was looking for. The name mostly showed up as Dr M, but once in a while it was spelled out. Musadabwe. The bedraggled doctor he had met at Dad's funeral. Joseph sent a text explaining who he was and asking if they might meet again.

The notes on the iPhone app took some deciphering. The logs were dated but coded in a cryptic shorthand, with test subjects labelled by number. Joseph had just cracked the key and was typing out the list of names – Chileshe K., Loveness J., Sylvia M. – on his laptop in the dining room when Gran walked in.

'Darling.' Her voice was thin as a string. 'Could you find something for me?'

She was in her usual outfit – a faded collegiate sweatshirt and a wrap *chitenge* skirt from Sunday market. She had worn it every day since the funeral, except for the days that Ba Grace insisted she take it off to be washed. Gran's eyelids were shadowed with purple and she seemed ruffled, her freckles shifting in her skin as she fidgeted.

'Are you too busy?' she said. 'With your schoolwork? How is—'

'No, no. I'm working on my own project,' he said. 'What is it you're looking for?'

'There is a—' She stopped herself. 'You know? I've been thinking. Since that conversation we had about the protests? "Rhodes Must Burn" and so on.'

'Fall,' he said.

'What? Oh dear. Yes, "Rhodes Must *Fall*".' She paced in a circle, picking at her cuticles. They looked raw. 'In any case, it has me thinking about these campus protests that went on at UNZA in the seventies, when – actually I was pregnant with your father at the time and I was in this group, The Reds, and we had a—' She stopped to catch her breath. She was panting slightly.

He stood up and put his hand on her shoulder. 'Are you okay?'

'Yes, it's just, I've lost something terribly important to me. A tape. Well – a book.'

'A book on tape?'

'No, it's – I was hoping you could find it for me? It *ought* to be in my bedside drawer but . . .'

Joseph guided her down the corridor, though she could navigate by herself – his hand on her arm was just for comfort. In the master bedroom, he could smell traces of her body, a maundering mauve odour. She stood by the door and waited while he rifled through the leavings in the bedside drawer: a crusty earplug, old and new fifty-ngwee coins, a plastic chequebook cover, a Scooby Doo sticker, a box of Lion matches, a rusty pin that said MIND THE GAP.

'It's a book. Quite small. Red,' Gran urged. 'Perhaps the tape fell out . . .'

A small red book. Like the one Dad had been reading the day after he arrived back home? The one he'd taken golfing with him and had in his pocket when he collapsed? The one that had come home from the hospital in a plastic bag that was now stashed at the bottom of Joseph's closet?

'I think I know where it is,' he said and sat Gran down on her bed.

He went to his bedroom closet and dug out the bag, then the book. He opened it. MAO-TSE TUNG. He turned past the title page and frontispiece and saw now that the rest of the book had been hollowed out and an old cassette tape was squeezed inside. He tugged it out and turned it over – it was labelled LIONEL. Just then, his phone buzzed. A text from Musadabwe: *hi jo! meet @ clinic tmrw. kalingalinga. nxt 2 rip kapenta.*

Joseph put his phone away, then took the book and the tape to Gran's room and placed them in her hands. She nearly swooned with relief, running her hands over the book, opening it and expertly slotting the tape back into its choppy cave.

'This is all very mysterious, Gran.'

'Oh dear, I suppose it is,' she smiled. For the first time since the funeral, she seemed happy.

'What's on that tape? And why's it got Dad's name on it?'

'It's actually his namesake. It's a recording of these meetings that a lecturer named Lionel Heath used to run on campus.'

'What were they about?'

'Well.' She tilted her head. 'It's—' She shook her head. 'It's hard to explain. I suppose I listen to the tape more for – the sound. The voices. The feeling. Of that moment in time.'

'What feeling?'

'Why don't I play it for you?'

✳

Kalingalinga had become a little city by now, concrete blocks with flat colourful faces, windows criss-crossed with white grids. There were signs everywhere – BE ON TIME TRADING, OBAMA SALON, NITE DANCING CLUB – and misspelt lists of services: *cooka, barba, filta, panting.* Items for sale lined Alick Nkhata Road: thatch coops and kennels, wooden tables and chairs, bricks stacked in Tetris-like heaps. Joseph parked Grandpa's car and got out and asked a Digit-All Time seller for directions. From Musadabwe's text, he had assumed the clinic was next to one of those fish stands loaded with ponging heaps of silver minnows, flies buzzing over sizzling flesh strung with latticed bones. But as the sign came into view – RIP BEDS & COFFINS LTD – he realised that *kapenta* was just the doctor's efficient if idiosyncratic spelling of the word *carpenter*.

There were two actual carpenters in the yard, both coated with white dust, a roiling sea of curled shavings at their feet. The older man wore goggles and gloves and was bent over a sawhorse, delicately applying a spinning blade to a log. The younger man sat on a turned-over oil drum, legs swinging, feet gonging, as he fiddled with a black box with a single phallic antenna. Nailed to the tree next to him was a *kifwebe* mask, a spine running down from its crown to form the bridge of its nose. Below it was a plastic version – the top half of a *chigubu* jug, its handle for a nose, its spout for a pout.

Next door was a blue building with a white base, like a schoolgirl in bobby socks. A satellite dish sat on its corrugated roof like a jaunty cap. The facade said ONE HUNDRED YEARS CLINIC and below that, in smaller letters, DR PATRICK MUSADABWE, and below that in even smaller letters: BA. BSC. DPHIL. MD. PHD. Lowest and smallest of all was a set of Chinese characters like squashed insects. The door was ajar so Joseph came in, gently knocking the frame.

He found himself in a corridor that ran the length of the building to the back door. To the left was a door labelled in white paint: EXAMINATIONING ROOM. Across from it, to the right was a modest waiting room, inside which a teenager in a grey school uniform sat behind a desk, desultorily thumbing his phone. There were three folding chairs against the wall, one occupied by a dark-skinned, big-boned woman wearing a white blouse, a pinstriped skirt with a side slit, and espadrilles. She looked up from her phone as he came in. She seemed familiar, not her face but her scent.

Joseph approached the schoolboy secretary and asked for Dr Musadabwe. Without looking up from his phone, the boy stood and left the room. He returned promptly, Musadabwe rushing in behind him, dressed in his dingy lab coat, his tattered stethoscope swinging.

'Joseph!' Musadabwe reached his hand out.

'Doctor.' Joseph shook it, ducking a wave of halitosis.

'Come!' Musadabwe paused and turned to the woman. 'Am coming just-now, love.' He grabbed Joseph's shoulder. 'It is velly-good to see you, young man. Come and see the lab.'

Joseph followed him down the corridor to the back door. They exited into a dirt yard strung with a clothes line bedecked in white – lab coats, towels, sheets. The laundry's sparkle belied the stench back here, which was chokingly putrid. It grew as they passed a set of crates.

'Testing animos,' Musadabwe explained as they stepped inside a small concrete building at the bottom of the yard. 'And this one is the lab.'

It was nothing like the labs at UNZA, which were shabby and chipped but functional. This was more like something you'd see in a post-apocalyptic movie, all bent tools and drifting debris. There was a black workbench in the centre, dusty pipettes and test tubes scattered over it. An incubator sat unplugged in a corner, its door ajar.

Musadabwe turned on the light – a bare bulb hanging from the ceiling – and motioned for Joseph to sit. Joseph perched on the one high stool, suppressing the urge to tidy up. Musadabwe ceremoniously pulled his stethoscope off his neck and placed it on the workbench – it looked like a snake with two heads set to attack each other. Then he leaned against the workbench, crossed his arms and ankles, and plunged right in.

'Andi so? Your father. He was a blirriant man, your father. He was telling me we can even have science in Zambia. It is a technico world, *hm*? These Americans – they are too greedy! And the Chinese now? *Mm-mm*. But they can help us. They can supply matelios and whatwhat, from this Sino-American Consosham. But even us Zambians, with our limited rezosses, we can come together! Andi use? Our heads!'

Joseph nodded.

'Now. This is the current state of the situation. The Virus has destroyed our country. Compretely and totally! Whole generations have been wiped down! Those plagues in the Bible? Those locusts, those boyos bursting on the skin – they were just prophecies of this disease!'

Joseph nodded again, a bit warily. He wasn't a huge fan of the evangelical craze in Lusaka.

'To make a kew-ah – how can we? The Virus compolomises the immunie system. So you cannot even do a normal vaxin. So maybe the solution? Don't kill The Virus compretely. Maybe just find some? Equa-biriam.'

Musadabwe uncrossed his arms and levelled his hands like a see-saw.

Equilibrium. Joseph nodded. *Commensalis.* Okay. Learn to share the table with The Virus.

'But The Virus, it is velly movious, changing-changing all of the time. You cannot swove this problem just like that,' Musadabwe snapped his fingers. 'No! It is a moving target! So we must also keep moving. Like Muhammad Ali, floating like a bee! Knock it off from the pass!' He punched his fist into his palm, then grabbed a scrap of paper on the workbench and plucked a Bic from his coat pocket. 'This?' He drew a circle. 'It is a human immunity cell. They are calling it? Tee. Cell.' He labelled it. 'And these ones,' he gave it a halo of sprouting mushrooms, 'are the receptacles.'

Joseph nodded. *Receptors.* He knew what these were from googling the abbreviations in his father's notes. Receptors and co-receptors sat on the outside of human T-cells. The Virus used them like portals to break into the immune system and take over. If one receptor didn't work, The Virus shifted to the next, like a general trying every gate of a walled castle. Musadabwe explained all this in his broken English, which oddly didn't seem to impede the clarity of his science.

'Andi so? There was some resatch in Kenya. It's now twenty years ago! It was showing that these women, you know, the women of the night,' Musadabwe blinked over the euphemism, 'they are highly exposed to The Virus. But they did not catch the full disease! The Virus, it was in the cells but at velly low logs, the same low levels that we need for . . . ?' He lifted his nose and waited like a teacher.

'Equilibrium?' Joseph answered tentatively.

'A-*haa*!' Musadabwe see-sawed his hands, slower this time, more dramatically. 'So these female populations had some natchuro immunities that made The Virus sustainabo. It was because they had a mutation on the respectacle that was preventing The Virus from attaching—'

'Oh.' Joseph sat up. 'The mutation blocks The Virus from getting in the T-cells!'

'Mm-*hmm.*' Musadabwe grinned. 'Their mutation was on this respectable,' he scribbled letters next to a mushroom on the diagram. 'See. See. Arra. Two Dashi. Sickisty-fo. Eye.'

CCR2-641. Joseph recognised the abbreviation from his father's messages and emails.

'But your father found a woman with a mutation on a ligand of another receptor as well.' He scrawled out another abbreviation: CXCR4Δ6. 'We are calling her the Lusaka Peshent. Andi so? If we duplicate both of her mutations in the general populations—'

'We can prevent The Virus from infecting our immune cells,' said Joseph. 'But' – he nibbled the side of his thumb – 'how do you duplicate mutations?' He was out of his depth now.

'A-*haa*! So, there is a technology now! Crispa!' Musadabwe wrote it out: CRISPR-Cas9. 'It targets the genes. You can make mutations at the DNA level. Crispa is simpo and affordabo.'

So why had this not been done before?

'Crispa is velly new. And you can make some mistakes. How do you mutate the genes without damaging other things, this-side-that-side? It is not easy. It is some kind of *mm*, genetical engineering? Because if we go along this path, we are not mutating The Virus. We are mutating our bodies.'

Joseph remembered the last memo on his father's phone, the words just audible through the wind on the golf course: '. . . the question then is whether to modify the genome of the host or . . .'

Musadabwe had now embarked on a begging rant. There was a Chinese study being run by a Dr Ling and Ling had said he would back Musadabwe, but new equipment was needed – did Joseph have access to his father's research funds? To buy a cell sorter? A new incubator? The mice could be ordered online—

Joseph's head was swarming. He needed to think. He needed to read Dad's notes and listen to Dad's memos and process them. He needed to zap each buzzing thought, pinch it between his fingers, pin its jerking body to a velvet plate, frame it behind glass and hang it on a wall with the others. Only then could he step back and see the big picture. He stood up and cut off Musadabwe's spiel by murmuring some vague promises.

'Fine.' The doctor clapped his hands once, resignedly. 'That is velly-fine.'

He led Joseph back through the fluttering white yard with its animal reek and into the dark corridor of the clinic. They shook hands at the front door. Joseph stepped out into the bleeding sunset and the teethgrinding drone of woodsaws at the woodyard next door. When he glanced back at the clinic, the doctor was gone, but Joseph caught a movement behind the window. It was the dark-skinned woman from the waiting room, staring straight at him.

He averted his gaze and turned around. There goes one of Dad's women, he thought, or rather one of his women of the night. Had they been his lovers or his patients or both? There had been a circle of sickness around Dr Lionel Banda – Salina and Mum and Farai and Sylvia. They all had The Virus. Joseph realised now that to be spared that intimacy was also to be deprived of it.

2016

'They called him The Black.'

'The Black?'

'The Black.'

'Hm. The Black? *Shuwa?*'

'Ya,' Joseph insisted. 'The Moor.'

'More what? More colour?'

'*Moor.* It's an old word for a black man. They spelled it M-O-H-R in German. I read about it online.'

'But he was black? *Shuwa?* Did you not tell us he was a Jew?' Jacob looked annoyed.

'*Mwebantu*, Ba Marx started all of the revolutionary movements!' God exhorted. 'Marching on the road of history, justice on his side. The black and the brown and the yellow: all of us must rise up!'

There was a pause.

'So – he was a *muntu?*' Jacob asked again.

'No, he was German. He was what they call *swarthy*. It was just his friends and family teasing: "The Moor is going underground. The silly old Moor." They called Engels The General.'

'What kind of friends talk like that?'

Joseph pulled up a picture on his phone. 'Just look at his face. It's definitely brownish. The hair is kinky. Thin lips, yes. But that is what they called a Negroid nose.'

Jacob peered at the phone. 'Ah you, that is just a tan.'

'*Mwebantu*, this is a tired debate!' said God. 'Shut your mouths.'

Jacob laughed and clapped God on the shoulder. 'Yes, *bwana*.'

Joseph left the woodyard and walked through Musadabwe's clinic to the lab in the back. The door was open and he stood at the entrance for a second. The floor of the lab had been scrubbed raw this morning. But the dust would soon return. It had already begun its inevitable drift from the yard. He thought of the old man and the young man next door at RIP Beds & Coffins, smiling at the lazy, hazy arguments they had cultivated over the past few months. Joseph had become a regular, stopping by on his way to and from the lab, smoking a joint or two, drinking a beer or two, chatting about the Marxist ideas he was learning from Gran's cassette tape.

Joseph washed out the beakers from this morning. He sterilised. A chicken from the crates outside made a popping sound. He sucked his teeth and went to see what was up. Musadabwe's newest schoolboy secretary was standing outside the door. The boy held the latest results out to Joseph with both hands, the insides of his elbows splayed taut. His uniform was green and stiff.

'How do you expect me to know you're there if you don't say anything?'

The boy shrugged, a smile flickering upward then subsiding into indifference. Joseph took the results and told the boy to change into *patapatas* before coming into the lab. Joseph spread the results over the workbench. He could just make out the numbers in the tables, flush against the borders, serifs overlapping. The boy was shuffling uneasily by the sink, awaiting instruction.

'Big results today, eh?' Joseph said wryly.

The boy stood with his hands clasped in front of him. His shaved head shone under the bare bulb, making him seem smaller.

'Don't you want to learn anything?'

The boy shrugged one shoulder.

'Lesson one. A virus eats its house from the inside. That's the only way it can survive.'

∗

I told you about the first trials a couple of emails ago, but I guess I didn't tell you about the second ones? In the second ones, the nodules burst from the inside. You can imagine the pressure we're under from Ling. Musadabwe keeps trying one way, then another. The specimens are all botched. There's no pain, I don't think, but there are mutations in the skin, and the bones start to curl up. I can hear them outside sweeping the ground – the sound of tumour-blasted feet.

Yeah, God's just a nickname, haha – the old man doesn't even believe in God. He lectures us about class politics so often that Jacob calls him bwana *just to piss him off. God the atheist,* bwana *the Marxist. Jacob works for him, technically, but he lacks a feel for carpentry. It's hard to admit but working with his hands may be all that a poor person of our generation can manage. Jacob stares at me sometimes. I think he wants to ask me about his mother. I guess I want to ask him about her, too. The Lusaka Patient.*

Naila. At night I dream of you, of your hands.

∗

Joseph lifted a mouse out of a wooden box, one hand holding the tail, the other gripping the neck. The animal bucked between these pincers, its body pulsing with panic. Joseph slipped it into a Mason jar, which was stuffed with tissue soaked in anaesthetic, drops clustering on the inner glass like dew. The mouse collapsed with a soft squeak.

'Come on out, now.'

He tilted the jar to tip it out again. He pinched its skin, then slid the syringe in. He eased the plunger down. After a moment, the mouse flinched once, twice.

'Wakey, wakey.'

It got up on its little rubbery feet. He cradled it gently in his hand and let it back into its box. He wiped the workbench under the hood, his stoned mind drifting in the slow circles his hand was making over it. He prepared the gel plate with buffer and agarose and ethidium bromide, slid it into the UV transilluminator, and took the old gel plate inside the clinic. The examination room was dark but for a blueish spotlight from Musadabwe's Digit-All Bead.

'What is this?'

'The latest gel.' Joseph put it on the table.

Musadabwe pointed his glowing middle finger at it. As usual, he started complaining, the words in his mouth moaning like trapped animals as he hemmed and hawed. Joseph waited for it to stop. The light from Musadabwe's Bead lit upon an irregularity in the gel.

'Why is this still here? Did you not redo it?'

'I'll try a new mouse.'

'We do not have lab mice to spare,' Musadabwe grunted. 'They are velly expensive!' He held his finger closer to the plate and scanned his Bead light over it again.

*

In the first test, the cells were too full – too drugged, I think. In the second, they lysed. What will the third test do? I'm losing my mind, Naila. These tests are supposed to move forwards, not backwards. I know I didn't finish my second term at UNZA, but I didn't really need to, I had learned more than enough to improve Dad's protocols. That's why Musadabwe hired me, right? At least that is what I thought. Now I'm not so sure. Sometimes I think he appreciates my work. But sometimes I think he just wants my money – which is Gran's money, really.

*

'The copper mines are nearly empty,' said Joseph.

'The British cleaned them out!' said God, picking at a back tooth with a matchstick.

The yard was scaly with wood shavings, some so tightly curled, their shadows made garland chains. Jacob kicked through them as he came in, carrying his latest toy. He squatted to open the cardboard box and they heard the creaking sound of styrofoam. Sunlight flashed over a black surface as Jacob inched the machine out. It clicked as he tugged it one way then the other, pivoting it back and forth. At last, it sat upright in the dust. Jacob pressed a button on a remote. The drone shuddered to life but stayed crouched on the ground. Joseph turned back to his conversation with the old man.

'The British colonialists were just highstrung. Too brittle, too cold.'

'There were hordes of them!' God laughed, marijuana smoke spilling down his body, rolling around his neck, massing from his mouth. 'This country caved when the *bazungu* came in.'

Joseph frowned, scratching his head with dull shame. He wasn't white or British but Gran was, and he sometimes felt an oblique guilt by association. The drone was squealing and buzzing now, rising slowly from the ground. Dust nipped at their skin. Jacob hunched out of the machine's way as it zoomed over his shoulder and hovered above the yard, propellers at full speed. Methodically, he brought it down, then went over and picked it up from the wood shavings.

'Our country is full of broken promise,' said God. 'But the promise never shatters completely – there's never the total disaster, the catastrophe we need to start the revolution!'

'That's sick, old man,' Joseph chuckled.

'Cooperating with the West after Independence only made us weaker. Why did we bother?'

'Uh, I think it was for the money?'

'No, they have just been waiting for our resources to dwindle. Vultures! We started this nation with potential. "A society of the people!" Kaunda said. But somehow we narrowed until it was just for the top three per cent. The capitalists replaced the colonialists. And now these foreigners take our minerals away and even shoot our miners. Every day their greed bites into our land. Soon there will be nothing left. We must wake up! We must stop dreaming! We are still on the ground. It is still night in this country. We are still on our knees. Time to rise up!'

God's face was wrinkled and his dreads were matted, but he was still quick and strong. His hands were busy now, rolling two new joints of *mbanji*.*

'This is how we put revolution in the body!' he laughed.

Joseph watched God with dreamy patience, waiting for him to light up.

＊

Have you heard of Jonas Salk? He was the American scientist who discovered the polio vaccine. He proved that we could use inactivated polio cells the same way we use inactivated tetanus and diphtheria cells to make a vaccine. Late in his life, in the 1980s, he even did some preliminary studies on a vaccine for The Virus. I was googling around and it turns out he conducted experiments on himself, and his wife and son were the test subjects for the first polio vaccine trial. 'I will be personally responsible,' he said. Good thing it worked! When they asked him who owned the patent on the polio vaccine, he said: 'Well, the people, I would say. There is no patent. Could you patent the sun?'

＊

'What are you doing with that thing?'

'Nothing,' Jacob replied without looking up.

God was sawing through a plank of wood. Now he pushed his goggles up. They held his dreadlocks back like a girl's headband.

'It better not be nothing!' he said. 'The General is waiting.'

The new drone model was propped on its back on an overturned oil drum, a brick underneath it to raise its head and protect its propellers. Its square belly was open. Joseph glanced around the yard at the remnants of Jacob's experiments. It looked like the aftermath of a battle scene in a *Terminator* movie.

'But why?' he tried again. 'Is that, like, a *real* drone? How much did it cost?'

Jacob glared at him and returned to his tinkering. After a beat, he spoke. 'I'm rebuilding it.'

'Why?'

Jacob narrowed his eyes and flicked his chin up. 'And you – why do you do those things in your *ka* lab?'

'Science.'

'So?' Jacob jerked his head at the drone. 'Same-same.'

✳

Joseph turned on the gas for the Bunsen burner. Four samples of canarypox – one had disappeared last week, he suspected Dr Ling had snatched it – were huddled in the wooden rack. The Petri dish was sitting on the workbench. He lit the burner. From a recessed part of his mind, he watched himself hold the inoculation loop in the tiny roar of the methane flame until the metal glowed a fierce orange. He cooled the loop in the agar with a hiss. The agar looked clean, the colour of Vaseline. He dipped the sterile loop into the open test tube, then scribbled it over the agar. He was making another culture to examine on the electrophoresis tray. He leaned against the workbench, watching himself dip and transfer.

✳

Salk wasn't the only one. Scientists love to experiment on themselves. The immunologist David Pritchard slipped hookworms under his skin. The cardiologist Werner Forssmann put a catheter in his heart. The chemist Albert Hofmann took the first ever hit of LSD on his bicycle ride home from the lab. I can see the appeal of testing yourself. It's all about the control. You control the whole experiment. You prove your commitment to your hypothesis. You observe symptoms internally and externally. You skirt the ethical morass of testing human subjects, if not the legal one. But I'm sure there's a loophole, the same way no one ever goes to trial for attempting suicide because you'd have to bring charges against yourself. It's all about 'the control' in another sense, too. If you give yourself a disease from a known source, you have a control condition – two patients with the exact same strain. One you test, the other you don't.

✳

The yard vibrated with the smell of fresh wood and friction.

'Maybe the Chinese will be the dawn of a new economy,' said Joseph. 'They'll light the way.'

'With kwacha and ngwee?' God snorted. 'And what about our free-doms? We are already falling back under the sway of totalitarian think-ing with the Chinese.'

'Yes, *bashikulu*,' said Jacob. 'If we want light, we must have fire! Burn out the disease.'

'What disease?' asked Joseph.

Jacob swept his hand through the air and began to walk away.

'Do not run from the argument, *mwana*,' God spat.

Jacob glanced at the glob of spit on the dirt. 'The foreigners are the disease. They are still in power.'

'That's superstitious nonsense,' Joseph clucked. 'You believe we're still under colonialism?'

'Me, I don't like the foreigners who come here. They just plunder our resources.'

'Most of the world doesn't even know who we are,' said Joseph. 'We're still very young, you know. This nation barely has a history or a working economy. We benefit from foreign aid.'

'Zambia is only young *because* of the foreigners.' God lifted his joint with delicate fingers. He sipped the burning leaves and winced with pleasure. 'They carved us up. They drew borders straight through the villages. Pulling tribes together from this side, that side. Joining us into Federation, splitting us again. It took some time to make one Zambia one nation.'

'Well, the Chinese aren't doing that,' Joseph shrugged. 'They first came here in solidarity. And now they have come to invest. They're building railroads and farms and airports. That can only help.'

'Ah? No. We cannot afford that kind of help,' said God.

✳

I've been listening to my dad's Memos, going backwards in time. The Notes are more useful, of course – he lays out the exact procedures to test the mutations. Musadabwe and I have essentially been replicating what he was doing, but faster now that we have access to CRISPR. It's changed the whole scientific landscape. My dad knew it would. You can hear it in his voice in the last Memos – the news really started to circulate about CRISPR in 2013. The term for what it does is DNA editing and it really is almost as easy as typing and deleting the words in this email. It's cheap now, too, but of course there's a patent war already.

Dad's Memos are more philosophical than scientific. He asks himself questions and answers them, like he's ventriloquising both Socrates and the sycophantic neophytes. He gives himself diagnoses. I'm looking for the moment he figured it out. I think he was testing the vaccine on himself. Like Salk. Did he test it on my mother too? On Jacob's mother?

＊

Joseph printed out the Wikipedia entry on 'Unmanned Aerial Vehicle'. It was eighteen pages long. He slid the printout onto the oil drum, next to Jacob's drone.

'You know I have Wi-Fi too?' Jacob said through gritted teeth. 'Like everybody else in Lusaka?'

'Ya, no. I just—'

Jacob pressed his middle finger to his thumb. A skewer of light shot out from the tip of the finger.

'You got beaded?'

Jacob crooked the fingers of his left hand at the top knuckle, casting a square of light onto the palm. He tapped this 'screen' with his right index finger. The Google home page appeared. 'See?' He extended his hand palm up. 'Even us poor people, we have Googo now.'

'Technology is no longer the preserve of the rich, eh?' said God. He came over from his sanding bench and peered down at Jacob's hand. 'How does this thing work?'

'Human skin is an electric interface,' said Joseph. He had seen a demo at the Arcades Digit-All shop. 'They embed a torch and a speaker in the finger, and a mic at the wrist – but you can also use a wristband. There's a circuit in the median nerve,' he pointed to the centre of Jacob's palm. 'The rest is conductive ink.' Jacob turned his hand over to show off the tattoos radiating across its back.

God shook his head. 'I like electronical guitar but I will never put electricity in my hand. The hand is man's saving grace. This part,' he pointed at his own median nerve, 'we call it—'

'The eye of the hand,' said Joseph.

'No!' said God. 'It is called the labourer's nerve. The hand is what we use to grasp tools to plough the earth! And weapons to fight the power! And instruments to play freedom songs!'

Jacob rolled his eyes, clicked off his Bead, and pointed at the Wikipedia printouts Joseph had brought. 'Anyway. I already read about drones online,' he said. 'It will not help my project.'

'Ba Marx wrote that the machine, it is a virtuoso,' God was musing. 'It has a soul! The mechanical laws are acting through the machine and these act upon the mind of the worker ...'

'What *is* your project exactly?' Joseph asked Jacob.

'A nanorobot.' Jacob crossed his arms. He was shorter than Joseph, but stronger.

'Whoah. The robots that they send through veins and arteries?'

'Ah, no. Not that small.'

'You mean a microbot?'

'Yes. That one. They are making them in USA already. The size of a fly. Or a bee.'

Joseph cast his eyes at the drone on the oil drum – the size of a pigeon. 'Okay.'

✳

I found Jacob's name in my dad's files. I've been going through the photos – they go back the furthest because every time Dad plugged his iPhone into his laptop, it downloaded his whole photo library. There's a 2012 album, from when he moved out – he took photos of his old documents to back them up. It's barely legible but I think it was a test. It says 'sample' and Jacob M. The result is negative. I guess he lucked out. Should I tell him? How do I even bring it up? 'Remember when our parents used to fuck?'

I mostly go over there to smoke with God and hear stories about freedom-fighting days, to talk about Marx – another self-tester, in a way. He wasn't really black but he certainly lived the poverty he was theorising. And yeah, I guess I'm a little curious about Jacob's 'drone project'. It does seem shady, as you say. But it also seems so unlikely, so kachigamba. *Does he really think he can pull it off?*

✳

Joseph stood above the woman of the night. He watched her for a moment then rapped his knuckles against the wall to wake her. Her eyelids shimmied up, her irises like solid black buttons. Her head fell forward and she began coughing. When the fit had settled, she blinked.

'Injections,' he said, placing a hand under her arm to help her up. Her skin felt damp.

As Joseph guided her to the 'Examinationing Room', she slurred at him. 'I know you,' she said. Her head drooped so far her chin almost touched her chest. Joseph sighed and kicked the door open. Musadabwe watched warily while he assisted her up onto the exam table.

'Drunk again, love?' Musadabwe smiled grimly.

Joseph handed a tray of medical equipment to the doctor and placed a bucket beside the woman, just in case. She was falling to pieces, her skin scorched black, her eyes slitted like buttonholes now. When Joseph moved towards the door, Musadabwe called out.

'Help me,' he said.

*

I didn't think we would get this far. We're nearly ready for human inocula-tion. The patients are hungry for it: whining and pleading with their big eyes. Ling wants us to gather more data first. It turns out he organised competing teams of scientists on either side of the Indian Ocean – he's essentially pit-ting us against each other, to force a breakthrough. It leaves a bad taste in my mouth. I know what you'll say, Naila – neocolonial neoliberalism, Ling just pushed our research back etc.

He held the Chinese results over Musadabwe the last time we met. Can you imagine it, all of us sitting across from each other in that hovel of a lab? Ling blinking slowly. Musadabwe singing his give-us-more-money song – Dad must have taught him that. They ignored me completely. Humiliating. I know the Virus vaccine is not technically my project but I've worked on it for months. I had to insist on even attending these meetings. I threatened to resign. Don't laugh. I know you can't resign from a job you never had. I know I got this far only because of my money. But I want to see it through. I'll rustle more out of Gran if I have to.

*

The sunlight had gone from dull orange to white heat, the day burning itself up. Joseph squatted on the stoop of the clinic, rinsing tools in a bucket. Students in pale blue uniforms strolled along Alick Nkhata. Joseph watched them with fond pity as he dried a beaker and the centrifuge tubes. He hadn't gone to his UNZA classes in ages, not since Naila had transferred out. The One Hundred Years Clinic and RIP Beds & Coffins were schools of a different sort.

Just as he finished drying, he heard loud voices next door. Joseph walked over to the woodyard, slipping through the gap between a dresser and a coffin. Jacob was leaning against a tree, jeans low on his hips. Joseph's eyes narrowed – Jacob hadn't come by in a couple of weeks. He was talking to God, who was facing away, a block plane in his hand.

'Isa kuno, iwe,' God called. 'Come closer if you want to ask for things! You need what?'

Jacob strode over to him and God's hand fell onto his shoulder. He gestured for Jacob to assist and they levered a plank onto the trestle. As God began shaving bits of wood off it, their words grew inaudible. In the bright midday light, the wood flakes looked like scraps of gold.

God stopped to point at the metal lumps around the yard. 'And what are these?'

'False starts,' said Jacob.

'You buy these machines and just break them,' God chided, picking up a discarded drone.

'I'm almost there, bashikulu,' Jacob protested.

'Almost!' God laughed and tossed the machine to the ground again. 'No, I'm not throwing kwacha away so you can build some more almost-robots.'

'I'll lend you the money.' Joseph stepped forward.

Jacob gaped, a laugh catching in his throat. 'I will not owe money to a stranger—'

'Ah, you!' God shoved Jacob towards Joseph. 'You need the money? So take it.'

✳

I never thought about that possibility. You think? Jacob is darker than both my dad and his mum, so I always assumed – although Sylvia's skin is artificially light after all. AMBI-valent, so to speak. And the genetics of skin colour do play out in unpredictable ways.

Naila. I miss you. There's a crack in my screen because Musadabwe's secretary boy dropped my phone, but I got your WhatsApp. Your new haircut is lovely. Why did you decide to dye it silver? I've never seen that before – it looks like a helmet. My Joan of Arc. You'll call me a fool for giving any of Gran's money away, especially to Jacob, and for drones at that. But he's aiming high, right? Striving for innovation! I sound like a muzungu. *Maybe you're right – maybe it's just guilt like he really is my brother. Is the selfie you sent from the rally you told me about, after the protests? You look so hopeful. So strong.*

✳

'Eye for an eye. Or is it tit-for-tat?'

Joseph reached out his hand.

'Are we *bazungu* that we must shake on it?'

Joseph blinked and lowered his hand. He leaned down, opened his satchel, and took out a paper bag with the money in it. 'Okay, here it is. Five thousand sharp,' he said.

He sat on the high stool, watching Jacob take the block of kwacha notes and count them out, slipping them onto the workbench. Joseph looked over the loan contract – he had printed it out this morning without proofreading it. Jacob counted the money again in that leisurely way of his.

'So,' Jacob said finally, pinching the bridge of his nose.

Joseph was at the sink, idly rinsing out test tubes.

'What are you doing in here with this Virus thing?'

Joseph looked at him. 'I've told you. Musadabwe and I are trying to cure it. We're scientists.'

'Scientists? *Nts.*'

Joseph folded his damp arms across his chest. 'What word would you prefer? Doctors?'

'What do you know about doctors?' Jacob sucked his teeth again.

'Yes, of course. Africans know *nothing* about medicine,' Joseph said sardonically.

Jacob pointed his finger in Joseph's face. 'I know your medicine is killing my mother.'

Rage beat across the air between them. Standing across from each other in this dark room had kindled something.

'Jacob. The Virus is killing your mother, not the medicine.'

'Your father is the one who brought her to this clinic.'

'He did not take her away from you.' Joseph released the words one at a time.

'You people are using her!' Jacob shouted. 'For experiments!'

'No! I don't know exactly how my father did his experiments, but we've only used animal subjects.' Joseph strode across the room and opened the door to the yard between the lab and the clinic, where they kept the crates of mice and chickens. His words cut through the smell of shit and bleach and dust, through the whimpers and squeaks of the animals.

'We take their T-cells out, genetically modify them with CRISPR, and put them back in.' The jargon tasted metallic in his mouth. 'They don't die, but I can see it in their skin, off-target symptoms from disabling the cells, black spots and patches from the mutagenesis. This is just what happens when we test it on animals. How could we use it on people?'

Jacob had turned away. Joseph stepped back into the lab. He grabbed a pen, signed the loan contract, and pushed it towards Jacob. Jacob's head was down, his hands on the money in his lap. He looked up.

'We shouldn't talk about your father.'

'He's gone anyway.'

'It happened a long time ago.'

'And your—?'

Jacob snatched the contract closer and signed, too. He stood, gingerly hitching his jeans up.

Over the two years since the funeral, Joseph had come to hate his father: a feeling which had clarity and could accommodate the admiration he'd once felt for him. Dr Lionel Banda had still left him this legacy, though: a trail of coded messages leading to a cure. Joseph had started with the truth – he and Musadabwe had tested only animals so far. But the rest was a lie. Joseph knew human trials would have to come eventually. He felt sorry for the Lusaka Patient and the other women like her. But to say sorry to her son would be tantamount to a confession, and Joseph would not face that until the study was done.

✳

Musadabwe is shutting the lab down. He told me to stop the experiments. I guess he reached an impasse with Ling – 'that Chinese trickster has robbed us!' – and the results from our lab are just going to be absorbed in the experiments at Huazhong. Our tiny data set will be lost in the midst of the discovery! Musadabwe has licked his wounds already. He says that he'll shift his focus back to treating Virus patients. That he can't stem the uneven tide of research, but he won't let these 'women of the night' succumb like dogs. He'll keep the clinic open as long as he can.

✳

Joseph shuffled through the dark, carrying a bag of lab equipment over his shoulder. He had paid for it – he might as well keep it. It dangled down his back and bumped as he walked unsteadily towards the wood-yard. He was high and delirious with fatigue from packing up the lab. He glanced back at the clinic, a last goodbye, and tripped. His bag flew and landed with a soft crunch. He fell slowly and heavily, tumbling down piecemeal, buttocks, then torso, then head.

All of a sudden Jacob was above him, looking down at him. On an impulse, Joseph grabbed at Jacob's ankle. He lifted it and tripped him and Jacob fell too, cut down. Which came first? Jacob's nails abrading his cheek? Or the quick punches to his chest? Jacob's eyes were wide, his teeth gritted. His face floated above as if Joseph had exhaled him: mocking and grinning and drunk. Joseph pressed his fist hard against Jacob's chest, his other hand around his wrist. Jacob wrapped his fingers around Joseph's, their hands a clutch of flesh and bone, sweat and skin. Laughter burst from his chest. The moon watched over them, a perfect circle.

✳

God sat at the base of the mopane tree, looking out. It was night. He would have to tell his grandson sooner or later. But for now he sat and watched Jacob and Joseph wrestle like children, wasted on beer or *mbanji* or both. The black boy looked silver, the yellow boy gold in the moonlight. RIP Beds & Coffins was otherwise empty but for a few new commissions – a bed, a coffin, a stool – standing like giant chess pieces, mired in curving shadows: a soundless, motionless standoff.

NyiiiiiinYiiinyiiiiiiinyyyyiiiiiiiinyiinyiiiiiiiiiNyiiiiiiiiinyinyiiiiiiiii. Munyinyi.

We're still right here, niggling near, nipping and nibbling in. You say we're vampires – bamunyama – because of our thirst for your blood. But we're more akin to the walking dead, a stunned dumb nation, a Zombia.

The concept of the zombie was born in the Kongo, then travelled to the New World on slave ships: nzambi (a god) or zumbi (a fetish) – either way, a thing beyond the living. Revived from the dead by a witch, a bokor, the zombie's a slave with no will. It can be sent to do labour or to murder a neighbour. An unkillable beast, it wanders the earth, doomed to vicarious evil. When a zombie attacks you, bites into your flesh, does it know what it's doing? Not really.

This is true for us as well. We carry ill but we don't really mean to. Fevered blood, hot blood, spicy blood, sour. Boiling inside the veins of the ailing, the minute we sip it, we know it. But by then it's too late: the agent's inside us and somewhat beyond our control. Viruses and parasites are small canny monsters: they take over our wishes completely. Possessed, blooddrugged, we are the third man, we broker between flesh and disease. Bad faith, bloodlust and anthropophily: such is the way of the mozombie.

Your beastly old tales know it all too well: we are Nature's great superfluity. 'What is this creature for?' you still cry, raising your fist to the heavens. We pollinate little and feed very few, and no predator needs us to live. The name of our species, Anopheles gambiae? It literally means 'no profit'. A deity slept on the day we sprang forth. We're an asterisk to Nature, a flaw, a digression, a footnote if ever there was one. We are not just an accident, but issue it too. Extermination trials go wonky. Toxorhynchites, they thought, would devour us, but they released the wrong species and we did not just survive, we thrived!

Joseph himself has learned this the hard way: his vaccine, founded upon a mutation, has foundered on capital's reef. But all sorts of things can slip through the cracks, especially genetically tweaked ones. Evolution forged the entirety of life using only one tool: the mistake . . .

Jacob

2009

Jacob lost his mother when her hair salon burned to the ground. After the Indian girl fell from the jacaranda tree, everyone trooped out into Kalingalinga with Uncle Lee as he carried her through the compound to his pickup. They drove off to the hospital, the girl and Ba Sibilla in the front next to Uncle Lee while his coloured son and wife – rollers still in her hair – squatted in the bed of the truck. Those who worked and lived at Hi-Fly Haircuttery & Designs Ltd returned in high spirits – they had saved a life! – only to find it being ravaged by ragged, roaring flames.

Ash swarmed around, black and grey and white like television snow. It smelled like a thousand supper fires, a thousand hairdryers. The neighbours were already trying to put it out, shouting commands, flapping blankets, tossing buckets of water. The salon girls scampered here and there, crying out. Jacob stood there helplessly and stared – not at the fire but at his mother, who stood equally fixed before it. Only when Aunty Loveness hugged her from behind did Mummy move, barely – her face trembled like a brushed string.

Only later, when the police told her that the fire had started at the electrical outlet, did she burst to furious life and turn on Jacob.

'You!' she spat at him. 'Always messing about with these wires and gadgets and A-B-C-D! Why can't you just be playing outside like a normal child?'

But playing outside like a normal child was exactly how the *mwenye* girl got hurt in the first place, Jacob thought. And it was only because she fell from the tree that they had all abandoned the Hi-Fly.

That night, he and his mother and Aunty Loveness slept outside, warming their bones against the flame-heated earth around the black husk of the salon. The next morning, they stuffed what was left of their possessions into plastic bags – Jacob was distraught to realise his aeroplane belt had charred – and began their exodus from Kalingalinga. He imagined that they would be zamfooting for hours to find housing, but after a short walk across the compound, his mother paused in front of the gate of a small breezeblock cottage and took his hand, gesturing for Aunty Loveness to wait.

'*Odi?*' Mummy called out as they ducked through a curtain at the entrance. It was dark and dank inside, and Jacob heard a faint blurbling sound like a storm drain, though it was not yet rainy season. An older woman, short and dark and round, got up from her squat in front of what looked like a crate of soft drinks. She was wearing a pink jersey and a faded *chitenge* wrapper with a pattern of binoculars with eyes on the lenses. She stepped towards them and he saw that she was ill – her own eyes were black and shut, her cheeks covered in a chalky rash.

'Ba Mayo,' Mummy said coolly.

Jacob looked up at her, then back at the woman. This was his *gogo*? He had never met her before but he had heard rumours about Matha Mwamba, Kalingalinga's famous crying woman.

'This is Jacob,' Mummy said and nudged him forward. 'Your grandson.'

Gogo reached out and patted his head searchingly. Mummy was speaking in a stilted Bemba, asking, or rather telling, his *gogo* to look after him. Mummy turned him to face her. She told him that she and Aunty Loveness already had a place to stay – she named a clinic – then promised that she would come back for him. She rubbed his cheek and made her exit. She did not say goodbye to her mother. She did not turn her head as she went, not even once.

✳

After a week or so, Jacob went looking for her, but dozens of clinics had sprouted up in Kalingalinga to treat The Virus. It felt like it took as long as its name to find the One Hundred Years Clinic, and when Jacob enquired, a man wearing a white coat and a rubber and metal necklace told him that there was no Sylvia Mwamba living there. Gogo didn't complain when Jacob returned to her home, stayed on for six weeks, five months, a year, two. She fed him and otherwise left him to his own devices. She didn't seem bothered by his presence but she didn't much bother about it either.

Jacob tried to make himself useful. He knocked together a bed and a table out of scraps from a woodyard. He sewed a protective canopy to spread over her tomato garden in the back. He rejigged an old filing cabinet so she could lock away her small moneys and convinced her to spend some of it to fit one wall of her cottage with a glass window, and to replace the old *chitenge* at the entrance with a wooden door.

His new home seemed empty compared to the hair salon. Gogo only had one seat, a school chair with the desk still attached, graffitied with the love poems of Musonda + Debbie; and one table, covered with a flowery plastic tablecloth, upon which sat a dented pot, a black pan, two cracked plates and a mixed family of cutlery. Several crates of old soft-drink bottles sat under the bed he'd built. He slept on a mat on the floor beside it.

Having long dwelt in two kinds of washing-day loneliness – being alone amongst the salon girls and being alone without them – Jacob now became accustomed to a third kind: spending a lot of time with one very quiet person. Gogo would wobble outside with the dirty linens and slowly lower herself to her knees in front of a plastic tub. She would suds them, beat them on a flat rock, rinse them in the bucket, wring them, then hand them to Jacob to hang on the line.

When they were dry, she would press them with the coal-filled iron, more to eliminate putzi fly eggs than wrinkles. They would fold together, doing that odd mirror dance – their arms stretching wide and coming together as they drew close, then apart, then close again – until the sheets were all bundled up in themselves. Just like his *gogo*. Though she sometimes made a low hum that he recognised as his name, her quiet, weeping presence made Jacob feel lonelier than ever, as if her solitude were contagious.

One Tuesday two years after he'd moved in, Matha's grandson came into the house, closed the door, and told her that there was a dead man in the garden. It was rainy season. The smell of mud and the smell of concrete walls hugged in the air like long lost relatives. The tin roof clattered.

The air was skittish with sheltering insects. Matha sat on a stool, head tilted so her tears ran off her face. She was shelling groundnuts, discarding the squeaky husks on the floor, preparing to make a special dish of *chibwabwa ne'ntwilo* for her grandson. She would roast the groundnuts and pound them; the pumpkin leaves were already boiling in a pot on the *mbaula*. Jacob came in and said, 'There's a man in the garden holding a piece of paper that says he is dead.'

Matha frowned and smacked his head for lying. Then she paused. She stood up and went over to her new window to look outside, but she couldn't see properly through the heavy rain. She patted the windowsill to find her matchbox of razor blades, opened the little drawer, pulled one out, and plucked its tip to check its sharpness. Then she swiftly ran the blade lengthways between her right eyelids. She heard Jacob gasp and rush over, but by the time he reached her, she had already done the other side, slicing through the tangle of lashes that usually kept her half-blind. She nipped a final knot and blinked wide. She stared out of the window until she was sure.

She went over to the bed Jacob had built for her and dragged a crate out from under it. She pulled out three soft-drink bottles – a Coke bottle shaped like a bishop chess piece, a Fanta bottle engraved with ridges that you could play like a *guiro*, and a Sprite bottle indented with fingerprints as if a baby had handled the green glass before it hardened. The bottles were full – not with bubbly black, orange or silver – but with a clear, still liquid. She picked up all three, reconsidered, and took just two. She walked to the door of No. 74 and opened it.

A man moved towards her through the downpour. Drops bounced off his body and crossed the falling rain, their clash shaping an aura. He stepped under the slim shelter formed by the jutting tin roof. His hair was long and matted in greying dreadlocks. A slip of paper hung from his slack fingers. Matha saw the scar on his neck. She reached across the threshold and handed him a bottle. He took it with a nod. They clinked and drank. He spat.

'Heysh, woman! But it's salty!'

Matha raised an eyebrow and drank again.

'May I have a beer instead?' asked Godfrey Mwango.

*

A few days later, the rain still clamouring on the roof of No. 74, Jacob found the dead man on the stoop, barefoot and muttering in a low steady current. His dreadlocks hung like different kinds of seedpods, some thin, some thick. He wore a tattered maroon suit with flared trousers and wide lapels. It had once been velvet but large mangy patches had worn away. Jacob joined him. Ba Godfrey handed him a Mosi – he didn't seem to notice or care that Jacob was fourteen.

'... radical! The Godfather of Soul! In Zambia! James Brown ...'

Jacob took a swig of beer – it tasted bitter and round like *impwa* – and tried to follow the meandering account of the concert. He latched on again when Ba Godfrey mentioned his *gogo*.

'... Lusaka to see Matha because I heard she was back from Kasama but then the lorry I jumped on in Choma broke down so I walked with the driver to a village somewhere there to find materials to fix the lorry. I have some mechanical knowledge from the Doctor, he taught us about revolution but also about these electronical things, I know how to fix an engine ...'

But when Ba Godfrey reached the nearest village, he had ended up drinking three or four cartons of *shakeshake* with the locals – this was unwise, he admitted – then he had made a bet and lost and had to work to pay it off and a white preacher had baptised him with cooking oil and put the host on his tongue – but it was a beetle, he vomited it up – and he had joined a church and played the guitar like KK but the white hanky turned black after KK lost the election—

Jacob knew about Kenneth Kaunda and his white handkerchief, but KK had stopped being president in 1991, six years before Jacob was born. Ba Godfrey was still going.

'... minibus stopped at Mazabuka but I found a bicycle. Then it broke but Ba Nkoloso taught us how to put the chain back on and ratchet it tight so I was riding fine but then a Land Rover hit me and I broke my leg and there was a hole just here ...' Ba Godfrey pointed to a deep scar, a ravine in his cheek.

A long night had followed – there was a *muzungu* woman and an Arab man who had vanished in a burst of kwacha and a boy who had brought him water and then the *muzungu* woman had returned but her hair had gone from black to yellow, from night to day. She had cradled his head in her lap and kept him alive until the *weeyo-weeyo* bus came.

Blinding white lights, the smell of *inswa* and Dettol, a fire, playing *nsolo* with a monkey that bit his thigh and snatched a beer out of his hand, a long dark plain lit by a single paraffin lamp ...

Jacob frowned, unsure if it was Ba Godfrey or the Mosi that had him buzzing with confusion. 'Who is Ba Nkoloso?' he asked.

Ba Godfrey's head swayed with the interruption, his lips trembling as he turned to Jacob.

'Ba Nkoloso?! A revolutionary! He said Zambia would go to the moon!'

Jacob's spirits sank. *Bashikulu* had wandered off the path again.

'Your *gogo* has not told you about Ba Nkoloso?'

'Gogo does not talk much,' said Jacob, wiping beer bubbles from his upper lip.

'Hm, yes,' Ba Godfrey laughed. 'She can be quiet, that Matha. But she is a fiery girl!'

Jacob looked at him. How strange to imagine that this muddy old man – skin riddled as dirt, wormy grey hairs in his dreads, that slug-like scar on his neck – had known Gogo as a girl.

'Ba Nkoloso taught us about history, politics, technology. And Matha – she even has math in her name! She was the smartest space cadet—'

'Wait, Gogo was ... a space cadet?'

'Yesss!' said Ba Godfrey. 'That is what I'm telling you! Listen.'

And on he went, opening two more Mosis for them along the way. This space story was bizarre but it was more coherent and detailed – oil drums rolling down a hill with cadets inside, the headquarters in Chunga Valley, the *Cyclops I* shuttle – and it could withstand questions, unlike his other stories, which crumbled at the touch like Jacob's clothes after the fire at the salon. By the time Gogo returned from the market, slouching under a Union Jack umbrella, Jacob almost didn't recognise her. So taken was he with the vision of 'Matha Mwamba, Star Afronaut' that his grandfather had painted – a young woman decked out in a bomber jacket, arms akimbo, a sparkle in her eye – that it had displaced the swampy, lumpy Gogo moving slowly towards them.

Jacob slid his empty beer bottle behind him and got up to help her carry her bags of unsold vegetables. Ba Godfrey nodded at her as she passed inside but stayed on the stoop, sipping at his Mosi, his feet half-sunk in mud. Inside, Jacob sat at the table and watched Gogo stash vegetables and a rotten wad of kwacha in the filing cabinet. Did she like selling vegetables? Did she miss being a space cadet? Gogo switched on the electric kettle he'd found for her in the dump and made them each a cup of tea. She sat with him and they sipped. Only then did Jacob ask her his most pressing question.

'You had *twelve* cats, Gogo?'

Her head tipped up with surprise. It was the first time Jacob had ever seen his grandmother's smile. She was missing some teeth but it was beautiful.

✳

Jacob was too young for a real job and too old to go back to school. His mother had never tried to get him a formal education, not that he wanted one – who would want to be a student with an itchy uniform and a ringwormy head, confined to a hot classroom all day, listening to the drone of a teacher who had barely passed Form II herself? Plus school was a dead end once you hit the dread wall of grade seven exams. Your best bet was to hustle – scrape some profit by hawking goods to those Zambians with better luck or richer relatives. You could grow those goods (vegetables, fruits, puppies). You could buy them on the black market (watches, hats, puppies). Or you could scavenge for them.

In the middle of Kalingalinga, there was a dump, a pile of rubbish even taller than the spires of the compound's homegrown churches, and with a stench so potent it lingered like a song stuck in your head. On the edge of the dump was the Auto Department, a vehicular grave-yard – a Mitsubishi more rust than red, a third of a Land Rover, a half-buried Beetle that resembled upended roots. The compound kids would climb inside these wrecks and 'drive', honking their noses, rev-ving their throats, their feet pumping invisible pedals as they looked through the paneless windows.

The kids sometimes used leftover scraps to build toy cars mod-elled after those husks. These wire cars and jeeps and trucks were like three-dimensional line drawings, each detail bent into perfect place – windscreen, wheels, gear stick, seats. To drive, you used a metal stick that interlocked with the front axle so you could steer it as you ran, the vehicle creaking ahead, its not-exactly-circular wheels leaving wobbly tracks in the dust. Over the years, as the dump filled up with better rubbish, these toy vehicles got fancier, updated with tin-can panels and rubber wheels and plastic headlights.

Jacob loved the Auto Department. Ever since he had discovered that half-wreck of an aeroplane at Lusaka City Airport four years ago, he had belonged to the electric world. He liked to make things in general, but nothing gave him greater pleasure than to galvanise them. No sound was more beautiful to his ears than the twitch-rattle-hum of an object coming to life in his hands. He could rejig a Discman, reassemble a foreign plug to fit a Zambian outlet, make a mixer spin its blades again by surgically removing a dead cockroach from its innards. But he lacked the bravado of the hawkers who strutted the roads, the 'amplifiers' who shouted the wares and prices of the market women. And what's the use of goods you can't sell?

✳

Matha had long intended to force Godfrey to taste the brine she had wrung from her pillow every morning for the last three decades while she waited for him to come back to her. Then he showed up in her garden with some kind of death certificate, took one sip, and spat it right out. The night of his return, Matha sent their grandson out to find his own supper and invited Godfrey inside No. 74. They sat side by side on her bed, their arms brushing. A paraffin lamp shot gold into a corner. It was quiet but for the two-tone chant of the crickets and the mutter of rain outside.

Godfrey was issuing a chain of words, strung together with no logic but chronology: *and then and then and then*. Matha barely heard him. *Where did you go? Where did you go? Where did you go?* she was thinking. Finally, he implored her directly, 'Matha, I was dying the bicycle was broken the Land Rover hit me ...' He trailed off. She looked at him. She bit her salty lips. She threw away her thinking and pulled his head to her chest.

They lay down together in her narrow bed. He didn't kiss her, but he touched her wet eyes with his fingers. She ran her hand over his matted hair and the silken scar on his neck. She removed her jersey and *chitenge* and petticoat. He kept his tatty natty suit on, unzipping his fly when the time came, as if to take a piss. Her thighs ached as they rolled open, a yawning feeling in the tendons. As they rocked together, a distant pleasure stirred in her. The bed was creaking. Her shoulder was bumping the wall. Godfrey finished with a shudder. He rolled over, zipped up and fell asleep. Matha lay still, an acidic ache in her belly, squeezed in the gap between the bed and the wall. She closed her eyes and tried to remember.

✳

At certain hours of the day, the traffic lassoing Kalingalinga tightened and knotted. In that listless slo-go, an albino girl would approach to beg through the windows. She was in her teens, bewitching and piteous both: her red-rimmed eyes looked raw yet exotic – *rare* in both senses – her scabby feet a special touch. *Bazungu* tourists and NGO workers in their cars were highly susceptible to her mewling. Little did they know that while they were busy mourning her plight and reaching into their pockets, the girl's brother was slipping his arm, dark and slight as a shadow, through a back window to pluck out a purse or a briefcase or a rucksack.

Once he had his spoils, the siblings would grab hands and race away into the compound, deftly navigating the alleys between lean-tos and shacks and breezeblock cottages. Sometimes, before darting off, the girl stole an *mbasela* from her benefactors – a little token to sweeten the deal. Just as the Brit or the Australian or the Israeli handed her one or two pin of kwacha, she would reach up and snatch the glasses off the bridge of their pointy noses. Sunglasses, prescription glasses, prescription sunglasses – these would all sell well.

When Jacob first met the albino girl, she was wearing three pairs: tortoiseshell frames propped in her blonde afro, gold-rimmed bifocals around her neck, and aviator shades over her eyes. Her brother, in a sky blue shirt with white writing and a picture of a crown, was loaded with loot too, straps criss-crossing his chest, bags dangling at his hips. One bag – a small black leather one – had the distinctive pout of a camera case. Jacob walked over and plucked it up from where it hung from the boy's shoulder. Jacob turned to the girl, who was clearly the boss.

'Zingati?'

'That *Aka kothyoka* thingie?' she said, her aviators blank. She named a price anyway.

Jacob unbuttoned the case, took out the camera and turned it over in his hands, dabbling at its buttons, fingering the loose lever. Then he knelt on the ground and pointed the lens at her.

'*Ah-ah*, it is not even digito,' she complained, meaning they wouldn't get to see a preview. But her brother posed, crossing his arms over his chest and making American westside signs. The girl gave in, putting a hand on her hip and her other elbow on his shoulder. Jacob looked in the viewfinder, then pushed the air to signal that they should step back. The moment they did, he got up and bolted, twice-poached camera in tow.

※

When they next ran into him, the girl cried bloody murder and the boy stomped around him like a Nyau dancer, hackles and fists raised. Jacob lifted his hands in surrender, then pulled out the camera. He had fixed the lever and replaced the battery with one from the dump.

'Not bad, hey?' the girl said, running her freckled fingers over it.

She looked at him through the viewfinder, gave a smirk, then turned, motioning for him to follow. The three of them strode through the compound towards the market on its periphery. Jacob wondered for a moment whether they were taking him to Gogo's tomato stall to report him. But instead the girl stopped in front of a stall that sold sweets in single units, down to the individual Smartie. The seller, listening to an evangelist bleating on the radio, barely raised her eyes as they clambered over plastic sacks to the back, where a canopy was spread on the ground. The boy lifted it with a flourish. Laid out in furrows was a cornucopia of plunder: a heap of spectacles like skewered bath bubbles, a sloppy stack of iPods and phones, a tangle of earbuds.

'So you can fix these kinds of thingies?' the albino girl asked, hands on her hips.

Jacob crouched over a heap of Nokias and picked one up with a grin.

Solo and Pepa were orphans. They had been passed between the homes of distant relatives so many times that no one remembered any more how they had got their names. Maybe they had been named 'salt and pepper' – the albino bright as light, her brother dark as night – without regard for which was which. Or maybe Solo was short for *pensolo*, the lead pencil to his sister's white sheet of *pepala*. They lived alone together now. They stole as a pair, ate as a pair, slept curled together like a sloppy yin yang.

Jacob was the first person they had ever let into their two-part existence. Within a year, their little Kalingalinga squad had developed a perfect system: Solo hunted for goods or pickpocketed them, Jacob patched them up, and Pepa got them sold. But then warnings spread among the expats to avoid the albino girl on the road past Kalingalinga. And the Auto Department started to run dry of spare parts to fix the things they stole.

There were rumours that there was better rubbish to be found, however. So-called E-Dumps had started to spring up all over Lusaka. These housed leftover gadgets, not from the rich, the *apamwamba*, the *been-to* class of Zambians, but from the places they had been to: America, South Africa, China, all of the countries that had run out of room to discard their obsolete and broken tech. These nations were now paying to ship their 'e-waste' to what they considered the trash heap of the world. Little did they realise they were jump-starting a secondhand tech revolution.

✳

In the midst of her plans for bitterness and grace, Matha hadn't considered that, when Godfrey came home, she might not stop crying. As it turned out, she simply carried on. Drip, drop, a shower, a squall, and in between, the seep of time. Had her man not come back? Had her love not returned? Yes but after that first night, she and Godfrey didn't have much sex or even much conversation. She felt obliged to feed him and give him a bit of money for beer. He mostly just sat on her stoop, drinking it and smoking *mbanji*, the rain leaving spiky splotches on his feet.

His grey dreadlocks, his laziness, his drinkardliness, made him seem like a dead man, even if that certificate he carried with him was in error. The rain had run the ink but Matha could see that it had been issued at a hospital in Mazabuka. Why had he been there? Why had he come back? *Where did you go? Where did you go? Where did you go?* Maybe, she thought as she stared at his back in the door frame of No. 74, he had just been away too long. Maybe their love had run all the way through the season allotted to it. Maybe even heartbreak breaks if you give it enough time.

*

'*Iwe*, Engineer!' Pepa shouted. 'Do not *kawayawaya*, just choose. This is not Pick-andi-Pay!'

She was standing on the highest summit of an E-Dump near Town Market, glancing over her shoulder in a halting rhythm like a stuck pedestal fan. She glowed like a beacon with her pale hair and pale skin, and she had the worst eyesight between them, but she was the only one responsible enough to be lookout. She didn't trust the guard they had bribed with a bottle of gin. And there were other gangs of techno-poachers too, some of whom carried big, heavy *ibende* – those wooden sticks for grinding grain could just as easily grind bones.

Solo raced up to her, holding a dusty black oblong over his head in triumph. He circled his hips, raised a foot, popped his hips twice.

'*Chongo iwe!*' Pepa whispershouted, squinting at her brother.

Solo hadn't said a word but he quieted his hips and brought the DVD player he had scored over to her, crunching broken glass, jumping nests of cables and skirting two PC monitors kissing screens along the way.

'Nice ... one ...' Pepa said, turning it over, caught up in admiration and calculation. They could easily resell it in Bauleni if Jacob could fix it. She called out to him again: 'Engineer!'

Jacob, crouched behind a leaning tower of keyboards a few yards away, ignored her. Pepa sucked her teeth and glanced anxiously over the concrete perimeter wall of the E-Dump, which was topped with broken glass.

'Jacob! *Tiye, iwe!*' she shouted. 'It's time to book! Solo—'

Her brother was already skittering down the spiky hill of plastic and glass towards Jacob.

'It is a toy. A choppa,' Jacob explained as Solo knelt beside him. Jacob turned it in his hands to show it off. It was white and spindly, about the size of a dove. He had found a shell-like controller nearby. Solo shrugged. It wouldn't bring much money on resale. Jacob glared at his friend. Of course a thief wouldn't understand. Once upon a time, Jacob too had been a mere thief. But machines had become more than money to him.

Jacob had been the driving force behind the reconnaissance mission to this gentrified wasteland. Ever since he had learned about the Zambian Space Programme, about how brilliant a cadet his *gogo* had been, he had become obsessed. Who knew technology was a family tradition – in his very blood! For the first time, Jacob could see a connection between his hands and his mind, and it was precious. He turned from Solo with disgust.

Just then, they both heard a commotion at the gate – the guard they had bribed was loudly blubbering excuses in Nyanja. The boys looked around for Pepa. She was already squatting behind a flat-screen TV, clutching her knees, her silver eyes flashing with fury and fear.

＊

Sometimes Matha eavesdropped on Godfrey and Jacob. The two males in her life often sat on the stoop together, Godfrey answering his grandson's questions between sips of beer. Matha would scrape salt from her ears with a matchstick, position herself at her table under the window and listen. Godfrey spoke like a living man when he reminisced – Zamrock songs on the radio, *A luta continua!* in the streets, miniskirts and bell *bontons* squeezing everyone's bums.

His talk often drifted to the Zambia National Academy of Science, Space Research and Philosophy. He hinted at the Academy's revolutionary underpinnings but never admitted outright to the espionage or the bombs. Instead, he told stories about Matha's cats – 'named after the disciples! I asked her, "And does that make you Jesus?"' – and about Ba Nkoloso's morbid pranks and even about her sister – 'Cookie was a too-pretty girl, that one!'

Not anymore, Matha thought pettily. Not that she would know. She hadn't seen Nkuka in years. And Ba Nkoloso had died in 1989. Matha had read about the funeral in the newspaper, the weeping politicians and the crowd of mourners at the Anglican cathedral – there had been plenty praise for his freedom fighting and no mention at all of his Space Programme. Listening to Godfrey's words carving a spiral into the past, it felt as if the great man and his dreams had risen from the dead.

Godfrey was vague whenever Jacob probed him about the actual technology, though: the *mulolo* swing, the *mukwa* catapult, turbulent propulsion. Matha frowned. Did Godfrey not remember the four stages of combustion? For months, she chopped vegetables or ironed clothes at the table by the window, her irritation gradually rising. Godfrey's dullard answers reminded her of her time in disguise at the Lwena Mission School, when she'd had to suppress all she knew for the sake of secrecy.

Then, one day, while sweetening her tea, Matha overheard Godfrey call a piston a pistol. It could have been a slip of the tongue, but she was so flabbergasted that her teacup was half full of sugar before she noticed. She searched for a pencil, then snatched up the only book in the place, the Bible that old Mrs Zulu had left behind years ago. Matha opened the front door and squeezed herself between the two useless males on her stoop. She turned to an empty page at the back of the Bible. And as they stared at her wet and furrowed face, Matha Mwamba sketched out a diagram of an engine.

✳

'Stop! Thiefies!'

A short man in an army uniform was racing towards the rackety mound of electronic waste, waving a black club overhead. The belt at his waist sagged under the weight of a holstered gun. The E-Dump guard they had paid off with Hendrick's gin stumbled along behind him, having obviously partaken in that liquid bribe. Shaking his head to sober up, he overtook the soldier and grabbed Pepa's *chitenge* to pull her down the rubbish heap and onto a patch of dirt. He knelt heavily on her back. She bucked and shrieked, her feet hammering the ground. Solo was cowering behind his DVD player, but the soldier knocked that shield away, swung at the boy's head with the club, and knocked him down.

The soldier turned to Jacob with a menacing look. Jacob curled away, cradling his toy helicopter to his chest as blows began to rain upon him. The beating was like the soldier himself – nasty, brutish and short. When it was done, he kicked at Jacob, bullying him over to where the other two were already lined up on their knees. Pepa was trying to hold her torn *chitenge* together. Solo's crusty swollen eye looked like an anthill. Jacob clutched his chopper, bruises throbbing on his back. The drunken guard stood swaying before them. The soldier strolled back and forth, snorting with contempt, his glittering cross necklace swinging with each step.

'Satanical children!' he shouted. 'Have you no *rrrispect*?! Stupit thief-ies! You do not know we can detain you like *that*,' he clapped his hands past each other.

The E-Dump guard nodded at this a little too hard and nearly fell over.

'Must we beat you again so you can understand?' the soldier continued.

At this, the guard stepped forward and slapped Solo's head.

'No!' the soldier complained. 'We must turn the other cheek!'

'Sorry, *bwana*,' said the guard, staggering back in confusion.

'I meant the other *cheeks*! Maybe their backsides can understand better than their brains.'

'Please, *bwana*,' Pepa begged.

'Turnaround, turnaround!' the guard said as if singing the playground song. He prodded them until they were on their hands and knees, bums rounding up behind them. Then he backed away as the soldier raised his stick.

'Don't! Come! Heeya! Again!' he shouted in sync with his blows. Solo and Pepa cried out with pain. Jacob stayed silent but the last blow knocked the helicopter out of his hands.

'What have we got here?' the soldier asked with slitted eyes and reached for it.

Jacob snatched it back with a snarl. The soldier laughed and raised his boot to kick him. Just then the guard vomited. The thin yellow gush splattered onto the ground and splashed up the soldier's boots.

As he stepped back in disgust, Pepa scrambled to her feet and pointed behind her.

'Can you see? The DVD machine?' she said. 'You can have, sah. We can fix it up.'

The soldier laughed. He stepped towards her and stood inches from her shaking body. They were nearly the same height.

'*You?* Can fix that?'

'No, but he can,' she pointed at Jacob. 'But not here.'

Pepa explained in a rush that the tools Jacob needed were in Kalingalinga. She could have lied about where they lived – Solo widened his eyes at her when she said the name of the compound – but Pepa was a savvy girl. The jewelled cross hanging from the soldier's neck looked expensive. His interest in the machine suggested that he had DVDs to play. She clasped her hands and promised the soldier that he could collect it, properly fixed, just-now, now-now.

'I want that one as well,' the soldier said, gesturing at Jacob's chopper. 'When it's fixed.'

*

It was dark by the time Jacob got back to No. 74 Kalingalinga. Matha was sitting at her table, pulling a comb through her salt-brittle hair when she heard him greet Godfrey on the stoop.

'*Ah-ah!* But what happened?' Godfrey exclaimed with a chuckle. 'Has there been a coup?'

'Ah, no,' said Jacob shyly. 'We had a small fight.'

'I can see you have some battle scars, young comrade!'

Matha had to stop herself from running outside. She stood by the window and listened as Jacob described scavenging in an E-Dump, getting beaten up by a guard and a soldier, bribing them with gin and stolen goods. When had her grandson become a *kawalala*? And Godfrey – *idjot* man – was busy responding with jokes and encouragement! Did he feel nothing for the boy? He hadn't even asked her about the pregnancy she had written to him about decades ago, as if he hadn't realised that Jacob's existence implied a mother somewhere, his daughter. Matha noticed that Godfrey's voice sounded clear and healthy now – staying with her had reinvigorated him, brought him back from the dead. And he had brought her nothing in return.

'Aha! Very resourceful!' he was saying to their grandson. 'In every society, Ba Nkoloso said, there are the haves and the have-nots and then there are the ones who are brave enough to *take!*'

Matha heard the clink of bottles and a pause the length of a sip.

'And your spoils of war?' Godfrey asked. 'How does this electronical thing work?'

'This one is the controller. I just have to get some batteries and fix—'

'Foolish boy,' Godfrey burped. '*This* one is not for *that* one. You have the wrong controller.'

'But they are the same colour,' Jacob protested.

'Can you not read, boy?' Godfrey laughed. '*This* one is Digit-All. *That* one is Panasonic. They do not match.'

There was a pause. Tears zigzagged down Matha's cheeks. The door opened and Jacob slunk inside. She took one look at his cut and swollen face and slapped him across it. Jacob stared at her, the shock in his eyes giving way to hurt. Without a word, he crept around her, unrolled his sleeping mat, and curled up under a blanket, his useless white toy beside him.

＊

Jacob opened his eyes to a pale blur. It slowly clarified into the geometric eyes of his new helicopter. He sat up, wincing at his bruises, and reached for it. The toy had some dents and scratches and was spattered with mud and blood. But it was still elegant, its surfaces smooth, its blades as fine as fish gills. The front windows were intact and you could see the pilot inside, a tiny white man with a cap. The sun rose higher and peeked into No. 74, casting the shadow of the toy against the far wall. Jacob spun its blades, watching the giant grey fins whir on the wall. He was sure he could make it work.

He trotted off to the public latrines and when he returned, he found his *gogo* sitting on her stoop. He wondered where Ba Godfrey had gone and why she had taken his usual spot. Her mouldy Bible was in her lap, a pencil in her hand. His helicopter was perched at her side, light as a bird on its skids. She beckoned him. He sat on the ground across from her, shifting on his sore buttocks. She opened the Bible and began drawing inside it, slowly and carefully, not with the swift strokes she'd used for those engine diagrams the other day. When she was done, she placed the book in his lap, then started as if recalling something, and turned it around so it faced him.

A feeling crowded between his eyes, salty and stinging and sharp. Jacob knew all about machines and gadgets. He knew that electricity moved in a strange jerky way, and that when it flowed into several things, it could be divided without loss, though that might make things overheat and spark out. But though he was now fifteen years old and though he could recognise STOP signs and the number 74 on Gogo's gate and the labels on his favourite foods, Jacob did not know how to read.

Gogo bounced a fingertip on the page and pointed at the helicopter to make her point: the same letters were on its nose. Jacob pulled the controller from his pocket and saw what Ba Godfrey had tried to explain last night. There were different words on the two gadgets. Jacob looked at his *gogo*, at her familiar rutted cheeks. Of course. Only Matha Mwamba, Star Afronaut, could teach him how to be a real engineer. He moved to sit next to her, keeping the book in his lap.

'Show me?' he asked.

And she did.

2012

It took a while before Jacob got that helicopter to fly. He found the right-sized batteries for it and the right controller to pair it with using Bluetooth. He unscrewed the belly of the toy to remove the circuit board. He resoldered the fritzed-out wires with his grandmother's help, Gogo wearing kitchen gloves so that her slick palms didn't short it. The mechanism was simple – lift and thrust – the goal even simpler: to fly. It should have been as easy as the moment in a dream when you realise gravity has no force and you step off a cliff and soar. But still the chopper did not rise.

Jacob couldn't figure out what was wrong. He would connect the controller and the toy – the two blinking in counterpoint – and press ON. The helicopter, now mottled with fingerprints, would shudder to life, the propellers on its head and tail drifting round, spinning faster and faster until they were whipping blurs. The helicopter would lift one skid at a time and hang in the balance. But then, every time, it would tilt over and tumble into the dust.

Meanwhile, Pepa was pressuring him about the DVD player.

'At least you can fix that one,' she said, hands on her hips.

It had been several months but she worried that the soldier with the shiny cross would show up at Kalingalinga any moment to collect.

'We do not have the right parts,' he said.

They were in the old compound dump, picking through dregs. Jacob tossed the husk of a car radio aside with disgust. 'We have to go back to the E-Dump in town.'

'Were you not beaten? Did you not see that gun? What if he is a Youth Leaguer?'

The nation's new president, 'King Cobra', was a rabble-rouser who railed against government cronies for being elitist and against Chinese mining companies for ignoring safety standards. When his Patriotic Front party had won the election last year, his Youth Leaguers had rioted in the streets. To the average Zambian, these young men seemed more like thugs than patriots.

'He looked like Defence Force to me.' Jacob shrugged and walked away from his friends and off towards the Auto Department. What did it matter? A man with a gun was a man with a gun. It wasn't that Jacob wasn't afraid of the soldier. He just felt helpless to do anything about him. Jacob wandered among the dead cars, their rusted frames like unburied bones. The Auto Department had been dry for ages.

A gruff voice called out to him. Jacob scanned the dump. It had come from a half-jeep – or rather from a shape inside it that now grew an arm. It waved. Ba Godfrey. Jacob hadn't seen his grandfather since the night he'd come home bruised and bleeding from the E-Dump. As he neared, he saw a blue, red and white carton in Ba Godfrey's lap. *Shake Shake.* Maybe that was why Gogo had turfed him out.

'*Mwana!*' said Ba Godfrey. 'How is it?'

'It is just okay, *bashikulu*.' Jacob stuck his hand through an aperture to greet him.

'So you see where I have landed?' Ba Godfrey gestured at the grove of defunct vehicles. 'In the graveyard after all.' He laughed. 'And what brings you to my humble boat?'

'Looking for parts.'

'*Aha!* For your choppa! Did you find the proper remote?'

'Ya. But I need some other things.' Jacob glanced over his shoulder. 'This place is clapped.'

'Mmm.' Ba Godfrey nodded. 'Have you tried that new *ka* wood pile?'

'Ah, no, I cannot use wood. I need tech.'

Ba Godfrey clambered out of the vehicle and brushed off the buttocks of his maroon flares. 'They have some good electronical things as well,' he said. 'Let me show you.'

They met Solo and Pepa again on the way. As Solo walked ahead with Ba Godfrey, listening to a lesson on the political history of dreadlocks – 'Ba Nkoloso would not cut his hair until Zambia was free!' – Pepa nudged Jacob and whispered in his ear.

'We do not have time to hang about with a *bashikulu*.'

Jacob shrugged, eyes fixed on the bedraggled hems of Ba Godfrey's velveteen flares. He felt an obscure solidarity with the old man, who had been banished to the Auto Department just as Jacob had been banished to Gogo's three years ago. Following Ba Godfrey they made one turn and then another until they were in a maze of *kantemba* selling cigarettes and Mosi. One more turn and they stood before a blue building with a white base.

It looked familiar. Jacob practised his new basic reading skills, mouthing the words: One Hundred Years Clinic. This was where the trail for his mother had gone cold. The place had been upgraded since then. Apart from the fresh paint job, there were security lights and a satellite dish and you could hear a generator chugging away in the back. Ba Godfrey was standing under a mopane tree a few yards away. 'There!' he pointed. It was a scatter of scraps, mostly wood but metal too, the leftover materials from refitting the clinic.

They didn't find what Jacob needed to fix the DVD player, but it was a trove nonetheless. Under Pepa's direction, the squad got to work dividing the stuff into piles – wood with rough edges like sugar cane, metal bars twisted like liquorice, a bent circular saw, some half-empty cans of blue and white paint. At the end of the day, they built a low grass fence to hide the stash and left Ba Godfrey there to guard it.

The old man settled right in. This was a softer spot to squat than the Auto Department, and more profitable: he whittled toys from bits of scrap wood and traded them for the booze and *mbanji* on which he seemed to subsist. Pepa decided it was a good place for them to hide their spoils until Jacob fixed the two machines she had promised the soldier. Solo was always happy to spend more time near Ba Godfrey, with his wild stories and rasta look. Jacob had his own reasons for wanting to keep an eye on the women going in and out of that clinic.

*

One morning, they found Ba Godfrey in particularly good spirits. He was sitting under the mopane tree, two drippy cans of paint open at his side, a plank of wood across his knees. He was using a leaf to coat it in white.

'Greetings, revolutionary youths!'

Solo and Pepa waved and set about sorting through materials. Jacob sat with his grandfather under the tree, fiddling with his helicopter. Ba Godfrey offered him a Mosi.

'Ah, no,' Jacob demurred. 'It is still morning.'

Pepa was shaking her head happily. 'I still cannot believe we found this place.'

'It is the *mulu*.' Ba Godfrey raised a piece of bark to point at the crumbly redbrown termite hill. 'It is our godsend! It has hidden the goods from everybody else.'

Ba Godfrey dipped the shard of bark into the can of blue paint, traced a short vertical line on the now white plank, and launched into a detailed treatise on the wonders of the African termite. You could use it for bait on a fish-hook or in a hunting trap. You could eat it for supper yourself, if you were so inclined. As builders, the termites were most magnificent. They constructed cathedrals, towers and spires, pillars and pavilions. You could use the material of their mounds to make clay bricks for housing. Their faeces fertilised grasses and crops and *bowa* ... Ba Godfrey trailed off as he leaned back to scrutinise his sign.

Jacob glanced at it, trying to read it. What was a 'rip bed'? And why was there an eight in the middle?

'You know,' Ba Godfrey mused, 'Ba Nkoloso used to teach us about these insects for political purposes. We must be like *ububenshi*! We must work together, busy-busy, building things. We must scrounge with intelligence, we must use what is around, even if it is our own wastage. Let us praise the termite! Although, we must be vigilant against them in our line of business.'

Pepa looked up. 'What's our line of business?'

'Furniture.' Ba Godfrey stood up, holding his sign. The three young people gathered around him to look at it.

'But what does "rip" mean, *bashikulu*?' asked Jacob.

'Arra eye pee. This is standing for Resting in Peace,' Ba Godfrey said. 'RIP Beds and Coffins. The perfect kingdom for a dead man to rule!'

'But *bwana*, are you really dead?'

'*Mwana*, that is what government says with official documentation. So it must be—'

Ba Godfrey's words were swallowed by the growl of a vehicle. A black SUV skidded around the corner of the clinic and parked, sending up a cloud of dust. They all stepped back, coughing and waving their hands. A car door swung open. Something bright flashed in the midst of the swirling red. It was a cross. The soldier from the E-Dump had found them.

☀

Jacob often had dreams about the crashed aeroplane he had stumbled upon at the Lusaka City Airport when he was a boy. Sometimes it became whole again and he was its pilot. Sometimes he woke up just as it hit the ground and burst into flames. But even though he had complete freedom to roam around Kalingalinga, Jacob had never tried to sneak into the airport across the road to see it again. That adventure, that straying, had occasioned Lee Banda's entrance into his life, which had in turn occasioned his mother's exit from it. The airport had come to seem a chancy, cursed place.

The number of aircraft that landed there had dwindled over the years. Only once in a while would a zipping or rumbling overhead signal that a private plane was arriving, bearing a shah or a minister or a 'special guest' of government. Security had amped up. The bougainvillea fence had been replaced with a concrete wall topped with a musical score of wires – definitely electrified – and someone was paying for a powerful generator: though power cuts happened all the time these days, the lights blasting from the walls at night never trembled or died.

'Over here!' Pepa seethed, her eyes flashing under those lights now.

The three of them were behind the perimeter wall of the airport. According to the soldier, this was in fact the back wall of a warehouse and if you dug into the soil underneath it, you could pull out the breezeblocks in the bottom two rows. Pepa pointed down at the telltale signs of wear in the crevices where they had been chipped loose. The boys knelt down and started digging into the tough dry-season dirt.

When the gap in the back wall was big enough, Pepa wriggled through it into the warehouse. Jacob and Solo waited for their cue. Instead of Pepa's soft whistle, they heard a screech and the cascading sound of falling boxes. Jacob jumped down and dragged himself through the gap, scraping his stomach.

'Pepa?' His foot hit something soft – 'Ow!' she said – then something hard.

'Am fine,' she snapped. 'There is a cat in here.'

Jacob pulled out his old Nokia, turned it on and waved it around like a torch. Its blue light floated fairy-like over Pepa's face, over the garish split in her lip from the soldier's last visit. She was lying under a pile of small white boxes. She sheepishly unearthed herself.

Jacob picked up a box. 'I. P-p-p ... *eepon?*'

'Oh, iPhone! I know those!' Pepa rose excitedly from her crouch.

Just then, Jacob's Nokia went dark and something swooped at their heads. Pepa squealed. Jacob felt something graze the tip of his ear, soft as Ba Godfrey's velveteen suit. Jacob turned his phone on again and cast the light around the room. A shadow flickered and fluttered among the bigger boxes stacked against the walls.

'It is just a bird,' he said as the phone went black again. The just-a-bird screeched. 'A bat?'

He felt Pepa's glare in the dark. Why hadn't he fixed the DVD player and the chopper in time? The short soldier had located them easily. Everyone knew the *chidangwaleza* in Kalingalinga: 'I just asked for the white *muntu*!' he'd laughed. When he had found them empty-handed in the yard by the clinic, he had recruited them to do this job in lieu of the electronics they owed him. Or rather, he had knocked them around for a bit – Ba Godfrey watching helplessly, tied to the mopane tree – until they had agreed to steal for him. They were the perfect *skinnymaningi* weasels, as he put it, to crawl through the hole in a wall.

'Come on,' Jacob exhorted Pepa now. Under the intermittent light of the Nokia, they ferried the boxes in the warehouse out to Solo through the gap in the wall. When they were halfway done, Jacob felt a flapping wind at his cheekbone. Pepa shrieked again.

'Enough!' she said and tore through the plastic wrapper of one of the iPhone boxes. She tugged the lid off, plucked the new phone from its bed and pressed a button on its top edge.

'Don't worry,' she said. 'We will leave it. I just need ...' She swiped right to open and up for the control centre and touched her finger to the torch app. 'Light.'

She placed the phone on the ground, pulled her jumper off, and they resumed ferrying. The next time the bat swooped at their heads, Pepa threw the jumper over it and down it tumbled. Jacob almost applauded. They continued their labour, ignoring the sounds from the corner – *flibberti-thump, flackata-bump* – and the jumper's manic flapping. When they had taken as many boxes as they could carry, Pepa wriggled out first. On an impulse, Jacob picked up the iPhone and aimed its light at the jumper. Two red pinpricks gleaming evilly through the weave. He shuddered, pocketed the phone, and birthed himself outside again.

※

That bundle of agitation with its beady eyes needled into Jacob's mind and stayed there. A few days later, he realised why his helicopter wouldn't fly. Just as Pepa's jumper had kept the bat earthbound, he had added too much weight to the helicopter when he had soldered the circuit. The moment it tilted too far, the airlift vacuum created by the spinning blade weakened. The balance of energy and mass was off. Jacob couldn't make the circuit board lighter now. So he broke a plastic window and pulled out the little pilot, who was bent permanently in a seated position as if taking a shit. Unburdened, the toy buzzed to life, lifted right up and flew.

It flew so easily that Jacob found himself chasing after it. He hadn't even figured out how to turn it off or how far it could go before the Bluetooth link severed – in the many months of trying to fly it, he had never needed to. His eyes fixed on the hovering chopper, Jacob pushed through Gogo's gate and ran down the guttered path, swerving around a wheelbarrow and darting down a narrow passage behind a nursery school. He raced diagonally across its yard, where the girls skipping rope stopped their chanting song and gaped up at the wondrous toy, then giggled as he bumped into a guava tree and fell on his bum.

The helicopter swerved towards the metal yard, where Ba Solomon's crew was busy welding, twisting, pounding and painting iron into playground equipment. Jacob stepped on a merry-go-round, leaving a footprint in the fresh paint, jumped through a swing, tangling its chains, bounced off a juddering slide. Ba Solomon gave a lazy shout, his boys laughing at the slapstick. The helicopter gusted higher, caught in an updrift. As he watched it rise, Jacob's competing impulses – to fly the thing and land the thing – suddenly both seemed pointless. He just had to let it crash. His hand went limp on the controller as he slowed.

The toy came sloping down, Jacob trudging after it. It had led him to the edge of Alick Nkhata Road, where a blue and white minibus was just pulling onto the dirt bank to pick up passengers. He watched the helicopter swoop down as if on the end of a heaven-hooked string. Just before it crashed into the dust, it nosed into the back of a woman in the bus queue. She turned to stare at the intruder at her feet. She was wearing stiletto heels and a tight *chitenge* skirt with a pattern of dollars, euros and yen. Her shirt was twisted, her lipstick smudged. Glittery nails curved around her bus fare. She looked up with a frown and blinked.

'Jacob?' she gasped dramatically. She shuffled forward in her binding and stilts and fell upon him. Jacob reluctantly accepted the hug. He hadn't seen Aunty Loveness since the Hi-Fly had burned down three years ago.

'You've grown, haven't you?' she smirked. 'What are you up to? Making trouble?'

'No, *ma*,' he mumbled, picking up his helicopter and hiding it behind his back.

'Madamu!' the bus conductor called. 'Please come up now so we go, eh?'

'*Iwe*, shuttup if you want my money,' she spat, slapping the air with a clutch of kwacha bills. She turned back to Jacob and smiled, her teeth bright as moons in the dark sky of her face.

'You should go and see your mother, darling,' she purred meanly. 'She misses you.'

Jacob swallowed. 'But Ba Aunty, where is she keeping up?'

'You haven't been to the house?' Aunty Loveness's laugh tinkled up then fell to a sigh. 'It is just *pa* Northmead. Paseli Road.'

Before he could ask for the house number, she had turned, her weave sweeping the air.

'Right, darling, I'm off. *Ciao*,' she said and stepped onto the bus, delicate as a queen in her stilettos. The conductor turned to watch her squeeze into a seat. 'Key to the grave,' he muttered. Then he swung the door shut in Jacob's face and the bus crept into the traffic.

⚹

That warehouse shipment of smartphones had come in to take advantage of the completion of the AFRINET project. Fibre cables now floated in the three seas around the continent like immense electric eels, zapping currents between servers and routers that spewed Wi-Fi into the air until a swarming, flashing stormcloud of it hovered over Africa. Korea and China and Japan had all caught Afrotech fever, flooding the market with cheap mobiles with built-in Wi-Fi ports. In a leapfrog of technology, the majority of Africans, the poor included, had access to the whole wide world through its web.

Jacob connected the iPhone he'd nabbed from the warehouse to AFRINET and searched online for Audis and Benzes; Solo watched Nollywood clips on YouTube. The boys had been swapping it back and forth for weeks before Pepa noticed. She was furious. Christian, as they had started calling the soldier with his dangling cross, had been satisfied with their warehouse heist. He had even rewarded them with a carton of Pall Malls, which Ba Godfrey had promptly resold. But if he found out that they had stolen from him, who knew what he would do to them?

'Are you not the one who opened the box?' Jacob accused Pepa.

'Just to see!' she protested. 'We could not do the job with that nasty thing flying at our heads! But I told you we must leave it there. Not start thieving-thieving.'

Jacob defended himself. It had been an impulse theft, the way Pepa herself had once snatched glasses off the sunburnt noses of foreigners.

'Solo, did you not say your sister took *mbasela*?'

Solo was too busy scrounging around Ba Godfrey's mat for bits of marijuana to reply.

'He pays us to steal *for* him!' said Pepa. 'Not from him!'

'Isn't he stealing from the *bwana* who owns the warehouse? How can he deny us the same?'

'*Waona manje*,' she said sullenly. 'That man has a gun.'

Solo sidled up and put his arm around his sister, the iPhone in his hand. The browser was open to a picture of a South African model, Refilwe Modiselle. Pepa's eyes widened: Modiselle was an albino too. Soon enough Pepa was snatching the iPhone out of the boys' hands every day, shouting 'Bags I!' and hunkering down to open her book-marked fashion blogs. And when Christian asked them to do another warehouse job, and then another, with nary a word about a missing iPhone, she decided he must have missed or forgiven it.

Over the next two years of working for Christian, the Kalingalinga squad skimmed a little off the top of all of their heists. They alternated who got first choice of *mbasela*. Pepa selected a sky-blue dress from a shipment of clothes. Solo took a neon boomerang from a crate of electronic toys. The siblings were surprised that Jacob let Solo choose that time – didn't Engineer want this-here remote-controlled car, or that-there robo-dog? No. Jacob saved his pick for a shipment of sports equipment. Aha! A bicycle! Pepa winked at Solo. But no, what Jacob wanted was a small white box labelled GoPro.

*

Jacob downloaded the GoPro app on the iPhone, then popped a battery in the eyeball camera and suctioned it to the bottom of his helicopter, right between the skids. He had to chip away six panels, the pilot's chair and the steering wheel to make up for the camera's weight, and the chopper still wobbled when it went up. But Jacob had become an expert at flying it and it was unexpectedly easy to navigate via the iPhone, which streamed the images recorded by the GoPro.

Jacob saw its flight unfurl from his seat on the stoop of No. 74. It was like watching a film of the compound taken from above. The dwellers of Kalingalinga went about their business, little black heads trailed by their shadows. The motley roofs of their homes resembled the *chitenge* patch-quilts people sold at Sunday Market at Arcades.

On a whim, Jacob sent the helicopter across the road to the Lusaka City Airport to meet its gigantic relatives, the parked aeroplanes with their drooping noses. It zipped between two barbed electric wires and over a rolling heap of oil drums. He saw the warehouse in a corner of the screen and instinctively veered towards it. He approached from behind, clucking at what a poor job he and Solo had done of concealing their digging under its back wall, then navigated around to the front. Four men were loading boxes inside. They wore green army uniforms and black belts sagging with guns. Soldiers. Rich ones – gold glinted from their necks and wrists and fingers and earlobes.

As he neared, one man whipped around and gazed right into the eye of the camera. Shit. Jacob started back and reversed. An eddy of action broke onto the screen – men yelling and waving gold-spined fists – then receded into a blur as Jacob lifted the chopper's nose up into the air and banked sharply left. Shitshitshit. He zoomed off, his heart pounding, and in a fever of acceleration, he overshot the compound. He caught a glimpse of Gogo's roof and himself on the stoop – a cross-legged splotch – and looked up just in time to see the helicopter fly overhead, the camera like a black moon in its white belly.

There was a warning sound and he looked back down at the phone. A low-battery window was covering the view. Sucking his teeth, he tapped the x in the corner to close it. The helicopter was still moving rapidly. Jacob recognised the green expanse of the UNZA grounds, the Goma Lakes set into them like giant mirrors. Arcades came into view with its white canopy like a cresting wave in the middle of the car park.

Then the building-buttoned maze of Showgrounds. The Manda Hill parking structure, grey and immense as ancient ruins. The green metal pedestrian bridge where Great East Road met Addis Ababa Drive, infested with Airtel and Digit-All ads.

Just after the Northmead shopping centre, Jacob made a right. Paseli Road. He didn't know the exact house number but it didn't matter – a boxy white frame came into view and he swerved towards it as if magnetised. It was Uncle Lee's old pickup, parked in the drive in front of a reddish L-shape – a roof – with a green lawn filling out the rectangle. Jacob descended and sent the chopper around the house, angling the one-eyed belly of the beast up to a window but he could see nothing through the curtains. His mother had always preferred privacy to light. Annoyed, he reversed from the window too quickly, ricocheted off the edge of the house and tumbled into the grass.

Jacob stared at the picture on the screen: sharp green blades jutting through thin white skids. He jabbed the launch button but the chopper shuddered uselessly against the ground. Shit. The low-battery window appeared again. He tapped it closed. A *chongololo* began slinking upward from the grass, probing a skid with its antennae, then creeping up it. What if he sent the chopper forward and up at the same time? He pressed both buttons at once, but this just sent the blades sputtering like an overturned plough. The knubby centipede was now curled around the skid – the vibration had triggered its spiral clutch. *Shit.* With this new burden, the chopper was once again too heavy to launch. A little white circle began to whir over the screen. Shitshitshit. Jacob stood up from Gogo's stoop in Kalingalinga, staring helplessly at the iPhone as it went black.

※

He ran to RIP Beds & Coffins to get the phone charger, which Pepa insisted on keeping there at all times. He found her alone, sitting under the mopane with a resting frown, rifling through an issue of *Mademoiselle*. With a sinking feeling, he noticed the telltale bulge under her tight blue skirt – she had stuffed something in her panties to absorb her menstrual blood. That bulge usually appeared along with the cloudy mood that dulled her silver eyes to grey.

'Pepa? I need the . . .' he began cautiously but he was interrupted by a shout.

Solo raced into the woodyard and stopped in front of them, panting and pointing behind him. Pepa stood with a sigh as the red dust storm approached. Christian's SUV rumbled towards them and crunched to a halt. Used to this by now, they stepped back, coughing. But this time, Christian did not come out to berate and instruct them. Instead, the tinted passenger window purred down and a gun nosed out from the darkness within. Pepa gripped Jacob's arm. Their stolen *mbasela* had been discovered.

With a curt clunk, the back door swung open. Solo, Pepa and Jacob looked at each other, then piled wearily into the SUV. Christian glanced at them in the rearview mirror, but said nothing, his gun resting in his lap like a subdued pet. The driver beside him wore civilian clothes and so many silver chains that he seemed caught in a net. Christian gave a slight nod, and the driver reversed the vehicle and sped out of the compound.

The three teenagers sat quietly in the back of the shadowy machine, with its cold air and metallic smell and glinting lights. Jacob heard Pepa's bare thighs unstick from the leather seat whenever she shifted. Christian was tapping his palm with a finger. Solo's eyes widened and he nudged Jacob, who peered between the seats. Christian's palm was lit bright blue – he'd had a Digit-All Bead implanted in his finger. The boys had read about the prototypes online but they had never seen one in person before. Christian glanced at the rearview again and they trained their eyes on the tinted windows.

They drove from Kalingalinga towards Kabulonga, from the compound to the suburbs, moving up in the world. Stone walls rolled by, their smooth facades hiding private schools and fancy motels and *apam-wamba* homes. Even the walls seemed to have their own gardens here – their barbed-wire or broken-glass crowns festooned with bougain-villea, strips of green grass stretching from their feet. Past Crossroads, near Leopards Hill Cemetery, jagged heaps of slate began to appear on the side of the road, stacked vertically like jagged grey flames.

Around New Kasama, the SUV turned onto a dirt road then, after a few minutes, swung into a stone driveway splotched with red ants' nests. The silver-strung driver parked and leaned back as if settling in.

Christian got out and walked off, waving his gun over his shoulder to beckon them. The three of them tumbled out and followed him on a path through lush hedges springing with purple and white flowers – a shocking abundance in the midst of dry season. Jacob had just decided that Christian was taking them into the bush to murder them when they came out into a fenced-off clearing.

Before them was a rectangular swimming pool, its inside painted the colour of shadow, a scatter of leaves poxing its surface. On the other side of it was half of a mansion. Concrete columns stood in the three corners, and there was a flight of steps in the fourth, but there were no walls or ceiling yet. Wave-shaped roof tiles were stacked along the edge of the garden. Though unfinished, the house was furnished, with armchairs and sofas and tables and even a bed. With no walls to hang from, the decor was spread out on the ground: 'African' paintings of bare-breasted women with pots on their heads, raffia-trimmed wall hangings, mirrors in gilt frames. Uniformed men prowled around, stepping cautiously around the strewn interior design. Le Grand Kallé muttered from speakers as tall as the men.

Christian walked into the open-air half-building, stepping politely through an empty door frame. They followed. A low voice issued a command and Christian stepped aside to disclose an older man sitting in a leather chair with wooden arms carved into pouncing lions. He was blueblack, bearded, bespectacled, his big belly taut under his army shirt. He gestured for them to sit on a white leather sofa across from him. They huddled together, Pepa's arms crossed over her breasts. Christian stood beside them, handgun at his side. The man, the big *bwana*, petted the lions' heads and smiled broadly.

'It is now a party!' he said.

They stared.

'Greet!' Christian ordered.

Solo shot to his feet and stepped towards the man in the chair to shake hands, but Christian grabbed the back of his shirt and pulled him down onto the sofa. 'From here!'

'Hallo, sah?' Solo said shakily.

'*Muli bwanji,* Ba General!' Christian corrected.

They all intoned the greeting. The General adjusted his spectacles but did not reply. He flicked his fingers over his shoulder to call one of

his men, who leaned in for a whispered instruction. The minion sauntered off and came back with a tray bearing glasses of a clear liquid,
which he served to the three quivering guests. The vodka went from
knife cold to searing in Jacob's throat. Pepa gulped it down, thinking it
was water, and started coughing. Solo sipped cautiously, then eagerly.

'So,' the General smiled. 'I hear you have been robbing me, *ehn?*'

The three of them glanced at each other, Pepa shaking her head
subtly in an 'I told you so' way. This must be the *bwana* whose warehouse Christian was stealing from. Christian had clearly brought them
here to take the blame for the missing loot.

'Toys, gadgetry,' said the General. 'Whatwhat, other things. Clothez,
camera, iPhoney.'

Jacob sat up, pulled the dead iPhone from his pocket and stretched
it towards the General. Christian grabbed it from Jacob's hand and ferried it to his boss.

The General pressed the silver button on the edge of the phone.
'What kinds of things are compound children doing with my phones?'
He sucked his teeth. 'Why is it not coming on?'

'The battery is finished, *bwana*,' said Jacob.

The General called for a charger. A guard brought a black square
covered with gleaming panels. Jacob stared with professional curiosity
as the guard plugged the phone into it and placed it in a spot of sunlight by the sofa. A solar-powered charger.

The General thrust his beard upward. 'You! Come here.'

All three of them touched their chests: *Me?* Christian hoisted Pepa
to her feet.

'But I am the one who took!' Jacob said.

The General waved his hand dismissively. Christian slammed the
butt of his gun down on Jacob's shoulder to shut him up, then grabbed
Pepa again and began dragging her to the General. She looked over
her shoulder, her pale cheeks blotchy, her eyes pleading.

'No, no,' the General smiled. 'They cannot help you, pretty girl.'

Jacob tried to catch her brother's attention but Solo was staring dis-
mally into his glass of vodka. The sky stretched flat and blue above the
roofless house. Rays of light skewed down, foreboding as blades. The
guards ceased their patrolling to watch. A few feet from the General's
armchair, Christian released his clutch on Pepa's shirt and spanked

her buttocks forward like a reluctant child. Pepa tripped ahead but stopped, eyes downcast.

'Come and say hallo, *kapompo*.' The General patted his thigh.

'She has injured me!' Christian said abruptly. He was staring at his hand, which was stained with red. Pepa's menstrual blood had leaked into the seat of the skirt he had just spanked.

'She is just on her period, *bwana*,' said Jacob, rising to his feet. 'It is not her fault.'

Christian sucked in a breath and raised his hand over Pepa. But he was too caught up in the taboo to touch her. He walked off angrily, shouting for a towel. Jacob approached Pepa and pulled off his t-shirt to give to her. She took it but didn't put it on. She was sobbing.

'Ah you, Jelita. Stop crying. We are happy that you are mature,' the General laughed. Pepa only sobbed harder. 'Go and clean yourself up.'

She raced off, covering her stained behind with Jacob's shirt, and crouched behind the sofa to put it on.

'And you. Hero,' the General said, his spectacles blank discs. 'Do you know what your galfriend's condition can do? It can cause a miracle! It can heal people who have The Virus.'

Jacob frowned. Growing up in a women's hair salon had accustomed him to periods as a fact of existence. Periods didn't heal anything, though they often seemed to come as a relief.

'... perfect specimen,' the General was saying. 'Have you tasted that creamy white skin?'

'What are you saying?' Jacob demanded. He always felt protective of Pepa when people mocked her for being albino, when they spat on their chests for fear of the hex of her.

Before the General could answer, a man burst into the clearing, yelling 'Ba General!' He skidded to a stop at the edge of the pool, then turned and ran into the house through an invisible wall. 'We have been spotted,' he panted. '*Pa* airport.'

Jacob's eyes darted to the man's hand – two gold stripes – and his earlobe – a bead of gold.

'Spotted by who?' the General stood up. He carried his big belly with authority.

'I do not know if it is police or government or what,' the man panted. 'But it is some *ka* flying thing, videotaping us.'

Just then, the iPhone flashed on, the black bitten apple in the white screen. Jacob and the General saw it at the same time but the General got there first. He reached down, picked it up and unlocked it.

'What is this?' He turned it towards Jacob. 'What have you put on my phone?'

The GoPro app was still open. A blurry patch on the screen shuddered into focus: a black circle, a white oval around it riddled with red cracks, a wet throat in one corner. It was an eye. Someone had picked up the crashed chopper and turned it over and was staring into the camera in its belly. Jacob looked at the General, unsure how to explain. He reached for the phone and guards on either side stepped forward, but the General raised his hand like Moses and they parted. The General handed the phone to Jacob, who turned and stood beside him so that they could both see the image. Jacob touched the launch button. There was a yelp on the other side of the screen as the chopper stirred to life and rose.

'Oho!' the General laughed. 'So that thingie at the airport was yours?'

The chopper was unsteady, a fly drunk on sugar. Jacob compensated by tapping between keys, yielding a shuddery hover over a black and white pattern – a tiled floor or maybe a duvet.

'You must bring this machine to me, *ehn*? In exchange for your white *ka* galifriend?'

As the chopper rose, the geometric pattern was replaced by a frowning face.

'Who is that?' The General darted his beard at the screen.

Jacob hesitated. But something – the look in her eye or the fact that she lived in that house in Northmead, without him – something made Jacob tell the General the truth.

'It's my mother,' he said, just as her hand swept through the screen and knocked it black.

※

That evening in New Kasama, as the sun departed, dragging a ragged train of orange and purple behind it, the General recounted the legend of his empire. Ever since Lusaka City Airport had been given over to the military, he had used his access to bring in goods hidden in the crannies of his cronies' flesh and luggage. Pills: pharmaceutical, recreational, both. Rough-cut diamonds and cobalt from the Congo. An assortment of consumer goods from Jo'burg and Hong Kong and Dubai, which he sold outside the tariff system. Recently, he had been looking to fry bigger fish, or rather, smaller ones. He wanted to shift his mode of transportation from aeroplanes to drones.

Drones were everywhere these days but the aircraft laws in most nations had not yet been adjusted to account for them. Drones had been used for reconnaissance during the Arab Spring. The US military was mapping the continent with them to burrow bunkers under the land. A drone airport was being built in Rwanda. The General's plan to use a fleet of them to secret goods over borders seemed dauntingly pricey, however. He was delighted to learn that you could make your own. He didn't understand that Jacob had just strapped a camera to a toy helicopter. He instructed Jacob to fetch it and handed over a wad of crisp clean kwacha for transport.

The money was tempting, but Jacob felt more compelled by the fact that, when the silver-strung driver drove him back to the compound that night so he could carry out his mission, Solo and Pepa stayed behind. The General, casually waving the steak knife he was using to cut his *nshima* and bream, said he would send the siblings home tomorrow. Christian handed Jacob a fresh t-shirt, then cuffed Solo on the head to bully him to the back of the house to wash the supper plates. The last glimpse Jacob got of Pepa, she was curled up on the sofa, his old t-shirt like a nightgown on her. Had there been drugs in her glass? Her pale cheek pressed to the white leather, her pink lips wet in slumber, she seemed like an animal that has fainted for fear.

2014

Jacob walked in on his mother breaking. Not breaking outwards into pieces, but shattering inward, towards the core. She was sitting on the floor of her kitchen, back against the wall, knees pulled to her chest, thighs as spread as her tight skirt would allow. Her chest was clutching, her shoulders jerking. In the ambient glow from the street lamp outside, he could see that tears had melted her make-up, muddying her collar and uncovering dark patches on her cheeks. On the floor were the honey-coloured shards of a broken Mosi bottle – no, five or six bottles. Her knees were rubied with scab.

Jacob toggled the light switch uselessly. There was no power cut in Northmead tonight. This was an unpaid ZESCO bill. He turned on the iPhone – the General had let him keep it – and scanned the room. No sign of his chopper in here. The light accidentally skimmed over his mother's face and she opened her eyes. She tried to get up and couldn't. Her eyes slid shut again.

Jacob hesitated, then put the phone away and went over to her. He knelt at her side and put his arms around her. She was lighter than he expected, so when he lifted her up, her bloody knee struck his mouth. He carefully wiped his face, then levered her up again as he rose to his feet, one arm supporting her neck, the other wedged under her knees.

He kicked open a couple of doors before he found a bedroom. As he carried her in, he recalled an image from five years ago: his mother cradling the Indian girl, just like this, and handing her over to Uncle Lee in the middle of the Hi-Fly. That was the day it had burned down. The day he had burned it down. He laid her on the bed, lifted half of the duvet over her, tucked her in. He didn't know when he had learned how to do this – no one had ever done it for him.

'Lee,' his mother croaked, her eyes stirring open.

'It's Jacob,' he said, looking around the bedroom. No chopper in here either.

'Lee,' she said again, urgently.

Rage lit his spine from its base to the top of his head. These tears. This drunkenness. This illness that was consuming her body. It was all for Dr Lionel Banda. Again. Her eyes closed and this time her breathing steadied into a sleeping rhythm. Jacob sank to the floor by her bed. He didn't care, he didn't want to care. He was just here for his chopper.

Jacob woke the next morning with the chopper in his face. His heart wrenched at the sight of it. It was covered in reddish smears, one blade bent out of shape, the GoPro dangling like a cartoon eyeball. Jacob's mother, who was holding it over him, was no longer wearing her tight skirt or her wig. She had bathed and was in an orange robe, her damp hair in knots. The lesions on her face and neck were clearer in the daylight. He reached for the toy in her hand.

'So it *is* yours?' She pulled it out of reach like a bully.

Jacob staggered to his feet, his joints cricking from sleeping on the floor. He was seventeen now and he loomed over her in her bare feet. But he was still her son and he tugged his t-shirt down self-consciously.

She looked him over sceptically. 'You want a drink?'

He raised an eyebrow, eyes straying to the chopper in her hand.

She gave it to him, rolling her eyes. 'Take it and go, or come and drink. Me, I don't care,' she said, then turned and floated out of the room and down the corridor.

He followed her into the kitchen. In the light of day, it looked emptier than Gogo's but in a rich-person way: a glass table, matching chairs, a single fern in a porcelain pot. The broken glass from last night had been swept from the floor. In a single motion, Jacob's mother sat and lifted an open Mosi to her lips. She gestured at the crate under his chair. He pulled out a beer and opened it against the edge of the table. He took a sip. It tasted beerier with his morning breath.

'So you've come to ask where I've been,' she said knowingly.

He shook his head. He fondled the chopper. He looked up and nodded.

'Well,' she swept the air dramatically. 'Been all over, darling. Ethiopia, Dubai. I even went to China!' She gave a stilted laugh. 'Sylvia Mwamba is a prize commodity. The Lusaka Patient.'

'You went with . . .' He paused. 'With Uncle Lee?'

At the mention of his name, tears sprang to her eyes. The unpredictable weather of grief – Jacob knew it well from living with Gogo, how abruptly it could whip a rain shower into a storm – but he was startled. He had never seen his mother cry before. There was a knock at the front door. She brusquely wiped her face and got up to open it.

Leaving his beer and his chopper on the table, Jacob haplessly trailed her again.

It was still early, the sun the colour of unripe mango flesh. The woman pouting her lips rudely at the door wore a grey trouser suit, the smell of perfume around her like a swarm. Behind her stood a big man in a brown suit with a short tie, his stomach straining his shirt buttons. And behind him skulked two men in dusty coveralls. The perfumed woman clearly already knew Jacob's mother. She flung some words directly at her – *squatting, bailiffs, thirty days* – and stomped off in her heeled boots to a waiting taxi, which promptly drove away. Jacob's mother put her face into her hands. The big man pushed past her into the house and pointed his workers towards the larger items in the sitting room – the settee, the coffee table.

Jacob turned to his mother. 'Mummy,' he said, and felt the strangeness of the word in his mouth. He tugged her hands from her face. 'They cannot boot you from your own house.'

'It's Lee's house,' she choked. 'He's—' She collapsed against the door frame as sobs overtook her.

Jacob backed away. Now he understood. Lionel Banda was dead and his family had come to collect. The workers were shuffling towards the front door, each holding one end of the sofa.

'Stop,' said Jacob, putting his hand on one worker's arm. 'We will move the things out.'

'Too late.' The big man strolled towards them, sipping Jacob's beer. 'She was given a month's notice.'

'*Bwana,*' Jacob pleaded. Then he remembered that he had the money the General had given him for transport. He took it out and pulled out several bills and stretched them towards the big man. The man looked him over, then pocketed the money.

'Go on,' he winked. 'Take what you can. I won't tell.'

As the workers proceeded to carry the sofa out through the open gate, Jacob darted into the house and started gathering what he could and packing it into the back of Uncle Lee's pickup truck in the drive. But the bailiffs had four hands and he only had two – his mother's were busy holding her face as she wept. Neighbours and bystanders soon sniffed out the drama and started taking the things the workers had left in the road. Jacob chased them off but then someone set the pile on fire. Jacob dashed around rescuing valuable items – electronics mostly – trying to avoid the feeling that he always seemed to bring fire into his mother's life.

She stood on the side of the road in her orange robe, screaming as the morning traffic honked and crept around the commotion. When all of the things in the road were packed in the pickup or gone or burnt up, Jacob guided her back to the house only for them to find the front door bound with a column of shiny new bolts. The bailiffs had changed the locks. His chopper was still inside. So were the keys to Lee's pickup, his mother informed him forlornly. Jacob used the dregs of the transport money from the General to pay for a taxi to take them to Kalingalinga. He didn't know where else to go.

✳

The General had not kept his promise to send Solo and Pepa home. As the days went on, Jacob realised that the General was holding them hostage until Jacob brought him the chopper. He couldn't call the police – just more men with guns – and the chopper was locked up in the Northmead house. Handling his mother's business had left his pockets too dry to purchase a taxi ride to New Kasama to explain things to the General. She had taken over his sleeping mat at Gogo's, so Jacob stayed at the woodyard with Ba Godfrey, waiting for his friends to come home.

Nearly a week passed before the hulking black SUV arrived with its halo of red dust. A back door clicked and swung open. Jacob and his grandfather approached the vehicle. In the back seat, where pale Pepa and sooty Solo were supposed to be, was a black and white box, labelled with a pointy-lettered word. Jacob made to climb in beside it, but the driver turned and glared, motioning for him to take the box out. Jacob lifted it onto the ground – it was surprisingly light – and shut the door. The SUV rumbled away.

Jacob knelt down to open the box, sounding out the letters on it in his head. Pandom?

'Is it a gift?' he asked his grandfather.

'It is a ghost!' Ba Godfrey laughed.

'No,' said Jacob as he tugged away the styrofoam packing. 'It is a drone.'

He recognised it from the Internet – the latest model from a Chinese company called DJI.

'What's this?' Ba Godfrey reached into the box and pulled out an envelope. It was thick with fresh kwacha bills. 'Two thousand, three thousand,' he counted. 'Ah, but this is not much.'

'No, *bashikulu*,' said Jacob. 'You have forgotten that they changed the currency.'

The kwacha had been redenominated last year, from multiples of a thousand to multiples of one. K3,000 was no longer equivalent to less than $1. It was equivalent to nearly $500.

'Oh!' Ba Godfrey's eyes grew wide. '*Iwe*, what did you do for this money?'

But the real question was: what *would* Jacob do for it? He was staring at the drone on the ground. It was a bribe and a temptation and a command all at once.

✳

Sylvia woke up on the floor of her mother's house. It was afternoon. The sunlight in the room was brazen and casual, pouring in through the new glass window and the cracks around the new wooden door. She watched the dust drift and flash in its rays. Turning onto her side, she pulled her knees to her chest, examining the wounds from the broken glass. The scabs had a comforting smell, like warm ngwee. Time passed. Even when the sun had snuck away, leaving the air to cool and the shadows to gather, Sylvia stayed curled up on the floor, not waiting, but not not-waiting, either.

When her mother came home a few hours later, her feet knocked right into Sylvia's legs. Sylvia yawned and stretched and said hello, her voice crackling with sleep. Matha sniffed and made a pot of tea. They sat across from each other at the wooden table – also new – and sipped tea from tin cups in a silence strung with unspoken words. Evening arrived: woodsmoke and cooking oil, homegoing footsteps, people talking and eating. Then the children went to bed and the bars woke up and night arrived: twinkling light and tinkling glass, bass tremors, people laughing and drinking. A juicy, drunken laugh splashed in through the window from a shebeen.

Matha sucked her teeth and Sylvia looked up. Since when? And so what if she had spent her life in that kind of place, enjoying the company of a man or two? At least she hadn't been stuck inside a room, crying over one. Her head shook no; Matha's head shook no. Their heads were like flowers swaying in the rain, like there would be no end to the back and forth. Finally, Sylvia stood and cleared their cups, taking them out to the tap in the yard – another upgrade to No. 74.

She squatted and washed up, the colliding tin cups making an open-mouthed echo, the gritty spray needling the cuts on her knees. Her thoughts struggled to float free but a string held them, kept them fluttering. *Where can I go? Where can I go? Where can I go?* It had been years since Sylvia had worked the profession, years since another man's mouth had clenched over her with pleasure. She was too sick now, anyway. Who would trust a face like hers, with its dark, rough patches? Many of her former clients had The Virus too, but they could afford the ARVs to pretend otherwise. She still didn't know who had given it to her, which anonymous man had carried death instead of life in his *amabolo*, banking the wrong currency in his money bags. Her precious mutations had only delayed the inevitable. The Virus had several sub-types and more than two ways to enter the body.

She shook the tin cups dry. Was it Lee? That man and his bloody promises. A house, a cure. His love. Even the smallest promise – that he would come to her before he died – he had even broken that one. She had learned of his death from the funeral announcement in the *Post*. The Anglican cathedral. No way would she have shown her face there or at the crematorium. Had his skin burned like bark? Like paper? *Where can I go? Where can I go? Where can I go?*

As Sylvia walked back to her mother's door, an image came to her. Aubergine skin, *impwa* eyes – Loveness, but from before Lee and his many varieties of drug, before the Hi-Fly, before their late nights at the shebeens and hotels. It was Loveness's young face, from when the two of them were just girls, sitting face to face, knee to knee, pulling together, bathed in that soft light from the plastic-bottle roof.

She had lost touch with Loveness years ago, somewhere between a Virus conference in Berlin and a Virus workshop in Holland. What had brought that memory to mind? Sylvia tried the door to No. 74 and found it locked. She sucked her teeth and banged her fist on it. Greed, maybe. That was what connected those two. Lee and Loveness both had no limits. They were the kind of people who eye your plate even while they're eating from their own.

✳

'Smaller,' the General said. He and Jacob were circling the swimming pool together, their composite shadow undulating on the water. The General had been talking to some government contractors and it seemed that they were more interested in surveillance drones than delivery drones now.

'Smaller will not be easy, *bwana*.'

'You have already given us miracles! My left-tenant, *ehn*?' the General laughed, his fillings a plague of metal in his mouth. 'I have provided. And you will provide, *ehn*?'

He put his arm around Jacob's shoulder and turned them to face the New Kasama house. It was crawling with its usual infestation of guards. The ground floor had a white facade now, though rainy-season mould was already reaching green fingers up it. The entrance had been fitted with sliding glass doors that reflected the garden and the pool and Jacob and the General standing side by side. The pillars still poked up into the sky, and hovering between them, where the second storey ought to have been, were Jacob's first prototypes: three bird-sized drones that he had stripped to the bone and coated with solar tape so that they could travel long distances without refuelling. They dipped and bobbed, flashing in the sun like monstrous dragonflies.

The glass doors beneath them slid open and Pepa emerged, wearing a navy-blue bikini and a green and pink *chitenge* knotted at her hip. Her gold hair was plaited in a zigzag *mukule*. A diamond necklace around her neck flashed in the sun. Jacob waved but she ignored him, like he was just another of the General's men. Perhaps he was.

By the time the General had sent the SUV to bring Jacob to the New Kasama house to show what progress he had made on the drone project, Solo and Pepa had been living there for two months. Solo's eyes looked as if they had been swallowed up – too much labour, too many beatings? No, Jacob realised. Drugs. One time, Jacob had managed to get Pepa alone but as soon as he was done apologising and conveying his worries about Solo, she'd replied with just two words: 'Too late.' But it wasn't too late. He had to believe that. He would prove it to her.

Now she walked to the deep end of the pool, untied and tossed her sarong, and jumped in feet first. Up, down, up – her sleek, riven head broke the surface. She wiped her hand down her face and began a gangly crawl through the water.

'Okay, *bwana*. I have some ideas,' Jacob said, turning away from her.

'Good,' the General murmured, still watching Pepa swim. 'I already feel richer.'

*

When Sylvia had returned to No. 74 Kalingalinga, she had brought with her a particular smell – faintly reminiscent of Godfrey or of Matha's fingers after she'd been gardening. It irked Matha. First, Sylvia had left her. Then she had dumped her son here. Now she had displaced him. Why had she come back? To show off her fancy robe and beery breath? Or her scarred skin and thin body? Wasn't flaunting your death a sin?

Over the last few years, Matha had developed some new opinions, or rather some new words for opinions that she had long held, about what was and wasn't a sin. Teaching her grandson how to read with Mrs Zulu's Bible had reintroduced her to its lessons. She had been surprised by how familiar some of the passages were. At first she thought this was just because of how people in Lusaka spoke these days – God bless this, bless you that, as if everyone were sneezing all the time. But then Matha remembered that Ba Nkoloso had taught her to read using the Bible. *The first shall be last and the last shall be first. Put thou thine tears into my bottle.* The words echoed back to her from her childhood. *For the love of money is the root of all evil.*

Returning to those mouldy old pages, she saw for the first time how angry God was, how He smote and browbeat his way through the Old Testament, and raged His way through the New: cursing fig trees and whipping money changers, daring people to consort with lepers and poor people, posing such a threat to government, they'd had to hang Him as a warning. It made sense to her that as a girl, her image of God Himself had been Ba Nkoloso – round black cheeks, storm clouds of dreaded hair, fearsome flashing eyes. Her image of heaven had been the clouds that he had asked to step out onto during his first flight.

Did he live in the clouds now? Was he looking down upon her from up there? She could hear his booming voice. Back straight! Eyes up! *A luta continua!* You squandered your whole life on that dead man Godfrey! What has become of my Star Afronaut? What has become of the Matha I knew? And what has become of her daughter?

✳

When Lee Banda's son started pitching up at the One Hundred Years Clinic next door to RIP Beds & Coffins, Jacob was puzzled. UNZA students did not intersect with compound residents unless they were reaching through car windows to trade kwacha for packets of fruit or Christmas ornaments. They might look each other in the eye, comfortably touch hands and even exchange thanks. But to broach the class barrier beyond this consumers' pact was rare.

Was Joseph slumming, enjoying the low life on the low down? Like father, like son. One of Jacob's few satisfactions in life was that Dr Lionel Banda was finally dead. He wasn't about to resurrect him by resenting this skinny, yellow boy, his ugliness spiced now with pimples.

But then Joseph started showing up at the woodyard itself. Ba Godfrey had managed to build RIP Beds & Coffins into a small enterprise, collecting scraps from the woodyards in Kalingalinga and knocking them into items of furniture that he sold on the side of the road. Returning from a meeting with the General in New Kasama one day, Jacob found Joseph sharing a joint with the old man under the mopane.

'Bwana,' said Jacob to his grandfather.

'Mwana,' said Ba Godfrey. 'This one is Joseph. He works at the clinic.'

Joseph coughed and woozily tilted his head up. 'Have we met?'

Jacob ignored him and reached down to pluck the joint from his fingers, then sucked on it so fiercely it singed his lips. He handed it back, holding the smoke in his lungs and sipping out a question to his grandfather – 'Has. The. General's. Driver. Come?'

'Not today,' Ba Godfrey said. 'But stay, comrade. We are discussing politics!'

Jacob sauntered off with a backhanded wave. He was not in the mood for his grandfather's chatter about the good old days of Marxist revolution in Zambia.

Evidently Joseph was, however, because he started coming by every other day on his way to and from the hovel at the back of the clinic, where he and Musadabwe were doing god-knows-what with chickens and prostitutes. Joseph didn't seem very serious about it. He mostly hung about RIP, smoking weed, calling Ba Godfrey 'God', and peppering Jacob with questions about his drone project.

It was not going well. Jacob had been experimenting with different drone models, trying to figure out the best ones to shrink down to miniature size. He purchased them online with the Standard Chartered bank card the General had given him, picking up the shipping boxes from the DHS off Makishi Road. But after nearly a year of work, RIP Beds & Coffins looked like a robot graveyard. Compound kids snuck in at night to strip the corpses, stealing metal and plastics to model little vehicles, just like the ones Jacob had once made in the Auto Department. Those old toys and these new ones – they were not so different. Except that Jacob not only had to make his look good enough to sell to *bazungu*, he had to make them fly, too.

He was running out of ideas. The websites on small drones were all geared towards research in universities or the military. With his limited reading skills, he could just about follow the findings – automated flight, hovering capacity – but he could not replicate them. He ordered more parts but they were stiff and heavy. His drones ceased to lift altogether, skittering in vain on the overturned oil drum in the wood-yard. It was his too-heavy chopper all over again.

※

Sylvia had stopped eating. It had been a gradual process. She started with medicine. Dr Musadabwe had hunted her down to No. 74. Just to see how she was doing, he'd said. Matha was at the market, so Sylvia let him in, suppressing her distaste for his skew afro and his stained lab coat and his threadbare stethoscope peeling like a snake's skin.

She had always hated the look in Dr Musadabwe's eyes when he examined her. It was not strictly clinical. It wanted something from her. Not sex or money. Data. She shrank from him. 'I'm fine,' she said. She refused the ARVs he offered, suspecting he would switch the pills with the ones he and Lee had conjured in that shack at the back of their clinic or the ones they had given her to ease the side effects.

Once she gave up medicine, it wasn't so hard to give up food. The resurgence of pain helped. It gripped her here and there over the course of the day, like an animal leisurely clenching its jaws around her body parts, its teeth puncturing her skin centimetre by centimetre, skewering her organs at the rate of a shadow's creep.

In this state of suspended agony, food was a distant notion, a *wait, what did I forget?* on the edge of the mind. Sometimes Sylvia would smell food or glimpse it – she might see a boy pass by the window with an ice lolly painting his lips blue – and wonder: *do I want?* But after a moment, she would snuggle right back into the clutter of her aching bones knowing the answer. *Nakana*. I don't want.

Jacob was taking a nap under the mopane one day when Joseph strolled up with a cocky grin and tossed a sheaf of paper at his feet. It landed with a smack and sent up a waft of dust. Before Jacob could speak, Joseph squatted down and made his case.

'I know, you've got this. But listen, this article is about the exact thing you're trying to make, and' – he held up a finger – 'it's only available online through UNZA.'

'*Futsek*, man,' said Jacob. He tipped his head back against the tree and closed his eyes. He heard Joseph walk away. A few minutes later, a voice woke him up.

'Foolish *muntu*. Where is your solidarity?'

He opened his eyes. Ba Godfrey was standing over him, licking the edge of a new joint.

'With that *ka* coloured? Ach, *bashikulu*, please.'

'You're going to chop off his head for having a drop of white blood? He's trying to help.'

Ba Godfrey walked off without offering Jacob a hit from the joint, which was the old man's version of a slight. Jacob picked up the article that Joseph had printed out for him. It had grown warm in the sun and black ants were crawling all over it, as if its letters had come to life. Jacob shook them off and slowly paged through it, trying to understand the complex words. He could barely make sense of the title: *Challenges Facing Future Micro-Air-Vehicle Development.* He squeezed his left fist and his new Digit-All Bead needled deliciously in his grip.

Jacob had been beaded a couple of weeks earlier, wearing his cleanest clothes and dabbing cologne behind his ears and marching into the shop at Arcades as if he weren't currently sleeping at a woodyard in Kalingalinga. Reckoning it was part of his technological research, he had used drone funds to pay for a full package: a Bead in his middle fingertip, a wrist speaker, and a permanent tattoo of conductive ink on the back of his hand. It had been worth it just to see the look on Joseph's face when he showed him – at least until Joseph had trumped him by explaining its mechanics to Ba Godfrey. Jacob grimaced. The guy *was* smart.

Jacob took the article and strode over to Ba Godfrey and Joseph, who were languidly chatting over the joint. He sat on a rock nearby and waited for a pause in their conversation.

'We're transforming the genes in the immune cells,' Joseph was saying. 'And that can cause a kind of butterfly effect. So the immune system might be attacking the skin cells, their melanin production. Skin conditions are often caused by autoimmune reactions and—'

'Auto-*what*?' Jacob interrupted.

'Autoimmune.'

Jacob rifled through the article in his hands. 'Is that the same as—' He held it out and pointed at a word on a page towards the end. Joseph leaned forward to read.

'Autophagous? No, that means – hey!' He looked up. 'You read it?'

'I can read,' Jacob said indignantly. 'A bit. But what does it mean? Auto like a car?'

'No, like automatic – on its own. Autophagous is something that eats itself.'

'Cannibalising,' said Ba Godfrey with a wise nod.

'Eh,' Joseph bounced his head side to side. 'More like *self-cannibalising.*'

'It is talking about eating why?' Jacob persisted. 'Is this article not about drones?'

'It's—' Joseph scanned the paragraph. 'The microdrone can use its own body for fuel.'

'But if it eats itself . . .' Jacob shook his head. 'Will it not be gone?'

'I guess.' Joseph frowned. 'Maybe it's using up just one part of its body. Or' – he grinned – 'maybe the drones eat each other.'

'*Eh-heh!*' Ba Godfrey released a plume of smoke. 'Cannibalising!'

He reached the joint back to the boys. But Joseph was translating in earnest now, Jacob sitting beside him, pointing at the words he didn't know.

Sometimes Sylvia would open her eyes to a blur stomping around, giving off a salty spray of words. What was her mother going on about? Oh, the smell. Sylvia had been using an old pot as a bedpan, too weak to make it to the latrines. How far she had fallen from her grand adventure as Lionel Banda's scientific breakthrough.

When the salon had burned down, he had taken her away with him, flown her all over the world. He had wined her in Paris, dined her in Shanghai, turning the Virus conference circuit into a bizarre medical honeymoon, a celebration of the Lusaka Patient. It was a thrilling title – her very *genes* were one of a kind – but an anonymous one. She had been probed and prodded, fed an endless assortment of pills, her insides like a jar of Smarties.

After his wife had divorced him for passing The Virus to her and their new child, Sylvia had thought things might change. In the end, Lee had left her to rot in that house in Northmead, while he went off and married some Ethiopian diplomat, just for the money, he'd said, just to sponsor his precious vaccine research. If that was the case, Sylvia had asked, then why was his new wife so pretty? No matter. Now he was dead. Now she was dying.

Why had Loveness not come? Sylvia could almost see her friend smacking her lips: *When did you give up, Syls? When did you become so sad?* Sylvia closed her eyes. I'm not sad, she thought as pain lackadaisically crunched into her back. I'm angry.

Armed with new knowledge, Jacob focused on addressing the main challenges that Joseph's microdrone article described – flight dynamics, energy conservation and navigation. He bought flexible solar strips for the wings, splurged on lithium batteries, experimented with laser sensors. He felt like he was nearing his goal but months of false starts had bled the Standard Chartered account dry. Truth be told, the Digit-All Bead he had bought for himself had been a stolen *mbasela* too far. He tried his grandfather first.

'After littering this sacred ground of manual labour with your electronical rubbish, you come and ask for money?' Ba Godfrey returned to shaving his plank of wood.

Jacob pleaded. All he needed was K5,000 – he was sure this light-weight lithium battery the Russians had just put on the market would work – but Ba Godfrey interrupted him, pointing at the skeletons of drones around them, berating him for his wasted effort.

Just then, Joseph walked across the yard towards them.

'I'll lend you the money,' he said smugly.

Hope rose in Jacob's chest like a kite but pride tangled its string and held it.

'No,' he said. 'I will not take money from a Banda.'

Jacob walked off, making his way to No. 74. Gogo did not have much kwacha stored in her filing cabinet, and he didn't go by her home often these days. But he was out of options. He found his mother sitting alone at the table, swaying slightly. She looked up and greeted him with a vague smile. He sat down across from her and nudged the plate of cold lunch towards her.

'*Nakana*,' she said and tried to stand, then collapsed back into her chair.

'You need to see a doctor.'

'Had enough of doctors, thank you,' she tittered, then broke into a cough.

'A real doctor,' he said. He looked at her. 'Not that charlatan.'

'Who? Lee?' she smiled. 'Shame. No, but he tried.'

'This medicine he gave you – it did not even work. He was testing you. Like an animal.'

'Maybe it could have worked. I stopped using it.'

'That family,' he fumed. 'They take everything away from us.'

'Not *everything.*'

'Your house,' he raised his fingers one by one as he listed, 'your body, your job—'

'My job?' A laugh rippled through her and she winced.

'Did he give you any money from his Virus vaccine? Did you get any proceeds?'

'No,' she shrugged and scratched a dark patch on her cheek.

He shook his head. 'You were just another lab rat.'

'No,' she frowned. 'I was the only one with *both* mutations. I was The Lusaka—'

The door opened. It was Gogo, dripping tears, carrying bags of vegetables.

Jacob stayed for supper. It was the first meal these three Mwambas had ever shared together. It was very quiet. His mother barely touched the food. Gogo furiously snatched hers into her mouth. But they somehow coordinated their movements – his mother reaching wordlessly and Gogo handing her what she wanted; Jacob pouring more water in Gogo's cup the moment it was empty; his mother adding just the right touch of salt to Jacob's meat. The air between them was tender when darkness fell. Gogo insisted that he stay the night.

Jacob had just achieved a restless sleep on the floor when a spasm in his hand woke him up. He switched his Bead to torch mode, cupping his hand to shield its brightness. It took him a while to see it because was it was nearly inside the light coming from his middle finger – a red bump next to his Bead. A mosquito bite. It must have interfered with the circuit. He clicked his Bead on and off, trying to still the zinging feeling, but it lingered, pulsing from the centre of his palm. He lay back down and closed his eyes and there it was. The key.

The Challenges Facing Future Micro-Air-Vehicle Development had to be considered all together. Jacob ran through them in his head. Flight: drone propellers were too stiff to account for the strange ways that air flows at such a small scale. Power: the balance of weight and energy had to be just right – the energy source for a microdrone could not be too heavy. Navigation: weight was also a problem here – the camera or lasers that would allow the microdrone to 'see' couldn't be too bulky. Could there be one solution for all of these problems?

The article had called this *multifunctionality*, but he hadn't understood what that meant until now. He had thought of it like a Bead, which you pressed in different ways for various functions – one tap for on and off, two to make it a torch, and so on. But this was more like the splayed network of nerves in his hand or the meal the three Mwambas had shared tonight, separate yet connected, synchronised.

He clicked his Bead on, crooked his left middle finger, and opened the Diagram app. With his right index finger, he drew over his palm, making a sketch on the virtual sheet. When he was finished, its lines were shaking because his hand was. It was the blueprint of a wing. Now he just needed money to make a new prototype.

✳

They made the exchange in the 'lab' behind the clinic. Jacob had thought he would resent it but it felt good to watch Lionel Banda's son hand over a thick wad of kwacha, cool and smooth as skin. Jacob counted out the bills twice. He barely paid attention to the contract or to Joseph's contorted words about the difference between experimenting on animals and people. Jacob felt that everything was coming to him now, everything that was owed.

He took a taxi to the New Kasama house a few days later. He hadn't been there in months, dodging the General. But now that he had good news to report, the General was out of town. Like teenagers without a chaperone, the guards were clustered around an *mbaula*, getting wasted and watching YouTube on their Beads, rifles in a casual heap like a woodpile. Solo sat alone in a corner, his eyes locked on something a centimetre away from his face, or a centimetre inside it.

Jacob found Pepa outside by the pool. She was wearing an emerald bikini and a big straw hat, and was rubbing sunscreen into her pale freckled belly. He had heard the rumour from the General's driver but he only believed it when he saw her stomach protruding like a watermelon. It was almost familiar – malnutrition had distended it back when she was a compound kid – but now it had a seam running down it, as if she might unzip any second. He pulled up a stool and sat beside her, watching her hand making mesmeric circles over her skin.

'Christian is somewhere there,' she said, pointing at the house. 'General is gone. *Big* business in Dar.' She raised an eyebrow and for a second, she was Pepa again, his cheeky friend.

'Hm,' he said. 'I will wait here with my own big business.'

'And what is that?' she smirked.

'I have done it,' he announced. 'I have the microdrone. It will be the smallest one ever.'

'Oh-*oh*?' she said and reached under her lounger for her drink. 'Took you long enough.'

Jacob scraped his stool close enough to smell the coconut of her sunscreen. He clicked his Bead on and stretched his left palm out to show her. It was hard to see in the sunlight, so he cupped his right hand over it and drew it to her face, as if they were kids and he was showing her a grasshopper. She peered inside the little cave at the picture of the wing glowing there.

'I call it Moskeetoze.' He spelled it out carefully.

'Why not just Moskee-*to*?'

Jacob had stolen the idea from nature. Insect wings are flexible but they have a built-in web of nerves, veins and arteries – this makes them stiff enough to flap. The nerves transmit signals for the wing to stroke and bend, which reduces drag. The veins and arteries carry blood – energy. The wing also has tiny hairs that help the insect navigate through touch. To make his microdrone, he would replace blood with fuel, nerves with circuits, and the tiny hairs with antennae that would brush the planes of the world and send Wi-Fi signals to the cloud – and to other microdrones. Together, Moskeetoze would move in concert, and if they ran low on energy, one could be sacrificed for fuel. It would be a swarm that ate itself once in a while to stay afloat.

'I'm impressed, Engineer,' said Pepa.

'Ya,' he grinned. 'It's fly, right?'

They breathed, eyes locked. He looked away first and saw the copper hairs curling out from the sides of her green bikini bottom. He clicked his Bead off and put his hands in his lap to conceal his erection. She smiled and picked up her drink, which was spitting softly.

'Malawi shandy?' she murmured. She reached it towards him. They both knew she was daring him to remove his hands from his lap. He took the glass from her hand and the hat from her head and put both on the ground. Then he grasped her face – her ear strangely cold under his palm – and kissed her. She kissed back readily, darting her sugary tongue into his mouth. She smiled against his lips to break away.

'And in my condition,' she chided and squirmed in her seat. There was a pause as they both remembered the General. 'You are going to make us so rich, Engineer.' She smiled sadly as she put her big straw hat back on.

*

It turned out there was no need to build a prototype. The General brought the men in suits to the New Kasama house – three Chinese, one Zambian, one American – and sat them around a table with Jacob. Jacob explained the wing design as slowly and clearly as he could. The five men whispered to each other, nodding tersely. A short while later, the General slid a piece of paper in front of him – the second contract Jacob had received this week. Jacob scrawled his name on it and the General handed him an envelope of cash. It was enough to live on for years.

They celebrated outside by the pool, which looked greensilver under the security lights. Jacob, Solo and Pepa smoked cigarettes and swilled Malawi shandies and danced to rumba, Pepa cackling as she held her big belly with her hands and circled her hips beneath it. She and Jacob exchanged vibrating glances all night and eventually snuck behind a bush to tangle fingers and lips, sending a surge into the throbbing knot at the centre of his body.

Hours later, when he got back to Kalingalinga and stumbled over to RIP to give Ba Godfrey the news, he saw Joseph walking out of the clinic, a bulky sack over his shoulder. Jacob was about to step forward and offer to pay the loan back when Joseph tripped and fell, the sack flying off him. Jacob was still thrumming with tipsiness, with the brush of Pepa's lips, the grip of the General's handshake. His muscles felt taut and alive. This strength seemed somehow correlated to Joseph's weakness. So rather than offering Joseph a hand up, Jacob found himself jumping him instead, wrestling with him until they were locked in a sweaty grip.

Jacob let go first and stood, smacking the dust off his thighs. Joseph was still on the ground, chuckling feebly. Jacob looked away. Across the woodyard, Ba Godfrey was sitting at the base of the mopane, watching them, a queer look on his face. Jacob walked over to his grandfather, navigating around a new chicken coop and a queen-sized bed. A freshly made coffin was standing on its end beside its maker.

'*Shani, bwana,*' Jacob said with a sloppy grin. 'And who is that one for?'

✳

No. 74 was electric with weeping. It seemed every woman in the compound had gathered there, their arms in the air, fingers trilling to what sounded like a sermon. Jacob pushed his way through the throng, urged forward by something less than love and more than curiosity. He had a desperate wish to see the body and believe. But when he managed to get through, a woman was blocking his view. She stood stock-still, holding a Bible open under the glare of the bare bulb, reading out from it in a hoarse shout. The words she spoke were unfamiliar and she threshed them out quickly, as if they tasted bad:

> *... locusts were like unto horses prepared unto battle and on their heads were as it were crowns like gold and their faces were as the faces of men and they had hair as the hair of women and their teeth were as the teeth of lions and they had breastplates as it were breastplates of iron and the sound of their wings was as the sound of chariots of many horses running to battle and they had tails like unto scorpions and there were stings in their tails ...*

The woman reading was short and round and dark. Her *chitambala* was halfway off, her grey afro in disarray, and her *chitenge* drooped low on her hips. Her eyes and mouth stretched wide as she poured forth her torrent of words. But what was most shocking – and the reason Jacob didn't recognise his *gogo* at first – was that her face was completely dry. And that was how he knew, that was why he believed. Sylvia Mwamba was dead and Matha Mwamba had stopped crying. Just like that.

Can mosquitoes and humans live peacefully together, can we forge an uneasy truce? Hover around each other enough and symbiosis sets in. Over moons, you'll grow immune, and our flus will move through you – a mild fever and maybe a snooze. This balance can even come to your rescue, defend you against rank intruders. As Simon Mwansa Kapwepwe once said, the lowliest creature, the tiny udzudzu, is what kept the imperialists at bay!

Thus when the whites first swooned to the tropics, they saw that the blacks never fell: the raging calenture that gripped the bazungu passed over the huts of the bantu. This place was The White Man's Grave. But it wasn't bad lands that caused their downfall – it happened on the seas as well. They say La Amistad's crew caught a fever, while the black mutineers were spared it. Was it African skin or sweat? It was neither. It was us, and a matter of time.

Reckon the wars, how a battleground festers: the British armies in the American South, the Japanese in the Pacific. Even the fall of the Roman Empire was due in part to our diseases. In every case, the nature of grace is that one side is simply more used to us. Call it invasion or world exploration: either way, it upsets this balance.

Your desire to conquer, to colonise others, is both too fixed and too free. Nothing escapes your dull dialectic: either it takes a village to live or to each his own to survive. Even your debate on the best way to be falls on either side of this blade. The social contract or individual free will; the walls of a commune must keep us close or capital must run rampant. That's how you froze your long Cold War, with this endless, mindless divide.

Our essence is somewhere between or besides. We flee but our flight is unruly and tangled, a haphazard hover, a swarm. We loiter a lot but we move over time, we do best when we choose to meander. Come and go, nor fast nor slow, but at a peripatetical pace. Be open to float over land and sea, beneath the communal sky, a throng, a flock, a sly murmuration – is this perhaps the solution?

Jacob's design might achieve this in time: a latticework drifting in tandem. But in the hands of those who are power disposed, what becomes of this socialish network?

Naila

2019

Lake Malawi at sunset. The sun was melting into the water, a simmering pot of gold. Twelve-year-old Naila sat in the sand, wearing her mother's old swimming costume. It was brown with little orange rectangles and fastened with safety pins to fit her slim hips and flat chest. Mother sat beside her, legs stretched out, green veins like tangled seaweed in her pale skin. Mother crossed her ankles and laced her toes, fitting one set into the interstices of the other, her best and only trick.

Gabriella and Contessa and Lilliana got up from their half-built sandcastle and ran towards the lake, hand in hand. At the shore, they dawdled and shrieked as the waves slurped up their toes and spat them out again. The wind dimpled the water. The girls splashed in and now Naila was with them. They floated on the rocking lake, their faces up to the glowing sky. They sank together, crossed legs for anchors. Tea party. Pinkies jutting, hands arcing, they sipped from invisible cups. Bubbles rose, stringing their lips to the air, necklaces losing their pearls.

Naila was alone underwater. A pin on her swimming costume popped open, hammocked down, nestled among the rocks. It glinted astral down here, but it would be dull metal once she pulled it out of the water. She reached for it, but it was too far away and then she couldn't move, her foot was caught. A pressure on top of her head, a hand, pushing her down, holding her under—

*

Naila gasped awake. Mother. She shivered. The air in the plane was so cold and brittle, it just might crack with the right kind of tapping.

Tapping. Someone was tapping on the lavatory door a few rows behind her. With a small whine like an inhalation, the door buckled open. The familiar smell of sugary soap and alien fart. Then the smell of shit, wide and deep.

'Yikes, right?' said the man next to Naila with an incredulous smile.

Oh no. She had already weathered a nine-hour flight and a four-hour layover. This second leg of the journey would be only six hours, but she was exhausted. The man in the middle seat hadn't been too bad so far, as far as flight companions go. Minimal fumbling, elbows politely retracted inside the armrests, a scent dominated by toothpaste, and blessedly quiet – until now.

She entered the conversation reluctantly. He was of Indian descent too, but they both spoke English, hesitant to broach language differences, which immediately convey class ones. She told him her name, about Zambia and its weather – 'still so mild, even with The Change?' he asked – and that she had just graduated from uni. He told her his name, which passed right through her head, and that he was an accountant for Cadbury Chocolate UK – he handed her a shiny purple business card. He was on his way to meet his bride for the first time.

'The first time?' A twenty-first-century arranged marriage. This should be interesting.

'Yeah.' He leaned in to speak confidentially. He had *lowered his standards a little* because he *really wanted a good woman*. Naila's eyebrow lifted. His fiancée currently worked for a phone bank in Chennai. Once they married, she could work as an administrative assistant for his father's garage in Birmingham. *She'll adjust really well.* Everyone in England had been *shocked* by his choice, *especially* his *mates*. His previous girlfriends had been *flashier*. More *stylish*.

'I'll show you.' He pulled out an Android – their Digit-All Beads had to remain off for the duration of the flight. 'So this is when we arranged things.' He swept a photo off the screen. 'And this is now. Not bad, right? More modern. She's cut her hair and now she dresses, you know ...'

He glanced at Naila to ascertain whether she did, in fact, know how modern Indian girls dressed these days, but her own fashion sense was currently hidden under a heap of aeroplane blankets. She felt seen, nonetheless, with her short, metallic haircut. She subtly fingered a pimple on her chin, which was surely a creamy button by now. She looked back at the Cadbury man's phone, at his future wife. The woman's expression looked more forgiving than camera-happy: *Okay, just one more.*

The meal began and the Cadbury man put his phone away. The carts trundled down the aisles, model-hot airline attendants explaining the options even though the passengers had already received a printed card menu in English and Arabic. Their row had already been served when Naila remembered that she had to take her birth-control pill. She reached awkwardly under her loaded tray table for her rucksack and pulled out the packet with its telltale calendar. The Cadbury man didn't seem to notice – he was busy ploughing into his chicken masala.

She took her pill with the water from the cupcake container, feeling a Pavlovian twinge of nausea. Morning sickness. How odd that the pill prevents pregnancy through trickery, making your body believe it's already pregnant. Like how vaccines use inactive cells to jumpstart the immune system. Or how she used to give Daddiji the TV remote with the batteries missing – only when it sat useless in his hand would he give in to his drowse, leaving Naila and her sisters free rein over the channels. Silly Daddy. Naila patted her womb. Silly body. She glanced at the Cadbury man, but he was eating his chocolate and raspberry fool, his eyes on his screen – the flashes over his face implied an action film. Why did she care what he thought of her? Was it just because he was attractive?

The attendants cleared the trays and dimmed the lights, the video screens casting an eerie glow over the cabin. Naila sat sleepless in that artificial dusk. She regretted taking her shoes off. Her feet were already swollen. She thought of Daddiji's feet, how she had washed them as a girl, carrying a shifty bowl of water to his hallowed, hollowed leather chair. He had washed hers once in return, when she was twelve. She had dropped a glass while doing the dishes and stepped on a shard. She had swept up, wiped off the blood and gone to bed. He must have seen it sticking out from the blankets. She had woken to a cool wet cloth on her sole, the tingling scrape of scabs being undone ...

Naila glanced at the Cadbury man. He had fallen asleep to his action movie. Grief flooded her then and she wept, grateful for the anonymous dark and for being in a place where sniffles are not unusual and people keep their eyes closed or locked on screens. 'It's okay,' said the

Cadbury man, her jolting stirring him awake. His breath was warm and stinky and human. Naila tried to corral her sobs, but he just nodded, his eyelids drifting down in gentle pulses. She wept against his shoulder as he dozed. He stroked her hair, murmuring the name of his modern bride-to-be, until he fell asleep again, his inevitable hand warming her thigh.

✳

When Naila had arrived back in Lusaka a week ago, she hadn't been sure that anyone would be at the airport to meet her. She had rolled her suitcase outside to where the waiting families were standing behind the barrier, sick with solitude, her eyes searching the crowd. Relief. There they were: her three sisters, arms around each other's shoulders, a twisted rope of beige limbs. Naila hugged them each in turn, then all of them together. The smell of their swaying black hair – spiced with sweat and product and their distinct yet harmonious pheromones – swelled her heart.

She was sporting a silver bowl-cut, but her sisters all wore their hair long now. This made her unreasonably happy, this proof that they had at last escaped Mother's business, if not her home. Laughing and chatting, the four sisters daisychained to the car park through the tunnel with the blue canopy and the flashing ads. They hopped into the old Mazda, Gabriella in the driver's seat, Naila beside her. It smelled spitty in here. She turned to the back.

'So we're going to shave our heads, right? For tonsure?'

'Mother is supposed to do that, not us,' Gabriella frowned.

'And has she?' Naila scoffed.

Gabriella stared ahead, hands on the wheel. Contessa opened her mouth, closed it. Lilliana sighed. The girls tossed their dark, wavy manes and fell silent, gazing out of their respective windows as Gabriella drove home. Naila was only twenty-two herself but as the eldest, her authority still muted them – which was too bad because she could have used a warning. As it was, she walked into the family home in Kamwala unprepared.

At first everything in the sitting room looked the same. The patchy orange carpet. Framed family photos infesting the walls. The American stereo system hulking blackly in the corner with its tangle of dust-furred cords. Workers steadily criss-crossing the room. And Mother, ruling over it all. She was unaccountably sitting on the back edge of the sofa, a heap of white hair between her knees. She was sorting it, issuing commands to the workers all the while. Naila's eyes fell on the packets of brown, red and yellow hair lying like dead fish on the sofa beside her – chopped and dyed and priced. If her sisters had quit the hair business, then how—

'So you decided to come home, did you?' Mother asked without looking up.

The pile of white hair between her legs twitched – Naila blinked – and a face nosed its way out from it, cheeks wrung with wrinkles, a sloppy smile between them. Naila rushed over and sat on the sofa and took Nonna's birdboned hand in hers.

Nonna Sibilla was Naila's accomplice. She had opened an escape hatch from this family by taking Naila to Kalingalinga that day ten years ago. Naila had fallen out of the jacaranda tree and into a new world. That world was dirty and scary and unclear – like being inside a dust storm – but it was real and she had loved it: the crowd of people running her through the compound, the speedy drive to the hospital, Dr Lionel Banda's flashing eyes, the smell of his cologne mingling with Dettol and soap, the stinging pull of the stitches, and the wet slime of plaster mummifying her broken wrist. Naila had loved it all and she loved her *nonna* for tossing her into it.

After that accident, Mother had put severe restrictions on them both, but Nonna had continued to smuggle little liberties to her granddaughter. Nonna had covered for Naila when she snuck out to clubs. Nonna had washed cigarette smoke and whisky sweat and semen from Naila's clothes. Nonna had given Naila financial support when she transferred to a university abroad. Nonna had encouraged her with curt, signed Whatsapps when Naila chose to major in political science. But Naila had neglected her grandmother over the past two years, as she began to spend more time at protests than in classes, and to take holidays with friends rather than home in Lusaka.

To see her intelligent, mischievous, rebellious grandmother reduced now to a pile of white fur, to see her fall under the axe of time and

Lovely Luxe Locks Ltd – it redoubled Naila's grief. She had lost her two closest allies in the war of her family.

✳

Ding. The cabin lights came on. Naila lifted her head from the Cadbury man's shoulder. He pulled his hand off her leg and smiled forgivingly, as if she had been the one to impose this intimacy. The flight attendants paced the aisles like antic tightrope walkers, with fixed smiles and mussed make-up. They were done with coddling. They snatched Naila's blankets and demanded her headset, they claimed her rubbish and chastised her tilted seat. Naila snuffled her apologies and slid open the window shutter.

It was midnight. Darkness above, darkness below, both littered with grains of light. Out there was a fatherland. The engines grew louder, heaviness swelled into the loftiness, and the plane began its leisurely downward spiral. It landed with a scorch and a wobble, slowed with a blustering sound, then swung grandly round. Digit-All Beads, now permitted, immediately strobed over the cabin, clashing like light sabres. The seat-belt sign went off and passengers popped up to queue in the aisles. Naila boycotted the rush and stayed staring out of the window.

Everything is always flashing at airports. But only at night do you really notice the pulse of it, like fireflies with their rhythmic pickup lines. Once, when she was nine, Naila had heard a fierce electrical noise coming from the transformer that translated between American and Zambian voltage for the stereo. She'd pressed the crusty orange wave of the off/on switch, and the lights on the stereo had faded, but the shrill buzzing had kept on. She'd found it eventually: a cricket, mottled as maize, clutching a power cord, still singing to its machinic mate.

Except, unlike the love signals of bugs, she thought as she tugged her rucksack from under her seat and shuffled into the aisle, the flashing lights at airports don't forge connections between the planes. They help them avoid each other's paths. What lonely lives machines lead. *You're one to talk. You touch and touch and remain untouched. Even by Joseph, who loves you.* Naila was at the threshold of the plane now, surrounded by the attendants' chiming goodbyes and democratic smiles. The Cadbury man was already striding ahead in the tunnel, disappearing into the eddying crowd. Onward. She, too, had a mission here. Naila stepped forward, her feet thick with the blood that had sunk there.

❋

Death had changed the Balaji family, the way the loss of one tooth leads the others to shift, to drift in the thick of the gum. The change was especially stark in Mother. Over the years, as Lovely Luxe Locks Ltd had grown into an empire, Isabella Balaji had cultivated an easy magnanimity in proportion to its success. Mother-the-boss reigned serene. But now she erupted out of this moneyed calm. She bustled about town, collecting payments the second they were past due, scolding negligent clients, firing workers on a whim.

Hidden away in a bedroom, Naila's sisters recounted all this, concluding with the scandal of the funeral. Mother had insisted on holding the service at the Catholic mission.

'With psalms!'

'They splashed holy water and everything.'

'But that's insane—'

'You weren't even here, Niles. You can't complain now.'

'I had finals! And even if I had been here—'

'Don't,' said Lilliana softly. She had been the most wounded by Naila's absence.

'Was there a casket?' Naila asked after a pause.

'A white one!'

'And gold!'

'Gold is fitting at least,' Naila snarked. The four of them giggled. 'Was she pleased?'

'Is Mother *ever* pleased?'

'She absolutely lost it when we got home. The workers were doing their thing—'

'No!'

'Believe you me! Full-on village-style wailing.'

Naila pictured it: the workers' howls perfectly calibrated to the measure of respect due to the deceased, to how poor the mourners

were, and how needy. None of them would receive any money anyway. The will was vague – that was how Mother had managed to get
away with a Catholic service – except for one key instructon.

'So when do we go?' Naila asked.

Lilliana closed her mouth. Gabriella stared. Contessa, the youngest,
gave Naila the news.

·'Mother wants to keep the ashes here.'

*

Naila was the last passenger standing at the baggage claim when the
scales of the carousel slid to a stop. Men in overalls pushed trains of
luggage carts and giant wooden brooms – brooms as big as Christ's
cross – over the shiny linoleum floor of the Chennai airport. Naila
perused the queue of black and blue suitcases that had been pulled off
the carousel, then gave up and headed into a small glass office.

There, another stunningly gorgeous Emirates employee told her
that her suitcase had not made the connection in Dubai. It was on the
next flight, which would arrive in about five hours. It was just past 10
p.m. If Naila waited for her bag, she would have barely enough time
to catch her morning train. She felt her eyes sting at the injustice. Was
Mother thwarting her, like some grey-eyed Greek goddess swooping
in to interfere?

'It's not just clothes and shoes in that bag, you know?' Naila said to
the official, pressing her breastbone against the high counter.

'Yes, ma'am,' the woman said, blinking her long lashes. 'But there's
nothing we can do.'

Naila parked herself on one of the plastic chairs in the baggage hall,
messing about on her Digit-All Bead until the next flight came in. She
joined the other passengers around the carousel, feeling like an interloper. Her suitcase was an interloper too, so scuffed it looked mauled.
Naila grabbed it, checked the contents in the ladies' room – thankfully,
it hadn't been disturbed by airport security – transferred the heavy box
into her rucksack and ran out of the airport.

*

'How can you betray him like this?'

Mother ignored her. She was sitting at the dining-room table, which was tiled with white receipts. She tapped listlessly at an ancient calculator, its buttons squeaking feebly.

'You know your Bead has a calculator, right?' Naila pulled up a chair.

Mother turned her hand over with a faint frown. 'I hate this thing.' The Bead in her finger and the circuit in her palm looked purple under her skin. 'Your father hated his too. He insisted that we pay full price to get them right away – "technology-technology!" – but his Bead always just got in his way.'

Naila's mind reached for him, sending seeking tendrils into the rooms of the house. *Where's Daddiji?* This was the feeling now. Not the anguish that had wrenched her when Mother had called to say he was dead. Just: *Where is he? Where?* thrumming over her skin ...

'When they set him on fire,' Mother was saying, 'his Bead didn't even burn. The crematorium gave it to me in a baggie – black bits and bobs. Like some kind of refund.' She glanced at the box of ashes sitting on the side table beside a bowl of Madrasi mix. 'And now Beads are free anyway.'

'Mother,' Naila urged softly. 'He wanted for us to take his ashes home.'

Mother's eyes silvered. She turned back to her calculator. Her hands grew busy again. 'The dead do not want for anything,' she said.

✳

In the taxi to the train station, Naila wrapped her arms around her rucksack and saw the driver's eyes harden in the rearview mirror. No, she wanted to explain, the precious cargo she clutched was not money. She put on her chattiest face and asked him questions to even the scales: You, me. Brown, brown. But the questions he returned – about her family, her education – unbalanced them again. Her discomfort at answering him disturbed her. According to Marx, the money form is an illusion – she ought to be able to talk frankly about it, no? The driver's eyes flashed from their caves. She was rich and female and African and he resented her. No doubt he would charge an unreasonably high fare. But then he didn't, and in her haste to catch her train, she forgot to tip him.

Naila and the dawn arrived at the train station at the same time. The sky looked battered, like beaten tin. It was ten to six but the station was already crowded. Voices scurried, rickshaw bells and car horns jangled, smells smoked through the gritty air. Knowing her Bead wouldn't work without Wi-Fi, Naila had printed her ticket in advance. Clutching it – the flag of a tourist, if ever there was one – she raced to the platform, brushing off the porters, her rucksack tucked under her arm, her roller suitcase bumping behind her over the uneven ground. With ten minutes to spare, she clambered aboard her train and panted her way to her seat.

The other passengers were mostly families: unsmiling fathers, doting mothers, children like small gods – smooth-skinned, bright-eyed, quietly aware of their power. No one spoke to her. Her ripped jeans and silver hair set her apart from them. Chai wallahs marched the aisles, croaking out their wares and fares. At exactly 6.25 a.m., the train jerked and slugged forward. This didn't feel like the India she'd read about in the news: authoritarian measures, class tensions, poor amenities, the threat of rape hanging everywhere.

The conductor strutted down the aisle, using his Bead to scan the tickets projected on passengers' palms. When he reached her, Naila handed over her printout, its corners curling in the humidity. He lifted his chin and refused it. Naila blinked at his rapid Hindi, helplessness sticking in her throat. The ticket had cost less than a meal at the uni canteen but TripAdvisor had said that it was essential to have a reserved seat. Finally, 'Bead, Bead,' the conductor said in English and she shook her head and turned hers on to show him that it didn't work here – but then of course it did. He rolled his eyes, scanned the QR code in her palm, and marched off.

That her Bead worked in India was a relief – it would be much easier to get around. She should have known her SIM would sync automatically with a local network. After all, developing countries had all got Bead-fever first. Digit-All had been savvy. Instead of calling these technological gadgets *chips*, the company had marketed them as *beads*, which sounded smooth and round and ever so 'cultural'. After an initial high-cost roll-out to spark interest, Digit-All had partnered with local governments to distribute free Beads. The Third World had been ripe for them. Power cut? A torch in your finger. Poor schools? Google in the palm of your hand. Slow communication? A photo beats a thousand words: a Bead was also an eye.

Naila opened the camera app now, reversed it, and stared at the girl in her hand. She ruffled her greasy mop of hair, pinched her chin pimple – satisfyingly, it spat its ivory guts out – and plucked a remnant of *saag* from her teeth. She hadn't showered in days. This was starting to feel like a matter of principle: she was in mourning, she refused to be clean. She had three more hours on the train. Suitcase and rucksack tucked around her like a fortress, Naila closed her eyes.

*

She was inside a warped cage of grey limbs shot through with violet light. She saw the ground from up in the tree – dappled shadows over rooty ground – then at eye level, the dull planes of the earth, the purple wrinkles of fallen blossoms. She was curled up on her side. A pair of green trainers approached but then the shoes became brown feet, a woman's manicured toenails. She was being lifted, carried. A curtain parted. Steady, sure arms – a passage.

*

Naila woke to the tumult of Tirupati. It was not a quiet town, as she had supposed, given how close it was to a pilgrimage site. The train rumbled between narrow buildings with flat roofs and multicoloured walls, Telugu script crawling like creepers over them. When it pulled into the station, she disembarked with the other passengers and walked out to the main road, which was as busy as Chennai had been. There were no apparent rules or lights to obey: pedestrians shuffled around and between cars, their pace calm, their movements fluid – no jerks or pivots. Fooled by this rhythm, the friendly brown faces and the modern feel of the place, she decided to save the taxi fare by walking to the hotel a few blocks away. It was around 10 a.m. She had time to spare now.

She crossed the main road and entered a maze of alleys, rolling her suitcase behind her, eyes on the map in her palm. Autorickshaws paused putteringly to offer their services to her – 'No, I'm fine. Yes, I'm sure' – then zigzagged off into the traffic, waggling their bums. The alleys narrowed and disintegrated to ruts and rubbish. Cars and autos gave way to cows and chickens. The sun rose like the red in the Global

Climate Change thermometer. Her rucksack was a hot grasping thing on her back, her suitcase wheels crudded with mud, by the time she deadended in front of a house that looked like marzipan – matte pastel walls, slanted roof and windows. A cow lounged in front of it.

This was absurd. She was Zambian, for goodness' sake. And Indian, by descent at least. How could she be lost? The cow swung its tail and painted the back of her calf with a slick brown stripe of god-knows-what. Self-pity stung her throat again. A woman stepped out onto the balcony of the marzipan house, nursing a baby while talking into her Digit-All wristband. Naila asked for directions, and after a stilted English conversation and a dozen more labyrinthine turns, she found herself in a hotel lobby icy with air conditioning.

Her clothes stiffening as her sweat dried, Naila filled in the register. As she wrote the time, she realised she had managed to catch her train only to lose an hour getting lost. She rushed up to her hotel room, changed into a *kurti*, threw a shawl over her head, grabbed her rucksack, and went back down to book tickets for the temple. The concierge shook his head. It was far too late to buy a Special Entry Darshan ticket to see Sri Venkateswara today. But, he smiled, if she was willing to walk up the mountain, *darshan* would be free.

'How long is the hike?'

'Oh, just five–seven hours for *pada yatra*.' His head wobbled smugly. 'Beautiful views.'

'I'll book a car,' she mumbled. 'Tweather says it looks like rain. Early monsoon.'

The concierge wobbled his head again, as if he had expected this of a foreigner, then lifted his beaded finger to his ear to book her a car. She was considering running up to her room to stash the box of ashes in the safe when the driver walked in. He was in his forties, wearing jeans and a windbreaker. His Bead was flashing like a strobe – his torch function was stuck, he apologised. Once she was in the back of his Lexus, he gave a rehearsed speech into the rearview mirror:

'Temple is ultimately top of seventh hill of Tirumala, which we are calling Venkata. Tirupati is not this temple where you can do quickly *darshan* and go, no. Because in actual matter of fact every day there are thousands-thousands pilgrims who want to do same as you are asking and are looking for the ways and opportunities. There are very-many queues, Madam, but there are ways-and-means. If you have …' he rubbed his thumb against his fingers, sending his Bead light scurrying over the car, 'then black market is also happening.'

'No, I'll just do *darshan* tomorrow. But can I get tonsure today?'

'*Kalyana katta?*'

Their eyes met in the rearview, then his skittered over her silver haircut.

'Yes, I read online that it doesn't take long. And it's free, right?'

He nodded. 'This time of day, very-many queues at main complex. But I take you for doing *mokku* at cottage. A friend of mine is there and I'm getting very-good discount for you.'

He started the car and drove them through Tirupati's chaotic traffic, which sorted itself only slightly when they reached the queues of the Alipiri tollbooth. He dropped her off to get her passport checked and picked her up on the other side. Soon, the Lexus was spiralling up the mountain just as the plane had spiralled down to Chennai. Is the sky best traversed in circles? Naila felt drowsy. The slow spin, the lowhanging clouds, the green hills, the radio's soupy murmur—

'Temple of Tirumala,' said the driver.

She checked her Bead. The drive had only taken half an hour. The word *pilgrimage* had always conjured for Naila a desert – feet pocking into dunes as the sun laid itself to rest on a wide horizon – or maybe a forest – dense foliage from which a ruined stone temple would surface like a barnacled whale. But Tirumala was a complex of hefty buildings and broad avenues, great paved plazas, metal accordion fences everywhere for the queues. There were statues and fountains, gardens and BeadTime kiosks. It was as grand and officious as a capital city.

'Very rich temple,' the driver smiled at her surprise. 'Pilgrims donating weight in gold.'

'Ya, I read that it has more money than the Vatican,' she said. 'But I didn't think …'

He circled a roundabout and drove into the hostel area – tree-lined roads, two-storey buildings, clothes hanging to dry on the balconies. Families strolled around, looking clean and alien with their freshly shaved heads. He parked on an incline in front of a small building and gestured for her to go inside. Naila got out and walked up to it. A sign outside pictured a dozen items circled and crossed out in red, including shoes, a beaded palm, a camera and a suitcase. Naila pulled off her Adidas and set them beside the cairn of black sandals outside the door.

Fluorescent lights, white walls, and windows with metal grills all gave the scene a medical cast. The floor was concrete grey and sluiced with hair like marbling over its skin. The feeling in the room was animal and wet. Everyone seemed pleasant and calm. Along one wall, male barbers in all white sat cross-legged, directly across from the female barbers who wore saris in a jungle's worth of pattern and colour. Pilgrims of matching gender knelt facing them, heads bowed to be shaved.

Naila joined a queue on the women's side and the pilgrim in front of her turned and smiled, head gently rocking. The barber they were lined up for wore a satin fuchsia sari with white geraniums, its beauty contravened by the banal plaid towel on her lap. Her own hair was pulled back into a long braid. She worked quickly, silently, one hand gripping the bowed head before her and tilting it incrementally, the other holding her blade, which swooped in swift arcs towards her, from neck to crown to forehead.

When it was Naila's turn, the barber frowned and interrogated her with bits of pungent Telugu, spitting words like clove seeds. The newly shaved pilgrim from the queue translated: 'Barber is asking you why, Madam. Are you a widow?' Naila bit her lip and nodded. The barber made an acquiescent gesture. Naila knelt and bent her head. The blade was cool and made a slivery sound. She watched her silver hair waft into the plaid towel and onto the slick slate floor. This was so very different from Mother's 'harvests' for Lovely Luxe Locks Ltd. The air in the room shifted like clouds across Naila's scalp until it was bare sky. When her head was completely shorn, it rose up all on its own.

The barber beckoned the next woman in line. Naila stood and stepped aside, touching her scalp, looking at the scrolls of fallen hair. According to custom, it would be donated directly to the god – she did not have to take it to him. Daddiji's debt had officially been repaid. But in reality, she knew, her hair would be weighed and sorted and distributed to one of the wig factories in Tirupati. Someday it might mingle with another woman's hair on yet another woman's head. Anonymous, profitable, generous – was this the gift economy her *nonna* had aspired to when she had sponsored the Hi-Fly salon?

The driver was leaning against a wall outside, smoking a *beedi* with another fixer. Like a bad boyfriend, he took no notice of her haircut and kept chatting. Naila put on her trainers and saw her rucksack sitting at his feet. He handed it over and scolded her for leaving it next to the open window of the car.

He took her to the pavilion to do a bit of tourist shopping. Naila mounted the broad steps bordered with stalls selling medicine and bangles and key chains and Tirumala t-shirts – mementos of loss, of having given something away. At the top of the steps was a station where people were burning coconut. Naila stood in the midst of that nutty, sooty smell, wondering if Daddiji's ashes – in the box in the bag on her back – were stirring, sensing burnt friends nearby. She looked out at the white temple and the gold temple beyond it, where tomorrow she would visit Sri Venkateswara. She clicked on her Bead, held her middle finger up, extended her arm to zoom, and narrowed her eye professionally. She tapped her index finger and thumb to take the picture, then examined the photo in her palm. Figures were cavorting on every inch of the temple's facade. Even the walls here had people.

＊

She knew she was supposed to wash immediately, cleanse herself of the barber's contamination. But instead she went back to her hotel room, stripped off her sweaty *kurti* and underclothes – her bra and panties like kelp – and slid under the sheets. Her newly bald head felt tender. She tried to ignore the operatic mosquitoes drifting around her. They looked like flecks of ash. *Ashes to ashes, dust to dust.*

What had it been like? Had Daddiji fallen asleep feeling fine and woken up to spasms and death? Perhaps he had eaten supper spiced up with Rivonia mango chutney, then some Earl Grey, a nap in his leather chair with the taste of bergamot on his tongue, and then – what? Spasms and death? Mother had found him. Had she tried to shake him awake? Had she knelt at his feet? Had she washed them before they took him to the mortuary, before they slid him into the furnace at the crematorium? *Ashes! Ashes! We all fall down . . .*

Naila woke up with her bladder half full, a comfortable ache. She turned on her Bead and ran through her messages. Four from Joseph –

gawd, so needy – one from Gabs just checking in, and a linked article from Tabitha: 'Revolution is a Slow-Moving Riot'. Naila started reading it, then gave up – insects kept flitting in her face, drawn to her Bead. She got up to pee, and already in the bathroom anyway, she finally relented and took a shower, the water thrilling against her bare scalp. She threw on jeans and a long-sleeved shirt to go out for dinner. She put her passport in the safe and tried to shove the rucksack with the box of ashes in there, too, but it was too big, so she slung it over her shoulder. Better safe than sorry.

Stealing Daddiji's ashes had been easy. Mother hadn't hidden the box. If anything, she'd flaunted it, leaving it on the sideboard so she could gesture to it while making her macabre jokes. Getting here had been more difficult. Naila had used up all her savings flying back to Lusaka from uni. She had eventually found an old bank card of Daddiji's stashed in the back of a kitchen drawer – there was very little left in the account but it hadn't expired and it had a credit line with just enough for a plane ticket from Lusaka to Chennai via Dubai.

Naila stepped out of the freezing hotel lobby into the steaming hot night. She checked Tweather for Tirupati. 97°F. Jeez. She clicked 'like' to confirm the temperature with her Bead's own measurement. As she made her way to the busy main drag, Tirupati glowed around her, as if lit with burning crops. *Chitemene.* Did farmers still do that? Burn it all down to start over? Tracing her route to the well-rated restaurant she'd found online, Naila came to a big, white building with an electric sign that said HANK YO. It looked colonial – columns and balustrades and palm trees and a fountain – but it was strung with gaudy lights. She heard drumming and saw people in traditional garb, their Bead lights dancing. A wedding? A wake? Bodies were being lifted and carried. It felt human and alive and just out of reach.

She opened her Maps app but the location service wasn't working – the blue circle kept drifting across the lines in her palm. She stared blankly at a road sign. She was lost again. She was on a bridge, in the middle of a crowded pedestrian path, autorickshaws buzzing past like flies. She slung her rucksack down and knelt to dig inside it, searching for the printout of her hotel reservation, which had a tiny map on it. She stood and aimed her Bead at the rumpled paper, looking up now and then to orient herself. There. She had found herself. The restaurant was a few yards away. When she reached down to pick up her rucksack, it was gone.

✳

Sitting in the Tiruchanoor police station, a yellow building with a clutter of motorbikes parked outside, Naila bowed to her fate. She put her elbows on her knees, her bald head in her hands, and whispered to the floor. *You win, Mother*. The place was full of police officers – men wearing tan uniforms with short-sleeved shirts, big black belts, and bulky caps. They all had moustaches and nothing to do. A lipsticked grandmother sat on a bench, weeping, dabbing her eyes with the edge of her periwinkle sari. A man in a loincloth lay on another bench, passed out.

The woman behind the counter called her name and Naila approached the glass window. She was handed a registration form on a clipboard with a chewed corner. She looked it over.

'Ya, I don't know my passport number,' she said. 'My passport's in the safe at my hotel.'

'We can quite simply scan your Bead, Miss,' the woman said. Naila stuck her finger under the glass and the woman touched her own Bead to it. As both Beads beeped, Naila thought, as she always did, of Adam and God in the Sistine Chapel.

'The officer will be with you shortly.' The woman gestured for her to sit again.

Naila slumped back onto the bench next to the *dhoti* man. Glances hovered around her like bugs. Naila was used to this by now. She was mixed and itinerant; she was Zambian here, Indian there, foreign and uncomfortably female everywhere. The weeping grandmother rose to her feet and shuffled to the glass window. After an exchange in Hindi, the official handed the old woman a key with a dented Coke can for a key ring. She shuffled over to a door in the corner and let herself in.

Naila had made this trip to fulfill the promise Daddiji had made to Sri Venkateswara when she had fallen from the jacaranda tree in Kalingalinga. Before he had arrived at UTH and learned that she had only a fractured wrist, Daddiji had bargained for her life with *mokku*, the hair on his head. But he had never returned to India to bequeath it, even though he had worked all his life precisely to afford luxuries like international air travel. In the end his bank card had paid for a plane to circle his ashes up and down in the air, for a Lexus to drive them up and down a mountain. The one thing it could not pay to do was to bring them back to life, restore what was lost.

The grandmother shuffled out of the bathroom and shut it behind her. She was no longer weeping. She returned the key and headed straight for the exit, her nose lifted imperiously. The moment she was gone, a brown trickle crept out from under the bathroom door. Everything ground to a halt. The official came out from behind the glass, shaking her head, marching to and fro, ordering a miserable-looking cleaner about. The *dhoti* man stood arms crossed, frowning. The smell was profound – so incomprehensibly rank and pervasive that Naila was forced to breathe through her sleeve.

It was another half an hour before things had settled down enough for a police officer to usher her into his office and take her statement.

'So, Miss Balaji,' the man with the moustache began. 'Anything of value in this stolen bag of yours?'

2020

Joseph first took Naila to the New Kasama house on her lunch break. It was like he was trying to keep the visit short. She had been back in Zed for a year and they had fucked their way to a kind of intimacy. But he seemed to want to lock her down now that his Virus experiments were over. She had become his sense of purpose. As he sped down Leopards Hill Road, she gazed out of the passenger window, avoiding his covetous glances, those green eyes tugging at the side of her head. She ran her hand over the cropped hair there, her rings clicketing over the cuffs riddling the outer rim of her ear. Her hair had grown back at its usual rapid rate, but she had kept the sides shaved since Tirupati, as a souvenir.

He turned off Leopards Hill onto a dirt road and pulled into a cracked driveway strung with weeds. They got out and she followed him down a path that wound through a jungly garden. A humming entered her ears. At first it swelled in gentle pulses but as they walked on, it filled every crevice of the air. It was deafening by the time they stepped into a clearing. It was coming from a cloud of insects hovering over a swampy pool across from a half-built house.

Joseph had told her that the owner, some big-shot army general, had been appointed to a government position and moved to an official state residence before this one had been completed. It looked like it was slinking back to nature. The columns poking the sky were streaked with bird droppings. Bushy reeds grew up the mildewed facade, which was reflected to infinity by the fallen glass from a shattered sliding door. They walked around the unswimmable pool – the swarm seemed to follow them like eyes in a painting – and crunched through the shards into the darkness of the ground floor.

The electric hum was louder in here, as if amplified by speakers. They picked their way through rubbish towards a slant glowing tube – from a skylight, she thought, until she looked up and saw the jagged edges of a hole in the ceiling. She tracked the light down again and blinked as it parted, curtain-like, to reveal a man reclining in a pool lounger. He was shirtless and barefoot, his jeans low on his hips, his face featureless in the brightness. His thumbs fiddled with a black box on his stomach. Smoke swirled around the tube of light like serpents around a staff.

Naila had been asking to meet Jacob for ages but Joseph had been reluctant to reintroduce them. Now, as Jacob stood and walked towards them, torso rippling with muscles, she saw why.

'Ati bwa?' she grinned.

'So you have come to punish me?' he grinned back, still fiddling with his box.

'What are you talking about?' Joseph asked stupidly.

'You forgot,' said Naila. 'He frikkin knocked me out of that tree.'

The hum intensified by a notch and she glanced around. The darkness had encroached. She leaned her head into it and saw that it was swarming with little black bits. The hum stopped and there was a brief skitter – a rain shower on a tin roof – as the air cleared and brightened.

Naila knelt, clicking her Bead on to investigate the bits scattered over the floor. She picked one up and held it in the beam of her Bead to examine it. It was tiny, its limbs metallic but flexible. She half expected it to come to life. The smell of weed crept around her and she looked up. Jacob was standing over her with a joint in his hand.

'Microdrone. I am the inventor.'

His voice was stridently casual. He took a hit, his cushiony lips pulsing offbeat with the copper tip of the joint, and strolled over to confer with Joseph. They walked together to a set of steps in the back corner. Naila put the microdrone in her breast pocket and followed them.

Up on the roof, Joseph sat in a rotting armchair, Jacob on a stool the shape of a barbell. Naila walked over to the hole in the roof and peered down. The empty pool lounger below cast prison-bar shadows. The guys were quiet, sipping whisky and sharing the joint. Naila intercepted it and took her due, then stepped to the edge of the building to look out at the swarm moving in elastic circles above the pool.

'Drones are frikkin scary, men.'

'You can't stop technological progress,' said Joseph.

'Progress?' she said. 'Progress is just the word we use to disguise power doing its thing.' Naila let the joint drop but before she could put it out with her shoe, Jacob leapt up and snatched it from under her sole. She watched him walk away, admiring the muscles in his back.

'Here we go again,' said Joseph. 'Between Niles and my gran, it's like I'm still at uni.'

'Maybe you shouldn't have quit,' said Naila. 'Maybe you would have made more *progress*. You could've been the one with the scientific breakthrough.'

'Fuck you, Niles,' said Joseph.

Jacob raised his eyes at the squabbling couple. Naila smiled to herself. This was an act – Joseph was bitter about his wasted vaccine research, yes, but he never cursed at her, not even in bed. Jacob lit the joint again, cupping his hands around his mouth to keep the wind from snuffing it.

'The Chinese fucked us,' Joseph was muttering, nudging his toe at an empty beer bottle, sending it rolling. 'They stole our work and then they stole the credit for it.'

'Why you so frikkin racist, men? It's bigger than "the Chinese". It's the Consortium.'

'The Sino-American Consortium?' Jacob asked slowly, as if the words were new to him.

'You've seen the SAC clinics? They're giving out free beta vaccines for The Virus.'

'Better than what?' Jacob frowned.

'No, *beta*. You know, like alpha beta delta?' said Joseph. 'A beta version means a trial.'

'Beta version,' Naila scoffed. 'They should just say black version. They're testing it on us.'

'Oh-*oh?*' Jacob said softly. Naila couldn't read the expression on his face.

'Human trials are the only way science can move forward,' said Joseph.

'Ya, and black people have always made great guinea pigs.' Naila crossed her arms.

'You're always crying paternalism but development is a good thing,' said Joseph. 'Take AFRINET and Digit-All. Those technologies helped us leap ahead with free Wi-Fi for all.'

'Oh yes, *bwana*,' she clapped her cupped hands, 'thank you please for foreign investment!'

'These foreigners take out more than they put in,' said Jacob.

'Exactly!' She raised a finger. 'They only gave us free Beads because electro-nerve technology uses melanin. Again, they were *testing* them on us. If the product is free, you're the product.'

'But if you are so against Beads, why do you have one?' Jacob turned his on and fixed her with its beam. She couldn't see because it was flashing in her eyes but she knew the pinprick light was crawling over her face as he scribbled his fingertip at her. Was he pulling her pigtail?

'Ya, Niles. In fact, aren't you about to bead us all?' Joseph asked sarcastically.

She turned her back and stared out over the lumpy green view of Lusaka. From out here, you could barely tell they were in a city. Joseph was explaining the new government-sponsored roll-out of National Registration Beads to Jacob. 'No more laminated green ID cards. We all get chips in the finger instead.'

'But what if you have already got a Bead?'

'You still have to come in to the Reg Office,' Naila said over her shoulder, 'for an update.'

'She knows all about it. She works there.' Joseph's voice was insufferable.

'A job is a job,' Jacob said appeasingly. 'It is not so easy to find a job in Lusaka nowadays.'

'So what are these for anyway?' Naila pointed at the drones over the pool.

'Security,' he said.

'Surveillance, you mean?'

Jacob tutted. He fiddled on his Digit-All, then stood and cast a screen onto the rooftop. With his hand splayed in the air, light streaming from it, he was a beautiful bare-chested wizard. Naila dragged her eyes to the video, a moving scan over rocky grasslands. People appeared, some holding signs, others holding guns, all of them shouting.

'Ya. I know about drone photojournalism. But is that really what these tiny-ass drones are for?' She pulled the microdrone from her shirt pocket and held it out to Jacob on her palm.

'I made the wings with solar tape.' He smiled admiringly down at his creation.

'What does that have to do with what you're using them for?'

'Niles!' Joseph piped up. 'It's just technology, it doesn't have morals built in.'

'And what *are* your morals?' she asked Jacob, locking eyes with him.

'Well, he sold the Moskeetoze design to government, so you can guess,' Joseph sneered.

'I made these ones on my own,' Jacob said, looking in her eyes. 'I can use them for whatever I want.'

'It was still a mistake to sell them to the powers that be,' Joseph said pedantically.

'Everybody makes mistakes. I make mistakes all the time,' Naila laughed and broke eye contact. 'It's a frikkin pastime. I don't even know how to drink a glass of water any more. It's like a wet t-shirt contest every time.'

Jacob cracked up, his stomach muscles clenching. Naila watched him. She'd always loved to make a man laugh.

*

Naila and Joseph quarrelled on the drive back to her office, a fight like a sneezing fit – automatic, expulsive. Combined with the weed, it left her with a headache. They had hit the end of lunchtime traffic and by the time they reached the turning off Independence Ave, the inroad was jammed. Joseph kept inching forward in bursts, a rhythm not unlike the accusations he was lobbing at her as she stewed in silence. *Flirting with him! Mocking my research! Arguing for what?!* One more, she thought. The car jerked. Naila got out, slammed the door and trotted the last few yards from the car to the Department of National Registration, Passport and Citizenship.

Everyone in Lusaka just called it the Reg Office. It was a long concrete building, its yard riven with staggered queues, which you could see even when no one was there because the shuffling feet had ruddied the dirt. The shortest queue led to a barred window in the outer facade, where a *dwanzi* of a clerk told people which of the other queues to join. Depending on why you were here, he might direct you to Marriage or Death, or to the long and tired Birth queue. Most people ended up in the longest queue of all, the generically named Reg Queue.

By noon each day, the Reg Queue had crept out of the gate and halfway up the road, its ragged tail curling around the fence. Naila thought of it as a kind of crooked mural of Lusaka. Old men in dark suits; young men in lighter suits; young women in skirt suits; old women in *chitenges* patterned with staplers, stars, turtles, forks. Hawkers ran alongside, singing out prices for apples, shoes, BeadTime and bubblegum.

Old green Reg cards littered the ground, with torn or curling edges, text worn to cipher. Sometimes, people played the game of sifting through them for relatives, friends, younger selves. They often treated the queue itself as an incidental reunion, calling out names, asking after kids, chuckling at the old gossip, gasping at the new. Only occasionally did someone naïve pitch up and start asking loud questions: why had she been asked to report? Why did her card need replacing? Where was the manager? What was registration even *for*?

Hearing the shouts, Naila went to the doorway of her office – Electronical Administration – and tried to make out what was happening in the Reg Queue. In the midst of the bodies twisting like water, arms raised with indignation, she caught a paler splash: a *muzungu*? A coloured? No, the shouting woman today was Chinese, although her voice sounded Zambian. As Naila approached the trouble, she saw that the woman was decked out in touristy gear – cargo pants, a t-shirt, and black sandals that zebra'd her feet.

'*Futsek!*' she was shouting at the guard. She insulted him, called him a *muntu* and an *idjot*, tried to stomp her flexible sole down on his boot.

'Madamu, please come down,' the guard said worriedly.

The Reg line had deviated into a loop, around them.

'What is going on here?'

A high voice with a tremor to it: the chirp of an ailing bird. Miss Cookie, who was rumoured to be in her seventies but still refused to retire, usually stayed in her back office all day. This was a dark, cob-webby room that looked as ancient as she did and seemed to concentrate all the bureaucratic energy of the place, as if the rest of the Reg Office had secreted out from it eons ago, diluting as it spread. Her office had no label and she wore no name badge – Naila wondered if she even had an official job title – but everyone at the Reg Office seemed to accept Miss Cookie's dominion as if it were the sky itself.

Today she was wearing white flats and a faded teal polyester trouser suit, her spectacles sitting on the top of her head like a modernist tiara. As she neared, the knot in the queue loosened and explanations erupted. Miss Cookie patted the air until everyone quieted.

'This man is just doing his job.' She pointed at the guard, who nodded vigorously. 'And you do not need to insult people, Mrs . . . ?'

'Makupa,' said the Chinese woman, lifting her chin.

'Oh-*oh*? You see.' Miss Cookie turned to the guard. 'She even has a Zambian husband. You have come for registration, Mrs Makupa?'

'*Eh-eh*.' The woman reached into her bumbag. 'My beth setifi ket is samweya heeya.'

Miss Cookie took the wrinkled sheet and wrangled her glasses down, Caucasianing her nose. '*Mmm!* Born in Siavonga! So Mrs Makupa, do you already have a Reg Card?'

'It expired and they did not let me vote! Nexti time,' she raised a finger, 'it will be different.'

'Yes, one man, one vote. That is very important,' said Miss Cookie. 'We are sending renewals to Miss Naila here for our new electronical programme.' Miss Cookie put her hand on the woman's back to guide her towards the office. But Mrs Makupa planted her feet.

'Why am I being singode out? Where is the big *bwana*?'

Naila winced. Miss Cookie let her hand fall from Mrs Makupa's back and rose to her full height. She swung her glasses back up to the top of her head, like a queen crowning herself.

'I am Nkuka Mwamba,' she said. 'I *am* the *bwana*. This young lady will be beading you.'

'*Beating* me?' Mrs Makupa squealed.

'I thought government doesn't want us to call it beading?' Naila whispered to her boss as the three of them proceeded to Electronical Administration. Miss Cookie shot her an evil look and huffed off to her dungeon.

Naila led Mrs Makupa – 'Am Mai, you can call me Mai' – inside the office and offered her a seat. Then she stupefied her by flooding her with the technicalities of the beading process and the details of the consent form. Mai listened closely and asked just one question: 'It is flee?'

Naila nodded and unlocked the cabinet and pulled out the Digit-All beading equipment. She tugged her rubber gloves on and unwrapped the hygienic syringe, peppering Mai with jokes and chitchat along the way to distract her. Mai became almost girlish, bantering back, giggling at Naila's snark about the guard's stinky uniform. They were both still laughing when the blood began to spray.

'I'm *so* sorry!' Naila pressed a square gauze firmly to the finger. 'I've never hit a vein.'

Mai was curiously calm, given her tantrum in the queue. 'It is fine,' she sighed. 'Am used to blood. I wek at a fishery.'

※

'So we know,' Joseph said as Naila rolled over to light a post-coital spliff, 'that everything that goes on in the mind is the result of a physical process.'

They were in her Ibex Hill flat. He was explaining how Jacob's Moskeetoze worked.

'Light waves hit the lens of the eye, sonic waves hit the eardrum, texture agitates skin cells. Neurons themselves transmit biochemical signals that may derive from the genetic code of an ancient virus …

Anyway, most of our mental activity is made up of the actual move-ments of physical things. But human *consciousness* isn't physical. It can't be measured.'

'Not even like IQ or with a CT scan or whatever?'

'No, IQ measures intelligence, not consciousness – and all it really tests is your ability to take tests, plus it has a long history of racial bias. I thought you would have learned about that—'

'Ya, whatever. Okay so, consciousness is what then?' She flicked ash off her tit.

'It's something *beyond* the physical – it's a meta-phenomenon. So if the physical activities of the mind are like insects, then consciousness is the swarm. Or maybe the hum that—'

'Oh, like Tabitha's job at Tweather. Their tag line is something like "A Hive for The Change".'

'Yes, a hive mind is the same concept. We used to use satellite imagery and meteorology to do the weather before The Change. But now that global warming has made the weather so erratic, it's more efficient for us to get live updates. So, we might say each person's tweet about the weather wherever they're standing in the world is like one neuron firing. Tweather gathers them together to create a shifting data map.'

'So Tweather is like the consciousness of The Change?'

'Yes. And Jacob's Moskeetoze have a kind of consciousness, too, because they communicate.'

'Huh.' She took a drag off her joint. 'So how come you know all this?'

'I was an early investor,' he said. 'I gave him a loan for his first design. He sold that prototype to the General, but he's building some new models, and now that I'm not working on the vaccine, I help out with his ideas. It's not official but we're kind of family—'

'So you guys are a swarm?' She smirked. 'Do you share his consciousness?'

'No,' he snapped. 'You don't *share* consciousness with someone, you *form* one together. I can't even know for sure that you have a conscious-ness, that we see the same—'

'Ugh.' She tipped her head back against the wall. 'Not this again! *Colours exist.*'

'We can never get outside our own minds. I can never know if my blue is your blue.'

'But,' she straddled him, 'I know that you know that I know when you're about to come.'

She crushed the spliff in an ashtray and ground her pelvis against his. The thin layers of underwear between them quickly came off and they were at it for the second time that morning. To prove her point, Naila stilled her hips when he was close and moved achingly slow, inching them towards a staggered climax: her first, then him.

She swung off him, pulled her panties back on and watched him dress, measuring how his body had changed since their first time in the UNZA hostels. He had filled out and his skin had cleared and tightened, as if it had just been waiting for the flesh to come.

He stepped into the bathroom. She lifted her laptop onto her bare thighs. She had missed her phone date because of that second bout but Tabitha's icon was still up – videochat was her preferred retro-techno medium. Naila clicked on it and the app made its bleeps and bloops, like a cascade of underwater bubbles. The call failed – a bubble burst in a shower of coins – then Tabitha tried to call back and failed. They went back and forth for a while, easing into conversation through technological commiseration. Finally Tabitha glitched into view.

'Sup, bitch,' she sang. She was topless, doing her make-up, using the laptop camera as a mirror.

'Hey girl hey.'

'Howzit in the boondies?'

'Dull as fuck. You coping without me?'

'Meditating helps.' Tabitha stood up and turned around. She was wearing midnight-blue yoga pants spangled with stars. Her constellated bum hitched left-right, then bounced twice.

'Twerking is meditating now?'

'Darling,' Tabitha turned back to the screen and sat down, 'it's the absolute best way to decode the mysteries of the womb. Unleash yourself. You need to awaken your cunt.'

'I just came twice in one hour. How's that for awakening?'

'Where is he?' Tabitha's eyes scanned around. 'I know you didn't do it yourself, you lazy bitch.'

'Taking a piss.'

'Hmm, good hygiene.' Tabitha returned to applying her lipstick. 'I hope he did you right, girl. It's important to let only the best energy into your *kundalini*.'

'You're definitely using the word *kundalini* wrong.'

'Wha'evs.' Tabitha delicately kissed her lips inward, spreading the copper. She reached off-screen and grabbed a purple mug with white letters that read: DECOLONISE YOUR PUSSY.

'Where did you get that?' Naila laughed.

'This?' Tabitha sipped from the mug. 'It's turmeric tea from a Nubian village.'

Joseph came in, his hair a gleaming cap, his green eyes sparkling with damp. He leaned over and craned his head around the laptop screen to wave. 'Hi, Tabs.'

'Greetings, black b-b-b-brother,' she replied, her voice laddering with the bad connection.

He straightened out of her view, cupped his hands under his chest and jiggled them with a questioning look.

'Ya, she's topless,' Naila intoned. 'Avert your eyes lest the sight of nipples blind you.'

He twirled his finger at his temple. Tabitha was in the middle of a story about Nubia.

'. . . missed my flight from Cairo to Jo'burg and this Sufi tech guy was like, "Dude, go see the real pyramids." So I took the train fifteen hours to this Nubian village where you can still drink Nile water and see the pyramids – the real ones, not the whitewashed ones. The lengths people will go to erase the blackness of our ruins! So anyway, I'm the only one in the pyramid tomb, in its, like, womb, right? So I start communing, do some yoga and shit, and right as I'm really getting into it, the lights just – *psheewww*. Power cut. A minute later they came back on and I was like, "I've been fucking acknowledged."' Tabitha sipped. 'So I bought this tea to, like, preserve that feeling? It's part of my decolonial diet.'

'I miss you so frikkin much,' Naila pouted.

'My heart twerks for you too, love. Right, let's see it.'

Naila propped the laptop on the bed and stood up. She tilted the screen to catch her image, then turned and pulled the back of her panties down, unveiling the patch of brindled skin.

'Ugh, you're a goddess. Look at that *ay-ass*,' Tabitha Minaj'ed the word into a squeak. She peered closer. 'Beautiful,' she concluded and sat back. 'Fucking. Vintage.'

Naila craned her neck to look at the fresh tattoo. It was a row of thin vertical lines of different weight, tiny numbers nudging up into them from the bottom edge.

'What price comes up when you scan it?' Joseph laughed from across the room.

'You can't scan it,' said Naila. 'The lines are meaningful but not, like, capitalistically.'

'You know what?' Tabitha was nodding. 'I really respect that you didn't do a QR code.'

'Oh, yeah,' Joseph rolled his eyes. He was pulling his socks on. 'A barcode is so much classier.'

'Uh, it makes it clear that she's critiquing late capitalism rather than neoliberalism, which is, like, infinitely more available for revolutionary inversion? But also, Nilotic, you don't want a code on your body that someone can *actually* scan. That's fucking terrifying.'

'Tabs, I need to tell you something,' Joseph called out as he put his shoes on. 'Don't pop a vein but ... You're on a computer. Right now.' He stood up. 'You might even work for the Internet?'

'Is he being funny?' said Tabitha. 'Listen JoJo, I'll let it go because you've straight mapped my girl's g-spot. But truth? The Web is dark. It's all fake smiles and *blahblahblah* we're changing the world, but underlying it all is just a big, poisonous, capitalist fuck you—'

'Bye Tabs!' Joseph cut her off as he walked to the door, then turned and mouthed to Naila: 'Don't forget dinner.'

Naila nodded and sat back on the bed. He shut the door.

'What's his problem? Testing a new butt plug?'

'Taaabs,' Naila moaned. 'I can't leave. I think I've been dicknapped.'

'Grrrl, I've been there.' Tabitha was tweezing her eyebrows. 'Sometimes I think I *live* there.'

'The dick isn't even all that – I've just trained it. Like a pet snake. A *kundalino*.'

Tabitha snapped her fingers to make Lilliputian applause. 'So what about the, uh, friend?'

'Jacob? What about him?'

'"What *about* him?"' Tabitha echoed Naila in a mocking singsong. 'You seemed . . . intrigued. And if I know my Nilotic, one man will not satisfy the beast.'

'Uh, that dude makes frikkin drones. Ew.'

'And?' Tabitha glanced up into a corner as if a thought had flown into the room. 'You know what? You should hook Jacob up with yours truly. *We* would have loads to chat about. Technologically speaking, of course.' Tabitha grinned, unveiling her purplish gums.

'Anyhoo!' Naila rolled her eyes. 'How's the job?'

'Tweather?' Tabitha shrugged. 'It's just numbers, darling. It's all just numbers. But it's the future, too. The revolution may not be televised, but it sure as fuck is gonna be programmed.'

'Mmm. Jacob said something about that the other day.'

'Oooh!' Tabitha clasped her hands. '*Jacob* did, did he?'

'Fuck you, men,' Naila said sheepishly. 'It was just kinda smart. He was like, if everything's online now – banking, government, military ops – and the power cuts, what do we do then?'

'Oh that's easy, darling.' Tabitha pressed her middle finger to her chin to turn on her Bead, lighting her smile from below. 'Then it's just a matter of to bead or not to bead.'

＊

Naila had been avoiding this dinner with Joseph's grandmother for months. Now that it was finally happening, it felt both formal and frenzied, like a job interview on New Year's Eve. Joseph's grandfather had passed away a couple of years ago, from colon cancer. They were living off his UNZA retirement bursary and the money that Joseph's Aunt Carol sometimes sent from her conservationist work in Malawi. Naila could tell the Bandas were barely making ends meet. The dinner table was set with elaborate place settings but the edges of the chairs were scuffed, the tablecloth faded and stained, the plates chipped and mismatched.

Joseph had decided on a French meal and instructed the worker, Ba Grace, to make it. She had taken over preparing meals after the old cook, Mr Sakala, had retired, but this was apparently not her forte – the *coq au vin* was *coq au vinegar*, the *boeuf bourguignon* was oniony biltong, the *au gratin* scalded the mouth. Everything tasted like Saladi cooking oil, which just made Naila long for the familiar dishes lurking inside these ones: *nkuku*, *nyama*, shepherd's pie.

'You're supposed to use olive oil,' Joseph said exasperatedly. 'Not just substitute—'

'Joseph, dear,' his grandmother cut in coldly, her eyelids like shut mussels. 'If you wanted the meal to come out differently, you ought to have cooked it yourself.'

The reluctant scrape of cutlery. Ba Grace was silent. She was probably in her sixties but, blessed with the perennial youth of black women, she was ageing at a snail's pace: a white hair a year, a wrinkle every other year. This seemed unfair next to Agnes, who was in her seventies, and whose face was like an old umbrella – all drapey folds and spiky bones and mouldy spots. They both stooped, though, and Ba Grace's hairline had receded.

'I cannot cook propalee with no pawa,' she said. 'I was having to use *mbaula*.'

'*Another* power cut?' Agnes's knife clanged on her plate. She shook her head. 'This load-sharing nonsense is a disaster. We're not sharing the burden of electricity, we're bearing it.'

'It's load shedding, not load sharing,' Joseph said. He just couldn't help himself.

'Oh?' asked Agnes, cocking her head in his direction.

'Load sharing,' he continued, 'is when you distribute power across multiple circuits to conserve energy. Load shedding is when you disconnect one source from supplying power.'

'That is a distinction without a difference,' said Agnes.

'No, it isn't,' said Joseph. 'We complain about load shedding like it's a choice that government is making. But it's the best they can do with the situation. Kariba Dam is failing.'

Naila forked a piece of chicken into her mouth. It was somehow both oily and dry.

'Don't be such a bootlicker, Joe!' said Agnes. 'Have you learned nothing from my tape?'

Naila nearly choked. She saw Joseph's eyes dim. She knew she should rescue him or keep quiet. But instead she found herself opening her mouth to argue against him too.

'I mean, Kariba Dam has been failing for years, men. That *is* politics.'

'The dam is failing because of gravity and The Change, not capitalism! The plunge wall—'

'But why hasn't it been fixed? Where did the money for fixing our infrastructure go?'

'To be sure,' said Agnes. 'Kariba Dam *was* cursed from the start. Thousands of people were displaced in the building of that dam.' She slowly ran her knife back and forth over a grey lump of beef, making it wriggle obscenely. 'The Italians did that.'

'The Italians?' Naila frowned.

Agnes paused her sawing and turned her head in increments towards Naila, as if her sharp nose were the hand of a clock. 'Yes. The Italian company that built the dam. Impresit.'

'Right,' Naila muttered. She knew that her grandfather, who had died before she was born, had worked at Kariba Dam but she had never learned its history.

'Oh dear, you have Italian family, don't you?' Agnes smiled, her closed eyelids gleaming. 'Don't mind me. There's blood on all our hands, really. The Brits are the ones who built the dam on the Zambezi instead of the Kafue. To keep the electricity near the mines, or perhaps I should say to keep the power near the money.'

'And now there's neither money nor power,' said Joseph.

'Ah, but these power cuts are velly bad,' Ba Grace chimed in, still stuck at the beginning.

'Government is talking with the Russians about building a nuclear plant,' said Joseph.

'The Russians. The Americans. The Chinese,' Agnes shook her head. 'It's the Cold War all over again.'

'Or the Scramble for Africa,' said Naila. 'The Sino-American Consortium owns the dam *and* the electric grid now.'

'Don't forget the clinics,' said Joseph bitterly. 'The SAC owns the vaccine clinics, too.'

✳

Jacob, Joseph and Naila – the three musketeers, the band, the squad. They were chilling together all the time now. They would sit on the roof of the New Kasama house, talking politics, drinking whisky and getting high, listening to that old tape from Joseph's grandmother – a British lecturer and Zambian students fervently hashing out the political dilemmas of the day: Kaunda's One Party State and his dodgy diplomacy with various Marxist factions during decolonisation.

It seemed like a utopia compared to what was happening in Zambia these days. The president – nicknamed Kalulu for the slick way he wriggled outside the law – had shut down a newspaper and arrested his critics: one for a rude toast, another for a Facebook rant, a third for overtaking a motorcade. He had sent police to raid a political opponent's home with tear gas and had him arrested for 'treason'. Spouting anti-corruption mantras, his party had nevertheless spent lavish amounts on personal business and government contracts. Most recently, he had banned a novel that laid his actions out plainly. Confronted with these human-rights violations, Digit-All had issued a fierce statement, threatening to retract their free beading programme from the country. Calling their bluff, Kalulu had simply shut off AFRINET access for a week, then announced a new tax on Internet calls. 'Bear with me if I become a dictator,' he joked at the Sino-American Consortium summit.

Over time, Jacob, Joseph and Naila solidified their respective positions on this state of affairs. Joseph – they nicknamed him Kofi – believed in incremental change through existent structures. 'Last election we had sixteen candidates on the ballot! That's progress.' Jacob – they called him Killmonger – had never voted, but his grandparents' revolutionary past had inspired him. 'Blow up the bridges and dams! We must bomb them until they listen.'

To Naila – she named herself Kali – this sounded like just another of those debates among men about how to defeat other men. She wanted to make protest art. She posted links on social media every day: graffiti in the West Bank; sculptures of politicians with distorted or missing penises; a gollywog cake served to a European minister of culture; a giant heroin spoon placed outside a pharma company. She glossed news headlines in all caps. TODAY IN NEOLIBERALISM. TODAY IN NEOCOLONIALISM. TODAY IN MISOGYNY. TODAY

IN PUBLICLY FINANCED CARNAGE. It was her daily assortment of astonishing outrage.

＊

The day the Chinese woman came back, Naila was slow-moving, cottoned from the world by a hangover. She had been up all night drinking and arguing with the guys about data collection and voter manipulation. Joseph was aghast at this distortion of electoral democracy. Jacob thought this kind of propaganda only went so far. Naila was sure Digit-All was involved. 'I have to quit this job before I have blood on my hands,' she kept saying.

Electronical Administration at the Reg Office was busier than ever, with four new clerks and dozens of waiting customers. It felt like a crowded clinic: discarded syringes cluttering up the bin, the smell of rubber gloves and antiseptic cream. Naila was filling out forms on a tablet.

'It is infected,' came the heavy bass accent.

'What?' Naila asked. A hand jutted in her face, reddish around the Bead, bluish in the palm. 'Does it hurt?' She reached out and the hand retreated skittishly. 'Can I—?' She looked up. 'Oh, it's you! Hello again.'

Mai blinked at her. 'Ya, hallo. It does not het. But—' She glanced around at the cluster of applicants in the office, then pulled up a chair and sat. She leaned in. 'It is frashing.'

'Flashing? Oh, that's just a program error.' Naila's smile made her headache twinge.

'But it is frashing,' Mai glanced over her shoulder, 'when I'm neeya those sack plesses.'

'Sack?' Naila paused. 'Oh, SAC? The Virus vaccine clinics?'

Mai flapped her hand to hush her. Naila fought the impulse to explain that The Virus should not be stigmatised, that treating the infected like pariahs was in fact—

'They are saying this Virus vaxini,' Mai leaned in further to whisper, 'makes you blek!'

Naila did a neck stretch to calm herself and caught sight of Miss Cookie strolling by the open office door with a young man – Naila did a double take. What was *he* doing here?

'Would you excuse me for a moment?'

'*Ah-ah?* No!' Mai sat tall in her seat. 'You must fixi this. Now-now.' She pointed at her palm, as if demanding that money be placed there.

'Okay,' Naila smiled broadly and winced again. 'Let's get you rebooted.'

She clipped the clothes-peg sensor onto Mai's finger and pulled up a terminal program on the tablet. Naila couldn't read code any more than she could perform a medical procedure – she had been hired for this job because of her political science degree – but she knew an error when she saw one. She took screenshots of the knots and gaps in the strings of characters and emailed them to Tabitha with the subject line: WTF? Then she started the reboot program on Mai's Bead.

'Why was this thing frashing neeya the clinic?' Mai pressed.

'I'm sure it was just a coincidence,' said Naila. Did she believe that? Beads had become ubiquitous. They were the nexus of emails, texts, social media, jobs, money – Beads could send and receive kwacha like Zoona, and some South African chains let you use them as credit cards. People even used Beads to vote. Why not public health too? Mai's Bead flashed three times.

Naila unclipped her finger. 'All set. Shall I escort you out?'

As they walked through the shadowed corridors toward the glare of day, Mai chatted about her fishery in Siavonga, how the workers spent hours playing on their Beads. The Change had brought new cycles of drought and flooding and either there was barely anything to fish or one species was overwhelming the others. When they were outside the Reg Office, Mai leaned in close.

'I hope you are not lying about those clinics,' she whispered, wagging her middle finger. 'If this thing tans me blek? You will be seeing me.' She turned and duckfooted away.

Naila sighed and scanned the yard with its riverine queues. There he was. Jacob was leaning against a tree next to a man with long grey dreadlocks – it was his grandfather. She had only met Ba Godfrey once, when she'd picked Joseph up from the woodyard in Kalingalinga. The old man looked accidentally fly in his orange corduroy flares and suit jacket.

'Children, children!' she mock-scolded as she walked up to them.

'Nayeela!' Ba Godfrey looked surprised. 'What are you doing here?'

Jacob nudged Ba Godfrey. 'This one is a big *bwana* here. She is the one giving us Beads.'

'It's just a pilot programme.' She ran her hand up into her hair, stroking the shaved fuzz on the side. 'What are *you* guys doing here?'

'Ya,' Jacob said, scratching his cheek. 'My *gogo* has been arrested.'

'Yikes, men. For what?'

'Revolution!' Ba Godfrey grinned.

'They say she set off a bomb,' said Jacob. 'We came to get money for the bail.'

Naila frowned. 'I thought you had money from selling off Moskeetoze T-M.'

'*Chapwa*,' Jacob dusted off his hands. 'I bought that New Kasama house for a woman. Ah, but she left me anyway for the boss.' Ba Godfrey put a commiserative arm around him.

Naila felt a swell of jealousy. 'Look, I wish I could help out with the bail but—'

The men looked at each other and laughed.

'No, *bwana*,' Ba Godfrey clasped his hands and wobbled his head apologetically – it was almost a *mwenye* joke – 'we came to get the money from his Aunty Nkuka.'

'Miss Cookie?' said Naila, putting a palm to her blushing cheek. 'That's my boss.'

'Ya?' Jacob shrugged. 'Anyway she has refused. *Ati* "Matha Mwamba is a spiteful witch with a demon for a daughter *chani-chani*".'

'That Cookie, she is a conservative!' said Ba Godfrey. 'But Matha? That one has a true revolutionary spirit! She was part of the Cha-Cha-Cha movement. Revolutionised by Ba Nkoloso, freedom fighter!'

'Nkoloso?' asked Naila. 'Wasn't that the guy who was going to the moon? I saw a clip online – that was reckless, men! Was your grand-mother an "Afronaut" too?'

'Ya,' Jacob nodded proudly. 'Even this one,' he clapped Ba Godfrey on the shoulder.

'Matha was hiding all these years,' Ba Godfrey said. 'Hiding her revolutionary light under the bushes. But now she has come up! She has woken up! Let me go again and try to persuade the sister to set her free, *enh*?'

He shook Naila's hand and strode towards the building. Jacob and Naila looked at each other – this was the first time they had ever been alone together.

'Soooo,' they both said at the same time and laughed.

Naila leaned towards him until her shoulder gently bumped his arm. 'You busy?'

＊

The New Kasama house was like a castle at night. Its columns and breezeblock heaps became towers and turrets, the sludgy pool became a moat, the frowsy garden with its racket of drones became a forest growing wild as beauty slept and siblings wandered. In the witching hour, the moonlight danced. The music danced. Naila danced. Jacob and Joseph watched her. They had been drinking for hours, listening to the radio, talking about Matha's arrest. She had refused the money that Jacob and Ba Godfrey had scrounged up to bail her out of Mukobeko Maximum.

'She will not leave without the other women,' Jacob said. 'She calls them The Reapers.'

'I thought it was The Weepers?' said Joseph. 'But why the hell are these women setting off bombs?'

'Nobody got hurt,' Naila pointed out. 'It was at night. And it was just one clinic.'

'Ya, the One Hundred Years Clinic,' Joseph said. 'Why did she bomb *my* old clinic, man?'

'*Kaya, siniziwa,*' Jacob shrugged. 'I cannot know her mind. I cannot think off of her behalf.'

'She's a revolutionary!' Naila yelled. 'This country has become a dictatorship. The rich are richer, the poor are poorer. Government is controlling us. And the worst part is – we *chose* this. We held our hands out to them and said PLEASE BEAD US! We can't even frikkin take them out of our hands or deactivate them. It's the perfect system to monitor us, to force compliance.'

Jacob nodded. 'I heard that in the Copperbelt, the miners are chopping off their fingertips.'

'That won't work,' said Joseph with disgust. 'They'd have to chop off their whole hands. But wait, why are we talking about Beads? Matha Mwamba blew up a vaccine clinic, not a BeadTime kiosk. That's not political. That's just preventing people from getting the treatment they need.'

'Need?!' Naila slurred angrily. 'First of all, it's not a cure, it's a vaccine. Second, it's a beta test. Other countries get cheap, generic ARVs and we get to be guinea pigs for an untested vaccine on a national scale. And third, this issue with Mrs Makupa's Bead makes me think they're going to use our Beads to force all of us to get the Virus vaccine, and that means fourth, the side effects are going to turn us all into frikkin leopards—'

'You sound like a bloody anti-vaxxer!' said Joseph. 'There's no scientific proof of those side effects and—'

'It is *your* vaccine then?' Jacob challenged him. 'The one you made with Musadabwe?'

'Our research was just a tiny part of what Ling accomplished at Huazhong.'

'So why are you now defending?' Jacob seethed. 'This guy? *Awe, apwalala.*'

'You're such a hypocrite, Niles!' Joseph paced the roof. 'You go on and on about colourism. And your friend, Tabs, always going on about *greetings black brother*—'

'What does that have to do with—'

'This alleged side effect everyone is protesting?' he went on. 'It's *literally* superficial. This terrible thing people don't want, even though it vaccinates against the most deadly and pernicious virus in the history of mankind – all it is,' he pointed at his arm, 'is a bloody tan!'

'It is not just a tan!' Jacob yelled. 'It is black patches! It is another disease, like leprosy.'

'Leprosy—' Joseph sputtered and slugged the rest of his beer as if to quench himself of wrongness. 'First of all, the condition is called melanism, and it's the reverse of the condition your girl has.'

'What girl?' Naila frowned.

'She is not my girl any more,' said Jacob. 'Pepa made her own choices, that one. And it is not the same as albino!' Jacob shook his head. 'To be black in this world is a curse.'

'A lack of melanin is no blessing either!' said Joseph. 'Ask your girl Pepa, or not-your-girl Pepa, whatever. Melanin is a biological advantage – it protects our skin and our neurons. It's an organic conductor of ions and electrons, which is why Bead circuits work better in dark skin.'

'Mmhm,' Naila nodded vehemently. 'The world hates black people but they *love* our biological advantages. Our skin, our bums—'

'"Our"?' Jacob started laughing. 'What do you mean "our"?'

'Laugh all you want,' she said. 'I'm African and I'm not white and in this world, that means I'm black. They don't like us but they wanna *be* like us. But,' she turned her back to them coyly, 'you can't put a price tag on this,' she spanked her own copious ass. The guys responded at the same time:

'You are the one who put a real price tag on it,' said Jacob.

'You literally can. It's called butt implants,' said Joseph.

The guys laughed and clinked their drinks. She saw Joseph frown slightly, but before he could ask about Jacob's comment, she shifted the conversation back to Matha Mwamba.

'Even our grandmothers are tossing bombs,' she concluded. 'So why are we doing nothing?'

*

She and Joseph fought about it the next morning driving back from New Kasama. It was dawn, the dark sack of the night slowly turning inside out, baring its pale inner surface.

'So, you told Jacob about your ass tattoo?'

She scratched her ear. 'Oh, ya, we were, uh, chatting about the historical shift from a barter to a money economy and I used my tattoo as an example of how capital converts every product into a social hieroglyph because, you know, a barcode looks like a sign that needs interpretation and—'

'And where was I during this little chat about commodity fetishism?'

'In the loo,' she said, looking out of her window. It was only six but the road was already thickening with cars. Slo-go traffic had become like heart disease in Lusaka, clotting its major arteries.

'Did you show it to him?'

'Would you think less of me?' She turned back to him, allowing her guilt to flip into indignation. 'Is that not frikkin refined enough for you?'

He twisted his grips on the wheel. 'I didn't say that—'

'STOP!' she yelled, pointing at the yellow triangle in the road ahead of them. He slammed the brakes and the car screeched to a stop, bucking forward, then falling back on its heels. They both looked in the rearview mirror. Luckily, there was no one behind them. He pulled the car around, skirting the traffic triangles cordoning off the stretch of tarmac. It was just an empty construction site but the near accident had stunned them awake. After a moment, Naila started laughing.

'What?' he grumbled, glancing in the rearview again.

'They spelled it wrong. They were supposed to paint STOP in the road. It says S-O-T-P.'

'Idiots.' He sucked his teeth. He still seemed shaky.

Naila turned to look out at Lusaka zipping flatly past.

'It's like the Mile of Crosses in Chile,' she said.

'The what?'

The typo in the road had winkled it out of her memory, where she had stored it years ago for an art history course called 'Tricontinental: Art in the Third World'. She explained to Joseph how, in 1979, the Colectivo Acciones de Arte in Chile had staged a protest against Pinochet by turning the dashed lines in the roads into crosses.

'They taped horizontal lines across them, turning those minuses into plusses. In one installation, they wrote *no* next to each one so it read *no mas*. No more.'

'Hmm,' he said, interested but still grumpy from their unresolved fight.

'SOTP,' she murmured. 'It almost sounds like an abbreviation.'

'Some of the parts,' he said.

'No, all of it – the whole thing sounds like an abbreviation.'

'No,' he said. 'I mean SOTP is already an abbreviation, for the Sum Of The Parts.'

'As in the whole is greater than?'

'It's a kind of business valuation. If a company has multiple divisions, you figure out what the divisions would be worth if it got broken up or acquired by another company.'

'What's a business valuation for?'

She already knew but at least they weren't talking about Jacob any more.

*

The idea took shape in her mind over the course of a few weeks. The next time she met up with the guys in New Kasama for their funny little three-way dance – fuming and fomenting and flirting – she tried it out on them. What if they changed all the STOP signs in Lusaka? Repainted them one by one? Or just taped over them with stickers that reversed the middle letters?

'But for what?' asked Jacob.

'To get the message out, to catch people's eye. The drivers, the pedestrians, the hawkers, the street kids, the expats, the tourists. Even illiterate people will notice that something is off.'

'No one here follows traffic signs as it is,' said Joseph. 'It'll just cause accidents.'

'Maybe,' she said. 'More likely a traffic jam, like when the robots go dead. But that's the point. This is how protest movements begin – activists swarm onto the roads and stop traffic. They bolt themselves to redwood trees and fences outside nuclear plants. They jam the circuits.'

'This sounds like recreational politics,' Joseph rolled his eyes. 'Gentrified protests.'

'The Civil Rights Movement in the US was all about logjams and blockades. Martin Luther King is the one who said "a riot is the language of the unheard". And the decolonisation of our country wasn't just boycotts and speeches. It was bombing bridges, too.'

'Zo'ona,' Jacob said. 'That was what they did during Cha-Cha-Cha.'

'What we need now is a riot from within the system. Okay, stay with me.' She told them the story of the weeping grandmother who had lost control of her bowels in the police station in Tirupati.

'What does your shitty travel experience have to do with anything?' Joseph asked.

'In a police station, something like that can wreak havoc – it's a different kind of bomb.'

'A stink bomb,' Jacob guffawed.

'Ya, it's funny, but that woman did more to fuck the police than any activist or politician could with ten times the effort. And she did it by making a mistake, by missing the target.'

'It's a stretch, Niles.' Joseph raised an eyebrow.

'It's like the basis of your vaccine. Insert mistakes into our genetic code so The Virus can't get inside our cells. We have to insert the errors into the system. Not with activism but with the *inactive*: the loiterers, the shitters, the unemployed – the idlers who jam the circulation of money and goods and information. A slow-moving riot. And we start with the signs on the road.'

'But so what does this SOTP stand for?' asked Jacob.

'The Sum Of The Parts,' said Joseph.

'No, no,' she said. 'I've been thinking it should be the State Of The Planet.'

The guys objected in unison, Joseph raising his hands to the heavens, Jacob clapping dismissively. They went in spirals for hours, riffing on the abbreviation as if playing a game, which, in a way, it still was. The conversation devolved into pettiness and jokes, trolling and trifling: a transcript of Internetspeak. This was how everyone talked these days – too many people with too many ideas and too many things to protest. But Naila convinced them that this was the beauty of using an abbreviation – they could always decide what SOTP stood for later. The first step was to generate buzz.

When Naila got to the house in Kamwala, she anticipated that her senses would be on high alert for Mother: her authoritative step, the smell of her perfume, her imperious voice: *And what are you made of?* But instead Naila found herself unconsciously reaching for her father instead – those tendrils seeking *Where is Daddiji? Where?* as she found her way to the bedroom. She knocked on the door.

'Nonna?'

Nonna Sibilla's bedroom was as clean and bare as ever – a bed against one wall, a small table under the window. She was under the covers, sitting up, idly plaiting the white hair spilling over her lap. It was Sunday. The workers were out, the girls brunching at Mint Cafe,

Mother delivering wig. Upon seeing Naila, Nonna gave a low grunt of pleasure and patted the bed. Naila sat.

'Nonna, I wanted to ask you about Grandpa. Nonno Giuseppe. His job at the dam.'

Nonna nodded, a smile gleaming under her white veil of hair. She listened as Naila explained what she needed, then directed her to some boxes under the bed, to one box in particular. Inside were green folders full of documents. Naila rifled through them. The pages were old and brittle, with jagged rips on the edges and ghostly ink between the lines. But they were legible. Naila paused over a diagram – arcs swooping across the page, tiny letters underneath: KARIBA DAM IMPRESIT 1957.

'It's—' She looked up. 'It's all here?'

Nonna smiled her veiled, gappy smile.

'Why did he take them from the office?' Naila had never met her grandfather but he seemed like a company man. It would have been strange to bring documents like these home.

'Federico,' Nonna Sibilla sang softly at her lap. 'Federico.'

Who was Federico? Naila's grandfather's name was Giuseppe Corsale – the name printed at the top of each page she held in her hand. Nonna sighed. Naila leaned down to kiss her forehead through the shroud of hair. Well, maybe it didn't matter how they had arrived or by whose hand. They were here – the blueprints, an X-ray of infrastructure – and now she had them.

✳

Matha Mwamba's court case dragged on – no one had been harmed but a vaccine clinic had burned down. Government did not take kindly to acts of terrorism, especially when the accused expressed no remorse. The story stayed in the news like a TV serial: *Kalingalinga Bombers. Banakulus of The Revolution.* International organisations took an interest and made Matha a human rights martyr. A media outlet called Chronics got an interview with her on the inside – 'Local Churchwoman Reignites Cha-Cha-Cha' – and when she mentioned an organisation called the SOTP, the word raced across the country like flame along a gas-soaked string.

Their little revolutionary squad had already revised dozens of STOP signs around Lusaka. As Naila had predicted, this had led to more traffic jams than car accidents. And slo-go had infected the city for so long that government couldn't attribute it to the altered signs. The effort to catch the perpetrators – the 'purple traitors', as one MP called them – dwindled and everyone just blamed the typo on illiterate municipal workers.

In the meantime, Tabitha had figured out how to hack Digit-All Beads.

'I should have used tabs,' she tutted. 'It's way more accurate than spaces.'

'What the fuck are you talking about?' Naila whispered. She was standing in a storeroom at the Reg Office, talking to Tabitha on her Bead. Her friend's face rippled on her palm.

'Don't worry about it, darling. Tech speak.' Pink bubblegum flashed between Tabitha's lips.

'Okay,' said Naila. 'Listen. They've started sending notifications for a National Virus Vaccination Programme – like I thought, they're using Beads to monitor compliance. That'll give us access to anyone the Reg Office has beaded.'

'Alright, what do you want the message to say?'

'Just the date and location for the rally. Kalingalinga. Twenty-fourth of October. 6 p.m. Oh, and: SOTP.'

'Have you queens decided what that shit stands for yet?'

'Jacob and Joseph still disagree.'

'*Do. They.*' Tabitha raised an eyebrow and blew a fleshy, veined bubble.

'Shhh,' Naila said guiltily.

Tabitha barked a laugh and her bubble burst. She cursed as she extricated the pink tangle from her nose ring with her fingernail. 'You catchin feelings for one a dem, darling?'

'I just – it's more like catching politics?'

'Sounds very current affairs. You better be making them both wrap it up.'

'I'm on the pill. Sort of.' Naila had been lax about taking it lately.

'Darling! All that male energy inside of you. That's why your father's been visiting you—'

'Ew. It's just dreams. And he doesn't even say anything, he just keeps ... circling me.'

'Mmm,' Tabitha nodded knowingly. 'Restless. Daddiji's roving, Nilotic.'

'This is absurd,' Naila shook her head. 'I'm gonna go.'

She clicked off her Bead. What if Tabs was right? What if Daddiji was still roaming around Tirupati, the stolen box of ashes passing from hand to hand, never at rest? Maybe that was the source of the *Where is he? Where is he?* that still vibrated in her skin whenever ...

Zzzt.

'Shit!' she gasped – her Bead had buzzed. It was a text: 'r u bizi?'

※

The rains had come, and this was a blessing. Luminous green bounded over the land, the drought was over, the crops would grow. The rains had stayed, and this was a curse. The roads flooded with twisting brown currents, cars drifting off like unwitting boats. Pedestrians clomped along in gumboots, the middle air a flotilla of umbrellas. Cholera and malaria swept through the markets and compounds. Kalulu sent his officers to boot the sellers off the roads – a cleansing. Those who protested were beaten and detained. Stalls stood bare. Downtown Lusaka looked clean and mournful.

The rain rattled down on the roof of Naila's flat in Ibex Hill, strumming a gentle vibration over her bed. It was a wet, silvery afternoon, an afternoon made for sex.

'I was only ten when my mum started the business,' she said, tangling her legs in the sheets. 'Boutique hair. But, like, selling the hair off our heads, you know?'

'This hair?' He threaded his fingers inside it and tugged gently, pulling her head back.

She just about kept from moaning. '*Leka*,' she said unconvincingly.

He let go and smiled. He was always amused when she tried to sound more Zambian.

'The workers thought the business was witchcraft.'

'Hmm?'

'Ya, be careful, men,' she flicked a finger against his chest. 'You might be dealing with a witch.'

He grabbed her finger and kissed the tip. 'You would not be the first.' He opened his lips to suck on it.

'*Iwe!*' She pulled it away. 'That's my Bead! You want to get zapped?'

He laughed and turned her hand over, kissed the back of it instead like a courtier.

'So what kind of *muzungu* witchcraft did they say your mother was practising?'

'Well,' she smiled, 'my Italian ancestors are famous for their *stregonaria ...*'

'Is *it?*' He rolled on top of her, holding himself up so their naked torsos just barely touched.

'Mmhm,' she nipped up at his lips. He still tasted of her – chalky and sour like baobab fruit.

He pulled away, teasing her. 'I am happy that your mother made a witchy business. And that your angry grandmother brought you to Kalingalinga. Because now look at us here.'

She flipped onto her stomach and arched her bum against him, teasing the stiff urgency there. Then he ruined it.

'Your grandmother had blueprints of the dam?'

She collapsed into the mattress. 'Sometimes I wonder if you're with me just—' She stopped herself. 'Ya, she did.' She spat a hair from her mouth. 'But J? What are you planning to do with them?'

He said nothing. Instead, he began scribbling on her back with his finger, a new habit of his. It drove her mad. She could never read what he was writing.

2023

A revolution always seems, in retrospect, like an eruption: a massive upheaval that overturns everything, flips the tables, shatters the sky, fractures the earth. No one talks about how long a revolution takes or how boring it can be, how it can slowly chew time with grinding teeth before gulping it down all at once. It consumed their lives for years – the supposed time of their lives, their early twenties – and in the end, it swallowed one whole.

One day in October of 2023, the city garlanded with blooming jacarandas, a great light flashed over Lusaka. In restaurants, waiting rooms, bars, market stalls, at Spar, at the bank, on minibuses, even in a handful of schoolrooms – all of these peopled places lit up with bluewhite brightness, as if daytime lightning had come in the window. But this flash came from inside, not outside. Everyone who had a Bead contributed to it. It cast upon their palms a place and a time and the mysterious letters: SOTP.

People were used by now to receiving government notifications through their Beads – about taxes, electric bills, elections, and, recently, the compulsory Virus vaccination appointments. But those messages had arrived individually, citizen by citizen, not all at once like this SOTP one. After everyone had recovered from the wonder of the simultaneity, some people went online and found a bare-bones website (www.theSOTP.com) with an RSVP form. The event, whatever it was – a rally? a giveaway? a concert? – would take place in a week, on Independence Day, in Kalingalinga.

Lusaka was perplexed.

'S! O! T! P! WADAZIMEEN TO YOU AND ME?!?!' sang around the schoolyards.

The *Mast* published a full-page ad: WHO IS THE SOTP?

Radio Phoenix brought in experts – a linguistics lecturer from UNZA, a rising hip-hop artist named KnockKnock, a government official and a Christian minister – to talk with DJ Jay Dee.

'So, me I think it means Surrender Oil Thankyou Please,' said KnockKnock.

'What oil? We are not Nigerians. Me, I think it stands for Seek Out The Praiseworthy!'

Callers into the show had equally outlandish theories. Maybe this was doomsday talk like Y2K or Twenty Twenty. Maybe it was about The Change. Maybe it was a coup, like back in '97.

'Do you remember those dangerous happenings? It was also around Independence Day.'

'Yes, but four days after,' the older government official corrected. 'Twenty-eighth of October.'

'*Ah-ah?*' KnockKnock exclaimed. 'The coup was operating on African time?!'

Laughter.

'But you people, that was not even a proper coup. Three men conquering a radio station—'

'If that was a coup, even our show today can be a coup,' said DJ Jay Dee.

Laughter.

'Alright, that's all we have today. Thanks, listeners. We'll see you at the S to the O to the T to the P. Whatever that ends up being!'

✳

Naila felt full to the brim. It was like getting likes or hearts or adds online – a flood of community feeling blinking towards her, albeit empty of content. Joseph was furious. The day of the radio show, he picked her up from work. He started ranting as soon as she got in the car.

'How the hell are we supposed to get a political platform together in a *week*, Niles?'

She flipped down the passenger-side visor and flipped up the mirror.

'Why the fuck did Tabs send out that message without consulting us about the date?'

Naila pulled her hair up into a bun and applied her Bruise lipstick.

'I told her to send it,' she said. 'We can't keep frikkin *kawaya-wayaring*. Are we going?'

He opened his mouth, closed it again. He drove them to New Kasama in silence. Jacob welcomed them at the broken front door with open arms, a big grin and an open bottle of whisky. They settled into their usual rooftop roles – Naila raising, Joseph dampening and Jacob ironising their spirits as they planned. They decided the best place to set up a stage was under the billboard at the CRDZ intersection. They could paint their message on it. But what should it say?

'Freedom,' said Joseph.

'Freedom is a capitalist illusion,' said Naila. 'It should say equality.'

'You people, it must say revolution!' said Jacob.

And then the guys were off arguing again. Naila settled back, stroking her palm to scroll through RSVPs – 379 people had already said they were coming. The comments section was full of jokes about what the letters stood for and whether there would be freebies. Free like Digit-All Beads and AFRINET Wi-Fi had been free. Addicted to aid, indeed. Naila smiled to herself. It was her vision in action – an infiltration of the capitalist circuits. Everyone was happily doing what they always did, joining in with their clicks. The SOTP had the masses. Now it was time for the swerve.

*

The day of the rally dawned sullen with heat. After lunch, Naila put on her green cotton *salwar kameez* patterned with little Black Power fists. She drove to Showgrounds to pick up a generator and the rental audio equipment and then on to Kalingalinga. The fever for malls that had gripped Lusaka in the first decade of the twenty-first century had spread to the compounds. She read the signs as she drove past: WALKERS MALL, JUBILEE MALL, NDEKE MALL, MADINA MALL. More the size of grocers, these buildings now lined the roads, as if they'd just devoured the wares that used to be displayed on the ground. Some had their escalators on the outside, for show. The painted signage had been upgraded, too – fluorescent screens advertising stock photos – though the names of the businesses still had their Zinglish charm: THUMBS NAIL HARDWARE, GOD KNOWZ HAIR SALON, THE HIGHEST BEEDER.

They had chosen the least busy part of Kalingalinga to set up, an empty field where two roads met under an old billboard. As Naila parked, she saw a raised platform ten feet above the ground. Jacob and

Joseph were crouched at its base, knocking together a set of steps up to it using tools borrowed from RIP Beds & Coffins. She winced – they had set up the stage on the wrong side. The plan had been to mount it facing east, under the blank back of the billboard, so they could paint their slogan on it. Instead, the guys had built it facing west, under the front of the billboard, which showed a multicoloured advert.

Naila got out of the car and walked up to the stage, passing through a football game in the field. Some kids had gathered to play, hoping for handouts or gossip. She beckoned for Joseph to come down from the stage, then took him aside to point out the mistake.

'Fuck!' He blinked up at the billboard, then whirled around with his hands on top of his head. His bare chest was sweaty from the exertion of lifting and hammering, and she could almost feel his rage beaming off it.

'We can't move the whole stage now!' he shouted. 'It's too heavy.'

The kids stopped kicking their plastic-bag football and stared at the angry coloured man.

'Then we have to take it apart and rebuild,' she said.

'What's up?' Jacob called out from the stage, standing slowly, hitching his jeans. He was bare-chested too. She pointed at the billboard. He walked a few feet forward, turned, and looked at it. He started laughing, his mouth snapping up at the sky. The kids giggled and pointed too, as if they got the joke.

BOOM POWER.
YOUR SMART DETERGENT CHOICE.

'I guess it is a message?' Jacob shrugged.

'It's an embarrassment.' Joseph shook his head and stormed off in a huff.

Naila raised an eyebrow at Jacob, but he was still looking at the billboard.

'You know what? We can fix it,' he said and loped off. He came back moments later, carrying a ladder, two cans of paint and a paint brush. The kids sat on the ground in a line in front of the stage to watch like it was field day.

*

Naila didn't see Joseph again until hours later. She and Jacob were climbing the steps up to the stage, holding either end of the giant speaker they'd rented. Joseph emerged in the distance, wearing a suit, carrying a sheaf of pages – a speech, no doubt – and his little red book. She and Jacob shuffled along the creaking wood planks and levered the speaker into place. She dusted off her hands as Joseph came up on the stage.

'Yikes. Where d'you get that Kaunda suit, men?' she said. 'Sally's?'

'It's not *salaula*,' Joseph said indignantly, looking down his chin at it. 'It's my grandpa's.'

Jacob was leaning over the edge of the stage, dousing his head with a bottle of water. He shook his head like a dog, flinging droplets. Naila stepped away, clucking – he was still covered in paint like a Nyau dancer from whitewashing the billboard. Joseph approached the mic and tapped it.

'Microphone testing. One-two—' His voice boomed then screeched and he ducked.

The kids sitting on the ground in front of the stage covered their ears – the littlest one covered his eyes. Jacob gave a shout and jogged over to a nest of cables by the speaker to fix the feedback. Naila went to stand next to Joseph at centre stage. The sun was setting right into their eyes.

'So you wrote a little speech?'

He looked hurt by the question. He paused.

'Are you fucking Jacob?' he whispered.

She glanced back but Jacob was rummaging in a duffel bag at the back of the stage. She laughed, her throat tight. 'Are you really asking me that right now, men?'

'Answer the fucking question, Niles.' Joseph's green eyes looked swampy.

Jacob came towards them, buttoning up his own secondhand Nehru jacket. He shooed them together, oblivious to the tension in the air. They stood next to each other – Joseph, Jacob, Naila – and he took a group selfie with an old iPhone.

Just before it gave its fake camera click, Naila noticed a boy standing in the football field looking up at them. So this was how kids faked taking pictures these days: not by bracketing their hands into a camera, but by raising a middle finger as if for a Bead selfie. Naila smiled. The boy smiled back. The sun glowered behind his head. He turned and then Naila heard it too: the rumble-drum of approaching feet.

*

The roads were chock-a-block with rush-hour traffic so the people flooded around the slo-go, trickling between the cars, and even clambering on top of them. Fed-up drivers left their vehicles in the road to join the surge of bodies. It was surprisingly quiet. People laughed. Babies squawked. Opportunistic hawkers called out wares and prices. Two news drones hovered above the compound with their truculent whine. But curiosity is not a loud sound and this was neither protest nor riot. It was more like an *indaba*, a gathering to discuss a problem, the problem pending until everyone has arrived.

Naila took a breath and glanced at Jacob and Joseph on either side of her. They were ready. Except – she looked behind them – they hadn't had time to paint their message on the billboard. It sat there, its all and nothing surface, that dumb blankness full of meaning. The slick paint was coppering in the sunset. Traces of a BOOM shadowed its surface. Jacob saw Naila looking at it and with a nod, he walked over to a can of blue paint, bent down, and levered its lid up.

He had only managed to paint a big sloppy S and half of an O by the time the crowd was complete. There was still some motion within it but no longer that of a gushing flood or a river breaking its banks – it was the shimmering of a dark, pensive lake. Naila stepped back. Joseph stepped forward. He shuffled his papers, sniffed into the mic and looked up.

'My name,' he began and the mic bansheed with displeasure.

The crowd reeled. Joseph stepped back. Jacob scampered around adjusting cables. Naila, sensing restlessness afoot, quickly stepped to a corner of the stage. She raised her fist and started a simple chant – 'S! O! T! P!' The crowd picked it up, delighted to be instructed. Naila saw the speed of sound as the chant travelled back – by the time it hit people twenty yards off, it had stuttered off-rhythm. It became an echo, then a round, then died away.

A sweaty target had spread on the back of Joseph's Kaunda jacket. He cleared his throat then hesitated and glanced back. Jacob, kneeling over a tangle of cables, motioned for him to go on.

Joseph turned to the mic and yelled furiously: 'My name is Joseph Banda!'

No echo. No screech. Just his high, clear voice. Relief hummed across the crowd.

'We have gathered here today,' he smiled, 'to—'

The sound cut completely and the rest of his sentence was drowned out by groans of pity and disappointment, which swelled and grew spiky with complaint. Joseph stepped away from the mic. There was a movement in the crowd, just visible in the purpling gloam of the sunset: a new contingent of bodies was wriggling through the masses, heading towards the stage. Naila heard a droning sound, punctuated by clapping: someone was singing a hymn.

'What the fuck is going on?' Joseph shouted.

'Power cut,' Jacob replied brusquely as he strode past and squatted at the front edge of the stage. An undulating serpent of bodies was squeezing towards him – all women, wearing all black – and now the head of the serpent emerged: a short, round woman in a cracked leather bomber jacket. Jacob reached his arms down into the twisting pit. The crowd knotted and boosted the woman up into his arms.

Joseph was yelling in Naila's ear now, clutching his undelivered speech. She brushed him off and ran forward to help lift the woman up onto the stage. Jacob's *gogo* got on her feet, tugged her jacket down and nodded her thanks. Then she turned to the crowd, pushed past the dead microphone and punched her fist into the air. The crowd erupted. When had Matha Mwamba been freed from prison?

'*Kwacha?!*' she called in a deep, guttural voice.

'*Ngweeee!*' came the response from the older members of the crowd, the ones who remembered.

'*Kwacha?!*' she called again, cupping her hand to her ear.

'*Ngweeee!*' came the response, sighing across the crowd to the ones who were learning.

Matha laughed with joy and her congregation of Weepers below the stage began to sing and ululate.

'Revolution now!' Jacob shouted. He grabbed his *gogo*'s hand and punched it high again, so their fists were raised together. The bolus of their hands glowed – the press of their fingers had turned on his Bead. Those closest to the stage took the cue, pinpricks of light flickering on one by one. It was nearly dark out and Naila now saw the speed of light, the scatter of Beads flashing on over the crowd, coursing into a galaxy. The crowd cooed softly at the nimbus it had made, like a big baby fascinated by its own hand.

Matha Mwamba stalked the stage, calling out, a natural-born preacher.

'One Zambia?!'

'One Nation!'

'*A luta?!*'

'*Continua!*'

The bits of light waved and trembled. Jacob switched his Bead to a megaphone app. Matha took his wrist and began speaking into it.

'And the first beast was like a lion,' she said. 'And the second beast like a calf.' She raised her voice. 'And the third beast had a face as a man and the fourth beast was a flying eagle. And the four beasts had each of them six wings about him and they were full of eyes within. What. Are. These. Mysteries?!' She cocked her head. 'Is. This. Not. Prophecy?!'

The crowd cheered wildly.

'End of days is here!' Matha preached. 'Have you not seen the winds of change rushing over our lands? Have you not seen the burning winds of Lucifer and Mammon? Bending heads and breaking backs across the world? In USA! In UK! In USSR! In China! And now even here in Zambia! Can you not see that the lion is war? That the calf is for fattening, because it is for slaughter? The third beast – it is the dictator in every land from Russia to Kenya, Zimbabwe to India. It is the face of man! On the body of a demon!'

Naila ran to Joseph and hugged him – forgive me, that hug said – and kissed him on the lips. 'We did it!' she shouted into his ear over the booming of Matha's speech.

'Did what?' He gestured at the crowd. 'Started a new church?'

She looked up into his eyes, eerie emerald in the crowd's Bead light. 'We got them here.'

'Ya.' He gestured at the billboard behind them, its half-message, its giant SO. 'And for what?'

'For that!' She gripped his face with both hands and turned it towards the glimmering lake of Bead lights. He shook his head within the vice of her palms.

'What do you want to say to them, Joseph?'

He looked at her. He swallowed. 'I want to tell them that our minds are free, even if our hands are tied by poverty,' he said, gaining confidence. 'That we can innovate! We can—'

'—horse is conqueror!' Matha was hollering. 'The red horse is murderer! The black horse is scales, the moneyed banker! And the pale horse, oh, the pale horse of death—'

A cry rang out: 'Police!' Matha broke off. Night had fallen and it was hard to see. Jacob pointed across the crowd at a flurry in the swimming constellation. There was a staccato echo: 'Police, police, police,' called the people. Uniformed men and women were blundering in from the sides, holding their weapons aloft. The crowd wriggled like a mess of worms as people tried to turn, to run, to stay – all at the same time.

Naila looked around. Joseph was frozen, staring at his unspoken speech. Jacob was squatting at the front edge of the stage with his *gogo*, who was conferring with her congregants below. The Weepers were a dark clot in the midst of the lights – they wore all black and many of them had missed the government roll-out of free Beads while they were in prison.

Matha cast her hand forward and they dispersed, spreading like inky tentacles from the stage, each sinuous line moving towards those who had infiltrated the rally. The officers were yelling and swinging. The Weepers were humming and swaying. Naila ran towards the steps, where she met Joseph and Matha. Jacob was still crouched at the edge of the stage. His eyes met hers just as he jumped down into the mass of people.

✳

Some said that if the SAC security forces hadn't arrived with their bullying guns, their shouts and their shoves, the Kalingalinga rally would have stayed peaceful. Respectful. No one even knew what they were there to protest! Others said that Matha Mwamba was the one who had disturbed the peace, incited the violence, that she had unzipped her bomber jacket and bared her breasts like Mama Chikamoneka. They swore that, right before she sent The Weepers back into the crowd – their wrists locked in front of them, demanding to be arrested – Matha had said: 'Burn it down.'

Naila's feet hit the ground just as it began to tremble. For a moment, she thought it was an earthquake, like the one The Change had brought in 2017. But the vibration was not coming from below. It was blasting from above – surpassing, total. The crowd was immersed in it, sounds were lost in it, the air was glitching with it. People stopped running and pushing and stood where they were, shocked by its sheer volume. Then their Beads shut off, all of them, all at once. Everyone stood in the blaring dark, their hands over their ears, their eyes looking up.

Naila saw the night sky vanish. It was so sudden that she gasped. It was like the stars had fallen to the earth, blossoms shaken off by a mighty wind. Or like a great black sack had swept across the sky and caught them up. Or like the sky had always been an onyx scroll with white Braille letters, and it had just swiftly rolled up tight. Something was up there above them in the sky, moving over the face of the crowd, blocking out the heavens. All around was the swell of that fierce, quivering vibration. A dark immensity lowered.

A wheezing grunt, a shriek of hinges, a crash of thunder – more than one – five or six in succession, some near, some far. The earth bucked the crowd off its feet. Naila landed on a woman, who scrambled out from under her and grabbed her son, who had toppled nearby with the impact. The gushing vibration abruptly ceased. The thing hovering above them had settled onto the ground – the slams had been its feet, hundreds of yards apart.

Then there was light. A blinding cone of it blasted down from the darkness above. The light captured the upturned faces of the crowd, their fallen bodies in unwieldy tangles. Human sounds started to come back to life: people called out to each other, men moaned in their bruising and wounding, babies cried, grandmothers shouted, women said *tuleya, mwebantu!* Car alarms wailed, honked, beeped, accompanied by the smash and tinkle of broken windows.

Then a new sound. At first Naila thought it was the congregants again, humming their way through the crowd. But this was closer to a ringing, the electric sound of pylons growing steadily unbearable. It looked like smoke was pouring through the air, cutting in and out of the cone of light. People shouted and the mother next to Naila pointed. Her boy nodded. *Mulilo*, he said. Fire.

But there was no burning smell, no searing heat, no flame. The smoke's syrupy sweep through the cone of light reminded Naila of a starling murmuration. It swung around, its ringing sound drawing near, then far, flooding thick, spiralling wide. Its outer edge swept past her and she saw tiny buzzing bits within it. Not smoke, microdrones. She heard the mother say it. *Udzudzu*.

Naila felt the cumulative touch of them on her face and neck – a whispering feeling, as if a furry wind were passing by. Then she felt the gentle needling. A dozen twinges, a hundred, a thousand, each no more painful than a normal mosquito bite. The swarm – they were Jacob's Moskeetoze, she was sure of it, the ones he'd sold to the government – had landed upon the crowd and begun to puncture them.

In and out of the blueblindingwhite cone of light, people ran and stumbled. Their clothes grew black under the swarm, as if turning to cinder. The boy beside Naila grew hairy with drones. His mother tried beating them off, but they bounced right back, or onto her instead. Naila cried out, for Jacob, for Joseph, for Daddiji – *Where is he? Where?* – and felt a queer tickle on her tongue and a webby film on her teeth. She hooked her fingers inside her mouth and pulled out a dozen tiny drones. She spat, then shut her mouth tight.

Everything went silent – everyone had stopped shouting once they realised the drones would fly into their open mouths. The swarm was so thick, the air so feverish with it, that Naila couldn't see. She cupped a hand into a visor, and still she felt the scrape of thin legs and wings on her corneas. Finally she wiped her eyes with her fingers and shut them too.

If the drones had been sent to subdue the crowd, they had served their purpose. Everyone was still, eyes closed, mouths closed, shoulders raised, arms wrapped around their bodies. Such a quiet conquest, a dark blanket cast over the people, gently chewing into them, bites stippling across the expanse of their skin. Minutes passed. Then the muffle began to loosen.

The swarm rose and swung again into its measured spirals, moving slightly faster now, as if lighter. Naila realised what this meant: the drones had not come to extract something from their bodies but to deliver something – Joseph's Virus vaccine, she was sure of it, the one he had made with Musadabwe – administered via the tiniest plentiest injections. Mission accomplished, the drones skittered up into the cone of light. The brightness gulped them steadily and then cut to black, as if the throat of light had choked.

The crowd stirred uneasily in the dark. People touched their skin instinctively, anticipating itch or ache, hunting for bumps, seeking a bodily script to read. All they found were painless welts, which would subside by the next morning. The effects of the mass vaccination would come later. Virus immunity for all. Black patches for many, nothing a little Ambi won't fix. But, for the next generation – the descendants of the vaccinated – there would be another illness entirely.

Just as the crowd began to gather in clumps of wonder and worry, everyone's Beads flashed on again. There was a collective chorus of relief. It was over. Was it over? Not quite. Again the shuddering blast – a redoubled earthquake or the distant pounding of Mosi-o-Tunya – and the people covered their ears, some with their forearms this time, crouched on the ground. No more, please. *Nakana*. Then a tremendous earthly flinch – more than one, a succession of five or six, some far, some near – as the macrodrone lifted off its feet.

In the light of the Beads, which seemed a dull glow after that harsh spotlight, Naila saw the thing's legs this time: massive curved arcs cutting through the night – two to the north and four in the distance. They lifted up and away from Kalingalinga, which was somehow still standing. The vibration dissipated as the great beast – the shape of a giant mosquito – rose up and flew away, restoring the constellation to the sky. The scroll of the night unrolled, flat as it ever was, its uneven Braille twinkling down. The black sack scattered its loot of light back across the universe again. And the vast night tree under which we all stand bloomed with stars once more.

Oldest friends, ancient enemies, neighbourhood frenemy foes. We're perfectly matched, Mankind and Moz. We're both useless, ubiquitous species. But while you rule the earth and destroy it for kicks, we loaf about, unsung heroes. We've been around here as long as you have – for eons before, say the fossils.

When man took up tools, we were right there beside you. When you left Broken Hill, we tracked you. Reckon the great men littered in our wake, or the wake of the fevers we carry: Dante. Vespucci. The King of Siam. De Gama. Three of the Medicis. Oliver Cromwell. The twelve-day pope. Lord Byron. Livingstone, of course. Behold the might of the mite!

There's naught like a nemesis for truth, they say, and this story does have a lesson. Your choice as a human may seem stark: to stay or to go, to stick or strike out, to fix or to try and break free. You limit yourselves to two dumb inertias: a state of rest or perpetual motion.

But there is a third way, a moral you stumbled on, thinking it fatal, a flaw. To err is human, you say with great sadness. But we thinful singers give praise! To the drift, the diversion, that motion of motions! Obey the law of the flaw! If *errare humanum est* indeed, then it follows that si fallor, sum.

As the Gnostic Gospel of Philip opined: 'The world came about through an error.' He probably meant God, but for good old Lucretius, this was a matter of matter. When atoms plummet like rain through the void, they deflect – oh, ever so slightly, just enough that their paths divert. From this swerve, called the clinamen, come collision and cluster, both the binding and fleeing of matter. Stephen Hawking once said, 'Without imperfection, neither you nor I would exist.' Every small stray opens up a new way, an Eden of forking digressions.

Don't forget the catch like Naila did, though: error slips through your hands if you grasp her. Error is slick and slimy and rich and she begets more errors at random. She's a real coquette, she'll take your bet – and fortune's forever behind her.

The Dam

The *Vulture*, a fishing boat, swung to her anchor with barely a shudder and was at rest. The wind had dropped, the water was calm, and being bound for Mlibizi, the only thing for it was to sit at the bar on the lower deck and wait for the day to turn. Lake Kariba stretched before them like the expanse of an ocean. Water and sky seemed welded together without a joint, and in the luminous evening, the other boats seemed to stand still in white clusters of sharp corners and varnished planes. A haze hung over the low shores, which ran out to land in vanishing flatness. The clouds were growing dark in the distance, condensing into a mournful gloom, over the largest man-made lake on earth.

Mai was their captain and host. The three of them affectionately watched her back as she stood at the rails looking out. On the whole boat, none of them had even half her authority. She was their pilot, trustworthiness personified. It was hard to remember that their work was not out there in the melting surface of the water, but behind them, within the brooding face of the dam. Between the members of the SOTP, there was, as would be expected by now, a revolutionary bond. Besides holding their efforts together through long periods of stagnation and fear since the rally, it had made them tolerant of each other's flaws – and convictions.

Joseph had bagged the only cushion on deck and was lying under the only blanket. Jacob, eager to get started, had already taken out the box of microdrones, and was toying architecturally with them. Naila sat cross-legged, leaning against the base of the bar. Her cheeks were sunken and had a sallow tinge. Her back was so straight, she had a severe aspect, and with her arms dropped, the palms of her hands outwards, she looked like an idol. Mai, satisfied that the boat would not stir, made her way back and sat amongst them. They exchanged a few words lazily. Afterwards there was a silence and, for some reason or other, they did not speak about the next stage of the plan. Still tired and wired from the previous night's mission, they felt meditative, fit for nothing but placid staring.

The sun set, dusk fell upon the lake, and lights began to appear inside the holds. A guard tower, a three-legged thing erect on a mud-flat, shone intermittently in the distance. Here and there, you could see the jagged outlines of bare branches emerging from the surface of the lake, the drowned trees of Gwembe Valley still reaching for the sky.

'And this also has been a dark place.'

Joseph's remark was not at all surprising. It was accepted in silence. None of them even took the trouble to grunt. And presently he continued, very slowly.

'I was thinking of the olden days, when the British first came here, a hundred years ago. Imagine the feelings of a local chief – what is the Tonga word? – a *muunzi*, chased suddenly to the north; run over the land across the region in a hurry and put in charge of one of these settlements that the white men – a lot of useless men they must have been, too – had built for 60,000 villagers in a month or two. It must have seemed like the end of the world, the soil full of lead, wood that burns too much smoke, ground hard as a rock. Chased from the Zambezi, without stores, under orders. No riverbanks, no marshes, no trees. The Tonga became scavengers, nothing to eat for a fishing culture, nothing but dirty water to drink. No *bukoko* beer, no escape. Scattered, a people lost in a wilderness, like a needle in a stack of hay. Cold, swamp, storms, disease, isolation. Death skulking in the air, in the water, in the bush. People dropping like flies.

'Oh, yes – the Rhodesians did that to the Tonga people! Did it very hastily, too, no doubt, and without thinking too much about it either, except to brag that they had pushed it through in time at least – the building of the Great Kariba Dam! And maybe they were encouraged by keeping their eyes on the chance of a promotion to the Federation government at Salisbury at some point, if they had good friends in London and survived the political situation. But what of our young Tonga, banished after training to be a prefect or a tax-gatherer or a trader even, wanting to mend his fortunes? Sent into exile, marched through the bush, put in some inland settlement. He must have felt the savage conditions, utterly savage, closing around him, squashing that yearning that stirs in the spirit, in the minds, in the hearts of all men. There was no preparation for such misery. He had to live that way without understanding why, which was just as detestable. But it had a fascination, maybe, that started to grow. The fascination of oppression – the growing regrets, the longing to escape, the powerless disgust, the surrender, the hate—'

'Mind you,' Naila cut in, lifting one arm from the elbow, the palm of the hand outwards, so that, with her legs folded under her, she had the pose of a Buddha preaching in American clothes and without a lotus-flower – 'mind you, what ruined this country was efficiency – the British worship of efficiency. The first settlers weren't smart or royal. They were not *kings*. The empire was a frikkin sham. They were *colonialists*, and for that you only need brute force – nothing to boast of when you have it. Power's just an accident that depends on the weakness of others. They grabbed what they could get for the sake of it. Robbery plus violence, aggravated murder on a big scale, and bloody *bazungu* going at it blind – men tackling men in the dark. The conquest of Africa, which meant stealing it from those with a darker complexion and flatter noses, is an ugly thing, men. Even worse was the idea at the back of it, not curiosity or love, but just belief in an *idea* – something they set up, and bowed to, and sacrificed us to—'

She broke off. Flames had begun gliding on the lake: small green flames, red flames, white flames, pursuing, overtaking, joining, crossing each other, then separating slowly or hastily. It was the lights from the fishing boats that continued to pass in the deepening eve upon the lake. They looked on anxiously – had they done all that was needed to be done?

*

After the Kalingalinga rally, they had watched the video footage from the news drones over and over, trying to see when things went wrong, when they took that unaccountable turn for the worst. The problem was that everything went black at a certain point – the moment night fell and everyone's Beads cut out and the macrodrone covered the crowd with its vast, vibrating shadow.

'Why did we pose a threat?' asked Joseph. 'They didn't even know what we were protesting.'

'*We* didn't even know,' Naila muttered, as she pulled the video bar on her palm back to rewind. They were watching from her Bead, which was projecting the footage onto a wall at the New Kasama house. They had been holed up there since the rally, trying to regroup.

'Look.' Naila pointed.

They looked. A sea of bitty lights, then a hoarse sea of darkness washing over the scene.

'We've seen it a million times,' Joseph said exasperatedly.

'Yes, but—' She pressed pause. 'Why did all our Beads cut out at the same time?'

'Power cut?' Jacob shrugged.

'No,' Naila mused. 'Our Beads kept on working after the microphone cut. Remember the lights?'

'Yes.' Joseph stroked the beard he had been growing. It covered his acne scars and made him handsomer. 'Beads are powered by our nervous system so they don't need to be charged.'

Naila turned off her Bead. 'They must have shut them off, through the cloud.'

'AFRINET still works when the power is cut?' asked Jacob.

'Yes,' Joseph said. 'AFRINET servers are plugged directly into the grid at Kariba. They don't ever shut down, even when our devices do, even when there's load sharing.'

'So, we can never truly take control of our own Beads,' said Naila, head in her hands. 'Government can always hack them through the web and we're stuck with them in our bodies.'

'Unless we cut off our hands,' said Joseph with a low chuckle. 'Or blow up the grid.'

Naila rolled her eyes. 'But if we blow up the grid, how will *we* even access the Beads?'

'Drones.' Jacob stood up.

Naila and Joseph exchanged a look. Drones had turned out to be the most nefarious tech of all. But Jacob was walking around, explaining that his drones didn't need the cloud.

'They communicate with each other with Bluetooth. And they are solar-powered.'

'So,' Naila said slowly. 'If Beads are powered by our bodies and drones by the sun ...'

'Our Beads can communicate without the cloud.'

They discussed various ways they could go about it. They could use Bluetooth to create virtual private networks that would get around the government's control of the Internet. They could string a chain of communication from drone to drone to reach air towers outside the borders, and tap into Wi-Fi from one of the seven countries that surround Zambia.

'None of this matters unless we target the grid and shut down the cloud.'

'The electrical grid isn't just the cloud, guys,' said Joseph. 'It's people's lives. We need to make sure we warn them.'

'It is okay, comrade,' Jacob laughed. 'We are used to power cuts in this country.'

＊

Months of planning later, their mission was ready. It was plugged into each of their Beads.

SALUTE:
Size: Three-member squad.
Activity: Plant transmitters in 3, 4.
Location: 16.5221°S, 28.7617°E. Kariba Dam.
Unit: SOTP.
Time: 22.10.23 1800 hrs Central Africa Time.
Equipment: Rope, harnesses, ascenders and aiders, anchor gear, carabiners, webbing and slings, abseil devices, gloves, helmets, Gore-Tex suits, tent.

Naila had driven into the dam during the late afternoon, posing as a tourist, a gear bag in the boot crammed with equipment – to scale down the gorges for fun, she would have said, had she been asked. Tons of people came here for extreme sports these days – ziplining and bungee jumping and white-water rafting and mountain climbing. In the end, the security guard had waved her in without question, shaking his head at her choice to do her tourism in the rain, hurrying back to his booth to get out of it himself.

She inched the Mazda through the gates and along the top of the dam, rain sweeping over the windscreen. She looked to the left and the right – the precipitous drop on one side, the lake's tremulous surface on the other, as if respectively epitomising the sheerest of vertical and horizontal planes. When she reached the south side, she pulled into a shadowy corner of the visitor centre car park, right next to a statue of Nyami Nyami, the Tonga god. It had a spiral body with a long curved head like the alien from *Alien*. Naila turned on the heating system to fog up the windows. Then she looked in the rearview mirror.

'Okay,' she whispered.

'It is hot in here!' Jacob sat up from the back seat with a grin, pulling off the blankets he'd concealed himself under. He looked like Black Panther in his Gore-Tex suit.

'Please leave the heat on.' Joseph sat up from the floor, coughing feebly. His wrinkled black outfit made him look like a disgruntled server at Debonairs Pizza.

They waited quietly. An hour later, Mai stepped out of the visitor centre, in gumboots and a wide-brimmed hat that brought out the Chinese in her by connotation. She would drive the car out, pretending to be Naila – an easy match, beige skin, black hair – so that the parked car wouldn't give them away. Mai hopped in the vehicle, and they hopped out and crept to the boot to take out the gear bag. Jacob knelt to peel off the faux licence plate, revealing a second plate underneath, and rapped the boot with his knuckles. The brake lights glowed red, then vanished as the Mazda crept off to the exit gate at a snail's pace.

They headed up into the hills to wait for nightfall. The forest was green and heady, drunk on rain. It stormed the whole afternoon and they were glad for their camo-coloured tent and their helmets – Joseph had insisted on them although the black ones, on back order, had taken longer to arrive. The rain stopped just as the sky dimmed from lavender to slate, the cloud cover blotting out the sun and the moon. The sun was due to set at 18:05. At 18:00, they left. They would have thirty minutes before the security lights came on.

They headed for the dam, the curving 2,000-foot wall with its six sluice gates like lidded leaking eyes, rust-coloured stains yawning down under each of them. They jumped the gate and snuck along the top of the dam, hunched over, cleaving to the low wall. The sky growled and flicked out a silvery tongue but held its spit. When they reached the middle of the dam, Jacob started placing cams and nuts in cracks. Joseph held back, crouching and handing Jacob anchor gear and rope. He was afraid of heights. Naila wasn't a big fan either – she'd been slightly skittish ever since her fall from the jacaranda tree – but she distracted herself by tightening her harness. Jacob handed her the ATC belay device and jumar. She girth-hitched a sling to her harness and threaded her rope through the ATC. Then she straddled the wall, took a breath, and lowered herself into the chasm.

❋

She zipped down – *Zhrrrrrr-rrrrrrrrrrr-rrrrrrr*-fuck she had lost control of the rappel-*rrrrrrr-rrrrrrr-rrrrrrrrrrrrr-rktch* – until the knot at the end of her rope finally stopped her. She gasped at the jolt to her crotch and waited for the swaying to stop. She looked up at the dam, which merged strangely with the sky – the same dark grey – and made her feel like the whole world had tilted vertical. A knot of puke rose up her oesophagus. Then there was a flash of light and she saw the seam dividing the dam from the sky.

She swallowed. Was that lightning? *Mmmhmm*, the sky rumbled in confirmation. Two more flashes above, smaller and more permanent: the guys' Beads. She turned hers on too and glanced at her fingerless, palmless glove – she'd cut out a square patch in the centre for her Digit-All screen. 18:11. Shit. She switched her Bead to torch mode and scanned up the dam towards the sluices. There.

She raised herself up slowly. *Zhr. Rrr.* A minute later, she was hovering in front of the two middle sluice gates. They were enormous – almost thirty feet across – each with horizontal metal grids and a jutting lower lip of concrete. Between them was a ten-foot wedge-shaped wall. Her goal was to place a transmitter in each one. The rain started spritzing again. She unzipped her hip bag and pulled out the first transmitter. She activated the magnetic clamp on it and reached out for the sluice, but it was too far – the curve of the dam's edge suspended her a few feet away. She heaved herself towards the dam, grunting as she kicked her leg out uselessly. Fuck. She tilted her head back. The rain touched soft fingers to her face. She clicked on her Bead. 18:14. Sixteen minutes. She dialled Jacob's Bead.

'Sup, comrade,' he whispered.

'I'm too far from the dam. I need you to rock me.'

'I got you,' he said. She could almost hear the smile in his voice at the implication.

She heard Joseph's anxious voice – 'What the fuck is going on?' – then the line cut.

She felt herself swaying side to side and spinning as if Jacob were pushing her on a tyre swing. She giggled. The rain fell harder. She turned to the sluice as it zoomed towards her, reached out her hand and stuck the transmitter to a metallic protrusion on its inside wall. She tugged the rope – *next* – and Jacob tugged it back – *Roger*. She felt the vibration of the rope above as he dragged it ten feet against the edge of the dam to pull her in front of the other sluice.

The rain was pouring now and she could barely see. She couldn't get a grip on the zipper of her hip bag, either. She pulled off her glove with her teeth. She unzipped the bag with her bare fingers, pulled out the second transmitter and turned on its magnet. She tugged the rope twice, hoping Jacob would understand the command. He did – she began to sway to and fro now, nearer to the dam each time, until finally she reached out her arm and—

Zhrrr – she slipped down and her knuckles slammed into the concrete wall below the sluice, ripping off a layer of skin. Shit. *Zhrrr* – she dropped down another foot. She hadn't tightened her autoblock enough and was sliding down the wet rope. She tightened the knot, licked the blood off her knuckles, and pulled her glove on again. She gritted her teeth and jugged up. As soon as she reached the right height, she tied off and locked this time.

Zhrrrrr-rrrrrr-rrrrr. Puke glubbed up again like wax in a lava lamp, but it wasn't the sound of her slipping down her rope this time. Someone else had abseiled down and was hovering beside her.

'Jacob?' she whispered. 'Thank frikkin God.'

She turned on her Bead. Green eyes flashed towards her.

'You were in trouble,' Joseph shrugged with a trembly smile, then gave a high-pitched sneeze. The echo of it ricocheted around them. At least it sounded like a bird.

'*Shhh,*' she shook her head. 'I just have to do the second transmitter.'

As if on cue, her rope began to sway again. Joseph gave a yelp – *that* sounded human – then hushed as he realised Jacob was manipulating her rope from above. She slammed the transmitter into the second sluice and swung back towards him. Joseph grinned at her, as if he had accomplished something too. Then he cocked his head.

'Would you have preferred it if Jacob had come?' he asked but before she could roll her eyes, the floodlights clunked on. *Zrk-zhr-rrr* – she immediately started jugging up. There would barely be enough time to get out before security noticed two giant spiders clambering up the wall of Kariba Dam.

✳

This morning had felt both weary and wary. After a restless night camping in the forest, they had snuck out at dawn and boarded Mai's fishing boat, the *Vulture*. They had dozed the afternoon away on board, Mai telling stories about Kariba Dam, Joseph and Naila turning them into philosophical treatises on the nature of colonialism. Finally night fell and they sat in silence, drinking and waiting. A light flashed and they turned, half expecting to see a bigger boat coming by, maybe the *Matusadona*. But then the light flashed again from above, and now the thunder came, as if the sky were clearing its throat.

'You people,' said Jacob. 'We must be serious. Are we sending these machines tonight?'

Another flash. Rain bristled the air. The thunder requested their attention once more.

'Okay,' said Naila. 'Let's do this.'

They crowded around a small table nailed to the deck, where Jacob was seated in front of the box of drones and a heavy-looking black controller. He had programmed the Moskeetoze to seek the transmitters they had planted inside the dam's sluices. Within minutes, each sluice's inner surface would be lined with their tiny bodies. Sluices often got jammed this way with detritus like leaves or sticks that the workers had to clean out, so the infiltration had to be subtle. Thousands of drones would creep into them over the course of the night, just enough to cause a malfunction.

'So they're ready?' Naila asked.

'Whenever we are.' Jacob pointed to an unmarked button on the controller. They stared at it, then at the tinselly drones in the box beside it.

'You have warned the peepo?'

Naila looked around, blinking. She had almost forgotten Mai was here.

'Am asking because that is what the *bazungu* did wrong the fest time with this same dam,' Mai said. 'They did not give the peepo proppa warning.'

'Ya,' Naila nodded. 'The effect will be a nationwide power cut. That's the warning.'

'It is okay,' Jacob smiled at Mai, charming her. 'This time, we know what we are doing.'

'Actually, we don't.' Joseph's lips slid past each other. He was leaning against the table. He was tipsy and Naila could smell the sour flu on his breath, like *chikanda*.

'Ach, shuttup, man,' said Jacob. There was no anger in his voice, just irritation.

The storm winds were starting to make the lake rock, which was making the boat pitch.

'Look, I know the rally didn't work, but we have to be careful about direct action,' Joseph grumbled. 'It always just harms the people it's supposed to help. We're shutting down a dam that provides electricity for millions. Mai is right. We should send out a warning now.'

'We've gone through this, babe,' said Naila. 'We're shutting it down just long enough to jam the cloud. Then we'll send a signal out to coordinate a resistance movement, and get everyone plugged into SOTP so we can operate outside government surveillance.'

'But remember the history of this place?' Joseph squawked. 'Remember Project Noah?'

'Operation,' Naila and Mai corrected at the same time.

'And that was just animals!' Joseph protested. 'We're risking people's lives.'

'You did not seem to mind risking people's lives when it was for the Virus vaccine,' said Jacob.

'That's not the same.' Joseph shook his head. 'Look, we're brothers here, man—'

'We are not brothers!' Jacob shouted and got to his feet.

Lightning crackled the sky – a brief, incomplete shatter as if in the surface of an obsidian vase – and pale light bounced off the wooden surfaces of the boat. The rain began to come diagonally through the open sides. It was already raucous on the surface of the lake. Jacob and Joseph were arguing across the table bolted to the deck, yelling over the noise of the storm. Bead light striated the air. Naila shook her head and strolled to the bar to pour herself another drink. Mai followed, her hands on her hips.

'What is this bluther stuff all about?' asked Mai, eyeing the men.

'Who knows?' Naila shrugged and handed her a G&T. They toasted carefully – the boat was still pitching. Glass clinked, lightning flashed, and one man punched another in the dark.

'Shit.' Naila put her glass down and ran over to break up the fight, placing one hand on Jacob's arm and the other on Joseph's chest, repeatedly shrieking a single word – STOP! But her voice could not compete with the rain or their tussling. Mai watched the three revolutionaries slipping around on the wet deck, fighting for the upper hand.

Finally, there was a heaving pause, lit haphazardly with electric light – man-made and natural, Beads and lightning. Jacob was seated at the table again, panting. Joseph was standing across from him. Naila had wrapped her arms around Joseph's chest from behind, hugging him or holding him back, her cheek pressed to his shoulder. Mai sipped her G&T.

'Pussy,' said Jacob. He said it quietly but it cut through the noise of the storm.

'I'm not fucking afraid,' said Joseph, sounding afraid.

Naila groaned and let go of him. The storm held its breath. Jacob reached forward and at the same moment Joseph reached his hand out to the table. CLICK. It seemed as if the storm were exhaling again but as the sound zithered up and out and began ringing round, it was clear that one of them or both of them had pressed the button on the controller. The drones ascended, glittering bits rising from the box. Mai pointed at the swarm with redundant wonder. They watched the drones go, scattering their murmurous sweep over the water, looking like pixels, then like ash, then like smoke. Naila turned her head and vomited.

'*Mwebantu!*' Mai stepped forward. 'My boat!'

'It does not matter who pressed it,' said Joseph. 'It has been pressed.' Then he applauded and persuaded everyone to smoke some *mbanji* in celebration. Jacob agreed reluctantly. Naila mopped up her vomit with a rag, on hands and knees like a servant. When she returned from washing her hands in the loo, Joseph grabbed her and started slow dancing.

'You see?' he kept saying. He was playing an old WITCH song through his Bead. His high had cheered up his drunkenness. He danced badly, switched his hips back and forth as he spelled out the old band's acronym: ' "We. Intend. To. Cause. Havoc." You see?'

Naila chuckled throatily and let him spin her. Jacob was watching, sitting on the floor, leaning against the door to the head. Mai sat on a bench with her legs splayed, sipping at her drink. The rain stopped and the clouds cleared like chorus girls to let the moon shine. They would dock in the morning and send a message from the SOTP across the hacked Beads, inviting the Zambian people to join Cha-Cha-Cha 2.0.

✳

Dawn. A cup of melted ngwee. The deck washed and wet. The birds were snickering. The cabin was strewn with sleeping bodies, felled by fatigue and liquor. Except in one corner: soft plaintive moans, like a baby enjoying milk from a nipple. Mai woke up and saw them. A man was sitting with his back against the low wall of the deck, his face in darkness, legs stretched out on the ground. Naila was astride him, her hips leisurely shoving and shifting. Her hair was tied up, her ponytail swaying. Her back was bevelled on the sides like a banjo. On her bottom, there was a tattoo like a thin skyline and along her spine, a set of characters. Mai tried to read them but it wasn't Chinese nor another tattoo. It was a queue of drones, thirty or so, lined up along her vertebrae, perched there, plugged in, or drinking. Mai gasped.

Naila turned and her eyes swam into view, vague with sex. Sunrise spread behind her so she was backlit and glowing. The man panted urgently, out of view but for the jeans garrotting his calves. As she moved, Naila kept her head turned over her shoulder, riding blind, a smile curling her nostril. She seemed to know that she was being watched. But Naila's eyes were hazy, as if behind clouded glass, as if some part of her were locked inside a private room, through which she was delicately rummaging, seeking her pleasure.

She shuddered. The lake trembled. Mai heard a groan and turned away from the lovers. But the sound was too broad and low to be human. The approach of the swarm? No. The sound was vibrating her bare feet through the wood. The hoofbeat of water trotting to a gallop. Mai rushed to the lee of the *Vulture*. She craned her head towards the familiar thin grey curve on the horizon. It was not there.

'The dam!'

A wall of twisting mist rose where it had been, where it should be.

'It's gone!'

Naila was suddenly beside Mai, a *chitenge* wrapped around her, tucked under her armpits, her skin beaming out a humid pulse. Mai recoiled – Naila was still practically haloed with sex but her eyes were switchblades glinting in the morning haze. No fear, this one. The men crowded in behind them now, both in jeans and bare-chested, rank with sleep and sweat. Which one had been under Naila's shoving buttocks just a moment ago? Mai couldn't tell. They all leaned over the side of the boat, tense, concentrating on the smoke in the distance.

'But – there was no warning, no alarm, nothing.'

Mai felt the tug, the urging strain of the boat under her feet. She looked down over the edge. The speed of the water was visible, frothy darts and pleats in the brown cascade.

'The anchor!' she shouted. 'It will not hold!' She raced up the staircase to the pilot house.

*

Instead of causing a simple malfunction, the drones had blocked the sluices completely. The waters had risen and tumbled over the dam. Beneath the boat, Nyami Nyami was tossing his whirlwind hair, arching his spiny necks. The Great Zambezi was flooding. Lake Kariba would soon become a river. The Dam would become a waterfall. And miles away, the Lusaka plateau, the flat top of Manda Hill, would become an island . . .

'We need to get off the boat!'

'Can we even get to the shore?'

They yelled to each other, pointing uselessly. Dawn fanned her golden fingers. A mockery, that blank brightness above the rising chaos. The sound of the water was growing louder by the second, thundering, unharnessed. Was it a victory? Or a havoc? They had heard no sirens, received no panicked announcements over the radio or over their Beads screaming SABOTAGE!

The *Vulture*'s engines came to life: a jerk and a rumbling under their feet. Mai in her pilot house gestured for them to put on life jackets. Joseph dug the boxy vests out from under a bench. They shrugged them on and sat, the excitement in their eyes edged with triumph and fear. The boat began to rock, knocking back and forth indecisively. They felt friendly sprays of water against their bare backs, gentle blurbles spilling up through the cracks in the deck, rivulets fleeing over their feet.

The engines purred, then tantrummed over the roaring water. The racket rose and rose, the boat shaking as if it might explode. Another jolt as Mai set the windlass to pull up the anchor. The buzz below yawned down and ended in a low boom, as if something had plunged to the lake bed. Things grew quieter: the engines had stopped. Then the feeling of an earthquake, slow and liquid and rolling – with the anchor released, the accelerating current was dragging at the *Vulture*. It groaned and tilted heavily.

Gravity swung sideways. They stumbled to their feet. The boat lurched roughly in the other direction with a heaving, consequential thrust. They fell, flung by the bucking pitch of the deck. Their hands grabbed for anything within reach, anything to right the world. They skidded and tripped. Their mouths opened and closed in the great roar, fish out of water. Then another fierce lurch, a sheer sideways shove. A great straining and all around, the plucking, tearing, snapping sounds of wood breaking. *Chishamanzi!* The waters broke. The Zambezi came curving in, fountaining in arcs as it crushed down upon them.

*

Sputtering, feeling herself flung in two directions, Naila reached out and her hand landed on some wooden thing – she clutched it. Part of the boat. No. It flexed – an arm. She fumbled her hand into a grip, yelling into the void. Water veiled her vision. She pawed at her face with her other hand and saw the round dark skull at the end of a shoulder slip under the waters gushing into the boat. The head re-emerged – it was Jacob, his mouth the shape of panic. His eyes grew wide as another swell peaked and collapsed, tossing him away from her, their link severed.

Naila slithered sideways over wood, the skin of her arm and hip and hands gathering splinter and fire. Suddenly she was in the air, a flash of light, of flight. The plunge: the blaring rush of noise swallowed up in an abyssal suffocation. Then a skimming slant up through the busy water, the life vest dragging her up to the surface. A belch as the bubbling around her burst into sound. Gasping. Spewing. The torrents devouring her again. She lunged desperately, here, there, seeking air. The life jacket was buoying her but she could not keep her head above the water long enough to breathe. The surging, twining current kept submerging her. After one long plunge, the dull pain in her lungs began to sharpen. A terrible exhaustion fell over her, veiling her from her will, tempting her: just let go. Just let . . .

CRACK. She heard her knee break before she felt the fire crunch into the bone. Rage flashed through her and she flung out at whatever had slammed into her, skinning her hand as she tried to loop her arm around it. She pulled up and her head broke the surface. She gasped alive. The leafless tree jutting above the water was rough but she clung to it, keeping it in a chokehold until she could wrap her naked legs around the trunk – her *chitenge* had long washed away. The sun dazzled down. The water boomed and pounded past her. *Papu*'d to the tree, panting, she scanned the swarming bright water.

Through the prism between her eyelashes, she saw the hills around the lake, those plush green blankets draped over the sloping banks.

To the south, the white mist was thick as a wall. The *Vulture*'s shattered remains drifted and spun in the brown, rushing water. Above, tiny specks flew, scattering in every direction, then coalescing into a flock that zipped and zoomed in saltatory shifts across the sky, changing direction abruptly like those old computer screen savers with Bézier curves. Naila's arms and legs were cramping. Fighting the current was sapping her strength. The water leapt and tumbled, its thick tresses caressing her as

Shhhkkkrrrkakingkakinkakingchchchch*ding*ding*ding*shhhtzzzzzzzzzzt.
ERROR. HTTP 404 FILE NOT FOUND. WE ARE HAVING TROUBLE
RECOVERING THE FEED. CHECK YOUR MONITOR AND TRY AGAIN.

Excuse us. We're sorry. Please pardon our dust. It appears that we have a problem. The feed has cut, interrupted abrupt, and the culprit? Nowhere to be found. O Error! It seems, while extolling your virtues, we have made some mistakes of our own. For one, we're not sure that we are who we said. Are we red-blooded beasts or metallic machines? Or are we just a hive mind that runs a program that spews Wikipedian facts?

Pondering this query – who are we really? – we discovered another mistake. We searched entomology, *the study of insects, but* etymology *popped up instead. It's all fine and good, we looked into the root,* etymology *means 'search for the truth', its origin is* etumos *– oh no! There we go! We're doing it again! Straying, swerving, stealing. (Nostra culpa to the Bard of* Nostromo, *by the way.)* Traduttore, traditore, *as the Italians say. Or as the Internet says. In fact, any facts, any stats that we've stated? There's just no vouching for their veracity. We deviate, drift . . . oh, how we digress. We're semantically movious, too.*

Are we truly man's enemy, Anopheles gambiae, *or the microdrones Jacob designed? If that's who we are, then this tale has explained our invention. The problem is that we'll still never know because . . . we've joined up with the local mosquitoes. We get along fine, but can't tell us apart in this loose net of nodes in the air. We just buzz about and follow commands and live lives of tense coordination. Half insects, half drones; perhaps all drones or none; maybe something between will emerge. But what a joke! What an error! What a lark indeed! A semi-cyborgian nation!*

Here's one more question: are we really a we? *Or just a swarm in the swarm? Worse, is this* me?! *Was it the dread* royal we *all along? And is that the meaning of SOTP? Oh what a shame, that they rotted so quickly: the fruits of the new Cha-Cha-Cha.*

Those fiery young bolshies tried to blow up the dam and take down the government that way. But their blueprints were old, their calculations too tight, and they'd made no concessions to chance. Indeed, their mistake – their Error of Errors – was simply forgetting the weather. Tabitha had warned them all about The Change, and that season was ultra-disastrous. The rainfall that came was ten times the norm and the damned wall was already failing. When the drones blocked the flue, the Zambezi pushed through, and Kariba Dam tumbled down after.

The bodies of water spilled their banks within days and soon the whole country was drowned. The gorges and valleys were rivers and lakes, the escarpments were lost under waterfalls. Electric grids failed, people fled from their homes. The flood flowed broad and washed out the roads, making streams and canals of the tarmac. Traffic slowed down, then stopped altogether. Passengers waded, then swam.

Lusaka survived, that dusty plateau, as its own city-state. Kalingalinga became its capital. A small community, egalitarian, humble. People grow all of the food that they eat. There are a few clinics, and one or two schools. Beads are used for barter and voting. And in its midst our lone survivors, Naila's two lovers, now old. Haven't we told you? She died giving birth, but her son doesn't know who his father is.

We are here, too, in this warm, wet future. What keeps us going? Our arthropod flesh or our solar-strip skin? Perhaps it's the same old difference. The best kind of tale tells you you in the end, unveils the unsolvable riddle. Wait! Did you hear that? Don't leave us just yet! They're suddenly all speaking through us – Naila and Jacob and Joseph, their parents, and all of their ancestors, too – with a crackling noise like old radio waves, here is their terminal message:

Time, that ancient and endless meander, stretches out and into the distance, but along the way, a cumulative stray swerves it into a lazy, loose curve. Imagine the equation, or picture the graph, of the Archimedean spiral. This is the turning that unrolls the day, that turns the turns that the seasons obey, and the cycle of years, and the decades. But outer space too, that celestial gyre, the great Milky Way, turns inward and outward at once. And so we roil in the oldest of drifts – a slow, slant spin at the pit of the void, the darkest heart of them all.

✳✳

Acknowledgements

The Old Drift includes many fictions and quite a few facts. 'The Falls' chapter borrows heavily from Percy M. Clark, *The Autobiography of an Old Drifter* (London: G. C. Harrap, 1936) – all racism his. Other works consulted include: Milisuthando Bongela, 'Tech artist bends the net to create decolonial, spiritual therapy for the spiritual age,' *The Mail & Guardian* (28 July, 2016). Beppe Fenoglio, *The Twenty-three Days of the City of Alba* (1952), tr. John Shepley (South Royalton: Steerforth Italia, 2002). Ilsa M. Glazer, *New Women of Lusaka* (Mountainview: Mayfield, 1979). Jan-Bart Gewald, Giacomo Macola and Marja Hinfelaar, eds, *One Zambia, Many Histories: Towards a History of Post-colonial Zambia* (Leiden: Brill, 2008). David M. Gordon, *Invisible Agents: Spirits in a Central African History* (Athens: Ohio UP, 2012). Karen Tranberg Hansen, *Distant Companions: Servants and Employers in Zambia, 1900–1985* (Cornell: Cornell UP, 1989). Panpan Hou et al, 'Genome editing of CXCR4 by CRISPR/cas9 confers cells resistant to HIV-1 infection', *Scientific Reports* 5:15577 (20 October, 2015). David Howarth, *The Shadow of the Dam* (London: Collins, 1961). Christina Lamb, *The Africa House* (London: HarperCollins, 1999). Austin Kaluba, 'Zambia Down Memory Lane' series, UKZambians (www.ukzambians.co.uk). Clare Pettitt, *Dr Livingstone, I Presume? Missionaries, Journalists, Explorers, and Empire* (Cambridge, MA: Harvard UP, 2007). M. Marmor et al, 'Resistance to HIV Infection', *Journal of Urban Health: Bulletin of the New York Academy of Medicine*, 83:1: HIV Perspectives After 25 Years (1 January, 2006). Darryll J. Pines and Felipe Bohorquez, 'Challenges Facing Future Micro-Air-Vehicle Development', *Journal of Aircraft* 43:2 (March-April, 2006). Saritha Rai, 'A Religious Tangle Over the Hair of Pious Hindus', *New York Times* (14 July, 2004). Andrew Spielman and

Michael D'Antonio, *Mosquito: The Story of Man's Deadliest Foe* (New York: Hyperion, 2001). Research that I conducted at the National Archives of Zambia, in newspapers and journals from the sixties and seventies, and via interviews for my *New Yorker* article, 'The Zambian "Afronaut" Who Wanted to Join the Space Race' (11 March, 2017) also made its way into the novel.

Snippets from the following songs appear in the novel: Larry Maluma's 'Chakolwa (Drunkard)' (1984); Whitney Houston's 'How Will I Know?' (George Merrill, Shannon Rubicam and Narada Michael Walden, 1985); Billy Ocean's 'Get Outta My Dreams, Get into My Car' (Billy Ocean and Robert John 'Mutt' Lange, 1988); Soul for Real's 'Candy Rain' (Ali Shaheed Muhammad, Hamish Stuart, Dwight Myers, Malik Taylor, Owen McIntyre, Samuel Barnes, Jean-Claude Olivier and Terri Robinson, 1994).

A novel this long in the making draws around it a veritable swarm of souls. Some categories overlap; I name you each only once. My warmest thanks to:

The classmates and instructors of writing workshops I took with Lan Samantha Chang, John Crowley, Mitchell S. Jackson, Jamaica Kincaid and Katharine Weber. The members of my writing groups over the years: Alisa Braithwaite, Case Q. Kerns, Julia Lee, Christina Svendsen, (Cambridge); Tej Rae (Lusaka); Nadia Ellis, Swati Rana (Berkeley). My residency hearts: Allison Amend, Liz Greenwood, Fatima Kola, Carmen Maria Machado, Janet Mock, Kiran Desai and Seema Yasmin. My Berkeley students and colleagues, especially Scott Saul.

Callaloo for publishing 'Muzungu' (an early version of 'Isabella 1983') and Alice Sebold and Heidi Pitlor for selecting it for *The Best American Short Stories 2009* (Houghton Mifflin Harcourt, 2009). Binyavanga Wainaina, Margaret Busby, Osonye Tess Onwueme and Elechi Amadi, for selecting me for *Africa39* and publishing 'The Sack' (Bloomsbury, 2014). Margaret Busby and Candida Lacey for publishing 'The Living and the Dead' in *New Daughters of Africa* (Myriad, 2019).

The Berkeley Institute of International Studies for the 2012 Robert O. Collins grant to brush up on my Nyanja and Bemba. The 2010 and 2015 Caine Prize for African Writing for shortlisting 'Muzungu'; awarding the prize to 'The Sack'; giving me the space to write 'The Man With the Hole in His Face' (an early version of 'Thandiwe 1996');

and (re)publishing them in the respective *Caine Prize Anthologies* (New Internationalist). Nick Elam for telling me that I was already a writer in the Douala airport. Nick Stanton for being my Virgil through the media. The 2015 committee – Zoe Wicomb (chair), Zeinab Badawi, Brian Chikwava, Neel Mukherjee and Cóilín Parsons – and Lizzy Attree for forgiving my cheekiness.

Berkeley for giving me a job that lets me write. Sangam House, Ledig House, Chaminuka, Hedgebrook and The Ruby for surrounding the creation of this project with beauty, time, deliciousness and solidarity.

My generous fact checkers and providers: Samuel Bjork, Glenda Carpio, Roy and Sarah Clarke, Federico Ferro, Mubanga and Juanita Kashoki, Georgina Kleege, Adam Morris, Audrey Mpunzwana, Ilse and Jacob Mwanza, Suwilanji Ngambi, Mukuka Nkoloso Jr., Shailja Patel, Ranka Primorac, Bartek Sabela, Robert Serpell, Duncan Smith and Shanti Thirumalai. My last minute proofer Kyler Ernst.

My teams at Janklow & Nesbit and at Hogarth for being extraordinary machines. Will Francis for escorting me around London; Molly Stern for gallantly swooping in. Poppy Hampson and Alexis Washam for taming this monstropolous beast and ushering it into the world with such patience, precision and love. Greg Clowes for fixing it up. Kai and Sunny for dressing it up. Michael Taeckens for introducing it to everyone with panache and grace.

PJ Mark for finding me, sticking by me, and always knowing exactly what to do and when – you are kismet itself.

My earliest editors: eagle-eyed Margaret Miller and gimlet-eyed Mike Vazquez.

My readers, my sisters, my graces: Michelle Quint and Zewelanji Serpell and Ellah Wakatama Allfrey.

My other family members, friends and boos for your love and support along the way.

My mother, Namposya Nampanya-Serpell (1950–2016), who knew who I was before I did, and never stopped believing. Mama, this book is for your joy. It isn't the story of the invention of the alphabet ('Ay! It's a bee!') but at least it begins with a Z.